FOR ELIZABETH AND LORCAN,

WELCOME ON A JOURNEY
TO THE FIRST YEARS
OF OUR GREAT COUNTRY.

JOHN SLADE
DECEMBER 2004

BOOTMAKER TO THE NATION
The Story of the American Revolution

Dr. John Slade

Maps and Illustrations
by
Carolyn Peduzzi

WOODGATE INTERNATIONAL

BOOTMAKER TO THE NATION
The Story of the American Revolution

Copyright © 2002
by
Dr. John Slade

ISBN 1-893617-06-8
Library of Congress Control Number
00 136346

FIRST EDITION

Cover photographs by the author

FICTION / HISTORICAL / AMERICAN REVOLUTION

WOODGATE INTERNATIONAL
P.O. Box 190
Woodgate, New York 13494
USA
www.woodgateintl.com

WOODGATE INTERNATIONAL
www.woodgateintl.com

The Thirteen
Colonies
1774

Canada

Quebec

Halifax

Montreal

1. New Hampshire
2. Massachusetts
3. Connecticut
4. Rhode Island
5. New York
6. Pennsylvania
7. New Jersey
8. Delaware
9. Maryland
10. Virginia
11. North Carolina
12. South Carolina
13. Georgia

Mississippi River

Proclamation Line of 1763

Wilmington

Charleston

Savannah

St. Augustine

N
W — E
S

0   100   200   300
Miles

Foreword by Samuel Adams

As my cousin John well knew, the Revolution that brought an entirely new nation onto the stage of the world, and planted an entirely new dream in the hearts of all people, began with a people who demanded not land, nor wealth, nor power, but freedom from tyranny. The farmer, the cobbler, the blacksmith knew right from wrong, and demanded to live according to what was right. They did not wish to be soldiers, but free men. They did not wish to be conquerors, but equal men. They did not wish to be aristocrats, but men who knew the profit of their own hard work.

These were the "rabble" whom I encouraged, the rebels whom John represented in Congress, the men for whom Thomas Jefferson wrote his sacred text, the "winter warriors" with whom General Washington defeated the most powerful army and navy in the world. These were the common people, who rose above their common lives for eight and a half years of privation and anguish and grief, until their triumph gave to the world an unprecedented form of government. Its charter began with three words, unknown during all previous centuries of human history, "We the People."

This book, about a common cobbler, about a farm girl, about a carpenter, about a widow and her son, and about the Commander in Chief who loved every soldier, every citizen, more than he loved himself, asks the reader today to continue the fragile American "experiment" with the same integrity, and determination, and mindfulness of the world beyond our shores, that once guided the good people who forged, more for posterity than for themselves, the golden chalice of freedom.

Acknowledgements

I am profoundly grateful to the following people
for their professional support,
and for their encouragement over the years.
You enabled me to live, and work, in two different worlds:
the demanding, complex world we live in today,
and the unique epoch of America in the 1700's.
You made the machines work,
you helped with the history,
and you provided me with the bedrock foundation
of your encouragement.

Marilyn Thomas

Mary Helen and Major Ed Jones

Raju Katari

Inger Petterson

Dick Eiger

Ruth Johnson and Jon Simonsen

Susan Marie Chappelle

Åge Lind

Carolyn and Jack Peduzzi

Contents

Maps

Prologue

Benjamin.

10 July, 1826
The old farmhouse
Lincoln, Massachusetts

Today the news has come that our John Adams, and our Thomas Jefferson, both in their time patriots fit to be hung, and both in their time Presidents fit to be honored to the end of human endeavor, have gone to their eternal rest. They went together, one on his farm near Boston, the other on his mountaintop in western Virginia, fifty years to the day after they had signed our Declaration of Independence. Aye, together with Congress, they wrote and signed that revolutionary document, then they sent it to the King, telling him in bold clear English that I, and my sons-to-be, and their sons after them, could stand equal to any other man upon this earth.

On the same day, July 4, 1826, within hours of each other, were they both gone, as if they had waited, watching from the north and watching from the south for half a century, to see whether the unprecedented dream which they had wrought with words, and we with blood, could actually take root upon a continent prepared for us by the hand of God. Their twin hearts beat until the fiftieth Fourth of July, like the twin hearts of a brace of oxen who pull the plow through virgin earth, until they can pull no more.

The news arrived (by word of mouth across the States far quicker than by post or broadsheet) that Adams and Jefferson have left us. We are on our own now.

So I come to think, a man of seventy-one myself, that on this warm evening in July, the milking done, I would set pen to paper (not unmindful of the presumptuousness of my task) to tell the tale of rebellion and war and victory. I would like the many progeny to whom I will bestow not only home and farm but nation itself, to know at what cost, in treasure and love and anguish, the blessings of American nationhood were bought.

I would like my seven grandchildren, and their children after them—as well as "the unborn millions," as General Washington often called them—to understand the gift they have received. So that as they turn their eyes to their own future, they may sow not only seed but a certain wisdom into the land.

Therefore I sit at the kitchen table with a freshly sharpened quill. By daylight and by lamplight, if the good Lord give me strength, I shall chronicle the years between 1774 and 1783, the decade during which this nation was born.

Genevieve sits in her rocking chair across the table from me, facing not me but the open window for its light upon her knitting. As she once taught a boy from London how to ride a horse, so I once taught a farm girl from Massachusetts how to write with a fairer hand than my poor scrawl. She has agreed to set upon paper her full share of our distant history, reaching, she says, back to 1763.

For she saw it all, as well as I. And she ought, I think, to have her say.

PART I

In His Majesty's Service

Chapter One

Benjamin York, his page.

To begin at the beginning, we must turn back, far far back, the thick ledger of years, to the time when I was a lad of eighteen in London, apprenticed as a cobbler to my father. Skilled I was at cobbling a pair of workman's shoes, and skilled I was becoming, as I followed my father's example, at fashioning a pair of gentleman's boots.

I honored my father and my mother, kept the peace with my siblings (especially on the Sabbath), and had reached the age when the comely glance of a cooper's daughter had instigated my courtship for her hand. My single dream was to be wed with my beloved Elspeth, and to raise our brood on the basis of my earnings as a cobbler of the finest gentleman's boots in the city of London.

But then, in April of 1774, from that comfortable home and hearth, by the hand of the Devil, I was snatched.

"I'll take them boots."

A hand grabbed for the shiny black boots which I was carrying to a customer's address off Oxford Street. Determined to thwart the thief, I clutched Papa's newly-made boots to my chest, spun away from the hand grasping my arm and began to run up the cobblestone lane toward home.

But I hadn't run two steps before someone in a blue seaman's jacket kicked his foot between my legs and sent me sprawling. My first thought, while I lay with my face on a gritty paving stone, was that I had scraped the boots which I had spent much of an afternoon polishing. I couldn't deliver them now, and Papa would be most upset when I returned home with the damaged boots and not a pence of money.

A buckled shoe gave me a kick in the shoulder as a voice above me shouted, "Up with you, lad. You're in His Majesty's navy now."

I sprang up like a wildcat. While one arm clutched the boots, I cocked my other arm to land a blow on my assailant. For I understood that it was not the boots they were after, but myself, and were they to succeed, my life was over. A seaman in a blue jacket, his weathered face grinning at me, danced quickly back beyond the range of my punch. I thought to turn and run once more, when hands grabbed both my arms from behind.

Now another blue jacket stepped out from an alley, holding a raised cudgel. The vicious look in his eye bade me to understand that he would gladly crack open my skull. Though I roared for help, not a soul would come to my aid; rather, the cowards up and down the busy lane scurried away, mindful not to be caught as well by a navy press-gang.

To struggle was useless, but still I might argue myself free. I begged them to understand that I was but an apprentice cobbler, and that my family depended on every ha'penny I could earn. I'd been sent by my father to deliver these boots, and if I did not return home . . . my mind recoiled with horror at such a thought, for my family would surely believe that I'd been murdered in the street for a pair of boots.

Seeing that my argument had no effect on my sneering captors, I shouted with desperation, "You can't take me!" Then I stood up tall and glared at the seaman with the cudgel. Summoning an authority which I knew not I possessed, I announced, "I will not allow it."

With a guffaw, the brute jabbed me in the stomach with his club. Grunting sharply, I doubled over into an unbreathing knot of pain. I would have collapsed to the cobblestones, but hands still gripped my arms from behind. The bully with his club mimicked in a high shrill voice, "I will not allow it!" As laughter erupted around me, I realized that I was in the midst of half a dozen men.

Now two more of the King's hirelings stepped into view. One was clearly a naval officer, for he wore a long blue coat with white facing and white cuffs, a black hat with gold trim, a sword at his hip, and tall black boots. He stood some distance from me, his attention not on me primarily, but on the men of his press-gang (lest one of *them* should attempt to escape).

The other villain stood directly in front of me. He wore a shabby blue jacket over a filthy white shirt, and a battered black hat without any gold trim. The officer, as I later learned, was a lieutenant; his unwashed underling was a bosun's mate. The first, despite his higher rank, was but a minion; while the second, a petty officer who craved the dignity of power, was the Devil himself.

While working at my bench in my father's shop, I often glanced up to see the faces of customers who addressed Papa at the counter. I had learned with a quick reading to know who meant to trade with us in good faith, who meant to try to barter down the price, and who meant to give us trouble with excuses rather than prompt payment.

But never, as I watched my quick and clever father handle all manner of Londoners from top to bottom, had I encountered a visage like that of the petty officer who stood now before me. His countenance was so filled with hatred and contempt, that I could not help but understand it was not me whom he hated, but all men upon the earth.

Reaching toward me with his grasping hand, he growled, "I'll take them boots." I glanced down at his shoddy shoes. His toes showed through one of them. This was no high-born officer whom I faced, nor even a yeoman's son who'd become an able-bodied seaman. The man gripping Papa's boots—I had not yet let go of them— was almost certainly a gutter-born convict who had been offered the navy or the noose. He now wore a blue jacket that would never be an officer's coat, a white shirt that would never be an officer's shirt with frills at the neck, and a black hat that would never be trimmed with gold. He glared at me with the sneer of a man for whom no revenge would ever be enough.

I submitted, like a slave to his chains. As my captor snatched Papa's boots from my hands, I felt with a crushing despair that my life had ended. My dear mother, my aging father . . . What of my plan of taking over Papa's shop, and of caring for my parents in their old age as well as they had cared for me as a child?

And what of my beloved Elspeth? We were to be married on the coming New Year's Eve, that we might ring in 1775 as man and wife. To disappear, without a word to her!

I struggled anew, but the rogues behind me wrenched my arms all the more tightly. The brute with his cudgel warned me, "Come quietly, or we shan't mind dragging you."

As the gang of bullies led me on that warm April evening along increasingly unfamiliar streets, I mustered the presence of mind to ask, "Where are you taking me ?"

"To the ship, you damn fool."

I searched around me for the officer, but he had disappeared. As had the petty officer, with my boots.

"But where," I wanted to know, "is the ship taking me?"

"To Boston, lad," replied a blue-jacketed seaman with satisfaction. "We're taking General Gage and His Majesty's troops to Boston, to teach the bloody rebels a lesson they'll never forget."

To Boston. To America! I kicked and twisted, and swore with words I never before had dared to use. But the scoundrels held my arms tightly behind my back.

Finally, knowing my rights, I roared that I was English-born and in England I would stay . . . until the cudgel crashed down upon my head and gave me a moment of hideous pain, then sent me, for all I knew, to the land of the dead.

೮౧

Chapter Two

I awoke in a tumbril, atop a load of grain sacks. Whether I had been carted to the wharf, or dragged there and then tossed into the wagon, I did not know. But as I lay on my back staring skyward, I beheld what seemed to be a giant spider's web: a tall, complex lattice. Its lower portion was lit by flickering lanterns; its rising strands reached up to snare the stars.

I realized that I was looking at the rigging of a frigate. I lifted my head (though it ached with every move) and peered over the side of the tumbril. A dozen cannons jutted at intervals through the length of the long black hull.

Papa would never forgive me for sailing on a warship.

But Papa would never know.

Sailors clamored up a gangway from the wharf to the deck. Barrels stood along the pier. But I spotted nobody watching me. Thinking I might leap to my freedom, I tried to gather my legs beneath me, but discovered that my feet were bound with heavy rope and lashed to a post of the tumbril.

A face peered down at me as if I were a hog in a pen at market.

"The cobbler's awake, 'e is," called my guard to the frigate's deck.

"March 'im aboard, then. 'E's in the forward orlop with the others."

"Right." With a satisfied leer, the bluejacket unbuckled my shoe. When I sat up to protest, he slapped me across the face with the sole of my own shoe. "You'll grip the rigging better barefoot, lad," he told me as he tugged off my other shoe. "In a month, you'll be a regular monkey up there, you will."

He untied my ankles and ordered me to climb down from the tumbril, then he marched me in my stockings across the gangplank onto the frigate's cluttered deck. Dozens of sailors were busy at their tasks. Not a one bothered to glance at me.

My rum-wheezing guard shoved me toward a brass railing wrapped around three sides of a large square hole in the deck. He told me to climb down "the ladder," as he termed it. I made my way carefully down a steep set of stairs, to a deck lit by lanterns hanging from the ceiling. The long cramped room was swarming with men, and pungent with the stink of beasts who had long forgotten what it means to bathe.

As I hunched over to keep from banging my head on the beams, I saw once again the enormous black cannons, mounted on heavy wooden carriages along both sides of the ship. Their barrels jutted through square open hatches.

They could hang me before I blackened my hands, and my soul, with gunpowder.

A yank on my arm started me down a second flight of stairs to a lower deck, where countless hammocks were slung in rows from the ceiling. Crowded beneath them were another hundred sailors, some leaning over trunks, some sitting on the floor. I wondered how so many men could possibly live on a single ship.

My guard ordered me down a third stairway. As I descended to a deck much darker than the others, he closed a hatch over my head. I found myself locked in a small, odd-shaped room without portholes, lit by a single lantern on a crate. I breathed no longer the stench of human sweat, but an evil dampness laden with the smell of bilge water, caulking tar, and the decay of something rotting. (The stink came from rats which had been clubbed, then dropped into the bilge). As my eyes opened to the purgatorial darkness, I discerned uplifted faces of men seated on the floor: young men like myself in tradesman's aprons, in the work clothes of a farmer who had come to market, in the rags of a beggar. Here were my brethren in hell, whose families knew no more than mine about our fate.

A bluejacket stepped forward into the lantern light: the petty officer who had stolen Papa's boots. Looking down, I recognized immediately the boots which Papa had so laboriously and lovingly fashioned. The thief might well have been up on deck, taking a last look at the lit windows of London, at sweethearts waving farewell, at cathedral towers rising toward the stars, were it not his pleasure to be here below as gaoler in a dungeon, where he could savor the stink of our terror, the stench of our hopelessness.

Growling at me, "Look there, boy," he pointed toward a narrowing of the dark room, a coming together of the two sides of the hull, and thus, as I guessed, the bow of the ship. "That way lies Boston!" he roared, and then his boot, Papa's boot, struck my knees and sent me sprawling among the lads on the floor.

I thought then that I knew hatred. I thought, as I got back on my feet (bowing my head beneath the low beams) that I hated the villain who stood between the lantern and me, his face completely black, his knotted fist waiting for my slightest move. Hatred burned in my heart, a lad's heart which had before never known more than occasional irritation or mistrust, a heart which had always believed that no matter what wrongs it encountered, Papa and the hand of God would set them right. But my heart now burned with a fierce determination that I would have my vengeance. I would have those boots back, scuffed or not; and I would have my freedom, no matter what port I found my freedom in; and I would beat that thieving blackguard until he crawled, bleeding and whimpering, and begging for mercy.

I stepped toward the safety of the bow, then sat on the hard deck, my back against the damp hull. I felt myself powerful with hatred.

But as I was an apprentice cobbler, so was I still only an apprentice patriot.

I watched Papa's boots climb the steps, heard their new owner thump his fist on the hatch. The hatch swung up. The boots climbed to the deck above us, then disappeared. The hatch fell back in place with a loud bang. An iron bolt slid fast.

Our wretched lot sat motionless in the dim glow of the lantern. We were about thirty lads. Scattered, murmurous voices now broke the silence. I paid no mind to them. I had my own thoughts to attend to.

As soon as we arrived in Boston (I knew not how long such a voyage would take), I would escape from this frigate, then seek an American ship preparing to sail to London. I knew not how I might pay my way back, but I hoped the captain would have some work aboard that I could do. Or perchance I might find a captain who would transport me to London, trusting my word of payment (from Papa) when we arrived. My father, I had no doubt, would gladly pay my ransom, though I would insist on paying him back from my wages, every shilling.

We all looked up together in the lantern light, for we heard a scrambling of feet on the deck above us. Muffled shouts . . . and then a tremor of the hull that went right up my spine: we were moving. We had no porthole through which to catch a last glimpse of London. No way of calling out our names to someone on the wharf, begging them to inform our families of our departure.

When the hull listed to the left, we became as silent as death: the sails up in that spider's web now caught the night breeze. We could hear the wash of water along both sides of the hull, above our heads. Therefore we had no portholes, nor any other source of fresh air: because our dungeon was below the surface. For all that anyone in London knew, our bones were rolling in the current along the bottom of the Thames.

The lantern flickered, smoked, and burned itself out. I sat on the floor in blackness so absolute, I could not see the man seated beside me, nor even my own hands when I spread them in front of my eyes.

The air became increasingly foul as water in the bilge below us sloshed about. And as various men relieved themselves as best they could. When the ship began to rock upon waves fetching up the river, a growing number of prisoners vomited onto the floor, rendering into our presence whatever had been their final dinner in England.

The clanging of the ship's bell, muffled by the three decks above us, chronicled the slow passage of the night. It bespoke of life and activity and purpose in that world above our tomb, our grave, our crypt. Feet thumped across our ceiling. In our fetid darkness, we breathed heavily, and gagged, and one of the lads wept like a poor lost child.

The ship abruptly heaved steeply onto its right side, and so it stayed. We crawled across the floor to readjust ourselves. We had sailed beyond the river's mouth and now caught a much stronger wind blowing across the broad waters of the English Channel. Heavy waves slapped and gurgled against the hull. The bow plunged and rose and plunged again like a battering ram against the sea.

We were leaving the waters of home. We were bound westward across the vast oceanic waters of the Atlantic, toward, God willing, the American port of Boston.

ॐ

Chapter Three

The iron bolt above us slid free; the hatch creaked open. A voice shouted down, "Up with you, lads. Up on deck, every blessed one."

Like cadavers rising to our feet, we assembled around the steps. Mute and apprehensive, we stumbled into each other with the rolling of the ship. None of us dared climb up through that dimly lit hatch, yet none wished to endure another minute in our dungeon; thus when the voice roared down, "*Up* with you, you despicable devils!", we scrambled up the steps.

On the deck above us, I glanced about at hammocks that bulged with sleeping men; the hundred hammocks swung together as the ship rolled. A shove sent me up more steps to the cannon deck. The cannon barrels had been pulled into the ship. The square hatches were shut.

Then we climbed—like prisoners rushing to their freedom—to the topmost deck, where I took a deep breath of sea air and squinted in the blinding sunshine of a blue-skied day. The sun nearly straight overhead proclaimed the hour as roughly noon.

My first thought was to look beyond the rear of the ship, hoping that the coast of England might not be too far off. Though I had never learned to swim, I entertained the idea of throwing myself overboard, then somehow floating my way home. But, for the first time in my narrow life, I saw nothing around me, in every direction, but rolling blue water.

We were herded against a waist-high wall across the front of the ship, then told to face "aft." Spreading my bare feet for balance on the heaving deck and gripping the wall with one hand, I stared up at three rectangular sails on the first mast, their huge gray-white bellies filled with wind. Then I spotted, spread along horizontal poles that held the sails, several dozen men in blue jackets.

A crow might perch on the outer end of a limb, but even a crow will move toward the trunk should a strong wind begin to blow. But those men, spread like sparrows against the blue heaven, rode the outermost limbs of a trunk that heaved and rolled and pitched with every wave that heaved and rolled and pitched the ship. Should a man miss his footing and tumble from that towering mast toward the merciless deck, or the only slightly less merciless sea . . . I lowered my eyes, unable to consider any further such a fate.

I surveyed the frigate's long deck, where two or three dozen men were working at various jobs. They wore blue jackets, they were barefoot, and they called now and then to each other as they tightened a rope leading up to the sails.

Toward the rear of the ship stood a row of red-coated soldiers with white belts criss-crossed over their chests. Each soldier held a bayoneted musket. Standing nearly shoulder to shoulder, they were clearly guarding the half-dozen officers on an elevated deck behind them from the crew on our lower deck.

Papa had stated sternly to each of his four sons, "No boy of mine will grow to be a soldier." Following our six years of schooling, he had apprenticed each of us to a trade, that we might never be driven by destitution into the ranks of the King's armed ruffians. My father read to us from the Good Book every evening after supper, and would not abide even a sharp word in his household. We lived in peace and friendship, and expected peace and friendship; I knew of no other way.

Now here I was, a prisoner on a warship among His Majesty's troops. I would be forced to labor, no doubt, for the soldiers who would soon aim their muskets at the rebellious colonials in Boston.

Better, almost, for Papa to believe that I'd been murdered, than for him to know that I was sailing toward one of Britain's countless battles.

While growing up, I had been as aware as the next person of the troubles across the Atlantic. The patience of the British people had already been well worn by the surly ingratitude of the American colonials, when we learned of their "tea party" in Boston's harbor. It was the work, so the talk went on the streets of London, of idlers and rabble. "Shall the King's word not be law?" asked our newspapers with fierce indignation. "Or shall the shouts of an unruly mob become law?"

I must truthfully say that I shared little of that indignation. For as a lad in love with Elspeth, I cared no more about the riots in Boston than I did about the wars of ancient Greece which I had studied briefly at school.

As I felt no allegiance toward these British brutes who had impressed me into their navy, so I felt no allegiance toward English-speaking rebels across the sea. I had no part in their dispute, especially should that dispute come to blows between King and colony.

I stared at the line of redcoats, soldiers as rigid as their muskets, the cockades on their hats alternating with the points of their bayonets. Never, for any reason, would I become a soldier. I was my father's son;

never would I bring shame or dishonor to our family's compassionate patriarch.

There was more: a further reason. How many times had Elspeth commended me on being "the gentlest of men?" If such was my nature, and if such could earn me the pledge of my betrothed (the wisest, finest, most charming creature on God's good earth), then unthinkable would it be for me to abuse her trust. When I returned to London, I would return as pure a lad as when I left.

Turning now to look at my fellow prisoners, I saw lads of more or less my own age, their clothing disheveled and their faces distraught. One brave boy began to protest in a loud voice, addressing himself to a cluster of sailors working nearby. He helped to print a newspaper loyal to the King, he declared, and by the ink on his apron, I believed him. But he had remonstrated for no more than half a minute when the petty officer stepped forward—our ugly friend from the night before, who seemed to take a special interest in us. With nary a word of warning, the brute struck the lad such a blow that the boy reeled against another lad and crumpled to the deck. Not a one of us offered a hand to help him, so great was our shock, and our terror that we might be next.

"Petty Officer Hench you'll call me," stated our imperious churl, strutting on legs clearly at home on the rolling deck, "and you'll learn to call me that with *respect*." He stomped the heel of Papa's boot to emphasize the word "respect."

Then Hench pointed, "You shorter ones to starboard. You taller ones to larboard. And you middling creatures athwart the beam."

Having been tall for my age since I was a stripling of twelve, I stepped toward the left, or larboard side of the deck. Shorter men gathered together to the right, and those in the middle remained in the middle. The printer, spitting blood, began to crawl toward the hatch. Hench gave him a kick in the ribs, then ordered the shorter men to drag him into their group.

"Right, then," growled Hench. "Below with you for a proper set of togs and bit of bread. Then to work with you!"

We were herded back down the "ladder," though only as far as the second deck below, where the purser's mate issued us outfits suitable for labor at sea: ill-fitting shirts, worse-fitting trousers, a bit of unwashed red rag to serve as a scarf, and a seaman's blue jacket, faded, patched, and torn. We stowed our London clothes in a pair of empty trunks.

We were then ordered to sit at a rude sort of table, set between snoring hulks of men slung in their hammocks. We struggled to keep our places along two benches while the ship tossed us toward one end of the bench and then the other, and tossed as well our bowls of soup, bricks of bread, and mugs of beer. Not so easy to raise a spoon to my lips, I discovered, especially with any soup still in it.

Barely finished with our meal, we were ordered to our jobs. The ten shortest lads were sent back down to the dungeon to swab it of our filth, then to fumigate it with vinegar and brimstone sprinkled over buckets of hot coals. That vile procedure brought them choking up the ladder for a breath of stagnant air.

The middle lads were given bricks of stone. They were to scrub the floor of the hammock, or "berthing," deck. Their hands and knees were soon worn raw by rubbing the flat stones over a mix of water and sand.

The seven tallest, myself among them, were ordered back up to the "weather" deck. We assembled in the sunshine near the bow, there to wait upon Hench's pleasure. With a shrill piping of his bosun's whistle, he summoned a half-dozen blue-jacketed seamen from the deck further aft. He let them do the choosing as they paired up with us, teacher with student, as I understood. My tutor was a well-built fellow taller even than I, a bright-faced man who seemed to find something humorous in our proceedings, for a lively smile rarely left his sunburned visage. He gave me a wink of welcome, and so let me know that among the beasts and brutes aboard this frigate, I might find at least one friend.

Then, "Away aloft!" roared Hench. To my astonishment, our tutors bid us follow them up the rope ladders and into the rigging!

My teacher strode toward the uphill side of the deck and gripped a thick black rope that rose steeply to a point half-way up the first mast. He leapt onto the waist-high wall running along the side of the ship, and from there scrambled deftly up a rope ladder. "Always climb the windward ratlin's," he called down to me. "Then the wind at your back blows you into the lines you're gripping."

I walked uphill on wobbly widespread feet to the edge of the ship. The sea slapped the hull below me; ropes and sails creaked and rumbled in the wind above me. I clutched the thick black rope with both hands, then hoisted myself awkwardly up onto the wall. There I grabbed a second heavy black rope, one of many with rope ladders laced between them. I stared down again at the rush and splash of waves washing a few yards below my feet. One tall wave reached up as if to snatch me.

Looking upward, I stared at a confusing multitude of ropes that rose into the spider's web of rigging. Each rope seemed to have some appointed task among the sails, but I could make sense only of the rope ladder leading to a platform halfway up the mast.

"Trust the black lines," called down my teacher, "never the white. Black is standing rigging, white is running rigging."

My hands gripped the thick black vertical lines while my feet tested each black rope step before I placed my weight on it. I glanced neither up nor down, but only at the length of ladder between my hands and feet. Thus I crept by increments upward.

I had never been higher in my life than the balcony of our church. And there I had sat on a sturdy bench behind a sturdy wall, with the good Lord minding my safety and His angels ready to catch me. Now as I climbed higher and higher into their realm, I wondered whether those snug, comfortable angels of Westminster Parish ever ventured so far to sea.

The rope ladder rolled with the ship, leaning me forward toward the mast and then backward over a long drop to the deck. The ladder also shook sideways as the bow rose and plunged and battered through the waves.

We climbed together until we stood side by side just below a small platform wrapped around the mast. My friend—for friend he must be, or never would I survive the increasing gusts of wind—informed me that this first time, I might climb up through a square hole in the platform, "the lubber's hole," as the safer route. While I groped and twisted and nudged inch by inch up through the hole, my friend deftly scampered up the "futtock shrouds," as he called them, leading around the platform's outer edge.

Immensely relieved to stand upon that solid platform—though it heaved and pitched far more than had the deck below—I gripped the mast with both hands and caught my breath. Barely able to look down, certainly unable to peer up, I stared instead out at the rolling blue ocean, framed by the edges of billowing sails . . . and felt a boyish exhilaration at finding myself a sailor at sea. No more the cramped, stuffy cobbler's shop. No more the pall of coal soot besmudging London's air. No more the tiny world of my neighborhood bounded by its all-too-familiar lanes. I took a deep breath of briny air and almost cheered "Haloo!" to the sea that had both captured me, and set me free.

"Come along, then," called my companion as he swung gracefully onto another rope ladder, rising from the outer edge of the platform, a narrower and steeper ladder than the first. Peering up, I saw that we were not yet halfway to the top of the mast. I almost asked if he meant to climb all the way to the top, but he was now so far above me that I would have to shout my question.

Letting go of the mast with one hand, I grabbed hold of the second ladder. Gripping its heavy rope tightly, I stepped cautiously across the rolling platform until I stood at its edge. Then, my heart thumping, I swung myself out around the ladder, and so *beyond* the platform, and set my foot on the first rope step. Or "ratlin'," as he had called it.

I started up. The vertical ropes were not as thick as those below. The wind tugged at my blue jacket and snapped the tip of my scarf.

The sides of the ladder converged until I had barely enough room to insert my increasingly sore feet. I was vaguely aware of other men in the rigging around me, but I dared not take my eyes from the ladder to which I clung.

I came to a pair of short horizontal braces attached to the mast. My companion stood atop one of them, grinning down at me. Once again I twisted and wrenched my way from the peak of the ladder up through a narrow gap onto sturdy footing (if sweeping back and forth in the sky was sturdy). Standing on a brace, I gripped the ropes of yet another ladder, narrower and steeper still.

Mustering some small measure of courage, I gave my teacher a confident nod. We were now as high as the bottom of the third sail. The enormous billowing expanse of canvas blocked our view of the sea ahead of us. A contrary gust suddenly caught one edge of the sail and caused a thundering rumble. My grimace of fright—I thought the entire ship might shake apart—prompted a laugh from my companion. Though I did not yet know it, I had just heard the laughter of an angel.

He pointed down. Reluctantly, I looked down the mast and saw the ship far below. It looked sturdy enough, its cluttered deck busy with men. I could hear snatches of orders blown away in the wind.

But viewed, from our elevated perch, as a vessel plying its way across a blue ocean that seemed to reach to the ends of the earth, our frigate appeared to be but a tiny bit of carved oak.

"You're nearly a topman now," said my companion as he swung onto the ratlin's of the third ladder.

This ladder was nearly vertical, following close up the mast. It moved in not two but three different directions at the same time. It rolled with the ship. It jolted sideways. And, now no wider than my shoulders, it began to twist, swiveling me first one way and then the other. Panting with fear, I wrapped my arms around the shrouds and hugged them to me.

"Come along," called the voice above me. "The lads are waiting."

Glancing up, I saw four men standing to the right of the mast, and two to the left. They stood along a rope slung beneath a horizontal pole that supported the uppermost sail. All six stared down at me as I clung to the ladder and swung and bobbed and swiveled. Clearly my companion and I were to join the two men on the left side of the mast, making a team of eight.

Their arms were wrapped over the top of the horizontal pole. The pole seemed to be sturdy, about ten inches wide, and stable, with the weight of the sail hanging from it. Another ten feet up, and then I too could wrap my arms over the pole while I stepped out on that footrope. If I had thought for a moment about *why* I would stand along the pole, I could not have nudged myself upwards even one ratlin'. But I thought only about *how* to do it: I stepped upward when the rolling ship leaned me toward the twisting ladder, clutched the shrouds tightly when the ship rolled me backward. I was determined that I would join the men above me. I would no longer be a solitary, lost, terrified prisoner, but a member of eight men with a job.

My eyes reached the level of my teacher's bare feet, spread on the slung rope. "Come up a bit more," he said to me, "then call out, 'Laying on larboard!' so we know you're stepping onto our footrope."

That made sense, for they would surely feel my weight on the rope, and if they were working, and I suddenly jolted their footing . . .

I climbed to the very pinnacle of the ladder. Stared at the thick horizontal pole, stared at the meager footrope. Stared again at the pole. Three men now stood along the left half, and four stood along the right. My own spot, just left of the mast, was clearly waiting for me. I called out, "Laying on larboard!" Then I stepped with one foot, and reached with one hand, from the ladder to the footrope and pole. The footrope gave slightly, but it held me; I could feel men shifting their feet further out. The horizontal pole, about belly height, felt reassuringly sturdy. I stepped with my other foot, grabbed with my other hand. Crouching a bit, I wrapped both arms over the pole and hugged it against my chest. I was at my station, as high as a man could possibly be in the rigging.

I didn't dare think that I was actually to *do* something up here.

I heard murmurs of welcome. Glancing in both directions, I nodded at men who regarded me with a measure of approval.

We had climbed up the mast behind the bellies of three sails, but now that I stood above the topmost sail, I could look ahead at the vast blue ocean stretching all the way to . . . to Boston.

"Come a bit further out on the yard."

Yes, I was still standing right beside the mast, whereas my counterpart to starboard stood a good four feet out.

Hardly believing that my hands and feet behaved as well as they did, I shifted to the left—my heart thumping against the pole—until my friend said, "Aye, now you're home."

I looked up, almost straight up, at the final spike of the mast: it rose another ten or fifteen feet. Above it, the huge blue sky reached from horizon to horizon, all the way around.

Something stirred in me, something from church: I was breathing not simply air; I was breathing from the sky, from the winds that swept over the face of the deep, from the firmament itself.

"Now listen," said my companion, "for you've got to learn every cringle and clew as well as you knew your shoe buckles. The deck near the bow," he pointed down to the spot where I had stood, "is the forecastle, or 'fo'c'sle' as we say. Furthest aft is the quarterdeck, where the officers plan their next war. Between them is the waist of the ship."

The frigate jolted over what must have been a steep and heavy wave; the four of us along the spar jounced, and dropped, and then rose again. I began to trust our sturdy perch in the sky.

"Now, the ratlin's we climbed were the lower shrouds, then the topmost shrouds, and finally the topgallant shrouds, leading to the topgallant sail. But we say the word . . . t'gallant."

I repeated, my voice sounding thin in the wind, "T'gallant."

"Aye. The platform you stood on, that's the fighting top, where the marines station themselves as snipers if we strike upon a battle."

A battle? Once again I heard my father's words, speaking with stern finality, "No son of mine will grow to be a soldier." Perhaps up here, high in the rigging, I could escape the muskets and the swords and the cannons.

"You're atop the foremast, on the t'gallant yard," he slapped his hand on the pole which I gripped, "to larboard. Them rogues," he winked at me as he nodded toward the four men on the other side of the mast, "are to starboard. And your job," he reached over the yard and patted the huge bellied gray sail beneath us, "is to help furl and set and trim the t'gallant sail."

Though the cobbler in me cringed with apprehension, the newborn sailor in me understood that life in the rigging must be immeasurably better than fumigating the dungeon, or scrubbing a deck with a flat block of stone. I'd learn to furl and set and trim, and otherwise keep myself out of harm's way.

"There's many a man aboard the *Lively* who's never been above the fighting top. There's some who don't dare set foot on a ratlin'." Tossing his head toward the other men along the t'gallant yard, he declared, "We're the kings of the frigate. In fair weather, anyway. But when foul weather is brewing, we bundle sail and tie our gaskets with every bit of strength, or Hench'll have our hides."

"Hench?" I understood with sharp disappointment that the petty officer's authority reached to the top of the mast.

"Aye, you're better riding a half-furled t'gallant in a hurricane, than to cross words with Hench."

I glimpsed in my friend's blue eyes a look of pain, and something more . . . as if whatever Hench had done to him, the capable man beside me had responded not with self-assurance, nor with anger, but with a helpless despair. For a moment, I stood beside a bruised and grieving child.

Then he pointed. "Look there." The sunlit sparkle returned to his eyes as quickly as it had vanished.

I looked beyond the starboard edge of our sail, then I grinned when I spotted it: a white sea gull, the largest bird I had ever seen, flapping lazily a short distance beyond our yard and *below* it.

"Now look behind you, lad, and say farewell."

I peered back as best I could, but the sail behind us blocked the view directly backwards. Though I searched the sea on both sides of it, I spotted nothing noticeable.

"The starboard quarter." My friend pointed back to the left.

I searched the horizon until I finally discerned, faint in the sea mist, a low gray-green stretch of land. "England?" I asked with excitement. I was glad for at least a final glimpse of home.

"Cornwall," he said with satisfaction. "Land's End."

I stared a while longer at the ghostly wisp of shore. Then I turned to him and asked, "You're not sad to say farewell?"

"My bonny Elizabeth proved fool enough to marry another man," he told me. "Tore my heart out, she did. Tore my heart out and fed it to the crows." He spoke with anger tinged with sadness, though a sadness far less severe than the grief, the devastation, the despair which I had witnessed when he spoke about Hench. The sadness was in his heart, but the grief had been in his soul.

Turning toward the horizon beyond the bow, he proclaimed, "I'm bound for Boston, I am, for to find me a Boston beauty!"

I thought of Elspeth, of the anguish she must no doubt be suffering today, thinking me murdered for a pair of boots. Could she possibly guess that I'd been impressed into the Royal Navy, and that even here high in the rigging, my heart still beat with unfailing love? "Not me," I stately firmly. "The first thing I'll look for in Boston is a ship to take me back home to my Elspeth. We're to marry on the eve of the coming year."

My friend unwrapped one arm from over the yard and held out his hand. "Then, congratulations. My name's Nathaniel Ash, and I'll be the man to help you find that ship."

Squeezing the yard with my left arm, I cautiously let go with my right, then I reached my hand across my chest and shook Nathaniel's strong, work-hardened hand. "Benjamin York, I am." And so aloft in the rigging of His Majesty's frigate, where never yesterday would I have believed I'd find myself today, I met the man, the lad, the child, whom I would come to love as the most unselfish friend I had ever known.

A friend, deep and true, for his heart knew naught else. From those five weeks aboard the frigate, when he protected me on deck and aloft, to the day a year later in the colony of Massachusetts, when he offered up his life in the stead of mine, he taught me to look beyond all the evil heaped upon my own heart, that I might see the goodness in his, and in the world.

Even more: he gave me an entirely new life. For the day I buried Nathaniel Ash, was the day I buried everything I had been, everything I had believed and felt and loved. And then I turned to a new belief, and to a new love, both of which filled my poor battered heart until it nearly burst.

"Right, then," said Nathaniel. Leaning over the yardarm, he patted his hand on the sail as if it were the flank of a favorite horse. "Let's have a go at furling."

I had no time to protest that my bare feet were beginning to ache from the footrope that dug into their soles (though I eased the weight from one foot to the other), for Nathaniel looked quickly left and right, "Ready, lads?"

"Aye," called the others along our spar, though not a one bothered to look toward us.

Nathaniel cupped his hand to his mouth and called down to the deck behind our mast, "On deck!"

A voice called up, "Deck aye!" I could see by the upturned face that it was Hench.

"Ready to furl the t'gallant!" called down Nathaniel.

Hench burst forth with a series of commands to the crew on deck, some of whom sprang to the lines coiled along the hull. Hench then called up again to Nathaniel, with a flurry of words in English that made no sense to me. Nathaniel called out orders to the topmen along our spar.

Then he instructed me, "Reach down and grab two handfuls of sail. As I call the cadence, haul it up and lay it over the top of the spar, then set your belly on the canvas and reach down for two more handfuls. That way we pile the sail atop the spar in even folds."

I watched the other men as they leaned over the spar and reached down as far as they could to grip the fluttering canvas. But to do so meant to let go of the spar itself. And to haul the sail up onto the spar . . . what would be holding *me* up, save for a wobbly footrope beneath my horribly aching feet?

"Hold onto the sail," said Nathaniel, guessing my thoughts. "It's not going anywhere, except where we want it."

I paused, breathed, stared down past the sail at the bow far below. Should I fall, my bones would surely be shattered on the deck. Hench would have me tossed overboard—still alive or very dead, it mattered not—before Nathaniel knew my father's name and address. Thus, never could he one day tell Papa that yes, in a heedless manner aboard a royal frigate, I had been quickly led to my death.

Nathaniel reached down with two strong sun-browned arms and gripped the sail. I unwrapped one arm from around the spar and reached down. Then, mindful of every roll and lurch of the ship, I leaned my belly over the spar and reached down with my other arm. I tried to grab two handfuls of sail, but the heavy canvas, though no longer as taut as it had been (for the crew below had loosened the lines), was still full of wind and rumbling as it fluttered. I made several attempts before I managed any sort of grip.

"Ready, *haul!*" shouted Nathaniel. The seven topmen hauled up their portions of the sail, laid their canvas neatly over the top of the spar, then pressed their bellies on the fold and reached down for more.

I, however, could barely lift my portion of unbelievably heavy, flapping canvas. Nor had I the slightest notion of doing as they had done: while they hoisted, they leaned back away from the spar—leaned back toward the long windy abyss between us and the deck—so that nothing supported them during that precarious moment but the jouncing footrope and the madly tugging sail.

"Ready, *haul!*" shouted Nathaniel.

I did manage this time to lift my portion of sail an inch or two, though more with Nathaniel's help than with my own strength.

"Ready, *haul!*"

By now I had enough slack sail (drooping between what the other men had hauled) that I did manage to lift a bit of it up onto the spar, and to lay my belly over it.

"Ready, *haul!*"

Thus we brought up, fold by fold, the t'gallant sail, until only the "foot," as Nathaniel called it, remained below the spar, dangling with lines to the deck.

My arms were soon so tired that I wondered if I would be able to hold onto the spar. But their discomfort was nothing compared to the ache in my back from the bending and lifting. I could not fully stand to straighten my back (unless I let go of the spar). Finally, despite the tucking and tightening of the sail that continued on both sides of me, I crouched on the footrope while gripping the spar and thus was able to straighten my back and briefly ease the pain.

"Gaskets!" shouted Nathaniel. The others now wrapped short ropes around the sail atop the spar, holding it in place.

Nathaniel glanced down at me where I crouched and stretched. "Now watch how I fasten this gasket with a loop that I can quickly pull free."

I stood up and, aching a bit less, watched him as he tucked a loop of rope under the gasket coils, with its end sticking out so that he could—as he demonstrated—yank it sideways and pull the loop free. The rope might then be unwrapped from around the sail. "In weather, or at night," he explained, "your gasket has to hold tight, or pull free, as you want it."

In weather? Up here in a storm? At *night?*

Nathaniel helped me to wrap the short rope in front of me around my portion of the sail. He watched as I tucked the loop, then pulled its end—three times—until I knew how to secure my gasket. Thus the London cobbler learned his first nautical knot.

Nathaniel now called down to Hench; Hench roared orders to the crew on deck. The sailors tightened lines and secured them, then neatly coiled the ends of the lines and hung them along both sides of the ship.

But no sooner had the deck crew finished their job than Hench again roared orders: the lines were slackened, and the eight topmen, myself included, pulled free our gaskets and let the sail drop. It rumbled and fluttered and filled anew with wind. As the lines were tightened on deck, I understood that our furling the sail, and then setting the sail, had not been essential to the ship, but rather a lesson for me to learn from. (And if I learned it not, I'd soon be down with my brothers from the dungeon, scrubbing a deck with a slab of stone.)

Setting sail was a far easier job than furling sail; the canvas simply dropped into place. Nathaniel showed me how to bundle and tie my gasket rope, so that it hung down the back of the spar without getting tangled in any of the other ropes.

Then he called to our fellow topmen, "Lay down to deck!"

My counterpart called out, "Laying off starboard." He stepped from his footrope to the ladder. I understood with immeasurable relief that we were done with the sail and under orders to climb down the to the deck.

"Laying off larboard!" I called. Then carefully, cautiously, incrementally, I reached with one hand, and then one foot, for the ladder. I shifted my weight from the footrope to a ratlin', brought my other hand to the ladder, managed to find a foothold for my other foot. Once on the ladder, I closed my eyes and said a short vehement prayer, "*Thank you.*"

Down we climbed, the eight of us together. Most of the men scampered past me when we reached the broader middle ladder, though all gave me a nod of greeting, and several complimented me, "Well done, lad."

Nathaniel climbed down the bottommost ratlin's beside me, then he swung deftly to the deck.

I climbed awkwardly down from the ladder to the wall, then to the rolling deck . . . and savored how good that flat sun-warmed deck felt beneath my bare feet. Never had the cobblestones of London felt so steady and reassuring.

Nathaniel led me to an upright barrel lashed to a post near the ship's brass bell. He dipped a battered tin cup through the open top of the "scuttlebutt," then we savored, passing the cup back and forth, several draughts of oak-flavored water.

"You'll do all right," he said, his blue eyes sparkling with approval.

"I most heartily thank you," I replied.

He glanced around the deck and spotted Hench. Then he led me in the opposite direction, to the side of the ship where the lines from our sail were tied and coiled.

We now began our second lesson as I struggled to learn the name and job of each line as it rose from its "belaying pin," then disappeared into the web of lines above us: fore t'gallant clewline, fore t'gallant inner buntline, fore t'gallant outer buntline, then we jumped over several other coils and lines to the fore t'gallant halyard, a much heavier line. Should I be on deck, explained Nathaniel, whenever orders were called to ease, trim, or furl a sail, I must jump to exactly the right line and know beforehand what orders I was awaiting.

Every sail on the frigate had its twin sets of lines, larboard and starboard. So, with another glance toward Hench, we crossed the rolling deck and now followed upward with our eyes the starboard buntlines and clewline, though once again they quickly evaded me as they intermingled with other lines and then disappeared into a pulley: which line it was that emerged from that pulley, and leading where and to what, I could not follow, although Nathaniel pointed and explained most precisely.

I began to believe, with Nathaniel as my teacher, that I might survive the voyage to Boston. And thus manage to find the first American vessel home.

ॐ

Chapter Four

The apprentice cobbler became an apprentice seaman. At any time day or night, Hench might shout down the hatch, "Foretopmen aloft to furl the t'gallant!" I'd jolt awake in my hammock, swing my feet out and grab my blue jacket. I'd hasten with my mates up two companionway ladders, step lively across the deck to the windward side, leap upon the gunnel, swing onto the shrouds and scurry up the ratlin's. As we neared the fighting top, I'd scorn the lubber's hole and instead follow Nathaniel up the futtock shrouds.

I hurried up the topmast shrouds on my increasingly leather-soled feet, continued without a pause up the t'gallant shrouds to our yard. With careful efficiency, we'd layout along the footrope. Nathaniel led me to the very end of the spar, where he stood on his own small separate footrope, called a "Flemish horse." I stood beside him, with two men between me and the mast. From asleep in our hammocks to alert at our stations, I doubt we used even two full minutes.

Our job was to furl the angrily flapping t'gallant while we kept an eye on storm clouds approaching. I had not been long aboard the *Lively* before I could guess whether rain or wind or both blew toward us, and how long we had before the first wet blast made furling the huge sail an almost impossible task.

Fair weather brought the call from Hench, "Trim and make sail!" Up we climbed to our yard, where we cast off the gaskets. I grew to love the sound of unfurling sails: they flapped until they grew taut, full-bellied, their silence a signal that they had caught the wind and put it fairly to work.

By watching other men in the rigging—on the fore topsail yard below us, or on the yards of the mainmast aft of us—I began to recognize a well-furled sail, or a flapping clew that would unfailingly bring a barrage of curses from the bosun up to the seamen who must immediately fix it.

From our perch on the t'gallant yard, Nathaniel pointed down toward the bow and taught me the settings of the fore-and-aft sails rigged between the bowsprit and our foremast: the fore staysail, the outer jib, and the flying jib. All three reached as far forward as they could to catch every bit of wind.

Then, pointing down aft of our yard, he taught me the settings of the three triangular staysails rigged between our foremast and the mainmast. They caught the wind that passed between the two masts.

And so the sails continued, from bowsprit to spanker boom, from the fore course to the stargrazer, catching every puff of wind.

While walking the deck, while climbing the rigging, and while swinging and sweeping with the other lads high above the sea, I studied the path of every line (not rope, mind you, but line) as it rose from cleat or belaying pin on deck, passed through blocks of a dozen kinds (themselves attached to another set of lines), then angled upward to earing cringles and clew garnets. To reef tackle on the topsail. To bowline cringles. My eyes learned to follow skyward every line belonging to the foremast, the mainmast, and the mizzenmast. (The latter rose from the officers' quarterdeck; I could not stand at its base as I could the other two.)

On deck, I learned the work of sheets and braces in trimming the sails (pulling the sails to an angle that best caught the wind). I learned the work of halyards to hoist or lower the yards.

And of course, I learned from my mates a half-dozen knots and where to tie them, some to hold for but a moment, staying a halyard until it was secured; some to fasten two lengths of line together; some to keep the end of a line from running through a block; and some merely to serve as intricate decoration in a round mat on the table where a man set his rum cup.

Nathaniel and I and our fellow topmen served watch together, four hours of duty, in one of three shifts. We served our four hours aloft in the rigging, or, if the sails were trimmed and the wind steady, we served on deck at any of a dozen chores: we spliced lines together, chipped rust off an anchor chain, caulked the deck with oakum and tar, and tarred the shrouds. We might separate from each other fore and aft with our tasks, but whenever Hench bellowed at us, we jumped as one and set to our new duties before he had cause for one word of complaint.

Our watch was followed by eight hours of rest, asleep in our hammocks (by day or night), or at the table with our messmates. Best of all, Nathaniel and I would stow ourselves in whatever nook we could find (often we sat hidden between cannons on the gun deck), where a few minutes were ours to mend a button and swap thoughts on the day's events.

The ship's bell, mounted on the weather deck where those in the rigging as well as those below could hear it, rang out the half hours, up to eight bells for a four-hour watch.

Three bells might mean to a man slung in his hammock below decks that he had another four bells of slumber before a hasty meal and then his watch.

On the other hand, three bells might mean to a man aloft in the rigging, soaked in a driving rain as he struggled with bruised fingers to shorten sail, that he had another five bells until the eternally distant eight. Until then, he would shift his sore feet back and forth on the wet footrope, hunch his sore ribs over the yard that punched him in the chest with every pounding wave, and squint his eyes warily at the end of the line he was supposed to grab while it flailed and lashed like a berserk bullwhip. He would shout over the howl of the wind and the wail of the rigging, as he relayed orders down the yard to the next man. And the next man, who but a short time ago had been a tinker, a tailor, a silversmith, and who prays in English, Dutch, Polish, or Senegalese to his long-remiss god, shouts back with his own particular curse that he *is* trying to "layout cheerily," be it a bit difficult in the mouth of a gale.

During the first week especially, I sorely longed for my mother's porridges and puddings. At the table in the berthing deck with our fellow topmen, Nathaniel and I picked our way through "bargemen in the biscuits," as we called the dead weevils that journeyed as stowaways in our hardtack bread. We picked our way as well through bowls of burgoo, an oatmeal gruel in which the weevils were served boiled. We dined on pea soup, made from dried peas; followed by pea soup, made from dried peas; followed by pea soup, made from dried peas. Most of the lads liked pea soup, because the weevils did not. We also feasted on salt horse, as we called the salted beef, and a poor tired bony horse at that, often simmering in a stew called lobscouse, where it swam about with potatoes, onions, and more dried peas.

We relished a certain notorious pudding that resembled no pudding any man on board had ever known. But neither could we ascertain what it might otherwise be, so we termed it "Jenny Prine's Pudding" after a poor child who had been murdered some half-century ago, and whose grave was robbed the day after her funeral (some say by medical students, while others affirm the macabre deed was done by cooks in the service of His Majesty's navy).

We washed down these fine meals with a gallon of beer a day, and a gill of watered rum. The lad from London, who had never touched anything more than a cup of Mama's Ceylon tea, grew most fond of his daily swig of spirits from Jamaica.

Nathaniel and I occasionally consoled each other with a heartfelt declaration shared by our messmates: after swallowing down a salted cod that seemed to have died a dozen deaths, we lads of the foremast t'gallant, gathered around our dark, dank and crowded table, a deck below the cannons, two decks below fresh air and sunshine, would hoist our battered mugs of beer and roar our allegiance to each other:

> "A messmate before a shipmate,
> a shipmate before a stranger,
> a stranger before a dog,
> and a dog before a soldier!"

Thus we topmen declared our eminent superiority to all those lesser mortals aboard the *Lively*, especially the rabble and layabouts who never left the decks, and who thus never knew the gallant freedom in our world aloft.

8○

Chapter Five

Now I must turn our attention to the most powerful personage on board, and to the purpose of pressing every strip of sail most efficiently to the wind, so that the *Lively* might reach Boston as soon as possible.

General Thomas Gage, commander in chief of all British forces in North America, was now returning from a visit to London, where he had spoken in person with His Majesty King George III. For nine years, from 1765 to 1774, the thirteen American colonies had insulted the King with their defiance. General Gage had orders to put an end to any further rebellion. The colonials were to submit to the sacrosanct authority of Parliament and Crown.

Married to an American wife named Margaret Kemble, and more familiar from his seventeen years in the New World with American politics, American trade, and the American coastline than most native-born Americans, General Gage would take a stern and knowing hand to His Majesty's American children.

In particular, he would punish the Bostonians. Four regiments of British troops were now aboard transport ships making the same 3,000-mile voyage across the Atlantic to the port of Boston. These professional soldiers would close the port until the rebels paid for the tea they had dumped into the harbor. Further, the port would remain closed until the rebels, chastened by the firm but merciful hand of their King, swore allegiance to the Crown, the Parliament, and to their Mother Country.

This much I had learned from my messmates. We did not, however, see General Gage himself until our fifth day at sea. Following eight bells that morning, Nathaniel and I had just started up the rigging when a stir on the quarterdeck drew our eyes toward the stern. "Gage," whispered Nathaniel. And there he was, unmistakable in the finery of his red uniform, gold epaulettes and shiny gold gorget. He inspected a small swivel gun atop the larboard quarterdeck gunnel. The ship's officers gathered stiffly around him. For before them stood the commander in chief who would bring America to her knees.

Nathaniel and I paused in the ratlin's to watch. (Hench must have been watching as well, or he would surely have cursed us and sent us aloft.) General Gage crossed the quarterdeck to inspect the starboard swivel gun. He was making certain, no doubt, that should any American warship meet him on the high seas with the intention of curtailing his mission, he could quickly acquaint the rogues with a bit of His Majesty's grapeshot.

"Perhaps," I observed to Nathaniel, "he's walking on worn shoe leather, as my father would say."

Puzzled, Nathaniel replied, "He probably wears the finest boots aboard this ship."

"Not quite," I said, knowing well the quality of the boots that Hench now wore.

But then I explained, "General Gage, acting on the King's orders and in the King's name, sails westward on a ship crewed by shopkeepers, farmers and thieves. In a crew of a hundred and sixty, at least half have been impressed from the streets of London. Many of the lads have come straight from prison, and glad they are for a breath of fresh air. Fully a fourth of our crew have never been to sea before, never tied a sheepshank, never trimmed a jib. We've got men at the halyards who don't speak a word of the King's English, and boys so young that we have to lift them up to their hammocks. The carpenter's a Dutchman, the steward's a Dane, and the surgeon's a drunk." General Gage now inspected the compass in its binnacle. "If that's the best our King can do, then he's walking on worn shoe leather, and any sharp pebble on American soil is going to be felt."

"Never mind," whispered Nathaniel with a laugh. Turning from the quarterdeck, he stared instead at the sea beyond the bow, his blue eyes bright with expectation. "Benjamin York shall soon be aboard the first frigate headed home, back to the arms of his faithful Elspeth. And Nathaniel Ash shall be reefing the skirts," he grinned with delight, "of his Boston beauty."

Then up we climbed, and bruised and wrenched our fingers through another watch, while we dreamed of the soft curls we would one day touch, and of a rosy cheek, a gentle hand.

Thus occupied, we left the royalty and rebels to their bickering.

☙

Chapter Six

We were about three weeks out from London when the worst storm of the voyage struck our vessel.

Awakened in our hammocks during the early morning hours, we knew the weather was turning foul: the ship rolled more heavily and pounded into the troughs, swinging and jouncing us. Nearby in the darkness, someone was retching into a bucket.

At six bells, we topmen swung our feet down to the heaving deck, with half an hour to struggle through a rolling breakfast, then half an hour to spend on the fo'c'sle, inspecting the sea and sky while we waited to use the head.

One by one we stepped over the prow's bulwarks, then climbed down into the head: a walled-in, V-shaped chamber forward of the hull and below the bowsprit, where four seats with open holes let us drop our loads into the sea with some degree of comfort and no degree of privacy, while the waves, especially in heavy weather, splashed up and washed the seats and those sitting upon them quite clean. Better, at least, we cobblers and tinkers and chandlers consoled each other, than using a bucket in some dark airless corner of the berthing deck.

On the morning of which I speak, the bow rose and plunged so heavily that the first lads to use the head soon cried out for their lives. When they climbed back over the bulwarks, their trousers and half their shirts were soaked with sea water. The four holes had spewed like fountains: a man in the midst of his business had to grip the seat with all his might. Their tribulation brought a somberness to our assembled visages. One by one we undressed, then we stepped as naked as Adam, or four Adams, over the bulwarks and into the head. We both relieved ourselves and bathed, some with a yelp of fright, some with a hearty laugh.

We returned to the fo'c'sle feeling most refreshed.

Nathaniel kept a weather eye on the darkening sky ahead of us and to the south. He looked up at our t'gallant, rumbling—as all the sails now rumbled—in gusts that shook the frigate from above as the waves shook it from below. "They ought to be furling," he said, loud enough for all of us topmen, and Hench, to hear. "They ought to have furled an hour ago."

No blame on Hench it was, for he stood his watch the same as us, and had no right to tell another bosun's mate how to perform his job. And with seven bells already rung, better to let fresh lads wrestle with a monster of flapping canvas, than to ask lads tired and cold since four in the morning to labor at such a job.

Still, as Nathaniel had said, the officer on watch should have furled that t'gallant, and several other sails, an hour ago. Aye, better a messmate than a shipmate.

When the brass bell clanged eight times, we started up the ratlin's. With every heave of the ship, the ladder slackened, then snapped taut; by tightly gripping the heavy shrouds, I could just manage to hang on. Though the other lads climbed up quickly past the thundering sails, Nathaniel climbed slowly just above me. When finally we reached the fighting top, I struggled up through the lubber's hole.

We heard Hench roaring orders to the crew on the foreyard: they were not to reef, but to furl. We heard him shout to the men laying out along the fore-topsail yard: they were not to reef any further, but to furl. Then he roared to us topmen as we struggled up the t'gallant shrouds: we of course were to furl. Since the entire foremast was to furl, we understood that real weather was coming.

I had reached halfway up the t'gallant shrouds. The mast swung so wildly that I could only hug the swinging, jolting, twisting ladder to my chest and hang on.

"Come along, Ben!" shouted Nathaniel above me. "Wait for the trough, then take the next step." He meant the thump of the bow into the trough; then we had a second or two while the bow rose smoothly up again.

"York!" I heard from below. Hench had spotted me. "Lay out and furl, you motherless bastard, or you'll feel the knot!"

"Up with you, Ben!" shouted Nathaniel. "The lads have taken the outermost. You'll stand between me and the mast."

Drawn by Nathaniel, driven by Hench, I worked my way upward. Rocking forward, then rocking steeply back in great shuddering sweeps across the blackened sky, I crawled from ratlin' to ratlin'. I staring at each hand, each foot, as I moved it up a step. Shouts from above and orders from below were lost in the rising roar of a storm that was all but upon us. Glancing over my shoulder, I saw white churning waves beneath a black churning sky. Cold pellets of rain stung my cheeks. I turned my face away from the wind.

I knew what was next: the wind would rip open the t'gallant, tear it to shreds, then lash me with a snap of thundering canvas. Lash the skin from my face, and me from the rigging.

I fought another step upward. One of the topmen, Michael, called down, half encouragement, half curse. The t'gallant rumbled like a monster in a rage. A hand gripped my collar, Nathaniel's, tugging me upward. I stared at his wet bare feet on the footrope, inches from my face. Another step, another, then I stared at his snapping white trousers. I hauled myself up another ratlin', until I stared at the yard itself.

"We need you, Benjamin," shouted Nathaniel, his mouth to my ear. "I'm sorry, but we need you now."

"Laying out larboard," I called weakly. Driving rain stung my face. I had to squint in the darkness as I reached one foot from the ladder to the footrope slung beneath the jouncing yard. Hugging the yard as it heaved and thumped, I slid my feet along the rope and slowly inched out from the mast.

Each man stared down at the shuddering, thundering, snapping sail beneath us. We must either furl the t'gallant to its last square foot, or relinquish it, perhaps with the mast, to the blast of battering wind.

Hench . . . we no longer heard Hench. Wind shrieked like banshees in the rigging. The sail cracked and roared. But we had no need for Hench. Two of the lads, Adam and Hank, had once sailed to Halifax in a North Atlantic gale. As long as the crew on deck could steady the braces and hoist the clews, we topmen could gather, bit by thrashing bit, the furious demon beneath us.

The monster had its own tricks. As did the wind. They fought and brawled like two cats in an alley. The wind jumped from one side to the other, snapping the sail with a crazed ferocity.

I was reaching down with both arms for another handful of canvas, when the yard suddenly jumped and thumped me in the jaw.

I stared down dully, my arms wrapped over the yard but otherwise dangling. Scarlet strings trailed down the gray thrashing sail. I had no idea the blood was mine.

Nathaniel wrapped his arm behind me, squeezed me firmly against the yard. He shouted into my ear, like an angel delivering an annunciation amid the furies of hell, "*Elspeth*, Benjamin! *Elspeth*, Benjamin! *Elspeth!*"

I kept to my feet. My legs did not crumble. My dangling arms somehow gripped the monster's spine.

But we were not working. We gave our work to other men. Adam and Michael shifted toward us, two men working where four should have been. Reaching down with hands that grabbed and clutched and hoisted, they managed to gather sail, to hold it beneath their bellies, so that a smaller and smaller t'gallant thrashed beneath us.

At last the monster succumbed: bound by gaskets, imprisoned within its own folds, it thundered no more. Despite the unrelenting scream of the wind in the rigging, the sail's welcome silence eased our beating hearts.

With both sails furled below us on the foremast, and all sails furled behind us on the mainmast and mizzenmast, a lone triangular jib on the bowsprit pulled the entire frigate. The ship rode easier, shuddered less, though her bare poles still raked the sky.

A bosun's whistle called up to us: we could go down now.

Nathaniel asked me, "Can you step to the ratlin's?"

"Aye," I nodded, dripping blood on the furled sail. I felt his grip loosen slightly as I shifted my arms, shifted my feet. Ethan, from the starboard spar, had crossed over to help. I grabbed hold of a shroud, reached one foot to a ratlin'. With Ethan bracing me, I managed to step onto the tiny swiveling ladder.

The shrouds did not slacken and snap as much as when the mast had carried sail. Watching my feet, my hands, my feet, I climbed downward, downward. Ethan scrambled down past me, then stayed just below me, guiding my feet with his hand when I seemed at a loss.

Nathaniel climbed down beside me. When we reached the fighting top, I leaned against the mast and rested. The lads all said a kind word to me as they headed down, never mind they'd done my work.

I eased myself down through the lubber's hole. Nathaniel beside me, Ethan still below me, we made our way down the lower shrouds, as steady as bedrock compared with the rigging above. I set my foot on the gunnel. Ethan stood ready to brace me, or to catch me. I swung awkwardly down to the deck, the pitching, yawing deck, where I tumbled in a wet exhausted heap, unable to keep my feet beneath me.

"York!" I heard Hench roar at me. My blurry eyes stared at the black toes of the boots my father had made. "For dereliction on your watch, you shall be flogged."

I heard Nathaniel shouting words of protest. One of those black boots backed away, swung forward and struck me in the head.

No angel this time kept me from letting go my grip.

☙

Chapter Seven

I awoke, drenched in cold rain on the weather deck. Lying on my back, I was rolling steeply from shoulder to shoulder as the hard deck tossed beneath me. I struggled to sit up and discovered that my feet were shackled in irons. I was a prisoner, serving punishment for dereliction on my watch.

Raising a cold hand to my face, I felt my aching jaw: it was swollen and horridly sore from its blow by the yard, but not broken.

The side of my head was scraped. I remembered Hench's boot.

Looking fore and aft through heavy rain that swept across the ship, I saw the deck was deserted by all but myself. Searching further astern, I spotted three misty figures at the wheel on the quarterdeck. Not a man up in the rigging. I had been left alone in irons, just abaft the mainmast, to face the storm unprotected and alone.

There I lay through the long wet day, unfed, with naught to drink but what I could lick from the planks of the deck. Seamen in oilskins occasionally appeared from the hatch. They went about their duties, drawing taut a slackened line, lashing fast a flailing block, with nary a greeting. One of my messmates did manage, while making his way across the deck toward the head, to hand me from his shirt two hardtacks and a cold potato. I devoured the potato, then took tearing bites from the rain-dampened hardtack.

When Hank returned from the head, I asked, "Where is Nathaniel?"

He whispered harshly through the rain, "In irons below."

"In irons!" I exclaimed, outraged.

But Hank hurried to the companionway and disappeared. Perhaps Hench was somewhere watching.

The food brought a degree of strength to my limbs, and clarity to my thoughts . . . and anger to my heart. I burned with a growing rage, a rage that far exceeded the anger I had felt during that first horrid night in the dungeon. To put me in irons . . . Well, I had managed to climb down from the t'gallant alive. A small indignity hardly mattered.

But to put Nathaniel in irons! The man whose arm like an angel's wing had wrapped around me.

Was it Hench alone who had ordered this punishment? Or—my mind by tentative increments began to reach further—were there other officers involved? Perhaps General Gage himself, determined to reach Boston with all possible haste, had ordered our shackles.

Were there no limits to what the officers of this frigate, disregarding every sense of justice, were able to do to the crew?

Were there no limits to what His Majesty could do with the men he caught on the streets of London?

Never before in my cobbler's life had I asked such questions.

But now, imagining Nathaniel down in the black stinking dungeon, tossing on the filthy deck as a shackled captive, I wondered what sort of King, and Parliament, and aristocracy of naval officers they were who could treat in such a foul and despicable manner a man as kind and cheerful and brave as Nathaniel.

As dusk darkened into night, the rain diminished to a drizzle.

Some hours later, a cold wind from the north blew across the deck. Dark figures climbed the shrouds to set the fore- and main-topsails. At the eight bells of midnight, I spotted the first star to appear, winking as the mizzenmast swung back and forth across it.

Shivering horribly, clenching my teeth to keep them from chattering, I thought I would surely freeze before morning. Perhaps only my anger kept me alive.

Though I knew it not at the time, while I tossed unceasingly and shivered through that long frigid night, the rage in my young heart etched itself into my soul.

Shortly after seven bells the next morning, I heard a drummer beat a repeated cadence on the quarterdeck. Sitting up slowly, for I could barely move, I looked toward the stern. I was blinded by the yellow sun blazing just above the taffrail.

As my eyes adjusted to the glare, I saw the usual rank of red-coated marines standing shoulder to shoulder athwart the ship, just in front of the steps to the quarterdeck. Each marine held a bayonetted musket while standing at attention. But this morning, each marine was staring at me.

Behind the marines and several feet above them, a large group of officers was gathered on the quarterdeck, naval officers in blue and marine officers in red. Searching further, I spotted General Gage, standing, as always, near a small cannon.

Looking around me, I saw a great number of blue-jackets—most of the crew—assembled along the larboard gunnel, all the way forward to the bow. Turning my head slowly to look toward the other side of the ship . . . my eyes fastened upon a man, Nathaniel, with the wrists of his outstretched arms tied to the mainmast shrouds, He wore no shirt, clearly in preparation for a flogging. His head drooped forward. He seemed barely able to stand. "Nathaniel!" I called. He showed no response.

Four marines came to fetch me. They unfastened the shackles, drew me up to my feet, then marched me on legs that hardly held me to the larboard shrouds, opposite Nathaniel. We now stood back to back, the empty deck between us. I suffered no fear, nor any renewed outrage. Rather, as the marines pulled off my sodden jacket and shirt, then tied my wrists to the shrouds, I gloated.

Whip me with your lash. Tear the skin off my back with your cat-o'-nine-tails. Do the same to my brother Nathaniel. So do you sink in your foul offense as the Devil's minions. As the Devil's kin. And so do we two rise up in a bond of loyalty that no bastard officer can touch.

My heart grew in that moment. If I could have spared Nathaniel's back by taking twice the punishment upon my own, I would gladly have done so.

I stared out between the ratlin's at the roughly rolling sea. Gray waves rose up to catch the light of the sun. I felt an exultation that comes only from a flow of boundless love.

When the first lash suddenly struck, pain etched deep into my back. I glared over my shoulder at my assailant: Petty Officer Hench, who regarded me with unfettered hatred.

A sharp word came from an officer on the quarterdeck. Hench backed away.

I heard a reading of some military regulation, which I scorned to follow.

A roll of the drum. The sound of Hench's boots crossing the deck to Nathaniel. The ugly sound of the lash.

"Be strong, Nathaniel!" I called over my shoulder. "Be strong!"

Hench's boots thumped across the deck . . . and then I tensed and staggered at the blow of the lash, twice as fierce as before.

Ah, that lash was sweet at it burned across my back. It wove a bond of blood between myself and the man now moaning behind me.

Back and forth strode Hench, as if across a stage upon which both officers and seamen could watch him: the first, as he no doubt hoped, with admiration and envy; and the latter with terror, for they witnessed what awaited them, should they shirk their duty.

Neither Nathaniel nor I gave Hench much satisfaction. Nathaniel, though groaning with dull anguish, was too senseless to cry out. And I, though my back was scorched by the flames of hell, no more than gave a muffled gasp.

The cry I waited for—the prolonged scream that would rend the night and awaken the dead from their graves—would be Hench's. *That*, I vowed to Nathaniel in my soul, I would one day accomplish in a feast of revenge.

Our messmates later told us that we took twenty blows apiece. I had, at the time, no awareness of how long I stood, and then slumped, dangling from my wrists.

Unbound from the shrouds, we were dragged across the deck and lowered down a ladder. Dragged and lowered down a second ladder. Down a third ladder, where we were dumped on the orlop deck. Face down in the stinking darkness beside Nathaniel, I knew we were back in the dungeon.

With the last of my strength, I lifted my cold hand and laid it over Nathaniel's. My fingers dug between his fingers.

Then, out of the rain, out of the cold, with a seed of hatred planted in my breast, I slept.

છ

Chapter Eight

A swabbing of vinegar on our backs twice a day was all the medication the ship's surgeon would afford us. Though my wounds burned anew with each treatment, as if red coals were sowed in furrows across my back, I knew, as the pain eased slightly day by day, that I must be healing.

We were not, I discovered, in the dungeon, but in the same forward hold that had once been the dungeon. The dank, fetid, airless room, lit by a single whale oil lamp, was now the frigate's sick bay, its floor covered with rotting straw, its plank beds occupied by a dozen men. One lad suffered from a broken leg, another from horrid cramps in the lower belly. There were several cases of the dreaded ship's fever. An ancient one-legged gunner, who had often boasted that a French cannonball took him at the knee during a battle in the West Indies, now suffered from an oozing rash climbing from his foot up the other leg.

Nathaniel had been laid in the damp straw beside a man sweating with wide-eyed convulsions. Gently, I shifted Nathaniel onto my thin pallet of straw, then I lay upon his. I now listened to Nathaniel moaning in his sleep to one side of me, and the rattle of death on the other.

Like a beast, our pain clawed us every time we moved. We lay just above sloshing putrid water in the bilge, and on the same deck with the penned hogs. The sick bay, located in the bow, took a constant beating from the sea. Our beds dropped and banged and shook with every trough. Water thumped and washed above us, water seeped down the inner hull. The straw was forever damp.

Get well or die. Such was the medical code of His Majesty's navy.

Without portholes in the orlop, we knew no day or night. Though I sometimes heard the muffled clang of three bells, or seven bells, I never knew what they meant. Our messmates were forbidden by Hench to visit us. They were thus unable to bring us food and fresh water. Or news from topside.

Every few hours, I awoke Nathaniel to give him his bowl of broth and cup of tea. He said little. His eyes stared from depths of fear, like the eyes of a badly beaten child. He was so weak that I had to help him hold the bowl, hold the cup.

I had a new duty now. I knew that if I lived long enough to walk the fo'c'sle again, to lift my face to the sunshine, to breathe the fresh sea air, then Nathaniel would live.

But if I died, he too would soon be wrapped in a shroud of torn, worn-out sail, with a cannonball at his feet, then dropped over a gunnel into the sea.

So for Nathaniel, I lived.

After a week's time (our messmates counted the days), four red-coated marines, choking and coughing through the rags they held over their mouths, climbed down the ladder into the hold. They stepped carefully over men who sprawled on the straw, as if they would not soil their white trousers by touching anything so foul. I stared up at faces neither pale nor gaunt. The four marines were real living men who had decended to the underworld of the dead.

Two of them lifted me, and two of them lifted Nathaniel, up to our feet. His head drooped forward, his mouth hung open, his eyes were closed; he did not respond to their rough shaking and curses. Desperate that they might drop him back to the floor, I called his name over and over, gently but firmly—"Nathaniel! Nathaniel!"—until finally my voice reached into the gloom of his soul. Lifting his head, he looked at me, haggard, broken, but alive.

The marines had to lift us up the steps of the ladder. Up another set of steps. And then . . . I stared up at sunshine pouring down the hatch. The marines lifted us, though my feet were working now, up the last ladder to the fo'c'sle, where they lowered us to our knees. I braced Nathaniel, helped him to sit. He leaned against me. We stared at the life around us.

At eight bells, our messmates came down the rigging and greeted us with a hearty welcome. After a quick trip below, Adam gave us each a cold potato. I bit into mine, gnawed at it until it was gone. Nathaniel simply held the potato in his pale hand.

The sunshine, more than anything else, brought life back into my blood.

But it was those faces crowded around us, Ethan and Hank and Adam, Michael and Eb and Sir Garth (as we called him), that brought back life into Nathaniel's blood. His slack face quickened, his blue eyes brightened. He reached up his hand to take the many hands offered to him.

Never have I forgotten those six men who helped Nathaniel to stand once again on his feet, and to walk the rolling deck. Two have stayed with me through a lifetime of friendship. Two were snatched by the war. And two have vanished, their fates unknown to me. But toward all six, I hold a golden treasure of gratitude in my heart.

We stood no watch that day, though Nathaniel and I took our meals with the lads. Hench had ordered two other men into the rigging in our stead. We saw the brute on deck, but he never deigned to meet our eyes. He treated us as if we should be dead.

On the third day after our return to the weather deck, a lieutenant ordered us both back to work, though not up in the rigging. Instead, Nathaniel and I joined a surly gang of men who toiled on the fo'c'sle at repairing sails and clews and reef points. This new employment suited me well, for the sailmaker's tools fit easily into my cobbler's hands. I learned the use of several types of marline-spikes (iron pins over a foot long) as I opened and separated the strands of a rope I was splicing. I grew adept at the pricker (a shorter pin with a wooden handle) which we used to make holes through the sailcloth. Soon I could run a roping needle along its course more quickly—and neatly—than any other man in our gang.

Nathaniel and I were at first not given a palm leather, which the other men wore to protect their hands. It served as well as a rawhide thimble when forcing a needle through the heavy cloth. Our congenial mates seemed to be waiting, during our first days of work, to see whether Nathaniel and I would live or die. When we did not die, a Scotsman named Broyle reached into a canvas sack and handed me two palm leathers. At my word of thanks, he merely nodded.

I learned the sail tailor's trade by watching Broyle. Then I became a teacher to Nathaniel. With dogged determination, he learned to make an awkward stitch. I took the long seams, while he strengthened the corners.

We gained back our strength, until we too could howl in protest at another bowl of Jenny Prine's Pudding. The lads told us they were watching now, while aloft, for the first sight of land. When we reached Boston, surely our fortunes must improve.

I tried to jest with Nathaniel about his Boston beauty. I reminded him of his promise to help me find an American ship bound for London. But his smiles came no longer from his once jovial heart. Rather, his brief glances conveyed a momentary brightness in which he himself had no faith. Whatever it was that dwelled deep within him, he wished to hide it from even me.

We sewed our sails together, ate our weevils together, bedded face down on the deck together, climbed over the bulwarks to the head together, and stared out at the sea together, with the unspoken friendship and loyalty and absolute devotion of—though I did not yet know it—two soldiers surviving together through a war.

꿍

Chapter Nine

With four hours on watch and eight hours off, and our duties with the roping needle steady but uncumbersome, Nathaniel and I had a good amount of time to gaze over the frigate's gunnel at the sea and sky.

I had never before seen the ocean, nor even the mouth of the Thames. And though I had occasionally delivered a pair of boots to a customer dwelling on Hampstead Heath, northwest of London, where I could look up at more of the hazy sky than I could see from the lanes and parks of the city, never before—never once—had I watched the sun as it rose in a blaze of scarlet.

Never before had I watched rolling gray waves as they caught the sun's fiery gold. Never had I basked for peaceful hours in the sun's morning warmth while I did my work. Never had I watched the sun's full and stately arch across the entire southern sky.

Never before had I considered the sun as my daily companion.

I had never before admired the great diversity of clouds: their flat bottoms, their towering billows, their shades of gray and white. Nor had I ever admired a cloudless sky: a pure, deep, and unblemished blue over the entire dome of heaven.

And certainly, never in my brick-and-cobblestone lifetime had I stared so fascinated, so delighted, and so entranced, evening after evening, at the sunsets beyond our bow. Some were yellow-pink as the sun melted into a mist over the sea. Some were muted maroon as the sun delved into a bank of heavy clouds. And one was so magnificent—rippling clouds of brilliant red covered half the sky—that even the old salts came up on deck to watch: in the midst of all that fire, the huge red-gold sun hovered, triumphant and beckoning, over the still-unseen New World.

Despite all I had suffered, I came to feel grateful that I had been snatched from my tiny walled-in shop. I had been shown, at least this once in my life, how much there was on God's great earth that could make a man's heart rejoice.

Yes, and more. I discovered aboard the *Lively* that never before had I known the night. One of the older sailors, from Plymouth, encouraged by my curiosity, pointed out Polaris, the north star. I marveled at its steadiness, directly to starboard and halfway up the sky, while the other stars wheeled up from the sea behind us, coursed through the rigging above us, and disappeared into the sea ahead of us.

Nathaniel's favorite heavenly light was the ever-changing moon. One clear evening—early in the voyage this was—while we were climbing the rigging, a full moon, pale yellow, floated just above the sea off our stern. The day had been blustery, but now the wind was settling; we were to spread our t'gallant to the night breeze. We took our places along the yard, loosened the gaskets and let the sail drop. With a full moon astern, our t'gallant became a billowing bag of light.

As the moon arched across the southern sky, determined to catch up with our frigate and surpass it, the shadow of our foremast swung across the moonlit deck. Nathaniel, standing at the yardarm, pointed toward the sea opposite the moon. There lay the dark shadow of our mast and its three sails upon the moon-silvered sea.

As the moon rose higher, those three black rectangles crept ever closer to the ship. At seven bells, the moon was so high overhead that we could see our own shadows: eight dark spikes above the t'gallant shadow, not quite as tall as the spike of the mast. Like a row of carefree boys, we waved, and roared with mirth when our row of shadows rolling on the sea waved back.

The moon waned on the following nights. The ever-thinning bowl turned itself slowly upside down, pouring out what little light it still held. When it vanished from our watch entirely, we topmen stared up from our great height at stars so sharp and bright, we might well have reached up and plucked them until we had filled our pockets.

And then Nathaniel discovered, beyond the bow at dusk, a thin bone-white crescent in the darkening turquoise sky. From our perch aloft, we watched that slender tilted bowl as it dipped into the sea, filled with salt water, and slid gracefully under.

Later that same night, the approaching storm shook us awake in our hammocks. We saw no more of the moon during the wretched week that followed.

One evening during our first week back on deck, the clouds in the low gray sky began to break open. Nathaniel spotted a full-bellied moon: greater than half, but not yet full. It shone so brightly that the clouds around it glowed with a fringe of radiant white.

His uplifted face lit by moonlight, he smiled, "There be the ripe round belly of my Boston beauty."

And so, I thought, I had my Nathaniel back.

Chapter Ten

An increasing number of gulls swooped and glided on their long white wings above our ship, a sure omen that the coastline was near.

General Gage appeared more frequently on the quarterdeck. He stared westward toward the North American continent, still hidden beneath the horizon, where he had served his King for many years, and where he no doubt intended to serve for many years to come.

He would soon take the government of the colony of Massachusetts entirely into his own hands. In doing so, he would frighten the twelve other colonies into obedience to their King. Or such was the plan.

Little did General Gage suspect, as he paced the *Lively's* quarterdeck, how successful he would be in uniting the thirteen wayward colonies in resistance against their King, forever.

And of course he could not know, as he stood in his polished boots beside a small swivel cannon, occasionally raising a brass telescope to his eye, that those rude Bostonians would, in a little over a year, stand up bravely against three British assaults on Breed's Hill. Their courage would send Gage sailing home to London in disgrace.

"Land ho!" cried a topman. Men poured up from below. But from the deck, we could see nothing beyond the bow but the featureless gray edge of the sea.

Nor could we see anything more through the long afternoon. The "land," we decided, had been a cloud sighted by an eager sailor.

The birds, however, were a sure sign. As more gulls gradually gathered into a flock that followed the *Lively*, we knew we must be close.

All hands aloft had been told to look sharp for other ships, and thus a rumor swept our frigate that we might be fired upon by an American privateer as we approached the port of Boston.

That evening, the topmen furled all but the reefed topsails; with so little canvas to the wind, the frigate, creeping slowly forward, would stay clear of the coastline and shoals until daybreak.

That night, our lads aloft in the rigging spotted no lights along the western horizon. But they came down at eight bells, midnight.

At two bells, five o'clock in the morning, Nathaniel and I stood up from our blankets. We hurried up to the weather deck so we could stare westward in the pearly glow of dawn.

A great number of men came up from below, until all three watches were crowded along the gunnels. Topmen stood along every spar, searching westward. On the quarterdeck, officers in red and blue stood near the ship's wheel, staring toward His Majesty's colonial realm. All of us, from captain and general down to deck swabbers and powder monkeys, stared ahead into the gray mist, seeking the first tinge of green, the first hump above the horizon . . . the first sighting of the New World.

The gulls, and now a few terns, circled and swooped in a noisy flock above the *Lively*. The undersides of their long wings caught the rosy glow of the sun rising beyond our stern.

"Land ho!" boomed a voice in the rigging. Barely had we taken our next breath, while staring hard at the horizon ahead, before a voice on the fo'c'sle called, "Land ho!" Others took up the cry. And now I too was able to see, at the very edge of the gray-pink Atlantic, a faint gray-green smudge. I grabbed Nathaniel's arm as I proclaimed, "America!"

He glanced at me, his blue eyes exultant. Then he stared, as we all stared, at the increasingly distinct gray-green hill that stood above the expanse of brightening sea.

Bosun's pipes trilled. "Trim and make sail!" The three masts blossomed with billowing sails in perfect trim. Our frigate leaned with the wind. The splash of water along the hull grew stronger. We felt ourselves coursing as if at full gallop toward a new land, a new beginning, a new life. Though my thoughts all during the voyage had been directed toward returning as soon as possible to London, to my family, and to Elspeth, my heart now pounded with an unanticipated eagerness. I ached with a sudden keen desire to set my foot on the firm earth of the New World. Perhaps I would return with my bride to America, where, in "the land of opportunity," as so many called it, I would seek my fortune as a cobbler.

We spotted more hills; they became increasingly distinct from each other. We pointed toward a distant sloop that paid us no mind as it headed south and vanished.

We gazed at the long unbroken line of the coast, green with trees. (We imagined their lush springtime blossom.)

And now I spotted the tall thin vertical white arrow of a church steeple. There in that church, I promised, I would kneel and thank God that despite all we had suffered, Nathaniel and I had survived.

The remainder of the day was much like a dream. It was so unlike our previous five weeks at sea that, on watch and off, we had to remind ourselves that the land which had revealed itself to us—just beyond our grasp—was truly real.

We spotted a half-dozen white steeples. Now we could see the red brick towers beneath them. Tacking slowly starboard and larboard on a serpentine path through a maze of islands and rocky shoals (our captain was apparently well acquainted with the approach), we entered a harbor busy with small boats. We studied a row of buildings clustered on what appeared to be an island: some of them wooden, some of them brick. All were reminiscent of buildings back home in England.

And now we could see people, Englishmen, working on a long pier that reached far into the harbor.

Yes, *there* was the fabled Boston, seat of the rebellion, home of a crude and unprincipled rabble who thought themselves better than the long-patient citizens of Britain. The Bostonians had forgotten that valiant British troops had fought on their behalf against the French, against the Spanish, against the heathen savages. And now the ungrateful scoundrels refused to pay for the tea which they themselves had dumped into this very harbor.

And yet, as I stared toward that pier with over a dozen vessels moored along it, and at the tiny figures who loaded and unloaded them, I had to admit that no American had ever lashed my back with twenty stripes. No American had stolen me from my home. No American now strutted imperious in my father's fine boots.

୫୬

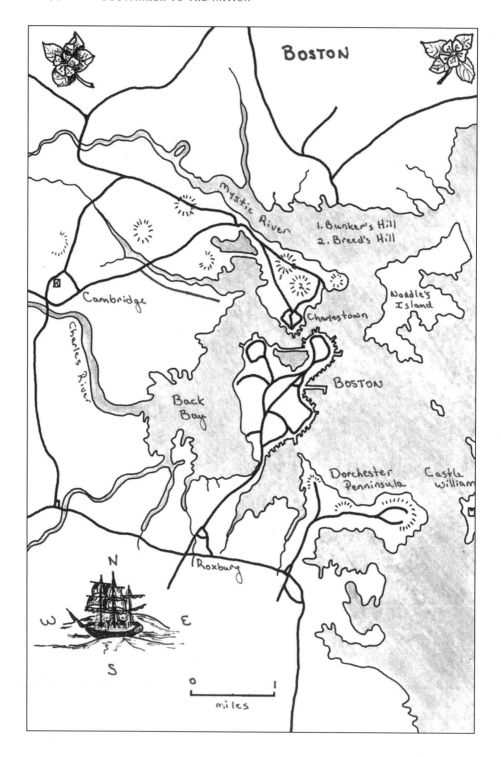

Chapter Eleven

We anchored in a broad, island-filled bay, close enough to Boston that we could see individual shops and warehouses along the wharves: the wharves which General Gage would close on the first of June.

One of the *Lively's* eight-oared cutters was lowered by block and tackle to the water. Then Hench ordered our mess to the oars, Nathaniel and I with them. We climbed down a wooden ladder hanging against the frigate's hull; we stepped, as Hench bellowed at us, not on the cutter's seats but on its bottom; then we took our places, each man at an oar.

General Gage descended the ladder and boarded our craft, the hilt of his sword gleaming in the morning sunshine. He took his seat in the bow, behind our backs as we sat facing the stern and Petty Officer Hench. Now a lieutenant and a corps of marines also boarded. They seated themselves toward the bow, thus forming a heavily armed guard between the General and the lowly crew.

We rowed the cutter across choppy water to an island with two log forts built upon it. (This was Castle William Island, the British headquarters in Boston.) After landing General Gage at the island's dock—where he was received with drums and fifes and a trooping of the guard—we rowed the cutter back through the chop to the frigate, with Hench, the lieutenant and the marines still aboard.

I will add that while I waited in the cutter for my turn to climb the ladder up the *Lively's* hull, I reached over the side and dipped my hand into Boston Harbor. Thus, though I had not yet set foot on the New World, I had baptized my hand in its waters.

That was Friday the thirteenth of May, in the year of our Lord, 1774.

Then, a thing most strange happened. We waited. And we waited. Through four long and dreary days and nights (we caught now and then a whiff of apple blossoms from shore), we waited while General Gage was on Castle William Island, conferring, it was rumored, with Governor Thomas Hutchinson, whom he was soon to replace. Thus a crew of a hundred and sixty men aboard the *Lively*, with no sails to trim and make, no jibs to furl, now idled about the deck and grumbled increasingly as we gazed at the American continent, just beyond our reach.

We felt ourselves to be useless, forgotten, and trapped. Long and hard we had toiled to bring General Gage to his new post. Yet rewarded we were for our labors by naught but an extra ration of watered rum.

On the blustery morning of the seventeenth of May, we rowed the cutter back to Castle William Island, where we fetched General Gage, well-wrapped in a long black cape against the weather. Following orders bellowed from Hench, we rowed with the wet wind in our faces for about two miles to Boston's Long Wharf, jutting several hundred yards into the harbor. Personages of authority had assembled on the pier to greet General Gage. As he climbed a ladder from the cutter up to the pier, cannons fired a volley of salutes back and forth between the *Lively* and batteries on shore.

Accompanied by drums and fifes, General Gage and the distinguished leadership of Boston walked along the pier (between a sparse crowd of silent spectators), then up an adjoining street (King Street, as I later learned), to a dignified red brick building, its white tower capped by a golden cupola. (The State House, the seat of British government on shore.)

Though now so close to the New World that, sitting in my rain-soaked blue jacket, I could touch with my hand a barnacle-encrusted piling of the wharf, we were ordered by Hench, the commander of our little cutter, to row cheerily back to the *Lively*.

Where again we waited, bored, impatient, surly and brooding, beneath the sunny springtime skies of May, for two tedious weeks. We watched as several transport ships arrived, from England and from Halifax, with the four regiments of His Majesty's troops who would enforce the closing of the port. We watched, some in silence and some with curses, as their fleet of cutters rowed the red-coated soldiers to the pier. Those men were able to stretch their legs on solid ground, to eat (as we imagined) fresh bread and fresh meat, and to drink fresh water. And they were able (as we further imagined) to gaze upon the pretty faces of the women on shore. We began to realize, while gnawing our hardtack, guzzling our bilge water, and glancing wearily at each other's grizzled faces, that we might never set foot on land.

Like the sails and spars and blocks, we were mere equipage aboard ship. We might tomorrow be posted to Halifax, without the slightest idea why.

On Wednesday, the first of June, we heard bells tolling throughout the seaport of Boston. Tolling as if for a funeral. Not a single ship departed from the long pier. Nor did we discern any activity on the other, smaller wharves. We saw no carts drawn by horses, no unloading of barrels and crates. Instead, redcoats marched in small units up and down the wharves. Redcoats marched out to the end of the long pier and back. Beneath the mournful tolling of church bells, we could hear, drifting across the harbor, the roll of British drums, the shrill piping of British fifes.

Some of the lads aboard the *Lively* recognized a somber march. The British were playing "The World Turned Upside Down." They were taunting the Bostonians, who now found themselves crushed beneath the military boot.

Boston Harbor was closed to all traffic, including my American frigate back home to London. Nathaniel was no closer to his Boston beauty than he had been on the night of that full-bellied moon.

We waited. We chafed. And we wondered if there was any end to what the British would steal from us.

ℬ

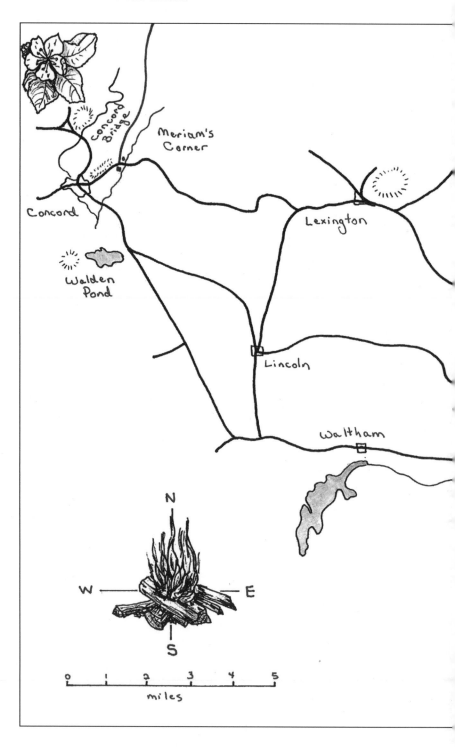

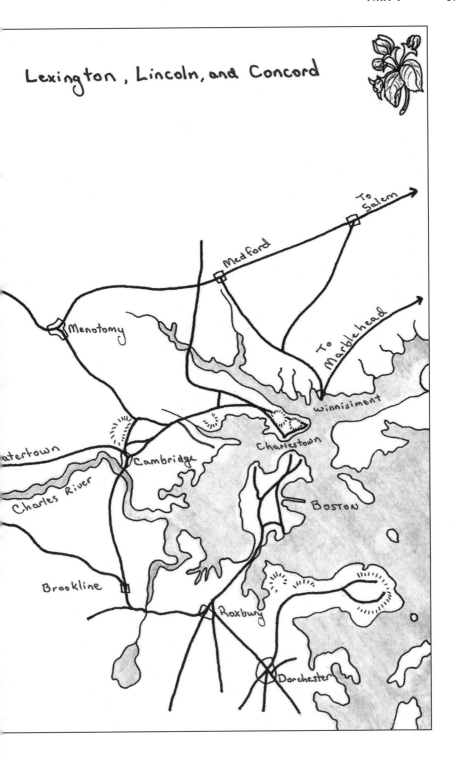

Chapter Twelve

Genevieve York, her page.

I had thought, while Benjamin spent an entire week scratching with his tireless quill, that he must have finished the entire Revolutionary War and sent the British back to their arrogant little island. But having read through his nautical pages, I see that he hasn't gotten any further than Boston Harbor. And I see also that we have ahead of us a job that will likely keep us at this table right through the winter. Then he had better not complain about holes in his old mittens, for I shan't have time to knit him new ones. Because if he can fill up half a ledger with a tale about his voyage to the war, then I shall certainly pen a page or two about my girlhood on a farm near Boston.

In 1756, Britain went to war with France over their colonial empires in the New World.

And in 1756, I was born in Lincoln, Massachusetts.

That war was called by some "The Seven Years War," and by others "The French and Indian War," because for seven years, British troops and their American allies fought French troops and their Indian allies for possession of the northern wilderness of Canada (rich with beaver furs), the western wilderness of the Ohio River Valley (rich with farm land for settlement), and the sugar islands of the West Indies (where great fortunes could be made from sugarcane grown by slaves).

In 1759, the church bells in London nearly wore themselves out as they rang for victory after victory. The British boot now proudly trod on British Canada, on the British banks of the Ohio, and on British sugar islands sprinkled across the sea. The British navy ruled the Atlantic and the Caribbean, and British armies marched invincible from Halifax to India.

The Treaty of Paris in 1763 brought (as we then thought) a full and formal peace to America. Though I was only a child of seven, I remember Papa's toast at this very table during our celebration dinner. Raising high his tankard, he declared, "Long live our glorious King George, and his worthy minister Sir William Pitt!" For together, those two gentlemen had rid our country of the threat of French Catholicism, and they had saved us from the rampaging savages whom the French had paid with beads and rum for collecting our scalps.

Proud to be Englishmen, Americans ordered carriages and clothes from London, read British newspapers, quoted John Milton, John Locke, and the King James Bible, and drank their ale at The King's Inn. Never did we miss a hearty toast on the King's birthday.

But then came startling news from London: Parliament had established the Proclamation Line of 1763. Determined to avoid any further conflict between the unruly colonials and the Indians further west, the British Parliament had drawn a line (on their own maps, at least) from Hudson Bay to Florida, stretching along the top of the Appalachian Ridge. The Proclamation of 1763 not only forbade the colonials to move west of the line, but ordered settlers already west of it to leave home and move back east.

Suddenly, after a century and a half of English settlement in the New World, and without any discussion between the Mother Country and her colonial children, we Americans were told that we could not cross the Appalachian Mountains. That long ridge now stood like a wall between the colonies along the Atlantic seaboard, and the wilderness further west. We were forbidden to settle on land where the soil was deep and black. Land which awaited the settler's axe, the settler's plow, the settler's cabin, the settler's church. Land where a great number of streams and rivers led to the fabled Ohio River, and then to the great Mississippi. The Proclamation Line of 1763 gave the Indian savages formal title to all that land, and told us colonials to leave those barbaric tribes undisturbed, forever.

More bad news arrived from London.

At the end of the French and Indian War, Britain was victorious, but badly in debt.

The British decided that since they had spent all that silver and gold to protect their children in America, then those children (an industrious and prosperous people) should be called upon to help pay the debt. And the best way to do that, figured the British Parliament, was to place tariffs, or taxes, on various goods traded between Britain and America. The Revenue Act of 1764 began a decade of tariffs and bitter argument. The Americans claimed they had fought the French and the Indians just as much as the British had, and thus they had squared their debt. The Americans saw these new taxes as a way of squeezing more money from the colonies, and they weren't about to give up a single principled penny.

During the bitter decade between 1764 and 1774, British customs officers collected very little money. On the other hand, American shop-keepers and farmers and craftsmen became exceptionally well educated in the fields of economics and politics.

I was nine years old when Parliament passed the Stamp Act of 1765.

Papa read the news to Mama from the *Boston Gazette*. They both grumbled all through dinner at the thought of a British tax on every piece of paper, whether a newspaper or a marriage license or even a pack of cards.

But they more than grumbled at the news (passed by word of mouth from farm to farm as the *Gazette* had been passed from hand to hand) about riots in Boston against the Stamp Act. Papa and Mama were outraged at the mobs of drunkards who roamed at night through the streets of Boston, threatening British customs officials. One mob broke into Governor Hutchinson's home, where they destroyed his fine furniture and threw the books of his library out through broken win-dows into the muddy street. My parents certainly had no love for cus-toms officials, but neither could they condone brawlers from a tavern who threatened the lives of our fellow Englishmen.

These riots were the doings of the so-called "Sons of Liberty." And a rogue by the name of Samuel Adams was rumored to be the leader behind the mobs.

As a little girl of nine, I was learning my place in the world at Mama's side: I was proud of my spinning, and delighted to be knitting my first pair of stockings for Papa. But young as I was, I listened with fascination to the talk around our dinner table—among my parents and two older brothers—about a Stamp Act Congress, the first meeting of its kind in America. The representatives of nine colonies had gathered in New York City to protest the new taxes. The delegates declared that they would no longer buy British goods. *I* had no British goods, except for a pair of crimson ribbons which Papa had bought for me to tie my braids. I otherwise wore homespun, as did every other farmer's son and daughter in the towns of Lexington and Lincoln.

No one listens to a grumbling farmer, and few will pay serious at-tention to a rioting mob. However, the colonials did have one voice to which Parliament paid heed. Benjamin Franklin, who represented the

Colony of Pennsylvania in London, now spoke in the House of Commons on behalf of *all* of the thirteen colonies. He warned the British government that because of the Stamp Act, bad times would only become worse. Unless the Stamp Act was repealed, Americans would boycott British goods. British merchants would suffer greatly. Franklin knew that if the British ever understood anything (a not frequent happenstance in those times), they did at least appreciate earning a profit from the colonials.

So Parliament repealed the Stamp Act. King George and his loyal Parliament decided that the obstreperous Americans could have their way, in most matters at least, with the notable exception of their cup of tea. The King, a lad of twenty-eight in 1766, acting through the guise of his ministers, insisted that every cup of tea, imported from Britain and brewed in the colonies, must pay its penny toward relief of the war debt.

Despite the lingering tax on tea, the Americans viewed the repeal of the Stamp Act as a victory. The good news was brought to Boston by one of John Hancock's cargo ships in May of 1766. The news spread within days to remote villages in western Massachusetts: clear words from the colonials had caused the King to back down.

Papa took the whole family in the farm wagon to Boston for the celebration—even me, the daughter. Church bells rang jubilantly throughout the city on that warm afternoon in May. People paraded and cheered and visited with each other in the streets. And for the first time in my young life, I heard cannons fired. Though they fired only blank shots over the harbor in honor of America's proud victory, their roar shook me to my bones. No one, I say, *no one* who has not stood near a cannon when it fires (our family stood among the crowd of hundreds on Griffin's Wharf), can ever guess at the power of its thunder. (Of course, I did not then know that I would live the first six years of my marriage, and bear two children, within earshot of two armies and their thundering artillery.)

That evening, people carried oiled paper lanterns through the streets of Boston. Boys climbed a huge old elm called the Liberty Tree and hung hundreds of lanterns in its branches. Sir William Pitt's profile in white paper was illuminated by candles in the windows of many homes. For with brilliant speeches in Parliament, Sir William had defended our American rights.

That night on Boston Common—a broad grassy park in the center of the city—the Sons of Liberty built a tall obelisk made of oiled paper with lanterns inside. The obelisk stood high above the crowd, glowing valiantly in the night and shining on our multitude of faces. That tower of light represented our strength, our unity, our determination.

As the grand climax of the celebration (organized, people said, by Samuel Adams himself), fireworks shot into the sky above the dark Common, blocking out the stars with their bursts of color. They silhouetted the tall black elms and maples, and lit with red and blue and crackling puffs of yellow our upturned faces.

One descending spark landed on the paper obelisk and set it afire. The enormous crowd of city shopkeepers and country farmers cheered the growing flames. We each felt in our heart that we had managed to preserve the flame of American liberty.

Nine years later, in April of 1775, muskets were fired at Lexington and Concord. For though the Stamp Act was repealed, other Acts followed, each trying to tax us in one way or another, without giving us a voice in Parliament. We endured ten years of anger because our rights were trampled, and ten years of apprehension, of fear, of horror, at the thought of a civil war.

Our family drank bee balm tea to avoid paying the tax on imported British tea. I remember Mama brewing the leaves of the wild, red-flowered bee balm, and how much we all liked (or said we liked) its mint flavor. We were most satisfied to brew our *own* American tea.

We bought no more crimson ribbons. Papa read to us every week from the *Boston Gazette*. And now while I knitted, I pondered such things as the rights of British citizens, the authority of our Massachusetts Charter, and the simple fairness of choosing our own judges in our own courts.

Mind you, these were not discussions for men alone. Looking back now from 1826, sixty years after 1766 (in a new century, a new era, a new way of life), I am profoundly grateful that I grew from girlhood into womanhood at a time when a woman's voice counted. Though I could read but slightly, and write not more than my name (and that at my own instigation and practice), closely did I listen when Papa read from the *Gazette*. And heartily did I agree with my parents that any neighbor who took the side of the Crown, was no longer a friend of the Byrnes.

❧

Chapter Thirteen

But something else happened during those tempestuous years, something wonderful, something extraordinary. I might merely have learned to knit stockings, and helped my mother in her herb garden, and looked for a boy who could catch my fancy. Yes, and I might well have stayed home on the farm during the coming eight years of war.

When I was a child of five, my father would take me riding with him on Lady Rose. He would lift me up and set me on his saddle, swing up behind me, wrap his arm around me, then gently trot across the farmyard. We trotted out through the gate and down the lane until my worried mother could no longer see us. Whereupon my father would kick his heels, and I would kick my little heels too, and his chestnut mare would canter with the most wonderful gliding bump-a-bump-a-bump. Imagine, we would ride all the way to Lexington, where Papa would tether Lady Rose to a post on the green, then we would step through a door into the Buckman Tavern, its dining room dim and smoky and fragrant with roasting pork. Feeling grown and worldly, I would have my cup of cider while Papa drank his tankard of ale and talked with the other men about corn and rain and the price of goats.

When I grew older, Papa would take me with him all the way to Boston. Most times we rode side by side on the seat of the wagon. On those market days, he would barter corn and potatoes for sugar and nails. But sometimes we would ride to Boston in the saddle together on Lady Rose, his arm snug around me. And on those special days, Papa would make his mysterious rounds through the cobblestone streets, buying nothing, bartering nothing, but speaking quickly with a half-dozen men. I remember the thump! thump! thump! of the printing presses in the shop where Papa spoke with Mr. Edes and Mr. Gill. We always visited Mr. Paul Revere in his silversmith shop, where I admired the most beautiful forks and spoons and sugar bowls. At the huge marketplace in Faneuil Hall, we sold no eggs, but read the latest broadsheets tacked to the wall. Rather, Papa read them aloud to me, while I listened to catch the meaning of the news from New York City, from Philadelphia, from London.

I came to understand more and more of what I overheard between

Papa and his friends. Sitting in the saddle with Papa on the way home, I would ask him questions, and he would kiss me on the top of my head and do his best to explain the difference between a good tax and a bad tax. I realized that apart from the world of corn and wheat and pumpkins and milk cows and chickens, apart from the world of Lincoln's new white meetinghouse and Lexington's blacksmith shop and Boston's noisy crowded streets, there was another world, one that existed far away in England. Somehow, the king on the other side of the ocean was a part of our world, and he and his ministers were meddling in our affairs.

More and more often on our visits to Boston, Papa and I tied Lady Rose to a post outside the Old South Meeting House, a stately red brick building with a towering steeple, used on the Sabbath as a church, and on other days as a place where men crowded together in the pews and up in the balcony to listen to someone shout at them from the pulpit. Mr. Samuel Adams, whom my father had come to greatly admire, was especially clever at addressing the assembled mechanics and wharf workers and farmers. There were usually several freed Africans in the crowd, and a few women, and always a cluster of children with whom I could whisper and point, picking out this man and that to stare at for his fine clothes, or the patched hole on the seat of his trousers. I say that Mr. Adams was especially clever, for though I could not always follow his arguments, they never failed to rouse the crowd of men until nearly everyone was shouting from the pews.

Papa and I usually took our supper at the Green Dragon Tavern, on Union Street near the millpond. Papa tethered Lady Rose among a dozen other horses from city and farm, then we entered a boisterous room crowded with men drinking their ale and smoking their clay pipes. We sat with five or six of Papa's friends and dined on Irish stew, or baked cod (my favorite). I noticed that the serving girls often gave my handsome father the eye, but I gave *them* the eye and chased them away. Papa was more interested anyway in talking with a strange man who had been a great lawyer in his day: he had been the first person to stand up to the King's magistrates in Boston. But lately he talked and talked without stopping, about ideas that even Papa admitted he could not follow. The lawyer was named Mr. James Otis, and the men around the table treated him with respect, for he had shown them how to stand up to the British bullies. But then he went mad.

Riding home one night beneath the bright stars—Lady Rose was trotting across the narrow Neck that linked the almost-island of Boston with the broad countryside around it—my father told me, "Genevieve, your brother Henry knows his crops and his carpentry, and your brother Judd knows his cows and oxen, and such men we need. But the good Lord seems to have given me a girl who is learning her alphabet from broadsheets, and her common sense from men whose ideas will one day sail across this land—sail across it as if on the wings of an eagle."

I won't say that I fully understood what Papa meant, for no person, man or child, could then have understood what America was to become. Yet it is true that by the age of ten, I had learned about the Stamp Act, and then the repeal of the Stamp Act, with the qualification of the Declaratory Act of 1766. Papa read aloud that qualification to us one evening in the Green Dragon: it declared that even though no taxes would be required on newspapers and all such paper goods, the King and Parliament still retained the authority "to make laws of sufficient force to bind the colonies and people of America in all cases whatsoever."

"Bind us!" roared Mr. Otis, thumping his fist on the table and nearly toppling the tankards.

Looking back now sixty years, I see that Papa was right. Little Genevieve had the wondrous privilege of growing up among eagles.

∞

Chapter Fourteen

I was eleven when Parliament passed the Townshend Acts; they required us to pay duties on British imports as an "external tax" rather than an "internal tax." But a tax was a tax, and thus our meetings, boycotts, resolutions, and threats of violence began anew.

I was twelve years old, in September of 1768, when Parliament, responding to our unrelenting resistance, sent a fleet of warships loaded with troops to Boston Harbor. The soldiers disembarked at Long Wharf and marched with their muskets into Boston. They had come to enforce the hated taxes, and to protect British customs officials from the mobs. The red-coated soldiers marched through Boston's streets by day and by night, their fifers and drummers making no end of noise. The "lobsterbacks" drank most of their pay, and tried to sully our women. Our boys threw snowballs and our men muttered curses.

When I was fourteen, a boy named Christopher Seider was killed on a street in Boston during a dispute over tea. It happened in this way:

In the North End of Boston, the Sons of Liberty gathered in front of a shop which they believed was violating the boycott on British tea. They posted a hand-painted sign on the front of the shop,

"THAT IS AN IMPORTER OF TEA."

A Tory neighbor, Ebenezer Richardson, tried to tear down the sign. A gang of boys threw snowballs at him. When Ebenezer retreated into his house, the growing crowd outside—another of Boston's many mobs—began to throw rocks at his windows. Ebenezer's upstairs window swung open. The infuriated man aimed his musket down at the crowd and fired. Christopher Seider was wounded, so badly that he soon died. A second boy was struck in the hand and leg, though he survived. The mob dragged Ebenezer Richardson out of his house and tightened a noose around his neck. William Molineux, a leader of the Sons of Liberty, did not want his men involved in a lynching. He called to them, "To your tents!" At that well-known signal, the Sons of Liberty and the gang of boys vanished for home. Ebenezer staggered back into his house, where he perhaps calmed himself with a cup of British tea.

Samuel Adams made good use of Christopher Seider's murder. Mr.

Adams arranged the grandest funeral that had ever been held in Boston. The boy was buried as a hero, as a patriot, as a martyr.

Papa and I rode into Boston on February 26, 1770 to attend the well advertised funeral. No one else from our family would come with us. Mama wanted nothing to do with Boston's mobs, whom she blamed for the poor boy's death. Henry was building a barn for a neighbor and did not want to lose a day of work. Judd, my sweet-tempered giant of a brother, had no interest in Boston's ruffians. He would spend the day in our barn, soothing an ox that was calving early.

But Papa and I both wanted to be in Boston. The soldiers had been marching through the streets for sixteen months now—bringing "order" on one hand and creating no end of difficulties on the other—and the rumor was out that they might try to stop the funeral.

Of course, Mama argued with Papa the night before.

"We shall stay clear of any mob," Papa reassured her.

"But the soldiers!" she protested.

"For over a year, the soldiers have not fired a shot. The only true danger, Caroline, is our enslavement in the grip of the British." Placing his hand on my shoulder, he added, "If this girl wishes to savor the taste of freedom, then the good Lord will protect her."

Brooding, but silent, Mama made pork pies for our dinner tomorrow in Boston.

We were up with the dawn. Papa rode his Lady Rose. I was old enough now to ride Henry's horse. We met a great number of people along the way, on horse, on foot, and in their carriages, from Concord, from Lexington, from Cambridge, from dozens of neighboring farms. Most of the people were quiet as we approached Boston Neck, their fear well hidden by their determination to honor the boy. And to affirm their rights.

Mama needn't have worried. Samuel Adams organized a funeral with hundreds of schoolchildren marching behind the hearse, followed by Boston's dignitaries in their elegant carriages. The long procession moved slowly from the Liberty Tree to the Old Granary Cemetery, where Samuel Adams, speaking to a silent crowd of mourners, called the boy a "little hero and first martyr to the noble cause."

I did not personally know Christopher Seider, and though the sadness of his burial imparted itself to my heart, I did not weep. But the sight of so many schoolchildren stirred me deeply. I was becoming more than a curious girl watching adults have their arguments. I began to fear that somehow this argument with England would reach even me.

I was glad to leave Boston that evening, relieved to ride the fifteen miles back to our peaceful, snow-blanketed cornfields; to our farmhouse with a lantern glowing in its window; and to Mama, tears running down her cheeks as she swung open the door and ran out to us.

After warming ourselves with her potato soup, Papa, Mama and I followed Judd out to the barn, where he showed us his newly born calf, peacefully milking.

A week later, on the cold snowy night of March 5, 1770, another mob gathered in Boston. This time, however, they confronted not a mere Ebenezer, but a squad of armed British soldiers.

The throng of shouting men threw snowballs and snow-covered rocks at a lone British sentry on King Street in front of the State House, close to the military barracks. The sentry called several times for help. Captain Thomas Preston led six red-coated grenadiers out of the barracks. The squad of soldiers faced the mob with loaded muskets and fixed bayonets. Alarm bells began to ring in nearby churches, bringing many more people into the street. The crowd jeered the soldiers, "Fire and be damned!"

Someone in the crowd threw a heavy stick of wood. It struck a grenadier named Hugh Montgomery, who fell on the icy cobblestones and dropped his musket. Grabbing for his weapon, he stood and fired into the mob. Other grenadiers fired, although Captain Preston had given no orders to fire. Within seconds, four Bostonians lay dead on the trampled snow, and six lay wounded.

The terrified crowd fled into the adjoining streets. Captain Preston shoved his grenadiers' muskets into the air and shouted, "Cease firing!" He marched his men across the emptied street to the barracks, then ordered a drummer to summon the entire garrison.

Once again, William Molineux prevented a further catastrophe. While British troops formed on King Street and faced a rapidly growing crowd of outraged Bostonians (who shouted but threw no ice-covered rocks), Molineux banged his fist on the State House door and demanded to speak with Governor Hutchinson. Allowed inside, he told the Governor that the crowd, as yet unarmed, would go home peacefully only if the soldiers returned to their barracks. Hutchinson opened a State House window and called down to Lieutenant Colonel Carr, who ordered his troops off the street.

The citizens of Boston lifted their wounded and their dead from the bloody snow.

Boston remained deadly quiet throughout the night.

Once again Samuel Adams organized an elaborate funeral, and once again Papa and I witnessed Boston on a day of mourning. Ten thousand weeping, angry people, from a city of sixteen thousand, followed four black coffins from the Liberty Tree to the Old Granary Cemetery. Samuel Adams made sure that his ten thousand listeners knew whom to blame for the four murders.

Nine days after the Boston Massacre, a fifth man died of his wounds. Samuel Adams organized yet another funeral.

With a boy and five men now in their graves, the citizens of Boston burned in their hearts with a rage far deeper than the anger they had felt about taxes. The red patches of blood in the snow on the night of the Fifth of March, 1770, was a sight they would never forget.

I will here record an observation which John Adams, cousin to Samuel Adams, penned many years after the Revolution: "Not the battle of Lexington or Bunker's Hill, not the surrender of Burgoyne or Cornwallis, were more important events than the Battle of King Street, on the 5th of March, 1770. On that night, the foundation of American independence was laid."

෴

Chapter Fifteen

For the next three years, Boston needed a period of calm. The mobs, the taunts, the killings, now gave way to a time of weariness and disgust among many who once had sided with the Sons of Liberty. Enough of politics, they said. People began to import the elegant goods from England which formerly they had scorned. Even John Hancock, the wealthiest man in New England (who more than once had rolled out his barrels of rum onto the Common during Samuel Adams' rallies for liberty), now imported the very finest of British clothing on his ships, for sale in his shops.

On our farm in Lincoln, we wore homespun and drank Mama's bee balm tea. We sowed corn and wheat, preserved wild strawberries and fat tomatoes, and stored a growing abundance of potatoes in our root cellar. Judd hummed with his deep voice to his ever-growing herd of milk cows. Every spring, he hitched the plow to his two oxen, then across the fields he dug long deep furrows. Henry, following close behind, planted the best of the seed from the year before. Papa planted his potatoes, pruned his apple trees, shoveled soil into mounds for beans and squash. Mama kept her kitchen garden, and her herb garden, and her chickens. And I, true to my nature, was everybody's helper, with a hand in everything.

My favorite job was to work with Mama in her herb garden, a fragrant patch along the southern side of our farmhouse. Mama's lilies grew in the back row, their orange blossoms jubilant in the sunshine against the dark weathered planks. Her white daisies grew as a hedge along the front. Both the lilies and the daisies had been brought, as bulbs and seeds, by ship from England, long before the boycott. The daisies we called "bruisewort," for they made a salve useful in healing cuts and wounds.

Mama planted chamomile in our garden; she made the tiny white and yellow flowers into a poultice for swollen joints, and for sprains of an ankle. Chamomile was also useful as a sedative tea for babies in the neighborhood who would not sleep. When the flowers were mixed with the dried leaves of thyme, peppermint, sage and rosemary, then sewn into a cheesecloth bag and dropped into the hot water of Saturday night's bath, they imparted a perfume and a balm that made me feel as healthy as a ripe red apple.

Mama had learned about her herbs from an elderly woman in the village of Lincoln, who in turn had learned from an Indian woman of the Massachusetts tribe, before her people had been pushed into the hills to the west. Thus, when I made a bee balm tea for Henry—who had been working in the rain and now sweated in bed with a fever—I felt as if I were brewing an ancient medicine that must surely cure his pains and chills.

When I pressed the red sap from a bloodroot, then used the red dye to color my coarse linen ribbons, I felt as if I did with my red-tainted hands what women had done for centuries before me. My adornment, worn in the stead of fine English ribbons, made me feel in a girlish way close to those wild people who had lived in Massachusetts before us. Thus I felt a little wild myself.

But the most wonderful, most memorable, and most exciting event, during those three years of peace between the Massacre in 1770 and the Tea Party in 1773, was the arrival of Sir William.

Papa wanted me to have my own horse, rather than borrow Henry's, for Henry had taken it into his head to court a girl in Concord, and so his horse was entirely undependable. Papa did me the great honor of riding his very own Lady Rose to a neighbor's farm, without telling me (I was weeding pumpkins that day), where Lady Rose promptly and unbashfully (as Papa later told me) presented herself to the fastest stud stallion in the parish.

Only months later, when Lady Rose's slowness at the trot became apparent to me, did Papa place my hand on Lady Rose's chestnut ribs and tell me of her great secret.

Judd helped with the foaling. Papa helped with the breaking and training. I provided a bounty of apples, and a skilled hand at the reins. My yearling, chestnut red with a white blaze and three white stockings, was the gentlest and steadiest horse on the farm. *And* by far the fastest. Henry's Betty had held that honor, until one summer evening when I trotted out from a dark forest onto the Concord road, surprising poor Henry. The moon was nearly full and Henry was on his way to pursue his courtship. Determined as he was to leave me far behind him, Sir William and I were at Delilah's front porch in Concord a full half-minute before Henry arrived, sweaty and disheveled, and very much perturbed with his little sister.

As a girl of sixteen, I would finish my chores without fail before supper, eat a quick meal (my mother scolded me not to gulp), then dash from my chair out the door to the barn. I hefted and cinched my own saddle. Fastened the bridle. Led Sir William out the barn door into the fresh evening air. Then I swung up onto his back, my favorite place in all the world to be. With a tap of my heels, Sir William and I trotted toward the gate. We trotted down the lane . . . until I no longer heard Mama's worried voice. Then Sir William, with the faintest touch of my heels, would stretch into a canter, and now into a thundering gallop . . . and Genevieve Byrnes would sail like an eagle above those rhythmic pounding hooves.

I loved the American land, rolling past along both sides of the road on an August evening: the wheat fields filled with crickets, the tall corn rustling with a breeze, a cattle pasture graced by the call of a whippoor-will. I was sure that the darkening earth and brightening moon, and the heavy fragrance of freshly cut hay, and my exuberant friendship with Sir William, were all that a young woman could possibly want on such a night to hold in her heart.

ᛞ

Chapter Sixteen

But by December of 1773, the patriots of Boston would no longer tolerate even the tax on tea. They saw it as a lever that could pry open the door to all sorts of tyranny.

On December 16, 1773, Samuel Adams led his Sons of Liberty, my father included, on their first act of organized rebellion. Disguised as Mohawks, their faces blackened with burnt cork and lamp soot, they boarded three British cargo ships at Griffin's Wharf and ordered the captains to unlock their holds. With axes and hatchets, the Mohawks smashed open three hundred and forty-two chests of imported British tea, then dumped the fragrant leaves overboard. Boston Harbor thus became a saltwater teapot.

Though several British warships rode at anchor nearby, with Royal Marines on board, no attempt was made to halt the bold destruction of British property. The Mohawks worked in a silent and orderly manner for well over an hour. Then they crossed the three gangplanks and marched along the wharf toward home to the cadence of a lone colonial fife. On all three ships, the Mohawks destroyed only tea. They did not touch so much as a crate of other cargo.

I remember the faint smears of soot on my father's face, dark patches which lasted several days, for he was reluctant (being a bit proud of his part in the rebellion) to wash them away. Nor did Mama speak a word of protest, though we young ones either washed our faces before supper, or we went without.

Paul Revere, his face perhaps showing traces of soot, rode with the news of the Tea Party all the way to New York City, then on to Philadelphia. He brought back the encouraging revelation that patriots in Charleston, South Carolina had unloaded crates of tea from several British ships, but then deliberately stored the crates in a damp cellar, where the tea soon rotted.

On Christmas Eve, a week after the Tea Party, the Byrnes family savored many steaming cups of wild wintergreen tea, each cup sweetened with a dollop of Judd's honey.

In January of 1774, and then in February, in March, and in April, Boston waited nervously for the King's response to its Tea Party. We knew that Parliament would not let such willfulness go unpunished.

During those quiet months before the blow fell, Samuel Adams and a doctor from Boston named Joseph Warren arrived at our farmhouse in the doctor's carriage, for a cup of Patriot Tea and a lively talk long into the evening with both Papa and Mama at the table (yes, at this very table), so that Mr. Adams and Dr. Warren could learn, as they said, "the numbers and inclinations of the farming folk" as far out as Concord.

Samuel Adams I remember best. He looked old, though Papa said that his palsy had brought age upon him. His hands shook, but his voice was strong and steady as he recounted for us the latest news from London, as well as news from the other twelve colonies. I was astonished that one man could know so much. In exchange for whatever little he learned from us, he taught us so much more.

His eyes would sometimes blaze with resentment; sometimes they would stare at something the rest of us could not see. But I remember best, and shall always cherish, one moment at the end of his visit. He turned to me, a young woman of eighteen, and his tired eyes twinkled as he reached across the table and touched my hand. "You're the equal of a king," he told me. "With your braids and bib apron, you're the equal of a king."

I blushed, couldn't speak a word. But from that moment, I never doubted the truth of what he said.

The response from London arrived aboard Captain Shayler's frigate on May 10, 1774, in the form of a legal document to be read in the State House to our municipal authorities. The Boston Port Bill, signed by His Majesty King George III, declared that Boston's entire wharf and harbor would be closed to all commerce on the first of June, until the tea had been paid for.

Further, the Bay Colony's charter of 1691, sacred to generations of citizens in Massachusetts as a guarantee of their rights, was declared to be without further authority. A military governor would assume full control of the colonial government. British courts would now replace American courts, with obvious consequences.

Further, the old Quartering Act, which had expired in 1770, was renewed: His Majesty's troops were to be quartered in whatever private home, warehouse or factory the military governor thought to be suitable, for as long as he thought to be necessary. Thus, the troops sent by the King to close the port of Boston were to be housed in the private homes of Boston.

Further, Parliament had passed the Quebec Act, which extended the boundaries of Quebec, a Canadian province in the distant north, as far south as the Ohio River and as far west as the Mississippi River. Equally appalling, the Roman Catholic religion was legally sanctioned in that vast territory. The curse of an omnipotent king was now compounded by the threat of a meddling pope.

Though the wealthy Tories of Boston welcomed the King's firm hand, most people in the seaport were shocked: all sixteen thousand citizens would be punished for the work of a few dozen men on the night of the Tea Party. Shops would close, ships would not sail, and thousands of workers would lose their jobs. A multitude of families would face destitution. This was more than a tax: this was economic devastation.

Accordingly, on Friday, May 13, 1774, the very day that General Thomas Gage, the new military governor, sailed into Boston Harbor aboard the *Lively*, Samuel Adams presided at a tumultuous meeting in Faneuil Hall at the harbor's edge. The hall was so crowded that many people had to stand outside and listen to Samuel Adams' booming voice through the open windows. Papa and I arrived early enough that we were able to stand near the back of the Hall. (Papa stood behind me with his hands on my shoulders so that I should not be toppled by a shove from the crowd.)

We heard Mr. Adams read point by point through the Boston Port Bill. Then we heard him ask the people of Boston if they would pay for the tea. Papa and I were heartened by the roar of thousands who voted, "Nay!"

Samuel Adams now read a circular letter which he had written, a letter to the other twelve colonies (he was a master at writing to everyone, whether local farmers or Virginia patricians), asking each colony to organize a complete boycott of all British goods. The crowd in Faneuil Hall roared its approval, "Aye!"

Mr. Adams read further from his letter: "Now is the time when we should be *united* in opposition to this violation of the liberties of all." Boston, he declared, should not "be left to struggle alone."

"Do you hear that, Genny?" My father sounded doubtful. "We're asking the others for help." Never before had the thirteen colonies been united on anything, save in their unrelenting distrust of each other, as they squabbled over borders, over river rights, over unsettled land to the west. Most of us in Massachusetts felt far closer to our fellow citizens in England, than we did to the slaveholders of Virginia.

The Port Bill was reprinted in Boston with a heavy black border around it, as if it were a funeral notice. Paul Revere rode with copies all the way to New York City, and then on to Philadelphia.

When he returned to Boston he brought word from a Committee of Correspondence in Philadelphia, suggesting that all thirteen colonies meet at a Congress there sometime soon. Yes, it seemed that Boston, despite her mobs, might truly have the support of the other twelve colonies, all of whom feared that the port of New York City, the port of Philadelphia, the port of Charleston, might be the next to be closed by a decree from the King.

By signing the Boston Port Bill of 1774, King George III did more to aid Samuel Adams and his rebellion than Samuel himself had been able to do during the entire past decade.

∞

Chapter Seventeen

On the last day of May, Papa announced that tomorrow he would ride to Boston alone, to see what would happen when General Gage closed the harbor at noon. "We might well be at war by one o'clock, Genny," he told me. "Boston at war is no place for a girl to be."

Stunned by his betrayal, I told Papa (for I never hid a thing in my life), that I would ride Sir William to Boston, and that I would cross the neck *before* him. I had heard years of talk at this farmhouse table and at the Green Dragon Tavern, and I would watch the lobsterbacks myself as they turned our Boston into a military hostage. As I hid nothing from anyone, so I wanted nothing hidden from me. I was as much a patriot as anyone.

My father stared at me for along moment while my mother insisted that I would *not* be allowed to go. Today, half a century later, when our minds have turned to smaller things, a father might well tell his daughter, "No. Stay here at the farm with your mother. The both of you must remain safe."

But in those times, in those fearful, vibrant times, my strong and determined father said to his equally determined daughter, "Yes, come. We will *all* go, in the wagon. For nary a marriage, nary a child born, but will carry with it a blessing or a curse from Boston on this first day of June."

The next morning at dawn, Papa hitched both Lady Rose and Betty to the wagon. He and Mama climbed onto the buckboard seat. My brothers and I sat on a seat in the wagon's bed behind them, as we did every Sunday morning on our way to the meetinghouse in Lincoln. But today was not the Sabbath, and we were prepared to hear not a sermon, but possibly the first firing of muskets in a civil war.

The ride to Boston took a good deal longer than when Papa and I rode our Lady Rose and Sir William. Yet during those hours from sunup—when we left our peaceful, beautiful, orderly farm—to mid-morning—when we crossed the narrow neck—we hardly spoke. If war was coming to our country, then we would know with our own eyes precisely how it began, and we would meet it as a family. I will add that neither my father nor my two brothers had brought their muskets.

In the wagon behind our seat were to be found only a basket of chicken pie, which Mama and I had packed to save us the expense of eating in town, and a jug of Papa's apple cider.

But I was wrong. We did go to church. The bells of nearly every church in Boston were tolling, slowly, mournfully, and the doors of nearly every church were open. The first of June had been declared by most of the clergy as a day of fasting and prayer. So we hitched Lady Rose and Betty to the rail outside the Old South Meeting House. Our men took off their hats as we entered. We stood in a pew as a family, and we bowed our heads as a family, in prayer shared with the people of Boston. We stood in a congregation of several thousand, every one of us dressed in homespun.

Perhaps because so many churches were open on that frightening, unpredictable Tuesday, and perhaps because Samuel Adams kept a tight hand on his unruly Sons of Liberty, not a shot was fired, not a stone was thrown, when General Gage's redcoats marched in squads along the wharves of Boston, making sure that every shop and warehouse was closed at noon. Our family stood on the cobblestones at the end of King Street, staring out at Long Wharf: we watched as dozens of men and boys, newly jobless, walked in a silent, sullen, straggling parade along the pier toward town, some of them glaring at the soldiers with their bayoneted muskets, some staring straight ahead and thereby refusing to acknowledge the presence of the ordered ranks of troops. Papa gave several of the men whom he knew a silent nod of encouragement.

Out in the harbor, General Gage's triple-masted warship, flying a huge red British flag, was anchored so that one broadside of cannons aimed at our town, and the other broadside aimed toward the channel leading out to sea. Not so much as a rowboat stirred on the quiet water of our harbor.

And then . . . people went home. Workers and spectators vanished behind their closed doors. Our family departed as well. We rode in our wagon for several more hours into the late afternoon. On that day of fasting, we did not eat from our basket of provisions.

Henry's attitude toward the Sons of Liberty changed completely. He had always scoffed at the mobs, at the "ruffians and scoundrels," as he called them, "a shabby bunch who had no business in Boston's politics." He had even scorned, though silently of course, Papa's part in the Tea Party last December. But now having seen for himself the quiet and orderly people of Boston, saying their prayers on the day the King took away their jobs, Henry came to a new understanding. He looked at me as we jounced along side by side on the wagon seat—I sat between my two brothers—and I could see a trace of admiration in his eyes, in spite of himself. "You and Papa been watching this come for years, ain't you?"

"Yep," I replied, a bit cocky as a self-proclaimed Daughter of Liberty, "I've had more than one bowl of Liberty Stew at the Green Dragon."

"And you knew it warn't just mobs," he said, with the cautiousness of a man who still had a lot of thinking ahead of him.

"Papa and I haven't seen a mob yet. But we've been to the Old South Meeting House a good many times."

Now Judd nudged me from the other side. "That Tea Party, I hear, been as orderly as a church picnic."

"Hmm," I nodded, letting the fact speak for itself.

Judd wrapped his powerful arm around me and gave me a squeeze. "Then maybe they can keep it so."

Yes, we all hoped on that long, pensive ride back to our farm, that somehow, despite four regiments of redcoats marching through the streets of Boston, despite General Gage's warships bristling with cannons in our harbor, despite the brooding rage of men out of work as the summer, Boston's busiest time, was coming upon us, and despite a King and his ministers who, year after year, plagued us with their ignorant, petty tyranny . . . we still hoped that warnings and resolutions traded back and forth across the Atlantic, rather than shots on American soil, would bring a lasting end to the troubles that no one wanted.

And yet, looking back, I see that apart from a few statesmen like Sir William Pitt and Edmund Burke, John Wilkes and Colonel Isaac Barre, all of whom supported us valiantly with their speeches in Parliament, there were few people in London who read the situation with any degree of wisdom. The King and his ministers were like an arrogant gang of foolish boys: bothered by a few wasps, they knew no better than to throw stones at the hive.

ॐ

Chapter Eighteen

Benjamin York, his page.

Boston Harbor became our world. The closing of the seaport meant that all traffic, even the ferry across the narrow strait from North Boston to Charlestown, was forbidden. The *Lively's* cutter became a patrol boat with a lieutenant and a dozen marines aboard, and we eight topmen at the oars. Of course Hench rode imperious in the stern. He was captain, at last, of his own vessel. Ever on the lookout for small craft that might attempt to carry cargo or passengers to an American sloop hidden among the islands, Hench ordered us to bend our backs in this direction and that, from Castle William Island to Governor's Island, and then across to Shirley's Point, so we could inspect its deep northern cove. We rowed along the lee of Snake Island, then pulled to the bays and backwaters of Hog Island, and Noddle's Island. But never did we spot so much as a boy fishing from a rowboat.

We rowed in the blazing summer sun, when the harbor's blue water became absolutely flat with barely a breeze to ruffle it. And we rowed on days of such pummeling rain that we had to bail the cutter. Boston Harbor was often choppy with contrary winds, off the land and off the sea, and then our rowing became especially tiresome.

One early morning of heavy fog, we became stuck on the mud flats near Dorchester Neck as the tide was going out. There we sat, our cutter in the muck, our oars useless, while the sun rose as a pale yellow ball in the thick mist. The dozen red-coated marines, sitting in the stern sheets between Hench and the lowly rowers, first cursed us, then took it into their jolly heads to reach over the side, scoop up a handful of black muck and cast it onto our chests and faces. Hench presided over this merriment like a king on his throne. The marines were armed with muskets and knives, so we topmen could do no more than wipe the stinking muck from our cheeks.

The sun slowly burned off the fog, but then it made us sweat most miserably in the damp heat. We could now see the four green hills of Dorchester Neck, and even a few cows grazing upon them. Sir Garth, a farmer in his former life, noted how well-fed and clean the cattle looked, walking free upon the land, rather than fenced into a trampled pen, as were his cows back home.

As the tide flowed out of the harbor, we watched the edge of the sea creep away from our ever-expanding island of mud. A flock of terns swooped around us as they snatched up tiny silver fish trapped in pools on the mud flats.

We cast an occasional eye at Hench, who, through all those hours of heat and thirst and hunger, said not one cordial word to us. Rather, he surveyed with regal satisfaction the glittering harbor, empty of all but a few fishing boats, commissioned by the British to provide dinner for the officers.

Beneath June's midday sun, we watched the sea creep slowly back toward us across the rippled mud . . . until tiny lapping waves reached our cutter. Encouraged, the marines sang a boisterous medley of bawdy songs, until at last our cutter shifted, wobbled, then floated free. We dug the blades of our oars into the muck beneath the shallow water as we pulled in a silent rage toward our prison ship.

Hench enjoyed these voyages so greatly that he obtained permission (from some bored and indifferent officer) to make occasional trips without a lieutenant and marines on board. Hench especially liked to meander surreptitiously at dusk toward Charlestown wharf—a few hundred yards north across a narrow strait from Boston—where he had somehow established contact with a Tory merchant who supplied him with a nightly bottle of West Indian rum. The merchant, perhaps the obliging proprietor of a Charlestown tavern, would climb down the wharf's ladder to our cutter, take a bottle from his gunnysack and hand it to Hench. Our worthy captain always paid the man with good British coin. As he pulled out the cork with his teeth, the merchant disappeared up the ladder.

Then, having broken the King's law (which forbade all commerce in the port of Boston) Hench would roar at us, "Pull, lads, pull! I fear there's a smuggler sneaking about the back of Noddle's." Not a single swig of rum did he offer us as we bent our backs and ferried him like an emperor on his galley along the northern coast of Noddle's Island, where not a smuggler was to be found.

Seeking some way to better our lot, and being quick with a needle and a bit of old sailcloth, Nathaniel and I made eight haversacks for ourselves and our messmates. Into these we stuffed a ration of hardtack (by now so stale in the *Lively's* hold that we might well have tied a line to a sack of biscuits and used it as an anchor). We brought a cask of water aboard the cutter, though it was still ship's water, stale and tainted with scum.

We did not sing, as sailors often do at their work. We hardly spoke to each other during those four hours of rowing here and there, everywhere and nowhere, affording Hench, at long last in his dreary life, the opportunity to enjoy a bit of paradise.

In July, transport ships arrived from England with more troops for Gage. We watched as longboats ferried company after company of armed soldiers in their bright red coats from the anchored ships to Long Wharf. We watched as the troops marched up the pier and into town. Meanwhile, we who had sweated under the hot American sun for two months, had not yet set our feet on the American earth.

Hunched over our dark mess table one evening at supper, Michael whispered bitterly, "Lads, pack your London togs in your haversacks. Our next trip to Charlestown, I say we bid our Hench adieu with an oar over his skull. Then we'll climb the wharf ladder, shed these rags, dress properly, and discover for ourselves the New World."

It was a bold plan, for should we fail in the attempt, or later be captured, we'd surely be flogged. Or worse. And yet . . . after a moment of silence over our rancid lobscouse, every one of us to a man agreed that on our next trip to Charlestown, we would make our escape.

Though I lacked a pair of boots, I still possessed everything I had been wearing on my last evening in London, for my clothing, washed and folded, had been stowed in a chest on the berthing deck. Into our eight haversacks I now sewed a flap, forming a hidden pocket inside, and there we secreted whatever apparel we had worn when we first came aboard the *Lively*. Some extra biscuits, and what few pence we had managed to keep from gamblers and thieves on the ship, and we were ready to take our chances in the colony of Massachusetts.

We arrived at the Charlestown wharf as a clear evening, with a fresh breeze from the north, was darkening into night. A half-moon shone high overhead. Hench was in the best of spirits, for he anticipated a balmy moonlit cruise into Boston's Back Bay, and then, as he growled to the rum merchant at the bottom of the ladder, "a paddle up the Charles River to take a closer look at the village of Cambridge."

His illicit business swiftly accomplished, Petty Officer Hench arranged himself comfortably on his throne in the stern and took a long swig of Jamaican rum. (Most certainly not Yankee rum.) Then he roared at us to bend our backs toward the Bay.

But we hadn't rowed ten rods before Michael stayed his oar above the water and called, "Petty Officer Hench, might I have a drink of rum?"

Hench glared at Michael as if the vilest wharf rat had dared to speak to him. Then our captain took a swig of rum, stepped forward from the stern (over the empty seats where the marines should most certainly have been posted that night), and spat his mouthful of rum at Michael, wetting all the lads on the aftermost seats with his contemptuous spray. "Drink that if ye would," growled Hench, pleased with this opportunity to show us what dogs we were.

"Petty Officer Hench," called Michael, wet but undaunted, "one swig, please, or I shall be obliged to tell the captain on the *Lively* about your illegal rum, purchased in flagrant violation of the Boston Port Bill, that noble decree conceived and signed by His Majesty King George the Third, glory to his name." Michael pronounced each word with crisp and haughty self-righteousness. The rest of us stared at him with admiration, and at Hench with apprehension. The moment was coming.

Hench blinked at the courtly language. But he did not care a whit for such a threat, because never could a lowly seaman approach the very captain of a ship with a reproach against a petty officer. Hench saw an excellent chance to give a man a beating. He snarled, "I'll flog you twenty lashes tomorrow, I will."

"Hench," grinned Michael, "you've an arm so weak, I doubt I'd feel the tickle."

That was all the Devil needed. Stepping forward from seat to seat between the lads, Hench raised his fist to show a scoundrel the strength of his iron arm.

But barely had he passed the second thwart before the lads behind him were upon him, striking his knees and thus dropping him with a crash onto the hull. In the blink of an eye, seven oars were raised from the water: their blades were hoisted high into the air and their grips were thrust down by fourteen arms of iron, mine included, as the lads bludgeoned the skull and back and buttocks of the monster whom we hated.

Only Nathaniel did not join us, though not a man questioned him for that.

When Hench no longer fought, or moved, or moaned, we slipped our oars back into their oarlocks and pulled mightily toward the wharf. Leaving Hench drooling blood onto the floorboards, the lads scrambled with their haversacks up the ladder. I delayed my escape for a final feast of revenge.

I pulled the worn and scuffed boots, Papa's boots, from Hench's feet. I set the boots neatly side by side on a thwart. Then I tore off Hench's filthy stockings. I grabbed his knife from its sheath on his belt. Gripping one naked foot in my hand, I cut a deep red line from Hench's toes to his heel, and then a deep crosswise gash behind his toes, where the foot rolls against the ground. Grabbing his other foot, I carved a second bloody cross, cutting even deeper. Hench never flinched, and I thought he might well be dead. But were he alive, if ever again he walked, he would remember us with every step he took.

Tossing the knife overboard, I rinsed my bloody hands in the water. Then I grabbed my haversack and the pair of boots. With the sack on my back and the boots tightly clutched in one arm, I climbed up the sturdy ladder to the pier.

Glancing about, I saw our messmates tearing off their blue jackets and ragged trousers, and donning the fine London clothes from their haversacks. Then singly or in pairs, they dashed across the wharf and disappeared into dark alleys between the warehouses . . . toward the rooftops and white steeple of Charlestown.

Only Nathaniel stood waiting for me, bare-chested, wearing his London breeches.

I cast my hated blue jacket into the harbor, ripped the soiled and stinking shirt from my chest, then freed my legs from the tar-smeared seaman's breeches. All the while I searched again and again in the moonlight up and down the wharf, anxious for the sudden appearance of His Majesty's troops. Though most of the soldiers patrolled the streets of Boston, I knew not if some company might patrol the village of Charlestown as well. If caught with cast-off jackets all around us, and our officer perhaps dead in the cutter, we'd be hung from a yardarm by noon tomorrow.

Pulling on my clean London breeches, I whispered to Nathaniel, "If I'm captured, you run." Buttoning, I added, "All the way to Philadelphia."

"Damned if I will," he grinned, tying behind him the strings of a leather apron. "We'll swing in the breeze together, we will."

As I tucked in my cobbler's shirt, I had a moment's pleasure, for I was becoming my old self again. I pulled on my stockings, then thrust my feet into Papa's boots.

Suddenly I felt enormously powerful, as if Papa's spirit had joined me and I could now run forever.

"Ready?" asked Nathaniel as he stood up from buckling his shoes. The tall carpenter wore his smock and breeches, and his scuffed leather apron.

"Ready," replied the cobbler.

We glanced down at Hench, a dark moonlit heap across the thwarts of the bobbing cutter. Then we walked quickly, warily, into a dark alley between two warehouses.

The sea and its prison ship were behind us. The great American continent lay ahead of us. And our hearts were determined to find our freedom, together.

ॐ

Chapter Nineteen

During the weeks before our escape, Nathaniel and I had carefully observed, while rowing along the coastline of Charlestown peninsula (and keeping a watchful eye on carts and horses travelling along the shore), that two roads left the village of Charlestown. One road ran west along the southern shore to a narrow neck, then it crossed a bridge of land to the mainland of Massachusetts. The other road led northeast a short distance, then curved around a large hill; it continued west along the northern shore, past a second, taller hill, to that same neck. While the first road was shorter, we would have to walk through the village before we reached it, and we might well be discovered either by British troops or by a Tory loyal to the King. Better, we agreed, to take the longer road through the countryside. If we could manage to cross the neck before dawn, we would hide in a woods and sleep through the day. The following night we would walk further west, to some village far beyond the reach of His Majesty's troops. Nathaniel assured me that he was not particular about her being a *Boston* beauty. A good farm lass would do quite as well.

Stepping silently in Papa's boots, I followed a cart lane to the right, eastward, slipping behind the warehouses just above the wharf. We could hear voices from the next street . . . heard the hooves and rolling wheels of a wagon . . . heard the cry of a baby, the cooing of its mother, inside the open window of a clapboard house.

At the end of the lane, we peered cautiously from the shadow of a warehouse toward a few dark shanties, the vague shape of a stone wall, and the moonlit grassy openness of a broad field stretching into the night. We saw no road leading from the wharf along the coast. We decided, whispering back and forth, that the road must leave the village further inland. If we angled across the grassy field, we must surely meet the road running east. Then we need but follow it as quickly as we could, our ears ever cocked for approaching hooves.

With a dash, we left Charlestown behind us. We clambered over the stone wall, then ran across level ground (soft beneath our feet and thus probably sand flats above the sea) at an angle toward where we hoped the road must be.

The grass deepened, until it reached our knees. We ran at a steady but not exhausting pace, until suddenly we tumbled into a ditch which neither of us had seen in the darkness. We tumbled headlong, though without injury, to its damp bottom. Whatever thoughts I had entertained about traveling secretly across the wild terrain, I now abandoned. Better to hasten at some risk along a road, than to struggle we knew not where, perhaps into a swamp, and not reach the neck before dawn.

We climbed up the steep sandy wall of the ditch, then hurried again through deep grass. We had traveled perhaps a quarter of a mile when, with great relief, we spotted ahead of us a dark road running parallel to the coastline. Halting where we stood, we searched in both directions in the moonlit dimness. We listened carefully above the rasp of crickets for any voice, or cart, or horse. Certain that we were alone, we hurried across ground that became increasingly firm, until finally, feeling a measure of success, we stepped onto the road. A glance at each other, a nod, then we strode together eastward along the lane with growing confidence.

To our left now rose the tall black hump of a hill, blocking the stars behind it. We knew not its name, only its shape and location as we had often seen it from the cutter. Nor did we know the name of a second hill, further inland. (One year later, the names of Breed's Hill and Bunker's Hill would be branded with a hot iron into my soul.)

I glanced up at the half-moon that lit the road ahead of us. Then I looked at Nathaniel, who at that moment was looking at me. Though neither of us spoke, I could see in his eyes that he too marveled at what we were doing: we were walking, as carpenter and cobbler, as two free men, on the soil of America.

But here I must lay down my quill. I cannot, with such pain in my heart, go on. Perhaps tomorrow, I shall tell the tell the tale further. For if only to do justice to Nathaniel, I must take us both to Lexington in April 1775, and to Concord, and to the horror of the march back to Boston.

But for now, I must stop. Because Nathaniel might be here today, penning *his* view of the War, were it not for what happened to us later that night in July of 1774, upon the moonlit Charlestown road. I cannot, just yet, walk any further.

Of Nathaniel, friend Nathaniel, guardian Nathaniel, I ache to ask the same haunting question which later I would ask many times of many men and women: Why did some of us live through the War, while hundreds of others, thousands of others, people equally good—and often far better than the rest of us—died a brutal death?

War brings questions of Justice, and Divine Purpose, as we seek to find hidden in all that chaos and terror and devastation some measure of sense, some small bit of understanding. But though the War brought to me many things, including an angel named Nathaniel, it rarely brought me answers.

We needed to wait for men like Washington, like Jefferson, like John Adams and James Madison, to provide some deep and lasting meaning, after all those years of turmoil and death.

&

Chapter Twenty

Benjamin York and Nathaniel Ash, our page.

The road passed around the foot of the first hill. The hill's broad dark slope rose like an uplifted pasture, so that a cow might start at the bottom feeding on clover, work its way up through a bountiful growth of grass, and finish at the top with a midnight nibble on the bottom corner of the moon.

Beside the road stood occasional thickets of trees, their trunks coal-black, their leaves glistening faintly in the moonlight.

We came to a fork in the road. The right branch led east toward the sea. (We could faintly hear waves rolling along the shore). The left branch led west toward the second hill, a tall black hump against the stars.

Without pausing, Nathaniel and I continued on the westward fork, toward the American continent. But we had taken barely ten steps when a voice behind us called, "Halt right there or we'll put a musket ball through your backs."

I made no attempt to run, for I was unwilling to risk Nathaniel's life. I did glance behind me and saw two musket barrels, long stripes of silvery gray in the moonlight, reaching out from a copse of trees near the fork. The two bayonets gleamed especially bright. But the men who held the muskets were hidden in the shadows.

"Turn away!" shouted a harsh voice.

Turning my back to them, I faced the far-off hills of America, a black rolling landscape lit here and there by faint sparks of amber light: a sanctuary forever just beyond our reach.

"Now take off everything you're wearing."

They wanted not us, but our clothing?

Then I understood: we were almost surely at the mercy of two deserters in uniform, who wished, as Nathaniel and I had wished but half an hour ago, to shed the apparel of His Majesty's enslavement, then to hide themselves in the clothing of two common craftsmen. They would become us, leaving us to hang from a noose in their stead.

Nathaniel unbuttoned his carpenter's smock. I did likewise with my cobbler's shirt.

"Toss them back thisaway."

We unshouldered our haversacks and set them on the road, then took off our shirts and tossed them behind us. I could hear a stirring in the trees; one man was undressing while the other aimed his musket at our bare backs.

"Now your boots and breeches."

Once again, I relinquished Papa's boots to a thief. I had worn them for less than a mile on the American earth. Out of respect for Papa, I did not toss the boots behind me, but stood them together, toes pointed westward.

"*And* your breeches."

I unfastened the waist buttons, then felt a flush of angry embarrassment as I bared my bottom to the two rogues behind us. I now wore only my stockings, their soles dirtied with dust from the road.

Nathaniel took off his stockings and threw them behind him. He stood absolutely naked in the moonlight, his face hardened, grim.

"Now walk, and keep your eyes forward until you reach the college in Cambridge."

I heard a rude laugh, and more stirring of leaves.

Nathaniel and I walked quickly down the road, wishing to be well beyond the range of their muskets. After some hundred yards, I paused to take off my stockings. I'd be damned if I was going to ruin them with stones and dirt. Better, like Nathaniel, to continue our journey toward America as two noble savages.

When I heard the faint sound of boots behind me, I looked back. Were the soldiers after us with their bayonets? No, they were running in the opposite direction. I watched my moonlit shirt disappear along the lane toward the sea. Perhaps the two scoundrels had stolen a rowboat. They would make their escape across the Mystick River to the mainland, and freedom.

Nathaniel and I had little choice but to cover our nakedness with a pair of cast-off breeches. We returned to the fork in the road, where we found, as I expected, two complete British uniforms scattered in the dust: white linen shirts with ruffles at the neck, dark reddish-black coats with lighter facings, and white breeches. There were also two plumed hats, their upturned brims embroidered with a royal crown and insignia.

Our haversacks were gone.

In exchange for my boots, I'd been left a pair of buckled shoes with worn heels and holes along the seams.

Nathaniel spat with disgust as he pulled on a pair of well-worn breeches. He buttoned their waist flap and then the front flap, though he left the legs unbuckled at his calves.

I did likewise with my own ill-fitting pair. They were damp, and pungent with the odor of a man who had rarely bathed.

Nathaniel found his stockings in the road. I still had mine in my hand. We pulled them on, then each of us stepped into a pair of castoff shoes. For a moment, I felt a cobbler's impulse to repair them properly. But of course, my tools were in London.

I lifted a ruffled white shirt from the road, shook off the dust, then put the shirt on. I felt as if His Majesty had once again gripped my arm with his firm hand.

We left the coats and hats in their scattered heaps.

Having been my old London self for a brief half-hour, I now stood on the road as someone with whom I was completely unacquainted: someone clad fully in white—a luminous white in the moonlight—and thus someone readily visible to any military patrol out tonight in search of two deserters.

Should we roll in the dust to darken ourselves?

Should we try to make our way as hidden as possible through the heavy grass?

Nathaniel looked at me with that same determination I had seen up in the rigging: no matter what winds blew our way, we would somehow prevail. "I will be who I am," he said, "until I am no more."

And so, two pilgrims in white, we began to walk westward along the road. My fears were gradually outweighed by his confidence. Both of us were silent, our buckled shoes marching in step.

The moon and stars, old friends from our nights aloft in the rigging, accompanied us. No matter what else befell us, they would never betray us. The bright constellations which had rolled beyond the *Lively's* bow, now rolled over the rumpled black terrain of Massachusetts.

Half a mile down the road, we approached the second hill, a long loaf rather than a broad knob, and the taller of the two. The road rose along its flank, giving us a better view of the Mystick River, glimmering in the moonlight to our right.

Above us to the left, the sea breeze whispered through dark grass.

Below us to the right, a seagull, flapping up the river on ghostly wings, gave one brief cry.

*　*　*

And then Nathaniel spoke. The man in luminous white walking beside me quietly asked, "Benjamin, what shall we do with our freedom?"

We were still far from free, though I did not want to say so. Better to keep silent and walk quickly in these worn-out, too-big shoes. Once we were across the neck, and about twenty miles inland . . . we could begin to think about freedom.

"Benjamin, I want to walk far enough west that I can find a village without a church. There I shall work as a carpenter, and not for the King's shilling. I shall work as a carpenter, and as a cabinetmaker, a craftsman of tables and chairs. Yes, and I shall carve a rocking horse for every child. And as I work in that village, I shall give of my time and give of my tithes to build a church."

He regarded me with a pensive look, as if he were thinking not about his church, but about me.

"I shall frame the walls and frame the roof, and I shall frame a humble steeple. I shall frame tall pointed windows along both walls, so that even this early skeleton will say to people, 'I am a church.' "

I imagined that tall empty framework, standing near a cluster of rude houses. Air laden with the scent of forest and farm would drift through it, and the sun would shine down through the open roof.

"I shall cover the walls with planks of whatever wood this Massachusetts will offer. I shall cover the roof with sturdy shingles fastened with heavy nails. Then a floor shall I lay, of heavy planks, that I shall smooth with my plane until the floor is fit for the feet of farmers and mothers and pilgrims, and for infants taking their first steps."

Nathaniel stared ahead at the dark horizon rolling beneath the stars. I did not understand all of what he was telling me, nor why. But I knew that among the hundreds of customers who had entered my father's shop, some of them gentlemen and some of them rogues, and most a bit of both, never had I met a man like Nathaniel.

"I shall fashion a dozen pews to the right, and a dozen pews to the left, with an aisle between them. They shall face a tall pointed window, still without glass. As all the windows along both sides shall be without glass. At the back of the church, two pointed windows shall flank the door frame, a very large door frame. I shall build a great door, with a latch, but no lock."

He reached his hand and touched my back, just a touch, enough to remind me of the arm that had kept me safe up in the rigging.

"Here to this church can anyone come, by day and by night. On Tuesday as well as on Sunday, as if every day were the Sabbath. Here can they sit in the quiet. And here shall I ask them, 'Did you dip your cup in the well of freedom?' "

His fingers lightly touched my back.

"And while they consider, I shall ask, 'How far did you journey to offer that cup as a gift?' "

Nathaniel reached out his arm and swept it slowly, encompassing all the sleeping land before us. "Not as I have fattened my purse, but as I have passed the cup of freedom to another, have I prospered."

And so, though I knew it not, did I speak with my first American.

‭ℬℭ‬

Chapter Twenty-One

The road descended down the flank of the long hill. Ahead of us I could see the narrow neck between the moonlit waters of the river and the bay: a dark bridge between two breeze-rippled pools of pewter.

Further ahead, on the Massachusetts mainland, I could see a tiny square of amber, perhaps the lit window of an early-rising farmer. Or of a mother whose child was sick. Or of a poet working on his verses.

Or of an apprentice cobbler, cobbling shoes for his bride-to-be.

I asked Nathaniel, "What about your Boston beauty?"

He looked at me with a peaceful smile, as if in his heart he kept a bounty of peace, enough to share with all the world. "She will come. One day as I measure and hammer and plane, she will come. She will put the pieces of colored glass into the windows."

The road now hooked to the left and joined the southern road from Charlestown, a broader, rutted road, clearly the thoroughfare from the village. Pausing at the junction, we searched in both directions. We scanned as well a nearby mill pond, looking for anyone in a rowboat, for anyone walking along the dam.

Reassured, we followed the new road westward and soon came to the neck. We crossed the thin barrier of land, the air strongly tinged with brine. My heart thumped with hope as the dark land now broadened before us. The road stretched ahead toward that lit farmhouse window. Toward the dark rolling summits. Toward Nathaniel's village.

But we had barely begun our journey on the mainland of America when a voice shouted behind us, "Halt!"

Had Nathaniel run, I would have run. But he stood absolutely still, and so did I, for neither would risk the life of the other. He lifted his eyes toward the yellow half-moon over the hills.

We heard a stirring, other voices.

"About face!"

Slowly we turned around. I saw now, in a woods near the bank of the river, a small hut obscured in the shadows. Stepping out from a door into the moonlight was a British soldier with a musket, aimed at us.

Three more soldiers hurried out from the hut, clad in white shirts and breeches much like our own, so that we were six of a kind. Their muskets leveled at our chests, they shouted a barrage of questions that left no doubt they considered us to be the two deserters.

Our confused attempt at an explanation—that we were citizens of Charlestown, both of us laborers at the wharf—altered their opinion not a whit. For we wore the standard shirt and breeches of His Majesty's infantrymen. And we knew not, upon close questioning, a single dwelling or tavern in the village of Charlestown.

The soldiers bound our hands behind us, then they marched us back over the neck. We were to lead them to where we had cast off our coats. Thus, walking eastward, Nathaniel and I followed the same road we had just so pensively trod: up and down the flank of the long hill, darker now in its own shadow as the moon leaned westward; then past the shorter hill, until we stood at the spot near the fork in the road where we had been forced to undress. The coats and hats lay on the ground exactly as the runaway soldiers had left them.

Our hands were untied. "Put on your uniforms, you dogs!" I tried to tell them the true story, or at least part of it, about the deserters who took our clothes at gunpoint and then fled along the other fork toward the sea. My effort earned no more than a glance from one of our captors toward the darkness to the east.

"Where are your muskets?" asked the sentry, still reveling in his triumph of capturing us. "Where are your cartridge boxes?"

"They took their muskets with them," I explained. "You should be looking—"

"Silence!"

They bound our hands again behind our backs, then they marched us, dressed in woolen coats and plumed hats as His Majesty's troops, toward the village of Charlestown. I suffered during that walk a most hideous dread, for well might they find our dead Hench at the bottom of the cutter.

Charlestown—the village that a year from now the British would set ablaze by firing red-hot cannonballs at it from the *Lively,* until every building was destroyed in a raging conflagration—lay sleeping beneath the stars. Not a dog barked as we passed among the dark houses. The church steeple rose with silent dignity into the moonlight; perhaps an angel or two were still awake.

We followed a lane to the wharf. With a quick downward glance, I saw the cutter was gone. Nathaniel and I were saved from hanging as murderers, though we might still wear the noose as deserters. All around the pier were strewn our jackets and navy breeches, exactly as we had left them. I knew not what to say.

Nathaniel stared straight out over the harbor, his face frozen with an understanding far beyond my own.

Commandeering a rowboat, our captors ferried us across the narrow strait to a wharf at Boston's North End. I had departed London as a prisoner, and now I entered Boston as a prisoner: first as a sailor, now as a soldier.

Our hands were untied so we could climb a ladder from the rowboat up to the pier. Then our hands were bound again behind us, with an extra lanyard tied between my hands and Nathaniel's.

We walked along the cobblestone streets of Boston, lit by streetlamps as bright as those in London. We passed brick houses fringed by well-tended gardens; passed the shops of a blacksmith, a silversmith, a hat maker, a cobbler; then we passed a brick church with an exceptionally tall pointed steeple. (Nine months latter, in April of 1775, a boy would send a signal from a window of that steeple to patriots watching in Charlestown: two lanterns, for the British were beginning their foray by sea.)

We walked past a stable smelling of horses, a tavern smelling of beer.

We met a squad of redcoats on patrol. With no consideration for the sleeping Bostonians (nor certainly for our own feelings), the soldiers raucously taunted Nathaniel and I as deserters who deserved to be taken straight to the gallows. A window swung open in the upper story of a nearby house. A man in a nightshirt called out his complaint. The rude cursing he received from the redcoats taught me in a single brief lesson the nature of the bond between us Englishmen and our American brothers.

No comfort it was, as we marched toward our fate, that we passed a cemetery with uneven ranks of headstones, their faces black in shadow, inscrutable.

We arrived at an open rolling pasture with a dozen milk cows clustered upon it, in the center of Boston. Two rows of trees planted in an orderly manner formed a lane along one side; other trees, older and taller, stood here and there across the broad terrain. At the far end of the pasture stood neat rows of tents, their white peaks sharply defined in the moonlight.

My captors spoke with a yawning sentry, then we crossed what I later learned to be Boston Common: a pasture, a park, and now a military encampment. Another sentry guided us to a tent, somewhat larger than the others, with a canopy extended in front of it. Our four guards now addressed a third sentry, who stepped inside the tent and apparently awoke an officer, for we heard an irritated grumbling. The sentry stepped back outside and glared at Nathaniel and me, two criminals whom he might just as well run through with his bayonet.

The officer finally appeared, fully dressed in coat, hat and sword. After listening to a long and confusing tale from the four soldiers who had captured us, a tale woven piecemeal as each of the four interrupted the others with his own bit of detail, and which included their finding first us, and then the uniforms which we now wore, and then the blue jackets and navy breeches on the wharf, no not the Boston wharf, the *Charlestown* wharf . . . the officer ordered his sentry to bring him a lamp.

The sentry fetched a whale oil lamp hanging from a post nearby. The officer ordered Nathaniel and me to hold out our hands. We did so, and the officer scolded the "bla'gards" who had brought us all this way, showing them the tar on our fingers. Clearly we had escaped from a ship, not from a regiment.

The officer stared at Nathaniel and me in the light of the lamp. I wondered anxiously if he knew about Hench.

He declared, "You'll do." Turning to his sentry, he issued orders that we were to be taken to an infantry tent, guarded there through the night, then brought back to him in the morning.

Without a word to us (or from us), and without even a brief nod of gratitude to our four captors, who had a very long walk ahead of them, the officer returned to his tent.

Nathaniel and I were led by a new group of guards into the village of tents. We followed a lane between the orderly rows; every guy line was taut, every peaked roof was straight. Here slept His Majesty's mighty army, a lion in the midst of Boston's lambs. But how would the lion fare, I wondered, when winter arrived with a foot of snow?

"Halt." Our hands were unbound. We were told to enter one of the tents. Opening a flap, we discerned, by the dim glow of the moon, ten straw beds on the ground, with eight men sleeping upon them. The guards encircled our tent. Those to the west cast their restless shadows on the canvas.

Nathaniel and I were taking off our hats and coats when one of the eight soldiers leapt up with a shout. In an instant he had a knife at my throat. When I shrieked, he hesitated. Then he snarled at me, "You ain't Higgins!"

Nor, as the other seven soldiers ascertained when they too jumped to their feet, was Nathaniel their messmate Brown. They had little interest in who we really were, but remained vehemently disappointed that we were not Higgins and Brown, who, as they told us, had won every shilling at cards that could be had from a good many lads in the regiment. Then the villains had disappeared past the sentries with their loot.

Nathaniel and I, exonerated, were welcomed to share a straw bed. Then almost as quickly as they had risen up, the eight lay back down in their straw-covered blankets. They soon filled the tent with the deep tranquil breathing of sleep.

Nathaniel looked at me as we knelt and took off our buckled shoes. "Freedom," he said quietly, "is as precious as a man's next heartbeat."

But still we had each other. We were bound by far more than the lanyard they had tied between our hands.

We stretched ourselves upon two blankets. I remember thinking that despite all the recent calamity in my life, the straw bed was far more comfortable than my narrow, tightly-hugging hammock aboard the frigate.

Like an enormous, dark and peaceful wave, exhaustion rolled over me. I relinquished all thoughts of tomorrow, to tomorrow.

Our backs on the American earth, we slept.

৪০

Chapter Twenty-Two

Genevieve, with a proper bit of history.

Our American Revolution in the 1770's was the vigorous progeny of an earlier revolution in England during the 1600's.

A fervent group of church reformers, known as Puritans, whittled away at the hierarchy of church authorities. They preferred decisions made within their own local churches to the dictates of an Anglican bishop. Further, as they had a covenant with God, and would accordingly obey His laws, so did they form a covenant, or contract, with each other. They pledged to obey whatever laws they themselves developed as a religious community.

The more radical Puritans extended their philosophy into the realm of government. They proposed the extraordinary idea that every man ought to have a voice, a vote, in determining the nature and representation of his government. Wishing to eliminate all political and economic inequalities, these Puritans declared that government should be based on a covenant, a written constitution, an "agreement of the people," in order to protect the natural rights of all people, as given to them by God.

The powerful kings and wealthy aristocratic landowners fought to uphold the authority of the Church of England, and to preserve their own authority and privileges. Following years of strife and repression, several groups of Puritans boarded ships and sailed for the New World, where they could establish their own communities and govern themselves according to Puritan principles. One group settled in Jamestown, Virginia in 1607. Another group settled in Plymouth, Massachusetts in 1620. In 1630, over nine hundred men and women sailing in seventeen ships entered Massachusetts Bay; these Puritans founded Boston and a half-dozen nearby villages.

Our forefathers kept their word: they granted most citizens in America a far greater measure of equality than Englishmen had ever known in Britain. The Virginia Assembly of 1619 was elected not by wealthy landowners, but by all men seventeen years of age and older. In 1620, forty-one Pilgrim men signed a compact aboard the *May-flower* before they stepped on shore, forming their own cornerstone of self-government. The Massachusetts Bay Company, with its own charter, set up a commonwealth with an elected assembly. Neither the British king nor his Parliament had any significant influence on the assembly's decisions.

Other Puritans settled in Rhode Island, in New Jersey, in Maryland, in Connecticut, and as Quakers under the guidance of William Penn, in Pennsylvania. The Puritans gradually established themselves in all thirteen colonies. By 1770, roughly eight out of ten churches in America had been founded on Puritan principles.

A century and a half of settlement enabled the Puritans to sink their roots deep into the American soil. In Britain, the crown traveled its stormy journey from king to king, until it settled on the head of George III in 1760. Rather than watch his empire unravel, King George was determined to keep the American colonials fully obedient to British rule. But the colonials, descendants of those early Puritan revolutionaries, were determined to preserve, for themselves and their posterity, both their chartered rights as Englishmen, and their natural rights as the children of God.

Another thread, a very strong thread, is woven into this tale.

The ability to read was much more widespread in America than in England during the years leading up to the Revolution. Pamphlets, books, broadsheets, and newspapers traveled from hand to hand throughout the colonies, enabling farmers, shopkeepers, school teachers and tavern owners to discuss developments in the world of politics. Many Americans were familiar with the classical writings of the Greeks and Romans, on democracy, on law. Americans read articles by modern European philosophers, including the great English writer John Locke, whose book in 1690, *Two Treatices on Government*, stated that all men were equally entitled to their natural rights, primarily the rights to life, liberty, and property. Locke wrote that government, defined and limited by its contract with the people whom it governed, must protect these natural rights, rather than threaten them. Should a government fail to fulfill its purpose, then the people retained the right to establish a new government.

Locke's clear summation of ideas propounded by a few radical thinkers in the seventeenth century enabled those ideas to reach a widespread audience in the eighteenth, the Century of Enlightenment. From Paris to St. Petersburg, from London to Philadelphia, from the House of Burgesses in Virginia to the Green Dragon Tavern in Boston, people talked with great conviction about their rights.

The Puritans brought with them from England a candle of liberty. Though that candle had been all but snuffed out in Britain by 1770, the great-great-grandchildren in the colonies of Massachusetts and Virginia and South Carolina and New York were kindling their bright flame into a blaze.

∞

Chapter Twenty-Three

Genevieve, returning to the summer of 1774.

Papa had worried whether the other colonies would support Boston when its port was closed. Would New York and New Hampshire turn their backs on the mobs of Boston? Would other seaports conspire to increase their profits by taking the business that Boston had lost?

Would the other twelve colonies be frightened by the arrival of the King's troops, or emboldened?

During the summer of 1774, the citizens of Boston were profoundly heartened, for the other colonies quickly unified in their generosity. North and South Carolina sent ships laden with rice; the barrels were unloaded at Salem, a seaport up the coast from Boston, then carted at night to the marketplace at Faneuil Hall. Canadians who supported the American rebellion sent ships laden with wheat and corn. From farms along Hudson's River, from villages along the Mohawk, from warehouses in New York City, wagons of food, coffers of cash, and letters of support crossed the neck into Boston every day.

Israel Putnam, a farmer who would later become an officer in the Continental Army, drove a hundred and thirty sheep from his farm in Connecticut all the way to Boston. Putnam traveled over a hundred miles with his flock before he herded them across the neck and along Orange Street (where grateful Bostonians cheered him) to the pasture on the Common.

In August, news arrived from the House of Burgesses in Virginia, the seat of colonial government, that a plantation owner and former military officer named George Washington had stated publicly, "If need be I will raise one thousand men, subsist them at my own expense and march myself at their head to the relief of Boston."

Virginia, to the surprise of many, became Boston's most courageous ally. Back in May, when the Virginia Assembly first heard about the Boston Port Bill, the Assembly declared that in support of its "sister colony," June first would be a day of prayer and fasting. When the British royal governor, Lord Dunmore, consequently dissolved the rebellious Assembly, the Virginians were no more intimidated than Samuel Adams would have been. They moved their deliberations from the

State House in Williamsburg to the nearby Raleigh Tavern, where the Assembly boldly proposed that representatives from all the colonies should gather at a "Continental Congress" to discuss the closing of Boston Harbor, and other matters crucial to the thirteen colonies.

When this proposal reached New York, the colonial government there seconded the measure, then suggested that Boston should choose the place and date for the Congress.

In a meeting behind locked doors in Salem, Samuel Adams noted that the closing of a local seaport had become a matter of continental importance. He suggested that the Congress meet on September 1, in Philadelphia, a city in the heart of colonial America.

With enormous courage, Samuel Adams continued to hold his boisterous public meetings in Faneuil Hall, not more than a five-minute walk from General Gage's headquarters at the State House. On August 9, General Gage, Commander in Chief of all British forces in North America, sent a courier to inform Samuel Adams that his meetings were illegal under British law, and must therefore cease. Without hesitation, Samuel Adams sent the courier back with a message for General Gage, saying that the session now in progress was not a new meeting, but a former meeting which had been adjourned before Gage's arrival in Boston, and which was now merely resuming and thus entirely legal.

Though Adams and the other Sons of Liberty could hear troops of soldiers marching on the cobblestones outside the Hall's windows, the patriots continued to make plans, to draw up resolutions, and to write a multitude of letters to the other colonies.

General Gage could close the port of Boston, but he could not control the colony of Massachusetts. Frustrated by his limited number of troops, he waited for additional regiments to arrive from Britain before he made his first military move.

On August 10, 1774, four delegates from the Massachusetts Bay Colony—Thomas Cushing, Robert Treat Paine, and the cousins Samuel and John Adams—rode in a carriage past Boston Common. Looking out the carriage windows, they could see rows of white tents, cannons in an artillery park, a squad of armed redcoats setting out on a patrol of the city. They could see as well, on a flagpole mounted atop the Common's tallest hill, the British flag flapping in the wind off the sea.

Perhaps the four delegates tipped their tri-cornered hats with a polite farewell to the enemy's encampment, as they began their journey across four other colonies to the Continental Congress in Philadelphia.

Meanwhile during that summer of 1774, out here in the country-side, Papa, Henry, and Judd were meeting with a dozen other farmers once a week on the Lincoln green, where they marched with freshly oiled muskets as a company of militia. Our neighbors elected my father, John Byrnes, as their captain. Should the redcoats try to extend their tyranny beyond the confines of Boston—should they try to disrupt the patriotic meetings taking place in every country village—they would be met by a quickly mustered company of "minutemen." These ordinary citizens were ready to lay down their plows, ready to leap from a warm bed, ready (though no one boasted of such) to offer their lives, should they be called upon—at a minute's notice—to defend their rights by force of arms.

And myself? As a young woman of eighteen, I was proud of my two brothers, immensely proud of my father . . . and secretly as afraid as my mother that our three men might one day have to stand up to the dreaded redcoats.

I don't think I thought much further than that.

We had our arguments with Britain, we had our dreams for ourselves, but who could really know the terrible cost of war?

Until, abruptly, we were called upon to pay it.

❧

Chapter Twenty-Four

Benjamin, in Boston, a soldier.

Captain Simms informed us the following morning that Nathaniel and I would be trained to replace Higgins and Brown. He offered no explanation, though he did add, "In any case, should you choose not to serve in His Majesty's Tenth Regiment, you will be returned to the navy as deserters."

Our appearance back on the deck of the *Lively* would no doubt quite please Hench, were he still alive.

Seeing no other option, Nathaniel and I declared our willingness to learn the drill, though in our hearts we raged against it.

Thus we spent our first day in the seditious town of Boston as two British soldiers wearing the full uniform, including cartridge box and canteen, haversack and bayonet scabbard, and an absurd plumed regimental hat. All morning we marched hither and yon across the grassy Common while our sergeant roared commands and curses at us. We also learned to stand properly: heels close together, toes turned out, our meager bellies drawn in, our humble chests puffed out, shoulders squared, head turned a bit to the right, while keeping our right hand at the side, palm to thigh, and holding with our left hand a firelock (as the British called their muskets) that pointed skyward and was propped against the shoulder.

We then poised our firelock. And cocked our firelock. And went no further than that on the first day, for at noon, a drum called the troops to assembly.

Standing in a straight rank with our tentmates, deep within a large formation of several hundred troops who stood at attention in precisely squared rank and file, Nathaniel and I stared at two empty nooses hanging from a crudely built pair of gallows. Stunned, terrified—shivers of fear ran through me as never before in my life—I was certain that at the next moment, Nathaniel and I would be marched at bayonet-point from our rank to that scaffold, then ordered to mount the steps. Never mind that we had deserted from the navy: we were deserters, and would serve as an example. Glancing at Nathaniel, I saw not fear in his face, but a child's look of horror.

My minutes of helpless dread were abruptly ended when two men, one dressed in my cobbler's clothes and Papa's boots, the other dressed in Nathaniel's carpenter's smock and leather apron, were marched ahead of an armed guard toward the scaffold and up the steps. I glanced again at Nathaniel and saw his blue eyes filled with tears. They were not tears of relief, nor even tears of sympathy; this man, this child, this angel, wept at the baffling cruelty he was forced to witness.

The two men, one wailing for mercy, the other dropping to his knees, were held upright by soldiers who gripped their arms while the nooses were slipped over their heads and tightened around their necks. I thereupon closed my eyes, and can relate no more, save for the sound of the ropes snapping taut, and of Papa's boots kicking each other in a diminishing struggle. And then silence. The soldiers around us seemed to have stopped breathing.

An officer dismissed us. One of our tentmates patted Nathaniel on the back as a bit of encouragement. He must have noticed Nathaniel's pale staring face. But Nathaniel was by then looking far beyond two men dangling by their necks: he was staring through a keyhole at the world of human evil, and he knew—yes, he knew—that the door was about to swing wide open.

I never saw Papa's boots again. Or rather, perhaps I saw them, but did not recognize them, if they were appropriated one of His Majesty's officers.

Who I was then, as a lad of nineteen in Boston, I could hardly have said. I was neither Benjamin York nor Higgins, and yet a bit of both. The cobbler had been stolen from me, but I resisted the soldier with all my heart. My hands gradually lost the dark stains of tar and gained the odor of firelock oil and gunpowder. The soldiers and the Bostonians around me spoke English, yet I was a foreigner in a strange, cruel, and unpredictable land.

Our tentmates, light infantrymen of the 10th, Royal Lincolnshire Regiment (distinguished by red coats with yellow facing and cuffs), usually called Nathaniel by the name of Brown. He said so little, that perhaps it was easier for them to regard him as the Brown they had known, rather than the silent stranger whom they would apparently never know.

Nathaniel and I had no thought of attempting a second desertion. We continued our daily drilling, learned to handle a cartridge, how to prime, how to shut the pan, and every step thereafter, until our fingers and arms ached with the weight of our firelocks.

Not a day passed that I did not remember my father's words, "No son of mine shall ever be a soldier." Never did I rid myself of a burning shame at what I was doing. Nathaniel and I vowed to each other, on our first afternoon in camp, that never would we fire at any man, American, British, or otherwise. And though we were made to mount our bayonets and thrust them into the breast of a Yankee scarecrow, never, we vowed, would we impale any living man. Better, we agreed, to throw down our firelocks and run from the field of battle, risking our captain's lead ball in our backs, than to be forced to the crime—never mind its military masquerade—of murder.

Or so we said, hoping to preserve on Boston Common some empty remnant of decency.

Meanwhile, in order to preserve our necks, and to learn a bit more about this American world around us, we stood with our heels together, toes turned outward. We took proper care of our flints. And we plunged the bayonet into a torn and shredded scarecrow.

&

Chapter Twenty-Five

Genevieve Byrnes, Daughter of Liberty.

In September of 1774, my father received a copy of the "Suffolk Resolves," penned by Dr. Joseph Warren, the very same Dr. Warren who had visited our home with Samuel Adams. I have preserved Papa's copy to this day, keeping it flat and dry at the bottom of our linen drawer. Yellowed and a bit tattered now, it reads with the clear and passionate language that farmers and shopkeepers and ropemakers and fishermen spoke during those fervent years.

The British Parliament had closed the port of Boston and dissolved our colonial government. Responding to these Intolerable Acts, as we called them, delegates from Boston and the other towns in Suffolk County met in Milton on the 9th of September. By unanimous vote, the delegates proposed three powerful strategies: they urged the citizens of Massachusetts to cease paying taxes to Britain, to cease trading with Britain, and to organize local militias to prepare for war. The Suffolk Resolves, distributed to the other counties in the colony, were fiery, treasonous, and immensely popular.

As I now read through this treasured document for the perhaps the hundredth time, I find phrases that sprang from our hearts, phrases that we cherished in our souls. We fought not for ourselves alone. Remembering "our venerable progenitors," who first settled the "savage and uncultivated desart," then "bequeathed the dearbought inheritance" to our generation, we felt that we had "the most sacred obligations" to pass the twin gifts of land and freedom "unclogged with shackles, to our innocent and beloved offspring." We defended our rights not for ourselves alone, but for the "unborn millions" who would follow us.

This concept, that we were but one generation in a long line of American generations, was so important that the delegates repeated it. We had "an indispensable duty which we owe to God, our country, ourselves and posterity" to "defend and preserve those civil and religious rights and liberties, for which many of our fathers fought, bled and died, and to hand them down entire to future generations."

As for the hated British Parliament: "The streets of Boston are thronged with military executioners" who had been sent from England by "a wicked administration to enslave America." We had the choice to "tamely submit," or to "arrest the hand which would ransack our pockets."

Against the "obstinate and incorrigible enemies to this country," stood "this numerous, brave and hardy people," who were urged to "use their utmost diligence to acquaint themselves with the art of war as soon as possible," and to "appear under arms at least once every week." Our militias should not provoke conflict; rather, they "are determined to act merely upon the defensive, so long as such conduct may be vindicated by reason and the principles of self-preservation, but no longer."

Further, "we would heartily recommend to all persons of this community, not to engage in routs, riots, or licentious attacks upon the properties of any person whatsoever." Rather, "in a contest so important, in a cause so solemn, our conduct shall be such as to merit the approbation of the wise, and the admiration of the brave and free of every age and every country." No more mobs, no more riots. We would show ourselves as worthy of the world's admiration.

Copies of these Resolves were printed, then distributed to "our brethren in the country" of Massachusetts. One copy was delivered by Paul Revere himself to the First Continental Congress in Philadelphia. Many of the delegates in Carpenters' Hall were stunned, for they had not advanced in their thinking to the point of war. Most still considered King George the Third to be their rightful sovereign, and hoped to find some compromise with his wayward Parliament.

Nevertheless, the Suffolk Resolves quickly kindled their spirits. On September 18th, Congress endorsed them not as a mere statement from one county in Massachusetts, but as the voice of all thirteen colonies: the feeling and temper of the land.

John Adams, our delegate in Philadelphia, wrote after the vote of endorsement, "This day convinced me that America will support Massachusetts or perish with her."

The bold resolutions of that first Congress, which met for fifty-one disputatious days, were transmitted to every town and village of all thirteen colonies. Congress adjourned in October, with the understanding that it would meet again the following May, if necessary.

Thus, in the autumn of 1774, American democracy was nurtured in a multitude of town meetings. Resolves were carried by horseback across colony borders. A farmer spoke, the Congress listened; Congress spoke, a farmer listened.

All these events proceeded with a dignity and a courage which would honor us, as Dr. Warren penned, "to that latest period, when the streams of time shall be absorbed in the abyss of eternity."

To which I say, Amen.

∞

Chapter Twenty-Six

Benjamin and Nathaniel,
in His Majesty's 10th Regiment.

From July of 1774 until April of 1775, for the duration of nine months, we served as soldiers in an army which the King had sent from Britain to discipline and regulate the colonial population. But the army was confined to the tiny peninsula of Boston.

His Majesty's soldiers, bored and contemptuous, often gathered outside a meetinghouse on the Sabbath. They interrupted the service inside by bellowing sarcastic verses of "Yankee Doodle." The minister and his congregation, thus taunted during the most sacred hour of the week, either strove to forgive their enemies, or burned for revenge.

During that anxious autumn and winter, reports and rumors, rumors and reports, ran through the encampment that the Americans were preparing for war. We heard about militias drilling on village greens, about muskets and gunpowder and even cannons hidden in barns, about illegal meetings attended by angry throngs of people in every town and village, and about Committees of Correspondence that sent their plans, information, and resolves to other Committees of Correspondence, not only in Massachusetts, but throughout the entire thirteen colonies.

We felt a web of resistance wrapping around us, growing stronger by the week.

During those nine months of waiting—of waiting for we knew not what—we looked to better ourselves as best we could. The winter was especially mild, the warmest, said Bostonians, they could remember. Thus our quarters were far less dismal than they might have been. The troops were restless, drunken and often sickly, but at least we were not frozen corpses upon our straw beds.

Though gifted in a strange way in his heart, Nathaniel had no more schooling than a carpenter's simple arithmetic. Of his own name, he could write only an unsteady N, followed by a dot, as if there were no more to him than that.

Always a keen student myself (though my own schooling had ended at the age of twelve when I apprenticed to my father), I found great pleasure in teaching a student equally keen. From a bookseller in Boston named Henry Knox, I bought a child's first reader. Nathaniel proved surprisingly apt with words. He soon graduated to more difficult books, at such a rate that Mr. Knox kindly took back our used books at half the price. That worthy gentleman further obliged us by having available the next book, and the next, in a steady sequence. Mr. Knox was ready whenever Nathaniel became ready.

Every day, I read to Nathaniel from the *Boston Gazette*, until by November, he was reading the *Gazette* to me. We did likewise from the Book of Genesis, and from the four Gospels. Nathaniel read with a warm and earnest tone, as if he had finally found his voice.

I kept the promise I had made aboard the *Lively* on the day we sighted the steeples of Boston. Unable to attend services with the officers at King's Chapel, Nathaniel and I attended the Old South Meeting House, not far from the Common. Though we wore our scarlet uniforms, we were mutely welcomed, or at least tolerated, by the families who filled the pews. I said the same prayer every Sunday: I thanked the good Lord that Nathaniel and I had survived our crossing on the frigate, and I asked that we might somehow find our way free from the war that we knew to be coming.

Though Nathaniel had no one in England to whom he might write a letter, I searched for every possibility to send a letter to my family, and to my beloved Elspeth. Meeting, one day near the wharf, an Irish sailor who was soon embarking for Bristol, I entrusted him with a letter which I hastily wrote on a sheet of paper purchased from Mr. Knox. I signed the letter with a false name, lest the navy learn of my whereabouts and come to fetch me back to my old friend Hench. As I never encountered that sailor again, I knew not if my letter ever left the port of Boston, or if he simply pocketed my shilling.

I sent another letter with a farmer from Salem, with whom I secretly spoke near an apple stall in the Boston marketplace. I offered him a substantial number of shillings to take my letter with him and to place it aboard a ship from Salem to London. He spoke most cordially with me, and seemed sympathetic, but again I had no way of knowing whether my letter ever made its way to a ship.

The most wretched day of that long and aimless winter was the last day of December 1774, which was to be our wedding day. As man and wife, Elspeth and I were to greet the new year. Instead, I greeted it with several thousand roaring drunkards, few of whom made it back to their tents that night before they collapsed somewhere in the snowy grass. I felt myself a prisoner within the confines of Bedlam.

May no man upon this earth ever suffer the agony of regret, and grief, and helpless love for my poor abandoned Elspeth, that I suffered when cannons aboard the *Lively*, still anchored in the harbor, fired twelve shots at midnight to announce the new year. Even Nathaniel's arm around my shoulders could not stop my weeping.

The early warmth of spring brought a tremendous restlessness among the troops. If they were here to punish the Americans, then let them have a commanding officer who would order the punishing. They were heartily tired of "Old Lady Gage," who again and again appeased the Bostonians, and punished his own soldiers, in order to maintain some degree of peace between the two.

And then the trudging pace of history suddenly quickened. On the sixteenth of April 1775, the naval sloop *Falcon* arrived in Boston from London with orders for General Gage. Written by Lord Dartmouth in January, in response to Gage's grim appraisal of the situation in and around Boston during the previous autumn, the letter reflected little understanding of the dangerous level of bitterness between British troops and the seething Bostonians in the spring of 1775. Lord Dartmouth, three thousand miles away from the fists and taunts and curses in the streets of Boston, severely disappointed General Gage by informing him that the King was not sending the 20,000 additional troops which Gage had requested. As Lord Dartmouth wrote, "I am unwilling to believe that matters are as yet come to that issue."

However, Lord Dartmouth instructed Gage to "arrest and imprison the principal actors and abettors in the Provincial Congress (whose proceedings appear in every light to be acts of treason and rebellion)." Thus, Gage was to capture both Samuel Adams and John Hancock, and to ship them to London where they would stand trial.

Lord Dartmouth further stated, "It will surely be better the conflict should be brought on, upon such ground, than in a riper state of rebellion." In other words, better for the war to begin now, than when the traitors were more fully prepared.

With this letter in hand, General Thomas Gage, after nearly a year as military governor of the colony of Massachusetts, now planned his first major military action.

He would send seven hundred troops, commanded by Lieutenant

Colonel Francis Smith, a fat and slow but reliable officer, on a march to the village of Lexington, and then on to the village of Concord, with a dual purpose: the troops were to capture the rebel leaders Adams and Hancock, and they were to gather or destroy any military stores which the rebels might have hidden. The seven hundred soldiers were to leave Boston at night, in secrecy, in order to arrive in Lexington before dawn.

By sending several hundred troops into the countryside, General Gage, who had struggled with admirable diligence to keep the peace in Boston, would now, quite unaware of what he was up against, throw a very large rock (as Genevieve would say) at a hornets' nest of American patriots. The hornets would pour out, the hornets would rage, and their stings would be felt for the next six and a half years.

And we, Benjamin York and Nathaniel Ash in His Majesty's light infantry, were a part of that rock.

Chapter Twenty-Seven

On Monday, the 17th of April, 1775, just before a changing of the guard at midnight (Nathaniel and I stood atop Beacon Hill, yawning mightily as we completed our watch), news spread through the garrison that a night patrol on Long Wharf had noticed unusual activity in the harbor: several British warships, including our *Lively*, were launching their cutters and longboats, then floating them off their sterns. A launching of so many transport vessels clearly indicated an impending movement of troops.

On Tuesday morning at muster, Nathaniel and I were informed by Captain Simms that we—and we alone among our tentmates—were relieved of all further duties for the next several days. When I summoned the temerity to question why, Captain Simms replied that since we were more sober and industrious than the others, we would be detailed to a special detachment. More than that, he admitted, he did not know.

Rumors spread from company to company all day Tuesday, as several hundred men were relieved of their duties, but ordered to stay in camp. And no one, not even our officers (or so they claimed), knew why.

Were we to board a ship and sail for New York City, to close that seaport as well? Were we to sail for Philadelphia, and there prevent any further congresses from meeting? Were we perhaps to sail much further south, to the West Indian islands, there to join the British fleet in some dispute with the French?

And what if Nathaniel and I should be rowed in a cutter back to our *Lively*?

Or—the most worrisome possibility of all—were the troops to march across Boston's Neck onto the mainland of America, and there enforce by sway of arms the laws of His Majesty's dominion?

Were we to meet the farmers face to face, with the hope that they would turn and flee?

Having walked the patrolled streets of Boston for nine months now, having heard the shouted insults, suffered the rocks and snowballs . . . aye, having looked upon the bitterness and rage and unhidden hatred in the eyes that glared at us, Nathaniel and I wondered whether a thousand farmers might not encircle our island fortress one night, while a few rogues in Boston lit the town on fire. What choice then, but to board the ships and flee?

But most of the British troops cared not a whit about a thousand armed farmers. The soldiers were certain that the untrained rabble, when confronted by His Majesty's professional and superbly armed regiments, would simply turn tail and run home to their cornfields. The first redcoats had landed in Boston in September of 1768, six and a half years ago. Though most of those soldiers had been replaced by other troops, the soldiers in Boston now felt they had waited long enough. They had shown patience enough, forbearance enough, and it was time to punish the rebels with a well-sharpened bayonet. "Time," declared Isaac Butler, one of our tentmates, "to spice our daily swill of rum with a bit of Yankee blood."

Nathaniel and I had slept for no more than an hour in our tent on Tuesday evening, April 18, when we were awakened by a hand quietly shaking us. Our sergeant gestured that we were to rise silently, gather our gear, and leave our sleeping mates behind. Outside the tent flap, beneath a cloudless sky sprinkled with stars (the same April stars that had shone above our westbound frigate a year ago), we were formed into silent companies. A rising three-quarter moon lit our faces: some were enlivened with eagerness for whatever action awaited us, some stared dully at the ground.

We soon marched across the Common to a beach on Back Bay. There we saw a fleet of cutters and longboats assembled in the bright moonlight, each boat manned by sailors at the oars. Nathaniel and I peered from boat to boat, searching for Hench. I wondered with sharp anxiety if fate were about to bring us together again, he with his knife, I with my firelock and bayonet. But neither of us spotted his malicious face among the crew in the clustered boats.

While we waited on the beach, we enjoyed the springtime warmth of that April evening. We gazed across the black water at the distant lamps of Cambridge. Word gradually spread through the troops that we had no embarkation officer, and thus no orderly plan for boarding the boats. Finally a Lieutenant Frederick Mackenzie, adjutant of the 23rd Regiment, took it upon himself to load his two companies into several boats, although his soldiers then sat a small distance offshore, still waiting.

Following that example, the other companies began to load into boats, until several hundred men, Nathaniel and myself included, sat afloat near the shore, while several hundred more men, the boats being full, remained standing in silence on the beach.

It seemed a poor beginning to whatever we were doing.

Lieutenant Colonel Francis Smith, our commanding officer, at last appeared on the beach. He was a pudgy fellow who strutted slowly about. He ordered the boats to take us across the bay to the far shore. Nathaniel and I, who had spent two months at the oars of our cutter, now rode without effort as infantrymen. Our bayonets, like hundreds of other bayonets slowly crossing the bay, pointed upward at the stars and gleamed in the moonlight.

Nathaniel laid his hand upon my arm and nodded. There, two boats over, sat Hench in the stern of his cutter. He was a bit hunched over, perhaps from his beating. We knew he must be gloating, on this night of military maneuvers, for he was captain of his own troop transport vessel.

My rage at that monster still burned in my heart. Yet I was glad that we had not managed to murder him. We bore no guilt, had not sinned against the Lord's commandment which forbade us to kill another man. Nor, I promised myself anew, would I ever transgress that sacred law.

Once across the Bay—a journey north of about a mile—we did not come to any sort of wharf, but disembarked onto sodden ground. Rather, not ground at all, but the Bay's bottom at low tide. East of us, on higher ground, stood a few dark farm buildings. Further north, a low black finger of land jutted into glimmering water.

The boats, as soon as they were empty, paddled back to fetch the remaining men.

To our increasing disgruntlement, we on the western shore did not march toward higher ground, but instead waited with our shoes in the chilly mud, while the tide, then in young flood, gradually rose up our ankles to our knees. Despite the folly of our situation, we waited no less than two hours upon that shore, until it no longer was a shore: we stood in the Back Bay itself. The men, grumbling with vexation, were ordered to remain silent.

Even after the remaining troops had been ferried across, we *still* stood waiting in the water, the cold Atlantic water of early spring, while it rose ever further up our legs. Our arms ached at having to hoist our firelocks and other gear above the rising surface.

At last, well after midnight, the boats finished their third crossing, laden with cargo. We knew not what that cargo might be, until it was unloaded into the arms of wading men: bundles of food. The soldiers discovered the provisions to be naught but stale bread (not from Boston but the hold of some ship). Most of them cast the hardened loaves to whatever fish or ducks might later find them.

The moon had by now passed beyond its zenith. It was ahead of us, lighting our way, when finally we were ordered to march toward solid ground. With a good deal of trouble, I managed to keep my sodden shoes upon my feet as step after wallowing step I pulled left shoe and right shoe up from the mud. The soldiers ahead of us had the pleasure of walking on simple flat mud, whereas Nathaniel and I, and especially those troops toward the rear, struggled awkwardly to walk on and in and through deep holes in the muck.

It seemed an even worse beginning to whatever we were doing.

Gaining solid ground, we continued westward across sandy flats. In our stockings and shoes, we brought a good portion of the Bay's muck with us.

We passed dark farm buildings to our left, and a slender moonlit creek on our right.

Our spirits lifted when finally we reached a road. Though dark, and leading we knew not where, it was at least hard and smooth and dry. We assembled into a column, then we marched four abreast for perhaps a mile, advancing southwest toward the lamps of Cambridge.

But before we entered the village, we met a junction in the road. Rank by rank, our long column wheeled to the right. Now marching northwest, we headed back into the dark countryside.

Far to the west, above the rolling black horizon (as if prowling from peak to peak among the stars), the Great Bear was watching us. Perhaps with a silent growl of warning.

Nine months ago, while crossing Charlestown Neck on a warm moonlit night, Nathaniel and I had hoped to follow a country road westward toward our freedom. Now, on just such a road, we could only glance at each other, and wonder what our first night, our first dawn, upon the continent of the New World would bring.

છ૭

Chapter Twenty-Eight

Benjamin, on

LEXINGTON GREEN

We passed a freshly plowed field beside the road, black in the night and fragrant with upturned earth. Beyond it glowed a pale moonlit cloud of white blossoms in an apple orchard. We heard the chirping of birds as they flitted amorously from tree to tree, too busy with their flirting to bother with sleep. The beauty of a new, fresh season brought to mind most painfully my Elspeth, who should by now have become my bride, and with whom on this warm springtime night I should be walking, hand in tender hand, beneath the jubilant stars.

Our column had marched not more than a mile beyond Cambridge when we heard, dimly in the distance ahead of us, the ringing of a church bell: a prolonged, insistent ringing. A minute later we heard scattered shots, followed by more distant shots: muskets fired in relays to send a signal fanning out across the countryside. Not a soldier among us needed any explanation. The rebels knew we were coming. Several times during the past year, they had quickly answered the alarm when His Majesty's troops had marched outside of Boston. They would no doubt answer it again tonight.

Perhaps they knew better than we did the goal of our expedition. We were, by my estimate, no more than seven hundred men, marching blindly, each man with a heavy rucksack, a canteen of water, a firelock and thirty-six balls of shot. Whereas they, in an hour's time, might well number several thousand. And each American no doubt knew the roads, the hills, the streams, the swamps.

Perhaps, at the next bend in the road, they awaited in a dark copse of trees with a cannon.

Our column passed through the silent village of Menotomy, where not even a barking dog noted our passage.

We knew not, of course, that along this very highway several hours before, both William Dawes and Paul Revere had galloped to warn the rebels that we were coming. "The regulars are out!" they had shouted at the windows of every house along the road. "The regulars are out!"

Thus the silence of Menotomy indicated not that the villagers were sleeping, but rather that they were watching from behind dark windows and stable doors as we marched into their trap.

Our 10th Regiment marched in the vanguard of the long column. We were therefore able to see most clearly when three British officers rode toward us. We heard them tell Major John Pitcairn that they had captured an express rider named Revere, who told them that several hundred rebels had gathered further up the highway to confront us. The news was whispered back through our ranks.

Not long afterwards, we spotted a carriage coming toward us, then heard the gentleman riding within say that six hundred rebels were now assembled in Lexington—the next village up the road—and that they were armed and set to oppose us.

This news, passing back through the troops, engendered a wave of belligerent murmurs. Despite the tiresome march, the soldiers seemed most eager to advance upon the enemy.

The moon had by now disappeared beyond the western hills. The faces stretching back behind me were dimly lit by starlight. Who would live and who would die before the day was over, we knew not.

For myself, I wanted to cast away my firelock and bayonet, to tear off my clumsy rucksack and cartridge box, to toss away my red coat with its multitude of bothersome buttons. Then I would leap over the stone wall flanking the road.

Nathaniel and I would cavort like two colts across the dark meadow toward the pale nimbus of an apple orchard. There among the trees we would lie upon the earth, breathe the scent of fresh blossoms, peer up through the petals at the stars . . . and wait for the war to be over before we bestirred ourselves from a very long nap.

The sky behind us was beginning to glow with a hint of dawn when Major Pitcairn ordered us to halt. Lexington was now a short distance ahead. We could see a few scattered houses and barns at the edge of the village, though no lights in the windows.

We were ordered to prime and load our firelocks. As I performed the practiced movements, and heard behind me the click and rattle of seven hundred soldiers doing the same, my heart pounded with dread. To speak with Nathaniel was now impossible. We could only look at each other and know that we had decided, months ago, that whatever we did, we would do it together.

Seven hundred rammers slid down the long barrels, pushing the charge of powder and ball into place. The noisy rammers then returned to their fastenings along the barrels. Weapons were shouldered. Silence settled along the column.

The birds in a nearby woods, however, were warbling and chirping and trilling their mightiest, for their hearts knew naught but the joy of a brightening day.

Major Pitcairn, mounted on his horse, ordered us forward at double time. Our hundreds of shoes hastened with a vast uniformity.

As we entered the village, we heard a drummer ahead of us, beating an urgent Assembly. We also heard distant shots, serving either as a warning or a summons.

At a fork in the road, we were ordered to the right. Passing between a large stately tavern and a three-story meetinghouse, we stared ahead at the enemy, formed in two ranks on a broad triangular green in the center of the village.

There were no six hundred rebels waiting for us.

No more than seventy men and boys, all of them armed, stood in two ragged rows. An armed Negro stood among them. I spotted a farmer of advanced age, holding a musket; his hat lay upside down on the ground between his feet. None of the rebels wore any sort of uniform. Rather, they were dressed as if to plow their fields that day. A boy with a drum stood at one end of their line, though his drum was now silent.

Two or three dozen other villagers, men and women both, stood along the edge of the road, some sheltered behind a stone wall, some behind a rail fence. Others watched from the windows of houses around the green. One young woman stood in the open doorway of her home. These spectators watched the long column of redcoats now snaking from the road onto the green, there to confront the sons, fathers and grandfathers of the village.

Major Pitcairn formed the companies of the 10th into a battle line across our end of the green, three ranks deep (Nathaniel and I in the second rank), directly facing the colonials. No more than fifty yards separated our firelocks from theirs.

We could have proceeded along the road we had been on, for none of the rebels blocked it. We could as well have followed the left fork, which passed behind the meetinghouse, flanked the green, and then continued through a cluster of houses. A crossroad connected the two roads at the far end of the green. It seemed to me that seven hundred British troops with readied firelocks and fixed bayonets might well have marched past seventy armed farmers, at little risk. Aye, we might well have marched our column entirely around the green, forming a three-sided wall. Then we could have commenced our negotiations.

Instead, Major Pitcairn chose to form the van of our column into three ranks that paralleled and outnumbered their two ranks. The head of the long red snake was now ready to strike.

Major Pitcairn ordered us *not* to fire unless he gave the command. We stood, Englishman facing fellow Englishman, looking into the eyes of those who spoke our language; read our Bible; proclaimed, as yet, allegiance to our King; and who until recently had fed Londoners with their corn as we had clothed them with our wool.

Major Pitcairn shouted at the rebels from his horse, ordering them to lay down their arms and disperse. Their own officer may likewise have ordered them to disperse (upon seeing the great numbers of troops opposing them), for some of the farmers were now turning their backs toward us and walking, or hurrying, away. However, some of the rebels moved not at all from where they stood, their muskets raised and ready.

A shot to our right made my heart jump.

A puff of black smoke billowed over the green, perhaps from the firelock of a soldier at the end of our ranks, or from a villager behind the fence. Or perhaps, quite possibly, from a window of the tavern.

In the next instant, the British troops fired a full thundering volley at the colonials. Then with a roar, the soldiers charged. The sweeping mass of redcoats paid no regard to their officers, who shouted at them to cease firing and form. Perhaps as they reloaded and fired, they could not hear the officers. Or perhaps after a winter of waiting, after years of waiting, after the snowballs, rocks and curses, the soldiers were ready to slip the leash and show the rabble their teeth.

Several villagers, running for safety, tumbled forward with a ball in their back. Others stood their ground and fired bravely at the oncoming soldiers. The elderly farmer toppled where he stood. As he struggled to reload his musket, a half-dozen British soldiers plunged their bayonets into him with savage force. Then they pulled their blades free and ran after any other rebel still opposing them.

Clouds of black smoke covered much of the green. Nathaniel and I, our feet frozen to the ground where we stood (neither one of us had fired a shot), witnessed a scene of madness: red-coated devils dashed about in the brimstone and smoke of purgatory, bent on a wild feast of butchery. Their harsh voices intermingled with the cries and shrieks of the villagers.

Major Pitcairn rode back and forth across the green, shouting at his troops to cease their firing. He drew his sword and beat it downward as a signal. The soldiers swarming around him paid him no mind, but fired and reloaded as quickly as they could. Colonel Smith, arriving now upon a field of chaos, called for a drummer, who beat "to arms, to arms," until the firing diminished. With great reluctance, the troops gradually formed into their companies.

Everyone looked about to see who had been hurt. One British infantryman had been slightly wounded by a ball. Major Pitcairn's horse had been hit, though lightly enough that it still carried him. Otherwise, His Majesty's troops, Nathaniel and I included, remained unharmed.

A dozen colonials, however, lay before us on the green. Several, including the Negro, moved in pain on the ground. Some lay absolutely still. One man was crawling feebly across the grass toward the house at the far edge of the green, where his wife and child stood shrieking and wailing in the doorway.

We overheard several officers arguing that we had best turn back toward Boston, for we were sure to meet more rebels down the road. But Colonel Smith insisted that we would carry out orders, which were to proceed to Concord. However, he did send a rider galloping toward Boston to ask for reinforcements.

At the request of several grenadiers in the 10th Regiment, Colonel Smith allowed the troops to fire a victory volley (as was traditional in the British army following a victory on the field). The soldiers readied their weapons. The blast of a hundred firelocks in one thunderclap was the loudest noise I had yet heard in my life. A great billow of smoke drifted across the green in the sunshine, obscuring for some moments those who lay upon the ground.

The men then cheered with three huzzahs, announcing to the world their triumph.

That done, we were ordered to march, accompanied by the music of fife and drum, toward the road on our left: the highway to Concord.

Samuel Adams and John Hancock, having been warned earlier that night by Paul Revere, were fleeing from a house in Lexington at the same moment that British troops were marching into the village. Riding in Hancock's elegant carriage, they were close enough to the shooting to hear it clearly. Samuel Adams, who had worked day and night for over a decade to strengthen American resistance to British tyranny, was overjoyed when he heard the firing of muskets on Lexington's green. The endless waiting was over. Now the Americans could show their muscle.

He declared to Hancock, "Oh, what a glorious morning it is!"

He did not know, as Nathaniel and I did, marching past the bodies, that His Majesty's troops left eight men dead behind them, and nine wounded, including the young husband who crawled to his doorway and died in his wife's arms.

ℰℭ

Chapter Twenty-Nine

Benjamin, at

NORTH BRIDGE

I had eaten nothing since supper on Tuesday evening. I had slept but an hour before the sergeant awakened us. I had marched in wet shoes through most of the night. I had witnessed our first skirmish, the first firing of muskets in deadly earnest. I had seen corpses on the grass, their shirts stained with blood. And I now wondered how far Concord might be, and whether I would reach the village before I fainted on the road.

I glanced at Nathaniel. He stared straight ahead as he marched, his face determined, as if with a clear decision.

On the road ahead of us, a throng of rebels now appeared in the early morning sunshine, some fifty to a hundred of them, armed with muskets. Spotting us, and no doubt estimating our numbers to be much greater than theirs, they halted.

Our column continued to march. When we had narrowed the distance between us to a hundred yards—the edge of musket range—they turned their backs upon us and began to parade ahead of us, leading us toward the village of Concord. They apparently had no knowledge of the killing on Lexington green, and seemed to suffer no great fear of us, for we heard the cadence of their drum and the piping of their fife, playing most brightly.

We answered in kind: our drums and fifes livened the morning with several rounds of "Watkin's Ale." Our marching increased with the quickness of the tempo.

Thus we marched in a parade of fools following fools, ever deeper into their country. The news from Lexington they would soon learn; and we would learn . . . that we were a long way from home.

In the village of Concord, a cluster of tidy houses along a junction of several roads, Colonel Smith divided his troops. He ordered one company to guard a bridge to the south, so that no rebels might pass over it. He ordered six companies, ourselves included, to guard a bridge to the north. The grenadiers remaining in the village would search for military stores hidden by the rebels.

We marched north for about a mile, passing through farmland, until we came to a bridge arching over a narrow river. We spent a quarter of an hour crossing four abreast, company by company, over the bridge. Then three of the six companies detached and continued under Captain Parsons along the road toward a rebel farm, where arms were said to be hidden.

The remaining three companies assembled under the command of Captain Walter Laurie on the west side of the bridge, the river at our backs. A broad hill stood ahead of us and to the right, with a large farmhouse on its crown. During the hour that passed, a growing number of armed rebels gathered upon that hill, clearly with the intent of watching us as keenly as we were watching them. Our uneasiness deepened as their numbers increased, until they were perhaps four hundred or more.

Yet we did nothing. Our officers, hesitant to take any action, merely conferred again and again among each other. We might have constructed some sort of breastwork, preferably on the far side of the river, so that we might defend ourselves while preventing the rebels from passing over the bridge. But no, we merely stood in the warm sun on that April morning, our stomachs growling, our legs weary, our minds wondering whether anyone, from Colonel Smith in Concord to General Gage in Boston, to the King himself and his ministers in faraway London, knew what we were doing.

Suddenly we heard a rising murmur from the hill; looking up, we saw the rebels pointing toward Concord. We looked in that direction and saw smoke rising from what must have been a fire of considerable size. The murmur on the hill grew into a clamor of angry shouts, then the rebels swarmed down the slope toward us. Their fife and drums played a sprightly tune, "The White Cockade." They had no bayonets, but otherwise they were fully armed.

Captain Laurie sent a courier running to Concord to ask Colonel Smith for reinforcements. Then he ordered us to retreat across the bridge. We did so in a most confused manner, losing our ranks and to some extent our companies, for we felt the rebels were drawing quickly upon us. We therefore established no proper ranks on the other side of the bridge. Rather than extend our flanks in both directions along the river, we huddled in a tight cluster on the road, the men toward the rear thus unable to fire should the order be given.

Lieutenant Lister and a few of his men tried to pry up planks from the bridge, hoping to bar any further passage by the rebels. But as the farmers in their brown shirts and tri-cornered hats rapidly approached, the lieutenant retreated to our side.

The Americans halted at their end of the bridge, no more than a hundred feet from our end. They were close enough that I could see a variety of feathers adorning their hats.

That morning on Lexington green, British troops had faced a much smaller number of colonials, some of whom showed their willingness to retreat by turning their backs and hurrying away. But now at North Bridge, our two hundred soldiers were outnumbered by four or five hundred, and the colonials showed no inclination to retreat. Rather, they glared at us from across their bridge with the angry determination of men willing to die for family, land, and liberty.

Two shots, clearly from our side, made sharp splashes in the water. Despite shouts from Captain Laurie to cease firing, a third shot, again from our side, struck a man on the other side of the river. Men on both shores watched him collapse.

An American cried out, "God damn it, they are firing ball!"

Had they thought we were ranged against them with only blanks in our firelocks?

Once again, without orders, the British troops fired a full volley. And once again, Americans met their sudden death—struck this time through their chests and not their backs.

The rebel officer shouted, "Fire, fellow soldiers, for God's sake, fire!"

The volley of their muskets firing upon us, in a roar that lasted for several seconds, was a rumbling thunderclap. Soldiers dropped to the ground around me. Others turned and ran in wild retreat. The breeze brought a cloud of black smoke across the river. Though we could see the Americans but poorly, we could now hear their shouts and the pounding of their feet as they charged across the bridge. Grabbing my arm, Nathaniel spun me around and pulled me until I too was running with the panicked troops who fled from the surging rebels behind us.

The Americans stopped, however, a short distance beyond the bridge. Glancing back, I saw them gathered around several of our dead. They taunted any of our wounded who tried to hobble away.

Then I heard a cheer from our own men. Looking in the opposite direction, I saw a company of reinforcements marching along the road from Concord. Most of the troops were well ahead of their officer,

Colonel Smith himself, strutting with portly slowness. Heartened by the approaching troops, our men re-formed into ranks.

We did not, however, march back upon the rebels at the bridge. Rather, to the bewilderment of our troops, we abandoned the bridge—and the three companies who had left us to search a rebel farm. They would have to return by way of that bridge. Without detaching even one company to support them, we followed our incomparable Smith in an orderly parade back to the village of Concord.

Behind us, bleeding into the American earth at the foot of North Bridge, lay a dozen of our wounded and dead—men who had been abandoned by His Majesty's officers.

☙

Chapter Thirty

Colonel Smith dined at a tavern in Concord. The grenadiers searched for military stores, and found but little. They burned what was burnable and dumped the rest, primarily lead balls and barrels of flour, into a mill pond. Only three cannons were found, which the grenadiers damaged by knocking off their truncheons.

We in the light infantry stood in formation on the main road through the village. We occasionally marched back and forth from one end of the village to the other end, for two hours. We were increasingly faint with hunger, and mindful of our long march back to whatever awaited us in Lexington. We thought, too, of the much longer march back to Boston, where, God willing, we would not have to wade again through the muck bottom of the Bay.

At last, Colonel Smith, his ample belly bulging a bit more after his hearty dinner, gave the order that we should form into our column and march upon the road toward Boston. The hour was now past noon, as I judged by the sun high overhead. We had been on our feet for fifteen hours, without sleep or proper victuals. But Smith, smartly mounted upon his horse, would have us home in time for his supper.

We marched warily, with no beating of drums, no trilling of fifes. A company of light infantry swept with a flanking motion through the village cemetery on a ridge to our left. Advancing along its crest, the flankers guarded our troops on the highway from the American rebels who were now (as we learned from an officer advancing among the tombstones) crossing a pasture in large numbers and moving ever closer to the highway ahead of us.

We came to a junction with a road heading north. Across that road stood a large white house and a barn; the house was wrapped by a hedge of lilacs so heavily in bloom that we could smell them even from the highway.

The company of flankers, coming to the end of the wooded ridge, descended to the highway and joined the main column.

The Americans, having crossed the fields behind the ridge, now hid themselves behind the house, trees and barn. Nathaniel and I watched the rebels as they scurried in countless numbers toward the fringe of the road ahead of us. There they disappeared behind a farmer's wall of stone.

Nathaniel suddenly gripped my arm, against regulations, for he should have been holding tightly to his firelock and facing straight ahead. "Benjamin," he said, looking at me with that strange gaze of his. "Bury me as a Quaker, Benjamin, for such I am. In my heart abides no ill toward any man."

Then, his eyes brightened, as if we two stood alone upon a quiet country lane on a sunny afternoon in April. He told me, "Benjamin, seek that of God in every man, and thou shan't go wrong."

A hundred muskets suddenly fired upon us, from house and barn and trees and wall, as if a dozen thunderbolts struck the earth where we poor mortals stood. A gust of leaden balls tore through us, dropping men all around us. Nathaniel gripped my arm tightly as he stepped between myself and the farmhouse. Then with a leap, he threw himself upon me and bore me down with his awkward weight. I crashed to the ground with Nathaniel draped over me. Soldiers' feet were dashing past us. Men shouted above us. Thunder came now from both sides of the road as the rebels swarmed around us like hornets.

I knew from the heavy way he lay upon me that Nathaniel was dead. His face was pressed against mine, yet I felt no breath. His arms were sprawled outward in both directions on the hard dirt of the road. I wrapped my arm over his back, laid my hand on his . . . I jerked my hand away with a grimace. Slowly, protectively, with the mere beginnings of grief, I laid my hand back down in his warm blood.

Hugging him thus with one arm, I let go of my firelock. Then there I lay, as motionless as Nathaniel. Because for me, after a full year of madness, the King's war was over.

They could capture me. They could hang me. I did not care. Let me, I would ask, first bury Nathaniel. Then they could shoot me and bury me beside him.

ॐ

Chapter Thirty-One

Genevieve, meeting the man
who would become my husband.

I must return to the evening of Tuesday, April 18, 1775: to the time before I and my family became citizens in a colony at war, in a state at war, in a nation at war.

Dr. Samuel Prescott, a physician from Concord, had been courting his fiancée in Lexington on Tuesday evening. While riding toward home, he met both William Dawes and Paul Revere on the highway. They told him the British regulars were out and asked him to help spread the alarm. As a high Son of Liberty, he of course agreed.

The three riders had traveled only a short distance toward Concord when they were spotted and pursued by a patrol of British officers. Dr. Prescott managed, by leaping a stone wall on horseback, to escape. He galloped across the fields toward Concord, keeping well south of the highway, and so passed Samuel Hartwell's farm in Lincoln. He aroused our neighbor, who sent his son Joseph to ring the bell of the Lincoln meetinghouse. To that urgent clamor did I and my family sit up in our beds. Within minutes, Papa, Henry and Judd were on horseback with their muskets, and gone.

Before he left, Papa bade me stay home with my mother. Not yet a soldier, I acquiesced. Mama and I kindled the fire with fresh logs, made a cup of tea, and did what women have done for centuries, and did it poorly. We waited.

Though we opened a window toward the road (the window beside the table at which I now write), we heard no other sound through the night than the spring peeping of frogs in our pond. And, toward dawn, the chirping of the first robins.

We managed to eat a bit of bread as our breakfast, but neither Mama nor I took so much as a spoonful of corn mush, though by habit we had heated it.

(Because of that eternal night, followed by that eternal morning, I was determined for the next eight years to follow the war within sight and hearing of the cannons. Better by far to be cold and hungry and weary in your bones, but certain that a soldier whom you love is alive . . . than to be warm and snug at home, but deathly worried that he is somewhere hurt, bleeding away his life.)

Mama and I milked the cows. We fed the chickens. Then I fed and curried Sir William. Did I pray? I think that Mama prayed enough for the five of us.

The sun had passed its zenith; we had been waiting from midnight to noon. Mama and I were outside planting peas in the garden—keeping ourselves busy with a ritual of normalcy—when we heard a sudden and prolonged clap of thunder to the north, somewhere close to Concord. Despite Mama's wail of protest, I was quicker than Papa, quicker than Judd, quicker even than Henry, as I saddled Sir William and galloped out of the farmyard. They might have been minutemen, but I was beyond the gate in less than half a minute.

The roar of muskets continued, growing louder as I galloped along the road from Lincoln toward Concord. Sir William's hooves pounded across the bridge over Mill Brook, then we came to the broad highway leading west into Concord, and east toward hills clad in springtime green. I saw not a soul in either direction, though I noticed footprints of a great number of people who had walked in both directions.

Reining toward the steady blast of muskets—toward Lexington—I galloped no more than a mile before I slowed Sir William to a canter, a trot, a walk. For there in the road ahead, where the highway divided at Merriam's Corner, I saw red-coated bodies sprawled in the dirt.

As Sir William walked closer, snorting nervously, I recognized three older men from the Concord militia. They were guarding several wounded redcoats. Mr. William Smith pointed his musket at a soldier and spoke roughly to him while the bleeding man struggled to drag himself to the edge of the road.

Up the bank of a nearby creek came my brother Judd. He held no musket in his hands, but a tin pail and a dipper (which perhaps he had found at the Merriam House well). Glancing at me with a grim nod, he crossed the road and knelt beside the soldier crawling beneath the bore of Mr. Smith's musket. Ladling a draught of water, Judd offered it to the redcoat, who stared with disbelief first at the ladle brimming with water, and then up at Judd. The soldier reached with an unsteady hand and brought the ladle to his lips. He drank eagerly, then muttered, "I thank you, sir."

Standing up with the empty ladle and looking about, Judd's gaze rested upon a strange sight: in the middle of the highway, a soldier, the red wool of his coat glistening with blood, lay face down upon another soldier, dead upon his back. Both of their faces were turned away, as if, partners in a dance, they had taken a bullet through the both of them and had died in the same moment.

Judd stepped toward them. He set down the bucket and dipper. Then, with his huge hands, he reached for the uppermost soldier. Gripping the man beneath his shoulders, he lifted the limp body, then shifted his grip so the soldier lay draped across his arms. Judd looked at me for a moment, his eyes filled with a baffled sadness. The farmer who had raised and butchered livestock all his life, the minuteman who had trained to defend his liberty, now held a dead soldier in his arms. He began to walk with his burden toward the side of the road.

My heart, my very soul, jumped inside me when we heard the other dead soldier speak, "His name is Nathaniel."

Judd turned to look at the soldier who slowly sat up in the dirt. The soldier stared at the corpse whose head and feet dangled from Judd's arms. He paid no attention to the musket which Mr. William Smith now aimed at him.

"I should like to bury him," said the soldier, "but I have no shovel."

"Stand with your hands away from your pockets!" shouted William Smith, pleased to have captured an unwounded soldier.

"If you could bring me a shovel," said the soldier quietly to Judd. He stood up, paying no mind to the barrel of the musket inches from his chest.

Eleazer Brook of the Lincoln militia stepped close enough to the soldier that he could spit him. "Your murderin's over," he snarled, "ye damned butcherin' lobsterback!"

The soldier turned his head slowly to stare for a long moment at Smith and Brook. Breathing more and more heavily, as if he really had been dead but was now demanding his share of the breath of life, the soldier glared at William Smith and declared, "I hate them."

He looked at Brook. "I hate them," he repeated with a sharper edge, "more than you could ever begin to hate them."

He stared down at the blood on his hand, the hand which had been wrapped over the other soldier's back. He held up his red palm toward the disconcerted Smith and told him, "You may have fired the ball, but the British made you do it."

Reaching now for the leather strap across his chest, he lifted it over his head and tossed his black cartridge box onto the road. Eleazer Brook snatched it up.

Lifting a second strap over his head, the soldier cast away his empty bayonet scabbard. Eleazer Brook grabbed that too.

His hands working more and more vehemently, the soldier opened his red coat, yanked his arms from its sleeves and threw it down in the dust. His fingers working deftly, he unfastened the buttons of his red vest, then threw that too upon the dirt.

In a mounting rage, he untucked his white shirt, pulled it over his head and threw it at William Smith's feet. The soldier's naked back was toward me for but a moment, because he now turned his back toward Smith, but in that moment I saw the ugly red welts.

"Twenty lashes on the ship!" he roared over his shoulder at Smith. Pointing at the dead soldier in Judd's arms, he cried even more fiercely, "And they gave Nathaniel twenty lashes as well!"

Smith raised the muzzle of his musket toward the sky. Still unsure as to what to do with this peculiar redcoat, he knew at least that he had no ordinary prisoner.

The soldier walked toward Judd. He lifted Nathaniel's dangling head in his bloody hand. Staring in anguish at the slackened face, he bent down and kissed the dead soldier's brow.

Then he addressed himself to Judd, "I have no shovel."

"I shall bring you a shovel," I said.

He turned to look at me for the first time, seeing a young woman in homespun, mounted on a chestnut horse.

I told him, "I shall fetch a shovel at the farm."

"Thank you," he said, his voice firm and filled with gratitude.

I reined Sir William toward Concord, kicked my heels to a canter. Thinking already beyond a shovel, I saw in my mind a length of white bed linen, now folded in my dowry trunk, which I would bring as a winding-sheet.

I told Mama that Judd was well, that Papa and Henry had followed the battle toward Lexington. She sat at the table and looked at me, though she did not say anything. Her hands were folded on the family Bible. She waited.

I found two shovels in the barn and lashed them both behind Sir William's saddle, for I knew that Judd would want to help dig the grave. Then, from a bush of lilacs outside the farmhouse door—their violet flowers had bloomed early after the mild winter—I snapped off a half-dozen fragrant branches for a bouquet.

As I rode back toward the highway, I worried about Papa, I worried about Henry. Both would fight today's battle until the last shot was fired. I worried about Mama, who might well tomorrow be a widow.

Those worries were immersed in the lingering shock, the horror, the revulsion of seeing so many dead people sprawled on the road. Though the girl of nineteen had cringed at the sight, the woman of nineteen was hardening to the task ahead.

We would try to help one soldier who was clearly not our enemy. For the others, we could do nothing more than dig a proper grave.

As I rode a second time toward Merriam's Corner, I saw that Dr. Timothy Minot had arrived with his carriage from Concord. Kneeling in the grass beside the road, he was bandaging the arm of a redcoat. He glanced at me, nodded, returned to his work.

William Smith had departed, perhaps following the faint sound of musket shots, now far up the highway toward Lexington.

In the pasture behind a stone wall, Judd stood looking down at six red-coated soldiers who lay neatly beside each other, waiting for their graves.

Deeper into the pasture, the soldier without a shirt stood near his friend, who lay on his back in a white shirt and white breeches, his hands folded over his chest. Nathaniel's red coat and waistcoat had been tossed onto the ground nearby. Nathaniel would not be buried as a soldier, but as a man in blood-stained white.

I dismounted and tethered Sir William to the budding branch of a maple. Then I unlashed the two shovels.

Judd and the soldier worked for an hour in the rocky soil, carving a deep hole with good squared walls. Both men sweated heavily in the afternoon sun. The soldier's welts became redder as he dug and cast the dirt up into the grass. Neither man spoke.

When they were done, as they determined with a look and a nod to each other, they hoisted themselves up from opposite ends of the grave. The soldier wiped his hands on his trousers; Judd knelt and wiped his hands on the grass. I unfastened the bolt of linen from my saddle. While the soldier supported Nathaniel's head and Judd lifted his body, I wrapped Nathaniel in the clean white cloth.

Then the soldier jumped back down into the grave. Judd lowered the wrapped body into his uplifted arms. The soldier crouched as best he could in the small space and gently laid Nathaniel upon his back on the damp rocky earth. The corpse looked like a clean white cocoon.

The soldier hoisted himself once again out of the grave. Then we three stood together for a long time, peering down at the man whom we hesitated to cover with earth.

I offered, "Sir, let my brother and me do this for you."

He looked at me. Never had I seen a man so broken, so lost.

Then he seemed to remember something, something from which he took some comfort. He asked me, "Do you know a Quaker prayer?"

I considered, for though I knew a good many prayers, I knew not if any were especially of the Quaker faith.

Judd now spoke with the same firm voice that he used in the barn to calm cattle frightened by the scent of a wolf. "See ye by the Light within, and so shall break a glorious day."

"Amen," whispered the soldier. He stared down into the grave a moment longer, then he walked away. He stood beside the stone wall, his welted back toward us as he stared at the blood on the road where Nathaniel had fallen. He bestowed upon Judd and me the trust, and the honor, of casting down the earth upon his beloved friend.

Judd and I knelt beside the long dark mound and smoothed it by sweeping our hands back and forth over the dirt. I walked to the stone wall near Sir William and picked up the bouquet of lilacs, their scent strong in the warm afternoon.

I walked along the wall to the soldier. "Sir?" I said as I offered him the flowers.

He took them, his eyes thanking me. He walked back to the grave, where he knelt and laid the lilacs on the fresh dirt.

Thus began our marriage with a funeral, and thus began our love with grief.

When the soldier stood, my brother and I looked upon an orphan lost in a strange and brutal country. Judd reached out and touched his arm. "Sir, will you come home with us? We would be honored if you would sit at our table and break bread with us."

Four boys from Concord stood behind the wall and whispered excitedly as they pointed at the dead redcoats. Judd spoke with them. They accepted his promise of payment, took our two shovels and began the job of burying the six soldiers.

Their chatter was too bright, too brave, for my ears as I mounted Sir William.

Judd invited the soldier to mount his Bonny. I noted with surprise that Judd had to show him how to put his foot into the stirrup. Judd walked beside Bonny, leading with the bridle, while the soldier, who had no understanding of the reins, leaned forward and gripped the front of the saddle to hold himself steady.

Judd walked, holding the bridle, during the long hour of our slow journey home. Sir William seemed to understand, for never once did he attempt to hurry from a walk to a trot.

Perhaps we needed time to say a prayer, a long and thoughtful prayer, that the distant musket shots (now so faint that they must surely be near Lexington) might not be the sparks of a winding fuse leading to the powder keg of war.

&

Chapter Thirty-Two

As we approached the farmyard gate, the soldier gazed up the lane at our brown, weathered, two-story farmhouse. A wisp of smoke rose from the brick chimney. "I thank you," said the soldier, speaking to both Judd and me as he stared ahead at what was probably the first American home he had visited. "I do most deeply thank you."

The door opened and Mama hurried out in her blue dress to meet us. She wrapped her arms around Judd, whose broad shoulders were twice the size of hers. She did not weep, but her gratitude was clear: of her three men, she had at least one of them home.

Then she turned to the stranger. Though she had no understanding of who he was, she told him, "You are welcome."

The soldier, shy and polite, bowed slightly to her. "Thank you. I thank you. I . . . am Benjamin York." He seemed not to have arrived at the farm, but suddenly to have awakened there. Discovering that he wore no shirt, he was too embarrassed in the presence of strangers to say a word more.

Judd stepped into the house, leaving Benjamin with Mama and me in the yard, the three of us utterly mute as Benjamin roamed his eyes over the lilac bush. He stared at the piebald chickens strutting about. And then, his brown eyes lit by the late afternoon sun, he stared at the apple orchard beyond the garden. The blossoming trees formed a fragrant cloud of white.

Judd returned with one of his old shirts, a cast-off from his younger years, before he had muscled into his full growth. He handed the shirt to Benjamin, who nodded his gratitude.

When Benjamin reached his arms into the broad sleeves, then lifted the huge shirt over his head, I almost laughed, for he looked like a child lost in a gunnysack. His head reappeared; his lower face was browned by the sun, his forehead was white where he had worn his military hat. He pulled the shirt down around his waist: it was more a coat than a shirt. The shoulders drooped down both sides. But Benjamin nodded again, much gratified.

Mama laid an enormous table for her starving threesome, as if starved herself for something to do until her John and Henry came home safe.

And so, quietly, almost peacefully, we broke bread.

Following dinner, Judd heated pot after pot of water over the fire, then carried each pot out to the tin tub which he had placed in a spot of privacy behind the barn. Offering the readied bath to Benjamin, he handed him a block of soap and a towel.

When our guest appeared shyly half an hour later from behind the barn, he wore Judd's shirt and a pair of Judd's old breeches, the latter tied around the waist with a length of rope. He wore as well, without stockings, his buckled shoes.

Judd was waiting to return to the highway: he wanted to see that the British soldiers had been properly buried, to pay the boys, and fetch home the shovels. But before he left, he led Benjamin upstairs to his own bedroom, where he bid him to take some rest.

Benjamin slipped off his shoes and lay upon the bed. He reached up his hand to take Judd's hand in friendship, and to say once again, "I thank you."

Judd told me that by the time he had answered, "You are most welcome," Benjamin's eyes closed, his grip slackened, and he was asleep.

Mama waited into the evening without serving supper, with the hope that Papa and Henry might return. Well after dark, the table still bare, Joseph Hartwell, the boy who had rung the Lincoln meetinghouse bell almost a full day ago, knocked on our door. On his way home from Cambridge, he was kind enough to stop for a minute to tell us that Papa and Henry were fine, though they would not soon be returning home to Lincoln.

They were encamped with several thousand other minutemen— "Yes," Joseph insisted, despite our incredulity, "several thousand"—in the fields around Cambridge and all along the shore of Back Bay. Some had brought tents, although most of them (such as Papa and Henry) would sleep in their clothes on the ground near a campfire. The steadily growing encampment was filled with farmers from Waltham, Sudbury, Framingham, Woburn, Newton, Reading, Billerica, Watertown, and even Winnisimet. These thousands of patriots had left behind their homes and their plows—now, in planting season—to join the men from Lexington, Lincoln and Concord.

Gage's army, seriously battered all along the road back to Boston, had withdrawn across the neck to the peninsula and was now all but surrounded. Boston was an island fortress under siege. Joseph's father, too, had remained in Cambridge, waiting with the others to be formed into a proper army.

Proud to have brought news of such a victory, Joseph accepted a cup of cider, then he hurried off to the Farrar homestead with his good tidings.

Mama and I decided to serve supper. While we set bowls of beef stew and a platter of bread on the table for the four of us, Judd went upstairs to awaken Benjamin.

Again we ate a quiet meal. We of course said nothing to our guest about victory or defeat. Profoundly relieved that her men were safe, Mama stared at the table beyond her plate and more than once suddenly smiled, as if in her reverie she had just sighted Papa riding up the lane.

I too felt an immeasurable peacefulness, for surely now the British would sail away and leave us alone. Enough men had paid with their lives today for all the years of contention and turmoil. Let Boston be Boston, with its busy wharf and laden ships, and without its military camp. What need had any of us for the further curse of war?

Judd offered more stew to Benjamin, and more bread, more cider. He asked, "Would you mind a cup of bee balm tea? We have some dried leaves in the cellar from last summer."

"Yes," answered Benjamin politely, though I think he knew not one tea from another.

Then, straightening in his chair, he asked Mama, "Would you have some paper and a pen, that I might write a letter to my family?"

That we did, for during the past years, Papa had frequently copied certain phrases from the broadsides and resolves which had been passed to him by hand, and which he likewise passed on to another high Son of Liberty.

Papa kept his pens and ink bottle in the table drawer. While Mama cleared the plates, I took out several sheets and laid them neatly upon the table, then set Papa's ink and pen beside them. I placed a whale-oil lamp beside the paper.

"I thank you," said Benjamin. He held the quill pen and gazed at it as if it were a marvel in his hand.

He turned to me and asked, "Do you know the date?"

"Wednesday, the nineteenth of April, 1775." I watched his hand as he swiftly wrote the letters and numbers across the top of the paper. (I was trying, as was my habit with Papa, to see if I could read them).

Then, embarrassed to be spying so closely, I turned away. I went out to the well to draw fresh water for his tea.

He wrote for nearly an hour. I saw once when glancing at him that he wept while he was writing. He had filled a good number of pages when he turned to me and asked with hesitant politeness, "Might I be able to receive a letter from my family at this address?"

"Of course," I said, and wherefore not?

"Then, what would this address be?"

I thought for a moment; I had never before addressed a letter to our family. "John Byrne's farm . . . that is my father . . . Lincoln, colony of Massachusetts. That should bring a letter here, and then . . ." I did not know where Benjamin might be four months from now, when a letter from his family in . . . I knew not where he lived in England. So I said nothing further, while he wrote Papa's address at the bottom of his last sheet of paper.

Folding the pages, he asked, "How might I post this to London?"

Never having posted a letter, but knowing of course that the port of Boston was closed, I could only suggest, "Perhaps a ship sailing from Salem could take it for you."

"Aye," he said with a nod of agreement, "and might you have a bit of sealing wax?"

Never had I seen Papa seal a letter with wax. For whom did he know beyond Boston, to whom he might write a letter? "Perhaps," I suggested, "the postal office in Salem might have some wax."

"Aye, most certainly they will."

He stared at the letter in his hands. "I have not a penny on me, for I left my few shillings in our tent on the Common. And I dare not post the letter myself, for fear of being a third time caught. "

A third time caught? But I asked no questions. Rather, I promised him, "Your letter shall find an American ship bound from Salem to London, and not a penny do we ask." I felt quite bold to make such a decision on behalf of our family.

"I thank you," he said, bowing his head with gratitude. Then he wrote his family's address in London on the outside of the folded sheets of paper, and handed the letter to me.

And so, here at this table fifty-one years ago, Benjamin York wrote a letter to his mother and father, telling them that he was alive, and in America.

Four months later, a letter from his family returned to him (as well as another letter, folded within, from his fiancée). Their letters eventually found him, though not here in Lincoln.

We were both in the Cambridge encampment by then, starving the

British who were trapped in Boston. Benjamin and I had volunteered as soldiers—yes, I counted myself a soldier as well, for I rode by day and by night as a courier—in General Washington's Continental Army.

The next morning, the twentieth of April, 1775, I cantered on Sir William past Merriam's Corner, with its fresh graves . . . then through Lexington, where a dozen houses were draped with black . . . then through Menotomy, where the worst of the fighting had left scores of people dead.

I took the fork northeast toward Medford and the coast north of Boston. Despite the pall of death upon the land, I felt a bit pleased that Judd would this morning inform Benjamin, when he awoke, that Genevieve had ridden with his letter to post it from the port of Salem.

∽

PART II

The Siege of Boston

Chapter Thirty-Three

Benjamin York, or someone who
once was Benjamin York, or who is becoming
Benjamin York, in the colony of Massachusetts,
soon to become the State of Massachusetts.

Although desperate to return to Elspeth and my family, whom I missed most painfully, I did not hasten to Salem to search for a ship back to London.

And although fiercely determined, on the day I tossed away my British firelock, that never again in my life would I become a soldier, I became an armed and fighting Continental regular for the next six and a half years, from the Battle of Breed's Hill in June of 1775, to the Battle of Yorktown in October of 1781.

How did such a change of heart take place? Nay, a change of soul, to the most inner depths of who I was, and am.

During April, during May, and the first half of June, I was an eager student: I learned in a brief two months about my legal rights as an Englishman; about the taxes and tyrannies which my American hosts had suffered during the past ten years; about the enslavement which surely awaited them unless they defended their rights. I partook in long and passionate discussions at the encampment in Cambridge with Henry and Genevieve and Mr. Byrnes (who bade me call him John). I spoke as well as with a growing number of soldiers from the colonies of Massachusetts, New Hampshire, Rhode Island and Connecticut, men who had arrived to help us besiege the British in Boston. One by one, I cast away the lies which I had so willingly accepted in London. And one by one, I examined the facts which these Americans presented to me in such a cogent manner. Until finally, I came to a decision.

I decided that I could not fetch my Elspeth from England and return with her to this New World, while other men fought for the freedom that we would enjoy. Nay, I would have to earn that freedom myself, before I could fetch my bride.

*   *   *

But war is a form of madness. All whom it touches, risk losing to some degree their gentleness, their compassion, their better instincts. Even their firmest principles.

How little did I understand the words which I myself had shouted, "I hate them more than you do."

During those two months between the skirmishes in Lexington and Concord on April 19, and the savage battle on Breed's Hill on June 17, I was two men, one hidden deep inside the other.

I was driven by seething rage, by untempered hatred, rather than by some newfound love of liberty. Apparently calm as I conversed with Henry while we built a hut together, and with Genevieve while I helped her at the campfire, I was—deep inside—a madman: a madman hidden even from myself. Never would I have suspected in myself such rage, such hatred, stored like barrels of gunpowder deep in the hold of a frigate, a frigate sailing before a brisk wind directly toward enemy waters.

Thoughts of Elspeth diminished, and imperceptibly vanished. For I would have my revenge. Aye, a brutal vengeance, in payment for my impressment, in payment for my lashing, but most deeply of all, in full payment for Nathaniel's death. I recalled the night before Lexington, when one of the grenadiers waiting on the beach had bayoneted a barking dog to silence it. Nathaniel's death had meant no more to Pitcairn and Smith and Gage and the King than the death of that poor dog.

Aye, better a dog than a soldier.

Never once during those two fervent months at the encampment in Cambridge did I ask myself whether Nathaniel would have demanded revenge. I did not seek his guidance. I left unconsidered his refusal to raise a hand, or an oar, against Hench.

I merely waited, while I approached steadily closer and closer to the enemy: I moved like a sniper crawling on his belly through the deep grass of a sunlit meadow, his musket hidden beneath a bright canopy of daisies and buttercups and sunflowers . . . until, behind a stone wall, he slowly rises up and takes aim between two boulders . . . then with cold and sudden savagery sends a ball of lead into the heart of a mounted officer bedecked with a red coat and sword and gorget. The officer's heart stops beating as he topples from his horse. And the sniper gloats as he crawls on his belly like a serpent back toward his camp, savoring the taste of his hatred.

So I drew ever closer to the British army that huddled in Boston. I became once again a soldier, clad now in homespun, armed with a farmer's fowling piece, awaiting my chance to slaughter the despicable

Hench . . . or any of his brother officers.

Whether or not I myself died on some battlefield, was to me of no consequence.

A madman values only the moment, and not the eternity beyond.

Boston was a virtual island, surrounded by water save at the long and narrow neck. The island-city was cupped by an irregular crescent of land, roughly ten miles long. To the north of Boston, across a narrow channel, stood the two hills on Charlestown peninsula: Bunker's Hill and Breed's Hill. To the south, again across a narrow channel, stood several hills on Dorchester peninsula. To occupy any of these hills with substantial artillery would enable the American army to control Boston, and much of the harbor by threat of bombardment. But the Americans encamped along that ten-mile crescent, with Cambridge as their central headquarters, had no such artillery.

Major General Artemus Ward, commander in chief of the spontaneous American army—20,000 men from four colonies had gathered in response to the Lexington-Concord alarm—recommended that some of our troops occupy the hills and neck of Dorchester peninsula; even without cannons, they could at least build some sort of fort.

But Major General John Thomas, commander of the southern half of the crescent, refused to occupy Dorchester; he feared that he would thus weaken his lines on the mainland. His troops blocked the potential route of attack across Boston Neck, and they defended the village of Roxbury. Should Roxbury fall, Cambridge would surely be next.

So the Dorchester hills remained as they were, a quiet pasture for cattle and goats.

To the north, Charlestown peninsula also remained unoccupied by troops, until, on May 13, Major General Israel Putnam of Connecticut marched nearly three thousand Americans across Charlestown Neck. The column paraded up Bunker's Hill (one hundred ten feet tall), down across the grassy saddle and then up Breed's Hill (sixty-two feet tall, according to a local map). On the broad top of Breed's Hill, Putnam drilled his troops in clear sight of both the British army a mile away in Boston, and the British navy in the harbor.

Major General Putnam, or Old Put as his men called him (for he was fifty-three years old and a veteran of the French and Indian War), then marched his men right down Breed's Hill and into Charlestown. From the wharf, the soldiers called out to the officers and crew aboard the warship *Somerset*, taunting them. Neither side fired a shot, but most of the inhabitants of the village of Charlestown, fearing that they now resided upon a potential battlefield, loaded their families and goods into wagons and hurried west across the neck to seek refuge in villages further inland.

(Events soon proved the wisdom of their evacuation, for one month later, on June 17, the four hundred buildings of Charlestown would be burnt to ashes.)

In Boston as in Cambridge, officers argued whether or not to fortify the hills to the north and south of Boston. General Gage finally decided to occupy the heights of Dorchester, then to march his regiments to Roxbury and Cambridge. Thus he would break the siege.

But as the British had their spies in Cambridge, so the Americans had their spies in Boston. Information was brought to General Ward's headquarters at Harvard College in Cambridge that General Gage was planning to attack to the south on Sunday, June 18.

Ward knew from his spies that several transport ships had recently arrived in Boston, bringing the number of His Majesty's infantrymen, grenadiers, and marines to ten thousand well-armed, well-trained, well-organized troops. Ward also knew that he had under his own command twenty thousand poorly armed, poorly trained, and dismally organized farmers, shopkeepers, tanners, church deacons, candlemakers, coopers, smugglers, and indigent spectators, as well as an uncountable throng of wives, sweethearts, and ladies of pleasure.

Three of Britian's most experienced generals had arrived from London on May 25 aboard the warship *Cerburus*: Generals John Burgoyne, Henry Clinton, and William Howe. The King had thus sent to General Gage both the muscle and the brains, in troops and officers, to show the arrogant rabble of Massachusetts, as well as any rebels in the other twelve colonies, that Britain would continue to rule . . . and America would continue to obey.

General Ward knew that he was soon to feel the might of the most powerful army in the world, backed by the most powerful navy in the world. In accordance with a unanimous vote by the Committee of Safety in Cambridge (his political advisors), General Ward decided that Bunker's Hill "be securely kept and defended; and also some one hill or hills of Dorchester Neck be likewise secured." Ward would send out his troops on Friday night, June 16: the Americans would be in position on Saturday, June 17, the day *before* General Gage planned to attack.

*   *   *

A word about the family who took me into their protection. Never did the Byrnes tell anyone that I had deserted from the King's infantry. So many men had come so suddenly from so many places into the camp at Cambridge, that no one bothered to ask.

For two months, beneath the springtime sun and the springtime stars, I shared a makeshift tent made of sailcloth with Henry, John and Genevieve Byrnes. I shared their blankets, and cooking fire, and an old fowling piece that Henry had loaned to me. (Judd stayed on the farm with his mother, to plow and to plant, and to defend, if necessary, the family homestead.) Henry, John and I were formally mustered into a Massachusetts regiment; our duty as "regulars" extended to the end of the year. Genevieve accompanied us as cook, seamstress, and washerwoman.

John and Henry Byrnes welcomed me as a fellow soldier, though both remained suspicious, especially Henry. I well understood: I had marched too recently under Smith and Pitcairn to earn their trust. Even if I were not a spy, how warmly could my heart possibly beat for their cause? Though every volunteer was needed, they kept a wary eye on me, and would probably have been gratified if one morning at muster, I did not appear in the ranks. Henry would have called me, with a sour shrug, "A deserter twice over, a vagabond, gone to settle, more than likely, over the hills and into western Pennsylvania." Whoever Henry had no use for, he dismissed with a sneer.

Genevieve did what Genevieve does best, though I could not have known it then. She watched, silent, cordial, taking care of her two men, and taking care of someone part friend, part stranger—she was equal in her manner toward all—until the moment when, unsuspected by anyone, she rode at full gallop in exactly the right direction, to exactly the right place, with exactly the right message.

ॐ

Chapter Thirty-Four

Benjamin.

On Friday, June 16, 1775, Captain John Byrnes told our company (of which he had been elected captain), to pack a blanket and food for a full day in our haversacks, then to assemble on Cambridge Common at six in the evening. Our captain did not say why we were to assemble.

One thousand two hundred chosen men (including a number of Negroes, like a dash of pepper mixed in with a goodly sprinkling of salt) assembled at six o'clock on the common near Hasting House, General Ward's headquarters. The troops were led in prayer by no less a minister than President Langdon of Harvard College, who asked God's blessing upon our souls as we marched forth to defend our beleaguered country. We were then, all twelve hundred of us, placed under the command of Colonel William Prescott of Massachusetts, a veteran, like many of our officers, of the French and Indian War.

Standing with my fowling piece and haversack deep within the ranks of men, listening to voices speaking a different English from the English I had always known, I felt as if I passed along from moment to moment like a chip of wood floating down a river toward my destiny: I was now an American soldier fighting for American rights, and I would do as the Americans did. Then, when all this was over, I would become myself again, whoever that was.

We waited on the common while the June evening darkened into night. From our tent in a pasture just north of Cambridge, Genevieve had brought a loaf of bread and a jug of cider. The four of us eased our restlessness with a final meal, eaten as we stood and spoke quietly with each other.

Genevieve could have no doubt, after Lexington and Concord two months ago, that her brother and father, marching now into a civil war, might never return to the mother and wife waiting for them in Lincoln. When we heard the tolling across Back Bay of a steeple bell in Boston, counting the hour of nine o'clock, then heard Colonel Prescott ordering us to form in ranks, Genevieve kissed her father's cheek, kissed Henry's cheek, kissed my cheek, all without a word. Then she walked through the ranks of troops and disappeared into the darkness.

Ordered not to speak, the troops marched east out of Cambridge, then followed the same road upon which, as a British infantryman, I had marched west toward Lexington.

We marched past the spot where Nathaniel and I had slogged with muddy feet out of the Bay's muck bottom. Grateful I was, as I marched now with the Americans, that our officers seemed to know what they were doing.

Passing the dark knob of Prospect Hill, we took the fork to the right and so continued to Charlestown Neck. I saw once again the hut from which the British sentry had spotted Nathaniel and me. The sentries standing before the hut tonight did not wear red coats with crisscrossed white straps. Rather, they wore the drab dark clothing of men who might otherwise have spent the day hoeing weeds in a potato patch.

We marched across the neck, no more than thirty feet wide at high tide. At the junction, Colonel Prescott sent a captain with seventy men along the main road toward Charlestown, to serve as sentinels in the deserted village. Should the British detect our movements and send troops in boats across the channel, sentries hidden along the wharf would be the first to warn us.

Our column now advanced along the road up the western slope of Bunker's Hill, the same road on which Nathaniel had spoken to me about building a church. We heard hoofbeats approaching from behind. Major General Putnam rode past us and joined Colonel Prescott and Colonel Richard Gridley, a fortifications engineer, at the head of our column. Though we could not hear their words, we could see that the three were engaged in a discussion which entailed a good deal of disagreement. From the long crest of Bunker's Hill, they pointed toward the broad crest of Breed's Hill, then toward the village of Charlestown, toward the wharf of North Boston, toward the lights of warships in the harbor, then again toward the broad black crest of Breed's Hill. Clearly, as our halted column of over a thousand men waited, our three officers were arguing over what to do with us.

They must have made their decision, for we continued our march down Bunker's Hill, across the saddle, then up the western side of Breed's Hill. There on the fairly flat crest, Colonel Gridley laid out the lines of our fortification.

The stars shone clear and bright above us. Far to the east, the great horse Pegasus galloped over the black Atlantic. The silent troops turned their faces and listened intently when a distant bell in Boston slowly tolled a count of twelve.

Shovels were unloaded from wagons that had followed our column. Colonel Prescott, speaking quietly, did not order us, as would a British officer, simply to dig; rather, he explained to us how to dig a trench and then erect a wall along the angling sides of a redoubt. At dawn, he said with a tone of encouragement, the British peering up from Boston would discover our completed fortress.

Aye, farmers could dig. Farmers could move rocks. Farmers could pass a canteen filled with rum from man to man.

Colonel Prescott ordered a breastwork—a trench with an earthen wall chest high—built down the slope to the north of the redoubt. The breastwork would stop the British from sending a flank around our fort.

No moon that night. Only the stars, peering down as they passed above us, wondering what we mortals would do tomorrow with our New World.

We were discovered in the first pale grayness of dawn, shortly after the tolling of four o'clock. The *Lively*, standing in the channel midway between Charlestown and North End, suddenly fired several shots at us. Every man among us on Breed's Hill felt his heart jump to his throat. The ship's gunners had gauged their range well, for though they did no damage to the walls of our redoubt, one of their cannonballs sailed over our southeastern wall and struck a man's head, taking it neatly from his shoulders. Colonel Prescott, standing nearby, found himself splattered with blood and brains. A large number of men left their posts to stare at the headless corpse.

I knew the man. He was Asa Pollard from the village of Billerica, northwest of Boston. He had shared a cup of ale with me and a leg of mutton on a spit, one evening at his campfire. He cared not where I came from, asked not my reasons for mustering. He took me not as a stranger but as a friend, and told me about the elderberry bushes in a hedgerow behind his farm. He made wine from them. He invited me to visit him "once the British are done a-whoring." He wanted to share with me the "blue-black nectar" that he kept in a cask in his root cellar.

Officer Hench, no doubt on deck and staring up at our redoubt, would surely have been pleased to know that the *Lively* had fired a fatal shot.

As I stood among a cluster of shocked and murmuring men who stared down at Asa's headless body, that hidden person deep inside me began to emerge.

Colonel Prescott, seeing that the gruesome death had disheartened a number of his men, ordered a hasty burial outside the redoubt. He then climbed atop the parapet which we had erected. He walked along it with his sword drawn, in full view of the British artillery, while he urged us to keep at our digging.

When the huge orange sun rose over the shimmering Atlantic, we had not done more than half the work required to fashion a proper redoubt. With our Colonel's brave encouragement, and the *Lively's* unrelenting bombardment, we dug even deeper.

At nine in the morning, cannons mounted atop Copp's Hill, at the northern end of Boston, began to fire across the channel at us. We soon had the satisfaction of discovering how well our earthen walls held up to the 24-pound cannonballs that crashed into our fortress. Dirt sprayed into the air, but we were otherwise little bothered. Colonel Prescott, undaunted, continued to walk atop the parapet with his sword drawn.

That morning and much of the afternoon were spent preparing for the expected British attack. By the tolling of church bells in Boston, nearly twelve hours passed between the shots fired at us by the *Lively* at dawn, and the first assault of infantry sometime between three and four in the afternoon. The British allowed us to complete the trenches and parapets of our redoubt, with salient angles and properly aligned flanks, according to the excellent plan of Colonel Gridley. The British also allowed us to complete our breastwork, its outer flank protected by three *flèches* (as we called them by their French name): angled parapets pointing like arrows toward the river. Beyond these fortifications, a stone wall topped by a rail fence was bolstered with bundles of freshly cut hay, completing a sturdy barrier from the hilltop down to the beach. Even across the sand, our men built a wall of rock, using stones from nearby hedges. General Thomas Gage, in such a hurry while aboard the *Lively* to cross the Atlantic, now dawdled through the long morning and much of the afternoon, perhaps conferring with his officers, perhaps waiting until the tide was right, while our twelve hundred men dug and built and counted their cartridges.

General Gage also enabled a steady flow of reinforcements from Cambridge to walk across Charlestown Neck. The braver of these fresh and rested men joined us behind our parapets, while the more timid, much greater in number, lingered safely behind on Bunker's Hill.

We built no breastwork to the south of our redoubt, for Breed's Hill dropped steeply to a narrow plain that bordered the back streets of Charlestown. Our sentinels there, facing Boston, would later in the day reverse themselves and become snipers guarding our southern flank.

The British maneuvered their warships into position. The *Glasgow* and later the *Symmetry* sailed into the northern corner of Back Bay, from which they could bombard Charlestown Neck with their cannons. Two gondolas, rowed by sailors and mounted with artillery, paddled into shallow water closer to the neck. Though their grapeshot deterred some reinforcements from crossing the open bridge of land, it was far less effective than a landing of British infantry would have been at that vital point.

The *Lively* held her position in the channel off Charlestown. Two other frigates, the *Falcon* and the *Spitfire*, moved further north. Three powerful warships now ranged their cannons along the broad eastern end of the peninsula.

Quite another thing was happening during these early salvos. The *Lively's* first shot had awakened Boston. As the morning advanced, and British troops in full uniform marched through the streets toward the wharves, people began to assemble on Beacon Hill, then on the roof-tops, on the balconies of meetinghouse steeples, and in the rigging of ships moored along the piers. From our fortress on Breed's Hill, we looked south across the channel at an audience of hundreds, staring north at *us*. They were waiting for the battle to begin. Waiting to see whether the British, or the colonials, would stand victorious atop the hill at the end of the day.

In the village of Braintree, several miles south of Boston, Abigail Adams stood on a hill with her seven-year-old son, John Quincy. They were able to hear the cannons (and would later watch the flames and black smoke of the British attack). Thus our sixth and current President of these United States, now residing in the nation's capital in Washington, saw with his own eyes and heard with his own ears the first battle of the Revolution. In his boy's heart, he learned on that day the terrible price of liberty, and the greatness of men determined to pay the price, no matter how powerful the enemy might appear.

Before I relinquish the quill to my Genevieve, I must note a certain military maneuver that was *not* attempted. Every soldier on Breed's Hill knew that were the British to occupy Charlestown Neck with troops, thus cutting off our escape (as well as all possibility of rein-forcement or rescue), General Gage could have starved us until we marched down the hill as his prisoners. A landing of two or three companies of grenadiers might well have changed the fate of Colonel Prescott's twelve hundred men, of Boston, of the colony of Massachusetts. And of the other twelve colonies now meeting in Philadelphia.

But General Gage gave command of the attack to General William Howe, who preferred simply to march his troops up the slope of Breed's Hill and thus chase the cowardly Americans from their tiny earthworks. Farmers and shopkeepers would never stand up to His Majesty's finest troops.

ॐ

Chapter Thirty-Five

Genevieve, still in Cambridge
with a father, a brother, and a friend
on Charlestown peninsula,
a mother, a brother, and Sir William in Lincoln,
and me not about to sit still and mend a button.

Major General Israel Putnam was more often than not on a horse. During the morning of Saturday, June 17, 1775, he rode to General Ward's headquarters in Cambridge. He rode out across Charlestown Neck and up to the crest of Breed's Hill, where he spoke with Colonel Prescott. Old Put then rode back to General Ward's headquarters and recommended that fresh troops be sent to man the earthworks, for the men who had spent all night digging them (including Papa, Henry, and Benjamin) were by now exhausted.

General Ward was reluctant to move any of his troops from either Cambridge or Roxbury, for he feared a British attack across Boston Neck. He did agree, however, to send a courier riding to Medford, north of the Mystic River, with orders for Colonel John Stark: Stark should send two hundred of his Connecticut troops to assist Prescott on the Charlestown lines.

A good plan, certainly, but the general's young courier, whom I encountered at the paddock (where I was wont to observe the horses as some means of quieting my restlessness and worries), was a blacksmith from Framingham, to the southwest of Boston, who knew not, when I inquired why he was saddling a horse in such a hurry, the shortest route to a bridge across the Mystic River. Nor did he know which fork to take toward Medford. As he had the orders, and I had (from my many night rides upon Sir William) the proper route quite clear in my mind, I requested that he order me a horse saddled. Mindful of the importance of his mission, and finding no other person about the paddock who knew of Medford from Menotomy, or one bridge from another over the Mystic, the young courier grudgingly acquiesced to a woman as his guide.

The slowness of a groom at saddling my horse prompted me to buckle the cinch and fasten the bridle myself. When the lad cursed me for my forwardness, I taught him a half-dozen words which I myself had learned (though never before put into use) from an Irish blacksmith in Concord. The groom, his ears pink, departed from the barn, leaving the horse to me, and me to my work.

North out of Cambridge I rode my sleepy mare, the sullen courier beside me, ducking his head every time the cannons on Copp's Hill fired a shot at Charlestown. I quickly found the shortcut to the river, managed to goad my nag from a dozing trot to a bumpy canter until we reached the bridge. Once over the river, she settled back to a stubborn trot and cared not whether the King or our high Sons of Liberty should win the war today. Had I been riding my Sir William, I could, in the time I spent upon that mare, have enjoyed a cup of tea with Colonel Stark before we presented him with his orders.

We did at last arrive in Medford, and quickly found Colonel Stark's headquarters. He assembled and marched his men immediately. I had the pleasure of riding behind their column back to the bridge, then along the river to Charlestown Neck. I dared not cross the neck because of a thick and steady barrage of cannonballs from a number of British vessels positioned beyond the mill pond. It was not for my own life that I feared, but rather that of the poor miserable beast which I rode, for she was not mine, and I had not her owner's permission to risk her on a battlefield. Therefore I returned, most reluctantly, to the paddock in Cambridge, where I unsaddled the mare and patted her rump as she walked with a sigh back to her hay bin.

Now on foot, I walked the two miles back to the Charlestown Neck, where a great crowd had assembled at the western end: spectators from nearby farms who would venture no further, and soldiers under orders from no one, who stared with horror at the cannonballs and volleys of grapeshot flying over the neck.

Shoving their way through the crowd were soldiers who had just dashed across the neck from the peninsula. They had decided that cannonballs were far less worrisome than the British redcoats now crossing in boats from Boston. A cannonball had no brains, one frightened deserter told me, but a bayonet knew its business.

Though as a Daughter of Liberty I felt it my duty, and my right, to proceed across the neck to the fortress on Breed's Hill, and there to find my place beside my father, I had no musket. Further, I knew for a certainty that Papa would be much discomfited by the appearance of his daughter on a battlefield. I therefore remained on the more sheltered side of the neck, though somewhat apart from the churning turmoil of soldiers and spectators.

I was determined, however, most fiercely determined, that if the battle today did not send the British back to England, I would walk to our farm in Lincoln, where I would tell my poor mother what news I knew, then put a saddle on Sir William.

If a proper courier on a proper horse was what our army needed, then I, a fair-faced lad in my brother Henry's old clothes, would provide Major General Artemus Ward with a courier who could gallop through a thunderstorm at midnight and find any officer of any regiment on any road within thirty miles of Boston.

∞

Chapter Thirty-Six

Benjamin York,
standing with Henry Byrnes behind a parapet,
the two of us covered with dirt,
armed, hungry, thirsty, dead tired,
and ready to fight
for our own very different reasons.

THE BATTLE OF BREED'S HILL

The men watched, from our fortress on the hilltop, as cutters were launched from all the warships, including the *Lively*, then rowed to Long Pier and several other docks along Boston's wharf. We watched through the afternoon as those cutters brought their loads of red-coated infantrymen and grenadiers across the channel, first to the beach at the easternmost point of the peninsula, then later to a beach closer to the village of Charlestown. We watched His Majesty's troops form in their neat scarlet companies in the fields above the beaches. We watched as they marched in rectangular blocks toward the base of our hill. We could see, as they approached with the afternoon sun shining on their perfect ranks, the white belts crisscrossed over their red chests. Oval brass gorgets shone brightly on the upper chests of the officers. We watched the hundreds of glinting bayonets, pointing upward toward the heaven where they would send our souls.

We could hear the British drummers, measuring the brisk pace of the march. Their steady cadence would disappear for some moments beneath the blast of naval cannons, then become audible again, slightly closer, slightly louder.

We could hear the fifes, those shrill birds of death.

Aye, but what the Americans could not see (neither Henry at my side, peering over the top of the parapet, nor John who had taken a post along the breastwork) were the faces of comrades, the faces of friends. I had spent nearly a year camped on Boston Common with those red-coated infantrymen who now stood at the base of our hill. I had drilled with them, stood watch with them through rain and snow and fog and driving sleet. I had supped with them at their campfires, shared with them a cup of cider, a mug of ale. I had attended services every Sabbath with them. I had tended them when sick, as they had tended me when sick. Together we had cursed our officers, had cursed the weather, had cursed the lowly colonials. And together we had swapped stories of sweethearts and families and favorite meals back home in England.

Were these the men I was called upon to slaughter today?

My sharp eyes easily distinguished the yellow facing and cuffs of my own 10th Regiment, forming just above the beach along the river. Among those scarlet rectangular formations of infantry, my tentmates no doubt marched. Down there were the men who had welcomed Nathaniel and me in the place of Higgins and Brown. (Unless they had all been killed on the road back to Boston.)

Was I now to lay down Henry's fowling piece, bid him and Colonel Prescott a silent farewell, then slip out the back entry of the redoubt? Was I to aim high, firing as often as every American to my left and right, but sending my lead balls toward the empty heavens?

Or was I (as for a moment I had a strong impulse to do) to climb upon the parapet where minutes before Colonel Prescott had stood, as neither a soldier with the Americans nor a soldier with the British; nay, not a soldier at all, but a simple man whose battered heart could no longer accept the madness that never seemed to stop?

And if I shouted down the hill to the British, and if I shouted to the Americans behind their earthen wall (and if I shouted as well up to the good Lord who may or may not have been in attendance today), what would I say?

At some point during the last blurred and frantic hour of digging before the battle, Dr. Joseph Warren, whom I had once heard speak most passionately in the Old South Meeting House, strode calmly into our redoubt dressed in his civilian finest, as if he were on his way to the Governor's Ball. He was greeted by cheers from the men, who were greatly heartened to see a man of such high esteem among them. Though Colonel Prescott offered him command of the redoubt, Dr. Warren insisted that he was but a volunteer. He took a position with a musket at the parapet, some five yards to my left, in the eastern salient where the British infantry were likely to strike first.

Minutes later, we heard down on the grassy flats behind us our own American drums and fife, playing "Yankee Doodle" as Colonel John Stark and his Connecticut volunteers filed across a pasture and took their places along the stone wall that extended to the river. So it was Stark's men who would stand against my 10th Regiment. Colonel Stark himself, as we could clearly see from our hill, stepped out in front of the stone wall even as the 10th was forming in the distance. He walked about twenty paces, then stuck a stick into the ground. As he walked back to the wall, we understood that his men were to wait until the front rank of redcoats had reached that stick before they fired their first volley.

At a distance of fifty feet, they could not miss.

A church bell in Boston tolled three times. It was three o'clock on a sunny Saturday afternoon . . . when a man might well be fishing in the Mystic River, his bare feet buried in the warm sand of the beach.

Or when a man might well be standing in the tall grass atop Breed's Hill, with his arm around his best girl while they look far out to sea and dream of a future as blissfully happy as the moment they now savor.

Or when a man might well be patching the roof of his house in the village. A house that he received from his father, who received it from his father before him.

That church bell in Boston rang three deep and somber times: it tolled the fates of two thousand men assembled at the base of the hill, and tolled the fates of two thousand men atop the hill.

For when the bell rang the hour of three, General William Howe gave his British troops the order to attack.

We were ordered by Colonel Prescott to hold our fire.

The infantry of the 10th Regiment advanced in a column along the narrow beach. The grenadiers of the 10th Regiment advanced in three long ranks through the grass toward the stone wall.

Infantry from the 5th, the 52nd, the 38th, and the 43rd regiments (as I clearly recognized them from their uniforms) advanced across the broad plain toward our hill. We could hear their dozen drummers, their scattered fifers, like the rumbling growl and shrill breathing of some great beast moving toward us. We could hear shots from snipers in the village, shots that sounded tiny and flat compared to the roar of naval cannons in their now increasing barrage.

Colonel Prescott, walking behind us inside the walls of the redoubt, ordered us to hold our fire.

Up the hill the British redcoats marched—a few of them stumbled over stones hidden in the grass, some suddenly tumbled into a ditch, but they quickly resumed their ordered ranks—until they were close enough that I began to recognize faces, faces of men whose names I knew, faces in which I saw a grim determination to clear the hill of the vermin which now infested it. Officers with drawn swords led the ranks. But something more compelled the redcoats: years of training, years of waiting, years of honing their bayonets, now urged the troops confidently on. I saw such a fierce eagerness in their eyes, that were their officers to release them, few of the soldiers would have turned to descend the hill; most would surely have surged forward to savor the supreme satisfaction of thrusting their bayonets into as many American hearts as possible.

A wall of scarlet hatred advanced toward us, only fifty yards from us now, their drums trembling the very air we breathed. Colonel Prescott ordered us to hold our fire.

We could hear the rhythmic swish of their feet advancing through the deep grass.

I no longer considered whether to flee, or to fire high, or to commit my soul to God. I had been two men since the day Nathaniel died, and I now without a thought cast off the man to whom he had spoken about building his church. If madness is a poison that a soldier must drink, then I readily emptied my cup.

I leveled my fowling piece toward the chest of an officer, a tall burly fellow named Bartholomew Hampton, who had often scolded our men during drills, "I'll send ye off with 'iggins and Brown, I will!" Though those two scoundrels had brought us much misfortune, still I hated to hear their names besmirched, as if they were more useful dead than alive. What had they been but lads like the rest of us, snatched from their lives and made to—

"Fire!" roared Prescott. The very earth against which I leaned my chest shook with the roar of our muskets. Oh, did my heart not leap with joy when the officer at whom I aimed whirled around, then down the hill he tumbled!

The redcoats fired in return, but we were by then down behind the wall, reloading while those who stood behind us fired a second volley. Smoke like a thick fog billowed over the parapet. Through it came shrieks, orders, shots.

Down on the plain by the river, the 10th Regiment must have reached Colonel Stark's stick, for we heard now the roar of muskets far to our left. The entire wall and breastwork opened fire. When I peered over the top of our parapet, I saw four hundred yards of billowing smoke. I would not have been surprised if I had seen the earth itself open up with a tearing roar.

Through the smoke drifting in front of our redoubt, we could see the redcoats who had been marching toward us. Their ranks had halted. Men were writhing in the grass. Officers waved their swords and urged the troops forward. Our muskets fired at them no longer in volleys but in a constant blaze of fire. The scarlet targets in roiling black smoke stepped forward two or three paces and then crumbled. I fired in a wild ecstasy of rage at their chests, whooping, as Henry whooped beside me, with each man I sent sprawling.

And then the redcoats, disregarding those few officers still alive, turned and fled as fast as they could manage down the hill. Several of our men called out that we should pursue the retreating bastards. I myself was of that notion, for already I could feel my hands picking up from the grass a regimental firelock with its seventeen-inch bayonet. Then show me an officer still alive!

But Colonel Prescott ordered us to maintain our positions. Not a man went over the parapet in pursuit.

I saw to my right a patriot sprawled dead at the foot of our earthen wall. I had not a moment's pity for him, nor any other thought save that I would have his musket and cartridges before someone else discovered the prize. No one contested the weapon as I grabbed it. I was back beside Henry in less than ten seconds with both my old fowling piece and the far better musket. By my hurried count, I also had fifteen cartridges in the fellow's box. I reloaded both the musket and the fowling piece. Then I glanced at Henry, his face blackened with smoke, his cheeks smeared with dirt. I saw in his eyes a look of approval.

During those minutes of quiet while the British retreated down the hill, I walked to the north side of the redoubt and peered over the parapet to see how the breastwork and stone wall had fared. I saw that hundreds of redcoats lay on the ground; some were moving, some were shrieking in pain. Almost all of them lay in a scarlet band twenty yards from the breastwork, twenty yards from the wall. They had marched directly toward the muzzles of our muskets, and when they were close enough that no farmer who shot at squirrels could possibly miss, we had fired.

Had I not deserted from the 10th, that would have been me dead on the beach. Or shrieking for Elspeth, with a ball in my belly.

For a moment, I felt in my heart some degree of pity for my fellow infantrymen, perhaps a drop or two when compared to what would have been Nathaniel's ocean of compassion.

Returning to my eastern parapet, I watched as boats brought more troops from Boston. No doubt the proud British officers would send their sacrificial men on a second assault.

The *Lively* now began to fire red-hot cannonballs—even from the hill we could see that they were red and not black—at the village of Charlestown. Flames soon leaped up from the rooftops, then spread from house to house, until much of the wharf and several streets were ablaze. The tall pointed spire of the meetinghouse became a torch lifted above the doomed village.

Driven from their hiding places, our snipers dashed west across the fields toward a stone barn, from which they continued to fire. But their retreat opened the way for the British to advance around the hill to our southern flank.

We could hear the crackling roar of the flames, fanned by an off-shore wind. Black smoke boiled up into the blue summer sky. Houses, barns, warehouses and shops all crashed to the earth; each building sent up a fountain of sparks.

We were fiercely thirsty, but entirely without water. During the morning and early afternoon, men had scurried down the hill with their canteens to fill them at a well in Charlestown. But our canteens now lay scattered and empty.

We waited for the second assault.

∛

Chapter Thirty-Seven

Benjamin.

British reinforcements ferried from Boston landed along the coast and formed into companies. The scarlet rectangles moved into position along the base of our hill, and on the plain in front of the breastwork and wall. They would do again what their fellow soldiers had just done: march under orders to their deaths.

More than anything I had yet seen, the second assault showed me what these Americans were fighting for: they could think enough to call out "aye" or "nay" at a meeting; they could think enough to consider, as they did so often in their own newspapers and broadsheets, the future of "the millions yet unborn"; they could think enough to stand or run. Whereas the infantrymen and grenadiers in His Majesty's army, though frightened, though fierce with contempt, marched like trained beasts to their slaughter. The Americans fought for their freedom to think.

We watched the redcoats as they started up the hill . . . watched them step over the wounded and dead as if their fellow soldiers were naught but logs on the ground.

We held our fire until the front rank was thirty yards from us.

I stared down the barrel of my musket at an officer, for that much remnant of conscience I still had left.

"Fire!" shouted Colonel Prescott.

Our volley signaled a volley all along our line, from the hilltop to the beach.

After reloading as quickly as I could (choking on the smoke and spitting dryly), I fired at whatever scarlet soldier was still on his feet, marching toward us, standing frozen, or fleeing back down the hill. From my year of drilling in Boston, I fired three shots, sometimes four, to Henry's two, and I knew to fire low.

Had I a six-pounder cannon, I would not have paused a moment in loading its barrel with grapeshot. I would have fired a giant blast through a dozen men, sending their shreds of meat and shards of skull flying across the grassy hill.

For the madness of war is hatred, and hatred is a sickness, and on that madness I thrived.

Once again the British faltered. Once again those still on their feet staggered back. And once again the Americans proved to themselves that they could stand up to His Majesty's troops.

Before the third assault, we counted our cartridges and determined throughout the redoubt that we had nearly exhausted our powder. The men loaded with lead ball, with stones, with nails from an old fence. We were now no more than a hundred and fifty men in the redoubt, for a few of our men had fled, some had gone to support the breastwork, and some had peered over the parapet at the wrong moment and now lay in a bloody heap.

Were we to use the last of our powder before we stopped the third assault, the war would no doubt come pouring over the walls around us.

We had noticed before each of the first two assaults, and now saw most acutely before the third, that a great crowd of our fellow soldiers, fully armed, stood atop Bunker's Hill to our rear. Staring toward us with as much interest as the spectators on the rooftops of Boston, they would come no further. *They* no doubt had slept the night before. They surely had water in their canteens and cartridges in their boxes. Well might they have advanced along the saddle to support us in the redoubt, or down the slope to support those at the breastwork and stone wall. But though we could see Old Put upon his horse, riding back and forth along the crest of Bunker's Hill, waving his sword to urge the stragglers forward, few ventured even as far as the saddle.

Hearing British drums now begin their cadence, and hearing too the shouts of men along our wall, I peered over the parapet and saw the 43rd Regiment coming directly up the hill toward us. A flank of red-coats swung to the south, undeterred now by our snipers, who had been driven well behind us. The flankers were joined by several companies of marines under Major John Pitcairn, the same Pitcairn who had led us to Lexington's green. He was on foot now, for the British apparently had no boats to bring across their horses. The flankers and marines threatened to extend their line beyond our rear parapet: they might thus force their way into the redoubt by way of its single entrance. Or they could block our escape through that narrow gap.

Colonel Prescott ordered us sternly not to retreat until he gave the command.

We held our fire as the third assault mounted steadily up the hill.

The white breeches of the front ranks were stained with red from sweeping through blood-spattered grass.

I heard Pitcairn's familiar voice, below us and toward the right, as he ordered his marines to sweep further west . . . toward our rear.

Far to our left, British cannons opened a barrage. The cannons had been wheeled along the river until they could enfilade our breastwork: British cannonballs now swept lengthwise through our line of men. Many of the troops had left their posts; some fled toward Bunker's Hill, though most sought protection in our redoubt.

Amidst the clamor of new men surging into the fortress—some wounded, some shouting for water—Colonel Prescott ordered, "Fire!" We struck the British with our first volley.

Our second volley was even stronger, for the men pouring in added their muskets. The redcoats no longer advanced. But they stood their ground.

Then, without powder, many of our men could not reload. Sensing from the meagerness of our volleys that we were coming to the end of our powder, the British now charged forward the final thirty yards, to do their work with bayonets.

"Stand your ground!" ordered Prescott, though clumps of soldiers began to disappear through the gap. Whereas before we had been quiet and steady at our labor, the men now shouted and dashed about, calling "Here!" and "Here!" and "Here!" wherever the redcoats were nearing our walls.

My musket was empty.

I scrambled in the dirt, opening box after box (one still on the belt of a man moaning with his jaw shot away), as I searched desperately for any remaining cartridges. When a redcoat appeared at the top of our parapet, I dropped the musket, grabbed for the fowling piece and sent a charge through the soldier's face as he took aim at Henry. Dropping his firelock, the soldier tumbled backward over the wall. I leapt up and grabbed the barrel, swung the wooden stock snugly into place at my shoulder, leveled the barrel on the next redcoat to mount the wall and shot him as he leaped, striking him in the leg. He landed with a cry and fell forward onto his face, his firelock beneath him. With a shout of rage, I thrust my seventeen-inch bayonet down through his back. The man arched in hideous pain, and died.

As I pulled out my bloody blade, I saw Henry staring at me: he was so stunned that an officer with a sword could easily have cut off his head. Reaching down to the dead soldier, I rolled him over, grabbed his firelock with its bayonet and handed the weapon to Henry. "Don't get the blade stuck in their ribs," I shouted at him, then I turned to the next redcoat coming over the parapet.

Colonel Prescott shouted the order to retreat, for the redcoats were now climbing over two sides of our redoubt. Glancing back through clouds of smoke, I saw a crowd of men at the gap; some struggled to push through the others. Dr. Warren in his brocaded evening attire was swinging the barrel of a broken musket at a redcoat, who would easily have bayoneted the doctor had not Colonel Prescott run the soldier through the neck with his sword.

I had no thought of dying, not a moment of fear, as I dashed with my bayonet toward every redcoat coming over the wall: the instant he had fired his musket, I attacked. He could not shoot me as I lunged toward him. I had the advantage that my barrel and bayonet were already leveled at him and borne by the weight of my charge. If my blade came not free from his ribs, I stepped my foot on the corpse and yanked the blade free.

One marine managed to parry my blade. He then gave me a good nick in the arm with his own bayonet. But by then I was a demon, wild, shrieking, utterly berserk. I bludgeoned him with my stock until he dropped to his knees, then I brought the stock down like my oar upon Hench and crushed in his forehead.

I nearly bayoneted Henry when he grabbed my arm.

"Retreat, Benjamin, retreat!" he shouted at me. His eyes implored me to come with him.

Glancing, I saw that the gap was now free of the crowd of shirkers. Leading with my bayonet—the bloody and slightly bent blade like a great needle ready to stitch through any bit of red wool—I followed Henry through the gap to the open grassy hilltop behind it. Our men were dashing down the slope and across the saddle toward Bunker's Hill. British marines and infantry ran in pursuit, and I saw—many of us saw—the odd, heroic figure of Dr. Warren in his elegant yellow coat as he swung his sword to encourage us and then took a ball in the back of his head. Though several of our men paused in their flight to help him, the patriots' orator was dead. We left him wearing his silks in the dirt.

With a keen eye for a cartridge box at the side of any corpse, I managed to reload and fire several times before the growing surge of redcoats forced me to move down the saddle.

We heard a shout that Pitcairn had been hit. The flanking marines faltered. Prescott swept us westward with his sword, making no stand to the last drop of blood, but rather preserving his men as best he could.

With covering fire from Stark's men to our right, and covering fire from some unknown squad of Americans on our left, Colonel Prescott, Henry, and I walked, at the Colonel's steady pace, down the slope with the last dozen regulars to retreat from our redoubt.

Atop Bunker's Hill, Old Put on his horse attempted to stop the flood of men so that together we might hold the hill. But few listened to his ragged voice. I asked him if he had cartridges. He pointed me to a farmer who seemed to have done nothing all afternoon but stand facing our redoubt with a loaded musket and a box full of powder and ball. The farmer, his face and hands clean, his mouth open but not a word coming from it, readily let me lift the belt to his cartridge box over his head. He even handed me his musket. I thereupon took my stand atop Bunker's Hill and fired at the redcoats charging up the slope toward us.

Through the smoke and the blast and the roar I could hear Henry desperately calling my name. But not until I had emptied that leather box of all twenty-six cartridges did I even turn to look in his direction.

Old Put himself was by this time calling a retreat. We descended the backside of Bunker's Hill at Colonel Prescott's steady walk. I would have joined Colonel Stark's rear guard, would have asked the Colonel himself if he had a spare cartridge, but Henry would hear none of it. He had found his father on the back of Bunker's Hill, wounded with a ball in his arm. Henry was determined to get us both across the neck to safety, never mind who won the war.

So cross the neck we did, with bullets whizzing from behind us, and grapeshot and cannonballs sweeping sideways among us, some of them doing their work, so that men who had dug and thirsted and fought on Breed's Hill for the past eighteen hours now met their sudden death on the narrow earthen bridge that led to their campfire and tent and dinner and safety. We had to let them lie where they fell.

A short distance along the road toward Cambridge, beyond the reach of British infantry (which seemed to have halted at the neck), we approached a crowd of people. And there in that tumultuous throng of farmers and soldiers and women and even children, stood Genevieve, her eyes saying a prayer as she stared at the three of us.

She took her father's good arm to brace him, then led us around the crowd to the road toward Cambridge. None of us spoke. We had all of tomorrow to talk, or not talk, about the death we had seen.

We had gone but a short distance before Old Put rode up on his sweated and frothing horse. He leaned down from his saddle and put his hand on my shoulder.

"Good work, lad," he said to me, his voice hoarse but proud. His hand gripped my shoulder. "You're among the fittest of the patriots, you are."

Then with a nod to the others, Old Put rode back toward the neck.

We walked—dazed, silent, grateful, and despairing because of our defeat—the two miles back to our camp. Henry kindled a campfire to prepare some sort of dinner. Genevieve went to search for a doctor to attend her father.

I laid down in the grass outside our tent. For a moment I stared up at the lavender sky. Then I slept the sleep of the dead.

&

Chapter Thirty-Eight

Genevieve, no longer a girl of nineteen,
but now a woman of nineteen.

I finally found a doctor, at three in the morning, and bade him most insistently to attend to my father. The poor exhausted man removed the ball and put sulfur into the wound. Then my father, filthy, slept inside the tent beside Henry, also filthy. Outside the tent, mired less in dirt than in dried blood and gore, Benjamin slept beneath the tranquil stars.

I borrowed a horse from the paddock—nay, I stole a horse from the paddock—then rode at a canter beneath the fading stars to Lincoln and our farm. I awakened Mama and Judd and told them that our three men had survived the first battle of the war.

We ate a somber breakfast at dawn. I secretly gathered a bundle of Henry's old clothes. I saddled Sir William, and promised my mother to return often with news. Then I led the borrowed horse by a length of rope as I rode my Sir William out the gate and back toward Cambridge.

The rising sun shone brightly ahead of us on that Sunday morning. Sir William, in the best of spirits, pranced through the sleeping village of Lexington.

Yes, and more.

Somewhere deep within the turmoil in my heart, I was beginning to love the man to whom Old Put had given his blessing.

Benjamin, burning in the fires of shame.

I was awakened the following morning by blinding sunshine . . . to the remembrance, the horror, of what I had done. I stared at my hands, caked with blood, and at the sleeves and chest of Judd's once-clean shirt, now blackened with burnt powder and smeared with blood and something more. I raised my fingers to touch my face, brushed away flakes of dirt and dried blood. I thought I must look like the wolf that tears the flesh of its meal not with a knife and fork but with its teeth.

"I am Cain," I spoke aloud to myself, "who has slaughtered my brother Abel."

It was not my own voice I heard speaking. It was my father's voice.

Looking around me, I saw men at their breakfast fires. But I saw not Henry, nor John, nor Genevieve.

I stood, shielded my eyes from the glare of the sun over the bay. I noticed a blanket at my feet, which someone had placed over me.

"I am Cain, who has slaughtered my brother Abel."

Then I shall go to meet my brother Abel.

Leaving the encampment, ignoring those who stared at me, who called to me, I walked along the road which I had already walked too many times, toward the neck, the door, the gate, the passage.

I stared across the bay toward the two hills. Men stood atop them, men clad in red. Yes, I shall bury my brother Abel, and beside him can they bury me.

Hooves came galloping behind me.

"Benjamin! *Benjamin!* Where are you going?"

Opening my hands, I stared at their blood-caked palms as I walked.

The horse sounded as if it would run over me, though I stepped not out of its way. Then Genevieve was beside me, upon a reddish horse, her eyes baffled, and something more.

"Benjamin, where are you going?"

"I am Cain, who has slaughtered my brother Abel."

She swung down from the saddle, held the reins with one hand while she gripped my arm with her other. "Benjamin, Henry told me that you fought as hard as any man on the hill. He said that you're a true Son of Liberty."

"Aye," I said. "Nay," I said.

I walked, with her hand gripping my arm.

"Benjamin, where are you going?"

Why such a foolish question? I would cross the neck and climb the hill, where my English brothers, those still alive, would take me as their prisoner. A brief confession, then they would hang me. Or shoot me. Or bayonet me. And I would no longer have to live with myself.

Two American sentries stood in front of the hut near the neck. One of them shouted, "Halt!" But they could as well shoot me in the back as I passed them, and save the British the bother of hanging me.

Genevieve tugged at my arm as the sentry stepped in front of me, a stern look on his face. "Back to camp with you, soldier," he said, ready not to shoot me, but to bar my way with the barrel of his musket.

I shoved the musket so hard that the sentry stumbled backwards.

Genevieve cried, "Benjamin!"

The second sentry leveled his musket at me. "Halt! We've orders that no man passes here toward the British." He seemed more earnest in explaining his job to me than in stopping me.

I tugged my arm gently but firmly from Genevieve's grip. My eyes stared at the road crossing the neck.

And then I saw, thirty yards beyond the neck and walking toward us, a man clad in buckskin, the first such leather shirt and leggings that I had ever seen. He carried in his arms a British soldier who wore a scarlet vest but no longer his outer coat, and whose dangling arm and wobbling head indicated that the soldier was either gravely wounded, or dead.

Were I to walk any further, the sentry, should he shoot to stop me, risked hitting the man who walked toward us with his burden.

Genevieve stepped in front of me and stood squarely in my way.

The man in fringed buckskin, clearly wearied by the exertion of carrying a soldier from somewhere on yesterday's battlefield, crossed the neck behind her.

His eyes upon mine, the man paused. With his fair hair spread in tangles on his shoulders, and an intricate design in beads across the chest of his leather shirt, he seemed to have stepped out of a wild forest far to the west.

The soldier in his arms moaned enough to indicate some presence of life.

The man knelt and laid the soldier gently on the ground.

"Water, sir," he called to a sentry. The sentry lowered his musket and ran to fetch a canteen from the hut.

The man in buckskin, a man perhaps my father's age, looked down at the soldier, a lad no older than myself. He took the canteen with a nod of gratitude, lifted the soldier's head from the ground and tipped the canteen to his lips. I watched with unthinking satisfaction as the British infantryman managed several swallows.

The strange fellow now lifted his sunburned face toward mine and gazed at me with the faint crinkle of a smile in his eyes. "Help each other, and so shall you come to know each other."

I felt a wave of peace pass through me. The madness which I knew not as a madness, had never known as a madness, now lifted, leaving me feeling as a man feels when he has outlived a fever.

Returning the canteen to the sentry, the man lifted the soldier into his arms. He cradled the soldier's head against his leather chest, then stood up with his burden.

He stared for a long moment at Genevieve, her dark eyes no longer frightened, but somehow reassured, as she looked now from the man to me.

The stranger then told me, as easily and confidently as if he were telling me about tomorrow's weather, "When you are ready to marry this woman, I will wed thee."

Stepping around me, he walked with the wounded British soldier toward the distant breakfast fires of the American encampment.

I climbed down the embankment from the road to the mill pond, waded into water much warmer in June than it had been in April, and washed the blood from my hands. Cupping my clean hands into water that glimmered in the morning sun, I washed my face. I stepped further from shore, lifted the blood-smeared shirt over my head and tossed it away. The shirt sank slowly from the surface, like a drowning ghost, and disappeared.

Holding my breath, I dunked myself completely under, reached down and pulled off Higgins's too-large shoes. Pulled off the stockings.

I stood again, dripping, with my feet in the cool mud. I breathed the fresh morning air. Then I laughed as I looked over my shoulder at Genevieve. "Turn your eyes, girl!"

Whether she did or not, I paid no mind, as I unbuttoned and peeled from my legs the filthy, bloodied breeches. I cast them away from me, and they too slowly sank. As naked now as a Boston cod, I dunked and bobbed and splashed and laughed in the morning sunshine, freed of hatred, freed of rage, freed of an agony of loathing against myself. For surely there would be other soldiers, in scarlet wool, in homespun linen, who would need strong arms to carry them from the battlefield.

One of the sentries loaned me his night cloak.

Genevieve again held my arm, though not so fiercely now, as we walked together with her horse along the road toward the breakfast fires of the American encampment.

୫

Chapter Thirty-Nine

Genevieve, her page.

It seems to me that if my dear husband is going to write about every canteen and cartridge in the war, then we two old soldiers are going to be dead and buried long before this account is completed.

Well, I've got the quill now. So let me sketch neither the panorama of a battlefield, nor the panorama of history, but rather a few portraits: of Commander in Chief George Washington; of Private Henry York; of a minister named Johannes Kesslaer.

And of a man and a woman who courted and married—and conceived a child—at a time when no one knew who would sit at our campfire on the following evening, and who would be freshly buried.

General George Washington, forty-three years old, as a young man a surveyor and soldier in the American wilderness, and now a Virginia gentleman, was chosen by the Second Continental Congress in Philadelphia to take immediate command of the loosely organized army which had abruptly taken up arms against the British. He wrote a long letter to Martha, his wife at Mount Vernon, telling her that "the defence of the American cause shall be put under my care." The responsibility, he believed, was "a trust too great for my capacity." However, "as it has been a kind of destiny, that has thrown me upon this service, I shall hope that my undertaking it is designed to answer some good purpose." He enclosed a copy of his newly written will. Then he rode for six days in a phaeton pulled by two white horses to New York City, and thence to Cambridge, where he arrived without fanfare on July 2, 1775.

During his brief visit to New York City, General Washington met with the New York Provincial Congress. Its members did not hesitate to express the fear shared by many Americans throughout the colonies: Would General Washington, at the end of the hostilities with Britain, "resume the character of our worthiest citizen?" Or (unspoken in his presence) would he become, like so many military commanders before him, a dictator who might well turn his army against his own people?

General Washington's response to the New York Congress quickly spread—by newspaper as well as by word of mouth—north to the four embattled colonies of New England, and south as far as the backwater farms of Georgia, until most of the two million Americans who lived in our thirteen colonies, and perhaps a goodly number of the half-million slaves as well, had spoken and indeed memorized with satisfaction his very words.

Because he replied, "When we assumed the soldier, we did not lay aside the citizen." Like the old Roman, Cincinnatus, who left his plow beside a half-dug furrow to heed the call to war, Washington promised that when the conflict was over, he would return to his plow.

When General Washington arrived at the encampment headquarters in Cambridge, he was accompanied by his orderly, Billy, a slave whom he had bought seven years ago from a woman named Mary Lee. Billy Lee served faithfully as the general's servant through the next eight years of war. Then he returned to the Mount Vernon plantation and continued to serve as a slave, until finally, upon his master's death in 1799, he was granted "immediate freedom." William Lee was honored for his fidelity to his master, for General Washington's other slaves were not freed when he died. According to the General's will, they were granted their freedom only upon the death of his wife Martha.

Thus the Virginia gentleman who arrived in Cambridge to take command of the Continental Army intended, from the very beginning, to grant the fullest measure of liberty to his fellow citizens, and to grant not the slightest shred of liberty to his chattel slaves.

General Washington arrived in Cambridge on a Sunday. He moved into his quarters in the home of Harvard's president, Samuel Langdon. On Monday morning, the volunteer soldiers gathered in their untrained approximation of military formation in a pasture near our encampment, so the General could inspect his troops. He later rode north to inspect the troops of the left wing, and south to inspect the right wing. General Washington carried with him a telescope; from a dozen points along the ten-mile crescent, he studied the enemy in Boston.

While he rode his white stallion that day, and during the weeks and months of the siege, we watched him, came to know him, to like him. As he galloped—he rarely rode but at a gallop—from headquarters to garrison to redoubt to sentry post, he was stitching the thread that bound our little patches together into one American quilt.

General Washington was a tall man, even a little taller than Papa. He wore a long dark blue coat with buff facing and cuffs, and without a single military ornament or medal. Though many of our skeptical New Englanders expected the Virginia gentleman to wear the oval silver gorget of an officer, they were pleased by the lack of that aristocratic emblem. General Washington's authority was not in any gilt insignia, but in his bearing: he brought not pomp but dignity into our camp.

We immediately felt his insistence on military authority, military discipline. Officers and their men—often boyhood friends from the same village—no longer argued among themselves over every order: officers now gave out orders and soldiers carried out orders. And though a captain may have been a skilled barber back home, he no longer shaved his own men.

General Washington organized every aspect of our encampment. Privies were to be dug a healthy distance from our tents and log huts. No exceptions were to be made concerning their use.

Powder was never to be wasted in idle shooting, either at targets or at the enemy. (We did not know at the time—as General Washington knew all too well—how little powder we had.)

Our men labored every day, including the Sabbath, from four in the morning (using the very first light of dawn) until eleven in the morning, when they paused in their digging of endless trenches and their building of sturdy breastworks, for dinner.

But even before that early hour of four o'clock in the morning, the troops were roused out of their blankets; they ate their breakfast, then formed into regiments for the daily prayer, and general orders from our Commander in Chief. Whatever they had been before, our men were soldiers now, and soldiers working *together*.

&

Chapter Forty

Genevieve, still with her quill,
telling the tale of

THE GREAT HORSE RACE

While Papa, Henry, and Benjamin labored with their regiment, I would often visit the paddock near the encampment, where I fed and groomed Sir William. From the officers who kept their horses there, I learned that General Washington was recruiting express riders. Anyone who wished to ride as a courier was to present himself in Harvard Yard tomorrow morning at ten o'clock. All riders must be recommended to the General by someone in good standing, lest the rider turn out to be a spy.

I was determined to do something more for the Continental Army than sew on buttons for my three men. Sir William and I had found our calling.

I spoke with Papa, who had first lifted me up to his saddle when I was five years old. Without hesitation, he agreed to support me in my endeavor. And so the following morning, dressed in Henry's old clothes and his battered straw hat as Ebenezer Byrnes—a rustic lad of unassuming background—I accompanied Papa (his left arm still in a sling) to Harvard Yard.

I was dismayed to find a crowd of applicants gathered in front of General Washington's headquarters, well over thirty men, some with their horses, some without. Most of the horses were good steady farm horses, able at the plow, but certainly not the sort that Paul Revere would have chosen for his long gallop at midnight.

There was one exception. I cocked my ear to listen to the Irish voice of a young man with bushy red hair and a fine red beard, for he held the bridle of a magnificent coal-black stallion. That one horse, and that horse alone, might manage to stay with my Sir William for a good long stretch. It would not be speed, but stamina, that would determine the race in the end.

The white door of headquarters swung open and General Washington appeared at the top of the steps, accompanied by several officers.

The General seemed a bit surprised at the multitude of riders. His eyes glanced at several of the horses, then lingered, I noticed, on the black stallion. He conferred with an officer, who announced that we should step forward one by one with a person who would recommend us, so that our names might be placed on a list.

"Shall you speak for me, Papa?" I asked quietly, afraid that my voice might give me away.

"Aye," he nodded, clearly nervous himself in the presence of his Commander in Chief, "I shall speak for you."

As we waited, and shuffled forward, the both of us listened intently to the series of questions asked by the General's secretary: name, age, town or village, age of horse, familiarity with the roads and villages outside of Boston. Desired length of service.

The white door of headquarters again swung open, and to my great relief Old Put stepped out. He knew Papa well enough to vouch for him as captain of the Lincoln militia, yet not well enough to know about his sons and daughter. I nudged Papa. He stepped forward with a slight wave of his good hand to Old Put. The sunburned, wrinkled, congenial old general nodded with recognition, then stood for a moment beside General Washington until the General was done with his examination of the rider ahead of us.

Old Put pointed at my father and said to the General, "There's a born patriot, a man I'd trust with my life." General Washington gazed upon my father. Old Put, without even a glance at me, strode off toward whatever other duties awaited him.

"Name?" asked the General's secretary, a colonel seated at a small table.

"Ebenezer Byrnes, nineteen years old, my third son from Lincoln," answered Papa, pointing at me with his good hand, his voice as easy as if he were telling Mama how many eggs he'd found in the barn. "Sir William, a chestnut stallion with a white blaze and three white stockings, is four years old and can outrun a streak of lightning. My son has ridden every road, lane, and trail in Suffolk County more times than I could count." Papa bowed his head with respect to the General. "My son Ebenezer is ready to ride, your Excellency, for the duration of these hostilities. Until the last British soldier aboard the last British ship has departed for England, Sir, the boy is ready to ride."

My heart was thumping while Papa spoke. But when General Washington turned his blue-gray eyes upon me and stared—stared as if he would find the slightest sin in all my life—I stood tall and stared back. I remembered in that moment the words of Samuel Adams at our table in Lincoln. "You're the equal of a king," he had told me. "With your braids and bib apron, you're the equal of a king."

Well, my braids were hidden beneath Henry's old hat. And Sir William, I knew, *could* outrun a bolt of lightning.

General Washington nodded. "Thank you, Ebenezer. We'll see if a young lad can ride." He turned his attention to whomever stood behind me.

Papa and I stepped aside. We gave each other a silent glance of confidence. Then we waited together in the warm July sunshine for General Washington's decision.

Finally the last applicant, the Irishman, stepped forward and gave his name and particulars. He introduced himself as John Lally from County Cork, "but now from Dorchester, Sire, these past four years, and they haven't caught me to hang me yet, they haven't." He patted his restless black stallion on the shoulder, and could see for himself that General Washington appraised the excellence of the horse. "Came over with me as a colt, he did, " said John Lally. "Hated from the day he was born the British tyranny in Ireland. Hated the ship coming across even worse. But he loves the free roads of America, he does. Give me and Shamrock a message to carry, and we'll have it in Philadelphia two days before tomorrow."

"And who speaks on your behalf?" asked the General's secretary.

"Me mother back home in Cork," said John Lally sadly, laying his hand over his heart, "bless her soul in her grave."

General Washington, who had shown not a hint of judgment on his face during the thirty interviews, nodded cordially, then stepped aside to confer with his staff. We waited, thirty riders ready to swing into our saddles and gallop for the cause of liberty.

The General addressed the silent crowd. "I thank every man who has volunteered this morning." (He seemed to have forgotten already the one lad who volunteered.) "Colonel Ferguson will provide you with further instructions." Turning away, he climbed the stone steps and disappeared into headquarters.

Colonel Ferguson, standing behind the table, held the paper with our names on it. "General Washington needs twelve riders," he told us, "and we have here a list of thirty-four. The General has requested that you gather your mounts and meet me at the north end of the common in half an hour. You shall ride a course from here to Lexington, then on to Lincoln, and back by way of Watertown to Cambridge. The twelve first riders to cross the line shall report to headquarters."

Lincoln!

"Is there any man riding today who is not familiar with this route?"

If there was a man not familiar with the route, he certainly did not say so. Well, we would see.

"Then, gentlemen, in half an hour." The colonel carried his small table back into the house.

Papa and I hurried to our camp at the north edge of Cambridge, where I fetched the saddle and bridle from our tent. Then we hastened to the paddock in one corner of the common, where nearly every horse was being saddled. I whistled for Sir William.

We were soon ready to outgallop any bolt of lightning.

While we waited on the common for Colonel Ferguson to fire his musket and thus start the race, Sir William and I stayed well back from the tumultuous, tightly-packed herd near the road leading north. Let the riders open up between Cambridge and Menotomy. Pass the stragglers between Menotomy and Lexington. Keep to the rear on the road out of Lexington, to see who knew the turnoff to Lincoln . . . and who rode straight toward Concord. On the road to Lincoln, let the others tire out the leader. Trail the front three or four riders on the long winding high-way to Watertown.

Then let the thunderbolts fly all the way home to Cambridge.

Sir William was certainly ready. He pranced and pulled at his reins, wondering why we had waited four long years before we finally got down to business.

John Lally was at the front of the jostling herd, holding his position against any man who tried to push him aside. His red bushy hair would be an easy beacon to follow. Put his Irish fire behind me in the final mile and I'd be General Washington's man.

BOOM! roared the musket.

Sir William and I surged into a canter behind the thundering herd. Papa's voice called, "Ride, Ebenezer!"

Sir William had learned long ago not to tire himself too early. He could canter as if he had wings, saving his legs until the time had come to gallop. With barely a gleam of sweat on his chestnut shoulders, we passed the first dozen plow horses.

Leaving Menotomy behind us, I peered ahead through the dust. John Lally had stretched out a good lead on the road to Lexington.

Only three months ago, in April, the first battle had been fought along this road. Muskets had fired over the stone walls flanking the highway; redcoats had fallen where Sir William's hooves now pounded. I was grateful that we would turn toward Lincoln before we reached Nathaniel's grave.

I could see the rooftops of Lexington. People lining the road were cheering the first riders. (One of General Washington's officers had ridden ahead, warning people off the street.) Two of the riders took the right fork at the green, past Buckman Tavern, the long way around. But not, I saw as I reined Sir William onto the left fork and cantered past the meetinghouse and bell tower and school, John Lally, Irishman of County Cork, who clearly knew the shorter way through Lexington.

Aye, and he knew the turn to Lincoln too. Though the smart devil, he let a half dozen riders pass him while still a mile from the turn, and didn't four fools gallop straight on toward Concord, certain they'd be shaking the General's hand long before the Irishman did? John Lally rolled into that turn to Lincoln at a lazy canter, then I did the same, with three riders between us. Sir William sailed on wings, while we let those three do our work of pressing the leader. For fools are all eagerness, don't you know.

Lincoln appeared ahead: I could see the stately white steeple of the meetinghouse. And the ancient chestnut tree on the common, its trunk so huge that when I was a girl, we had needed twenty-three children holding hands to reach around it. Neighbors in sunbonnets worked in their gardens, women whose names and kindnesses and cantankerous ways were woven into the soul of my childhood. Our own farm was a half-mile south of the village crossroads, beyond the turn to Watertown. I would not pass it, would not see Mama and Judd if they were out today in the farmyard . . .

But Providence had brought Mama—both of them!—to the old cemetery across the road from the meetinghouse. Mama was pouring a pail of water on lilies she had planted on my infant sister's grave. Judd was kneeling, plucking weeds. He looked up at the sound of four riders galloping into Lincoln. Mama stood with her pail and watched as the riders pounded past her and swung into the broad turn, then raced in a rising cloud of dust toward Watertown.

Judd and Mama now turned and stared toward a fifth rider, a few hundred yards behind, cantering into their village. They no doubt recognized Sir William, but not the lad in Henry's old straw hat.

As I sailed in an easy rhythm past the cemetery, I called, "Hello, Mama!"

"Genevieve!" she called back, forever worried, forever astonished.

Sir William intended of course to head straight through the crossroads toward the farm. I let him know early with the reins that we too would take the turn left, following the others. Fine with him. He slowed as we approached the schoolhouse at the corner, rounded the curve with his customary grace, then opened his canter and quickly put the last houses of Lincoln behind us.

Sir William steadily shortened the distance between us and the four riders ahead of us. His chestnut body glistened with sweat. His great heart pounded (as I imagined) between my knees.

A mile from Watertown, at the big bend in the road, the three eager fools on their worn-out horses fell back behind us. The third shouted with encouragement, "Catch him! Catch him!"

Sir William watched that black stallion take the turn at the Watertown crossroads; he felt the reins telling him to do the same. He slowed enough to keep his footing, paid no mind to people yelling and waving their hats.

Fifty yards behind now, with a straight three-mile stretch ahead of us to Cambridge, Sir William outgrew himself and became General Washington's courier. I knew a gallop, and I knew a hard gallop, but never before had I ridden the gallop that now brought us ever closer to the thundering black horse just ahead of us. John Lally glanced back, whipped his horse with the reins.

For Papa was I riding toward the distant rooftops of Cambridge. For Benjamin. For America. And (hooves thundering, thundering, thundering on the free and precious earth) for my children, my children, my children. Knowing deep in my heart that the man whom Old Put had blessed with his hand would be the father, the father, the father.

Cambridge just ahead now. Harvard's tall rooftops beneath the blue July sky.

Sir William's neck at the black stallion's rump. John Lally shouting, fierce, fierce.

Half a mile ahead, a crowd along both sides of the road. Papa, who taught his little girl to ride.

Glancing at John Lally as I drew even with him, I saw that his blue eyes glancing at me had not a hint of anger in them, only a blessing, a blue Irish blessing, as slowly, slowly I pounded ahead of him. For the man surely loved a good horse.

A quarter mile now. A bell ringing brightly in Cambridge. The growing sound of people shouting. Not a fool in the road, the way wide open: just ride through.

Hooves behind me, ten feet . . . and falling back.

And then didn't Henry's old hat go flying off! The string held, for I'd put a new chin string on it myself. But the old sun-faded weather-worn hat from Henry's first days behind a plow must have gotten hit by a thunderbolt.

So we outran the thunderbolt, braids a-flying, braids unraveling, boy become girl become woman as now ahead of me I saw three men: Papa, stepping out from the crowd, shaking his good arm in the air. And beside him, hand cupped to his shouting mouth, Old Put. And then: a tall figure in a long blue coat, staring toward me with serene dignity, the General himself, needing no secretary now to see who it would be that would ride with his messages.

Sir William and I thundered past the first of the crowd . . . we sailed past the middle of the crowd . . . and we soared on eagle's wings past Papa, Old Put, and the Father of our Nation.

Still in the saddle, I walked Sir William around the common to let him breathe. John Lally appeared beside me upon his black stallion and reached out to shake my hand. "Tis a bonny lassie on a bonny fine horse," he declared with a jubilant smile.

(For the next eight years, John Lally rode, and I rode, as steadfast couriers; the message always went through, and the countermessage always came back to General Washington at his quarters in Cambridge, in Morristown, in Valley Forge, in Yorktown.)

When I saw Papa, I swung down from the saddle. There wasn't much we could say, for my hair looked like a wild woman's mane. We waited for Colonel Ferguson to decommission Papa with dishonor and send us both home to Mama.

"Well, Miss Ebenezer," said a gentle Virginian voice. I turned and looked up at the not-angry eyes of my Commander in Chief.

"Genevieve," I whispered, barely able to get the word out.

He leaned toward me with a gracious southern bow. "Well, Miss Genevieve."

He turned to Sir William and rubbed the nose of a most excellent horse.

"I believe," he said to me with a glint of gratitude, "there is not a British officer in the city of Boston who will ever outsmart or outride Miss Genevieve Byrnes. Please report to headquarters tomorrow after morning prayer."

"Aye, sir," I said, my first official words in the Continental Army.

General Washington turned to the other riders walking their horses.

Papa and I walked Sir William to the paddock, where we groomed my champion until he was cool and dry. Colonel Ferguson, appearing at the fence, told me that I should keep my saddle at the Harvard stables. Sir William would now be fed at government expense.

After lodging Sir William in his own stall at Harvard, Papa and I walked back to our encampment, where, at the campfire, Papa told Henry and Benjamin about my new job and how I had earned it.

I sat on a log between my brother and my friend and said not a word about my children's secret to anyone.

Especially not to the handsome sunburned man sitting beside me, laughing with delight at the loss of my hat.

ଚ

Chapter Forty-One

Genevieve, still her page.

An extraordinary change took place in Henry during the summer and autumn of 1775. On the farm, my hard-working brother rarely spoke about anything other than work. He never lingered at the supper table longer than what it took to finish his meal, before he was back to work in the barn. He had a hard look to him. Even during the months when he was courting Delilah, he rarely smiled.

Whether a sermon in the Lincoln meetinghouse moved him, or not, he never said. Whether a fresh April morning ever stirred his fancy, he never said.

But in the encampment at Cambridge, Henry found a hundred friends. He still worked as hard, but it was a different kind of work: he couldn't do enough for others. The carpenter became a teacher, who was never happier than when he was explaining by example, at another man's log hut, how to frame and hang a door, how to mortar a chimney, how to lay cedar shingles on a roof. He was glad to hammer together a sawbuck for a team of woodcutters. With some old planks from the side of a collapsed barn in Cambridge, he doubled the number grain troughs in the paddock. Give Henry two boards and someone to teach, and he became the most patient and thoughtful of men.

Previously a silent, diligent, dawn-to-dark farmer who counted every bushel of corn and every nail—and who would not have minded if in his entire life he never traded nor traveled any further than once a month to the market in Boston—Henry became a soldier, and a citizen. His thoughts reached out to his neighbors, and to Philadelphia. During that summer and autumn in the Cambridge encampment, Henry was no longer a farmer from Lincoln, but a citizen of the United Colonies of North America (as the Congress in Philadelphia called us). He ate his supper at the family campfire only occasionally; more often he took his plate of ham and potatoes and his cup of cider and wandered off to talk with the men around a Connecticut campfire, a Rhode Island campfire, a Virginia campfire. Henry, who during the past dozen years had shown naught but scorn for Samuel Adams, now returned to our campfire speaking like a veteran member of a Committee of Correspondence.

As the weeks passed by, Henry's ready laughter cheered the firelit suppers of countless soldiers. Henry had been a man who hungered for friends, without ever knowing how starved he was.

There in Cambridge in 1775, while our Continental Army was digging with shovels, training with muskets, and learning to salute, Henry outgrew himself. He outgrew building chicken sheds; instead he built, asking not a penny, roof after shingled roof on the log huts that would keep us warm and dry through the siege of Boston.

And he outgrew Delilah. She never came from Concord to visit him (or to see for herself the extraordinary events taking place in a new America). She did finally send a note to him, asking when he was going to come visit her so they could settle on a wedding date. He wrote back, "When the war is over," and that was the last between them.

Strange to say, but the summer after the Battle of Breed's Hill, and the autumn, and even the long winter, were a time of hope and promise. We'd fought one battle and we'd survived it. And now we had a real general who would turn us into a real army.

As colonials we were hardy oaks, but as Americans we were green sprouts. However, our nine months in the encampment at Cambridge, from June of 1775 to March of 1776, enabled us to put our roots down deep. Never before in the history of the thirteen colonies had so many people from so many places gathered in one spot for so long to work and eat and talk together, celebrate the September harvest together, celebrate Christmas together, and the New Year, and even, though it was no official holiday, the coming of spring.

We stared at the wild men in buckskin when they arrived from over the mountains of western Virginia, ready to enlist. We watched them shoot their rifles—not muskets, mind you, but a weapon with a long rifled barrel—at an old bucket so far away that some of us could barely see it, but we could hear the PANG! and see the bucket jump when they hit it.

We learned the latest dances from Willaimsburg, Virginia, taught to us in the flickering light of our campfires by gentlemen farmers who themselves had learned the minuet and "pas de bourrée" and "Kitty, Will You Marry Me?" from lords and ladies visiting (five years ago) from London.

We learned to savor, and to make for ourselves, a crab and codfish soup as people made it in Falmouth out on the Cape. We seasoned and simmered a mutton stew in the old style of the Dutch along Hudson's

River. We shared slices of oven-warm corn bread with the Virginians. And we roasted corn and squash over a bed of embers, as the settlers had learned to do from the Iroquois in western New York.

Yes, we *all* outgrew ourselves, as our determined men built earthen fortifications along the ten-mile crescent around Boston; as wagons brought food, clothing, and bedding from the countryside; and as we aimed our muskets at the redcoats and Tories clustered month after hungry month on their tiny island. We grew, until the children of the mother country were children no more.

In normal times (especially today, half a century later), most men know only their own pockets, the family Bible, and the names of a few friends and neighbors. But the glory and the privilege and the honor of living back then, was that we were all so much closer to each other, and to heaven.

Though Benjamin and I courted on a crescent of land that could at any moment become a battlefield (with a surge of redcoats marching toward us over Boston Neck), and though Judd and Mama struggled at home to do the work of five, and though an unknown number of our soldiers became horridly sick (and some died) before they learned to dig a proper privy, it was a good time, and a strong time, and a learning time, such as few generations are blessed to live through.

While our twenty thousand men dug and built their fortifications, they could look toward the sea and watch the British frigates that sailed with great frequency into Boston's harbor: ships from England, from Halifax in Nova Scotia, from British islands in the West Indies. These vessels brought (as we learned from our spies) food and soldiers and barrels of gunpowder. Our fortifications protected the villages of Roxbury and Cambridge, and they prevented the British from obtaining fresh meat, milk, eggs, and vegetables from the countryside, but they left open a broad passage to the sea.

True to his nature, General Washington wanted to challenge the most powerful navy in the world with a navy of his own. To this end, he commissioned fishing and trading vessels along the Massachusetts coastline to arm themselves and become "privateers." Our sloops and schooners were encouraged to attack any British supply ship not protected by a convoy.

After riding for two weeks on short errands, I had proven myself as trustworthy. The General began to send me on lengthier trips, no longer to a nearby redoubt on the Charles River, or to the small fortress on

Prospect Hill, but instead on twenty-mile rides to the coastal villages of Salem and Beverly and Marblehead, where vessels were being outfitted with whatever small brass cannons could be found. Inside Henry's old shirt, I carried secret instructions from General Washington to the ship owners, then carried reports of progress or difficulties back to the General. I rode by day, I rode by night, always as Ebenezer in Henry's old clothes (to fool any Tories and British spies). I wore a new old hat, made of leather, (a gift from Old Put), the sort of hat worn by a farm lad who had no use for the tri-cornered macaroni worn by minutemen.

As I learned about the beginnings of America's first navy, I also learned (as much as a courier might who met him almost every day) about our Commander in Chief. I received my orders in Harvard Yard in front of the General's headquarters, sometimes from an officer on the staff, but frequently from General Washington himself. He called me Ebenezer, treated me as an equal to every other soldier in his army. And as I earned his trust, he earned mine.

Returning late one afternoon from a ride to Marblehead, I was told by Colonel Ferguson that I would not be posted again that day. With an unexpected hour of liberty, I crossed the college yard and stepped shyly into the Harvard library. The large room was crowded and busy; at its many tables, officers examined maps, paged through thick books, and wrote in their ledgers. No one minded Ebenezer in his homespun shirt and Old Put's leather hat as he cocked his head to one side and slowly made out the titles of books along the shelves.

I found no primer, however. The students at Harvard College were well beyond their ABC's. Remembering Papa's encouragement while together we had read the broadsheets and *Boston Gazette*, I forged my way through three lines of Milton, then humbly closed the book and set it back on the shelf.

Looking further, I spotted a slender volume with gold letters along its leather spine: "Shakespeare—ROMEO AND JULIET." I had heard of the author, and thought that Juliet was a pretty name for a woman (if indeed Juliet *was* a woman). I pulled the book out from the shelf and opened it, but though I struggled through half a page of verse, I knew not who was speaking to whom, nor why.

But Benjamin might know who was speaking to whom, and why.

Benjamin marched off to work every morning in a patched outfit of Judd's clothes which I had fetched from home. (Being *older* old clothes, cast off by Judd at the age of fourteen, they were consequently smaller and fit much better.) But before he began to dig his daily portion of the breastwork between Cambridge and Back Bay, Benjamin took off his shirt. He did not want, he told me, to soil such a fine old shirt, made for Judd by Mama with buttons at the cuffs. And so, while the digging made for muscles in his arms and chest, the hot July sun baked him to a deep healthy brown.

Every day at labor's end, the men took turns in companies bathing in a bend of the Charles just behind the southern redoubt. I cannot say for Benjamin, but I certainly can for Henry, that in all his years on the farm, never was he so often clean.

The soldiers were assigned an assortment of duties: they stood watch as sentries along the breastwork, they melted into molds whatever lead could be found to make musket balls, and they dug (and dug and dug and forever dug) new privies.

Benjamin, however, although as occupied as every other soldier in camp, was determined to engage himself in something more. In August, while we sat one evening at our campfire after supper, our stomachs full but our eyes still feasting on the flames, he said to me, "The soldier must atone for being a soldier."

I looked at him, sitting beside me on one of four logs that formed a square around our fire. Henry and Papa sat across the fire from us, the both of them staring silently into the flames, wondering perhaps, as all of us wondered now and then, what sort of war this would be. I knew Benjamin well enough to know that when he spoke, he sometimes spoke from far away, but that he would come to fetch me to where his thoughts were wandering.

I laid another piece of wood on the fire. The stick was green, freshly cut, for an army has no time to season its wood. I had to poke at the hissing, smoldering pieces, huddling them together, so they might better kindle each other's flames.

"I know of no way," said Benjamin quietly, "of turning the cheek and winning a war at the same time."

Papa looked across the flames at us. "If you do find a way, let us know."

Henry too looked at Benjamin, but he said nothing.

"And I know of no way," continued Benjamin, "for an unfree man, or an unfree colony, to become free without demanding that freedom. Demanding, if necessary, with a sword and a musket and a fist. For such it is with men: we cannot understand that freedom given is a shared freedom."

He paused, watching me while I poked at the fire. Then he added, "If I must be a soldier, then I must be a soldier and something more."

"What more?" I asked.

What more, what more, what more? That question would haunt us through the next eight years of war.

It haunts us still today.

ॐ

Chapter Forty-Two

Genevieve.

The following afternoon, on a hot, damp, windless day in August, I took my father and Benjamin to Harvard College. I had a threefold plan: I hoped that Papa might have the doctor inspect his still swollen and tender arm, which had been in a sling now for two months; that Benjamin might meet the stranger in buckskin; and that I might begin my formal education.

We walked from the haphazard jumble of log huts and sailcloth tents in our encampment north of Cambridge to the order and dignity of Harvard Yard, a broad grassy courtyard flanked along three sides by the library, the classroom building (now military offices), the chapel, and the student dormitory (which housed most of the staff officers). The students and their professors had been moved for the duration to Concord; the entire college now served as offices, housing, and head-quarters for the Continental Army.

Behind the other buildings was the student infirmary, serving now as a hospital for the wounded from Breed's Hill. One day, while wait-ing in Harvard Yard for new orders, I spotted the doctor who had re-moved the musket ball from my father's arm. He was walking across the Yard and conferring closely with the stranger in buckskin. I fol-lowed them past the dormitory to the red brick infirmary, which they entered. Peering in through a window, I saw soldiers lying upon rows of beds in a crowded room. Thus I knew where to find the doctor for Papa, and the buckskin stranger for Benjamin.

But I did not take Papa and Benjamin directly to the hospital. I led them to the library instead. Their conversation diminished to silence as we stepped through the door into the room that smelled of books. A dozen officers were reading at various tables. I walked to the shelf where I had found Shakespeare. Papa reached with his right hand and touched the books, rubbing his rough farmer's fingers along their leather spines. Benjamin, turning his head sideways, whispered several titles, as if delighted to meet again a group of old friends.

I pulled *Romeo and Juliet* from the shelf and handed the book to Benjamin. He rubbed his palm over its cover, savoring the pebbly leather. Then he paged through the volume as if he knew exactly what he was looking for. Holding the book in both hands, he said, "Act one, scene five, in which Romeo first meets his beautiful Juliet."

Though several officers at a nearby table glanced in our direction, Benjamin paid them no mind.

"*Romeo,*" he said, naming the character who would speak.

And then that character spoke with a voice that came not only from the page, but from somewhere deep inside Benjamin.

"If I profane with my unworthiest hand"

(He let go of the book with one hand and gently touched my arm)

"This holy shrine, the gentle fine is this:
My lips, two blushing pilgrims, ready stand
To smooth that rough touch with a tender kiss."

I could feel myself blushing in front of Papa, but he never noticed, for he was watching Benjamin.

"*Juliet,*" continued Benjamin, his voice softening, yet losing nothing of its warmth and vitality.

"Good pilgrim, you do wrong your hand too much,
Which mannerly devotion shows in this;
For saints have hands that pilgrims' hands do touch,"

(He held up the palm of his hand toward me)

"And palm to palm is holy palmers' kiss."

Understanding his meaning, I, without hesitation, in front of Papa, reached up my hand and briefly touched my palm to Benjamin's palm.

We heard a flurry of applause from the officers' table. I blushed anew. Benjamin closed the book, but he did not place it back on the shelf. Instead, he walked across the room to the librarian's desk. Behind the desk sat a portly young officer, his attention upon the papers spread before him.

Benjamin apparently knew the officer, for he asked, "Mr. Knox, might a private soldier from the Massachusetts Sixteenth Regiment be allowed to borrow a book from this library?"

The officer glanced up, then said with surprise, "Mr. York!" He stood up from his chair, though it was a mere private who faced him. "I should say that you are most dependable."

Benjamin handed him the book.

Mr. Knox glanced at its title. "And a worthy fellow to read such a fine text." Clearly delighted to see Benjamin, he asked, "And how is your student? Nathaniel was his name, am I correct?" Then he shook his head, puzzled but pleased. "And how come you to be in our home-spun, and not in His Majesty's red woolens?"

Benjamin replied with a broken whisper, "I buried Nathaniel near Concord."

"I am deeply sorry."

"I have a new student now." Benjamin turned toward me.

I walked to the desk.

Mr. Knox told me, "You have a skilled and devoted teacher."

"Thank you. I'm sure he will be."

Mr. Knox sat in his chair, opened a drawer and rummaged about until he found a sheet of blank paper, a pen, and ink jar. He uncorked the jar, dipped the quill, then spoke the words as he wrote them, "Benjamin York, Massachusetts Sixteenth Regiment, would borrow upon his honor, Shakespeare, *Romeo and Juliet*, on August 15, 1775, to be returned . . ." Mr. Knox looked up at Benjamin. "One month?"

"Aye," nodded Benjamin, "one month."

"On September 15, 1775." He turned the paper toward Benjamin and handed him the quill.

Benjamin signed his name, the first time I had seen his bold and graceful signature.

Mr. Knox folded the sheet of paper and placed it in the drawer. Standing once again, he handed the book back to Benjamin.

"Thank you, sir." Benjamin bowed slightly, with that politeness which is his under all circumstances.

"Benjamin," said Mr. Knox gravely, "the place where we met so often, The London Book Shop, suffers its fate in Boston. I know not but what one of our cannonballs might by now have reduced my shelves to kindling. And all of my books?" He shook his head with a sadness verging on grief. "I can only hope that our British guests have put them to good use."

"Tis a mean time," said Benjamin. He rubbed his hand once again over the leather cover of his book. "Let us hope that one day we and the British might find the best in each other, and leave the rest behind us."

Our business completed, I led Benjamin and Papa out the library door into the hot, hazy sunshine in the Yard.

*   *   *

We walked past the dormitory and followed a street lined with neat clapboard houses (where perhaps the college faculty lived), to the red brick infirmary. A guard of soldiers was posted around it.

A sentry stopped us twenty feet from the door. I asked him, "Might we speak with Dr. Frazer?"

"Dr. Frazer is today in Roxbury."

"Ah. Then, is another doctor in attendance?"

The sentry hesitated, glanced at a sergeant standing nearby. The sergeant gestured with his thumb, "The reverend doctor is around back."

We walked along the front of the building, past a hedge of lilac bushes below its windows (the dusty bushes were long past blooming), then turned the corner and walked toward a large tent in a field behind the hospital. The tent was a patchwork of old sails supported by a rope slung between two elms. Though the sides of the tent reached to the ground and were anchored by rocks, the two ends were open. Thus we could easily look in and see the reverend doctor in buckskin, kneeling beside a Negro patient who lay not on a bed, but a bit of straw.

The doctor glanced toward us, saw Papa with his arm in a sling, nodded, then continued with his work.

I took hold of my father's good arm, to let him know that we would not leave. I knew not how he might feel to submit to the attention of a doctor who treated this other sort of people. But I did know that I had struggled mightily today to persuade him to see Dr. Frazer (for the proud, stubborn farmer felt that his arm of rights should simply heal itself), and I knew that I would have to struggle again tomorrow, when Dr. Frazer might or might not be in the hospital. So I held Papa's good arm to let him know: We shall wait our turn.

Benjamin stared at the dozen patients lying on the ground, all of them Negroes. He glanced over his shoulder at the sturdy red brick hospital behind us, then he looked at me. He said quietly, so that no one in the tent might hear him, "I'll wager that the redcoat is recuperating in a bed. While our compatriots from Breed's Hill lie here on the ground."

I replied quietly, "I'll wager you are correct."

The doctor stood up from his patient, then walked to the far end of the tent, where he poured water from a pitcher on a table into a bowl. He washed his hands with a bar of yellow soap (like the soap Mama and I made every summer). While he rinsed his hands, he looked out the open end of the tent toward an orchard of apple trees, their boughs heavy with ripening fruit. Beyond the orchard were more houses, then a stretch of the Charles River where it passed Cambridge.

The doctor turned and walked along the grassy aisle toward us, his blue eyes welcoming us. Blue jay feathers hung in the fringe across the chest of his leather shirt.

He said to Papa, "I am Johannes Kesslaer. And you have a wounded wing."

"John Byrnes," replied Papa, lifting his arm slightly in its sling. "I took a ball while I stood at the line below Breed's Hill. Dr. Frazer was kind enough to dress it. But it pains me still a good deal, and . . . but the doctor is out today, it seems, and . . ."

"Aye," said Johannes Kesslaer, reaching up to untie the knot on Papa's shoulder, releasing the sling. He gently unwound the bandages from Papa's upper arm, touched with his fingers the swollen flesh. Then he asked Papa, "Can you bend your arm?"

"I haven't for these seven weeks, but I can . . ." he frowned with pain, "try."

Moving his lower arm back and forth a bit further each time, Papa achieved several inches of movement.

Johannes Kesslaer asked, "And can you lift your arm as well?"

Papa tried to raise his elbow, flexing and lifting at the same time.

The reverend doctor ran his fingers along Papa's arm, squeezing it gently between his fingers and thumb. "Any severe pain, or just a general soreness?"

"Well," Papa considered, "no more than a soreness, I'd say. But a good strong soreness, I'd say as well."

"Aye, but I find no red streaks, no unusual swelling, certainly no running of pus. What your arms needs is to come out of that sling and to move. It will be painful as you stretch it toward what it used to do, but the best thing you can do with that wing is flap it."

I saw the first real brightness in Papa's face that I had seen in seven weeks. I don't think it was the pain of the wound that had subdued him (nearly quenching the fire that had made him captain of Lincoln's militia), but rather that he had to ask others to do nearly everything for him, a thing no man who had built his own barn and plowed his own land ever felt comfortable doing. Now that the doctor told him his arm was healing (was not turning green at the elbow, would not have to be cut off at the shoulder), and that all the arm needed was to be *used*, Papa quickly found his old confidence.

"*Thank* you, Doctor." Papa dug his good hand into a pocket.

"Oh, I am no doctor," said Johannes Kesslaer quietly, so that no one in the tent might hear him. "I am an ordained minister of God's word, and husband of a woman who taught me all I know about herbs and roots and the setting of a bone."

Papa seemed not to have heard a word as he offered the minister a pair of coins: two English shillings. "Please take this, Doctor, if it be enough?"

"More than enough, I assure you," said Johannes Kesslaer as he pushed Papa's hand away. "You take your tithe and bring it back as loaves of bread for these good men." He gestured toward his patients, several of whom were watching us, their eyes curious, frightened, unreadable.

Papa studied the man, as he always studied the face of those he considered to be more than ordinary. "Return with loaves of bread we shall. And we'll expect the doctor to supper one night," he pointed in the direction of our camp, "northwest corner of the pasture, near a scrub crabapple. Just ask for John Byrnes."

"I would be most honored. But now, I have dressings to change." Johannes stepped back into the tent. Halfway down the isle, he knelt beside a Negro who opened his tired eyes and stared at the reverend doctor.

Johannes Kesslaer, wearing a leather shirt and leggings, and leather moccasins, his long blond hair tied back with a leather strap, was here in Cambridge from some distant frontier. A frontier in the forest, a frontier in the soul.

Papa and I were turning to leave when we heard Benjamin ask, "How may I help?" His question was not to us, but directed into the tent.

Johannes Kesslaer looked up at Benjamin. He saw a tall young man wearing worn patched farm clothes; a soldier whom he had once met at Charlestown Neck, wearing clothes covered with dirt and blood and gore; a soldier who now stared at him with adamant determination.

"Yes. We need fresh straw. Any cut grass, any hay, that you can bring back in a wagon, we would be most grateful." Johannes added, "There is no smallpox here, no typhus. You would be safe. We too have wounds from Breed's Hill."

Benjamin stared at the reverend doctor.

Johannes told him, "Yes, you would be most welcome."

Benjamin handed me the book. He walked through the tent, passing between the patients on their mats of straw. He walked out the far end, perhaps hoping to find, beyond the apple orchard, beyond the houses, somewhere along the river, a livery with a wagon.

Papa and I walked back through the Yard and the common toward our encampment, Papa flexing his wing along the way. I carried the leather-bound volume which my Romeo had placed into my hands.

Benjamin, his note.

After some searching to no avail, I at last found a farmer and paid him from my soldier's pay to cut the grass in his meadow, grass thick with daisies and purple vetch and a good fragrant clover. "The army's horses," I explained to him (not wishing to reveal the true nature of my business), "are in need of good forage." I rented a scythe from him (such a thing never before had I handled). I had to rent as well his wagon, which I filled with armfuls of grass until it until brimmed with fresh bedding.

The farmer, Mr. Elias Whipple, agreed that I might return as often as I chose, for I had cut but one corner of his great field. I told him, "Your grass is good proof of your high patriotism."

With instructions from Mr. Whipple about the handling of his horse, I drove the laden wagon toward Cambridge.

The sun had nearly set when I reined to a halt before the open end of Reverend Kesslaer's Negro Hospital. I insisted that he allow me to unload the fresh grass into a heap, and then to gather with my own hands the fetid, damp, soiled straw upon which his patients had been lying, and toss this refuse into the wagon (to be emptied elsewhere). Each Negro did his best to sit up, or to shift aside, as I scraped up his old bed, then laid down a fresh bed of thick green grass and bright wildflowers.

After thus comforting fourteen injured men—some of their faces were familiar from our day up on Breed's Hill—I stood at the table while Reverend Kesslaer poured water from his pitcher so I could wash my hands.

Though he thanked me, I thanked him in my soul a thousand times over. I promised that I would return as often as my duties allowed me.

I dumped the filthy load in a remote woods, brushed clean the bed of the wagon with ferns, then returned the wagon to its owner.

I walked home beneath a young moon. Where the road neared the river, I paused to bathe myself, and my clothing. I must have spent nearly an hour in the river.

While I walked along the road into Cambridge, while I crossed the dark common, while I walked among the multitude of supper fires in the encampment, while I listened to the contented murmuring of men at their meals, and when I saw the silhouette of Genevieve leaning over her Papa as she poured him a cup of something hot, I felt, for the first time in almost four months, that Nathaniel was walking beside me.

ℰ℘

Chapter Forty-Three

Genevieve, describing our courtship.

Half of August. All of September. Two-thirds of October, 1775. In a military camp, closely surrounded by thousands of other people, with little time for each other. Such were the time and place of our brief but precious courtship.

Benjamin and I read to each other (each day I more flowingly) from the story of two lovers whose families were filled with hatred. We read almost every evening by the light of the campfire, while family, friends and strangers sat on a log, or stood close by and silently listened.

Whenever we were able—during the rare hour when we were both free from our duties—Benjamin and I would climb the grassy hill behind our encampment. From the hilltop, we could look down at the long line of our earthen fortifications, at the almost-island of Boston surrounded by the bay and harbor, at green islands scattered along the edge of the sea, and at the Atlantic itself.

Cannons in Boston occasionally spoke to our troops. Our cannons spoke in return. The faint shots of our riflemen spoke of the business of snipers.

On that hilltop, our sanctuary, Benjamin and I read to each other. We entered together a different world, a world where love struggled to prevail against ancient enmities, a world in which love discovered treasures forever hidden to those who feud and fight and hate.

At first, I had to read the same verse three or four times, until both my eye and my tongue had mastered the written words. But by the time we had reached Act Two (during the first week of September), I with only occasional help was able to read Juliet, while Benjamin with his rumbling rrr's read Romeo. We shared the other parts, Benjamin as my nurse and I as Tybalt. So deep we went into that sad and lovely tale that our daily speech took on its musical lilt, and certain words crept into our phrases at supper.

Thus a spirited garden we made for ourselves in the midst of war, a walled-in paradise, in which the nurtured seeds of love did sprout and bloom and flourish.

*   *   *

In mid-September, however, with the arrival of a letter, I thought I might have lost my Benjamin.

The afternoons up on the hill were cooler now; the evenings around the campfire were edging toward winter. On a Sunday afternoon, I rode Sir William home to Lincoln to share the latest news with Mama, to take a warm bath in splendid privacy, and to gather medicinal herbs from the garden for Johannes Kesslaer.

Mama and Judd waited until I had told them what news there was from camp. (Mama was especially pleased at the progress of Papa's arm.) Then she opened the table's drawer and took out a letter sealed with wax. "For Benjamin," she said as she placed it into my hands. "A rider from Salem brought it two days ago."

We ate supper while the letter lay unopened on the table beside me. I stared at the ceiling of my dark bedroom well into the night while the unopened letter lay atop the dresser beside my bed. The next day, I rode back to Cambridge with a bag of herbs, three loaves of bread, and the unopened letter in one saddlebag, and clean shirts and stockings for my three men in the other.

Benjamin was with his regiment when I arrived at our tent. A neighbor just back from sentry duty told me that the men were digging a new redoubt further down the Charles, almost at its mouth. Across the river we were building more breastworks, he continued, but I paid him no further mind as I went into our tent and sorted the clean shirts and stockings and laid them properly on Papa's blanket, Henry's blanket, and Benjamin's blanket. I placed a loaf of Mama's fresh bread on each bed.

Then I placed Benjamin's letter atop his folded shirt, where he would see it as soon as he returned to camp.

I rode Sir William to the hospital tent, where I gave the bag of a dozen different herbs to Reverend Kesslaer.

Trotting back to Harvard Yard, I reported to Colonel Ferguson. I was dispatched with a message for Colonel John Glover, a ship owner in Marblehead.

As I rode toward the coastal village, I knew that whatever message General Washington was sending to Colonel Glover, it would probably have less import on my life than the message which I had already delivered, and which Benjamin would find several hours before I returned to camp: the letter from his family in London. Containing, most probably, at least a note from his fiancée.

Benjamin, describing our courtship.

Filthy with sand and grit and clay and dirt, starving for my supper, I peered into our tent, thinking I might find Genevieve napping on (or now with autumn coming, beneath) her wool blanket. But instead I saw a letter on my own bed. Snatching it up, my heart nearly burst with joy when I saw my name in my father's neat writing. Already I knew that they knew, they *knew*, that I was alive. I'd not been murdered and dumped into the Thames, I was alive. I had given that great comfort to them, and in doing so I gave a profound comfort to myself.

I broke the wax seal, unfolded two sheets of papers, looked at the second sheet before I read the first to see—Yes, from Elspeth! I pressed that precious, sacred sheet of paper against my heart, feeling her gentle presence as if our last kiss were but yesterday.

However, I had read no more than her salutation (the first time I had seen my name in her handwriting) and her opening lines, when I was besieged by an increasing turmoil in my mind. Stepping out of the tent with the two letters, I climbed over a stone wall at the edge of the encampment. I glanced up toward the crest of the hill where Genevieve and I were wont to read to each other. Then I walked to a large gray boulder surrounded by smaller rocks in the adjoining pasture: a boulder which the farmer clearly could not move, and rocks which he and his forefathers for generations had dropped around it from the field.

Hidden behind the boulder, I sat on a rock and read, and read again, first the letter from my father, and mother, and even a few words from my younger brother who now could write.

And then I read the letter from Elspeth.

Her prayers were answered that I was still alive. In some strange place near Boston! When was I coming home? She had folded her wedding dress into a protective wrap of linen, had never given up hope. She, our families, the minister, would be ready for our wedding within a month, a week, a day after my ship arrived at the docks.

She wrote as if nothing had happened. As if her gentle lad had for a lark decided to hike to Aberdeen.

But I had been stolen from that life in London by her King. I had been lashed across my back by her King's minions. I had cherished my friendship with Nathaniel, until the brutes had marched him to his death. I had, with no officer's sword at my back, slaughtered an uncounted number of my own countrymen on Breed's Hill. I had met

Genevieve, and her family. I had met Reverend Kesslaer, and had spoken with Cato and Homer and Freedom and Prince.

I had looked anew at my King and countrymen. And I had looked anew upon America.

Hidden behind that cold gray boulder, I sat facing the yellow, the red, the huge red-orange sun as it touched the hills of Massachusetts.

I knew that Genevieve would be waiting for me in camp.

The sky had darkened to a purple-black before I stood, the folded letters in my hand.

I started back toward the campfire.

Genevieve.

When he came walking toward our campfire with the letter in his hand, he looked at me, and though his face was dimly lit by the flames, I could see that we were all right.

Papa was stirring rabbit and potato stew in a cast-iron pot over the low flames: anything to be using his arm. Henry was slicing Mama's bread with his hunting knife. Both of them looked up at Benjamin as he approached us, for we, at that late hour, had been watching for him.

"Thank you for bringing the letter, Genevieve," he said, holding it up. "It's from my family in London. They thank you." He looked now at Papa and Henry. "They thank you deeply for returning my life to me. My mother and my father," he glanced at the folded letter, then looked again at the three of us, "everyone in my family is profoundly grateful for what your family has done for me."

His handsome face lit by the flickering campfire, he stared down at me. I sat on a log with a knife and a potato, waiting for the rest of what he had to say.

"Genevieve, I look upon this military encampment," he swept his hand toward the fifty campfires scattered in the pasture, and the dark shapes of men sitting around them, "and I see more people doing one thing, one thing in which they truly believe, than I ever saw in London, where everyone scurries through the day in his own direction, on his own business."

Yes, the encampment was an unusual place, almost a village unto itself, where strangers became neighbors, and neighbors became friends, and all were there to defend their ancient rights as Englishmen.

"And I look toward the college," he nodded toward a multitude of amber windows that defined Harvard College within the village of Cambridge, "and I see not a mob of drunken rebels, but an outpost of learning in the New World."

Harvard College, the first college in America, had been founded in 1636, only sixteen years after the Pilgrims arrived. It had nurtured a great many minds, the minds of men who in their turn instructed and healed and enlightened and led a multitude of farmers and shopkeepers who never spoke a word of Latin.

"I look east toward the Bay, and I see a long black ribbon stretching from our redoubt on the Charles to our redoubt on Prospect Hill."

Not a fire burned along the breastwork, not a fire burned atop the dark heights of the hill, where hundreds of men stood watch.

"Every sentry, every gunner, every courier, stands at his duty not as a slave, not as a conscript, but as a volunteer."

Yes, every soldier in the Continental Army would certainly rather be home at harvest time.

He pointed across the dark bay toward Boston, its multitude of tiny amber windows clustered on what was almost an island, a tiny island all but surrounded by the American continent. The spark of a bonfire burned atop Beacon Hill.

"Genevieve, I could walk tonight across the neck and claim to be an escaped prisoner returning to my regiment. I could put on a red coat and I could fight for whatever it is they believe they are fighting for." He paused, then he added, "If they believe at all."

"Or," he pointed at the black Atlantic beyond Boston, "I could one way or another find a ship to take me back to London. To my family. And to Elspeth." Turning to Henry and Papa, he explained, "Elspeth was once my fiancée."

He stared into the flames, then shook his head. "But I would not be the boy she loves. I could no longer chat about the day's events, all of which occurred within her father's shop. I could no longer ignore the talk in my own father's shop about 'rebels and scoundrels in America.' I could not watch His Majesty and the loyal ministers ride past in their elegant coaches on their way from palace throne to country estate, without aching to throw a rock. And most certainly, I could no longer support my family by cobbling elegant boots for elegant gentlemen."

I felt at that moment an unselfish sympathy for Elspeth, because she was losing a most wonderful man.

"So, dear Genevieve, I shall ask Henry Knox at the Harvard Library for a pen and paper. I shall try to explain to my family, and to Elspeth, my change of heart."

Too much filled my own heart for me to say anything more than, "Thank you." My life, held in abeyance these twenty-four hours, was returned to me.

Benjamin asked my father. "John, may I continue to use your home in Lincoln as . . . my post office?"

"Most assuredly you may." Papa leaned forward and gave the stew another stir.

"Then," Benjamin leaned forward and peered into the steaming pot, "I know a soldier who's starving for his supper."

One week later, when Colonel Ferguson stepped out from head-quarters and handed Ebenezer a message to be delivered in Gloucester, Ebenezer handed the colonel a message for General Washington.

As the courier rode Sir William north up the rocky coastline (and watched the morning sun sparkling on the blue Atlantic), she imagined her Commander in Chief unfolding the sheet of paper and discovering, in Benjamin's handwriting, a wedding invitation.

GENEVIEVE BYRNES
and
BENJAMIN YORK
would be honored by your presence
on Saturday evening, October 21, 1775,
at 8:00 in Harvard Chapel
where Reverend Johannes Kesslaer
will perform the sacrament of marriage.

I had little hope that General Washington would attend.

However, the thirteen United Colonies of North America were to be, after all, founded on the principle of democracy.

&

Chapter Forty-Four

Genevieve, presenting the well-considered grounds for her decision.

When in the course of human events a woman decides to marry, a decent respect to the opinions of mankind requires that she should declare the causes which impel her to the joining together.

Benjamin wanted more than what most men wanted. He wanted to find the stranger in buckskin who had carried a British soldier from the battlefield. So together we found him, and much more.

While I grew up, I had listened to James Otis and Samuel Adams and other high Sons of Liberty. But when Benjamin and I met Johannes Kesslaer, and worked with him, we came to know a man whom even Samuel Adams would have learned from.

As Benjamin changed the straw in the reverend doctor's tent, as he changed the dressings on his patients, as he even bathed the men, the soldier became more peaceful, and the man more determined.

He returned home one evening (our newly built log hut was by then our home) after a day of drenching rain. While Henry and Papa slept in their bunks, Benjamin and I sat in front of the mud and wattle fireplace that Henry had built, talking, as we did every evening, about the events of the day. Benjamin told me—we had to lean back on our bench, away from occasional billows of smoke, for mud and wattle makes the poorest of chimneys—what Johannes had said to him that afternoon.

Wet gusts from the thunderstorm had been blowing all day through the hospital tent. Rain beat on the sailcloth and leaked through in many places. Benjamin and Johannes, standing together at the table, stared out the end of the tent at the wind thrashing the trees in the orchard. Some of the red apples had fallen from the tossing branches and lay glistening in the grass. While the tent rumbled so loudly that Benjamin could hardly hear Johannes speaking, Johannes said to him, "Be thou like the apple tree, which does not ask to whom she gives her apples."

There in our dry hut, in our windowless hut, in our increasingly smoky hut, beneath four sets of wet clothing hung on a rope above the hissing fire, Benjamin and I sat for a long minute in silence. Then he looked at me, and in his eyes I could see that he was ready.

He asked me if I would join with him to plant an apple orchard.

All the rest of me had by then, without telling him, said Yes. But when he spoke to me not only from his conscience as a patriot, and not only from his heart as a man in love, but from his soul as a man who would reach out his hand, his American hand, to all people—even those spurned and reviled and in chains—then I knew that the soldier who hated being a soldier would do more than lay down his musket at the war's end: he would continue to reach, he would continue to learn, he would continue to build. In a world where Benjamin would often not be welcome, he would continue to love.

I wanted the same. I was the same.

So I said, "Yes, I will plant with you a most beautiful apple orchard."

Benjamin, with my own well-considered grounds.

Because no thought of mine was complete, without her agreement or amendment;

Because a certain kind of love, dormant and hidden and unknown to me, awakened in my heart and tinged with its wild and powerful elixir every heartbeat, every thought;

Because "the fairest of the fair" was no longer a line from my grandmother's fairy tales, but a blessing Genevieve bestowed upon my eyes every morning at dawn;

Because, were I to die tomorrow, as very well I might, with a lead ball or bayonet through my heart, I would know, for one moment, an infinite anguish; and in the next, final moment, an infinite joy: because however briefly, I had truly lived.

For these reasons, my children and grandchildren, did I marry fifty-one years ago my Genevieve Byrnes, your mother, your grandmother, my life.

8○

Chapter Forty-Five

Genevieve.

OUR WEDDING

By eight o'clock in the evening on October 21st, dusk had given way to the full darkness of night. The air was chill and the stars were crisp, and Harvard Chapel (as I saw when Papa and I peered in through the open door) was lit with candles. The pews on both sides of the aisle were filled with guests. At the far end of the aisle, Reverend Kesslaer in a white surplice stood facing us, his countenance welcoming and confident.

Benjamin and Henry stood to one side of Reverend Kesslaer. Both of them wore the fringed linen hunting shirt that General Washington had recommended as the first uniform for our troops, and which Mama had sewn for the groom and best man. Poor Henry looked deadly serious, perhaps thinking how close he himself had come to marriage. But Benjamin's face nearly outshone the candles when he spotted me at the door.

I entered the chapel with Papa holding my arm. The guests turned to watch us as we proceeded up the aisle. The man who had lifted his little girl up to his saddle when she was only five, and who had taught her to read from newspaper articles written by Samuel Adams, was about to give her away to a man who had not been born on the American earth, and who volunteered as a soldier not to protect his birthright, but to give those rights of freedom and equality to his children.

When I reached my place beside Reverend Kesslaer—to his right, while Benjamin stood to his left—I turned to face our guests in the chapel. Papa now sat beside Mama in the first pew. She was smiling, crying, and threatening my steadfast composure. I wore her white linen wedding gown from thirty years ago—we had kidded and laughed all morning while we lengthened the hem and let out the bodice. But now, her tears glistened in the glow of the candles and I had to look at Judd sitting beside her, my broad-shouldered brother, as composed and serene as a Quaker prayer.

Glancing at the first pew in front of Benjamin, I was delighted and honored to see General Washington in his blue coat, his powdered hair pulled back in a queue. He returned my look with a smile both fond and amused.

To his right sat General Israel Putnam, who had laid his hand on Benjamin's shoulder after the horror of Breed's Hill, granting his approval to what Benjamin had done. Old Put winked with sly merriment at me, who this evening wore not the old leather hat as Ebenezer, but her long brown hair spread gracefully about her shoulders.

Sitting on the other side of General Washington, regarding me with sharp-eyed curiosity, was an older man (sixty-nine years of age), portly, bald, wearing an elegant russet coat with a ruffle at the throat, and spectacles. I knew who he was, for I had seen him walking across the Yard during the past four days in the company of General Washington and a cluster of other gentlemen, and I had heard the talk among the couriers: he led a committee from the Congress in Philadelphia, a committee which had traveled all the way to Cambridge to consult with the Commander in Chief. The committee would take back to Congress the General's recommendations regarding improvements in the Continental Army.

Thus I was honored at my wedding by the presence of a Member of Congress, a scientist known throughout both America and Europe (as the inventor of a smokeless cast-iron stove, and the lightning rod), a man who had been our colonial ambassador to the court of King George III, and a printer who had used his press to become America's most prolific patriotic writer: Benjamin Franklin himself.

Three such eagles now sat in the pew not more than ten feet from Benjamin; but at the moment they ignored the groom while they admired the grateful bride.

I looked with deep happiness at the guests who nearly filled the chapel. I smiled at old friends and neighbors from Lincoln, including the entire Lincoln militia. Most of my fellow couriers had come. John Lally wore a handsome frock coat and black cravat. Seated in the pew behind Mama and Judd, he looked upon me with such pride that one might have thought, save for his thick red hair and bushy red beard, that he was my eldest brother.

Benjamin's friends from the Sixteenth Regiment had come, some of them wearing the new fringed hunting shirts of coarse linen, some still in their old farmer's and shopkeeper's shirts and coats.

Candles burned in cast-iron candelabras above the wedding guests. The circles of flickering flames lit the hundred faces looking at me, at

Benjamin, and now at Reverend Kesslaer in his white surplice as he welcomed the congregation.

"Family and friends of Genevieve Byrnes," he said as he turned his tanned and sun-wrinkled face to look at me.

"And friends of Benjamin York," he said, turning to Benjamin, "we are gathered here today in the sight of the Lord to unite these two good people in the holy sacrament of marriage."

Reverend Kesslaer passed his eyes slowly over the guests on both sides of the aisle. Then, looking straight down the empty aisle, he held out his arms in their billowing white sleeves and beckoned with both hands, as if inviting someone still outside the door to enter. "Come in, come in," he called firmly, with the fullness of his ecclesiastical authority, that no one might gainsay his invitation.

The wedding guests, even General Washington, turned around to peer toward the rear of the chapel.

Shyly, with a multitude of people staring at them, a small group of Benjamin's Negro friends—the four men who had healed sufficiently that they could leave their beds and help to nurse the other patients—stepped silently in through the chapel door.

Cato wore a fringed hunting shirt much like Benjamin's, tied at the waist with a rope. Prince wore a fine white linen shirt and black wool waistcoat, which perhaps he had fetched from home for the wedding. Freedom (for such was his new name, and he would not tell us, told no one, his old name) was clad in a coarse linen hunting shirt. Homer wore a faded red military coat with pewter buttons, a coat from the French and Indian War, over his own gray shirt. (The coat belonged to Homer's master, who collected Homer's pay while the young slave labored on the battlefield and in the encampment as his master's surrogate soldier.) The four men sat together in the back pew. The congregation once again faced forward.

Reverend Kesslaer continued, his voice filled with the strength of his faith, "May the almighty Lord make His countenance to shine upon Genevieve, upon Benjamin, as they, in a time of grave civil difficulties, affirm their belief in the power, in the all-encompassing power, of their love.

"Without hesitation, without limitation, they offer a bond of love to each other. And they offer a bond of love to *all* who share this world."

He paused. He held no book of scripture in his hands. The thick, leather-bound Bible of Harvard Chapel lay on altar behind him.

"We sometimes forget to say our prayers. But the good Lord never forgets to say His. For an apple tree is His prayer, His supplication to us, asking us to bestow equally upon each other the gifts of service, gifts of kindness, as the apple tree bestows equally, without hesitation, without limitation, its gifts upon all of us.

"The Lord's bright sun, the sun that shines down equally upon all of us, is His prayer.

"The cool mountain stream that offers itself to our cups, equally, is His prayer.

"The meadowlark and the warbler and the hermit thrush, who sing for the magistrate passing in his carriage as for the farmer laboring at his plow . . . yea, all of the Lord's joyful birds who awaken us at dawn and brighten our day, sing His prayers.

"As you would have the Lord hear your prayers, so He would have you attend His. As you would have the Lord answer your prayers, so He would have you answer His.

"Therefore, be thou like the apple tree, that questions not to whom it gives its apples. Nor does it reserve good apples for some, and apples eaten by the worm for others. Beneath the bounty of the Lord's equal sunshine and the Lord's equal rain does the apple tree blossom, and bud into fruit, and slowly ripen, that every apple from its boughs may fit with perfection into every human hand.

"Accordingly, we gather together here today, so that the hand of this man, joining with the hand of this woman, may plant the seeds and nurture the trees and harvest the crop and share the bounty, without hesitation, without limitation, unto the end of their days."

He paused, then his voice boomed out to the congregation, "Thus, and only thus, can they know the fullness of love, and the fullness of each other, and the fullness of God. Amen."

Reverend Kesslaer asked Benjamin and me to stand before him. We glanced at each other as we took our places in front of the minister, and I in that moment understood something more than our mere human passage: I discovered a faith in human purpose.

No love so powerful between us was ours by accident. No rich and demanding opportunity, so laden with all the future years awaiting us, was granted to us by accident. Nay, not a single candle flickering in the chapel had been lit by accident. As love had brought Benjamin and me together, so love now bestowed upon us a magnificent purpose.

Unto the end of our days.

Speaking scripture by heart, Reverend Kesslaer performed the holy sacrament of marriage.

Bonded we were, Benjamin unto me and I unto Benjamin, by our vow of love and fidelity and devotion.

Bonded we were by the church's declaration of Benjamin and I as husband and wife. Bonded we were by our sacred kiss.

Holding hands, Benjamin and I walked together along the aisle while a hundred smiles bestowed their blessings upon us. We greeted our guests as they approached the chapel door. Mr. and Mrs. Benjamin York shook the hands of one and all.

Near the end of that long and patient procession—neighbors from Lincoln told me again and again (most of them unable to conceal their astonishment at my transformation) what a beautiful bride I was—stood General Israel Putnam. He offered us both his hearty handshake, and a kiss on the cheek for the bride.

Benjamin and I shook the hand of Dr. Benjamin Franklin, the sage of Philadelphia.

We shook the hand of General Washington, who had set aside the war for an hour to attend our wedding. Before we could thank him for coming, he had thanked *us* for the honor of inviting him.

My children, my grandchildren, when I set down the quill and stare now, fifty-one years later, upon the open palm of my hand, I can still feel the grip of those three warm and august fathers of our nation.

After the chapel had emptied and we all stood outside in the cool October night beneath the stars, Henry clapped his hands to gather our attention. He introduced the bearded man standing next to him, "This here is Nigel MacDonald, an over-the-mountain man from the wilds of western Virginia. He will now escort us with a bit of his Scottish music to the wedding dinner at our encampment."

In the glow of whale-oil lamps flanking the chapel steps, we could see that Nigel MacDonald wore a dark green hunting shirt, patched and worn: the genuine hunting shirt of a Virginia rifleman (after which the regimental shirts had been patterned). He carried an odd-looking thing in his arms: a cloth bag of green plaid, with an assortment of wooden pipes sticking out of it. Taking one of the pipes into his mouth, Nigel inflated the bag with his breath. Then he suddenly filled the dark Harvard Yard, and the night right up to the stars, with a musical wailing that sounded like a stuck pig shrieking a melody.

Nigel MacDonald, his pipes wailing mightily, led the bride and groom and all their guests across the Yard, across the common (the British surely heard Nigel's drones and skirls from atop Beacon Hill), to our encampment in the pasture, where hundreds of soldiers standing up from their campfires clapped and cheered us.

General Washington, called by duty at headquarters, could not join us for the full festivity. He did, however, visit with Mama for several minutes beside our campfire. She never forgot his dignity and charm as he complimented the mother by way of the "enterprising" daughter.

Before he departed, the General took my arm in a most gentlemanly manner and led me and Benjamin to the side of our log hut, where he himself lifted from the ground his wedding gift: a beautiful new saddle, crafted, so he told me, by his own personal saddler in Williamsburg.

Old Put stepped before me with a new bridle in one hand, a pair of saddlebags in the other.

Dr. Franklin placed into Benjamin's hand a shiny silver coin, one pound sterling, which we were to spend, as he said in his jovial way, on the firstborn child.

I could only whisper, three times, "Thank you."

A bagpipe and fiddles, alternating with drums and fifes, enlivened the night as wedding guests and congratulating strangers now feasted and toasted and danced by the light of fifty bright campfires, by the light of the festive stars, by the light of a late-rising moon.

Nor did the rejoicing cease when the honored couple secretly tried to disappear into their humble log hut. The moment Benjamin quietly opened the door, we were cheered and toasted and hailed anew with drums and bagpipes and several musket shots. More than one boisterous voice roared a request for a child at the end of nine months: "A new patriot in July!"

My husband and I blushed and bowed, then stepped into the snug windowless hut with six bunks and a fire blazing in the fireplace. (The fire and dry wood beside it thanks to Henry.) Benjamin pulled the heavy door shut behind us, slid the wooden bolt fast.

With quiet dignity, my husband held up his palm to me. In the warm firelight, Juliet held up her palm and with it kissed her Romeo.

Wrapping his strong and gentle arms around me, Benjamin kissed his Genevieve. And Genevieve kissed her Benjamin. For one night of privacy in our log hut, the uppermost bunk was ours.

Benjamin, his addendum.

As my father's apprentice in London, I had spent a year learning to repair shoes. I spent two years learning to cobble a pair of shoes (in various sizes), and three years learning to cobble a sturdy pair of riding boots. Even after six years, my father inspected every pair of shoes and boots that I cobbled before he would offer them to the customer.

Thus I am glad to say that as an apprentice father, I produced the beginnings of a son on the very first night.

ॐ

Chapter Forty-Six

Benjamin, a private soldier in the
Massachusetts 16th Continental Regiment
during the eleven-month siege of Boston.

We weren't ready, only we didn't know it yet.

Had we defeated the British in Boston, had we sent them sailing back home and ended the war in the spring of 1776, we would have continued as thirteen states, or as a fractious cluster of countries. One year of camping and training and fighting together may begin to knit the troops into a single army, but it does not knit the populations of thirteen colonies into a single nation.

Providence understood, I believe, that we had to struggle through eight winters. We had to fight, retreat, skirmish, and fight again and again, first for a year in Massachusetts, then in New York, New Jersey, and Pennsylvania, in New Hampshire, Rhode Island, and Connecticut, in Delaware and in Maryland, down south in the Carolinas, and in Georgia, and finally, following the longest march of all, on the coast of Virginia, before not only our American army but our American people had been fully transformed into citizens of a nation.

Had we defeated the British in Boston, we might have won the war, but we would have lost our future, a future built on the foundation of shared sacrifice, shared endurance, and shared beliefs. Every colony, every state, dug graves in which they laid their patriotic sons and daughters.

In October, 1775, a year and a half after our voyage on the *Lively*, General Thomas Gage sailed back to London. He had been replaced as commander in chief by Major General William Howe, the officer who had marched his troops three times up Breed's Hill, to their slaughter and eventual victory.

General Howe soon expanded the civil war in a most brutal manner. On October 17, the British frigate *Canceaux* sailed into Falmouth Harbor, up the coast from Boston. Captain Henry Mowat called through a speaking trumpet to men working on the wharf; he told them that he intended to destroy their seaport. Having given his abrupt warning, he allowed a few hours for a chaotic, partial evacuation, then he fired his cannons in a broadside at undefended warehouses, homes and shops. During a pause in the cannonade, he sent a crew of sailors in a cutter to the wharf, where they set fire to ships moored along the pier, and to any warehouses still not burning. Offshore winds blew the rising flames directly into the seaport. The fire burned all through the night, until nearly every building in Falmouth Harbor was destroyed by the raging conflagration. Several hundred people lost their homes, in October when winter was coming. Ships along the pier burned to the water, and sank.

When news of the savage bombardment reached Cambridge (two days after our wedding), a company of troops from Falmouth departed immediately to locate their families.

General Washington, in his report to Congress, called the British attack "an outrage exceeding in barbarity and cruelty every hostile act practised among civilized nations." No previous letter from the General to Congress had been so outraged at the enemy.

If General Howe intended by this naval attack to intimidate the colonies, he failed. As the news traveled south from seaport to seaport, Americans were not frightened, but furious. The patchwork of thirteen disparate colonies drew closer together, as the threads of their fury and determination stitched them increasingly into one fabric.

Throughout the autumn of 1775, women in every colony worked at their spinning wheels and at their looms, then they stitched with needle and thread: answering the call from the Continental Army, America's women sewed thirteen thousand homespun winter coats for the soldiers camping outside of Boston. Many of the seamstresses sewed their name and the name of their town into the coats, so that a sentry from New Hampshire, standing watch for four cold hours on a snowy November night, might know that he was kept warm by the generous efforts of his fellow citizens in South Carolina.

During the summer of 1775, the Continental Congress had written an "Olive Branch" petition to King George III, as their final effort to negotiate a compromise between the thirteen colonies and Britain. But in December of 1775, Congress learned that the King had refused even to read their petition. Responding to the hostilities at Lexington and Concord, and then at Breed's Hill, the King had declared in October to his ministers in Parliament that the American colonies were rebelling

"for the purpose of establishing an independent empire." He was therefore determined

> ". . . to put a speedy end to these disorders by the most decisive ex-
> ertions. For this purpose I have increased my naval establishment
> and greatly augmented my land forces. "

The King added, without as yet any further explanation,

> "I have also the satisfaction to inform you that I have received the
> most friendly offers of foreign assistance."

When this startling news traveled north from Congress and reached
us in Cambridge, we understood that we were not simply besieging
British troops in Boston: we were at war with Britain itself. The proud
ministers in Parliament had long ago turned against us, and now our
King had turned against us as well. Our final hopes for some agreement
were snuffed: the candle's tiny flame had been spat upon.

By order of our Commander in Chief, copies of the King's October
"Speech from the Throne" were tossed into a fire before the assembled
troops. Staring in somber silence, we watched a brief flurry of flames,
watched ashes drift skyward on the wind. We understood that we were
now engaged in what Americans had most feared: a civil war, neighbor
against neighbor, friend against friend, even parent against child, a war
in which the passion of love might now become the ferocious passion
of hatred.

While our regional colonial spirits were woven during that summer
and autumn and winter into one American spirit, a particular group of
people were all but excluded.

I learned from my Negro friends in the hospital tent that despite
their courage on Breed's Hill, despite their wounds from which they
slowly recovered, they were no longer wanted in the Continental Army.
In July, the Army's adjutant general issued orders to recruiting officers
that they were not to enlist "any stroller, negro, or vagabond." In October, the quartermaster general received orders to provide outfits of
clothing to all soldiers who would re-enlist, "Negroes excepted, which
the Congress do not incline to inlist again." Any Negro found "straggling" around the encampment was to be arrested and removed.

During the autumn, a group of free Negro soldiers courageously
gathered in front of General Washington's headquarters. Speaking to a
lieutenant who had come outside to meet with them, they asked for the

General's permission to continue their service in the Continental Army. General Washington considered their appeal; in December, he issued orders to recruiting officers, enabling them to re-enlist free Negroes (but not slaves). General Washington referred the matter to Congress, which replied in January, 1776 that only free Negroes who had already served might re-enlist; no other Negroes, free or slave, would be accepted into the Army.

The individual colonies passed their own regulations. In January of 1776, the Massachusetts militia declared that it would no longer accept recruits who were Indians, Negroes, or mulattos. In April of 1776, New Hampshire excluded idiots, lunatics, and Negroes from its colonial forces.

Cato, Prince, and Freedom continued to serve in the Continental Army as medical nurses under the authority of Johannes Kesslaer. Homer, a slave, was sent home to his master.

I had fought on Breed's Hill, where musket balls and bayonets cared nothing about the color of a man's skin. Though I had chosen to stand with the Americans in their rebellion, I now understood that these Sons of Liberty were blind in one eye.

The British did their best to turn the Negroes against the Americans (and thus the Americans against the Negroes).

In November of 1775, the British governor of Virginia, Lord John Dunmore, published a proclamation that promised freedom to all slaves who escaped from their masters and joined the Royal Forces. The news quickly spread throughout Virginia. Hundreds of slaves—and eventually thousands—escaped to the colonial capital at Williamsburg and to other British encampments. During the eight-year war, a great many runaways fought for the British, believing that by doing so, they were earning their freedom.

Virginia plantation owners who had remained loyal to their King, now changed their opinion to the degree that they lost their property. Lord Dunmore gained a horde of slaves to feed, and lost a multitude of white Loyalists.

The British governor managed, however, to turn a profit in the end. Lord Dunmore loaded a thousand of his Negro recruits onto transport ships, then sailed with them to various British sugar islands in the West Indies, where he sold the Negroes back into slavery, at a profit from which little expense was subtracted.

*   *   *

Strange that during those eight years of war, when we were learning to live without the British, we never learned to live *with* the Negroes. The number of Negro soldiers grew as General Washington felt an increasing need for reliable men who would serve to the end of the war. Regimental returns indicated that roughly five thousand Negroes served in the Army, some for part of a year, some to the last days at Yorktown. Negro soldiers fought in every major battle, and served as well as spies in the enemy's camp.

And yet, when the American Constitution was written in 1787, four years after the end of the war, the gentlemen assembled in Philadelphia still did not know what to do with their black Sons of Liberty.

૪

Chapter Forty-Seven

Genevieve York.

Two other ventures of great import (in addition to our wedding) commenced during that autumn of 1775. The Continental Army did not merely sit in its siege around Boston.

At the end of September, an expedition led by Colonel Benedict Arnold began a long journey northward, first by ship up the coast, then by canoe and foot through the unmapped wilderness of Maine (then part of Massachusetts). The goal of this invading army was to cross the St. Lawrence River and then to attack and conquer the city of Quebec. Another expedition, led by General Richard Montgomery, sailed north up Lake Champlain to attack Montreal. If these two strategic cities could be captured, then British Canada might become the fourteenth United Colony.

Meanwhile, General Washington needed artillery to dislodge the British from Boston. Last May (between the skirmishes at Lexington and Concord in April, and the Battle of Breed's Hill in June), the combined forces of Benedict Arnold from Connecticut and Ethan Allen from Vermont (then part of New Hampshire) had surprised the sleeping British garrison at Fort Ticonderoga on Lake Champlain. Without firing a single musket, the patriots captured both a vital fort on the water route between New York and Canada, and a substantial arsenal.

In November, while I was grooming Sir William in the paddock, I learned from John Lally, who knew everything about everything, that a detachment would soon leave our camp, bound for Fort Ticonderoga. The soldiers would load the captured British cannons and mortars onto sledges, then teams of oxen would pull the artillery train (as soon as enough snow covered the ground) on a three-hundred-mile journey to Cambridge. The oxen would have to pull their sledges over the wild Berkshire Mountains of western Massachusetts. The journey during the summer was daunting; during the winter, almost impossible.

I knew that Judd could talk his pair of oxen over any mountain, no matter what they were pulling, no matter how deep the snow. I knew as well that he wished to serve in the Continental Army, but not with a musket. I rode Sir William to Lincoln that very evening and told Judd about the impending expedition. He saddled his horse and rode with me back to the encampment, where he talked and made plans with Papa.

The next morning, Judd reported to headquarters, where he volunteered himself and his team of oxen. Papa returned to Lincoln to take Judd's place on the farm. Though Mama was fretful at offering another son to the war, she was profoundly relieved to have her husband home.

In late November, when there was still little snow on the roads, Judd gathered with the other drovers and their teams on the Cambridge Common. Led by Colonel Henry Knox (Benjamin's bookseller, who through reading had learned more about artillery than any other officer at headquarters), the drovers and their lowing oxen proceeded in a slow but majestic parade out the common gate, then northwest up a road soon trampled from snowy white to earthen black.

We couriers who watched them from the paddock hoped for their safety. We hoped they would return with the cannons before the British attacked. And we hoped for snow.

Benjamin York.

Our Commander in Chief often surprised us. Stories frequently swept through camp about what he had done that day.

One afternoon in December in Harvard Yard, a squad of Virginia riflemen began a snowball battle with a company of Massachusetts privates returning from the lines. Snowballs led to fisticuffs, the shouting brought reinforcements, and soon hundreds of men were brawling in the Yard. General Washington, returning on his horse from the redoubt on Prospect Hill, rode straight into the thick of the fight, swung down from his saddle, grabbed two soldiers by their coats and nearly shook their heads off while he shouted orders that quickly brought the fighting to a halt. The men were stunned by the sight of their Commander in Chief among them, and they were awed by the strength in his arms as he flung the two dangling soldiers in opposite directions. Never again was there such a brawl in our camp.

On another occasion, several officers were "hurling the bar" on the common: the men would throw a heavy iron bar like a spear as far as they could. General Washington rode over to them, dismounted and took the bar in his hand. To the astonishment of everyone watching, he cocked his arm and hurled the heavy bar a good twenty feet beyond the officers' furthest throw. As he swung back up into the saddle, he told them, "When you young gentlemen have equaled my mark, let me know, and I shall try the bar once again."

Perhaps most the most surprising habit for a Commander in Chief, and most welcome, were his nighttime visits to the breastworks. While a sentry stood at his post, staring over the windswept black ice on Back Bay toward a few scattered lights in Boston, he would hear footsteps crunching in the snow as someone approached from behind. The sentry would of course glance over his shoulder, expecting a messenger with fresh orders. He would instead see a tall figure in a long black winter cape, then he would recognize the stern and yet benign face of General Washington. The General would stand silently for long minutes beside the sentry, scanning the ice and the city in front of them.

Having shared the night, the cold, the war together, the General would say softly, "Keep a sharp watch, my high Son of Liberty," then he would turn and walk away into the snowy darkness.

Not a sentry ever dared to sleep at his post. And not a sentry ever forgot the burning pride in his heart when his Commander in Chief called him a "high Son of Liberty."

I know, because it happened to me, twice.

ॐ

Chapter Forty-Eight

Genevieve.

Though Henry continued to befriend soldiers from New Hampshire to Virginia, in one respect was his new cordiality limited. Having no experience with Negroes, he kept his distance.

He never entered the hospital tent with Benjamin and Johannes. However, he understood without a word from either of them that a tent would surely not do through the winter. He spoke with an officer; soon teams of horses were hauling logs into a field beside the tent. Henry cut and notched the logs himself, then with a company of volunteers (for any man who worked with Henry learned the trade of carpentry), he built not a log hut with six bunks, but a cabin large enough for twenty bunks, with a big stone-and-mortar fireplace at each end.

Henry cut and split firewood for the hospital right through the autumn and winter. He was polite with Cato, who occasionally came outside to fetch wood for the fireplaces. But Henry never paused in his work to chat and offer his friendship.

Benjamin.

One afternoon just before Christmas, Johannes Kesslaer met me at the door of our hospital. He stepped outside and pushed the door shut, then walked with me until we stood well away from the cabin's log walls. He told me quietly, "You are not to come back. You are never again to enter this hospital. We've got smallpox now."

"Smallpox!" I whispered. More dreaded than typhus, more dreaded than flux, was the unpredictable plague of smallpox.

The reverend doctor's voice shook with outrage as he told me, "The British sent prostitutes with smallpox into our camp. A dozen poor young women, who took a few shillings and infected our men." He looked across the snow toward Harvard's red brick hospital. "They've got twenty-two men inside, sick with the pox."

Then he glanced in the direction of Boston. "The British also sent runaway slaves with smallpox into our camp." He nodded toward his windowless cabin. "I have seven inside."

Prostitutes, and slaves. Could men really do this to other men, and women? Two seeds of fresh anger were planted in my heart. Their roots would grow deep. In the future I fought for, in the America I fought for, there would be—I vowed to myself—no prostitutes, no slaves.

"Benjamin, you must not come back." Johannes raised his hand toward my shoulder, but refrained from touching me. "I thank you for the work you have done here. But now you have a wife, and soon a child."

I asked, "Then, what else might a husband do? What else might a father do? For I am a soldier, and so I must be something more."

"Aye," he nodded, understanding. "Benjamin, when the good Lord would have something more of you, He will show you."

Then I would search. I would listen.

"Thank you," said Johannes, his words in the frigid wintry air a momentary white plume drifting in the sunshine.

He turned and went back into his log hospital.

Who, I wondered as I walked away, took care of those poor young women with smallpox?

&

Chapter Forty-Nine

Genevieve.

CHRISTMAS, 1775

On a cold, clear and windy Christmas morning, a morning that even the sun shining down brightly from a pale blue sky could not warm, Benjamin and I climbed to the top of the hill behind the encampment. There was as yet no more than half a foot of snow, so by stepping carefully, we were able to move steadily upward. At the summit, we stood huddled beside each other with our backs to the biting wind from the north.

Looking down to the south, we saw our sprawling encampment of snow-covered huts, with a spider's web of brown trails crisscrossing between them. Smoke no longer rose from fifty campfires, but from fifty chimneys.

Turning toward the east (Benjamin stood to my left, blocking the wind as best he could), we could see the backs of a dozen sentries standing guard along the brown slash of the breastworks, for not even on this sacred Christmas day could we lessen our vigilance against the British. Benjamin had already served his watch: he had stood for four hours in that trench with his mittens wrapped around the frozen iron of his musket. Stomping his cold feet, he had watched the stars rising in the east. He had watched the silver-gray glow that spread above the rooftops of Boston. And he had faced the sun as it rose to shine upon the world on Christmas day. When the sentries now on duty were relieved with the changing of the watch, they too would hurry to their huts, wrap their hands around their mugs and drink a Christmas wassail steaming hot.

Most of Back Bay was frozen, forming an irregular crescent of gray ice wrapped around Boston. Every soldier in camp had considered a surprise attack on Boston across that ice. And every soldier in camp had considered a surprise British attack across that ice in the opposite direction: at midnight, five thousand redcoats charging with bayonets toward Cambridge. That the British had not yet attacked was a mystery to us. Their hesitation, we surmised, resulted from our ferocity along the Concord-Boston road in April, and our tenacity on Breed's Hill in June. General Howe was afraid of risking his army a third time.

Looking across the moat of ice, Benjamin and I stared at the snow-shrouded fortress of Boston, where on Christmas Day no fresh turkeys roasted over the fires, no fresh eggs firmed up a pudding, no fresh beef was boiling. A great number of buildings had been torn down for firewood. Nearly every tree, including the Liberty Elm, had been cut down. No boughs of fresh evergreen would decorate King's Chapel, as they festooned the pews and pulpit of our Harvard Chapel.

Benjamin and I stood for a long time in silence, staring down at the world around us.

Then, with his right arm wrapped around my shoulders, Benjamin pointed with his left mitten (a blue wool mitten which I had knit for him) toward Boston.

"A year ago on Christmas Day," he said, "I was camped in a tent on the Common. Nathaniel and I sat on frozen stumps beside our campfire, reading aloud to each other from the Book of Luke, while drunken, lonely, bitter, despairing soldiers shouted and sang and stumbled around us. One man fell into a campfire and badly burned his hands and face. Another discharged his firelock and killed an officer in a nearby tent."

Benjamin, my ever pensive Benjamin, squeezed my shoulders.

"But this year on Christmas Day, I hold beside me the woman I love. The woman who harbors and nurtures our first child. Tonight I will sleep with my arm around her in our warm log hut."

Yes, in the midst of war, we treasured those snug nights in our hut. Treasured them defiantly against the madness of kings and generals.

"I look across the frozen bay at my countrymen in Boston, who today will read the same Scripture in their churches as we read in ours. And who will sing the same beloved hymns. And who will think of mothers and fathers and families, far away.

"And I wonder when we fools, having been taught the way of peace for over seventeen hundred years, will ever learn to lay down our muskets and take up the Book of Luke."

Benjamin stared beyond Boston, toward the unfrozen blue Atlantic, reaching to the horizon in the sharp wintry light. Surely he thought of his own family in London. This Christmas, he had the comfort of knowing that his family knew that he was alive. Alive, but a soldier.

We had learned, and learned most admirably, how to sow the seed, tend the sprouts, harvest the wheat, mill the flour, and bake the loaves of a dozen different kinds of bread. But would we ever learn to share that bread in peace?

Our cheeks stung by the wind, our feet growing cold, we started down the hill, kicking our shoes and spatterdashes through the dry powdery snow.

Mama and Papa had brought a Christmas feast from the farm. Henry would have a good fire roaring in the fireplace. Only Judd would not be with us. He was (we hoped) at Fort Ticonderoga, on the shore of Lake Champlain in New York, loading cannons onto sledges. And no doubt today giving an extra ration of feed to his oxen.

Papa would say the prayer before dinner.

Mama would glow with happiness as we feasted on her venison and corn pudding and mince pie and eggnog.

Henry would toast with cider to each of the thirteen colonies.

And after dinner, Benjamin would read aloud, by the light of the settling fire, from the Book of Luke.

8⊃

Chapter Fifty

Genevieve.

Thomas Paine's "COMMON SENSE"

On New Year's Eve, thousands of soldiers in the Continental Army rolled their clothing inside their blankets and walked out of camp, for their period of duty, "to the end of the year," had ended.

During the last months of 1775, recruiting officers had traveled throughout New England in search of fresh volunteers. On the first of January, 1776, new men, untrained and often unarmed, began to appear in camp.

Had the British attacked us on New Year's Eve, the war would have been over well before dawn.

If General Washington found any encouragement on New Year's Eve, it no doubt came from his wife Martha, who had arrived by carriage two weeks before Christmas. I admired her courage, for she had traveled all the way from warm Virginia to wintry Massachusetts, and to the field of war. A married woman myself now, I could guess her desire, in coming such a great and difficult distance, to bring some comfort to her beleaguered husband.

On New Year's Day, to hearten his army (and perhaps to disguise the chaos in camp), General Washington raised, for the first time, the flag of our United Colonies. Several soldiers had erected the mast of a schooner as a flagpole atop Prospect Hill, halfway between Cambridge and Charlestown Neck. Soldiers trained as tailors had found a large red British flag, with the Union Jack in its upper left corner. They sewed six stripes of white linen horizontally across the red field, thus creating thirteen red and white stripes. (We kept the Union Jack—formed by the red cross of St. George, representing England, and the white cross of St. Andrew, representing Scotland—as a symbol that proclaimed our willingness, even now, to remain within the British empire.)

Our new flag was raised to the top of the mast at dawn on New Year's Day, 1776. It flapped briskly in the wind off the sea, where every officer and soldier in Cambridge could see it, and where every officer and soldier in Boston could see it. We fired thirteen cannons in a salute. In camp and along the lines, our men roared with a cheer.

Despite a flag with thirteen stripes, the troops did not belong to a unified army. Most soldiers felt a far stronger allegiance to their home colony than to some sort of union. Privates distrusted any officer who spoke a dialect different from their own. Colonials still discussed their rights as Englishmen; very few discussed their rights as independent Americans. Our laws, our customs, and our language all reached back hundreds of years. Such a weaving of bonds was not easily unraveled.

Then the news arrived that on January 1, 1776, British warships had fired their cannons at Norfolk, Virginia, setting that seaport ablaze. Charlestown had been burned, Falmouth had been burned, and now Norfolk was destroyed. Every American port, whether along the coast or up a navigable river, could now expect the same British brutality. Our mother country had turned in a vicious rage against her colonial children.

But even that news did not shake us as much as the thunderclap in Philadelphia on the 10th of January, 1776, a thunderclap that rumbled north, south, and west in the following weeks, until every American household, tavern, meetinghouse and school shook with its force.

That thunderclap was an eighty-page pamphlet by Thomas Paine, entitled "Common Sense."

Thomas Paine was an Englishman who had failed at everything he had tried, including the manufacture of ladies' corsets. At the age of thirty-seven, he introduced himself to Benjamin Franklin in London. Dr. Franklin recognized a man of frustrated enterprise and talent; he wrote a letter of recommendation to his son William, who was then the royal governor of New Jersey. With that letter in hand, Thomas Paine sailed for America, and a new start in life, in October of 1774.

He became a journalist in Philadelphia, then editor of *Pennsylvania Magazine.* Taking a keen interest in his new home, he responded in print to the massacres at Lexington and Concord, to the first true battle of the war at Breed's Hill, and even to the contradiction of American slave owners fighting for freedom. Paine's quill did not limit itself to events in Pennsylvania, but reached out to all of the colonies, and to England as well.

During the autumn of 1775—encouraged by Dr. Benjamin Rush,

an early advocate of full independence from Britain—Paine organized his bold observations into the chapters of a pamphlet. "Common Sense" appeared in the book shops in Philadelphia on January 10, 1776. The first printing quickly sold out, for the stunning essay clarified, in clear and dramatic terms, what had long been churning in the hearts of most Americans. When the colonials read "Common Sense," they discovered in its paragraphs what they themselves had been thinking, but could not put so eloquently into words.

Reprinted again and again (until it sold over one hundred thousand copies in the first three months), the pamphlet spread into every colony and quickly reached our encampment in Cambridge. Disregarding the cold nights of January, Henry once again kindled the campfire outside our hut. Then, with twenty, fifty, a hundred soldiers gathered in a circle around the blaze, Benjamin read paragraph after paragraph in his clear and forceful voice.

Copies of "Common Sense" passed from hand to hand throughout the encampment, until nearly every soldier, every officer, knew a dozen sentences from of Paine's revolutionary argument by heart.

Above all, Mr. Paine gave us a purpose far beyond our argument over taxation. He wrote (as I read now from the yellowed copy which I have saved in the linen drawer all these years), "The cause of America is in great measure the cause of all mankind." Americans were not merely merchants and farmers enraged at our mistreatment by a tyrant and his tax collectors; we were the defenders of human liberties around the world. Our war over forms of taxation and the quartering of British troops became a war over the protection of sacred rights.

As I hold this precious document now in my hands, its pages so dry that while I turn them they threaten to crumble, I remember Benjamin's hands holding the pamphlet fifty years ago. Henry's hands held it, Papa's hands held it, Mama's hands held it, and the hands of twenty, thirty, fifty others held this pamphlet as well. "Common Sense" taught us to look anew at our King, and at all the kings before him, to the very first king, William the Conqueror, who crossed the Channel in 1066 and claimed the British throne by force of his sword.

Thomas Paine wrote:

"England, since the conquest, hath known some few good monarchs, but groaned beneath a much greater number of

bad ones; yet no man in his senses can say that their claim under William the Conqueror is a very honorable one. A French bastard landing with an armed banditti, and establishing himself King of England against the consent of the natives, is in plain terms a very paltry rascally original. —It certainly hath no divinity in it."

A page later, Paine added,

"Thirty kings and two minors have reigned in that distracted kingdom since the conquest, in which time there have been (including the Revolution) no less than eight civil wars and nineteen rebellions."

(He was referring to the English Revolution of 1688, not to ours of 1776.)

In summary, *"Of more worth is one honest man to society and in the sight of God, than all the crowned ruffians that ever lived."*

Thomas Paine then turned the attention of his essay from the scoundrels on the British throne to the people and purpose of America. He spoke to us not as colonials, nor as New Yorkers or Virginians, but as a people, unified both geographically and spiritually, and he showed us our special place in history.

"The sun never shined on a cause of greater worth. 'Tis not the affair of a city, a country, a province, or a kingdom, but of a continent—of at least one eighth part of the habitable globe. 'Tis not the concern of a day, a year, or an age; posterity are virtually involved in the contest, and will be more or less affected, even to the end of time, by the proceedings now. Now is the seed time of continental union, faith and honor."

Every farmer in America could understand the phrase "seed time." We were planting principles, laws, and rights, and we meant to have a bountiful harvest.

"The present winter is worth an age if rightly employed."

Every soldier standing around our campfire on a cold January night, listening to Benjamin read that sentence to him, felt a deep determination that the present winter *would* be rightly employed.

Our pamphleteer reminded us that we were not all Englishmen, nor descendants of Englishmen, in our colonies. Our people were from Holland, Germany, and Sweden as well. Thus there was little reason in our all being subject to the dictates of Britain's Parliament.

"Europe, and not England, is the parent country of America."

Further, the American continent had provided a sanctuary for those who fled tyranny throughout Europe.

"This new world hath been the asylum for the persecuted lovers of civil and religious liberty from every part of Europe. Hither have they fled, not from the tender embraces of the mother, but from the cruelty of the monster; and it is so far true of England, that the same tyranny which drove the first emigrants from home, pursues their descendants still."

He continued,

"But Britain is the parent country, some say. Then the more shame upon her conduct. Even brutes do not devour their young, nor savages make war upon their families."

As a final thrust at England, he added,

"There is something very absurd, in supposing a continent to be perpetually governed by an island."

Thomas Paine addressed the shopkeepers, mechanics and farmers of America in Biblical terms.

"No man was a warmer wisher for reconciliation than myself, before the fatal nineteenth of April 1775, but the moment the event of that day was made known, I rejected the hardened, sullen tempered Pharaoh of England for ever."

Thus he cloaked his argument with Scriptural power.

With reconciliation rejected, he wrote openly about independence from England, and heartily recommended that revolutionary decision to our people. He told us not to be afraid of severing our deep ties with the familiar traditions of the past:

*"If there is any true cause of fear respecting independence,
it is because no plan is yet laid down."*

He explained the many benefits that would be ours, were we to become an independent nation. We would not be bound to England in all her wars. Our trade with the other nations in Europe would no longer be controlled by Parliament. Our laws would be our own laws, not those imposed upon us by the King's ministers. He stated with wise foresight:

*"Independence is the only BOND that can tye and keep us
together."*

He recommended that we create our own constitution, and our own government:

"Can we but leave posterity with a settled form of government, an independent constitution of its own, the purchase at any price will be cheap."

He spoke not of thirteen colonies or provinces, but of something entirely new:

"the FREE AND INDEPENDENT STATES OF AMERICA."

Returning again and again from the local and the national to the universal, he encouraged us:

"O ye that love mankind! Ye that dare oppose, not only the tyranny, but the tyrant, stand forth! Every spot of the old world is overrun with oppression. Freedom hath been hunted round the globe. Asia, and Africa, have long expelled her. Europe regards her like a stranger, and England hath given her warning to depart. O! receive the fugitive, and prepare in time an asylum for mankind."

What man or woman among us could not respond when Thomas Paine told us,

"The birthday of a new world is at hand."

Not for anyone's individual freedom, nor even for our families and villages and colonies, were we now fighting. Instead, we fought for all of us together, even those still unborn, even those who lived far across the sea. That commitment to mankind was what made us Americans.

We were to hold up the flame of liberty for all the world to see.

Outside beside the campfire, inside our hut beside the fireplace, I read through "Common Sense" again and again. Along with the early broadsheets and the *Boston Gazette* which I had read with Papa, along with verses of Scripture in our family Bible, along with dramatic verses by Shakespeare, Thomas Paine's clear and bold sentences became a primer from which I learned to read.

With Benjamin's help, I studied its pages until there was not a word in the pamphlet that I could not understand.

୧୦

Chapter Fifty-One

Benjamin

In mid-January, 1776, the grim news reached us from Canada that the American attack on Quebec had ended in disaster. During a blizzard on the night of December 31, our troops assaulted the tall stone walls of the city—built like a fortress—but General Montgomery was killed, Colonel Arnold was wounded, and a great many of our soldiers were captured as prisoners. That defeat meant the loss of America's hope for a fourteenth colony.

It also meant the continued threat of a British attack from the north.

Perhaps most important to us in Cambridge, the defeat in Quebec meant that should we fail in our siege of Boston, the thirteen colonies, as well as the King and his ministers, would view our defeat as disaster following disaster. And with that, the entire war might collapse.

Genevieve.

In January, 1776. I lost my employment as courier.

Perhaps General Washington told his wife Martha about me. And about our wedding. And perhaps she asked him a certain question.

Every morning after breakfast, prayer, and general orders in our camp, I walked to the paddock and saddled Sir William, then rode him to Harvard Yard. There I waited with the other couriers for our orders. When, on the twenty-first of January, exactly three months after our wedding day, General Washington himself stepped out from Vassall House, his new headquarters, and beckoned to me, I felt very proud to have been selected from the other couriers.

Holding Sir William's reins, I stepped forward, ready to ride by day and night to Philadelphia and back, should my General request it.

"Miss Ebenezer," he said, looking down at me with a faint smile that I loved to see, "are you, perhaps, in the family way?"

The question stunned me. But I could not tell a lie. "Yes," I whispered.

"Then you are no longer to be riding your horse as a courier. I will not have you taking the risk."

"But . . . General Washington . . ."

"I am sorry. Your employment as courier is immediately terminated until a suitable time after the birth of your child."

I feared that next he would send me out of the encampment and home to the farm. I raged in silent protest. Never!

"However, owing to the trust which you have earned, I would be grateful if you would accept a post here in Vassall House. My letters must be copied before they can be sent to Congress, so that I retain a record of all correspondence. Your husband assures me that you are able to read quite skillfully, and that with minimal practice, you would rapidly develop your penmanship."

General Washington had spoken with Benjamin? Benjamin never said a word.

"Yes, I . . . would be most content with a position as a scribe."

"Excellent. I recommend that you take your fine horse back to the paddock, then report to headquarters. Please ask for my aide, Lieutenant Colonel Williams."

"Yes. Thank you, sir."

General Washington bowed slightly. "Genevieve, it is I who thank you for your integrity. That I can trust you is to me a treasure." He strode up the steps and disappeared into the yellow three-story mansion where today I would begin my new job.

I, who had not penned more than two hundred words in my life . . . I, on the secret recommendation of my husband to our Commander in Chief . . . I was now a scribe!

Well, that was worthy work for the mother of a patriot.

As I led Sir William back to the paddock, I felt most miserable for him, as if I were leading him to six months or more of confinement.

Benjamin.

"He done it again!" called the morning sentries when they returned to camp. Several times I myself, on duty from four to eight in the frigid morning in the forward redoubt at Phipp's Farm, saw him do it.

General Washington, riding the lines at dawn, would follow a snow-covered lane down to the edge of the frozen bay. Then, in full sight of the British in Boston, he would dismount and walk out on the ice. Standing close to where Nathaniel and I had stood in the muck at midnight, the General would stomp his boot on the ice, to see, as we guessed, whether it would bear the weight of his army in an attack on Boston. Though the ice at the outer fringes of the bay was thin (for there it met the tides and rolling surge of the Atlantic), the ice in the belly of the crescent was over foot thick. (We were told so by soldiers native to Boston: despite a brief January thaw, the winter had been a cold one, and on previous such winters, they would have to drill with an auger through fifteen inches or more of ice before they could lower a fishing line.)

At least one morning a week, General Washington walked out on the Bay and stomped his boot. The ice was ready. But the Continental Army, for reasons that only the General and his officers knew, stayed behind our earthen walls and never attacked.

Genevieve.

In February, Judd suddenly appeared at the door of our hut. He joined us for supper, then told us the story of his journey.

His detachment had reached Fort Ticonderoga in early December without much difficulty. There they found fifty-nine cannons, mortars, cohorns, and howitzers, but no gunpowder. They also found crates of lead, and some flints, for muskets.

Judd helped to build heavy-timbered wagons, loaded the artillery into them, then drove his oxen across a stretch of hilly ground from Fort Ticonderoga to the shore of Lake George, where the cannons were loaded onto flat-bottomed boats. The men rowed for several days, pulling against the cold wind and through the forming ice, to Fort George at the southern end of the lake. One scow sank in the choppy waves, but the mortars and cannon aboard lay close enough to shore that men wading into the freezing water could pass a rope around them.

At Fort George, the cannons were loaded onto enormous sledges. But the snow was not yet deep enough to begin the long journey south to Albany. So the men waited, watching the sky to the west.

"As if it were a gift from heaven," Judd told us, "snow began to fall on Christmas Eve. It drifted so deep we could scarcely walk through it.

But it gave us the road we needed. We drove our oxen along the west bank of Hudson's River—still open water—to the junction with the Mohawk. We followed the Mohawk west, upstream, to solid ice, and there we crossed.

"In Albany, we ate a kitchen-cooked meal. Then we sledded south along the western bank to good ice, and finally crossed the Hudson. Our parade of sledges followed the Post Road along the eastern bank, through the village of Kinderhook, where the descendants of the Dutch gave us a cheer and loaves of hot bread.

"The journey so far had been along good roads. But now we headed east into the mountains of Massachusetts, on a military trail cut through the forest by the British sixteen years earlier. Overgrown with trees and brambles, and barricaded by snags that fell in some winter storm, that trail slowed us to a few miles a day. We chopped and dragged, and chopped some more. Harnessed oxen to a tree to pull it clear, harnessed oxen to haul the sledge, harnessed oxen to pull the next tree clear.

"But the snow held, good and deep. The trail was so frozen that snow stayed snow, and did not trample to mud.

"We crossed most of Massachusetts during January. But we did not bring the artillery all the way to Cambridge. General Washington ordered everything hidden near Framingham until he was ready for those big guns. The British might break out of Boston to snatch our cannons." Judd laughed. "Cannons that belonged to the King!"

As he told his tale, I saw that Judd, like Henry, had become a happier man. He had finally found a job that called upon his strength. I think he would have been glad to heft a brass cannon onto each big shoulder, then walk with his artillery over the snowy mountains to Cambridge, while his unharnessed oxen ambled behind.

The following day, Judd returned to his oxen near Framingham. We did not see him again until the repaired, mounted, and polished cannons were hauled forward on their sledges in February, in preparation for their secret and sudden placement on Dorchester Heights.

℘

Chapter Fifty-Two

Benjamin, making fascines,
chandeliers, and gabions.

AN EMPTY VICTORY

Yes, we weren't ready. So the good Lord snatched away any sort of final victory, and gave us instead a long walk south.

Though the British continued to occupy Breed's Hill and Bunker's Hill to the north of Boston, they placed neither troops nor artillery atop the hills of Dorchester peninsula, to the south of Boston. They had a plentiful supply of cannons, both in Boston and aboard their warships moored in the harbor. But, mysteriously, they never rolled their guns to the top of the southern hills, a position from which they could have fired upon our Roxbury lines, as well as upon our troops guarding Boston Neck.

Nor did the British prevent *us* from claiming those hills. On the night of February 14, cutters ferried a company of redcoats across open water to the tip of the peninsula. The British set a few scattered farm buildings on fire, then returned to their fortress in Boston . . . and left Dorchester to us.

After waiting through an eight-month siege with little action, we viewed General William Howe as a most timid commander in chief.

Our own Commander in Chief, however, had us working day and night in preparation for a major action.

The ground was so deeply frozen that even with a sharpened shovel, we could dig barely more than an inch. Thus we could not build a redoubt on Dorchester's hills, nor could we dig a breastworks. And there was certainly no purpose in mounting our new cannons on the hills if we had no protection for our cannoneers.

Through these long months, General Washington recommended to his officers that they read as much as possible from texts on warfare. One of our engineers, Lieutenant Colonel Rufus Putnam, learned from a book about a French method of winter warfare: well before the battle, soldiers built a large framework, called a *chandelier*, which they placed into position, then filled with *fascines*, or bundles of sticks, and *gabions*, baskets filled with earth. Thus a protective wall could be erected above the frozen ground, a wall with narrow gaps for the protruding barrels of cannons. Secretly, well back from the lines, all soldiers not on sentry duty began to chop tree branches into short thick sticks, which were then bundled. We also cut and wove willow withes into baskets, then filled the baskets with rocks.

We filled wooden barrels, collected from every seaport and village around Boston, with sand and rocks. These barrels would be carted one night (along with everything else), to the top of the Dorchester hills. Should the redcoats attempt to march up the slopes against us, we would roll our barrels down to greet them.

We hoped, by occupying Dorchester Heights, to draw the British army out of Boston. Then, while they attacked us in the south, we would assault them across the ice from the north. We could attack as well by boat from the west, where the mouth of the Charles River kept a part of Back Bay open.

Our men were eager to bring the siege to a final battle: they wanted to destroy the flower of the British army, and then go home to their farms. Spring planting time was coming. The sun was arching higher every day across the southern sky. Early seeds, early tubers, had to be gotten into the ground.

And was Benjamin York to become a father while still a soldier on the battlefield of war?

So we prepared, and waited, and wondered, and hoped.

We heard that the chief physician of the encampment, Dr. James Thacher, had turned the mansion of the former British governor into a second hospital, in readiness. Two thousand bandages were prepared, as well as a fleet of hand-barrows to carry the wounded.

This was to be no poorly organized, leaderless battle on Breed's Hill. This was to be the first, supremely organized battle directed by our Commander in Chief.

On the morning of February 27, 1776, in the pale light of a frigid dawn, General Washington himself stood beside Reverend William Emerson, the army chaplain, during an especially fervent prayer.

Our General then addressed us. Sweeping his solemn gaze toward company after company, he spoke in a voice that reached every soldier.

"As the season is fast approaching when every man must expect to be drawn into the field of action, it is highly necessary that he should prepare his mind."

No British officer had ever told me to prepare my mind. They had simply told me what to do.

"It is a noble cause we are engaged in. It is the cause of virtue, and mankind. Every temporal advantage and comfort to us, and our posterity, depends upon the vigor of our exertions. In short, freedom or slavery must be the result of our conduct. There can therefore be no greater inducement to men to behave well."

The word "posterity" struck me forcefully. My child. Our child. Our American child.

Then General Washington warned us, his voice growing stern, "But it may not be amiss for the troops to know, that if any man in action shall presume to skulk, hide himself, or retreat from the enemy, without the orders of his commanding officer, he will be instantly shot down, as an example of cowardice; cowards having too frequently disconcerted the best formed troops by their dastardly behavior."

As we listened to this grim warning from our Commander in Chief, our excitement was tempered by a faint, unshakable dread: the war was approaching, and soon it would have each one of us in its unpredictable grip. No, we would not run as cowards; but what would we have to stand up against?

We wove and filled our gabions, and polished our muskets, through that day, and the next day, and the next, which was February 29, Leap Year Day.

On Friday, March first, we bundled the last fascines. On Saturday, March second, we filled the last barrels with stones.

Then at eleven o'clock on Saturday night (when Genevieve and I were snuggled in our bunk), cannons thundered from the redoubt atop Cobble Hill. Both of us sat straight up in bed, our hearts thumping as if some huge beast were pounding on the door.

Cannons fired from the redoubt at Phipp's Farm, further east and closer to Boston. We dressed as quickly as we could, then hurried outside in the cold dark night. Spikes of orange flame atop Cobble Hill jabbed into the darkness toward Boston. Each flame was followed by a delayed BOOM! We grinned to think how many British soldiers had sat up straight in *their* beds.

The cannonade continued all night. Campfires were lit throughout the encampment by men who gave up any thought of sleep. The British fired back from Beacon Hill and Barton's Point. Though their cannon-balls did little damage to our frozen earthworks, our cannonballs, as we guessed, must be destroying a growing number of houses in Boston.

We ceased firing at dawn on the Sabbath. During the service that morning in Harvard Chapel, Genevieve's hand reached for mine and squeezed it during the entire sermon.

The artillery, all of it northwest of Boston, resumed its barrage on Sunday evening with even greater force. The British brought most of their guns to the northwest corner of Boston. We fought a clamorous but generally ineffective duel until the following dawn. Orange streaks arched back and forth across the night sky, and for the first time in months, sentry duty was almost a pleasure.

Our firing ceased again on Monday, surely confusing the British as to our intention. Genevieve and I said little to each other that day, though while she mended a button on my coat after breakfast, I sat close by. And the moment she stepped out of Vassall House at the end of the afternoon, I was standing there in the snow to greet her.

On Monday evening at seven o'clock, Colonel Henry Knox began his third night of artillery barrage.

Also at seven o'clock—as soon as the night was completely dark—a second phase of the attack began.

Beneath a rising three-quarter moon, Henry and I assembled with our regiment in Roxbury, a village south of Cambridge. Our command-ing officer, Brigadier General John Thomas, told us that tonight we would raise two fortresses, armed with cannons, atop a pair of hills on Dorchester peninsula. Tomorrow, March fifth, on the anniversary of the Boston Massacre, we would be prepared to fire artillery that could reach anywhere in the city of Boston, as well as much of the harbor.

General Thomas warned us to work as silently as possible: no speech louder than a whisper, and certainly no firing of muskets.

We were gratified to learn that we would not spend the entire night building a fort, and then the following day fighting to defend it. We would not repeat our experience on Breed's Hill. Rather, fresh troops would replace us before dawn.

Our small army of three thousand soldiers, including a company of riflemen, marched in silence along the frozen, moonlit Dorchester road. At the junction with a lane leading out to the peninsula, we were joined by three hundred ox-carts loaded with chandeliers, fascines, gabions, and barrels, as well as bales of hay. And of course, the artillery. By eight o'clock in the evening (we could faintly hear, through the thunder of cannons to the north, the ringing of a church bell in Boston), our long, silent column was crossing the neck onto Dorchester peninsula.

Some of the carts stopped along the neck to unload bales of hay. Following whispered orders, a company of men built a wall of bales along the western and then the northern side of the angled road, both to hide our procession from sentries in Boston, and to protect us should we be discovered.

The riflemen spread themselves along the northern Dorchester shoreline, ready to fire across the ice and open water should the British attempt to attack.

But the troops in Boston (as we imagined) were facing northwest toward our artillery barrage, while they waited for the expected attack across the ice to begin. They never noticed, even in the moonlight, a wall of hay bales growing in the south.

Nor could they have heard, over the roar of their cannons, a drover's whip if he had cracked it at the flank of his oxen. But we did not risk even that: the drovers whispered to their enormous beasts, and patted their rumps, stopping and starting them as required, while our column of crunching feet and creaking wheels moved forward.

Henry and I marched with the first detachment up Forster Hill. The second half of the column moved on toward Signaltree Hill. As we climbed a snowy trail up the slope, our feet often slipped, but we did not mind: the British, if they attacked, would be slipping too.

Standing atop a flat dome of moonlit snow, we stared down across the frozen harbor at Boston; the city was shrouded in a heavy moonlit mist. A breeze, drifting from the west, carried a mist rising off the open black water of the Charles River: carried the mist in a long moonlit plume directly toward the city. Aye, we could see the white steeples rising above the radiant vapor. But down there in that fog, the British would have great difficulty in discovering our fortress.

The breeze carried as well whatever small sounds we made out to the black Atlantic.

The night was perfect. We were fresh and determined. The oxen and their carts traveled easily over the frozen road, even up the snowy trail. Providence seemed to bless us tonight in our endeavor.

We built our French ramparts. We readied our rock-filled barrels. We rolled into position six twelve-pound cannons. When Judd drove into the redoubt during the night—his team of oxen pulled a wagon loaded with cannonballs—Henry and I were able to speak with him. He told us, as he lifted a twelve-pound iron ball in each hand and set them on the ground behind a cannon, that he had explained to Colonel Knox that he would never fire a cannon. He would not even load it with a charge of powder.

He would help to bring a train of artillery across two frozen rivers in New York and over a dozen mountains in Massachusetts; he would repair the wheels of an artillery carriage; his oxen would pull a cannon into position; and he would return an hour later with a cart filled with cannonballs in a bed of hay. But he would not touch a keg of gunpowder, nor a fuse. Nor would he load a cannonball into the bore and then push it snug down the barrel.

Such were the decisions a man made, as he struggled to answer both the demands of his heart, and the demands of his country.

Colonel Knox understood. Judd tonight could finish the job he had begun at Fort Ticonderoga. He delivered his cannon—its brass barrel shone in the moonlight—and his load of cannonballs, to the men who would use them against the British.

Before Judd drove his oxen back down the hill, he turned to his brother Henry and reached out his huge hand. Henry, smaller, quicker, and certainly feistier, took his brother's hand and shook it. They looked upon each other in the moonlight with a bond of pride, not as farmers, but as soldiers. Judd had done his job, and now Henry could begin his. And neither one blamed the other.

A short time later, while we were building an *abatis* of sharpened sticks in front of our rampart, Henry nudged me and I looked up. Nearby was a tall rider on a black horse: General Washington, inspecting our fort as we built it. He rode around the entire perimeter, then rode down the slope toward the second hill, his dark figure visible against the bright snow for at least a hundred yards.

The distant ringing of a ship's bell every half hour in the harbor was like the voice of an old friend: eight bells at midnight, then one bell, two bells, three bells. . . . As promised, just after six bells (three in the morning), orders were whispered that we were to stack our entrenching tools: replacements had arrived. Tired, sweaty, and quickly chilled whenever we paused in our work, Henry and I were nevertheless disappointed that we must now abandon our sturdy fort.

We marched with the silent regiment down the hill, making room along the road for the silent regiment marching in the opposite direction. Near the bottom, we entered the fog. We could see no more than fifty feet ahead of us. I tightened my woolen scarf against the damp air.

As we marched the several miles toward Cambridge, the booming of the cannons to the north became ever louder. When we crossed the bridge over the Charles, we glimpsed, further upstream, some of the four thousand soldiers waiting along the banks of the river to board a fleet of rowboats and attack Boston's western shore. They would have to push their way through bobbing sheets of ice, and perhaps break through a mantle of ice along Boston's shore, while British infantrymen fired upon them. I wished the lads well, and greatly preferred our snowy hill.

Increasingly weary, Henry and I trudged with our regiment through the dark but busy streets of Cambridge. We crossed the trampled snow on the common to our encampment, where the men scattered to their huts. Genevieve, still awake, welcomed us at the door. She had a good fire burning and soup in a kettle.

By the time Henry and I set our spoons down on the table beside our empty bowls, and shuffled toward our bunks, we were both walking in our sleep.

&

Chapter Fifty-Three

Benjamin.

Our regiment was allowed to sleep the following morning, so that we might be rested when we returned to Dorchester hills at two in the afternoon.

At one o'clock, Henry and I stood with Genevieve outside our hut in the midday sunshine. We did indeed feel rested, though Genevieve had to give us both a good shaking at noon to rouse us for dinner. But this leave-taking, between brother and sister, between husband and wife, was very different from our parting the evening before.

Genevieve told us what she had heard. The British had discovered our two fortresses at dawn. All through the morning they had fired their cannons (while Henry and I slept like dead men.) But their cannon-balls, shot from an elevation just above sea level, could not reach the hilltops. The arching balls thudded without effect into the snowy hills below our ramparts.

Surely the British would launch their boats to attack us. Once again they would row from Boston to our beach, and once again they would march in bayoneted ranks up the slope toward our farmers' muskets. Would I survive another Breed's Hill? Would Henry?

Yesterday evening when Henry and I had prepared to march, I had felt a soldier's eagerness at finally going into action. But now, in the full daylight of a Tuesday afternoon—never mind that for some it was the anniversary of the Boston Massacre—I felt the foreboding, the dread, the prickly, unshakable fear of war. I tried of course to appear manly and confident as Genevieve and I said our last few words to each other. And Henry was a master at appearing manly and confident. But I knew, as I touched my lips to Genevieve's lips in our final kiss, that perhaps her husband, perhaps her brother, perhaps both, might not be coming home from Dorchester Heights.

We marched with our muskets across the broad neck of Dorchester peninsula, then climbed the back of the hill to our fort. Seagulls glided in the blue sky overhead. The sun shone brightly. How odd was the disjunction between nature's beauty and man's stubborn brutality.

As we took our positions along the ramparts, we could see British transport ships carrying red-coated troops from Long Wharf to Castle William Island, half a mile beyond the tip of Dorchester peninsula. Clearly, the British were preparing to attack from that island. Perhaps from Boston as well: across the neck, across the ice, or both.

Our own troops were still waiting along the banks of the Charles for their assault on Boston. More troops were waiting north of Boston, on Leachmore Point, across the ice from Barton's Point.

Several British warships, including the *Lively*, had maneuvered close to the edge of the ice in the harbor; they now fired their cannons at our forts. But a ship's artillery is mounted to fire at a horizontal target, not an elevated target. Thus their cannonballs had no more effect than cannonballs shot from Boston. However, should we be forced by an assault of infantrymen and grenadiers to abandon our hilltop, the *Lively* could easily direct its cannonballs and grapeshot at our retreat on the flatlands.

We watched an American artillery company moving fieldpieces out to the end of Dorchester Point, where they could fire, when the time came, at any approaching boat. Would more of us be ordered down, to meet the British at the beach?

While Henry and I waited through that long, cold afternoon, the world, in nearly every direction, seemed ready to explode.

Flood tide had been at noon. As the tide ebbed through the afternoon, it revealed the mud flats off Dorchester where Nathaniel and I had once been stuck in Hench's cutter. That all seemed to be years ago, in another lifetime. And yet, here I was still a soldier, holding my hated musket, ready to do a soldier's hated work.

Would the British, would the war, would the world, ever get itself unstuck from the black muck of belligerence?

As I stood with hundreds of soldiers along our ramparts, staring down at British preparations in the harbor for our mutual slaughter, I wondered how many soldiers during the past thousand years, during the past ten thousand years, had hoped that *this* war could be the last war.

Nathaniel. When will men like you ever sit upon the thrones of the world?

Once again, as it had been in June nine months ago, Boston became a city of spectators. People gathered on rooftops, on steeple balconies, in the rigging of ships moored along the wharves. They watched the cutters rowing redcoats out to the transport ships, watched the ships as they sailed to Castle William Island.

They no doubt looked up at us. Most of the Americans remaining in Boston were Loyalists, loyal to their King. They surely regarded us with hatred, for we had turned against the King, we had starved the Loyalists in Boston throughout the winter, and we had moved into their homes on the mainland. Now, by mounting our cannons atop the hills of Dorchester, we threatened their last hopes to return to the comfort and prosperity they had once known. The Americans who watched us from the rooftops of Boston would heartily cheer our slaughter.

How ugly was a rebellion. How much uglier still was a civil war.

The yellow-orange sun was lowering into the western sky. The churches in Boston had rung five o'clock. I was watching the *Lively*, about two miles away in the harbor channel. It seemed to be waiting for the tide to rise again, so it could sail closer to us and address us anew with its cannons. I hoped that as it approached, I might recognize Hench on deck, shouting up his blasphemy to the men in the rigging. I hoped that Nigel MacDonald, hidden behind a boulder down near the shore, might sight Officer Hench along the barrel of his rifle.

But night was soon coming, hours before the next flood tide.

And tomorrow . . . tomorrow and this war could bring us almost anything.

Henry touched my shoulder, then pointed along the snowy length of Dorchester peninsula. I saw nothing unusual, other than our other fort atop Signaltree Hill, due east of us. I looked further: British ships still huddled around Castle William Island. The red British flag flew over the fort; but the flag no longer flapped from west to east. It was now flapping toward us, in a steady gust of easterly wind.

I looked further: out beyond the silver-blue harbor and its islands, out beyond whitecaps rolling toward us on the blue Atlantic, way out along the horizon, somewhat to the north, a long wall of clouds as black as charcoal swept a veil of gray beneath it. Henry, a farmer with a farmer's weather eye, said to me, "Winter storm from the west, seek your nest. But winter storm from the sea, pray mightily."

Every soldier along the ramparts watched that dark bank of clouds as it steadily approached. We drew our coats snug against the first cold gusts. We were ready for a moonlit night in March, but not for a January blizzard.

The rising wind swept dry snow up the eastern slope of our hill.

The snow stung our faces as it whipped over the ramparts. I quickly put on my blue scarf and mittens.

To our great amusement, *we* now became the spectators, for the frigid wind swept the Loyalists from their rooftops. Three transport ships (which a quarter of an hour before had been running before a western breeze toward Castle William Island), were now striking their madly flapping sails (glad I was not to be up in the rigging) and trying to come about in the narrow channel.

The rising gale both churned up the harbor and brought towering waves rolling in from the Atlantic. A British cutter with a brass cannon aboard was blown, despite the men struggling at the oars, into shallow water over the mud flats. The boat heaved broadside to the waves; our men cheered when the cutter was swamped by whitecaps pouring over its gunnel. Those British lads were in for a long night at sea. At best, they might manage to shake hands with our riflemen along the shore.

Approaching swiftly, the black wall of clouds towered above us. The veil of gray proved to be pellets of frozen rain, sweeping almost horizontally with such force that we had to crouch behind the shelter of our ramparts. We tucked our musket breeches under our arms to keep our powder dry, then listened to the frenzied patter of ice pellets beating against our construction of sticks and earth. The huge orange sun, still shining upon us from low in the west, lit the snow and ice flying over our hill with a radiant pale orange glow.

Storm clouds swept over us, veiled the sun briefly, then swallowed it. The afternoon quickly became as dark as dusk.

Holding our hands to shield our eyes, we peered over the wall to see what was happening down in the harbor. The storm had thrown the British into chaos. We on the hill needed only to stomp our cold feet and hug our arms to our chests. But those poor souls crowded on Castle William Island, where spray from the crashing waves was whipped by the wind, were surely soaked in their red woolen coats. And the sailors scudding toward Boston, or desperately paddling their tiny boats (every cutter heavily laden with troops and artillery), would be fortunate to reach the docks and disembark with their lives.

Were General Howe and his suite of officers watching the storm from windows in State House? Or did they brave the weather and meet the retreating vessels along the pier? From either post, they watched the destruction of their finest plans. For months, for years—aye, since their first arrival in September of 1768—the British frigates had been masters of Boston Harbor. But now that they intended to sail no further than to one small island, and from there to the tip of Dorchester peninsula, the entire Atlantic seemed to have risen up in a rage to blow them back to the crowded, hungry, dismal fortress of Boston.

The nor'easter howled all through the night. We huddled against the shelter of our ramparts as sheets of rain, then snow, then rain again, swept over the wall above us. The men from the far side of the fort came to huddle in the lee with us. Officers crouched with their men, and we became that night a most democratic army. We shared what food we had in our rucksacks, what water we had in our canteens, what rum we had brought to get us through the battle.

To our astonishment (yet once again to our disappointment), new troops arrived at the redoubt's gate to relieve us. The night was so dark that we heard about them, by word of mouth racing down our lines, before we could see them. When they appeared, trudging against the wind across the open square of the redoubt, they looked like a horde of black ghosts, come to fetch us either to heaven or hell.

It was to heaven that they sent us. Too frozen to mind our exhaustion, too exhausted to mind how cold we were, Henry and I marched home a second time with our regiment, the wind at our backs pushing us across Dorchester Neck, then along the roads in swirling, blinding snow, toward our hut and our fire and a bowl of hot soup. And most of all, toward my Genevieve.

No manly and confident fortitude did I employ when she met us at the bridge over the Charles. I wept, she wept, and even Henry wept. For we were all three alive, and together. She walked with us, with our trudging regiment, through Cambridge and across the common to our encampment.

While the Atlantic raged, while the good Lord raged, and brought us, brought America, through another night.

On the following morning, the sun rose into a clearing sky, although storm waves continued to roll in from the sea. By midday, the British on Castle William Island were launching their boats, but not to attack us on Dorchester Point. The heavily laden, heavily rolling ships and gunboats and cutters ran with the surge to the docks of Boston.

No doubt their powder was wet.

His Majesty's troops did not attempt an attack, either that day or on the following days. We, meanwhile, on the night of March 9, built a third chandelier-and-gabion fort, this time on Dorchester Hill, a knob on the peninsula nearest to Boston. Our cannons atop that hill were so far forward that we could drop, so we told ourselves, a cannonball into General Howe's teacup.

From our three eagles' nests, we observed much frenzied activity on the streets and wharves of Boston. Redcoats and Loyalists alike were loading military provisions and household goods onto transport ships. We watched with astonishment as soldiers pushed cannons over the edge of the wharf into the harbor. Clearly, the British were abandoning Boston, and they were taking Americans loyal to the King with them.

But where would they sail to? Almost certainly, to New York City, where they could patrol Hudson's River and so divide New England from the central and southern colonies. The war had begun in Boston, but the real stranglehold was New York.

We wondered whether the British would burn Boston before they departed, as they had burnt Charlestown, and Falmouth, and Norfolk. Would the *Lively* fire a farewell broadside of red hot cannonballs at Boston's warehouses and churches?

The British navy—the largest fleet that had ever assembled in American waters, with twenty-two regiments aboard—appeared ready to sail on March 13. But heavy rain blew in from the ocean. Tempestuous weather continued for the next three days. Like gods peering down at earthly mortals, we along the ramparts stared down through gray sheets of rain to see what the helpless British would do.

Then on Sunday, the Lord's Day, the Sabbath, March 17, 1776, the sky cleared to a springtime blue and the wind reversed so that it blew gently from offshore, as if Providence—on St. Patrick's Day—would help the British out of the harbor and on their way.

Cutters ferried the last of the redcoats in Boston out to warships waiting in the channel. Cutters ferried the last of the Loyalists, families of men, women, and children, out to transport ships. (We guessed that a thousand Americans fled that day with the British. Most of them would never return to their Massachusetts homes.) When General Howe and his officers boarded the fleet's flagship, the other frigates fired their cannons in a most hollow salute.

Meanwhile, we patriots in the Continental Army marched openly around the heights of Dorchester. The proud cat was skulking off, while the brave mice were cheering.

We had not destroyed the flower of the British army. We had not finished the war. We hadn't even fought a real battle. The storm had fought it for us. We had won an empty victory, one that brought no guarantee of liberty and peace.

Nevertheless, on St. Patrick's Day of 1776, as we watched His Majesty's fleet heading out through the islands toward the open Atlantic, we felt unconquerable. Let them come back where and when the might. We would find the cannons. We would build the forts. And we would outwit them once again.

&

Chapter Fifty-Four

Benjamin.

But we still had to capture Boston. Had snipers been left behind? Were armed Loyalists waiting in their homes and shops, determined to defend their property? What about smallpox? Typhus? Had the British left behind their most deadly weapon?

Days earlier, General Washington had asked for a thousand volunteers who had survived smallpox. Led by General Israel Putnam, they would enter Boston ahead of the rest of the army, to inspect every street and building.

On March 17, while the last redcoats rowed away in cutters from Long Wharf, our troops rowed in flat-bottomed boats down the Charles River to the ice-clad shore of Boston Common. Thus as one army was leaving from the eastern side of Boston, the other was landing on the western shore.

From our ramparts, we watched American soldiers assembling on the Common. We passed an officer's telescope along the line, so that each private could see tiny dark specks ascending the snowy slope of Beacon Hill.

We heard no firing. We saw no flames.

Our troops soon appeared on the wharf. We heard a meetinghouse bell ringing at no specific hour: it was simply ringing, joyfully, its faint, bright voice reaching out over the harbor.

To our mystification, the British fleet sailed but a short distance beyond the outer harbor, then anchored in Nantasket Roads, forming a stationary parade of rolling hulls and swinging masts nine miles long. We traded guesses: Would the ships come about with a favorable wind and suddenly attack? Would they sail north to burn Salem? Were they waiting to race toward New York? Were other ships approaching from England?

General Washington rode across the neck into Boston on March 18. The remainder of the troops were finally allowed to enter the city on Wednesday, March 20.

Walking that evening through the town (I had the ironic pleasure of being Henry's guide), we saw how well defended the streets and hills had been with trenches, barricades, and cannon emplacements. Boston had truly been a fortress: had we attacked it across the ice, across the open water, across the neck, we would have been brutally slaughtered.

From my winter as an infantryman in His Majesty's service, I knew of a cobbler's shop, where the Loyalist proprietor had earned a handsome profit by cobbling shoes for the soldiers and boots for the officers of the occupying army. The shop was on Charter Street, just off North Street in the city's North End.

I led Henry to an overhead sign with a tall black boot painted on it. Beneath the sign, the door was locked. Peering in through a window, I could see a cobbler's bench and tools, and even a shoe upside down on a cobbler's anvil, its sole waiting for the last few nails to complete the repair.

I explained my plan to our company captain, who in turn spoke with Old Put, who not only gave permission, but arranged for a wagon, abandoned at Clarke's Wharf, to be brought to the front of the shop.

Henry took great pleasure at battering in the Loyalist's door with his shoulder. Then into the wagon we loaded tools, bench, lasts, boxes of buckles, piles of leather (most of the pieces uncut, though we found as well a dozen neatly cut vamps), and a barrel of nails (enough to sole a regiment). I now had a complete cobbler's shop.

For good measure, we peeked upstairs into the cobbler's quarters, then added both kitchen gear and bedding to our booty. No reason that Genevieve, five months with child, should struggle any longer without a proper griddle. She would appreciate as well a horsehair mattress, a goose down quilt, and a proper pillow with a proper pink, lace-trimmed pillowcase.

It was not until ten days after the retreat in panic from Long Wharf that the British ships finally spread their sails and headed . . . north. Not south toward New York, unless their first tack was but a feint.

(Only later did we learn that the ships had been laden with barrels of gunpowder and aristocratic furniture in such haste that the entire load had to be shifted and properly stowed before the vessels could sail on the open ocean.)

Meanwhile, General Washington had already sent a company of Virginia riflemen marching with all haste toward New York, to cause

what disturbance they could, should the British sail into the harbor . . .
until the General himself arrived with his Continental Army.

And so it came to pass that Private Benjamin York marched with
General Washington's undefeated army out of Cambridge on April 6,
1776, heading south for the seaport of New York. He was accompanied
by his good friend Private Henry Byrnes.

He was followed by his wife Genevieve York, a trusted scribe in
the employ of headquarters, who drove a cobbler's wagon pulled by Sir
William, in a train of well over a hundred supply and artillery wagons.

Benjamin York would be a soldier, and something more. When not
marching, when not standing duty as sentry, when not building a hilltop fortress and then staring down the barrel of his musket at the enemy, and when not firing upon that enemy and counting every shot a
sin that would stain him for the remainder of his life, he would gratefully serve as a cobbler. He would make and repair shoes for the soldiers who needed them, and boots for the officers who required them.

If the army had to march (to only the good Lord knew where), then
Benjamin York would do his best to enable his fellow patriots to march
in good shoes.

❧

PART III

The Torch Is Lit

Chapter Fifty-Five

Caleb York, born when our nation was born.

My mother and father tell me that because I was born in the same epoch, in the same month, and almost on the very day that our nation was born, I should describe the writing of that sacred document, the Declaration of Independence.

As a schoolteacher in Concord, I have gathered an ample library. Drawing upon my lifelong study, and reverence, for the Declaration of Equality, I shall begin.

THE DECLARATION OF EQUALITY

On April 12, 1776, one year after Lexington and Concord, and one month after the British fled from Boston, the colony of North Carolina sent a bold message to its three Congressional delegates in Philadelphia, instructing them to vote for independence from Britain.

On May 4, Rhode Island did the same.

On May 15, the one hundred and twelve members of the Virginia colonial assembly "resolved unanimously" that its seven delegates in Congress be instructed "to declare the United Colonies free and independent states, absolved from all allegiance to, or dependence upon, the crown or parliament of Great Britain."

On that same day, May 15, the Second Continental Congress itself, five days after convening in the State House in Philadelphia, urged "the respective assemblies and conventions of the United Colonies . . . to adopt such government as shall, in the opinion of the representatives of the people, best conduce to the happiness and safety of their constituents in particular and America in general." Congress was thus asking the thirteen colonial assemblies to replace the last remnants of British government with their own self-created governments.

On June 14, Connecticut instructed its four delegates to vote for independence.

New Hampshire did the same on June 15, as did Delaware.

New Jersey and Maryland soon followed.

In addition, counties, towns, and villages throughout America passed their own resolutions for independence. Militias and battalions passed resolutions. The New York Mechanics, a union of skilled artisans, passed its own resolution, as did three Grand Juries from South Carolina.

All of these courageous Declarations were posted by express riders to Congress, where a jubilant John Adams declared on May 20, "Every post and every day rolls in upon us Independence like a torrent."

On Friday, June 7, Richard Henry Lee, delegate from Virginia, the largest and most powerful of the colonies, read a three-part resolution to the fifty delegates assembled in Pennsylvania's State House:

> *"That these United Colonies are, and of right ought to be, free and independent States, that they are absolved from all allegiance to the British Crown, and that all political connection between them and the State of Great Britain is, and ought to be, totally dissolved.*
> *"That it is expedient forthwith to take the most effectual measures for forming foreign alliances.*
> *"That a plan of confederation be prepared and transmitted to the respective Colonies for their consideration and approbation."*

All three parts of this resolution were seconded by John Adams. Thus Virginia and Massachusetts harnessed themselves together to the great carriage of independence.

Several of the colonies, however, were still not ready to break away from Britain. They argued for further efforts at reconciliation, or that the proper time for such a momentous break had not yet come. Hoping for a unanimous Declaration of Independence, Congress postponed the vote on Virginia's resolution until July 1. During that three-week delay, delegates would seek further instructions from their home assemblies.

Meanwhile, Congress appointed a committee of five delegates from five different colonies to draft a formal Declaration, to be ready when needed. Because of his proven ability as a meticulous and yet graceful writer, Thomas Jefferson was chosen by his four colleagues to write the preliminary draft.

For seventeen days, between June 11 and 28, Jefferson sat in his second-story parlor on Market Street at a portable mahogany writing desk (his own invention), distilling with his quill the finest in Judaic, Greek, Roman, British, French, and American thought. He did not have in Philadelphia his library at Monticello, so rather than refer to various tomes, he wrote it all from his mind.

Of his efforts, Jefferson later stated,

> *"Neither aiming at originality of principle or sentiment, nor yet copied from any particular and previous writing, it was intended to be an expression of the American mind, and to give to that expression the proper tone and spirit called for by the occasion."*

Jefferson, thirty-three years old, presented his four large sheets of paper, covered with tight but legible handwriting, to John Adams, forty-one years old, and then to Benjamin Franklin, seventy years old, for their "judgments and amendments." Their editing was light; they cut nothing from Jefferson's document, though they improved some wording, punctuation, and spelling.

Meanwhile during that month of June, 1776, the British fleet sailed from Halifax to New York City. Additional ships sailed from England and Ireland, and from the West Indies, forming the largest war fleet that Britain had ever launched. By the last day of June, American soldiers looking out at New York Harbor saw hundreds of frigates at anchor. Their bare masts looked to one soldier "like a forest."

From his headquarters on Manhattan Island, General Washington reported to Congress that he was preparing his army for the impending British attack. His soldiers, however, were "extremely deficient in arms," and many of the men were recent recruits with little training.

On July 1, the news reached Congress that over fifty British ships were poised for an attack on Charleston, South Carolina.

With His Majesty's cannons now aimed at two major American seaports, Congress nevertheless continued its steady advance toward a unanimous Declaration of Nationhood.

On Monday, July 1, the delegates in Philadelphia once again took up Virginia's three-part resolution. Most of the day was spent in hearing the same multitude of arguments for and against a declaration of independence. Nine colonies were ready to vote Aye. But Pennsylvania and South Carolina still argued against the timing of such a declaration.

Delaware had only two of its delegates in Philadelphia, on opposing sides. And New York's delegates still operated under instructions to seek reconciliation with Britain.

Edward Rutledge of South Carolina, hoping to convince his fellow delegates to support a unanimous vote, asked for a postponement until the following day.

On Tuesday, July 2, Rutledge and the delegation from South Carolina voted Aye. Two of Pennsylvania's delegates abstained from voting, which allowed the remaining delegates to vote three-to-two in favor of independence. And Delaware's third delegate, Caesar Rodney, notified of the impending vote, left his plow, mounted his horse and rode eighty miles at night through a thunderstorm. He strode into the State House still wearing his wet coat and boots, and cast his vote, Aye.

Now only New York had not joined the other twelve, but its four delegates were willing to abstain from the final vote. Thus on July 2, after two months of intensive argument, Congress made its decision. Without a single colony voting against the measure, Congress passed "THE UNANIMOUS DECLARATION OF THE THIRTEEN UNITED STATES OF AMERICA." Despite the threat of a long and brutal war, the thirteen British colonies openly declared themselves to be thirteen independent States.

On July 3, John Adams wrote a spirited letter to his wife Abigail, at home on their farm near Boston:

> "Yesterday, the greatest question was decided, which ever was debated in America, and a greater perhaps, never was nor will be decided among men.
> "The Second Day of July 1776, will be the most memorable Epocha, in the History of America.—I am apt to believe that it will be celebrated by succeeding Generations, as the Day of Deliverance by solemn Acts of Devotion to God Almighty. It ought to be solemnized with Pomp and Parade, with Shews, Games, Sports, Guns, Bells, Bonfires, and Illuminations from one End of the Continent to the other from this Time forward forever more."

We have no record from Samuel Adams. Perhaps the fifty-four-year-old patriot, who for the last decade and a half had devoted his life toward this great moment, quietly bowed his head with a prayer of gratitude. Surely he reached his palsied hand and gratefully shook the hands of his fellow delegates. Perhaps in a crowded tavern that evening at dinner, he raised a toast to the Nation which he had fathered and nurtured from its very inception.

And perhaps later that night, too excited to sleep, he walked through the silent Philadelphia streets beneath the stars, while he marveled at the miracle which he and his countrymen had wrought.

But the work was not yet done. The Declaration itself had to be read and edited by the entire Congress, before it could be published. For a total of twelve hours, from Tuesday afternoon, all through Wednesday, and into Thursday, July 4, the fifty delegates went through Thomas Jefferson's four pages line by line, word by word. Since many of the delegates were lawyers, with a sharp eye for shades of meaning and variations of interpretation, they showed no delicacy as they altered and cut Jefferson's text. The author remained silent through his three-day ordeal. John Adams, however, fought for every word.

The Congressional editors cut about a fourth of the original draft, and changed about twenty-five words. They also added two references to God, so that Jefferson's references to "Nature's God" and "their Creator" at the beginning of the document, were joined by "the Supreme Judge of the world" and "Divine Providence" at its end.

One passage in particular was cut entirely: the clause blaming King George III for the slave trade. South Carolina and Georgia objected to any mention of slavery, for they considered it essential to their economies. Several of the northern states earned profits by shipping slaves from Africa to America; they too objected to the clause. It was therefore cut from the Declaration.

Late in the evening of Thursday, July 4, 1776, the entire edited document was read aloud one final time. Approved by twelve states, it was signed by the President of the Congress, John Hancock. The man whom the British had hoped to capture in Lexington (and to hang in London) signed the document with script so large that his signature was over four inches long.

Though the thirteen states had not yet defined their relationship to each other, they now took their places among the family of nations.

New York's assent finally arrived on July 19. On August 2, a copy of the unanimous Declaration, engrossed (handwritten) on parchment, was signed by delegates from all thirteen states. A few signatures were added later, bringing the total to fifty-five brave men who risked "our lives, our fortunes, and our sacred honor."

*   *   *

On July 8, the Declaration was read aloud to the public for the first time in the courtyard behind Pennsylvania's State House. Its author, Thomas Jefferson, left no record as to whether or not he was listening, or watching the reaction of the crowd.

On July 9, General Washington ordered the Declaration to be read aloud to his troops in New York City. Papa attended that reading, as he will later tell you.

On July 18, Abigail Adams stood with a crowd in the very square where British troops had once fired upon a Boston mob; on that sacred spot, she listened to the Declaration as it was read from a balcony of the Massachusetts State House.

Wherever the great document was read, church bells rang day and night, bonfires were lit on the commons, and tavern signs bearing any references to royal Britain were torn down and burned.

The news finally reached Georgia in mid-August. A coffin bearing King George's "political presence" was carried through the streets of Savannah in a joyous funeral procession.

The United States of America, the new nation in the New World, after one hundred sixty-seven years of fervent preparation, was finally born.

∞

Chapter Fifty-Six

Caleb, continuing as family historian.

I was conceived in October of 1775, in a log hut built by my Uncle Henry, in the encampment of General George Washington's Continental Army, near the village of Cambridge, Massachusetts.

I was two months advanced in my as yet unborn life when my mother and father stood atop a hill on Christmas Day and wondered whether I would grow up, or even be born, with both of my parents still alive.

I was not quite three months old in January of 1776 when, night after night, my father stood beside a campfire and read Thomas Paine's "Common Sense" to an audience of hundreds of soldiers, who went to bed night after night with their faith renewed.

I was just over three months old when Henry Knox and Uncle Judd arrived with enough cannons that David could now put a rock into his sling.

I was four and a half months old when my father, Uncle Henry, and Uncle Judd built a fortress of sticks atop the Dorchester Heights, while my mother waited and prayed in Harvard Chapel.

I was nearly five months old when Goliath boarded his boat and sailed in haste out of Boston. And maybe, though I cannot claim to remember, but maybe, while nestled in my mother's womb, I heard the bells of Boston ringing day and night in celebration.

I was five and a half months old when my mother drove the wagon south on the twelve-day march to New York City. Uncle Henry had built a frame of hoops, and my father had sewn a cover of sailcloth, so the wagon could serve my mother as a sort of home on wheels. Her horsehair mattress was nestled between my father's cobbler's tools and baskets of potatoes from the farm. Sir William pulled the wagon in a train of army wagons through the colonies of Massachusetts, Rhode Island, and Connecticut, to the colony of New York. Still unborn, I was now traveling further than my mother had traveled during her entire life. She tells me that she was uncomfortably aware of me during every mile of that long and anxious journey, for I was beginning to protrude into the world just beneath her hands holding the reins.

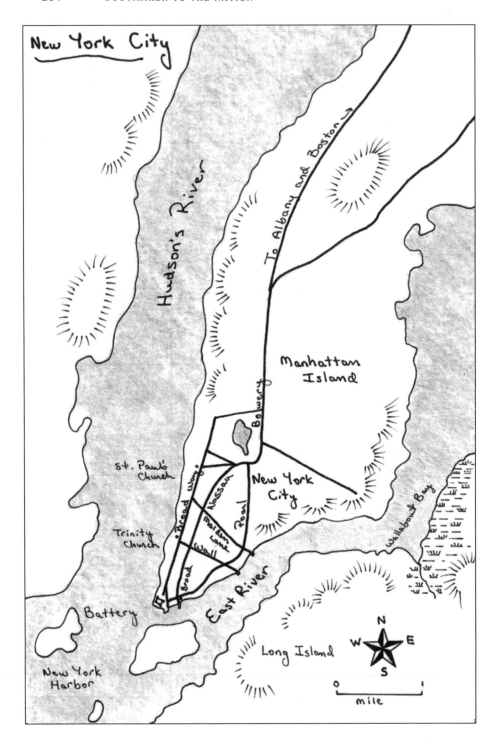

New York City

Hudson's River

To Albany and Boston

Manhattan Island

Bowery

St. Paul's Church

New York City

Broadway

Nassau

Maiden Lane

Pearl

Trinity Church

Wall

Wallabout Bay

Broad

East River

Battery

New York Harbor

Long Island

N
W E
S

0 _____ 1
mile

I was six months old when my mother crossed Kingsbridge onto Manhattan Island, then drove thirteen miles south to New York City at the southern tip. She found lodging in a three-story, red brick boarding-house called the Nassau Inn, on the corner of Nassau Street and Maiden Lane. The Inn was near General Washington's headquarters at Mortier's House, just north of the Battery, where Mama continued her duties as the General's scribe. She often worked at the same table with Lady Washington, who also copied some of the General's multitude of letters and orders and requisitions. The two secretaries helped each other to fathom the General's hurried handwriting. Mama received much welcome advice from Lady Washington, the mother of two grown children, concerning Mama's own impending child (me).

I was seven months old in May of 1776, when news arrived from London that King George had hired several thousand German soldiers to help him fight his war against the colonials. Though I at the time had little opinion on the matter, most Americans were outraged that their King, who had refused to read their Olive Branch Petition, now attempted to purchase a victory in America with mercenary troops.

I was eight months old, and kicking smartly, in June of 1776, while Thomas Jefferson labored at his desk in a rented second-story parlor in a brick house on Market Street in Philadelphia. For seventeen days in June, he wrote the phrases and arguments and justifications that had been kicking smartly in his mind for years.

I was eight and a quarter months old when, on June 29, the largest fleet of warships that Great Britain had ever launched began to arrive in New York Harbor, with the intention of capturing the city where we now lived.

I was eight and a half months old when, on July 3, 1776, nine thousand redcoats were transported in cutters from their transport ships to Staten Island, six miles south of Manhattan Island. They met no more resistance than a few muskets fired at them. The majority of the farmers on Staten Island were Loyalists, who welcomed the British troops with fresh milk, and meat, and vegetables in exchange for good British coins.

On the following day in Philadelphia, Jefferson's Declaration was approved by a Congress representing thirteen colonies. Congress thus became the still undefined government of thirteen States, each fully independent from Great Britain. On July 4, 1776, the King lost all of his colonies, and gained thirteen States with whom he was at war.

I was twelve days shy of My Birth when, at six o'clock in the evening on July 9, my father formed with his regiment on the common near his barracks (in the angle between the Broad Way and Bowery Lane) to hear an officer read to them the entire Declaration of Independence. The lieutenant had to pause frequently in his reading while the men cheered at their new citizenship, their new firmness, their new purpose. Never mind that New York Harbor was filled with hundreds of British war ships. Never mind that aboard those ships, thousands of redcoats threatened to attack Manhattan Island at any moment. Let the British commence their assault on the ditched and barricaded fortress of New York City. The proud defenders of American independence, American freedom, American equality, had whipped the British in Boston, and they would whip them again in New York.

Genevieve, at eight and a half months.

The owner of the clean and comfortable boardinghouse on Nassau Street, Mr. Elias Pennington, brought home one of the first broadsheet copies of the Declaration to appear in New York City (a copy actually printed in Philadelphia, then sold on the streets of New York before New York printers could replicate and sell their own copies). Being a man of great talent as an innkeeper, but of limited ability as a reader, Eli knocked on my door on the afternoon of Tuesday, July 9, and asked me (knowing that I kept a number of books in my room) if I would join a small company in the dining room, so we might each take a turn reading the broadsheet aloud to all assembled. I of course assented. After straightening my dress (more like a blue tent) over my enormous round belly (the dress a gift from Benjamin, from a shop on the Broad Way), I descended the stairs to the dining room and took my place with a dozen boardinghouse guests around the mahogany table.

Mrs. Patricia Pennington, so generous to me that she had become almost a sister, set a pitcher before me of cold water from the pump. On those hot days of July, with a most boisterous child kicking within me, I drank considerably more water than ever before in my life.

Eli, seated at the head of the table, began the reading. Holding the broadsheet with both hands, he declared,

"In CONGRESS, July 4, 1776, The unanimous Declaration
of the thirteen united States of America, . . ."

He then passed the document to a woolens merchant from Albany, and that gentleman read the first sentence. Thus we passed the Declaration from hand to hand around the table, each of us taking a turn (some in a most faulty manner) at reading the long but clearly stated sentences. As I proved to be the best reader among us, the Declaration, having gone once around the table, remained at Mistress Pennington's request in my hands, and I finished the reading.

In the opening paragraph, I was surprised and proud to learn that we, not as a nation, not as thirteen separate states, but as "one people," were "to assume among the powers of the earth" a "separate and equal station." We Americans were to stand together, equal to the French, the Spanish, the English, the Russians, as one of the nations of the world.

We were entitled to our new stature by "the Laws of Nature and Nature's God." Though we were new upon the stage of the world, our place, our role, our purpose, had been waiting for us.

We then had the graciousness to state: that if one people decided to separate from another, "a decent respect to the opinions of mankind requires that they should declare the causes which impel them to the separation." Thus, we regarded the other nations of the world not with belligerence, or with haughtiness, nor an inward-looking disregard for our neighbors, but with "respect." That attitude was to be the bedrock, the foundation, of all our foreign alliances: neither servility nor aggression, but "a decent respect."

When I heard the words of the second sentence, I was sensible that my heart beat with a more powerful stroke, thumping (or so it felt) both upon my ribs and upon the child nestled beneath my heart in my womb. Those unexpected words, "We hold these truths to be self-evident, that all men are created equal," had been written, I knew immediately, for my unborn son or daughter. Without thought or intention, my hands reached up and clapped together, catching those words, "all men are created equal," as they hovered above the table, holding them, and bringing them back toward myself that I might press them against my belly. The others around the table perhaps thought I had clapped my hands together in a sudden manifestation of prayer. And so in a way I had. For I acknowledged those five words to be divine: written with a human hand, but written by a man who finally, after these thousands of years, cast away his pride and turned his ear to God.

We were endowed by our Creator with "certain unalienable rights." That was a strange word—unalienable—in the conversation of parlors and taverns, but we all knew what it meant: what was unalienable was not able to be made a stranger to us. Such rights had been given to us by God, and could not be taken away. They must always be as much a part of ourselves as the breath of life.

Among our unalienable rights were "life, liberty, and the pursuit of happiness." The old phrase, repeated for a century by political philosophers, "life, liberty, and property," had been changed. The Congress in Philadelphia, speaking for the American people, had replaced the quest for property with a quest for happiness. Again, I felt a touch of divine intelligence. For even the lowliest among us would seek a better life for her children.

We now heard the astonishing statement, "to secure these rights, governments are instituted among men, deriving their just powers from the consent of the governed." We paused, then read the phrase again, "deriving their just powers from the consent of the governed." We knew what "just powers" meant: authority based on justice. Not on the whim of a tyrant.

Yes, we would build our own nation according to the consent of the governed, which was me. Benjamin. Mama. Papa. Henry and Judd. And the child who was kicking now with such sturdy thumps that I caught my breath, and blushed when Mistress Pennington smiled at me from across the table.

We would give our consent. Or withhold our consent. The document—which I held reverently in my hands—had given us, each one of us, a new voice.

And more: "That whenever any form of government becomes destructive of these ends, it is the right of the people to alter or to abolish it, and to institute new government, laying its foundation on such principles and organizing its powers in such form, as to them shall seem most likely to effect their safety and happiness."

Never before in human history had the architects of government given to the people permission to alter or abolish that government, and to replace it with one of their own design. We ourselves thus became the architects, and the builders, of our own political future. Here was an unprecedented faith in the abilities of the common people. No previous ruler had ever so believed in us, had ever so trusted us. Had ever so wanted us to succeed.

We read that no government should be overthrown for "light and transient causes." But when a people suffer from "a long train of abuses and usurpations," then "it is their right, it is their duty, to throw off such government, and to provide new guards for their future security."

Congress then listed a multitude of abuses and usurpations, most of them committed by "the present King of England." More than half of the Declaration of Independence was devoted to these twenty-eight charges, each one a slap in the King's face.

As I read them, slowly and clearly, I was taken back to my early girlhood, when Papa and I, at the Green Dragon Tavern, had listened to James Otis rage against the King. Mr. Otis was still alive, now living in Andover, but the poor man had lost his reason. How gratified he would be today to know that delegates from all thirteen colonies at last shared his opinion of our tyrannical King.

One stern accusation was directed not at the King, but "our British brethren." Though the American Congress had appealed to them, "They too have been deaf to the voice of justice and consanguinity." "The ties of our common kindred" must therefore be broken. Americans from now on would "hold them, as we hold the rest of mankind, enemies in war, in peace friends."

The Declaration concluded with a final paragraph, which presented to the world the name of our new nation: "The United States of America." Congress appealed "to the Supreme Judge of the world for the rectitude of our intentions." Every step in this political journey had been made with an eye toward the principles of God.

Then, "by the authority of the good people of these Colonies" (the *tenth* mention of the "people" in this document), the Declaration stated, "That these United Colonies are, and of right ought to be Free and Independent States." Specifically, "they have full power to levy war, conclude peace, contract alliances, establish commerce, and to do all other acts and things which independent States may of right do."

The war was thus no longer a civil war, but a war between nations. Further, as Eli Pennington noted, the United States of America now had full legal right to negotiate with France as a potential and powerful ally in our war against Britain.

In the final sentence of the Declaration, the delegates in Congress once again acknowledged their faith in God: "with a firm reliance on the protection of Divine Providence." They concluded with a pledge to their fellow delegates: "we mutually pledge to each other our lives, our fortunes and our sacred honor."

The final word in this address to mankind, to the King, and to the American people, was "honor." Their reputation, their honor, was so important to the delegates, so fundamental a part of their identity, that they termed it "sacred."

Congress had done far more than simply declare our independence; more than give birth to a free nation; more than define our fundamental rights. Our delegates in Congress had given to *the people* a profound responsibility. We were not free simply to pursue our happiness. We were granted our freedom only if we strove to guarantee that within our new nation, "all men are created equal." Yes, we had new freedoms, new liberties. But we also had a very new job. A job whose challenge we must accept, lest we sully "our sacred honor."

It was without a doubt the most difficult job in the world: to view each person as my equal. But in the performance of that job, in the daily striving, we would be superbly guided on our path toward life, liberty, and the pursuit of happiness.

And further, we would be guided on our path toward understanding the divine intelligence of our Creator.

When we had finished reading, Mistress Pennington served tea.

As an African woman with tribal scars on her cheeks set the cups around the table and then brought in the kettle, I began to have my first misgivings.

Benjamin, a most anxious father-to-be.

At six o'clock in the evening of July 9, when the companies of our regiment formed an open square on the worn grassy common in front of our barracks, we could only guess how Congress would formulate our break with Britain. Would Philadelphia take into its hands the power formerly held by Parliament? Would the thirteen colonies each go their own way, with little but the war to unite them? Would some powerful landowner assert his rights as our new king, in the guise of some title such as President? And would we, the soldiers, continue to fight and die so that ship owners and merchants could return to the old days of profits untroubled by taxes?

We assembled on that warm July evening, as the sun disappeared behind the rooftops and chimneys along the Broad Way, not to hear the latest list of resolves. We wanted to know *why* we were fighting this endless war.

As a lieutenant read with a voice loud enough for all to hear, we realized that the lawyers and landowners gathered in their assembly hall in Philadelphia had truly understood us. They seemed to have sat with us around our campfires night after night, to have listened to us, down to the last humble farmer and cobbler, as we spoke of our fear and our hopes, of our anger and our dreams. They seemed to have cast the old dusty history books into the flames, then to have penned something entirely new. Aye, they signed their fine names to that document in defiance of the King, but what they wrote, every soldier among us would have been willing to sign as well.

The soldiers interrupted the reading with frequent and hearty cheers. We felt emboldened, indignant, and vindicated: our defense of our American rights was justified by every phrase that we heard, and our mission on behalf of mankind was laid before us. The best minds in America believed in us, as did the Creator Himself. Every soldier among us felt a bit nobler, for our work would reach down through the ages.

Immediately after the reading of the Declaration, I stepped forward and asked my captain for permission to leave camp. As I had no duty until later that evening, he assented.

I hurried down the Broad Way, where the shops were closed but the lamps not yet lit, to Maiden Lane, which I followed a block east to Genevieve's boardinghouse. I bounded up the steps, then glanced into the dining room: Genevieve and the other boarders were just finishing their suppers. I spoke briefly with her, shared a hearty patriotic toast with Eli Pennington, then I took my wife by her hand and led her not up to her room, but out the door and down the steps to the street, so that we might walk in the lavender dusk as new citizens in our new nation.

As we followed Maiden Lane to Pearl Street, just above the docks, we spoke with excitement in our voices. And we savored in silence the gratitude in our hearts. The carts along the piers were quiet now. Men standing watch on the deck of a moored freighter gazed at Genevieve, perhaps glad after a long voyage to see a woman expecting a child.

My bride and I (for so I still liked to think of her) walked along Pearl Street past Wall Street (where the Dutch had built their protective wall of timbers across the island over a century ago), to Whitehall and the Battery at the very southern tip of the island. We did not look south toward the enormous fleet of British ships anchored in the harbor, but instead gazed westward toward vermilion clouds blazing above the shore of New Jersey, and their reflected russet sheen on the mouth of the Hudson.

We walked up Whitehall past the old fort with its four bastions, where Dutch sentries had once stood along the ramparts, where British sentries had once stood along the ramparts, and where I myself had a dozen times stood upon the ramparts, alert to the movement of every sail in the harbor. I had often wondered how well the old earthen walls would stand up to a broadside from the *Phoenix* or the *Rose*, but I said not a word of such musings to Genevieve.

We paused at the Bowling Green, a small park just north of the fort, where the Dutch, after a long day in their shops and counting-houses, had rolled their heavy balls across the grass and smoked their clay pipes and took a breath of air fresh from the sea. Standing outside a wrought-iron fence that wrapped around the Green, we stared with defiance at an equestrian statue of King George III upon a pedestal. As proud and regal as he looked, the King might well ride his horse down to the wharf and board one of his frigates for home. For that oval patch of grass was ours now, and his horse was not welcome to nibble even a blade of it.

As we walked up the Broad Way—the street lamps were lit, as were the windows in shops, taverns and mansions along both sides of the boulevard—a bell in the spire of Trinity Church ahead of us tolled eight o'clock. And then the deep bell kept ringing, joined by a choir of smaller bells in the steeple, as if the sexton could not refrain upon New York's first evening of independence from a bit of celebration.

Reaching up into the last glow of dusk, the stately white spire of Trinity Church rose twice as tall as any of the buildings around it, even those it faced on Wall Street. The spire rose far above the architecture of mere habitation and commerce, and thus pointed toward the heaven from which our blessings had come. Genevieve and I paused in front of the church and gazed nearly straight up at its towering spire, while its bells rang out over the city, over the harbor, over the sea.

Congress had given us much more than freedom from Britain. The delegates in Philadelphia had given us their blessing, as a father honors his child with a blessing of approval. Their vote for independence had also been a vote of faith. And for that faith in the common people, I felt profoundly grateful. The bells aloft in the Trinity spire tolled with a joyful cadence of celebration. But more: they tolled a joyful prayer.

Beckoned by those bells, people began to emerge from their door-ways. They mingled in the increasingly crowded street. Far up the

Broad Way, we could see that a bonfire had been lit on a corner of the common. Genevieve and I might well have strolled all night, listening as other churches now joined their chimes, but Mother (for so I had begun to think of her) was feeling her condition. Flushed and weary, she took my arm as we continued the last three blocks to Maiden Lane, and thence to the Nassau Inn. Its two lamps shone brightly over red brick steps rising to a handsome white door.

In the lobby, I commended my wife to the devoted care of Mistress Pennington, who accompanied Genevieve upstairs to her room. Back out in the street, I waved up to my bride in the window. In the glow of a lamp, she patted her belly and then waved to me, as if the both of them, mother and child, were bidding me Good Night.

With all my heart, I wanted to stay up in that small room with my wife, while she carried her burden through those last days and nights. But I could not, because I had to stand duty every night as a sentry: for four hours, I would stare across the dark harbor at the hundreds of tiny lamps aboard the British fleet, lamps by which the enemy sharpened their blades and oiled their firelocks.

I walked alone up Nassau Street to our barracks, and my musket.

That same evening, no more than an hour later, I stared down from a rampart of the old Dutch fort at a roaring mob of soldiers who tossed their ropes over King George and his horse, then pulled until they toppled the gilded lead statue from its pedestal. A boisterous crowd roared with approval as a soldier cut off the King's head by chopping with an axe into the soft metal.

The following morning at muster, an outraged General Washington reprimanded the troops for their breach of military order.

We learned a few days later that the lead of all but the King's head had been taken by ship to Litchfield, Connecticut, where it was melted down and then molded into tens of thousands of musket balls.

Thus did the Congress, and thus did the King, each make their contribution on the ninth of July to a people who would fight with a new faith in their hearts.

ℰ𝒪

Chapter Fifty-Seven

Caleb, almost born.

On the afternoon of Friday, July 12, nine days before I entered the world, two British warships sailed up Hudson's River in defiance of our ineffective cannons along the Manhattan shoreline. With a favorable wind and tide pushing them northward, the *Phoenix* and the *Rose* sailed well above the city. Had they been ordered to do so, they could have disembarked troops above us, thus trapping much of the Continental Army on the southern tip of Manhattan Island.

If frigates could sail up Hudson's River, they could likewise sail up the East River along the opposite shore of the long thin island. Two fleets of ships could easily surround us, then disembark both troops and artillery. Our entire Continental Army would be helpless.

My mother remembers the day those two warships sailed north of New York City as one of the worst in her long nine months of wartime pregnancy. For I might well, upon the day of my birth, have been born a prisoner.

However, American troops further up Hudson's River launched several burning rafts in an attempt to set the two British warships afire. As the flaming rafts drifted toward them, the *Phoenix* and the *Rose* both retreated back to their fleet in the harbor.

My mother spent the last two weeks of her pregnancy in complete confinement at the boardinghouse. She dared not, her time being so near, risk the sudden commencement of labor within the busy rooms of the General's headquarters. (Lady Washington had by now traveled to the safety of Philadelphia, for General Washington knew that a British attack on New York City could begin on any day at dawn.)

My father tried to visit my mother every day, between supper at six and sentry duty at eight in the evening. He tried to arrange for a doctor to visit her, but with over ten thousand American soldiers camped on both Manhattan and Long Islands, the few physicians who served in the army had little time for a pregnant courier.

So my father looked elsewhere. Thus my mother (and I) came under the care of an exceptionally skilled midwife.

Back in April, during the Continental Army's march from Boston to New York, the troops reached the bank of Hudson's River (which they then followed south to Manhattan Island). Johannes Kesslaer sent a message with Iroquois runners *up* Hudson's River, then westward along the Mohawk River, to his wife in their distant Iroquois village. She, a midwife of the Oneida tribe, Turtle clan, answered his summons by paddling downstream with her brother in a canoe, a canoe laden with medicinal herbs for the hospital that Johannes planned to establish in New York City.

She's Carrying Flowers and her brother, His Long Road, paddled with the current of the Mohawk, then with the current of the Hudson, until they approached, at the mouth of the enormous river, the strange habitation of the White Man. To the surprise of New Yorkers working on the wharf, the Oneidas in their birch canoe docked in a tiny space between two Spanish frigates. His Long Road stayed in the canoe with the cargo of medicine while She's Carrying Flowers, as undaunted by crowds and carriages on the streets of New York as she was undaunted by wolves in her native forest, accosted a dozen soldiers and officers, asking for Dokarames Tacher (Doctor James Thacher, chief physician of the Continental Army, the man whom Johannes had told her to seek). She found the Army surgeon at his military hospital in King's College on the Broad Way. He cordially directed her south down the boulevard: Johannes was tending his patients in a sail maker's loft near the Battery.

She's Carrying Flowers returned to her canoe and paddled with His Long Road to the Battery wharf. By asking repeatedly for "Minister Kasler," she found Johannes in his second-floor loft, where he was tending people of a sort she had never seen before. The Negro hospital was at one end of a huge room, a room otherwise filled with heaps of folded canvas and barrels of rope. The beds were naught but straw on the wooden floor. But a fresh breeze from the harbor blew in through several open windows. And the sun crossing the southern sky shone brightly into the loft.

She's Carrying Flowers became at once the chief physician of the Negro hospital. She opened her leather bundles, then simmered her teas not over a campfire, but in pots atop an iron stove. Though no one made an official tally, word spread through the summer of 1776 in New York City that a greater proportion of soldiers emerged healthy from the Negro hospital than from the Army hospital. This was perhaps because the Negroes were less crowded, perhaps because the mysterious herbs and roots which She's Carrying Flowers had brought were fresh from her forest. Or perhaps it was because she infused a calm strength into the spirits of her patients.

Outside of the Negro hospital, she had only one white patient, my mother. She's Carrying Flowers understood little of the White Man's ways; she certainly did not comprehend the economic and political causes which had brought their war to her country. But she understood sickness and the art of healing with an almost supernatural gift. She believed that if she could help to heal the White Man (or in this case, one white woman), then perhaps the White People, when their war was done, would help to heal the anger and fear and confusion between her people and theirs.

Her generosity, she believed, would not be forgotten.

When my mother opened her eyes at dawn on the morning of July 15, 1776, she discovered a black-haired woman wearing the same sort of beaded deerskin that Johannes wore, seated on a chair beside the boardinghouse bed, staring at her with dark and questioning eyes.

Behind the woman stood Johannes, who introduced her: he spoke first in words that my mother could not understand, then explained in English that his wife, She's Carrying Flowers, was a renowned midwife among the Iroquois people. (He was always to speak this way in his wife's presence: first in Oneida, and then in English. There was thus never a sentence that She's Carrying Flowers could not understand.)

Mama trusted the minister who had married her. Accordingly, she was willing to trust the midwife to bring her first child into the world.

After Johannes left the small bedroom, She's Carrying Flowers pulled down Mama's blanket and motioned for Mama to draw up her shift. She touched Mama's belly with such skillful and gentle fingers that Mama lay overwhelmed with serene gratitude.

I, no doubt feeling the touch of those pressing fingers, knew neither gratitude nor confidence. I simply kept kicking.

Caleb, making his triumphant entry.

On Sunday morning, the 21st of July, 1776, I announced myself with a vigorous wail, calling out the third-story window to the infant nation that another equal American had successfully arrived. Though no cannons boomed, no bells chimed, no hurrahs were cheered in the streets, Papa heard me from the downstairs lobby, where he had sat for several hours with Elias Pennington and Uncle Henry, sharing a deep, worried, fatherly silence.

Papa dashed up the stairs, tapped anxiously on the door, then waited for another several minutes while She's Carrying Flowers washed the howling infant with a warm herbal bath of her own making, wrapped him in a length of homespun linen, then placed him in the bed with his mother's arm wrapped around him.

Finally the midwife opened the door. My father, with Uncle Henry close behind him, entered the room.

Papa tentatively touched his finger to my wrinkled red brow. Then he leaned over me and kissed my exhausted, delighted mother.

Thus, though I was born into a nation at war, I was born as well into a family very much at peace.

Benjamin, a father and soldier both,
one foot in heaven, one foot in hell.

For exactly a month, until the great thunderstorm on the night of August 21, and the landing of British troops on Long Island on August 22, we lived in a world of waiting and worry. But we lived as well, Genevieve and I and our son Caleb, in a world of deep peace and immeasurable happiness. Aye, looking back I can say that we had pursued our happiness and we had found it: a rich, joyous happiness that neither Genevieve nor I could ever before have imagined.

During that same month, our life and liberty were threatened every day.

I don't know why the British waited so long. Their enormous fleet had arrived in New York Harbor at the end of June, but aside from the landing of troops on Staten Island, they made no move until the last week of August. We could only guess that General Howe knew, from his spies, how well we had fortified both the fringes of New York City and the Heights of Brooklyn on Long Island.

As long as we had farms and villages in America, we could find more men, more soldiers. But every soldier in General Howe's infantry had to be transported by ship three thousand miles across the Atlantic.

He had a great portion of the King's army at his command, but he also had a great portion of the King's treasury, not to be wasted. When finally he made a move, it would not be to win a battle, but to finish the war.

So Genevieve and Caleb and I—our family—had a month of peace together. I could usually manage to visit my wife and son every evening, between my hasty supper at six and muster for sentry duty at eight. During Caleb's first week, I sat in a rocking chair beside Genevieve's bed, talking and laughing with her while I tried to hold our wriggling infant. We kept the window open day and night, for a fine sea breeze filled the room. The window faced east, and Genevieve, from her bed, liked to watch the bright morning sun rising above the rooftops of New York while she nursed Caleb.

When Genevieve was able to get up and walk a bit, the first place she wanted to visit was the paddock on the common, for she missed her Sir William. On a fine sunny afternoon, we took (I carried) our week-old boy on his first journey along the bustling streets of New York, to meet his first horse. John Lally had been looking after Sir William; he was in the saddle cantering gracefully around the common when we arrived. Genevieve called to them. Sir William cocked his ears. The horse pranced over and affectionately nuzzled her. But when she took Caleb from my arms and introduced the fussy infant with tiny waving fists, Sir William's large eye stared with skepticism at whatever it was she was holding.

John Lally offered his congratulations. "My bonny lass has delivered another sort of message. Orders from heaven, sure."

Then he asked Genevieve, "While I'm exercising this fine horse, would you mind if I taught him to jump?"

"To jump?" asked Genevieve, intrigued.

"Aye, lass. A courier wants a horse that can jump. We can't always take the carriage road, can we? Sometimes it's across the field and over a hedge."

He nodded toward a low fence made of rails, about four feet high, standing in the middle of the common. "With your permission?"

Before I could say a word about Caleb's mother not needing a horse that could jump hedgerows, Genevieve answered, "Sir William could jump a rooftop if he had to."

John Lally spun away and cantered toward the fence.

They had no doubt been practicing, for Sir William sailed over the rails with an easy grace. By the pleased look on Genevieve's face, I could see that General Washington's courier meant to be back in the saddle as soon as she could, jumping stone walls and barns, and for all I knew, the moon.

While Caleb's father cobbled shoes, and changed the lad, and sang him to sleep in the rhythmic sanctuary of a rocking chair.

During that gift of a month of peace (or as much peace as two parents can have with a baby in the room), Genevieve and I sat at a table in the boardinghouse parlor and wrote a letter to Lincoln, then a letter to London, announcing the birth of our healthy child. (We mentioned in much less detail the mysterious pause in the war.) I did most of the writing, although Genevieve added her own note at the bottom of each letter, warmly greeting her parents, warmly greeting mine. We wanted to share our happiness by describing the small daily adventures in Caleb's young life.

We were determined not to let a mere war take that away from us.

Genevieve, a farm girl with a city-born boy,
far from home in New York State,
aching to show our Caleb to my parents.

There is the smell of the earth in the spring when the snow finally melts and the sun shines warmly on the dark naked fields.

There is the smell in the barn of oats and cows and leather.

There is the smell on an evening in May when the apple trees first open their blossoms, and we open all the windows so we can sleep with apple perfume drifting through the house.

There is the clean fresh smell when the first big drops of summer rain drench the dust in the yard.

There is the deep rich heavenly smell on a summer's night of the grass that Papa cut with his scythe that afternoon in the meadow.

There are all the blended smells in Mama's herb garden, when the August sun shines on it with the last of summer's baking warmth.

There is the smell as the pump fills the bucket with water from deep in the earth, a smell of stones, and of cold, and of time long ago.

There is the smell of Mama's applesauce simmering in a pot on the stove, mixed with the smell of wood smoke, and the faint scent of the soap on Mama's cheek when she kisses me.

There is the smell of maple leaves heaped on the ground, after they have lost their bright colors and have been wet for several nights of rain, when I shuffle through them on the way to the barn.

There is the smell of horse sweat on Sir William, and later in my clothes, when we have been galloping beneath an October moon.

There is the smell in the Lincoln Meetinghouse of old wood and candle smoke when we first walk in.

But the most beautiful of all, though I never before knew it, is the smell when I rub my nose back and forth in the tuft of hair on a baby's head.

8

Chapter Fifty-Eight

Benjamin, on 21 August, 1776,
the day and the night of the great storm.

19 October, 1826
Does she remember about
the day after tomorrow?
She hasn't said a word.

Never before had I seen a sky turn green. As I hurried that August afternoon up Broad Street to be with Genevieve, the sky above the slate rooftops and brick chimneys was a pale sickly green. A few thin clouds swept over the city from the west, portending some strange weather on its way.

I had been working all day with a squad of soldiers at the fish market dock, unloading not fish from a sloop, but long crates of muskets and kegs of lead balls which had been smuggled past the British fleet in New York Harbor. Exhausting labor it was, hefting up from the damp hold the heavy kegs of lead to lads on deck, who then carried the kegs across a gangplank to a waiting cart. Much fewer were the kegs of gunpowder; certainly not enough to fire all those lead balls.

The rumor on the wharf promised a frigate sailing from a Danish island in the West Indies, laden with powder for our garrison. It was due to arrive, we heard, last week, tomorrow, any day now.

No doubt the British troops camped on Staten Island had enough powder. And balls, and bayonets.

We kept a sharp eye on the harbor all through the afternoon, for a west wind blew with ever stronger gusts, until the choppy blue water became a turbulent gray. (We ourselves were in the lee of the island, out of the wind.) By four o'clock, when we were relieved by another squad of men, waves were breaking white as they swept toward Long Island. Not a single vessel sailed in the churning harbor; smaller craft were moored along the wharves, while the British warships trailed to the west under bare poles at the end of their taut anchor lines.

Whatever storm was approaching across the American continent threatened to blow half the British fleet onto the coast of Long Island, and the other half out to sea. Good riddance to them all. Let me take my Caleb and Genevieve back to her farm in Lincoln and there help

John and Judd to harvest the corn.

With our arms and backs mightily sore from hefting all those kegs of lead, the lads and I stopped at Fraunce's Tavern on Pearl Street for a bowl of hot barley soup. We treated ourselves to a bowl of blackberries and cream (the wild berries had been picked that morning, as Samuel Fraunce told us, in a meadow at the northern end of Manhattan Island). Of course, we partook as well of a tankard or two of ale.

I might well have fallen asleep in my chair, had I not been a man in love, so profoundly in love that every hour away from my son and bride were like an hour cast to the empty wind.

When we stepped out from the door of Fraunce's, we looked up with a weather eye and discovered the sky was green. "Lightnin', sure," said one of the lads. "This is Ben Franklin weather."

We hurried together up Broad Street. A pair of horses pulling a cart were exceedingly nervous; they could sense better than we could the sort of storm that was coming.

Beyond the crossing of Wall Street, Broad became Nassau Street. Soon I spotted the third-floor window, open, where my family dwelled at the Nassau Inn. My heart even today holds a warm spot for that sturdy brick building and its generous proprietors. Patricia and Elias Pennington provided my Genevieve, in the midst of an unpredictable war, with all the safety and dignity of a home.

I told the lads I would meet them at the barracks, for of course we had sentry duty that night. Then I hurried up the steps and swung open the big white boardinghouse door.

When I passed one of the boarders on the stairway, I nodded an embarrassed greeting, for I was truly begrimed with filth from the sloop's hold. But never mind: I hurried down the third floor hallway to her door (number 312, as I still recall), and I knocked the rhythmic greeting of an excited father.

"Come in!" she called with her lovely voice.

I pulled open the oaken door, saw mother and son sitting up in bed, Caleb on Genevieve's lap. As I stepped into the room, fragrant with the smell of clean linen, I too was home.

I sat in a chair beside the bed and listened with rapt fascination as Genevieve described the multitude of Caleb's doings since yesterday afternoon. Each nursing, each nap, each awakening during the night was a newsworthy event. Too dirty that day to hold him myself, I was content to watch my son squirm and yawn and blink on Genevieve's lap. Already I could see a bit of my father in the nose and eyes.

The blue curtains flapped at the window as a gust of cool damp air suddenly punched into the room. Looking out over the rooftops, I saw dark clouds scudding across that strange pale green sky.

"Weather coming," I said, though of course she knew it.

"Hmmm," she replied, with that brief acknowledgement we both used when referring to something we knew was there, but wished it weren't . . . like wagonloads of field artillery rattling up a cobblestone street. Like a fleet of warships clustered in the harbor. Like the winter that was coming, and the battle that would necessarily start before the weather grew cold.

She looked at me, her eyes sunken and tired from far more than nursing a squalling child every few hours through the night.

Then she asked a question which she had never asked before. "What was it like on the ship? Out on the ocean? What was it like . . . with just the sun and the wind and the waves?"

She knew about the flogging, of course. She knew about Hench and what he did to Nathaniel. About General Thomas Graves, sailing from London to close the port of Boston. She also knew how much I disliked talking about that voyage. I hadn't said a word about the *Lively* for at least a year.

She wanted to hear about something far away from sentries and barricades and cannons. Far away from waiting, waiting.

"What I remember best," I began, "is working with the lads up in the rigging." I smiled, thinking back to that exuberant time high in the fresh, constant wind, where a seagull's cry meant more to me than any voice down on deck. "During the first week, the poor cobbler ached in every muscle, every bone, from struggling to work the sail up there. My bare feet hadn't yet grown leather soles. My fingers gathered canvas until they were naught but bare nubs. My arms hurt so much from hefting the sail, they might well have fallen off my shoulders and clattered on the deck like sticks of firewood."

Genevieve's brown eyes were watching me, amused, intrigued, and full of sympathy. She seemed to have forgotten the gathering storm outside the window.

"But worst of all," I continued, rubbing my ribs, "every time we furled the t'gallant, we had to lean as far as we could over the spar, so we could grip handfuls of canvas. We leaned with the bottom edge of our ribs over that jouncing, jolting, thumping spar, and oooooh, my ribs were so bruised I could hardly breathe."

"You see, Caleb," said Genevieve, facing the infant toward me (though his blue eyes continued to wander here and there), "what your poor father endured on his way to finding us." Her happy eyes, filled with love, studied me, waiting for more.

"The sun and the wind and the waves," I said, for it was about them that she wanted to hear, "are out there every day, waiting for us. The same as blackberries are waiting for us in a meadow, and apples in an orchard. Freedom and beauty and bounty and joy. And if a man and a woman and a child do not partake of them now and then, it's a rebuke against the good Lord who made them."

I paused, for I was struck by an idea, an idea which I savored for a moment before I told her, "When our lad is old enough . . . and when trading sloops along the coast carry naught but timber and rice, tobacco and potatoes . . . I'd like to find a sloop at the Boston wharf that would take us out for a day at sea."

How her brown eyes brightened! For the first time in our marriage, we reached beyond my having to leave again, again, again for sentry duty; beyond the distant thunder of a cannon firing, beyond the flat crack of a sniper's rifle; beyond green firewood and a military privy and the trail of mud . . . We reached together toward that time when the sun and sea and waves might fill an entire day. Toward the time when a boy might point and shout with excitement at a dolphin leaping off the bow.

Toward the time when love between a man and a woman might flourish without the stranglehold of war.

The curtains shook like frenzied ghosts. Thunder rumbled far to the west, over New Jersey. When the first rain fell with a loud wet patter in the street, I jumped to close the window.

A flash filled the room, the street, the sky, followed by a crack so loud, the floor of the boardinghouse shook. Caleb shrieked. I latched the window, then turned to Genevieve. She hugged the wailing child and stared at me with a deeper fear than I had ever seen in her face . . . fear of far more than a summer thunderstorm.

And not a thing I could do about it.

At seven o'clock, the sentry had to leave to fetch his musket at the barracks.

At seven o'clock, the young mother might be a day, two days, a week from widowhood.

I sat down again in the chair, then I spoke with a voice that tried to hold in abeyance the thunderclaps beating on the tiny rooftops of New

York City, and the bolts of lightning that threatened every church spire, every ship's mast, every sentry standing guard with his musket pointed at the sky. "There was something more aboard the ship."

She watched me, her brown eyes believing in me.

"The frigate had two kinds of rigging, running rigging and standing rigging. The running rigging were lines that ran up and down through pulleys. They hoisted and lowered the sails, and trimmed the sails to the wind. The standing rigging were fixed lines that supported the masts. The standing rigging supported us too, for we climbed a web of steps woven up the shrouds."

Genevieve unbuttoned her shift and tried to calm Caleb by nursing him.

"The running rigging was white, whereas the standing rigging was black. The halyards were white lines, but the shrouds and ratlin's were black. Black with tar. That made life aloft simple: whatever was black, we could trust with our weight. But whatever was white might drop us, if we grabbed hold of it, like a bucket down a well."

A bolt of lightning flashed. Outside the tall window, wet with rain, rooftops flickered black and chimneys flickered red.

A horse whinnied wildly below in the street.

"At night, with a storm coming" I continued, "when Nathaniel and I climbed the ratlin's up to the t'gallant, the standing rigging—black— all but disappeared, while the running rigging—white—became dark gray. What we could see, we could not grab hold of. We could trust only the rigging we could *not* see. We'd reach, we'd step . . . and feel that a line was there before we'd put our weight on it. As the wind picked up and the sail flapped like a huge angry ghost, all we had to stand on, more than a hundred feet above the deck, was an invisible footrope we knew to be there in the howling night."

She stared at me, reassured. "Those black ropes," she said, cupping her hand over Caleb's bald head while he nursed, "they were your faith."

"Aye," I nodded. "Like black ratlin's rising into the stormy night. Like Nathaniel's arm behind me.

"Then take your faith tonight."

What else does a soldier have, as he walks—with a heart filled with aching love—out of a small clean room in a boardinghouse, along the hallway and down the stairs, then out the front door into furious rain on Nassau Street . . . when the time comes that he must fetch his musket?

*   *   *

Benjamin, wondering Why?

20 October, 1826
Tomorrow's the day.
Still not a word.
She seems to have forgotten.

Drenched from the sweeping rain and beginning to shiver, I walked across the soggy common, past the paddock, past the jail, past the workhouse, to the military barracks . . . as if the lowly soldier should be kept further away from the city than horses, prisoners, and debtors. Aye, better a dog than a soldier.

While I was changing into a set of Judd's old clothes—too big, but dry—Henry appeared at the door with something under each arm. "Try these," he said, offering me one of the bundles. "I found them in a shop on Water Street. They're what the fishermen wear when they're pulling their nets on the Newfoundland Banks."

I unrolled a stiff coat of oiled canvas, with a hood. I then unrolled a pair of canvas trousers, with heavy braces. In the center of the bundle I discovered a pair of tall boots, their leather slippery with what I could smell as bees' wax. Inspecting the boots, I noted the expert stitching.

"Three pounds, ten shillings," said Henry as he unrolled his own coat and trousers. "I traded the shopkeeper a few hours of carpentry. He wanted a set of shelves. So you don't owe me but five shillings."

Other soldiers in the barracks, preparing glumly for four hours of sentry duty in the rain, stared with envy as we stepped into our stiff canvas trousers, then donned our oiled coats. Henry and I grinned at each other as we pulled the hoods up over our heads: we looked like two monks.

"Keep your cartridge box under your coat," said Henry, "and your powder'll be dry to the end of Noah's flood."

There was a lot that I liked about Henry. He could find a pair of fisherman's boots that fit my feet and kept them dry, and he was glad to all but give them to me.

More than that: despite my English origin, and after a period of quiet suspicion, once he had made up his mind that I was who I seemed to be, no more and no less, Henry had fully welcomed me as the man courting his sister. His suspicion came not from an ill nature, but from an older brother's natural instinct to protect her. The last in the Byrnes family to shake my hand, he had been wary not on his own behalf, but Genevieve's.

Even more than that, I liked Henry, respected Henry, for a quality which few men possess: he was always ready to learn, ready to cast aside the old and to grow with the new. On a log beside a campfire, or in the barracks on a bench, he listened to hear the sense of what a New Yorker thought. Or worse, a Virginian. I am certain that if Henry could have put aside his musket and sat down for an hour with a redcoat from a farm in Yorkshire to hear his views, the discussion would gradually have moved from politics to sheep raising.

Henry seemed born to be far more than a yeoman and a carpenter, even the best carpenter in the parish. He had a gift for sizing up men, and for finding the best in them.

Every evening, soldiers on sentry duty split into two groups, one to guard the western shore of New York City, one to guard the eastern shore. The first brigade stood at their posts from Chambers Street down to the Battery, facing Hudson's River and New Jersey. The second brigade stood at their posts from the burial grounds beyond Rosevelt Street down to the Battery, facing the East River and Long Island. On different nights we stood at different posts, for some complained about the longer walk south, some complained about swarms of mosquitoes near the marsh to the north, and some complained, whatever they were ordered to do. Therefore in a democratic way, we all stood duty at a different post every night.

Our brigade followed George Street east to Water Street, where a squad of soldiers detached into the shipyards. The rest of us proceeded south, Henry and I mightily content in our cod fisherman's outfits as the torrents poured down. Four sentries were detached at every pier; our brigade was greatly reduced by the time we reached Albany Pier, where Henry and I and two other sturdy fellows from Massachusetts (for we still tended to cluster together) were posted to watch the harbor. The remainder of our brigade continued south another three blocks to the Battery, where they joined the brigade picketed along the Hudson.

In those days (though I hear no longer now), Boston, New York, and Philadelphia all had windmills along their waterfronts, where grain unloaded from ships could be ground into flour for the merchants of the city. A mill spinning gracefully in a breeze off the sea made a pleasant sight, for there the hand of nature worked in harmony with the hand of man, that bread might be baked and the children fed.

Such a mill stood on the shore near the Albany Pier, where its arms could catch a breeze off the harbor. But on the night of the storm, the blades were turned athwart the wind and tied with hawsers to iron stakes pounded into the earth. In the furious wind, the blades shuddered back and forth as they struggled to snap their lines: the windmill had become a shackled and maddened prisoner. Henry and I, standing in the lee of a warehouse, could hear the gears inside the mill as they creaked and clanked.

Each crack of lightning over the harbor lit the mill for a flickering instant. Its tall brown tower appeared sturdy enough, but the two upper blades looked like desperate arms reaching heavenward in supplication and despair. The canvas was tearing into rags from the skeletal frames and flapping in the wild wind.

Should the lines be torn from the ground, should the blades begin to spin, the crazed monster would whirl until it destroyed itself.

The harbor, too, was an unearthly sight. For long moments, it was hidden by the night, hidden by rain. But whenever a bolt of lightning stabbed the hills of Long Island, a broad silvery expanse of water briefly appeared. We could see every anchored frigate, every white wave, even the clustered houses of Brooklyn.

With each crack of lightning over Staten Island to the south, New York Harbor—filled with an immense fleet of warships—flashed into view for an instant. Then the harbor disappeared, replaced by sweeping rain and darkness.

I felt sorry for the lads crowded aboard those British warships. The hulls were no doubt rocking in the surge. A sailor had the choice either to remain below-decks and wait in line for a bucket (a bucket already full), or he could stagger up the ladder to the deck, then stand drenched at the rail, gagging and gasping and groaning while the storm roared around him. To roll under sail at sea was one thing, but to roll at anchor (as I well knew from my summer in Boston Harbor) could turn even the captain's stomach sour.

I wondered, as every soldier must at some time wonder, why we were doing this. Why should Henry learn as a soldier, rather than as a carpenter? Better by far that after framing a chicken coop, after framing a barn, he learn to frame the steeple and spire above a village meetinghouse, as Nathaniel would have him do. Better, given his friendly way with folks, that he become a selectman in Lincoln, than a sentry on a pier smelling of fish.

And certainly, the lads out on those warships had far more talent in their minds, their hands, and their hearts than the officers would ever let them use.

Hadn't we all enough to contend with in this world, without a war as well? On a night when the summer's worst thunderstorm threatened every building in the city and every mast at sea with its fiery bolts of lightning, must we also worry about cannons at dawn?

Didn't an equal number of soldiers, British and American, have a wife and child waiting at home?

The storm raged with a mighty wrath over the city, over the harbor. I wondered how much greater the wrath would be when the Creator, His patience finally exhausted, decided that He had had enough of our petty, relentless, blasphemous wars.

Relieved at midnight, Henry and I walked alone along Dock Street to Wall Street without seeing a single outdoor lamp still lit in the wind. The warehouses were dark, the countinghouses were dark; even the taverns were closed and dark. Henry and I, triumphantly dry in our rain jackets, seemed to be the only living souls in the city.

Near the corner of Wall and William, we paused to stare toward a certain spot in the dark. We waited for a flash of lightning, which soon accommodated us.

There on a pedestal directly in front of us (though veiled in silver streaks of rain) stood a statue which had *not* been toppled by an angry mob. The gentleman in bronze, with one arm raised as he spoke, was Sir William Pitt, the British minister who had defended our American rights in Parliament, and to whom very few had listened. Sir William gleamed in the flickering light . . . then disappeared back into the night.

Proud that he was my countryman, I had often paused at this corner to look with undiminished gratitude at his gaunt face. I had of course brought Genevieve here to see him. But tonight, during the first dark hour of August 22, 1776, I was granted no more than a flickering instant to look upon, to behold, to witness, that honored visage.

Sir William Pitt, Earl of Chatham, had told the Lords in Parliament, "The Americans are the sons, not the bastards, of England." But the British night overwhelmed him, and all of us with it.

Henry and I turned the corner at City Hall onto Nassau Street, then walked three blocks, past three gray, rain-shrouded churches, to the Nassau Inn, where every window was black. We knew which window was Genevieve's: third floor, second window from the southern end. There inside slept my wife and son; there inside slept nearly all that was precious in my life.

I turned to Henry, a dark face enshrouded by a black hood. "When kings are sent to milk the cow," I told him, "and mothers sit upon the throne, then shall we find our way toward the peaceable kingdom."

He stared at me for a long moment, until he said with a tone of self-reproach, "Damn me, if I haven't forgotten to build a cradle for Caleb."

"A cradle," I said, already thanking Henry in my heart.

He nodded—the black hood nodded—then we continued up Nassau Street toward the barracks.

Genevieve.   *20 October, 1826*
                                       No, I haven't forgotten.

Never forgot once, not in half a century.
Neither did he.

&

Chapter Fifty-Nine

Benjamin, 51 years after 21 October, 1775,   *21 October 1826*
and still calling her "my bride."   *Sunny day, cool.*

Today we set the war aside, as we set the war aside on that sacred evening in Cambridge fifty-one years ago. Today a lively fire burns on the hearth of our home in Lincoln, as it once burned in the mud-mortared fireplace of our log hut in the encampment.

Today the flame once kindled with green twigs, burns on seasoned logs laid over a deep bed of red coals.

We've almost more family visiting today than we can fit under the roof, but fit them all we will. Caleb brought a fifty-first anniversary gift for his mother, something I'd long forgotten about. He had kept it and treasured it when a boy: one of Sir William's old horseshoes, tossed aside by a blacksmith in West Point, New York in 1781, when the smith was putting fresh shoes on Sir William before the long march south to Yorktown. Caleb was five at the time. He loved to ride that horse with his mother as much as she had once loved to ride in the saddle with her Papa. When the smith pulled out the nails and cast the old scuffed and worn shoe into the dirt, Caleb snatched it up. He kept through all these years a horseshoe worn by Sir William during the War of Independence.

Aye, Caleb gave to his mother today a horseshoe knicked and scratched when Sir William had pulled a cobbler's wagon. And when he had carried Genevieve as General Washington's trusted courier.

Caleb couldn't have given his mother anything more precious.

Genevieve, blessed among women.   *21 October, 1826*
          Our day.

Today at two o'clock, before the family sits down to dinner, we will put on our woolen coats and ride in a parade of five wagons to the Lincoln Meetinghouse. There in the otherwise empty church, shall our family say a prayer.

A prayer for those who are no longer with us. Especially for a brother buried in the soil of far-off Virginia. Our years of peace, our years of abundant prosperity, can never replace the years which Henry willingly relinquished.

A prayer for the parents who brought Benjamin and me into this world. They did as best they knew, and now rest in England, and in America, two amicable nations.

A prayer for our children, and their children, and for all children who run joyfully on little feet upon this beautiful land. The Bible is the gift of God's wisdom, but a child is the gift of His heart.

A prayer of gratitude for the Quaker soldier named Nathaniel, who lay dead on top of Benjamin on the Concord Road. Because before Benjamin stood up, he took Nathaniel's heart into his own.

A prayer of gratitude for the Commander in Chief who asked for our obedience and earned our love. Despite occasional mistakes on the battlefield, he never let himself be less than what we all hoped to be.

A prayer of profound gratitude for a generation of men and women who likewise set aside their private lives. They learned to speak, with more or less conviction, the simple word, "mankind."

A prayer of gratitude for the land itself, an entire continent given to the world at a time when the world had done poorly with what it had. We continue, in many ways, to do poorly with our gift. The time will come—I can feel it—when our unrelenting sins against our Negro neighbors will anoint our brows with blood. Neither will our sins against the land's first people be forgotten by the Creator, though they, His children, have almost vanished. The land has been far better to us than we have been to the land.

And finally, a prayer of gratitude to the Lord in His heaven for considering us worth the effort. Maybe a little girl with red ribbons in her braids nudged Him beyond His skepticism. I know that Caleb's granddaughter Emily nudges me beyond mine.

May we all one day be nudged toward that promise, that pledge, that sacred oath, "All men are created equal."

And when our prayers have been offered, let Benjamin pull the rope and ring that old church bell. Let it ring, let it clang, let it peal, telling Lincoln, telling the hills of Massachusetts, telling the bright sun above, that upon this, the fifty-first anniversary of our wedding day, the bride still weeps with joy that her soldier husband came home.

℘

Chapter Sixty

Benjamin, recounting

THE BATTLE OF LONG ISLAND

When Henry and I awoke on Thursday morning, August 22, 1776, we stepped out the barracks door and discovered a fresh blue sky. The great sweep of the common was a patchwork of puddles. A man led his cow by a rope; perhaps she had run away during the storm. Soldiers hung wet clothing on a line slung between two elms. Carriages rolled along the Broad Way at the far edge of the common. The city had come to life. All we seemed to have suffered was a good drenching.

But grim news soon arrived from the wharf: the British were rowing thousands of redcoats in cutters to the port of Gravesend at the southern tip of Long Island. A sentry had counted seventy-five cutters, ferrying back and forth across the harbor. The landing of that many troops on Long Island was clearly the beginning of an attack.

Several thousand American troops were encamped on Brooklyn Heights. The ridge looked down upon Manhattan Island as Breed's Hill and Dorchester Heights had looked down upon Boston. Should we lose Brooklyn Heights to the enemy, we would quickly lose New York City as well.

Knowing I would soon be posted to some redoubt, perhaps on Long Island itself, I ran across the soggy common to the stables, where I hoped to find someone to take a message to Genevieve.

The paddock was bustling with grooms and saddled horses; officers dashed into the corral, mounted and cantered out the gate toward their posts. The wet ground had been churned to mud. I glanced about, but did not see John Lally, nor anyone else I knew.

Inside the stables, I found Sir William in his stall, stomping restlessly at the commotion around him. The stall where John Lally kept his black stallion was empty. I rubbed Sir William's soft nose, then I spotted a lad I knew, the Pennington boy, Ezekiel, who lent a hand at odd jobs around the horses, looking for the chance to ride one.

"Ezekiel!" I called. The boy turned toward me; he was buckling a halter. "Please, son," I hurried toward his stall, "can you take a message

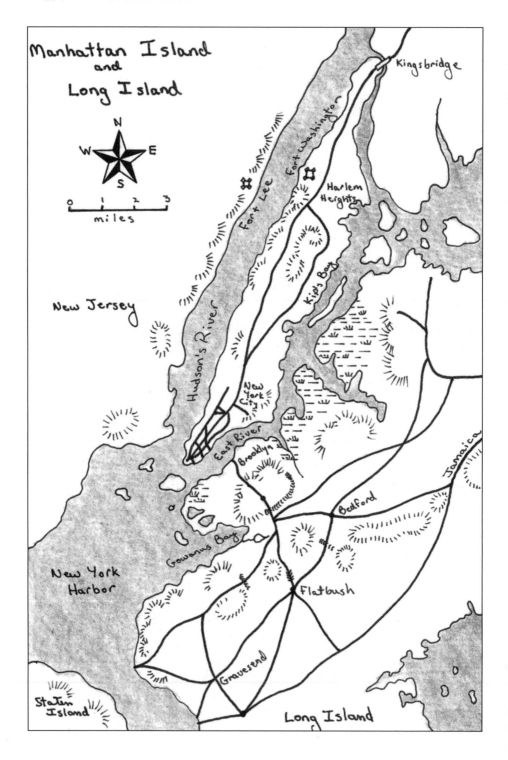

to Mistress York?"

"Yes sir," he beamed, glad to play a further part in the morning's military events.

"Tell her," I paused, wondering what to say, for soldiering is an unpredictable business, "tell her that I may not be able to visit her today. Tell her . . . that I'll be there as soon as I can."

I dug into my pocket for a penny.

"Thank you, sir." Troubled for a moment, Ezekiel explained, "I've got several horses to saddle. I won't be home until midday for dinner. Will that be time enough?"

"Aye, time enough, time enough."

Then I hurried out the stable door, toward the barracks, toward Henry and our muskets, and toward the poor doomed lads who were still in His Majesty's service.

Assembled with our regiment at the shipyard, Henry and I waited on a pier to board a flat-bottomed ferry. The passenger barge was one of several dozen vessels requisitioned up and down the shoreline to carry our troops across the East River to Brooklyn. Though we had not yet received any detailed orders, we guessed, as did everyone in the great milling crowd of soldiers, that we would reinforce the troops already encamped on Long Island. The men were justifiably nervous as they stared at the parade of tiny vessels crossing the broad river: the cannons of one British frigate could easily have scattered our ferries like a flock of ducks.

Equally worrisome, every man knew that we might well be crossing the water toward our capture and imprisonment. British ships could easily surround Long Island, then disembark redcoats wherever General Howe ordered them to land. Only the northern breeze sweeping down the river kept the British fleet at the southern end of the harbor.

Some of the soldiers argued, as we shifted slowly forward along the pier, that we should retreat from what was clearly a hopeless situation, set New York City afire, then march down to Philadelphia and there defend the Congress. General Howe could make his winter quarters in the ashes of Manhattan.

"What's the town anyway, but a nest of Tories?" demanded a tanner from Boston, where the Tories had been cleaned out five months ago.

I could have spoken up in defense of the Penningtons, patriots who asked a man's allegiance before they rented him a room. But I could not deny the great number of Tories in New York City.

I spotted Reverend Kesslaer standing with Cato, Prince and Freedom near the ladder down to the boats. The three Negroes carried, like the rest of us, a rucksack on their backs and a musket in their hands. The Reverend carried a rucksack, but he held in each hand an upright pair of poles, wrapped with worn sailcloth and tied with spirals of rope.

As Henry and I approached the ladder, I realized that the soldiers ahead of us, not wishing to offer a place in the boat to any Negroes, filed steadily down the ladder as if the four men watching them did not exist.

Henry too ignored the three Negroes as he stepped down the ladder. I paused—stood firm against a man shoving behind me—and waved to Cato that he should precede me. With a cordial nod, he stepped forward and climbed down the ladder, followed by Prince, then Freedom, and then Johannes. Henry looked up at me from his seat in the stern, then shifted a bit when Cato sat beside him.

I climbed down the ladder, stepped into the broad rowboat, then sat on a bench beside Freedom, a man some years older than myself. His musket, like every other soldier's musket, stood on its stock between his knees. He gazed across the harbor. A dozen more men boarded the craft, then our six rowers shoved off and paddled out onto the blue, wind-rippled river.

About halfway across, Freedom let go of his musket with one hand and trailed his fingers over the starboard gunnel in the water. He never dipped more than his fingers, perhaps wary that someone might accuse him of slowing the boat. But to touch the water, to feel it running through his fingers, seemed to fascinate him. His large hand might have been some sort of sea creature, delighted, after an extended removal, to be back in the water.

We disembarked at the Brooklyn wharf, then marched in a long, loosely formed column through the small seaport. We followed a rising road past farm houses and planted fields to the top of what folks called Brooklyn Heights, but I would have called just a row of low hills. We now saw for ourselves the line of earth and timber redoubts—said to be two miles long—which our troops had labored through the summer to build. The redoubts formed a far better fortress than what we had dug in one night atop Breed's Hill. The tall, thick walls appeared able to withstand a prolonged siege, even with artillery against them . . . unless they were surrounded, as well they might suddenly be. For where our regiment had just landed and marched, the British infantry could land and march too.

We did not relieve the troops in the redoubt, but marched through a well-defended breach in the ramparts, then continued southeast along a rolling highway. The midday sun shone warmly on our faces. When we reached a fork, a mounted officer directed us along a lane to the southwest.

Other regiments continued straight ahead on the Flatbush Road, or branched northward on the Jamaica Road.

We marched along the edge of a tidal swamp, the upper reaches of Gowanus Bay. On that particular morning, the tide was at ebb. Flocks of shrieking gulls sailed over the flats and landed on the black mud, seeking whatever creatures had been exposed atop the muck or trapped in a pool.

To our left was farmland, well drained. We passed an occasional clapboard house and its orchard. The apples (now toward the end of August) were full-sized and deep red. Some of the men reached over a fence and grabbed what they could while we marched.

Half a mile beyond the inner pocket of Gowanus Bay, our regiment joined the troops at a well built redoubt commanded by Brigadier General William Alexander of New Jersey. (He was more generally known as Lord Stirling, for he claimed a family title in Scotland.) As we set down our rucksacks beside the tents we would share, we learned from the soldiers in camp that we faced, some half mile further down the coast, seven thousand redcoats under Major General James Grant. The talk in camp was that Lord Stirling, some years ago, had been in the House of Commons in London during a debate on what to do with the rebels in the colonies. He had heard General Grant declare that with only five thousand men, he could march from one end of America to the other, restoring order along the way. Now Grant had seven thousand troops, while we had a mere sixteen hundred. Nor did we have artillery that might stand against the multitude of British cannons which had been ferried this morning to Long Island.

To the north of us, along a winding ridge, the regiment which had continued on Flatbush Road joined General John Sullivan's troops. A mile or two further north were General Israel Putnam's troops. Together we formed an outer wall of armed camps, while the long redoubt on Brooklyn Heights formed an inner wall. The two walls would prevent (or so we hoped) the British redcoats from reaching and then crossing the narrow river between Brooklyn and New York City.

Such was the plan, but a shift in the wind would enable the British fleet to sail right up the river. And then we might eat red apples until finally we waved a white flag.

Henry and I tented with nine fellows from Maryland. Henry had brought not spring water but rum in his canteen, and thus our welcome as reinforcements was itself reinforced by a hearty round of swigs.

That day, Thursday, and the following Friday and Saturday, we stood watch along the ramparts with fellows who pointed out the lay of the enemy's camp, the whereabouts of artillery, the directions of roads we could not see.

The weather continued fair. At night, we slept beneath the stars.

The British fleet had anchored in New York Harbor at the end of June. We in the American camps had waited through four and a half weeks in July for their attack. We had waited for three more weeks in August. Now, face to face on Long Island, we waited through a warm morning, we waited through a hot afternoon, we waited through a long, slowly cooling night, certain that the dawn must bring an opening blast of cannon fire.

The British and American camps were close enough that we could see the tiny orange sparks of their campfires. Surely they could see our fires as well.

How odd, this endless passing of phantom days before the sudden butchery.

Genevieve, on Henry's behalf.

Henry was a man of his times, who outgrew his times.

When the people of Lincoln were counted in a census of 1765, there were 621 citizens, mostly farming families, and 28 slaves. Several of the larger farms owned one or two slaves, although Judge Chambers Russell worked seven slaves on his estate. Some slaves were baptized into the Lincoln Meetinghouse; others merely attended. Slaves were allowed to marry; a man on one farm might take a wife from another farm. However, they continued to live separately.

The child of a slave couple could be sold by its owner. Joshua Brooks sold "a sartain Neagro Servant boy Named peter about one year and seven months old" for "the sum of four pounds." That was the same price as he might pay for a cow and its calf. Joshua Brooks was one of the founding fathers of Lincoln in 1754. He was later elected a deacon in the church. He sold the Negro boy to Josiah Nellson of Lincoln, a neighbor, and thus the boy's parents could upon occasion visit him.

Our own farm was small enough that Papa, Judd and Henry could manage the heavy work themselves, while Mama and I tended to the milking, the gardens, and the kitchen. I won't say that we were any more upright than some of our neighbors. Aside from glancing at a black face in the meetinghouse on the Sabbath, or seeing a Negro man repairing a stone fence at the edge of a cornfield, the plight or even the existence of slaves in our village rarely entered our thoughts.

Nor were they mentioned at the Green Dragon Tavern in Boston.

One might think that a hungry man would readily understand a starving man. But the hungry man's eyes are more likely fixed on the man seated at a well-provisioned dinner table.

For Henry, as for me and for Judd, Negroes were not merely strangers, but strange creatures, who spoke remnants of some African tongue, and a poor version of English. They were other, and they were lesser, and thus slavery was a suitable station for them. To be close to a Negro made us uncomfortably aware of that closeness; we didn't know what to do with it.

So Henry knew no more in that rowboat what to say or do when seated beside a Negro, than he had known in the Lincoln Meetinghouse had he stood near one by the door. As he had never shared a hymnal with a Negro, he certainly had no idea how to share a war with one.

છ

Chapter Sixty-One

Benjamin, listening to a man
whom some would have stoned to death.

On Sunday morning, August 25, 1776, Reverend Johannes Kess-laer delivered a sermon in a meadow behind the lines. The men who had spent the summer guarding the hills of Long Island had been without a minister; thus several hundred soldiers gathered on that Sabbath to hear him speak.

At the back of the congregation stood forty or fifty Negroes, some in small clusters, a dozen in one large group. Reverend Kesslaer spoke with a seasoned voice that carried to his most distant listeners.

Henry and I stood near the front of the gathering, squinting into the morning sun as we listened. A cool breeze from the north stirred the tall timothy grass and black-eyed Susans. Nearby, a meadowlark warbled. It was the sort of morning that might refresh any man's soul.

Reverend Kesslaer faced us in his fringed leather jacket, his long blond hair stirred by the breeze. He had neither pulpit nor Bible. We could see behind him our American camp and redoubt, busy with hundreds of soldiers at their tasks. In the distance, smoke rose from the breakfast fires of the British.

"What sort of man was Jesus?" asked Reverend Kesslaer, posing a question we had all heard and considered before. A compassionate man. A forgiving man. A man who was the Son of God.

"At the time that Jesus preached in Palestine, Palestine and Egypt had been neighbors for many hundreds of years. The two countries shared a border in the desert. Ships sailed the short distance back and forth on the Mediterranean. Travel from one land to the other was thus not uncommon. We know, for example, that when Jesus was born, his life was threatened by King Herod, and so his parents fled with the child into Egypt. They remained there 'until the death of Herod, that it might be fulfilled which was spoken by the Lord through the prophet, saying, 'Out of Egypt have I called my son.' "

Aye, we knew about the flight into Egypt. That was a solid premise upon which to build a sermon.

"Long before Jesus was born, his ancestors, the Israelites, endured a period of captivity in Egypt. They labored in Egypt, they suffered in Egypt, for four hundred and thirty years. Pharaoh 'set over them task-masters to afflict them with their burdens.' The Bible tells us, 'The Egyptians made the children of Israel to serve with rigor. And they made their lives bitter with hard bondage, in mortar, and in brick, and in all manner of service in the field.' "

Aye, that we knew as well. The years of bondage had been bitter years.

"The Israelites sweated and died in the sun-baked fields of Egypt, until the Lord spoke to Moses, and said, 'Go in, speak unto Pharaoh, king of Egypt, that he let the children of Israel go out of his land.' Moses spoke unto Pharaoh, but Pharaoh would not listen, until Egypt was stricken with plagues. When the king of Egypt lost his firstborn son, then did he release the children of Israel from their captivity."

And so the Israelites returned to the promised land, their home in Palestine.

Reverend Kesslaer paused for a long moment, his eyes searching every corner of the congregation.

"Now, in Egypt is a great river, the Nile, which flows out from the heart of Africa. The Nile is over four thousand miles long. Most of its water comes from the rains that fall on the land of Ethiopia. People have lived along this river since before the recording of time. Caravans have followed trade routes beside this river since before the recording of time."

A learned man is our Reverend. He has not always lived in a re-mote Oneida village far up the Mohawk River.

"The kingdom of the Pharaohs was rich and powerful. Because of trade routes by land and by sea between Palestine and Egypt, and be-cause of the great river that flowed from the heart of Africa, Egypt was able to purchase slaves from two different regions. There were slaves from the east, and slaves from the south."

I could hear a stir behind me. Where was this leading?

"What can we think of a people who spent four hundred and thirty years in bondage . . . in bondage, no doubt, with black Africans in bondage working the same fields? What can we think about the people who toiled where the waters of the Nile poured into the waters of the Mediterranean? What can we think of the people whom Moses led out of Egypt, six hundred thousand of them?

"Is it not possible," Reverend Kesslaer asked, lifting his voice so that every soldier in the congregation might not mistake his meaning, "is it not *possible* that the children of Israel took home with them to the promised land something more in their veins than the pure blood of Abraham and Isaac and Jacob? Is it not possible that they carried something more in their veins than the pure blood of Joseph, son of Jacob? For Jacob had been sold by his brothers into *slavery* in Egypt."

A murmur . . . a murmur of faint protest . . . traveled through the crowd behind us.

"When people labor beneath the lash, when people eat from the same gleanings and drink from the same well, when people bury their wives, or bury their husbands, and then seek a new mate, to survive—to survive in the heart as well as in the belly—do such slaves ask that their blood remain pure for four hundred and thirty years?"

A soldier stepped out of the congregation. With a look of disgust, he walked past Reverend Kesslaer, then returned to the redoubt.

The Reverend paid him no attention. "If we turn to the Beatitudes, as often we must, in Matthew, book five, chapter eight, whose voice do we hear?"

The voice of Jesus, of course, beginning his sermon on the mount.

" 'Blessed are the meek,' " called out Reverend Kesslaer, " 'for they shall inherit the earth.

'Blessed are they who do hunger and thirst after righteousness; for they shall be filled.

'Blessed are the merciful; for they shall obtain mercy.

'Blessed are they that mourn; for they shall be comforted.' "

Scripture that most of us knew by heart. Whether from London or from Lincoln.

"Are these the words of a man who speaks on behalf of the great and the rich and the powerful? Or are these the words of a man who speaks on behalf of the lowest and the least and the most wretched?"

I could hear angry murmurs now. Clusters of soldiers were walking away.

"Is it not possible that Jesus, whose lineage goes back to Joseph, who himself was sold for twenty pieces of silver into bondage in Egypt . . . is it not possible that Jesus understood the anguish of a slave? Of *all* slaves, who mourn, who are meek, who hunger and thirst after righteousness. And who, because they have nothing else to give, offer mercy to their fellow slaves."

Someone shouted, "You ain't no preacher!"

Others called out with rude agreement. The congregation began to break apart. Groups of soldiers walked past Reverend Kesslaer, glaring at him with anger and disgust. They returned to their campfires, to the redoubt, to their tents.

The Reverend stared straight ahead, toward (as I saw when I glanced over my shoulder) fifty Negroes who stood as still as statues, listening.

"Is it not possible that Jesus understood a slave's wretchedness, because he was more than simply 'thou Son of David?' Is it not possible that when he was nailed to the cross, the blood which ran from his wounds contained, from generations ago, the blood of slaves?"

Henry walked away, shaking his head.

Reverend Kesslaer held out both hands, as if bestowing a blessing upon those few who still listened. "Yea, I say unto you, that among the drops of blood on the brow of our Savior, blood drawn by the crown of thorns which he was made to wear, there were drops of African blood."

A soldier beside me shook his fist and shouted, "Blasphemy!"

But I heard myself say, with a voice so quiet that no one else could have heard, "Amen."

વ્ઝ

Chapter Sixty-Two

Benjamin.

On Monday night, August 26, 1776, we almost lost the war.

Fanning out from Brooklyn toward southern Long Island were a number of roads. Thus, fanning *in* toward Brooklyn were a number of roads.

These roads passed through a row of hills known as the Heights of Guan. Our encampment under General Sterling guarded the southern approach to Brooklyn. Further north, General Sullivan's troops and then General Putnam's troops guarded the roads where they passed through the central valleys. But nobody, as we soon learned, had bothered to guard the northernmost road through the hills: the Jamaica Pass.

Informed by his spies of this weakness in our line, General Howe sent ten thousand redcoats, led by General Clinton and guided by three Loyalist farmers, on a secret nighttime march up the eastern side of Long Island to Jamaica Pass, four miles above our camps. Finding no American troops, nor even sentries, in the Pass, Clinton followed a road southwest to the village of Bedford; the ten thousand British troops, still undiscovered, were now *behind* General Putnam's earthen fort. A detachment of redcoats marched even further, until they were behind General Sullivan's redoubts. The uncontested success of their maneuver must have astonished the British.

At dawn on Tuesday morning, the enemy hidden behind our lines fired two artillery shots, signaling to the enemy waiting in front of our lines that the attack had begun. The American troops, just kindling their breakfast fires, were baffled, shocked, horrified when they understood they were all but surrounded. Many of them retreated in panic toward the line of redoubts on Brooklyn Heights. But that retreat brought them directly into the hands of the enemy.

British officers had told their German allies (mercenaries who had arrived that summer in New York) that the Americans would give no quarter, would take no prisoners, but would bayonet every captured German on the spot. The Hessians accordingly bayoneted any wounded Americans they found lying on the field, and even stabbed men who attempted to surrender. American farm boys in battle for the first time were butchered by the dozens.

By steadily extending their forces behind our lines, the British cut off General Sterling's route of retreat. With no roads left open, we had a choice between a thick woods (where the British and Germans waited like wolves) or the tidal swamp (now filled with sea water at high tide) as our only routes of escape. While General Sterling and a contingent of men from Maryland and Delaware stood heroically as a rear guard against an attack led by Generals Grant and Cornwallis, the rest of us retreated as best we could through the swamp.

Men encumbered with rucksacks and muskets struggled to wade through black muck into murky water that rose from their knees to their waist . . . until grape shot or chains fired from British cannons threw them forward as bloody sinking corpses. A company of Hessians in blue uniforms drove our soldiers even deeper into the swamp, where many staggered and thrashed and then disappeared beneath the surface. British snipers fired from almost every direction. A man not more than six feet from me shrieked as he flopped backwards, the last of his cry mere bubbles rising from his blurry face.

Keeping the early morning sun behind us (and thus Brooklyn Heights roughly in front of us), Henry and I stayed close together while madness and death swirled around us. We had lost sight of anyone we knew. Skirting the deeper water, we struggled through knee-deep muck, falling so often that snipers probably could not distinguish us from the shore of the swamp.

We finally arrived, as did many who managed to survive thus far, at a broad stream that flowed into a millpond. In normal times, the mill made use of the tidal flow to turn its wheel. Now—British musket balls splattered into the water while our men tried to swim across—the mill wheel carried American corpses upon its revolving blades.

"Can you swim, Henry?" I shouted above the blast of British artillery.

"Never learned," Henry shouted back, gripping his musket as he stared at the roiling water.

I searched up and down the stream for a narrow stretch, or rocks to step on. Then suddenly I saw a man swimming across, not away from us, but *toward* us. He was swimming with his head lifted—we could see his Negro face—while his arms reached forward with a good strong rhythmic stroke. The swimmer approached a floundering soldier who held his musket over his head while struggling to keep his mouth above the surface, then he grabbed the soldier's hunting shirt. Freedom—for it was my friend from the hospital tent in Cambridge—reversed his course. With one hand gripping the soldier, he pulled with strong strokes toward the opposite shore.

Despite the barrage of British muskets, they reached the far bank. Freedom hauled the soldier up into the grass, where the man lay flat with exhaustion. Freedom unfastened a muddy hatchet on the soldier's belt, then dashed barefoot into a nearby woods.

I spotted Cato and Prince at the edge of the woods, wet and smeared with muck. They were shouting at Freedom, begging him to come with them, but he ignored them while he chopped at the base of a twenty-foot sapling. Working with swift agility, Freedom brought the tree down, then trimmed the branches from its crown. He handed the hatchet to Prince, grabbed Cato by the arm. Holding the slender trunk so that it balanced fore and aft in his hand, he hurried back to the bank of the stream.

Freedom handed the pole to Cato, then waded into the water where musket fire continued to splatter.

"Henry!" we heard him call. He must have seen us standing on the opposite bank, forty feet away across the flooded stream. Never before had Freedom spoken either of our names. But now swimming toward us with the grace and strength of a man at home in the water, he called again, angry at being ignored, *"Henry!"*

With musket and rucksack, Henry waded into the muck . . . pushed forward into deepening water . . . hesitated when he began to lose his footing . . . then Freedom grabbed his arm and yanked him into the creek. Freedom shifted his grip to Henry's collar and began to swim with him toward—as I saw now—the end of the pole that Cato reached toward them. Henry, flailing on his side with the musket held above him, did not see the pole. When Freedom reached it, he had to catch Henry's hand underwater and press it against the pole. "Grab hold, mon! Grab hold!"

Henry gripped the end of the pole. While Cato and Prince pulled him toward shore, Freedom began to swim toward me.

"Benjamin!" he called.

Holding my musket over my head, I waded into the stream. I was chest-deep when Freedom grabbed my collar and pulled me forward with surprising force. As I flailed on my side—with the musket above me and my awkward rucksack filling with water—Freedom pulled me with steady strokes, his legs kicking beneath me.

Looking ahead, I grabbed the end of the pole. Freedom released me; Cato and Prince drew in the pole as if it were a hawser on a ship. I quickly crossed the remainder of the stream to its muddy bank.

While Henry chopped down a second sapling and trimmed its branches, Freedom managed to bring three more of our men across the stream. He was just starting back to fetch a wounded lieutenant, supported under each arm by two men, when—the artillery coming ever closer—a length of chain fired from a British cannon tore off the top of Freedom's head. His body was thrown backwards in the water, so that half his face, little more than an open jaw, rose skyward. And then he sank.

On Breed's Hill, it had been Henry who pulled me away from the rampart and forced me to retreat. But at the edge of that stream, it was I who pulled Henry's arm and screamed at him, "There's nothing more we can do!" Our cartridge boxes were soaked; we could only flee.

The four of us, Cato and I and Henry and Prince, made our way through the woods—dodging a squad of Hessians—then we climbed a grassy slope to the startling sight of a neatly planted field of beans.

We gathered with other men lost from their companies. Then we ran and hid and dashed again toward the redoubt on Brooklyn Heights. There in the safety of the earthen fortress—never mind the chaos of shouting soldiers who expected the British to storm the wall—the four of us sprawled in the grass beside a wagon and panted for breath.

Rising to his knees, Henry vomited.

Lying on his back with his hand over his face, Cato wept.

The British did not attempt to overrun our line along Brooklyn Heights. General Howe ordered the attack to halt a few hundred yards from our ramparts. (No doubt his troops were profoundly vexed.) Was he unwilling to attempt another Breed's Hill? Was he confident that with the river at our backs and his fleet in the harbor, he had us trapped? Whatever the reason, after marching his troops all Monday night, and driving us back on Tuesday, he ordered his army to halt and set up their bivouac. We stared down from our redoubt at neat rows of tents in a huge British encampment; at regimental flags waving in the late afternoon breeze; at the smoke of supper fires.

Somewhere down there on the dark plain of Long Island were hundreds of our men, now prisoners of the British. And hundreds more, lying in butchered heaps.

Or drifting out with the tide.

The American soldiers posted all summer on Brooklyn Heights had limited tents and limited food. When their numbers were suddenly doubled by filthy, exhausted, starving men with little or no equipment, they could offer only a corner in a crowded tent and a handful of cornmeal.

After hearing the first artillery shots at dawn, General Washington had left headquarters and hurried across the river. Though the British might well have launched a second attack that morning on Manhattan Island, he brought three thousand fresh troops with him and took command of our desperate forces on Long Island.

We were cheered by his presence on Brooklyn Heights. The mood of panic greatly diminished. But truly, with the immense British encampment spread in front of us, and the vast fleet threatening our rear, there was little the General and his troops could do.

Some of our soldiers, despite earlier notions of patriotism, began to complain to each other. "Damn this war!" they muttered.

On Wednesday, August 28, the rain began, a heavy rain with little wind, falling from low thick clouds. Trenches behind the parapets filled with water, becoming long slender canals. Serving as sentries, Henry and I stood up to our knees in a trough of brown water; we wore our fishermen's coats, our ragged trousers, and no boots.

During that long dismal day, we watched the sodden redcoats as they began to dig an angled trench toward us, the first of a zigzag into which we could not fire our muskets, but which would enable hidden sappers to approach our ramparts. General Howe, using a traditional European method of warfare to "reduce our fortress," seemed to know every step of his business. In three or four days, the British would reach the foot of our wall. Then, if we did not surrender, a hidden column of infantry, bayonets fixed, would suddenly come pouring over the parapets.

The men declared at our meager supper that every cloud from here to the Ohio River had lined up to open its belly upon us. The only drinkable water was what filled a man's tin cup if he left it standing on a stump for ten minutes. Sleepless for almost two days now, cold and wet, the troops began to weaken with fevers. Dysentery from a lack of adequate privies became, for the first time, the scourge of our camp.

By Thursday, some of our soldiers—green farm boys, mostly, who had not been in Boston—were talking of surrender. A brigade from New York, reaching a state of mutiny, threatened the spirit of the troops around them. They were ordered down to the Brooklyn ferry and thence to Manhattan Island. Most of us scorned their lack of courage; some envied their departure from the site of impending calamity.

The gray day of endless rain darkened early. Deepening puddles crept beneath the sagging tents. Although we now had nine and a half thousand troops crowded along the two-mile redoubt, the British had twice as many troops. And our nine and a half thousand cartridge boxes were filled with wet powder. Sodden men sitting on sodden logs around hissing campfires became rings of mute despair.

And then, in the first blackness of night on Thursday, August 29, our officers, moving from one campfire to the next, stunned us with the news that we would soon be replaced by troops now waiting to ferry over from Manhattan Island.

"Replaced?" We were skeptical. "Not reinforced ?"

"Replaced," our captains told us. General Washington himself had given the order. We were to be ready at any time during the night to march down to the Brooklyn wharf to meet the boats.

That was the best news we had heard in our week on this hellish island.

After the hour when we should have eaten supper, and before the hour when we should have gone to bed, Cato and Prince found Henry and me lying on the wet ground beneath a supply wagon. Far from a campfire, we could hardly see their faces. The night was so dark that they no doubt could hardly see ours. And yet, they found us.

We shifted, making room for them beneath the wagon, out of the rain.

"His name was Thomas," said Cato, speaking with solemn deliberation. "He escaped from Jamaica. His wife and boy are still there."

I understood that Cato was telling us about Freedom. Telling us who the man actually was. Or had been.

Prince never spoke. In the darkness, I could tell by the angle of his head that he stared first at Henry, then at me.

Cato said, "Thomas fought in your war because he thought if you won your freedom from the British in Massachusetts, and in New York, you might win it for his people on Jamaica too."

Jamaica, a British sugar island in the West Indies, where most of Thomas's people—his wife and son—would be slaves.

"Even if you never freed Jamaica, even if you drove the British from America but forgot the Caribbean, Thomas wanted to be a free man in Boston. So he could work. So he could return to Jamaica and buy his wife and boy."

"Cato," I began.

"Never mind, Mister Benjamin. You just listen."

Hushed by a Negro who was enough of a man that he could let me know he had no need for my thoughts, I listened.

Prince stared at me.

"Thomas fought in your war. Thomas did whatever he could to help *you* fight. He wanted every American soldier to cross that stream."

The man who must have learned to swim as a boy in Jamaica, had done what he knew best to bring Henry and me across.

"Keep in mind, Mister Benjamin, as you fight your war . . . Keep in mind, Mister Henry, as you prime your musket . . . that every day, down on Jamaica working in a cane field, is a woman who will never know what happened." Cato and Prince moved toward the edge of the wagon. "She will wait. She will wait."

Then they were out in the rain, and gone.

Sometime during the long, black, timeless night, someone whispered into our tent that it was our turn. Henry and I mustered with our regiment, then marched in silence down the road toward Brooklyn. Staring ahead at the faint distant gleam of the river, each man nurtured in his heart a nugget of hope. Let the boats be there. Let other fools fight this war for a day or two. Let somebody else watch the British trenches creep toward them.

In the first gray glow of dawn, we passed through the village of Brooklyn—a few misty lights shone in the windows—then continued downhill toward the wharf. We were walking no longer in drizzling rain, but now through a heavy fog. Someone whispered that if the world got any wetter, we'd see fish swimming up the road.

Despite the order for silence, the men began to grumble when we spotted troops crowded on a pier—and no boats. Hushed by a sergeant, we clumped together on a shorter dock, and waited.

The fog seemed to be rising from the river. Troops standing on the pier and along the wharf appeared and disappeared in the mist like a silent milling throng of ghosts.

Emerging from the fog with barely a sound, an empty boat pulled up to the dock. The whaling skiff had eight rowers, but no soldiers aboard. Following the men ahead of us, Henry and I filed down the dock's ladder, then stepped over seats in the skiff to a place in the stern.

Not a soldier among us asked the obvious question: Where were the troops to replace us?

Our whaler was about to cast off when someone on the dock called down with a harsh whisper, "Wait!"

Peering up, we discerned in the fog two men standing at the edge of the dock, one white, one Negro, holding something between them. It was Johannes, and Prince. They knelt and lowered their long burden down to men who now stood up in the whaler to receive it. Cato was on the ladder, holding one pole of the stretcher.

The passengers in the whaler crowded toward the gunnels; a soldier with a bandaged head was laid on his stretcher between them.

The rowers readied their oars.

"Hold on," said Henry, standing up beside me in the stern. "We're getting out." He gave my arm a tug.

Though utterly baffled, I followed him. We stepped between the grumbling men, passed the wounded soldier who moaned as he rolled his head, then climbed behind Cato up the ladder.

On the pier, Henry said, "Cato, Prince, into the boat, please."

The two Negroes hesitated, glanced at Johannes.

He nodded. "Cato, Prince, into the boat. You've done your jobs, and done them well."

Cato led Prince down the ladder. They stepped awkwardly between the soldiers—who made little room for them— to take our places in the stern.

Someone muttered about having to sit with niggers. Henry quickly drew his knife out of its sheath; he knelt and pointed the blade down at the speaker. "One word from you, Connecticut, and I'll find you when I get across, I will."

A moment of silence, then a rower called, "Cast off."

The prow angled out from the pier. The rowers set and pulled their oars. The whaling skiff pivoted, then vanished into the fog.

During the next two hours, in growing daylight, Henry and I helped Johannes to carry eight wounded soldiers down from Brooklyn Heights to the wharf. Up and down the road we hurried, through fog rising ever further up the hill from the river. On each trip down from the redoubt, we were aided by soldiers who readily took turns to help us to carry the pair of stretchers. I was determined, as a former mender of sails aboard the *Lively*, to sew a hundred such stretchers.

General Washington stood at the end of the pier in the fog as the last of our troops (men who had been tending the campfires to fool the British), reported that the redoubts were entirely empty. The General's black cape was so wet that water dripped from its hem.

Our Commander in Chief waited until the last soldier had boarded a rowboat, until he too climbed down the ladder of Brooklyn wharf.

There were no replacements. General Washington had spread that rumor to cover our retreat.

Not a single man was lost during the night of August 29, 1776, as dozens of skiffs, sloops, and cutters—most of them crewed by Colonel John Glover's cod fishermen from Marblehead, Massachusetts—hurried back and forth across the river, half a mile wide, between Brooklyn's wharf and New York's shipyard, in the dark, in the rain, in the Providential fog that crept up the hills and enshrouded the redoubts. The fog was so thick that even at sunrise, the men on the ramparts could see no further than five yards from where they stood.

Our crowded skiff, paddling near General Washington's dory in the final crossing of the American armada, was halfway across the foggy river when British troops (whom we could not see) fired their muskets at us from the wharf. They had discovered our abandoned fires. They had no doubt raced down to the shore.

But too late. General Washington and the Continental Army had managed a brilliant retreat.

We had outfoxed even the magnificent British fleet, anchored in fog three miles downstream.

ॐ

Chapter Sixty-Three

Genevieve, who had been waiting, waiting.

There was a knock on my door. Dozing in bed (for I had just finished nursing Caleb), I called sleepily, "Hello?"

The door opened. There stood my husband, who had been gone for over a week, haggard, bedraggled, and filthy. But his eyes. Staring at me, then at Caleb, his exhausted eyes did not greet us, but stared as if to confirm, Yes, we were really here; Yes, he had found us; Yes, he was really home.

"Benjamin." I spoke to a man who seemed to have risen from a grave where he had been buried alive.

He stepped into the room (in wet stockings; he must have left his shoes at the door), leaned his musket in the corner by the wash stand, then he approached the bed, still not uttering a word as he stared at me.

I recalled the time when Benjamin and Henry and Papa had come down from Bunker's Hill after the battle. It was days before they began to be normal people again.

"Genevieve," he said softly. He seemed to stand behind a barrier, perhaps because he was so wet and filthy, perhaps because he was still unable to advance beyond what he had lived through.

I laid Caleb aside on the bed, swung my feet out and stood up in my yellow shift. I wanted to hug him, to clutch him—never mind that he looked like Adam, still half clay—but his hand held out to me was so tentative . . . as if he needed to touch me to be sure I was real. I took that earthen hand between my two hands and felt how cold it was, how desperate it was to squeeze my warm pink hand.

"Mister York, your bath is almost ready," called Elias Pennington. He peered in through the door, a pail of steaming water in one hand, then he disappeared down the hallway to a room with a big copper tub.

"Yes," said Benjamin, backing away from me. He had seen me, he knew I was here. Now he would clean away the battle, clean away the death, and let the steaming hot water warm his blood.

I waited for him. I could have gotten up and put on my finest dress and sat at breakfast with him. But I wanted to be where he had found me. He wasn't ready yet to reach any further into the world.

Eli peeked in once to tell me that Benjamin had fallen asleep in the tub. Patricia knocked a while later to tell me that he had fallen asleep over his porridge.

Finally the poor man appeared in the doorway, clean, and wearing a pressed shirt and trousers that Eli must have loaned him. He had a slight smile, a touch of brightness in his eyes.

He closed the door, walked around the bed, then climbed in and took Caleb into his arms. "Caleb, Caleb, no son of mine is ever going to be a soldier."

He kissed the infant's brow, then handed Caleb back to me.

He slid one arm beneath me, rolled onto his side, wrapped his other arm over me and kissed my lips for half a minute of passion and tears and heavenly joy.

Then he seemed to melt into the bed as he slept.

જી

Chapter Sixty-Four

Benjamin, recounting

THE INVASION OF MANHATTAN ISLAND

With a population of twenty-five thousand, the seaport of New York City occupied the bottom mile and a half of Manhattan Island. The upper twelve miles of the long slender island were covered by farmland, forest, and rocky heights. Now that the British were able to attack from several points on Long Island, General Washington shifted his troops. Although he could not simply abandon New York, nor could he risk the capture of nearly twenty thousand men on the southern tip.

He reduced the garrison in New York City to five thousand, then stationed five thousand soldiers along the East River, facing a possible invasion from Long Island. Further north, he posted regiments in three vital positions: along the granite bluffs of Harlem Heights, where they could block a British advance up the island; at Fort Washington, where they guarded Hudson's River; and at Kingsbridge, where they guarded the lone bridge that crossed from the tip of the island to the mainland.

Our troops were greatly dispersed. The British could attack almost any point of Manhattan Island with an army far larger than our own. Should we fail to fight our way free, we would lose not only the seaport of New York, but the war itself.

On September 3, the frigate *Rose* sailed up the East River, leading thirty cutters rowed by their crews. The cutters were beached along the shore of Long Island, clearly in preparation for an attack across the river.

On September 12, thirty-six more cutters rowed up the river. On the 14th, four warships and six troop transports joined the *Rose* at anchor near Kip's Bay.

Awaiting the attack by His Majesty's professionals were farm boys huddled in sandy trenches along the Manhattan shoreline. Most of them were temporary militia rather than Continental Army regulars. The unreliability of the militia had been well proven two weeks ago: following the retreat from Long Island, six thousand men (a major portion of

General Washington's army) in the Connecticut militia had packed their soggy knapsacks, ignored the pleas of their officers (and of their Commander in Chief) and marched home. Until the British army attacked Connecticut, they wanted no more of the war.

On September 12, General Washington ordered an evacuation of all but a rear guard from New York. (Henry and I remained in the city, under General Israel Putnam.) We were to hold the seaport with muskets and artillery until Harlem Heights had been properly fortified. Though we would soon abandon New York City, our Commander in Chief hoped to retain possession of the northern end of the island.

Genevieve rode north in the wagon with Caleb (not yet two months old) as part of a long supply train that followed Bowery Lane to the Boston Road. Some of the wagons halted atop Harlem Heights, where troops were massing. Some took supplies to Fort Washington. But Genevieve continued across Kingsbridge to Fordham Heights on the mainland, where, we hoped, I would eventually join her.

On the evening of September 14, General Washington moved his headquarters to the farmhouse of Charles Apthorpe on the Bloomingdale Road, about halfway up the island. He would thus be able to ride in any direction, depending on where the British chose to attack.

Henry and I once again guarded the fish market pier. Looking out at warships maneuvering into position throughout the harbor and up the river, we waited for the enemy to swarm toward us with brutal vengeance. The British had lost Boston, and now would they surely bloody their bayonets as they strove to capture New York.

Once again the British baffled us with their delay: they waited for two weeks on Long Island before they attacked.

General William Howe and his brother, Sir Richard Howe, admiral of the British fleet, were hoping to negotiate a peace with Congress. Though they could not acknowledge the legality of Congress, (Britain still spoke of the "colonies" and the thirteen royal governors), they invited delegates to meet with them. Congress, wary of this maneuver, appointed John Adams, Benjamin Franklin, and Edward Rutledge of South Carolina (men from the northern, middle, and southern states). The three patriots rode north from Philadelphia; on September 11, they were ferried by redcoats at the oars of a British barge from Perth Amboy, New Jersey to Staten Island, where they met with General Howe.

The British general expressed his great friendship for America; his family had been deeply honored by the monument which the people of

Massachusetts had installed in Westminster Abbey as a memorial to his oldest brother, killed while aiding the Americans in their battle with the French during the French and Indian War. General Howe then asked, "Is there no way of treading back this step of independency and opening the door to a full discussion?"

The three delegates stated firmly that the American people would never renounce their independence. John Adams reminded General Howe that the colonies had been unanimous in their vote.

General Howe walked with the gentlemen back to the barge. While serving as America's ambassador in London, Benjamin Franklin had spoken honestly and courageously to the British court as he described the damage done to American friendship. Today, General Howe, as Britain's military ambassador in America, had attempted to re-establish that friendship. But after almost a year and a half of war, it was far too late.

On Sunday morning, September 15, a warm and sunny Sabbath, British frigates positioned in the East River suddenly fired a broadside of cannons at the flank of Manhattan Island. Our farm boys fled like rabbits. The British soon launched their cutters: each craft was filled with redcoats bearing muskets and gleaming bayonets. The cutters crossed the East River against only scattered resistance; in one brief hour, four thousand enemy troops had landed on Manhattan Island. Were they to march a mere two miles to the west, forming a barricade across the island, they would trap the entire rear guard below them in New York City.

At his headquarters, General Washington heard the opening blast of cannons. He galloped toward Kip's Bay, where most of redcoats were landing, but soon encountered a panicked stampede of militia sweeping across the farmland. The General roared at the flood of men to take a stand behind a stone wall, but the terrified soldiers swept around his horse like a river around a boulder. Many had left behind their knapsacks and muskets, so they might run all the faster.

General Washington raged at the cowards. But though he shouted at them and even cursed them, never did he lash at them with his sword. Nor did he draw his two pistols from their holsters and shoot anyone in the back. Even in a mad fury, he did not harm the lads, some of whom had been in the army less than a month.

Finally he threw down his hat and shouted, "Are these the men with whom I am to defend America?"

The redcoats were by this time appearing from the woods a quarter of a mile away. (The trees were bright orange and yellow in their September glory.) The American militia, even the last stragglers, were by now well behind General Washington. Several of his officers begged him to ride out of musket range. But he sat motionless on his horse, deaf to all voices but his own despair.

The scene was so strange that the advancing redcoats, suspecting a trap, halted in formation in a pasture. They stared at a hatless officer, perhaps wounded though still on his white horse, who had not followed his troops from the field.

Daring to do what no colonel would do, a mere aide-de-camp (a battlefield courier named John Lally) rode up to the General, took hold of the bridle, then led our Commander in Chief off the battlefield.

We might otherwise have lost him there, a willing sacrifice to some vestige of his country's dignity.

General Washington quickly recovered. He galloped north through the bounding rabbits, then directed reliable detachments to guard the roads by which the five thousand troops in New York City would attempt to escape.

Meanwhile down in the city, we knew from the opening volley of artillery to the northeast that we had one hope: to race up the western edge of Manhattan Island before the British infantry marched across to Hudson's River.

Our retreat, ordered by General Putnam, was carried out with good discipline. Once again we escaped with most of our army intact. We left behind, however, more than half of our artillery, as well as wagons, tents, and kitchen gear, for the men fled with what they could carry.

General Howe—the ever cautious General Howe—once more kept his men reined in. They did not dash across the island, as they no doubt expected to do, but instead advanced only a short distance from the shore of the East River, then formed and waited for further orders.

We were therefore able to march at a rapid walk up the western roads to the encampment on Harlem Heights. Though disappointed that I could not find Genevieve that evening, I felt markedly better than I had felt standing (like a bit of fish bait) down on the fish market pier.

As the rabbits trickled in (although a good many headed straight for Kingsbridge and home), we gathered together on Harlem Heights the full miserable strength of our army. Two miles above us was Fort Washington. Five miles above us was the bridge that could take us, if we needed it, to the mainland. And the mainland, again if we needed it, could take us all the way to New England. Or Philadelphia.

Though some of the men who huddled around the supper fires that night regarded our loss of New York City with grim foreboding, others saw the day differently. Aye, the British slept tonight in our warm dry barracks. But we did not sleep as their prisoners inside the cold stone walls of the Battery fort.

We felt heartened. We had made a second respectable retreat.

And tomorrow was another day.

Genevieve.

With a child, a horse and a wagon, I spent September 15, 1776 on the north side of the Harlem river, listening to the faint roar of cannons far to the south. I was not alone, for our troops guarded both sides of the bridge.

If news arrived that I had lost Benjamin, as a corpse or a captive, I would have only one wish, and that was to be with him. I would ride the wagon south to his grave (if he had one) or to his prison. If a prison, a prisoner's widow would I become. I would follow him wherever they took him, with a child who would grow up outside the prison walls. Perhaps Caleb's father could see his son from a barred window.

If a grave, then torn would I be, between husband and child. If I could place Caleb into Henry's arms, I would, like Juliet, gladly join my Romeo in the sweet sleep of death.

Such were the wild thoughts loosened in my mind as I wondered, while grooming Sir William and nursing Caleb and staring at that empty bridge throughout that day, where between Pearl Street and the Harlem River my Benjamin was.

And whether he was still with me, or had gone to join Nathaniel.

Benjamin.

On the day after our retreat from New York City, we astonished ourselves. For the first time in the course of the war, our men stood up to British troops in an open field and forced *them* to retreat. Though the battle at Harlem Heights had little strategic consequence, and though we thereafter continued our retreat from Manhattan Island, leaving it completely to the British, we were nevertheless profoundly heartened by our show of courage.

Our fortified position atop the rocky bluffs of Harlem Heights was strong. During the preceding weeks, soldiers encamped there had built three long parallel redoubts across the island; the trenches and earthen walls were bolstered by rock walls built upon the granite. Only ships sailing up the two rivers could outflank us.

At dawn on Monday, September 16, the day after our rout at Kip's Bay, General Washington sent out a party of a hundred and twenty scouts to discover the position of the British south of us. Our men soon confronted the Forty-second Highlanders, a brigade of Scottish troops known as the Black Watch. They drove our scouts back into a valley, and thus it seemed that another retreat had begun.

But as the men encamped atop the rocks of Harlem Heights looked down on the skirmish, they heard a piercing insult: the British were blowing a fox horn, as if they had chased the poor fox down its hole.

General Washington, a Virginia fox hunter who knew that horn well, ordered a strong detachment of Virginians and Marylanders—accompanied by as many volunteers as wanted to fight—directly south to the Hollow Way as reinforcements. The General ordered a second detachment around to the left, where they could hide behind the rocks and thus surprise the Scots from the rear. The poor fox may have disappeared down its hole, but it had more than one exit. And the fox now hoped to fool the hounds.

Henry volunteered; I did not. Henry needed something to live for; I already had a wife and child. He needed to believe in himself, in our army, in our future; I already believed in our future, and ached for the day when we could begin to live it.

Before the flankers managed to sneak behind the Scots, they were discovered. But our men pouring down from Harlem Heights took with them a determination to recover the honor they had lost the day before. Though we fielded two thousand men against a Scottish, English, and Hessian force of five thousand, our men stood their ground in an open buckwheat field. Gradually they managed to push the faltering redcoats south toward New York City. Our musket fire was mixed with jubilant whoops of victory when the dreaded Black Watch, wearing kilts and tall black bearskin hats, fled in full retreat.

We might have chased them a good deal further, but General Washington suspected that General Howe had ordered reinforcements. Rather than allow his soldiers to rush into a trap, our General ordered an end to the attack and a return to Harlem Heights.

The men strode into camp as unvanquished heroes. That night, they celebrated with bonfires rather than campfires atop the rocky Heights, for they wanted the British to see the leaping flames.

Nigel MacDonald, whose Scottish ancestors had been slaughtered in 1746 by English troops in the Battle of Culloden, and who had no love for the traitors known as the Black Watch, stood that night atop a rocky cliff with his bagpipes. Lit by the flames of a bonfire, Nigel sent his wailing musical war cry down to the wounded hounds in the valley.

Genevieve.

As soon as he could, Benjamin found John Lally, who sent his own courier to find me north of Kingsbridge. The rider let me know that both Benjamin and Henry were safe at the camp on Harlem Heights.

They were out of the city.

They were safe.

They were safe.

☙

Chapter Sixty-Five

Benjamin.

THE BURNING OF NEW YORK CITY

As usual, it took very little to make General Howe extremely cautious. Following the fox hunt, he waited nearly a month before he made his next move.

We were therefore still encamped atop Harlem Heights on the cool, clear night of September 20, when a sentry spotted a red glow far to the south. The spark, for so it looked at first, rapidly grew in size, until we could have no doubt that the city of New York was burning.

The fire (as we learned from an English soldier taken prisoner later that week) began at Whitehall wharf, at the very tip of the island. A strong wind from the southeast, blowing off the harbor, drove the flames rapidly north: the worst of the blaze raged between the Broad Way and Hudson's River.

During the week before the attack on September 15, while all the troops but the rear guard were evacuating the city, the quartermaster's wagons had carried away every church bell in New York, even the bells of Trinity Church, so that we might later forge them into cannons. Thus when flames broke out on the wharf, no alarm could be rung to awaken New York's fire brigades.

The blaze advanced so rapidly that rather than try to extinguish it with buckets and water pumps, soldiers were ordered to tear down rows of buildings and thereby prevent the flames from leaping from one block to the next. The wind was so strong, however, that the flames jumped across every gap.

The conflagration reached Trinity Church on the Broad Way. Its white steeple became a torch towering above the city. After the outer boards had burned away, a blazing skeleton of inner beams pointed skyward in the night. The fire raged inside the church, flickering and flashing through tall windows, until the roof and steeple collapsed with an enormous explosion of sparks.

Saint Paul's Church, further up the boulevard, was spared. But King's College, a large building which the army had used through the summer as its hospital, was rendered into naught but ashes.

What started the fire, we never knew. A lantern might have toppled in a warehouse on the wharf. Perhaps a bitter patriot meant to deny His Majesty's troops warm quarters for the winter. We did learn that several suspects were hung without trial in a riot of vengeance.

Nearly five hundred buildings were destroyed, the entire southwest portion of the city, before the flames were finally halted the following afternoon.

While I stood beside Henry that night atop Harlem Heights, gazing south toward the fiery red glow ten miles away, I felt no joy in depriving the British of their seaport. Genevieve and I had loved that city. We had been fascinated, during our evening walks, by its astonishing diversity of people, by the ever surprising variety of its buildings, by its bustle and industry from dawn to late into the night.

Genevieve had felt so at home with the Penningtons. In that "nest of Tories," we had found the most decent of people.

Caleb had been born in New York. He had accompanied us on our strolls along Pearl Street and Wall Street, and sat with us (on my lap) on a bench on the Bowling Green. Caleb had gazed in his infant way at ships anchored in the harbor, at seagulls whirling overhead. He had met his first horse on the common. He had been bundled in my arms when Genevieve and I stood in reverent silence in Trinity Church.

No, I took no pleasure in watching our city burn.

I could only hope that we might one day return, the three of us, to walk its fascinating streets at some better time.

Genevieve.

Even from Kingsbridge, at the northern end of Manhattan Island, I could see the red glow, horrible in the night.

One wonders, so alone at such a time, how close we are to the final earthly apocalypse. To the final fiery judgment. Will, one night, we discover flames in towns and villages all around us, burning toward us? Will a whirlwind draw those flames—and our ashes—up toward the stars?

How well did we know that what we did, we did in the right?

A city in flames billowed red-black smoke, smoke that smudged the face of God as He stared down upon us.

God must turn His face away and shudder when confronted with our frightful doings upon the plain of war.

How easy it had been, as a girl, when I had ridden every Sunday morning in the family wagon to the white meetinghouse in Lincoln.

How difficult now—how profoundly frightening—when, in the name of some cause, we were burning churches.

℘

Chapter Sixty-Six

Benjamin.

Three weeks after the conflagration in New York City, General Howe finally resumed the chase. Rather than confront our fortifications on Harlem Heights, he ferried troops in a fleet of cutters up the East River and landed them at Throg's Neck. He no doubt planned that his redcoats would now march north of us and cut off our retreat.

However, the British marched into a swamp. At the lone bridge to solid ground, they met a detachment of Massachusetts muskets. After wasting nearly a week, General Howe loaded his troops back into the cutters, then rowed them further north, to Pell's Point.

Meanwhile, General Washington rushed his army across the bridge from Manhattan Island to the mainland (where I found Genevieve and Caleb, after a separation of a month). The Continental Army marched fifteen miles north to the village of White Plains, at a bend in the Bronx River, well above the British troops.

Acquiescing to the demands of Congress, and to the poor advice of his own officers, General Washington left nearly three thousand men at Fort Washington. Across Hudson's River stood a second fortification, Fort Lee. Vulnerable to assault from both land and water, these two posts would almost certainly be attacked before the end of the autumn campaign.

General Howe outflanked us at White Plains on October 28, but two days of heavy rain prevented a further and perhaps final battle. The driving torrents enabled us, on the night of October 31, to retreat further north, to Castle Hill on the Croton River, almost twenty miles north of Manhattan Island.

The British did not pursue us, but headed west to Hudson's River, then marched south toward Fort Washington.

General Washington left a body of troops at Castle Hill as a feeble barricade between New York City and New England. He marched the rest of us north to Peekskill on the Hudson's eastern shore. We crossed the broad gray river aboard barges on November 10, to Haverstraw on the western shore. We then marched rapidly south, parallel to the river.

General Howe attacked and captured Fort Washington in one day,

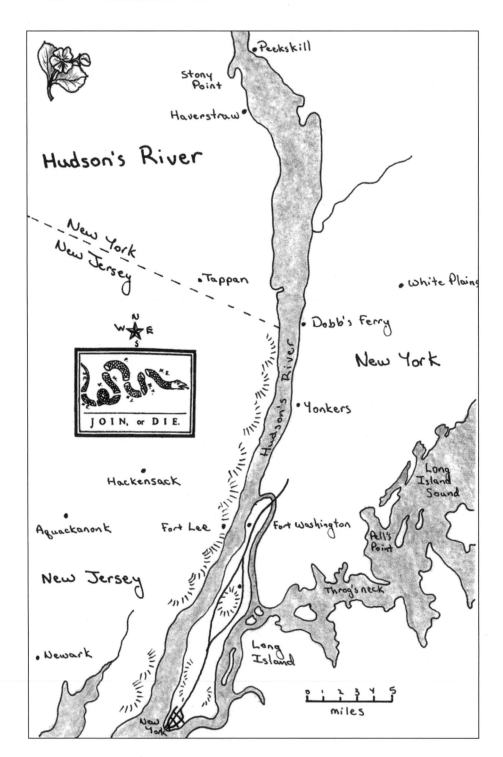

on November 16, then ordered General Cornwallis to cross the river at Yonkers and attack Fort Lee. We lost 2,800 troops and their artillery at Fort Washington; the soldiers at Fort Lee managed to escape. Hudson's River was now unguarded. It thus became a British boulevard all the way to Albany, where it met the Mohawk River to the west, Lake Champlain and its waterway to the north, and roads leading into Massachusetts to the east.

The British now pursued us in a race across New Jersey. Their front lines were often within sight of our rear guard. Snow had begun to fall. Militia volunteers abandoned the army by the hundreds. When we reached Newark, New Jersey on November 22, General Cornwallis was less than a day's march behind us. We had only three and a half thousand men, many of whom would depart for home on December 31, when their term of duty came to an end.

Our defense of New York City had been a disaster. We had lost that vital seaport. We had failed to prevent British ships from sailing up Hudson's River. And we had done so while thirteen States, and much of the world, witnessed our failure. Three hundred twenty-nine officers, and over four thousand soldiers, had been captured during the New York campaign. (They would now, though we did not yet know it, be slowly starved in the most hideous of prisons.) Thousands more of our men had died in battle, or of camp diseases, or had succumbed to the cold and rain and now the snow. We had left behind 218 cannons, countless barrels of gunpowder, tons of lead, and most of the tents and blankets that would have protected us on our humiliating retreat south through the early winter in New Jersey.

In addition to all this, the thousands of militiamen who disappeared toward home during that September and October and November of 1776, no doubt told anyone who would listen to them in their villages across New York, Connecticut, Rhode Island, Massachusetts and New Hampshire, that General Washington had been outmaneuvered at every turn, that the army was in rags, and that after the capture of New York City, Philadelphia, seat of the Congress, must surely be next.

Though we as private soldiers could know nothing about it, several of General Washington's officers were already turning against him.

And yet . . .

When, in early December, we crossed the Delaware River from

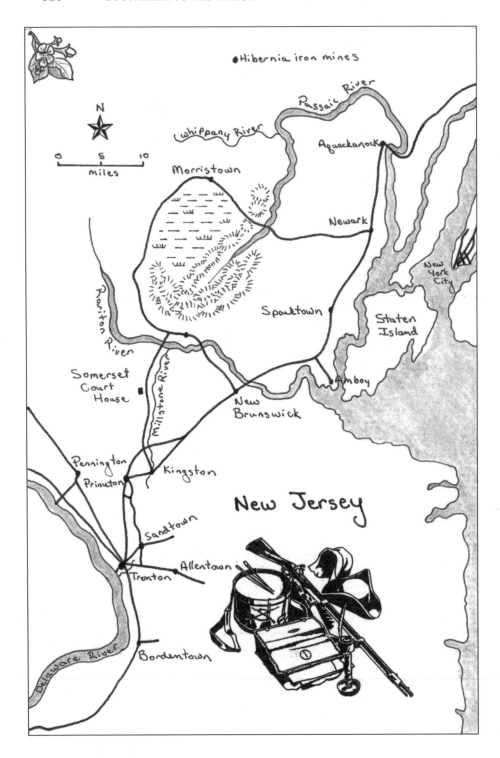

Hibernia iron mines

Passaic River

Whippany River

Aquackanock

Morristown

Newark

Spauktown

New York City

Raritan River

Staten Island

Somerset Court House

Millstone River

Amboy

New Brunswick

Pennington

Princeton

Kingston

New Jersey

Sandtown

Allentown

Trenton

Delaware River

Bordentown

N

0 5 10
miles

Trenton, New Jersey to the safety of the Pennsylvania shore (taking with us every boat on the New Jersey side so that General Cornwallis could not follow), we carried in our knapsacks something which no English or Scottish or Hessian soldier carried in his.

Aye, His Majesty's troops were well-dressed and well-fed, they slept in tents and in barns and even in homes along the road, and aye, the New Jersey farmers were glad, even eager, to trade fresh provisions for good British coins.

But in our knapsacks as we marched, in our knapsacks as we paddled across the ice-fringed Delaware, in our knapsacks as we chopped down trees in Pennsylvania and struggled to build crude huts before the full blizzard of winter was upon us, we carried folded, tattered, damp, and smudged broadsheet copies of our Declaration of Independence, bought for pennies in New York City during the bold summer of 1776, and treasured for a lifetime.

The British had a warm dinner for today, with little thought of tomorrow.

But while we chewed a crust of cold stale bread, we reached with our hearts and our souls toward a thousand tomorrows.

છ

PART IV

The Wildcat Pounces

Chapter Sixty-Seven

Benjamin, during
"the times that try men's souls."

As Providence had known in Boston that the thirteen colonies were not yet woven into one strong fabric (and so marched us off to further battles), so Providence in New York taught us a military maneuver that we were to use again and again, until we had won the war. And that maneuver was: to Retreat.

Our first lesson was in August of 1776, when we retreated across the river in the fog from Long Island to Manhattan Island.

In September, we retreated from the streets of New York City to the rock walls on Harlem Heights. In October, we abandoned the island completely.

Through the cold, rainy month of November, we retreated endlessly south through the State of New Jersey.

In early December, we retreated across the Delaware River into the State of Pennsylvania. Whereupon, for the first time in almost three months, the British and the Germans stopped chasing us.

Those three months had whittled General Washington's army from almost twenty thousand dispirited troops in New York City to five thousand starving refugees on the south bank of the Delaware.

We were cold, famished, and exhausted, wearing ragged summer uniforms, with no winter camp though the snows of December were upon us.

But we had learned our lesson well: the regulars in the Continental Army were masters of the orderly retreat.

Our Commander in Chief was learning as well (though of course we privates could not know it at the time). He was learning that his troops, when attacked by British infantry on an open field, would turn and run in panic. But if our men could stand behind the earthen wall of a redoubt, or even a farmer's stone wall, or especially if they could catch the enemy by surprise, they fought with a stubborn vigor.

General Washington was also learning to trust his own judgment, rather than the advice of his officers at headquarters. He learned when to retreat, despite the criticism and loss of faith that retreat brought him. And he learned, despite the warnings of weaker men, when to turn like a wildcat and pounce.

General Washington was caught, throughout the eight and a half years of war, between his determination to subordinate himself to the authority of Congress, and his determination to build an army that could ultimately outlast and outwit the British. He sent a multitude of letters to Congress (many of them copied by Genevieve), asking for supplies and payment for his soldiers, and asking as well for advice. He sought direction and guidance from that body of men in Philadelphia, distant from the battlefield though they were, in order to bolster them as the seat of the nation's government.

He thus learned to contend with a Congress who were contentious among themselves, cumbersome in the slowness of their decisions, and nearly hopeless in the crucial task of financing the war. Our troops and officers often went unpaid for months. We scavenged for what few chickens and cobs of corn we could find. We slept without tents in the rain. But though General Washington complained vehemently on our behalf to Congress, he never once turned against the body of men who had commissioned him.

He was learning as well to contend with the civilian population of New York and New Jersey, where a great number of Loyalists readily sold food, horses, wagons, and other supplies to the enemy. Determined to build a united America, even while he fought the war, General Washington did not send his troops to punish Loyalist farmers; instead he ordered his hungry soldiers to treat all civilians with respect. (The British, on the contrary, plundered farmers wherever they marched. They had little regard for any "colonials," friend or foe.)

Perhaps most important, General Washington was *willing* to learn, whereas the British officers thought they knew all there was to know about the art of war when they stepped off their ships. Our General was a new commander in chief of a new kind of army, fighting for an unprecedented cause in the New World.

He learned, and we learned.

But oh, our bellies were often empty. Our feet were tired and wet and nearly frozen along the way. And most of us, most of the time, were a long way from home.

During that early winter of 1776, while we retreated through New Jersey with His Majesty's well-equipped and well-fed army marching fast upon us, a new sort of union was formed. None of the soldiers had anticipated it. But a union it was, and neither winter storms nor British bayonets could sunder it.

We marched through the village of Princeton on December 2. On December 3, we reached the village of Trenton on the Delaware River. Across the gray, ice-fringed river was the State of Pennsylvania. We, and the army pursuing us, were now dangerously close to the Congress in Philadelphia. If General Howe ordered his troops to march past us and then attack Philadelphia by land, while the British fleet sailed up the mouth of the Delaware and attacked from the river, there was little we could do to stop them. By early December, the Continental Army looked more like prisoners released from a dungeon than American troops fighting for our nation's freedom.

The Connecticut militia had disappeared for home. The New York militia would march but a short distance beyond the borders of New York. The New Jersey militia had responded to our General's appeal with paltry numbers; they, in any case, would march no further than the borders of New Jersey.

Equally disappointing, hundreds of farmers in New Jersey had signed "certificates of allegiance" to the King. By doing so, they hoped that His Majesty's troops might steal only a horse or two, rather than every head of livestock. With our backs to the river, and Congress just beyond the river, our desperate soldiers began to wonder, Where were the throngs of patriots who had started this war?

During the years to come, we learned the same bitter lesson again and again: Few people could see beyond the boundaries of their farms, fewer still beyond the boundaries of their States. A good many Americans were willing to keep quiet while they waited . . . to hear who won the war. And while they waited, they prospered, quite willing to sell a chicken or a hog for a good British shilling.

Sometimes it seemed a marvel that enough of us remained to keep the war going. Often a third to half of the men were sick. After weeks of struggling to boil a pot of porridge with green wood in a drizzle, after weeks of trying to sleep in a wet blanket on the cold, wet ground, after weeks of fevers and aches and dizziness that were as much a part of daily life as marching with all possible haste, we had difficulty some nights to find enough healthy men to stand guard as sentries.

We marched with empty bellies and on bleeding feet wrapped in rags for one reason: because General Washington rode beside us. On that endless wretched retreat through New Jersey, and on all the wretched marches during the next five years, our Commander in Chief rode up and down the column, speaking quietly to the men, conferring with his officers. He was as wet, as cold, and as exhausted as we were.

Every soldier in the army knew: General Washington had been the last man to climb down the ladder on the pier in Brooklyn. He was in the last boat to leave Long Island, after all of his troops had made their escape.

Aye, though most of the American population was snug at home by the hearth, or gathered at tables in a tavern, talking about their love of freedom, we in that sickly, bewildered, despairing army began to know a different kind of love. Ours was a love that grew stronger every day, every month, every year. Despite the paltry fervor that filled our nation, *our* hearts formed a union, just as much—and maybe more—than the Declaration had formed a union. Because no matter where we had come from, Massachusetts to Virginia, a shop on a seaport wharf or a farm in a forest, we loved General Washington.

As long as he believed in us, we would believe in him.

From the Trenton wharf, we sent our baggage wagons across the Delaware River aboard a ferry to the Pennsylvania side. Then a portion of the army camped in Trenton, while a larger portion marched with General Washington the short distance back to Princeton, where we waited for General Lee to arrive with reinforcements from New York. (Thus for a few days in early December, I was in New Jersey with Henry, while Genevieve and Caleb were across the river with the baggage train in Pennsylvania. Never in the course of the war did those separations become any less painful. For though a man may attempt to predict tomorrow's weather, never can he predict tomorrow's war.)

General Lee did not show up with his six thousand troops. The British and Germans were meanwhile approaching in great strength. So we marched back to Trenton, boarded ferries and crossed the river. Our men paddled every boat on the New Jersey side, for miles up and down the river, over to the Pennsylvania shore.

On December 8, the redcoats appeared along the riverbank where less than an hour before we had been standing. They found not so much as a rowboat. But the river would soon freeze. General Cornwallis and his troops could then simply march across.

We spent the following days building crude log huts, of a much draftier and smokier sort than those we had built in Cambridge. Henry did his best for his sister and nephew, but with the enemy extended for several miles along the opposite bank, we spent much of our days and nights on sentry duty, with little time for carpentry.

The Pennsylvania farmers, like the farmers in New Jersey, would not accept paper money printed by Congress. Our neighbors placed no more value on our Continental dollars than they placed their faith in the Continental Army.

Congress fled from Philadelphia on December 13; the delegates felt safer further south in Baltimore. Thus they too showed their meager confidence in our Continental Army.

News arrived in camp that a British fleet had captured Newport, Rhode Island. Our small navy of privateers had lost one of its busiest harbors.

Chunks of ice were now drifting down the Delaware. The time would soon come when one cold clear night would provide the British with their bridge.

A few days before Christmas, Thomas Paine published another pamphlet. He had marched with us on the retreat across New Jersey; we had watched him, evening after evening, as he sat near a campfire and wrote his pages, using the head of a drum as a desk. Once across the river, he galloped south to Philadelphia to find a printer. His summons to the nation appeared in a newspaper, *The Pennsylvania Journal*, on December 19, 1776. A day later, couriers rode with freshly printed pamphlets to every state. Once again, Thomas Paine rallied us at a time when we had little else to cling to.

Copies of "The American Crisis" arrived in camp on Christmas Eve. As I had done in Cambridge, I stood in the light of a supper fire and read aloud to the troops.

> *"These are the times that try men's souls. The summer soldier and the sunshine patriot will, in this crisis, shrink from the service of his country; but he that stands it now deserves the love and thanks of man and woman."*

Aye, Mr. Paine had marched with us: well he knew the difference between summer and winter.

> *"Tyranny, like Hell, is not easily conquered; yet we have this consolation with us, that the harder the conflict, the more glorious the triumph."*

The mere mention of the word "triumph" gave a bit of strength to our spirits.

> *"What we obtain too cheap, we esteem too lightly: it is dearness only that gives every thing its value."*

We knew the dearness, the cost in suffering and sickness and death. We labored to accomplish something of profound and timeless value. Thomas Paine assured us,

> *"God Almighty will not give up a people to military destruction, or leave them unsupportedly to perish, who have so earnestly and so repeatedly sought to avoid the calamities of war by every decent method which wisdom could invent."*

True, not a man among us had wanted this war. Our Congress had sent repeated letters to London, seeking a reconciliation with King and Parliament.

Then God Almighty would surely support us through these cold dark weeks of winter.

On the following day, Caleb's first Christmas, General Washington ordered the troops to prepare with provisions for a three-day maneuver. We would depart from camp on Christmas evening after supper.

Genevieve, on Christmas Day, 1776.

In our tiny hut on Christmas morning, while a damp wind sifted between the unchinked logs and smoke from a hissing fire rose more into the room than up the chimney, Benjamin read from the Book of Luke. Henry gave Caleb a wooden bird that he had carved from a bit of pine—a chickadee with folded wings and the stub of a tail—small enough that Caleb could wave it in his hand.

After a bowl of porridge without honey, without milk, we stood outside in the snow beneath a gray sky with several hundred troops and listened to Reverend Kesslaer's Christmas service. The men were too sick, their feet too cold, for them to endure more than a brief reading, a prayer, and a blessing.

I returned to our shabby little hut with Caleb, while Benjamin and Henry mustered with their regiment.

When they returned to the hut and told me about their orders—a three-day maneuver—I was silent for nearly an hour. I could not speak.

I was fiercely angry with General Washington for taking away our Christmas. But I was determined not to say one word of remonstration or complaint.

Deep in my heart, I harbored the knowledge that no one, not the warm and well-fed farmers, not the Congress, nor even Mama and Papa, could possibly know what we endured, what we relinquished, what we were willing to do, for our country. Month after month, in state after state, we were becoming a people apart from all others. I feared that though our sacrifice might be the cause of a justified pride . . . it might one day as well become the cause of a divisive bitterness.

Benjamin spent part of that afternoon writing a letter, a Christmas letter to Caleb. He gave the letter to me and asked me to keep it until Caleb was old enough to read it.

The paper is now worn from so many handlings, so many readings. The ink, the thin cold ink into which Benjamin dipped his quill that day, has faded. But we can still read the words, as we read them every Christmas; or shall I say, as Caleb reads them every Christmas, after Benjamin has read from the Book of Luke.

Caleb has loaned his letter to me, for he is its keeper now, of course. I rub my fingers over paper that Benjamin bought in a shop in New York City, carried in his backpack across New Jersey, and wrote upon in Pennsylvania. From this old letter shall I copy:

25 December, 1776

My precious son Caleb,

I must say farewell to you this evening, though I expect and hope to return to you before the end of the year.

If I do not return, and you find yourself a boy growing up without a father, I want you to know that what I did, I did for you.

When I found your mother, I thought that I, though undeserving, had been blessed with all the happiness the human heart can know. But she would be the first to agree with me, that when you entered our lives, we both discovered a fuller and richer and far more joyful happiness. Even in this hut, a dwelling so poor, I hurt in my heart that you and your mother must live here . . . even in this hut, to be in the presence of you and your mother, and your Uncle Henry, and to know that we four are a family, provides me with a fulfillment, and gratitude, beyond measure.

So Caleb, take care of your dear mother, as the man in the family must do. Thank her for her courage. Thank her for a generosity beyond all practical wisdom. And thank her for cherishing a dream that belongs to tomorrow, rather than the trappings of ephemeral pleasure that belong to today.

May you live in a country that is free, and at peace.

Your father, with love.

∽

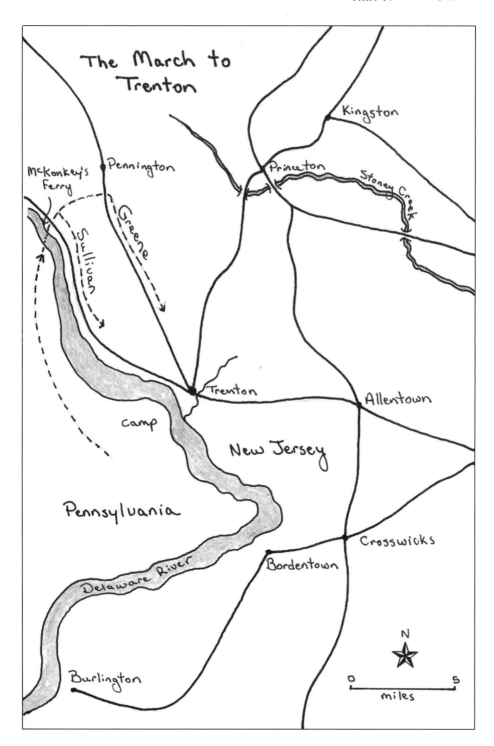

Chapter Sixty-Eight

Benjamin, on Christmas night, 1776,
marching toward

THE BATTLE OF TRENTON

Our column departed from camp during the last hour of daylight. As we marched toward a ferry nine miles upstream, the pale yellow sun ahead of us disappeared into approaching storm clouds. Wind buffeted our bowed faces, then stung our cheeks with a half-frozen drizzle. We hoped that as the evening grew colder, the sleet would become snow; enough snow, at least, to give us some footing on the rutted icy road.

Many of the men marching tonight would finish their terms of duty at the end of the year. General Washington was thus using his army while he still had one.

We reached McKonkey's Ferry, a broad dock jutting into the river. Peering into the darkness, we could see jagged sheets of ice drifting from left to right. Should any man fall into the Delaware tonight, that would be the end of the war for him.

As if responding to a silent signal, a fleet of long, flat-bottomed boats appeared from upstream, maneuvered by men standing at poles. Some of the boats bumped broadside to the dock. Others shoved their prows against the icy bank. Troops ahead of us clambered aboard, until roughly fifty sat crowded together on the bottom of each boat. Then the polers pushed off. The Delaware was apparently shallow enough that the crews could manage with poles rather than oars. A hundred feet from shore, the boats disappeared into darkness and sleet.

When our turn came, Henry and I stepped into a Durham ore boat, designed to carry iron ore from the hills of Pennsylvania to the furnaces of Philadelphia. Our shoes crunched on the gritty bottom. There were no thwarts, no benches. We sat on wet iron ore gravel. Each man pointed his musket toward the sky and wrapped his hand around the lock to keep it dry.

As the polers pushed off, I was astonished to see—I had to stare in the gloom to be sure—the face of Michael, one of our topmen on the *Lively*. We were under no orders to remain silent, and the crew called to each other as they reached with their poles to fend off chunks of ice, so I felt no hesitation in whispering, "Michael!"

He peered down at me and surely saw nothing more than a dark figure among fifty crowded dark figures. I wanted to reach up and grab his hand, but my hands were on my musket and his were on the pole. I could do no more than whisper, "'Benjamin, from the *Lively.*"

"Benjamin!" he exclaimed softy. Then he nodded at the other men pushing their poles against the river bottom. "Ethan, Hank, and Adam."

They stood on two narrow promenades along the gunnels. Yes, there in the darkness was Ethan's slender shape. And Hank's belly, which he had cheerfully pressed on top of the folded sail when we were furling. And Adam's enormous shoulders. For a moment I forgot that I was on my way to some unknown battle. Instead, I was delighted that tomorrow I could introduce Genevieve to four of the lads.

"We're with Colonel John Glover from Marblehead," said Michael as he leaned his weight against a sheet of ice so the prow could pass beyond it. "We took you fellows across from Long Island to Manhattan last August, but I didn't see you that night."

"Fog," I said.

"Hell of a fog!"

I glanced at Henry, wanting to share my discovery. But he stared at the other boats: ghostly barges clunking against sheets of ice.

Wind swept down the river, wet with sleet. The men hunched their shoulders, turned their faces away, retied a rag scarf. Some closed their eyes, for they had learned, as all soldiers learn, that even ten minutes of sleep can be a golden treasure.

Our boat crunched against the far bank. Before we climbed out, I whispered, "Adam!" He turned and looked at me with his ready smile, as if just yesterday we had shared a pint of ale.

Then I was over the prow and my feet were back on the State of New Jersey. We climbed a bank of frozen mud until we reached an icy road. Listening for our officers, we gradually formed into a column. But the column did not march. With our backs to a blizzard, we waited while the ore boats ferried back and forth, bringing over two thousand troops across the river. Our snowy column merely shifted forward as companies formed behind us.

The boats ferried eighteen pieces of field artillery, and then the horses that would pull the carriages. Well over an hour passed before finally we began to march, on frozen feet. And not one of us knew how far we would march before we got to wherever we were going.

General Washington rode up and down the column, the black cape over his shoulders covered with dark gray snow. He said not a word to us, but he did not have to. He rode with solemn confidence, and bestowed upon us the same.

After advancing no more than a mile, our column halted. We had reached a fork in the road. Some of the men slept where they stood.

Brigade officers whispered our password to us. Should a stranger appear out of the storm, he must say, "Victory or Death." As the phrase was passed along the column (men who slept on their feet were shaken awake and told the words), I knew that we had received more than a password. Never before had General Washington offered us such a choice. We were not marching toward some skirmish. The battle ahead would determine in some fundamental way the fate of our nation.

The column began to advance again. Our forces divided at the fork: General John Sullivan led a regiment to the right, along the River Road. We, under General Nathanael Greene, took the fork to the left and moved further upland. Thus we would converge upon Trenton—for so we now guessed our target to be—at two different points. Should one column be discovered as it approached, the other might still pounce with complete surprise.

General Washington accompanied our column. As did the artillery. In the windy darkness, we could hear the horses plodding behind us. General Washington rode up and down our line, speaking quietly to us, "Soldiers, keep by your officers. Keep by your officers." Aye, easy would it be in the whirling blizzard for a man to become lost without even knowing he was lost. We kept an eye on the dim figure of a captain ahead of us.

Victory or Death. Victory or Death. I heard the words in my mind as I marched my feet in time: Victory or Death.

How far had we gone? How long had we been marching? We had left camp before dusk on one of the longest nights of the year, and now the first gray light of dawn began to appear. Lifting our eyes from the rutted slush, we looked at the snow-clad backs of men trudging in front of us. Peering beyond them, we could see a long straight untrampled depression where the road lay. And there, far ahead, was that the shape of a barn?

One thing we knew: the wind howled from behind us, directly into the faces of whatever sentries might be watching for us. Our feet, even the horses hooves, were muffled in wet snow. We were not likely to be seen or heard until we tickled their noses with the muzzles of our muskets. And if the enemy had been celebrating Christmas the day before, we might even catch them in their beds.

I glanced at Henry, marching beside me. He looked at me. I saw an unshaven, blue-white face, with two dark eyes, more dull than determined, wrapped in a wreath of frost. I must have looked the same.

We heard a shout, not fifty yards ahead, "Der Feind! Der Feind! Heraus!" We had startled their pickets.

"Germans," whispered someone behind me. "Hessians."

We readied arms, marched briskly, every soldier now fully awake. We could see snow-blurred outlines of houses.

Musket shots. Theirs? Ours?

A voice behind us shouted, "Make way! Make way!" We jumped aside as horses pulling artillery carriages trotted past. The jolting bronze barrels dropped their tufts of snow.

General Washington deployed our brigades with superb efficiency. Henry and I, under General Stirling, followed the artillery to the most perfect location we could have found: we stood atop a slope at the crux of a V formed by the two main streets leading through town, King Street and Queen Street. Our cannons were quickly wheeled into position and the horses unharnessed; the bronze barrels now aimed right down through the heart of Trenton.

We had formed to the north of town. General Mercer's men formed along the western side. General Greene moved his troops to the eastern flank. Although a growing number of Hessians, some in blue coats, some in green, rushed out from the houses into the streets and fired at us, we quickly and without much trouble surrounded most of Trenton.

The southern edge of the village was bounded by the Delaware River and its tributary, the Assunpink Creek. Only a bridge over the creek offered a route of escape. Although we could see some Hessians racing across it, General Sullivan's men, who had marched along the River Road, were firing toward the bridge as they advanced. We would soon have the enemy entirely trapped.

The Hessians attempted to form their artillery on King Street, so they could clear us from our unprotected hill. But General Henry Knox, assisted by Artillery Captain Alexander Hamilton, was ready for them: with a volley of shots, our cannons cleared the street of soldiers. Then

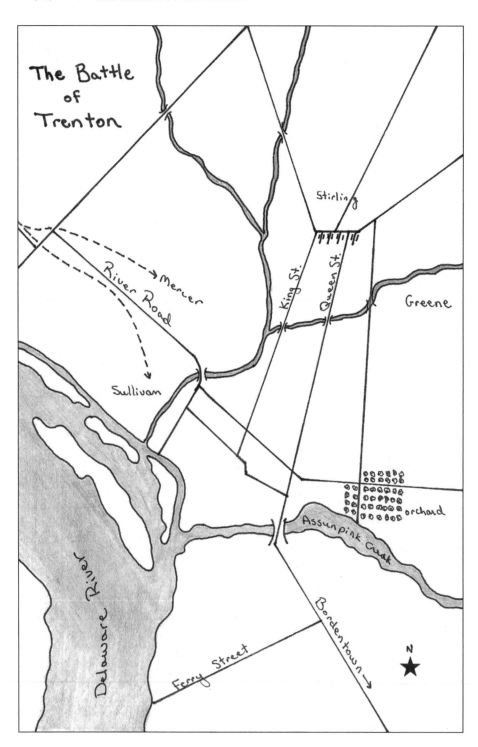

The Battle
of
Trenton

Captain William Washington, cousin to our General, and Lieutenant James Monroe (destined to become the nation's fifth president) charged down the street with a squad of roaring men and quickly captured the Hessian guns. Those of us still on the hill—as if in the front row of a theater balcony, looking down at the spectacle on a broad stage—could hardly believe our victory even as we watched it.

The Hessian commander, Colonel Johann Rall, appeared on his horse at the eastern edge of town. Waving his sword and shouting to his men, he tried to assemble them near an apple orchard. (The trees were black and bare against the snow.) One of our riflemen soon found his mark; Colonel Rall toppled from the horse. The Hessian troops milled in confusion.

A dozen more shots were fired. Then in the silence that followed . . . we realized we had just won our first battle. Here were the Hessian brutes who had given no quarter on Long Island: they had bayoneted every prisoner who begged for mercy. Now the butchers were *our* prisoners.

Well it was that General Washington maintained absolute control of his troops, for a good number of our men had lost companions on Long Island. They would gladly have given no quarter in return.

We were allowed to eat a brief breakfast from our knapsacks. Meanwhile, patrols went through every building in Trenton to be sure we missed no one hiding in a potato cellar, or in an attic. We heard that General Rall had been carried to a church, where he died as he lay upon a pew.

We learned as well that not a single patriot had been killed, and only four wounded. The Germans had lost twenty-two soldiers, killed and wounded. We had captured over nine hundred, including twenty-three officers, and we had acquired six field cannons and a thousand muskets. As important, we took from the Hessians hundreds of knives, swords, hatchets, side arms, and cartridge boxes. Everything was gathered with the strictest order, counted, then loaded into wagons.

Several barrels of rum were discovered, somehow untapped on Christmas day. But General Washington, who demanded discipline and dignity at all times, ordered them stove in with an axe.

As Henry and I walked the streets of Trenton with our company, gathering up enemy arms and stacking them in the beds of wagons (wagons requisitioned from the barns and stables in Trenton, and paid for with Continental paper dollars), we saw many faces watching us from windows. Few of the townspeople ventured out to greet us. Who knew but what the British might arrive an hour from now, and then might not another volley of grapeshot be fired down King Street?

And of course, some of the good citizens of Trenton may have prospered as hosts for three weeks to the Hessians. Then, better to stay inside with their shillings hidden under a floorboard.

Somewhat rested, and with a meal in our bellies, we marched our prisoners back along the road by which we had come. The Hessians were allowed to wear no more than what they had been wearing when captured. Some had sprung from bed when they heard the alarm, had grabbed a musket and ran outside with no more than breeches and a shirt. Last night's blizzard had diminished to a steady snowfall. Little pity did we feel for the butchers of Long Island as they trudged and stumbled, their arms wrapped tightly around their chests.

Soon, however, several wagons caught up with our column. The rear guard in Trenton had loaded them with Hessian coats, blue and green. As the wagons moved slowly up the column, soldiers riding in the wagon beds tossed coats, scarves, mittens, sweaters, even blankets to the desperate Hessians. The prisoners shoved each other as they called out in their strange language, held up their bare hands, showed us their shoes without stockings. While thus begging for coats and compassion, they seemed to forget that an hour ago they had been firing their muskets to kill us.

My sympathy for them did not increase when we passed two frozen corpses beside the road. Though partially hidden by snow, they were clearly recognizable as two of our own soldiers. Had they paused to sleep during the night? No one had noticed them.

While we marched through the morning, the low winter sun, veiled by silver-gray clouds, moved across the southern sky. To the north, snow clouds remained so black that the night seemed to be still in them.

At McKonkey's Ferry, the ore boats took both guards and prisoners across the Delaware. The chunks of ice were no thicker than they had been the night before, but the wind was much lighter. And of course we had daylight now. Nevertheless, our second crossing took much longer than the first, for we had nine hundred extra men to transport.

Searching for the topmen as we crossed the river, I spotted Ethan in a nearby boat. Calling to him, I inviting the four of them to visit our hut in the encampment. He nodded as he pushed his pole.

On the road approaching our camp, we were met by a large troop of militia from Philadelphia. Forming a guard, they herded our prisoners onto a road leading south. Toward what, we knew not. We were glad to be rid of those Hessians, those butchers with their bayonets who gave no quarter.

There was a jubilant spirit in our camp that night. Especially when we learned that two other regiments had failed to make the crossing. They both had orders to cross the Delaware further downstream, then to approach Trenton from the south; they would thus have guarded the bridge over the creek by which several hundred Hessians escaped. General Cadwalader had gotten his men across, but the fringe of ice along the far shore prevented him from unloading his artillery. So he ferried all of his troops back to the Pennsylvania shore. General Ewing, certain that boats could never get through the drifting ice, did not even attempt the crossing.

Aye, we had done the job ourselves. And aside from losing a few Hessians across that bridge (no fault of our own), we had managed the battle like professionals.

More important, General Washington had managed the battle like the Commander in Chief we needed him to be. There had been no thought of not crossing that river. There had been no thought of turning back. At Trenton, he had positioned every soldier and every cannon exactly where they needed to be. (Our General had excellent spies.) The battle had been quickly won without the loss of a single man. (The two who froze were lost not to the battle, but to the blizzard.) And we had conducted ourselves with order and with dignity: no butchery, no plundering. Not a single person looking out from those windows had reason for complaint. Not one chicken from its roost had we lifted, nor even one egg.

We had forced the British out of Boston. We had retreated across the river from Long Island to Manhattan Island without the loss of a single man. We had stood our ground at Harlem Heights. But today was the first time, the very first time, that *we* had the fleet which controlled the waterway. That *we* had outmaneuvered the enemy. That *we* had taken prisoners.

The news went out to the nation: after the loss of New York City, after months of disheartening retreats, after thousands of soldiers had walked out of camp and gone home, General Washington's Continental Army had stood up to European troops, and had won.

Genevieve, looking back.

Only later in the war did we learn that on Long Island, the British had told the Hessians that the *Americans* would give no quarter, and that to save themselves, they must bayonet us as quickly as they could.

Only later in the war did we realize that we had all become brutes, that we had all become prisoners: that the war had captured every one of us, and had made us brutish almost beyond recognition. Even when the war was over and it set us free from the battlefield, we were never again truly free.

Those German boys had been forced to leave their farms, forced to leave their families, forced to leave their country, their continent. They received enough pay to keep them alive in America. King George III paid for them, yes, but his silver and gold went to the German princes (the prince of Brunswick-Lüneburg, the landgrave of Hesse-Cassel, the prince of Hanau) who owned the land and the peasants who worked the land. We called the German soldiers "mercenaries," but a mercenary is well paid for his labor and his risk. Those poor men in their blue and green coats were no more than military slaves.

Of the thirty thousand German peasants who were shipped to fight the British war in America, twelve thousand found a grave, or a home, in the New World. An unknown number of Germans (the British rarely bothered to count) were buried in the American earth. Some survived the war (often because they deserted) and became farmers. Most of them sailed with their regiments back to Germany. A few men, however, returned with their families as soon as they could to find a home in the young nation that offered them both abundant land, and freedom.

Only later in the war, and in the years of forgiveness after the war, did we Americans learn to welcome our "enemy" home.

&

Chapter Sixty-Nine

Benjamin.

We heard a knock on our ill-fitting door (a vertical raft of slender logs lashed together). I pushed it open and discovered my four companions from the *Lively,* grinning at me. They looked healthy, rested, and well-dressed. With a whoop I invited them in, shook their hands, then introduced my fellow topmen to Genevieve and Caleb, and to Henry. The lads had brought with them a sack of huge potatoes. We were able to contribute a small slab of salted beef. With Henry's careful attention to the fire hissing and smoldering in the fireplace, and Genevieve's careful attention to the pot (while Adam held Caleb), we boiled for ourselves a bountiful stew.

While our feast simmered, Michael told us about their plans. They had found work with Captain Glover in the port of Marblehead, north of Boston, as topmen, and when necessary, as rowers and polers. But what they wanted was their own sloop, their own privateer, so they might serve their newly adopted America by capturing as many British vessels as they could. "We'll do unto the King's fleet as the King's fleet did unto us," declared Michael, who had been the first to suggest our mutiny, and the first to raise his oar against Hench.

Hank said he wanted to serve as chief cannoneer, if they could find at least one good brass cannon. Michael would serve as navigator, for he had an eye for the coastline, for the rocky shoals, for the stars. Adam quietly acknowledged that he would serve as captain. And Ethan stated that nothing would ever get him to come down from the rigging.

During supper, Ethan asked about Nathaniel. I told the lads, briefly, about our months of service in His Majesty's infantry. About the march to Lexington and Concord. About the moment when Nathaniel stepped between me and the musket that killed him.

A sad and bitter silence followed. Then we toasted Nathaniel, with what little cider he had, shared among seven cups.

When the four topmen, like four brothers, departed late that evening, I stood outside the hut's door and watched them disappear into the snowy darkness. I wondered if I would ever see them again.

I saw two of them. But not until after Yorktown.

*   *   *

On December 29, General Washington ordered the army to move across the Delaware into Trenton. With no need for surprise, we did not march for miles up the river, but crossed on Beatty's Ferry, which delivered men, wagons, horses, and artillery to the very edge of town. We made the crossing in daylight, with sheets of ice still floating along the river but no blizzard howling down from the sky. By evening we had moved into the warm houses—with our surprised but obliging Trenton hosts—where the Hessians had slept a few nights ago.

A cautious general would have stayed on the Pennsylvania side of the river, with all the room he might need for the next retreat. And from that camp we could, if necessary, have formed some kind of defense around Philadelphia.

But most of the soldiers in the Continental Army were due to leave for home at the end of the year: in two days. So General Washington had two days with which to pounce one more time.

He may also have moved his army across the river because Trenton was the site of our first victory. There on the battlefield where we had earned our laurels, he might convince some of his troops to stay with him just a short while longer.

Henry and I, and Genevieve, had stated clearly to ourselves, to our officers, and to our Commander in Chief, that we would remain in the Continental Army until the very end of the war. When the last British redcoat boarded the last British frigate and sailed back to London, then and only then would we turn our eyes toward Lincoln, Massachusetts.

But in that December of 1776, most of the troops (men from states north of New Jersey) felt they had fulfilled their duty, and that it was nothing less than fully honorable to leave for home . . . and a hero's welcome. Why risk another battle? Why risk another bout of smallpox or dysentery? Why risk ending up like those two fellows frozen by the side of the road?

In Trenton, our Commander in Chief almost had to beg for an army to command.

On December 30, Henry, Genevieve and I stood outside on a gray wintry afternoon, watching what might well have been the end of the Continental Army. And thus the war. And thus the nation.

In a field between the village and an apple orchard (the same field, filled with clusters of tracks in the snow, where the Hessians had surrendered), General Washington, mounted on his white horse, addressed a regiment of soldiers who knew that at midnight on New Year's Eve, they owed not a minute more to this miserable war. He spoke to the troops with friendship and pride, praising them for their victory. He promised that every man who would stay with the army for another six weeks would receive a bounty of ten dollars.

Then the General rode his horse to one side of the field. An officer ordered a drummer to beat for volunteers. We heard the stark, even burr of the parade drum, and then the silence that followed. . . . Not a soldier stepped forward. Not one. Samuel Adams would have wept.

General Washington rode once again in front of his troops. With a voice neither angry nor despairing, he told them,

> *"My brave fellows, you have done all I asked you to do, and more than could be reasonably expected, but your country is at stake: your wives, your houses, and all that you hold dear. You have worn yourselves out with fatigues and hardships, but we know not how to spare you. If you will consent to stay, you will render that service to the cause of liberty and to your country which you probably never can do under any other circumstance. The present is emphatically the crisis which is to decide our destiny."*

Having spoken not like a British officer, but as the American officer to whom I was devoted, General Washington again rode to the side.

Once more we heard a drum roll. We heard that steady insistent growl with our ears, with our chests, with our beating hearts. It told us: *Now* is the moment. The entire future was condensed into this single decision. We stood upon a stage, as small as a snowy field between an orchard and a village, as broad as all the world, and we wondered whether the actors would act.

The drumroll ceased, followed by a silence so deep, we might have heard the flutter and fall of every snowflake in the air.

One soldier conferred with another soldier, "I will stay if you will stay."

The other considered, "Six weeks. Planting time's not till May."

The two stepped forward.

They thereby tipped the balance against the tyrant and his Parliament, against British armies and British fleets, against writs of assistance and a tax on tea. Two unknown, unrecorded soldiers, one perhaps a farmer and the other perhaps a harness maker, in that moment stepped forward on a trampled field in Trenton, stepped forward into battles we would lose for Philadelphia, stepped forward into the sickness of fevers and flux and smallpox, and stepped forward as well in the brave commencement of a march that would take us, four and a half years later, all the way to Yorktown, Virginia.

When, in March of 1789, General Washington stepped forward onto the balcony of City Hall on Wall Street in New York City, placed one hand on a Bible and raised his other hand, then took the sacred oath of office as President of the United States of America, his step on that balcony began with the steps of two unknown men in the muddy snow of Trenton.

Several more soldiers stepped forward. A murmur passed through the regiment. One by one, two by two, then in clusters, soldiers in rags stepped forward.

Samuel Adams would have wept.

Nearly every soldier who was fit for duty stepped forward. Though they numbered in the hundreds and not the thousands (for we were by then not an army but the remnant of an army), we knew that the nation would live for at least another six weeks.

During the first three days of January 1777, our General became much more than Commander in Chief of the Continental Army. With Congress in flight to Baltimore, with none but the most determined soldiers in his army, and with (so we heard) eight thousand British troops marching from New York toward Trenton to take back that tiny village, General George Washington, in his venturesome youth a surveyor, soldier, and wildcat of the Virginia wilderness, now stripped off the cloaks of diplomacy and officialdom, and became a cunning fighter.

On the first day of the new year, knowing that the British army was approaching along the same road by which we had retreated in November and December, General Washington ordered his troops to move out from the warm, dry houses and barns and churches of Trenton, then to set up an encampment with tents and campfires in a field on the far side of Assunpink Creek, just south of Trenton, with our backs against the Delaware River.

Thus we would relinquish the town of Trenton, which we had so valiantly taken from the Hessian enemy, and give it to the British. And we would place ourselves where we seemed to be in a trap.

General Washington ordered a squad of snipers up the Post Road north of Trenton, to delay the British as they marched from Princeton. Our riflemen, firing from behind stone walls and trees, were pushed back relentlessly by the huge army and its flankers . . . until they at last took shelter behind the stone houses of Trenton itself.

On the afternoon of January 2, a regiment of redcoats surged into Trenton and forced the last of our riflemen to retreat across the fields toward the bridge over the creek. General Cornwallis then rode into the village and set up his headquarters on King Street.

We in the camp noticed something remarkable. Our riflemen had to retreat across the same small bridge that some of the Hessians had used in their escape. Stone pillars stood at each end, marking its location to anyone running toward it from a distance.

General Washington could have ordered an officer to oversee the retreat of the riflemen. General Knox had readied his artillery, with cannons aimed at both the bridge and at several shallow fords across the creek: should the British attempt a full assault, he was ready to fire upon them. None of the troops would have been surprised had General Washington remained at the rear of our camp, safe from British snipers, safe from British artillery.

But as our riflemen came dashing across the snowy fields toward the bridge, General Washington sat upon his horse on the Trenton side, as firm as those stone pillars, as firm as a statue of bronze.

Nigel MacDonald told us that as he ran toward the distant fires of our camp, his own Virginia rifle in one hand and the rifle of a friend who had just been killed behind St. Michael's Church in the other, he spotted the General waiting for him at the bridge. (Nigel and the other snipers had feared, while they fell back along the Post Road before the huge British column, that they might have been left behind if the General had ordered a sudden retreat across the Delaware. And then what would they do?)

General Washington, mounted on his white horse, his face stern and determined, was waiting for them at the bridge. To acknowledge their valor. To supervise their safe retreat. And, if necessary, to command the front line against a British assault.

Nigel ran so close to General Washington that as his feet reached the boards of the bridge, he could smell the breath of the General's horse.

Aye, our General could give a good speech to the troops. But he had a better way of showing us that together, we could accomplish any impossible task, until the day of victory.

Despite a few musket shots in our direction, the British troops did not attack our camp that evening. They moved into their warm quarters in Trenton and readied their artillery for the dawn.

General Washington ordered us to build campfires near the forward edge of our camp, easily visible from Trenton, and to commence digging a line of trenches (as if preparing for the morning's attack). He also ordered the train of supply wagons to follow a road south, in the darkness of night, to the village of Bordentown. Genevieve and Caleb departed with that train of wagons shortly after supper.

Our scouts reported that the British had left their baggage and a rear guard at Princeton, about eight miles north. The large number of redcoats in Trenton indicated a limited rear guard: a body small enough for us to pounce upon. We could then proceed further north, attacking British garrisons across New Jersey. We might not win the war, but we would win the confidence of the nation.

We would of course place ourselves in a most dangerous position, between General Cornwallis to the south, and General Howe somewhere to the north. We might well lose both the war and our nation's confidence if we were caught in a trap of our own making.

A general must have confidence in his soldiers, or he cannot take a risk. General Washington took the risk.

ᏸ

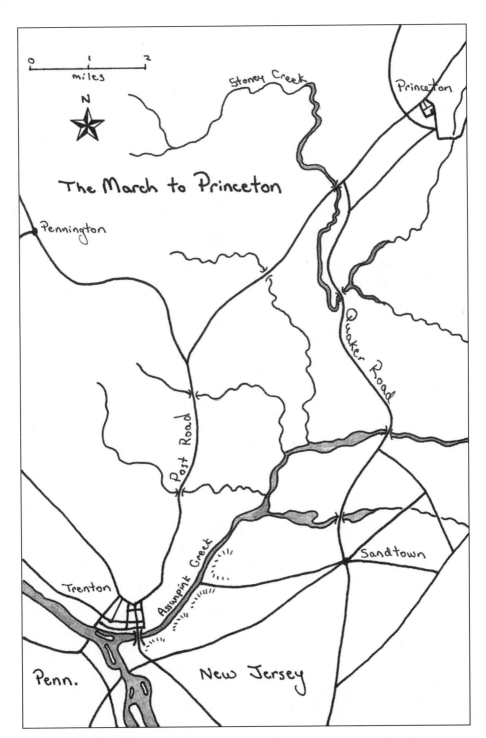

Chapter Seventy

Benjamin, at

THE BATTLE OF PRINCETON

Henry and I were awakened in our tent at midnight and ordered to prepare ourselves for an immediate march.

Beneath the first clear sky we had seen in weeks (bright stars but no moon), we set out in a silent column along a country lane leading to the northeast. We left roughly a hundred soldiers behind us in camp, to keep the fires burning, and to continue a noisy digging in the trenches. As far as the British knew, we were desperately preparing ourselves for their attack at dawn.

The night was windless, but deeply cold. Though the road was icy, it was frozen solid and so gave us better footing than half-frozen mud. The men were in good spirits. We had rested for a week after the battle of Trenton, we had eaten better meals than had been possible during our retreat, and we had dried what stockings we owned beside the warm flames of a fire. And now, on a brilliant winter's night, we followed a commander who seemed to know exactly where he was going.

At the dark hamlet of Sandtown, we turned onto the Quaker Road and now marched due north, parallel to the Post Road between Trenton and Princeton. In Trenton we had surprised the Germans. Would we now manage to surprise the British, His Majesty's very own troops? *That* was a maneuver which appealed strongly to our confident men.

And was it possible that we might this time take British prisoners? *There* would be news for the nation to feast upon as the new year commenced.

Once again, General Washington rode up and down our column, speaking not a word, but letting us know that when the first shot was fired, he would be there with us, firmly in command.

We crossed a bridge over a creek. We crossed a second bridge. While the column crossed a third bridge over a frozen stream, the sky to the east was brightening into a cloudless, crystalline silver-blue.

The rising sun, brilliant gold above gilded snow on the New Jersey plain, cast our long shadows far to the left: hundreds of slender gray figures marched like an army of giants.

Our shadows became shorter and darker as the sun rose, although they were still a good ten feet tall when we came to a fork in the road. The lane to the left led a short distance to a bridge on the Post Road over Stony Creek. The road to the right led another two miles to the town of Princeton.

General Washington detached General Hugh Mercer with a brigade of three hundred fifty men to secure the bridge and thus prevent General Cornwallis from coming to the aid of his rear guard in Princeton. Further, should any of the British in Princeton attempt to escape by the Post Road south, they would be caught by General Mercer.

The detachment split off. The remainder of our small army continued north toward the distant rooftops and spire of Princeton.

We had marched no more than half a mile when suddenly we heard shots near the Post Road. General Mercer had encountered resistance, but the heavy firing indicated more than a few sentries at the bridge: the volleys back and forth bespoke a full battle.

General Washington immediately detached a portion of our column as support. Henry and I, under Colonel Daniel Hitchcock, hurried with a company across a snowy field toward the battle.

We had advanced a few hundred yards when, to our horror, we saw a triple line of redcoats rushing toward us, no more than a quarter mile away, pursuing with their bayonets General Mercer's troops, who were in full flight. We had no artillery readied, no flank either to left or right. Our sparse line would soon be overwhelmed by a full regiment of fresh British troops.

General Washington galloped across the field in front of us, riding directly toward the fleeing men and the redcoats behind them. We could hear him shout, "Parade with us, my brave fellows!" Not march with us, not fight with us, but *parade* with us, as if we were stepping through our maneuvers on a village green before an audience of proud grandfathers and admiring girls. "Parade with us, my brave fellows!" he called again. "There is but a handful of the enemy, and we will have them directly."

Perhaps the panicked men thought that General Washington had diverted our entire column to support them. Perhaps his appearance alone was enough to hearten them. For when they reached our line, they turned and stood with us, loading their muskets while we fired a volley that brought the British bayonet charge to a halt.

More of our troops appeared from a woods behind us. Running across the fields, they were unwilling to miss a good fight. What had begun as an American rout quickly became a widening assault that threatened to surround the redcoats. General Washington galloped from one end of our line to the other, shouting encouragement as if he had waited twenty years for this moment. Though he was the most inviting target for the British on that broad, open battlefield, our General cared not a whit as he sent a body of men south to fill a gap, north to prevent a British retreat back to Princeton, and northwest on a long hook around the British to attack them from their rear.

We came so close to surrounding those eight hundred redcoats that they forced their way with bayonets across the bridge, then ran in full flight toward Trenton. I lost sight of Henry, for I was willing to guard the bridge over Stony Creek, our initial objective, whereas he seemed to want to fire one more shot down King Street.

Henry told me later (he never tired of retelling the tale to green re-cruits gathered around a campfire), that General Washington and the wildest of his wildcats chased the British for a couple of miles along the Post Road. The General, gentleman from Virginia, whooped as he galloped, "It's a fine fox chase!" Henry and a hundred others outran and captured fifty British prisoners (whose safety, even in the midst of a battle, General Washington ordered his men to respect).

Our troops would soon have met the full force of Cornwallis's five thousand redcoats, now thundering north up the Post Road toward Princeton, had not General Washington called a halt to the fox chase and turned our men around.

For there were more foxes in Princeton to bag.

As soon as the wildcats and their redcoat prisoners had crossed the Stony Creek bridge, we tore up the planks and positioned artillery a short distance up the road, to delay the British advance.

Then we hurried on to Princeton, a handsome town awakening at dawn to find itself a battlefield. We found the other half of our troops: they had surrounded one of the brick buildings of the College, Nassau Hall, where an unknown number of redcoats had taken refuge. The ever capable Captain Alexander Hamilton positioned a cannon: he fired two shots at the dormitory. Before the smoke had cleared from the court-yard, a white flag—someone's bed sheet—waved at the end of a pole outside a window. A minute later, a parade of redcoats marched out the door as shame-faced prisoners, while our men roared a cheer.

We had captured the town of Princeton. But General Cornwallis would soon force his way across the creek, and then it would be us who were quickly surrounded. To preserve ourselves, and our victory, we needed to keep moving.

Without pausing for breakfast, and certainly not for sleep, we emptied Nassau Hall of wool blankets, left untouched the British baggage, then marched, with our 323 prisoners, north up the Post Road toward Kingston . . . and the heart of New Jersey.

For the first time in weeks, we stepped to the rousing cadence of our drums and fifes. "Yankee Doodle" never sounded so sprightly and fine.

A month ago we had fled south along this very road, leaving behind our defeat in New York. Now we marched victoriously back into New Jersey, and neither General Cornwallis, whom we had completely outmaneuvered, nor General Howe, commander in chief of British forces in America, knew where we would pounce next.

The traditional rules of war directed armies to battle during the summer, to seek an encampment in the autumn, and to rest over the winter. (Before General Cornwallis had come chasing after us, he was preparing to board a frigate back to London for the winter, to be with his ailing wife.) But General Washington had changed the rules, and now no British garrison from Pennsylvania to Rhode Island could feel safe from a sudden attack. The Americans, fleet on our tired feet, could strike and withdraw, strike and withdraw, and the British would never be able to catch us.

☙

Chapter Seventy-One

Benjamin, approaching Morristown.

Our tired cold feet had their limits.

When we arrived in the village of Kingston on the morning of January 3, we had a choice. We could follow the fork to the right: that road would take us to New Brunswick, where the British kept a supply of military equipment, and, it was rumored, a fortune in silver and gold. Should we capture New Brunswick, the news would thunder from New Hampshire to Georgia, and it would thunder as well in London and Paris.

But our troops had reached the ragged end of their endurance. We had marched through the cold night; we had fought and marched again without breakfast. General Washington understood that despite the lure of a third victory, we had no strength to throw ourselves into another battle. So we followed the fork to the left and proceeded another ten miles, marching beside the frozen Millstone River, to a hamlet called Somerset Court House. There we built our fires, cooked our meager suppers, then wrapped ourselves in new wool blankets and slept like unburied dead men beneath the stars.

We camped for two days in Somerset Court House. We nursed our sick and wounded, turned our prisoners over to the New Jersey militia, and waited for the train of supply wagons in Bordentown to join us. (Our scouts watched General Cornwallis as he took the right fork in Kingston toward New Brunswick, then they alerted the wagoneers that the roads were clear.)

On the afternoon of January 5, 1777, I stood outside the village at the side of a frozen road, watching wagon after wagon approach in the long supply train . . . until I spotted Genevieve, with (as she spent much of the war) the reins to Sir William in one hand and Caleb in the other.

With a whoop, I began to run. I slapped Sir William a greeting on the shoulder as I passed him, then bounded up to the wagon's seat, took the reins in one hand and my wife with the other. My son was five and a half months old, and gave his father the grandest smile.

On January 6, we crossed the Raritan River, then marched to the west around the Watchung Mountains, snow-covered hills that rose and dipped gracefully beneath a pale blue sky. We hooked north along the edge of the Great Swamp, a frozen wasteland drifted with snow. We felt as if we were marching deep into wilderness.

Tramping wearily at dusk, barely able to put one foot ahead of the other, our muskets cold and heavy in our hands, we lifted our eyes as a murmur passed back along the column. Ahead of us, we saw a pair of steeples pointing like white needles into the dark turquoise sky. In the east, the first stars were appearing above the hills. To the west, a silver-blue glow shone over the rolling plain. But ahead, there, straight ahead: surely the two churches of Morristown were big enough that we could all sleep indoors tonight.

Genevieve, on Twelfth Night.

I must tell you about our arrival on the evening of January 6, 1777, when the army that had marched and fought and struggled and survived since the fifteenth of September finally straggled into Morristown.

General Washington had sent scouts ahead to ensure that the road was safe, and to alert the townspeople of our approach. Word of our bold victories at Trenton and Princeton had raced throughout the region well ahead of our scouts. The good people of Morristown, firm patriots in a state where many remained loyal to the King, were more than willing to welcome us.

We spotted the steeples of two churches: twin spires that caught the last glow of twilight, a most uplifting sight after traveling for miles beside a forlorn frozen swamp.

Our column marched into the village and formed as regiments on the snowy green, while the wagons halted along the roughly oval road around it. The tall windows of both churches were lit. As were the lights of every house. Dark figures approached, so many that it seemed every person in Morristown must have come out to meet us. Even small children, bundled in coats and scarves, stood quietly and admired our troops on that frigid night.

Captain Jacob Arnold (as he introduced himself) walked from wagon to wagon, instructing the drivers to lead their horses to several barns just north of—he pointed to a three-story building with its windows lit—"Arnold's Tavern." We could leave the wagons where they were. A guard of cavalry would be posted to watch them.

Following right behind Captain Arnold was a woman who invited everyone not caring for the horses to enter either of the churches, "Presbyterian," she pointed, "or Baptist."

Benjamin, appearing with his musket and rucksack beside the wagon, took Caleb into his arm (the boy was wrapped in a blanket, asleep), then joined a stream of weary soldiers trudging toward the open door of the Presbyterian Church.

I set the brake, climbed down from the seat and unharnessed my poor tired Sir William. My heart ached when I rubbed my hand over his chest: even with a mitten on, I could feel his ribs.

In the full darkness of night, we drivers walked our horses around the green toward the tavern. A dozen helpful men (and another dozen excited boys) led us to the barns, none more than a quarter-mile away. Because Sir William was officially a courier's horse (though I had been reassigned as a scribe), he was quartered in the couriers' stable. John Lally was already there with his Shamrock. That ever thoughtful man had requisitioned the stall beside him, pending our arrival. There was fresh straw, and oats in a trough. A boy would soon come by with a bucket of water. As I unbuckled Sir William's harness, he snorted with satisfaction.

For a moment, while I not only smelled, but paused to breathe, the rich fragrances of hay and horses and leather in the barn, I was a girl back home in the sanctuary of our own barn in Lincoln, where Papa at any moment might walk in leading his Lady Rose.

And then, only then, did I let myself realize how profoundly tired I was. The journey from New York City seemed to have taken years.

I curried Sir William. I made sure he did not drink too much from the bucket the first time the boy came by. And I watched—just stood and watched—with deep satisfaction as he nuzzled and ate the sweet-smelling oats from the trough, rather than frozen grass, frozen weeds.

I walked back through the brightly lit but quiet village. The green, its snow trampled by hundreds of feet, was all but empty. As I headed toward the Presbyterian church—its spire rose with silent dignity into the myriad winter stars—I savored a moment of peace.

I climbed on tired legs up the front steps. A girl stood outside, her eyes watching me above a scarf wrapped around her face; she opened the door for me. I thanked her, then walked into the warmth and lamp-light of a crowded, bustling church.

The floor was covered with straw. Never before had I been in a church with a floor covered with straw. Deep straw, over four inches thick, soft beneath my feet. I understood that here we would sleep.

As I walked up the aisle, threading my way through soldiers who unbuttoned their coats with nearly frozen fingers, I saw people wrapped in blankets on the floor between the pews, already asleep.

Toward the front of the church, on the side opposite the tall pulpit, soldiers gathered around a cast-iron stove. I could smell boiled beef, and potatoes, and Lord! Lord!, bee balm tea.

Benjamin, holding Caleb in one arm, offered me half a loaf of freshly baked bread. *Warm* bread. Yes, the mother should have thought first of nursing her infant; but no, the mother devoured her bread, biting off huge delicious chunks, needing no butter, no strawberry preserves.

The crowd of soldiers—a throng of creatures bundled in rags—became thicker as we advanced toward the front of the church, toward the stove, the food, the heat. And toward the altar table. I gazed at the candles beside a large open Bible on the altar, red candles, not white: Christmas candles.

Then I stared at something I had never seen before, certainly not in our meetinghouse in Lincoln (though perhaps such a thing could be found in Boston). There on the floor in front of the altar was a small replica of a stable, with cows that someone had carved, about four inches tall, standing in the straw. Peering closer, I saw sheep, and five or six figures of shepherds, quite distinct in their simplicity from the figure of a bearded man and a kneeling woman, who looked down upon a carved infant, wrapped in a bit of linen in a tiny manger.

The straw of the floor of the church reached from one end to the other, and mixed with the straw of that stable.

January 6, 1777. Twelfth Night, the eve of Epiphany. The eve when the Magi appeared before the Child. Yes, my children, on that night did General Washington's Continental Army find a sanctuary in Morristown, New Jersey. And what gifts we brought, what honor we proclaimed, what devotion we promised, you may judge for yourselves.

Benjamin and I shuffled through the crowd toward the stove. From tin bowls, we ate a beef and potato stew that warmed me for the first time since September. The soldiers no more than finished their meals (with mumbled Thank You's to the good people of Morristown, whom they would thank more fully in the morning), than they found a spot upon the straw and lay down with a Princeton blanket wrapped around their rags.

Benjamin and I found a spot near the foot of the pulpit. Benjamin went back out to the wagon to fetch our blankets. Caleb had his dinner while his mother, wrapping her scarf around the nursing child, struggled to stay awake. When Benjamin returned, he marveled at the brightness of the Milky Way, stretching over the black hills that wrapped around the village.

While we knelt and arranged our blankets, we noticed that our whispering was echoed and magnified by an octagonal sounding board above the pulpit. Benjamin joked that if Caleb awoke and yowled during the night, he'd surely awaken the entire congregation.

With Caleb asleep in my arm, and I snuggled in Benjamin's arm, husband, wife and child were settling with sighs of comfort between our blankets on the bed of straw . . . when we heard the ringing of bells—peaceful church bells—in the steeple high above us. And in the steeple above the Baptist Church across the green.

They rang no warning, no alarm.

The churches were tolling their bells to welcome us, to comfort us, to bless us, with a gentle, joyous, celestial lullaby.

As if the sextons, the villagers, the very stars themselves, were telling us, "Good Night, Good Night, Good Night."

ॐ

PART V

1777:
Gaining Strength
in Morristown

Chapter Seventy-Two

Genevieve, remembering the prisoners.

My children, before I tell you about our new home in Morristown during the winter of 1777, I want to tell you about the people who were not there. Hidden from us, they were the people who would neither fight another battle, nor rest peacefully in their graves. While we in the army sickened with smallpox, they sickened with every plague that man and devil both ever afflicted upon the victims of war.

Never forget the prisoners.

The Minutemen captured by the British on Breed's Hill, the patriots captured by the British in New York City and Fort Washington: they endured the cold filthy horrors of British prisons. From Boston, our men were shipped to Halifax, far to the north, where frost competed with scurvy in the Canadian dungeons. Some of our Minutemen were shipped to England, where for the next eight years they were beaten and starved by brutal guards who defended (as they thought) the dignity of the Mother Country.

In New York City, occupied by the British until November 25, 1783, our soldiers were jailed with thieves and murderers in Bridewell Prison. They were crowded into crypts beneath churches throughout the city, where their only companions were already in coffins. Many of the prisoners were kept in an unheated warehouse by the wharf, where the rats were plentiful from years of feasting. American officers were sometimes exchanged for British officers, but the farmer-soldiers were consigned for the duration of the war to the ravages of smallpox and yellow fever, scurvy and the bloody flux.

When the jails and churches and warehouses of New York City could hold no more, American prisoners were rowed out to rotting ships anchored in Wallabout Bay, just east of Brooklyn. As many as twelve hundred men at a time were forced to live and crawl and die between the decks of those floating dungeons, ovens in the summer, clad with ice in the winter. Corpses were carried up from the hold by men who craved a minute of fresh air, a glance at the sky, before they were forced below by the bayonets of their British and German guards. The bodies were buried on a nearby beach . . . where the incoming tide washed away the sand, and the outgoing tide washed away the floating, bloated cadavers.

General William Howe ran the prison system with his customary efficiency. He paid Joshua Loring, a Boston Loyalist, one guinea a day (an annual fortune) to supervise the jails, while the general slept with Mrs. Loring. This cozy triangle had commenced in Boston during the British occupation there; it continued in New York; and would eventually move further south during the occupation of Philadelphia.

Francis Hopkinson, a lawyer from Philadelphia who signed the Declaration of Independence, penned a song which made the rounds of American campfires:

> *"Sir William, he, snug as a flea,*
> *Lay all this time a-snoring;*
> *Nor dream'd of harm, as he lay warm*
> *In bed with Mrs. Loring."*

Thus our men fevered and starved and convulsed and died while Joshua Loring sold bread and potatoes meant for the prisoners, and General Sir William Howe roistered with his whore.

Remember, my children, my grandchildren, as you read about these years of the war, that while we marched, while we fought, while we baked firecake on a flat rock beside a smoldering log, while we slept three in a bunk and fourteen in a hut . . . while we celebrated Henry's marriage, and ourselves brought a second child into the world . . . while we cobbled shoes in the Morristown tavern, and a year later drilled in tattered remnants of leather in the Valley Forge snow . . . while year after year passed, 1777, 1778, 1779, 1780, until we marched south to the final Battle of Yorktown in 1781 . . . and then, even then, for two more years, 1782, 1783, until the Treaty of Paris was signed . . . the American prisoners were waiting.

Those poor men waited until finally, finally, General Washington's army entered New York City, and detachments were detailed to the jails, the churches, the warehouses, and the floating dungeons, to open the prison doors.

With a rag tied over his nose and mouth against the stench, your father descended to the lower decks aboard the *Jersey* in Wallabout Bay, and carried men in his arms up the steps into the sunshine.

ᘒ

Chapter Seventy-Three

Benjamin, a cobbler.

Morristown became our home for the winter. General Washington's initial plan, announced at a morning muster, was that we would rest in the village for a few days, then continue our raids against British and German outposts. But the size of our small army rapidly diminished as militiamen disappeared for home, and as Continentals vanished as well. By January 19, 1777, our Commander in Chief had no more than eight hundred soldiers, some of them wounded or sick. Unable to attack anything larger than a British platoon foraging for corn, and expecting fresh recruits in the spring, General Washington ordered the army to settle for the winter in Morristown.

We could not have found a better place. The village was sheltered behind a series of ridges known as the Watchung Mountains. We were protected as well by the Passaic River to the northeast, and by the Great Swamp to the south. To the west, the land presented few barriers; should the British attempt to attack from New York, the Continental Army could easily retreat into the New Jersey wilderness.

Our spies could watch the British on Manhattan Island, only thirty miles away. Scouts posted along the Watchung ridges could note any movement on roads running north and south. The troops in Morristown were within a day's march from New Brunswick, Amboy, and Newark, the three British posts on the mainland. We could readily march north toward New England, or south toward Philadelphia, as an emergency might require. General Howe and his redcoats may have chased us out of New York City, but now that they had it, there was little they could do with their new home.

In addition, the bountiful farms of New Jersey would feed our troops through the winter (or so we thought).

In order to hide from General Howe the fact that we were no more than eight hundred soldiers (whereas the British had over ten thousand troops in New York), we did not set up our tents in a tiny encampment. Instead, upon receiving permission from willing farmers and shopkeepers, General Washington billeted his troops in private homes, three or four soldiers to a house, both in the village of Morristown and along roads far into the countryside. We accordingly occupied a great sweep of the region. General Putnam spent the winter in Princeton with a handful of men. General Greene and General Stirling scattered their troops among farmhouses throughout the Watchung Mountains. Our Commander in Chief, a master of misinformation, sent out rumors that up to forty thousand Americans were poised behind the mountains, waiting to attack the first British regiment foolish enough to march north, west, or south.

On one occasion, a British spy was recognized at a table in the Arnold Tavern, downstairs from the General's headquarters on the second floor. Though several officers wanted to capture and hang the man, General Washington instead wrote out a formal return, tallying the number of regimental troops in the village at twenty thousand. One of the tavern wenches left the folded slip of paper beside an empty soup bowl on a nearby table. The peddler (so he fashioned himself) finished his platter of mutton, then quickly departed from Morristown on the road leading east. The slip of paper seemed to have vanished.

On another occasion, when Old Put allowed a lone British officer to enter Princeton (so that he might visit a wounded friend), he ordered his tiny company of men to march back and forth past the house where the gentlemen were quartered, giving the impression that the village was filled with American troops.

Our family found lodging with a blacksmith and his family in their home just south of the green. Genevieve, Henry, Caleb and I shared the unpainted, two-story clapboard house with Nathan Peabody and his wife Ruth, as well as with their daughter-in-law Susanne, and her son Robert, a lively boy of fifteen. Susanne moved into her son's bedroom, then insisted that we move into her room. Thus Genevieve and I, with Caleb, slept in her bed (her bridal bed as we later learned), while Henry slept on a corn shuck mattress on the floor.

After a week of politeness (standing up abruptly from chairs, and shifting out of the way in the kitchen), we all accommodated each other as comfortably as if we were one large, if somewhat crowded, family. Ruth was delighted, now that Robert had outgrown her ministrations, to take care of Caleb, half a year old, while Genevieve returned to work as General Washington's scribe.

In order to prevent the British from finding forage for their horses

or food for themselves in New Jersey (we could not prevent their foraging on Long Island), General Washington sent out parties of soldiers to
pounce upon the British, *after* they had loaded their wagons with baskets of corn, sheaves of hay, and sacks of potatoes. Our men developed
their military skills, and contributed to the Morristown pantry, without
having to convince the farmers of New Jersey that Continental paper
money was worth just as much as British shillings.

Thus a precedent was set for borrowing a bit of shoe leather.

With Ruth Peabody's permission, I set up a cobbler's shop in a tiny
lean-to built off the back of her kitchen, where preserves and potatoes
were stored. Heated well enough through the doorway by the kitchen
stove to keep the potatoes from freezing, and out of the way of all other
household business, with a single window looking out at a snow-clad
apple tree, the lean-to was perfectly suited as a cobbler's shop. I had
watched far too many soldiers march far too many miles with rags on
their feet, and I meant to cobble as many shoes as I could before we
marched again the following summer.

However, my supplies of leather, nails, and cobbling twine, taken
from Boston more than nine months ago, were limited. I had only a few
good skins left, including one ox hide for soles, and some scraps. So
one evening, when the seven of us were gathered around the table at
supper, I asked my host whether he knew of a good tanner, from whom
the army might purchase a supply of leather.

Nathan, a gray-bearded blacksmith of sixty with the strength of a
man of thirty, looked for a long moment at his wife Ruth, a slender
woman with a brow and nose and jaw of sculptured dignity.

She said quietly, "Ain't a one I can think of."

"Except Hosiah Reed, up on the Whippany."

"Ha!" she laughed with contempt. "For the King's gold guinea he
will."

Though I understood immediately that Hosiah Reed was a Loyalist,
I asked, "But does he have good leather hides?"

"Aye," nodded Nathan, "with twenty acres in beef cattle, four acres
in milk cows, and a roaming herd of goats, Hosiah takes a wagonload
of hides to New York City about every three months. And he ain't never
ridden back yet without a box of British tea in his wagon."

"A devil of a tea drinker he is," agreed Ruth, with a tone so bitter
that had Genevieve not been present, I think she might have cursed.

"How do you know," asked Henry, drawing his knife lengthwise
through the russet potato on his plate, "that he carts a box of tea in his

wagon?" Henry spoke with the evenness of an impartial judge seeking to assemble the facts. "Did you ever actually see a box of tea in his wagon?"

Nathan glared at him. "Didn't have to. Since way back during non-importation time, Hosiah come up to us after church, two, three times a year, just to ask Ruth and me if we'd like to join him for a cup of tea. 'Bought some fresh Ceylon,' he says. 'Just brought it home from Pearl Street.' Knowing, mind you, *knowing* that neither Ruth nor I would ever touch a cup of anything but what came from our garden."

Ruth slapped her hand on the table, startling me. "Letting us know he stands with the King, is all he's doing. Winter, summer, winter, summer, going on four years now: letting us know he stands with the King."

"Then Hosiah Reed is the man we're looking for," declared Henry. "If you would be kind enough to give me directions to the Reed estate, I would like to visit the tanner." He grinned at me. "Two or three wagonloads of leather ought to keep the cobbler busy right through June."

Two or three wagonloads! I would need an apprentice. I'd need *five* apprentices.

"You have a plan?" asked Nathan, intrigued with the boldness of his guest.

"We'll coax Hosiah with the King's gold guinea," said Henry, "then we'll pounce."

"Ha!" cheered Ruth. "Henry Byrnes, *you're* just the man we're looking for."

Susanne Peabody was watching Henry from across the table, watching him intently. She was a strikingly handsome woman, with dark hair and eyes nearly black. She rarely spoke. (Perhaps she was shy with guests in the house.) On the day we moved in, Nathan told me, briefly, that her husband, John Peabody, had been killed some years ago "up at the Hibernia iron mine." Nathan and Ruth had invited their daughter-in-law and grandson to stay on with them. Having nowhere else to go, she consented. But she was a quiet girl, "as well a widow might be."

Aye, Susanne was a quiet woman, though her bright eyes bespoke a lively spirit somewhere deep inside.

One other thing I knew about her. Every evening, when Genevieve and I were preparing for bed, we could hear Susanne talking with her son behind the closed door just across the hallway: they spoke some language other than English.

Genevieve now said to me, as if she had no doubt the wagonloads of leather would arrive, "I shall speak with General Washington, to ask if he might requisition cobbling twine and nails with the next shipment from Philadelphia."

The quartermaster could manage to pay for twine and nails.

But a wagon load of leather hides would be, to a barefoot army, like a wagonload of gold.

The following morning, Henry readied himself to transact business with Hosiah Reed. With help from a somber Nathan, who laid out his son's clothing on a bed, Henry wore John Peabody's Sunday shirt, coat, and beaver hat. Robert found, in a drawer, a pair of his father's black leather riding gloves.

When we all stepped out the front door into the January sunshine, we saw Genevieve trotting toward us on Sir William. She swung down from the saddle and handed the reins to Henry. He took them in his gloved hand, lifted John Peabody's polished boot into the stirrup, then hoisted himself up to the saddle, where he sat tall and proud against the blue sky: he looked most definitely like a New York commercial agent representing General William Howe's royal quartermaster.

In his coat pocket, Henry carried several official military orders from British regimental commanders in New York City, each order countersigned by the quartermaster himself, listing in detail the kinds and numbers of tanned hides needed by the Royal Army of His Majesty King George III, for the making of infantry, grenadier, and officers' footwear.

(Henry had been most impressed when his English brother-in-law wrote the requisition with proper British usage and flair. I even doubled the size of the G in George.)

It was at that moment, while Sir William pranced with eagerness, that we heard Susanne call up to Henry, "Au revoir, Henri. Bon chance!" He looked down at her, surprised, and pleased. No one had ever called him Henri before, with a fine French-Canadian accent.

With a nod to the cobbler, he cantered past the Baptist Church, then disappeared along a lane leading north toward the Whippany River.

During the remainder of the day, Genevieve worked at headquarters. I cobbled a pair of shoes for myself with what materials I had in the tiny shop off the Peabody's kitchen. Nathan worked at his blacksmith shop next door. Susanne walked with Robert to the Morristown schoolhouse, where she taught the children in the village their lessons.

Ruth, while watching Caleb (now crawling), mended the tatters in my hunting shirt and trousers, after their months on the march. (She mended Henry's clothing as well, and Genevieve's farm dresses. As the winter progressed, Ruth developed a steady business as seamstress for much of General Washington's tiny army. By the time we marched out of Morristown in May, nearly every soldier who had wintered in the village had a seam or a patch or a pocket which had been improved by Ruth Peabody's neat crisscross stitching.)

I got to thinking as I worked in the chilly lean-to, that if Henry truly were successful in his mission, I would need more than my own set of cobbling tools. If my (still unhired) apprentices and I were going to put shoes on the two hundred soldiers presently without them, and the four hundred more presently wearing worn-out remnants, then we would need at least a dozen sets of tools.

When Nathan came home for dinner that afternoon, I discussed the problem with him, then took him into my shop to show him my knives, hammer, anvil, and the other assorted implements of the cobbling trade. He held the small head of my hammer in his smudged and callused hand, a hand more accustomed to shaping the head of an axe, or the blade of a plow.

"This is forge work," he said.

"Hmm," I said, not knowing what forge work involved.

"There's a fellow with a forge up toward Hibernia."

I asked, "A patriot?"

Nathan turned the hammer in his fingers as if it were Caleb's toy. "He was John's best man at the wedding. He read from Corinthians at the funeral. You'll have tools from the finest ore that mine produces."

There was a sadness in his voice, the sadness of a father who never forgets that his son is dead. But an undying pride as well, a pride which had enabled him to offer his son's best shirt and wool coat to Henry that morning.

Some soldiers give their best until they are laid in a grave. But one, with his father's help, was able to reach from the grave and give what he could.

Henry returned at dusk, a successful but deeply saddened man. More than saddened: even frightened.

He told us—the moment he arrived, we all gathered in the parlor—that he had found Hosiah Reed's farm on a bend of the frozen Whippany River. With his own farmer's eye, he saw well tended chestnut fences, sturdy cattle in a large pasture along the riverbank, and a two-story clapboard farmhouse, painted white with red trim. Further up the river stood the original log cabin, with a new shingle roof; perhaps one of the sons lived there now. Lilacs grew around both the farmhouse and the cabin—twisted black branches reaching up from the snow—exactly as they grew around his own farmhouse back in Lincoln.

But it was the barn between the pasture and the house that Henry could not stop marveling at. Henry was a carpenter; he had helped to build a dozen barns in Concord, Lincoln, and Lexington. But he had never built a barn so large, so ornately trimmed, as Hosiah Reed's barn.

"It looked," said Henry, "as if a team of carpenters, who had spent their lives building churches and meetinghouses, finally decided to build a barn."

"Ayuh, that's Hosiah and his three sons," said Ruth. "If the Reeds built a rowboat, it would have two masts and a bowsprit."

"Well," continued Henry, "I tethered Sir William to a hitching post, then knocked on the big red door. When a dour-eyed gentleman opened it, I bowed and introduced myself as Richard Thorpe, Esquire. As soon as Hosiah understood that I'd been born and bred in New York City, he warmed up to me. When he understood that I was fiercely loyal to our King, he invited me in for a glass of Madeira. And when he took a look at the quartermaster's orders . . ." Henry turned to me with a sly smile, "You would have thought he held a signed and sealed epistle from King George himself. He saw in those orders an entire second barn, I'm sure: built symmetrically, with steeples, on the opposite side of his house. Hosiah lost no time in sending one of his Negroes to the tannery downstream, with orders to fetch his oldest son and a sample of oxen leather."

Susanne stepped quietly into the kitchen. She soon reappeared with a mug of hot cider. I could smell it as she walked shyly across the parlor and handed it to our commercial agent, seated on a parlor chair with his beaver hat now in his lap.

"I thank you," said Henry, taking the steaming mug by its handle, and taking as well (I could see it in his eyes) a whole new life into his heart.

"You are most welcome," she said in English with a lovely accent. Then she returned to her chair and, looking down, straightened her apron: brown homespun with a white hand print of flour.

Nothing hidden, nothing secret. Her son Robert sat halfway down the stairway, looking through the slender spindles of the banister into the parlor, watching his hero, watching his mother.

Susanne's mother-in-law and father-in-law had also watched her give that cider to the man who would not only outfox Hosiah Reed, but in doing so, would help General Washington's army to march in shoes soled with oxen leather.

"Squire Reed will need a couple of weeks," said Henry, "to gather enough hides from farmers and butchers around the region, and to give them a proper tanning." Henry handed me a parcel wrapped in burlap. "He promised two, maybe three wagonloads as good as what's there."

I unfolded the burlap, then inspected five samples of leather, each about as big as my hand, of increasing thickness, increasing stiffness, not a hole or a flaw in any of them. I rubbed them with my fingers, as my father would have rubbed them. I could hear his voice, echoed in my own words as I said to Henry, "These will hold a stitch for a good two years."

I passed the samples to Nathan. He saw in them perhaps the leather of a bellows. When he passed them on to Genevieve, she saw perhaps a well tooled saddle.

"But," said Henry, shaking his head as if still trying to believe what he had heard, "you should have listened to Hosiah Reed curse General Washington and the rabble in Morristown."

I saw the sadness in Henry's face. The worry, the fear. Since April of 1775, we had lived for almost two years in an army of patriots who left behind their farms, their shops, their families, to defend a freedom more precious to them than their lives. As we marched in our columns, raised and struck our tents, shared a meal around a fire, and aimed our muskets at the redcoats, we had lived with our own kind of men.

But today, Henry had stepped outside of the Continental Army. He had met one of his own countrymen who would never march—nor would his sons ever march—to defend the Congress in Philadelphia. To defend a New Jersey man's right, or a Bostonian's right, or a Virginian's right, to elect his own judges. To elect his own honest representatives to the State legislature. To determine for himself, and for his children, whether or not the western border of America stopped at the Declaration Line of 1763.

Hosiah Reed would never march to defend the freedom of his own people.

Henry turned to Nathan. "How many such men are there?"

"I cannot speak for more than the region," said Nathan, glancing, as he so often did, at Ruth for confirmation, "but within a day's ride of

Morristown, maybe a third are with you, a third are agin' you, and a third are looking for their chances one way or the other."

"And some just head west," added Ruth. "Good land for the taking, out west."

There it was. For two years, nearly, we had fought a war which, even if we won, we might lose, if our own people were not with us. The thirteen States could send the British army home, then fall to fighting among themselves, or worse, within themselves. So that all of our fine words about independence and equality, trumpeted to the world, would become nothing more than a boast and a sham.

Today we had eight hundred soldiers, volunteers from a nation of two and a half million.

And though we could not know it, within a month, many of those eight hundred, as well as a great number of the villagers in Morristown, would be near death with smallpox.

Neither Henry nor I, nor Genevieve, had really acknowledged before how tiny we were.

Robert stepped down the stairs into the parlor; he took the five samples of leather from his mother, then went back up the stairs, sat on a step and fingered each piece, still able to see us through the spindles.

"We agreed," said Henry, finishing his report of the day's business, "that I shall ride back in a week. Hosiah and I will settle on a date when he and his sons will drive their wagonloads to New York City. I shall ride with them, to be sure we meet with no difficulties along the way. And to insure full delivery of the goods for full payment in British specie. I have promised Hosiah that if all goes well, I would arrange a dinner for him with the royal quartermaster himself. At Fraunces' Tavern."

Henry smoothed the top of the beaver hat perched on his lap. "However, despite my best efforts, a brigade of Massachusetts infantry will surprise us before we reach the Passaic. The bandits, the rabble, the scoundrels, will steal from Hosiah and the King every scrap of shoe leather."

"Without a shot fired, we hope," said Genevieve.

Her brother agreed. "Without a shot fired, we hope."

ॐ

Chapter Seventy-Four

Genevieve.

Of course, before the men could march off on their raid, they had to ask their Commander in Chief for permission.

On the following morning, Benjamin and Henry accompanied me to headquarters. As we walked along the road around the green—the oval field was covered with a foot of fresh snow—we felt like three youngsters preparing to approach their father with a plan which they hoped would please him. But the father was stern and distant, and might well think them presumptuous.

Who, after all, were we, a scribe and two privates in the infantry, to suggest a military operation to our Commander in Chief?

We decided that I, when reporting for duty, would ask for permission to speak with the General. I would then present Benjamin (whom the General knew from our wedding) and Henry (whose hand he had shook in the chapel). Benjamin would explain to the General his plan for cobbling shoes. Henry would then explain his plan for obtaining the leather. I could at that point suggest that our quartermaster requisition the other necessary supplies from Philadelphia.

A good plan, unless General Washington abruptly sent us on our way.

As we walked toward the three-story tavern at the green's far end, we said little to each other. Instead, we mustered our courage to speak to the man whom many addressed as "your Excellency."

Benjamin.

The Arnold Tavern, with a pillared front porch for the summertime (its overhanging roof now heaped with snow), and a chimney at each end of the roof's peak for the wintertime (from which twin plumes of smoke now drifted), was, in January of 1777, as important a building to the future of our nation as the State House in Philadelphia, where Congress had declared our independence.

The ground floor was an alehouse, closed now to the public, where General Washington and his staff took their meals. The five windows along the second floor looked out from offices. The staff of scribes and officers working at the dozen tables (as Genevieve had told me) could look up from their papers and see the snowy green across the road, the village wrapped around it, and the distant hills. Beyond those hills was the expectant world where nations awaited the Continental Army's next move.

Genevieve worked in the office behind the middle window, now glazed with frost. General Washington's office was at the left end of the building. As the three of us walked in silence on the squeaking snow, I stared at General Washington's window and readied myself to be, within a few minutes, inside that very office.

Built onto the back of the tavern was a one-story addition, where until our arrival, dances had been held on Saturday nights. The large hall was now used for conferences with visitors who were not allowed upstairs, and for meetings held by General Washington with his staff.

Around the entire building stood a guard of twenty soldiers, five to a side. Each man wore a blue coat with buff trim over a red waistcoat, and carried a musket with a fixed bayonet. They were part of the General's Life Guard, carefully chosen soldiers who accompanied him everywhere he went. Though they knew Genevieve, the guards along the front stared warily at Henry and me as we approached the steps.

Genevieve gestured toward me, "My husband, Benjamin York," and toward Henry, "My brother, Henry Byrnes. They are here to speak with General Washington."

Without any greeting, or nod, or even a glimmer of acknowledgment, one of the guards opened the tavern's front door. We stepped into the alehouse, smelling of pipe smoke and roast pork, and this morning's porridge. Several officers were finishing their breakfast at one of the tables. As Henry and I followed Genevieve up a staircase, we passed several more officers hurrying down. One briefly greeted Genevieve as he swept past.

A corridor ran the length of the second floor, flanked by open doors. Glancing into a room, I saw several officers gathered around a table, pointing at positions on a map. In another room, I recognized Captain Hamilton in conference with General Knox. General Greene appeared from one room, hurried down the hallway and disappeared into another, papers in hand.

At the end of the hallway, we approached a guard standing in front of a closed door. Genevieve informed him that she was here to pick up whatever letters General Washington would have her copy. The guard stared at me, at Henry, said nothing.

"They are here on business," said Genevieve, "as cobbler, and scout."

The guard tapped quietly on the door, then stepped inside, closing the door behind him.

A moment later, we heard the General's strong Virginian voice, "Come in, come in." The door opened. We stepped into an unadorned office—nothing more than a small alehouse bedroom, without the bed. General Washington sat behind a cluttered table, facing the door. His eyes kindled with a moment's warmth as he reached toward Genevieve with a sheaf of papers. "Good morning, Miss Ebenezer." Then he said, turning to us with a look of recognition, "Benjamin. Henry." We both nodded—Henry even bowed slightly—with silent greeting. My heart was thumping; glad I was that Genevieve, not I, would speak.

"They have a plan," explained Genevieve calmly "to cobble as many shoes as possible for the army during our stay in Morristown. My husband Benjamin is a cobbler by profession. He is ready to train a number of apprentices to work with him. My brother Henry has located an excellent source of leather hides, though in the hands of a Loyalist who views the Continental Army with contempt. Henry has therefore posed as a British agent from New York City. He has agreed with Hosiah Reed, the tanner, to conduct him to the office of the British quartermaster in New York, where Mr. Reed will sell several wagonloads of leather for payment in British specie. We have come to ask for your guidance and permission, General Washington. We would like to arrange an ambush of those wagons on their way to New York, executed by a company of Massachusetts infantry, so that our men, and not the British, can be shod with good shoe leather."

General Washington glanced briefly at me, but studied Henry for a long moment.

"You have visited this Hosiah Reed?"

"Yes sir."

"Where does he live?"

"On the Whippany River, a short ride north of the village."

"So he is our neighbor."

"Yes sir."

General Washington turned to me. "Where will you set up your shop, with all of your apprentices? How many did you say?"

"We could fit five or six cobblers' benches in Nathan Peabody's blacksmith shop, where the stove would keep us warm."

"Five or six."

"Yes sir."

General Washington looked past us. "Guard." The door opened. "Please send for Captain Arnold." The door closed.

General Washington stood up from his desk and stepped to the large window. He looked out, as did we, at the fresh untrampled snow on the green, at the black skeletons of scattered trees, and the two spires of the churches.

The General was a tall man, something over six feet. His reddish hair, graying now, was tied back in a military queue. He wore a blue coat with buff facing and cuffs, with three silver stars on his epaulettes. He wore as well a pair of scuffed and creased black boots. When he spoke, when he moved, when he merely stood, he did so with a powerful dignity. As if, according to the requirements of the occasion, he could either lay his hand upon a man's brow with a paternal blessing, or draw his sword in a flash to cut off the head of the enemy.

We heard a brief knock, then the guard announced through the slightly opened door, "Captain Arnold, sir."

"Yes," replied the General.

General Jacob Arnold, tavern owner and captain of the Morristown Light Horse Cavalry, stepped into the office and saluted by removing his hat. "Good morning, General."

"Captain Arnold, you know our Genevieve York. Her husband, Benjamin York. Her brother, Henry Byrnes. They have proposed a raid on a neighbor of yours, a tanner, Hosiah Reed. You are acquainted with Mr. Reed?"

"Since I was a boy. We went through school together."

"And his political affiliation?"

"A Loyalist to the marrow of his bones. If I may say so, sir, he wishes a plague upon your Excellency."

"Right. I would be obliged if you and your cavalry would accompany Henry Byrnes on his proposed ambush. He will provide you with the details. He wishes to march with a detachment of Massachusetts infantry. I think that with your combined forces, we could accomplish our goal without any bloodshed to one of our neighbors. Am I clear?"

"Quite clear, sir."

General Washington turned again to the window for a moment of thought.

Looking out, I could see Susanne and Robert, with several children, walking around the southern end of the green toward the Presbyterian Church and the schoolhouse behind it. When the church bell rang eight times, they would be in their seats.

"Captain Arnold, one more question." General Washington turned from the window. "Might we use your dance hall for a cobblers' shop? We could have two dozen men working at their benches."

Two dozen men! I had never known a master in London to work with more than five.

Then of course we would need leather cutters. And bootblacks.

"Certainly," answered Captain Arnold. "My tavern, sir, is at your disposition."

General Washington nodded toward the door. "Let us take a look."

Captain Arnold led us out of the office, along the corridor and down the stairs, then he opened a door at the rear of the tavern and beckoned us into a large hall wrapped with windows. The room was cold—we could see our breath—for neither of the two Franklin stoves were lit.

General Washington turned to me. "Could you run your shop in this room through the next four months?"

I heard my father's voice as I spoke the very words I had heard him say so many times, "Yes, sir, we'll have the job done to perfection."

General Washington held out his hand. "Then I thank you, Benjamin, for providing the army with shoes. There is a desperate need."

I shook the General's hand, the hand that had waved his sword as he galloped back and forth in the thundering, terrifying, unpredictable battle at Princeton. "You are welcome, sir."

Now Genevieve asked, to complete the business, "General Washington, we shall have the leather, the benches and the tools, but we shall be lacking cobblers' pegs, twine, and needles. Might our quartermaster requisition these supplies from Philadelphia?"

We had fought at Trenton and Princeton not only to protect our Congress in Philadelphia, but to protect our source of supplies as well. With New York City now in British hands, and Boston too far away, we relied on trains of Conestoga wagons from Philadelphia to bring us tents, salted beef, gunpowder, and everything else that an army might need. With a population of forty thousand, Philadelphia was the largest of the American cities (and the second largest, after London, in the British empire). It was also America's most prosperous city, home to a multitude of craftsmen. Thus we hoped that since Hosiah Reed would supply the leather, Philadelphia might supply the needles and thread.

"Please make a list of your requirements."

General Washington added, speaking to Henry, "You are to offer neighbor Reed full payment in American currency. We do not wish to offend by stealing a tanner's wares. Please estimate the value of the goods. Our quartermaster shall provide you with an adequate supply of dollars."

"Yes sir."

The General held out his hand, then shook the hand of a private who was to become, in the course of the war, one of his finest officers. "I thank you for your bold and enterprising spirit."

"Thank you, sir."

Nodding his gratitude to Captain Arnold, General Washington walked toward the dance hall door.

The front door of the tavern opened; a cluster of officers stepped inside. In that moment, we could see—looking right through the tavern—bright morning sunshine on the porch, the road, and the snow that blanketed the green.

The guard at the front door hesitated before he closed it, then swung it fully open, so that General Washington might step outside.

We watched as the General crossed the road. He stepped into the snow on the green, which came halfway up his boots. He walked ten or fifteen feet, then he stood with his face lifted to the sun shining above the village.

Perhaps he needed a minute of respite from the clamor of duties inside headquarters.

Or perhaps, for one quiet minute, the farmer in him needed to stand as if at the edge of his field, counting the months before the low January sun rose high enough to melt the snow and warm the earth.

The General walked in a narrow loop back to the street, returned to the tavern and climbed the stairs. Already on the way up, officers addressed him with other, urgent business.

Genevieve led Henry and me up the stairs to her office, where we sat around the table which my clever wife used as her desk. I glanced out the window at General Washington's footprints in the snow. Genevieve laid the General's letters to one side of her desk, then readied a fresh sheet of paper. As I thought carefully through what I would need, and in what quantities, she listed each item in her graceful handwriting, under the title "Cobbling Supplies."

We had barely finished when John Lally appeared at the table. "Miss Ebenezer," he said with a grin, "are you posting me south to the great city of Philadelphia?"

"Aye," she smiled in return, "and no dallying with some tavern wench."

"No, mum."

With the folded sheet of paper listing supplies sufficient to cobble eight hundred pairs of shoes, John Lally was out the door and gone.

Henry and I, hearts brimming with gratitude, thanked Genevieve for her help. Then we descended the stairs, passed between silent guards and walked out into the sunshine. Crossing the road, I stared for a long moment at General Washington's footprints in the snow. Then I stepped carefully beside one of the clearest prints and reached down into it. Using my thumb and little finger as calipers, I measured the large print from toe to heel. Folding my fingers into a fist, I measured with my knuckles the width. I would have liked my ruler, but it was back on my bench in the lean-to. And I could feel the guards watching me. So I calipered, and knuckled, as Papa had taught me to do.

A good cobbler can gauge to within an eighth of an inch.

Genevieve.

Benjamin showed Henry the design and dimensions of his cobbler's bench, with a lid that lifted so tools could be stored inside.

Henry spoke with Nathan, who took the afternoon off so they could visit a sawyer whose mill was about a mile downstream from Hosiah Reed.

That evening after supper, using a corner of the blacksmith shop as his carpentry shop, Henry began to build the first bench.

He was assisted by an eager apprentice. For Robert, when not in school at his mother's stern insistence, followed Henry like his shadow.

ⅎ

Chapter Seventy-Five

Benjamin, on night patrol.

Henry rode a second time to Hosiah Reed's farm, where the two Loyalists planned the final details of their trip to New York City. On the night of January 24, Hosiah and his three sons would drive four wagons along an old timber road that met the Newark Road about two miles east of Morristown. They would thus avoid "that nest of Continental devils," as Hosiah called the village. (He had even stopped going to church. He honored the Sabbath with his family in their parlor, "where the Lord might look down upon us with naught unclean around us.")

Three of the wagons would be loaded with tanned leather. The fourth would carry butter, cheese, and smoked venison, all likely to fetch a fine price in New York City.

Henry, or "Richard Thorpe" as the Reed family knew him (he was a bit embarrassed to tell them that he had been named by his mother after King Richard the First, "the lion-hearted"), would meet them on the 24th at dusk, share supper and a glass of Madeira with them, then ride with them through the night to the quartermaster's office on Broad Street, which they expected to reach at daybreak the following morning. (They would travel at night to avoid any possible confrontation with "the rabble.")

At their dinner together at Fraunces' Tavern, Hosiah could speak with the royal quartermaster about an order for beef. "Either salted or boiled," Hosiah had told Richard, "or even fresh killed and frozen, if the British prefer it so." The January weather would enable Hosiah to cart into town twenty or thirty sides of frozen beef. "A soldier needs his meat," declared Hosiah, glad to make a profit by feeding the men who fought his war.

In the twilight on January 24, while Henry rode north toward the Hosiah Reed estate, thirty high Sons of Liberty from Massachusetts—accompanied by volunteers from several other states, including Nathan and Robert from the State of New Jersey—marched east on the Newark Road toward a pass through the Watchung Mountains. Our squad was led by Captain Jacob Arnold and his Light Horse troop of cavalry.

Thus we departed from Morristown with a detachment large enough to ambush a full British foraging patrol. "Poor Hosiah," grinned Nathan as we marched behind the clatter of horses, "he's going to think he's been ambushed by half the Continental Army."

The night became extremely dark. Heavy clouds covered the sky, and thick forest flanked the road. The weather was not cold, however, only a few degrees below freezing. The road was neither mud nor ice, but well packed snow. We had not marched more than half a mile before I unwrapped the wool scarf from around my neck, then opened the buttons of my coat.

The lads were in high spirits. We were surprised to discover how much we enjoyed being out on the road marching again, though now of course with warm feet and full bellies. We had become soldiers more than we had realized, for we liked our sense of purpose as we set out on a patrol. We liked marching together, listening together to every faint and distant sound, watching together for anyone who was not one of us. War is a great sin, but the friendship, even love, among soldiers is a blessing that can be found nowhere else.

The cavalry suddenly, upon a signal known only to themselves, moved forward at a trot, then broke into a canter of thundering hooves. We could hear them long after we could no longer see them . . . until the diminishing rumble of hooves vanished. We marched in deep silence, the road a faint stripe of gray snow.

Had the riders discovered Hosiah Reed ahead of us? Or did they have some plan which they had kept secret from us?

Uneasy, keenly alert, we listened for the sound of muskets.

Now we heard the faint but growing rumble of approaching hooves. The cavalry reappeared like dark galloping ghosts against the gray road. They reined to a halt and wheeled their snorting horses, then once more took their position at the head of our column. Though they felt no need to explain, the riders apparently had decided that a slow march with infantry was altogether too dull. Why not go for a bit of a gallop?

The road began to climb toward the pass through the Watchungs. Though we could hardly see it, for the night was so dark, a light snow had begun to fall.

The spruce towering above us, black spires against the charcoal sky, were much taller than the broad black crowns of maples and willows down on the plain.

Nathan touched my arm and cocked his ear. I too now heard a lone rider far behind us. The cavalry halted, and thus so did the infantry. Some of the riders turned their horses, facing us. None drew a sword or readied a pistol. The rider must surely be a scout.

As the hoofbeats approached, our squad moved to one side of the road to let the rider pass. He reined to a halt and reported to Captain Arnold. The infantry bunched forward to listen.

We were two miles ahead of Hosiah Reed, who was driving the first of four wagons. His three sons drove the others. Henry rode just ahead of them, keeping a watchful eye for trouble. "I cantered past them," boasted the scout, "so drunk I could hardly keep in the saddle while I sang a tender love song to my dear Lucille."

"Armed?" asked Captain Arnold.

"No one with a musket ready. They ain't expecting anyone."

Captain Arnold turned his dark face toward us, then surprised us by announcing, "You men from Massachusetts, this ain't your fight. You'll get your leather, but until then, I want you off the road and back behind the trees. No need for Hosiah to know you're out here tonight."

As we had no officer with us above a lieutenant from Roxbury, we were unable to contest Captain Arnold's order. After a brief discussion among us, the men of the infantry, disgruntled but obedient, stepped off the edge of the road into knee deep snow. Holding out an arm against boughs we could barely see, we trudged into the spruce. As Nathan and Robert followed in my footsteps, I heard Nathan tell me, "Jacob and Hosiah fought the French together. But Jacob hates a Tory."

We waited, silent, for a quarter of an hour. I stirred my feet in the snow, wrapped my wool scarf back around my neck. I hoped that whatever happened, Henry got out of the way before anyone fired.

What we witnessed that night—what we heard more than saw—was "the back country war." During the decade before Lexington and Concord, many colonials had feared a "civil war" between themselves and the Mother Country. But the real civil war emerged after Lexington and Concord, when neighbors who had shared generations of friendship were suddenly forced to choose between Loyalty, or Liberty. Families who had no quarrel with the King discovered that they had become "the enemy."

We heard wagons approaching: heard hooves, the squeak of an axle, the rolling crunch of wheels on packed snow. I felt once again the hideous dread that grips a soldier moments before a battle. But not, this time, for myself. I wanted shoes, not trouble. I hadn't come to Morristown to shoot my neighbor.

The lead horse stopped. That would be Henry. He must have seen the cluster of dark riders on the road ahead of him.

The wagons halted behind him.

Between the wagons and the cavalry, no more than a hundred feet.

One of the wagon horses snorted, perhaps catching the scent of cavalry.

"Neighbor Reed." It was the voice of Captain Arnold.

Hosiah Reed did not answer.

Henry called back with indignant belligerence, "State your name and business, sir."

"I am Captain Jacob Arnold, and you, sir, we know well to be an agent for the British. As such, you are now my prisoner."

"I am a loyal subject to my King," retorted Henry, "and you, sir, are a damned rebel. As such, you have not one whit of authority. Please stand aside and let us pass."

We heard cavalry swords drawn from their sheaths. Five riders moved forward, ready, should Henry attempt an escape, to pursue him until they cut him down from the saddle.

Henry snarled, "Damn you unconscionable scoundrels!" Then he turned to Hosiah Reed, for we heard him say, "General William Howe shall hear of this crime against one of His Majesty's most loyal subjects. You shall be compensated, Hosiah, for this indignity."

Surrounded by soldiers with their swords drawn—the silver-gray blades pointing straight up were more visible than anything else— Henry rode forward on Sir William. His dark figure merged with the troop of cavalry. The swords were returned to their scabbards.

"Neighbor Reed, " called Captain Arnold once more, "we offer you full payment for three days' use of your wagons."

"Payment in specie," answered Hosiah Reed, his first words.

"Payment in good Continental dollars," replied Captain Arnold.

Hosiah Reed spat.

"What do you carry in your wagons?" queried Captain Arnold.

A long moment of silence.

"Where are you headed?" asked Captain Arnold.

"Tis a public road," stated Hosiah Reed.

"Aye, but New York is not so public a city these days, now, is it?"

"Papa."

It must have been one of the Reed boys.

"Hush," snapped the patriarch.

"We are fully prepared, " said Captain Arnold, "to compensate you for whatever you carry in your wagons."

"Jacob, where are you taking my wagons?"

"Princeton. You have my promise, they shall be returned, with full payment, within three days."

"Am I to walk home?"

"Did you wear your shoes?"

"Three hundred sixty-two pounds for the goods I carry."

"Thirty-five dollars for the goods you carry."

"Jacob, the Great Jehovah looks down upon you tonight."

"And upon you and your sons, Hosiah Reed. Upon you and your sons."

Captain Arnold rode forward until his horse stood twenty feet from Hosiah's horse. "Keep to yourselves on the Whippany and we shall not bother you. But one more attempt, Hosiah, to carry provisions to the British, and I shall be required to send you and your family to join them in New York City. Now climb down from your wagons, please."

We heard a stir as wagon brakes were set, reins were tied, and feet stepped down to the road. "Scurvy devils," growled Hosiah.

One of the wagon horses pulled against the brake, then snorted.

No one said a word, no one moved, until the sound of feet walking toward home had vanished.

Then Captain Arnold said quietly, "Bring your platoon out to the road."

We trudged out from among the trees, stepped onto the road, brushed the snow from our breeches and spatterdashes. I walked over to the first wagon and lifted its canvas tarp. I could smell the leather better than I could see it: freshly tanned.

And without a shot fired.

Because we would follow the same road back to Morristown, and because we had no need to meet again with Hosiah Reed this night, we continued our march—four men from Massachusetts drove the captured wagons—up through the pass and then down a few miles to the frozen Passaic River. On the riverbank, the troops gathered firewood and built campfires. We warmed our hands and feet, of course. But the real purpose for the fires was to prepare a feast of roasted venison. Henry, a prisoner of war no longer, revealed for us (beneath a tarp over the fourth wagon) seven skinned and gutted deer carcasses, frozen; a keg of butter, extremely hard; and several crates containing blocks of cheese, also hard, but, as we pried up each lid in the darkness, most powerfully pungent.

The carcasses and the cheese yielded to our knives. We had no cooking implements; thus we soon appeared like a horde of barbarians as we dangled chunks of meat at the ends of sharpened sticks over the flames. We ate with our hands, our greasy faces grinning. The venison had been smoked with hickory, and not a man among us who did not thank Hosiah Reed for his smokehouse.

In the ring of soldiers around our fire, Robert stood beside Henry, roasting his strip of venison beside Henry's strip of venison. Robert snarled with a laugh, "'Damn you unconscionable scoundrels!"

Henry looked down at the boy. I could see in his smile that Robert had become far more than a carpenter's apprentice.

When the gluttons could eat not a morsel more, we marched home, and felt the great want of a drum and fife.

Arriving in Morristown well past midnight, we unloaded the wagons and carried the tanned hides through the tavern to the dance hall behind it. Lanterns were lit; I could see, waiting in a cluster beneath the black windows, Henry's flock of cobblers' benches.

Hosiah's four horses were led to a stable. His four empty wagons remained on the road in front of the tavern, gradually filling with the snow that fell more heavily now.

Most of the men went home as soon as the last of the hides had been brought in. Nathan, Robert and I were sorting through one of the piles (they counted hides while I marveled at the excellent quality of the leather) when General Washington walked into the hall, accompanied by Captain Arnold, General Greene, and Henry. It was then that I fully understood the responsibility I had taken on: our Commander in Chief had gotten out of bed in the middle of the night to see for himself the leather which I would turn into shoes for his army.

The General picked up one of the hides and inspected it on both sides. "Do you have enough, Benjamin?" he asked me.

"Yes sir. I gauge that we have well enough for eight hundred pairs of shoes."

"And your apprentices?"

"We start in the morning, sir."

"Excellent. "

He looked around the hall at a dozen heaps of leather on various tables; at the cluster of benches, waiting for their workers; at firewood stacked neatly beside each of the two stoves. Then, remembering a final detail, he asked, "You have your supplies from Philadelphia?"

"John Lally arrived with them yesterday, sir."

"Yes." The General's eyes kindled with warmth. "There is only one person in all the world who can ride faster than John Lally."

With a nod of greeting to Nathan and Robert, General Washington walked with Captain Arnold and General Greene back to the tavern. Henry gave me a glance before he too disappeared through the door; he had been invited to join the officers.

Robert, Nathan and I blew out the lanterns. As we passed through the tavern toward the front door, I saw the four of them—General Washington, General Greene, Captain Arnold, and Henry—seated at a table, a candle lighting their faces as they spoke quietly in conference. Captain Arnold had poured for them four tankards of ale.

The three of us—grandfather, grandson, and guest— walked home together in a deeply satisfied silence. I looked forward to telling Genevieve that all had gone well.

As we passed the Baptist Church, gray-white in the snowy night, it seemed to regard us with solemn approval.

છ૦

Chapter Seventy-Six

Genevieve.

During early February, 1777, we savored two weeks of peace.

If I had a minute or two between letters, I would leave my desk, hurry down the stairs, then stand quietly at the back door and peer into the hall where Benjamin worked as a master cobbler with twenty-five apprentices at their benches. Wearing his leather apron, he bent over a soldier from Massachusetts, from New York, from Virginia, showing a man often older than himself how to stitch the "vamp" (the piece of leather from the toe to the tongue) to the "counter" (which wrapped around the heel).

Benjamin then crossed the room to check the work of the cutters. Standing around several tables with their knives, they carefully cut the leather into different shapes. Some cutters made soles from thick ox hide, short enough to fit the smallest men, or long enough to fit the heftiest cannoneer. In those days, there was no left shoe or right shoe, but only variations in length and width. The two soles of a pair of shoes were thus identical.

Cato and Prince began as cutters, but by the second week of February, each man had graduated to his own cobbling bench. Prince proved to be especially talented with a cobbler's needle.

As Benjamin walked along the row of whittlers, each man held up a block of pine that he was carving into a "last," shaped in the form of a human foot. The cobblers fit their vamps over a last, which must be neither too thin nor too fat. While the whittlers carved lasts to match every foot in the army, a pile of curled shavings grew at their feet.

After the cobblers had pegged the heel into place, they put a brass buckle into each shoe. The soldiers themselves would punch two holes into each strap, or "latch," of the counter, then pass the latches through the buckles and secure them on the buckle's pointed prongs (thus ensuring a proper fit).

The shoes were blackened and waxed by a half-dozen soldiers with little ambition, who enjoyed a good long chat while they worked.

The completed shoes were then shipped (sixteen pairs packed into a cheese crate) upstairs to the quartermaster at his desk. He recorded each crate in his ledger, then distributed the shoes to the troops.

The tavern's dance hall was well warmed by the two stoves. The windows looked out at snow-covered fields and scattered farmhouses. (The windows also looked out at the soldiers of the Life Guard, who occasionally, while they paced in their trenches of snow, glanced inside with perhaps a bit of envy.)

The big room was filled with the sounds of hammers tapping their tiny pegs, of someone sharpening his knife on a whetstone, of a soldier humming an old song from home. It was filled as well with the scent of leather, the scent of pine.

Benjamin would glance at me with his handsome smile, then move on to the next cobbler.

I was not the only one who enjoyed peering into that room. Every now and then General Washington himself would stand at the door. Though Congress was bickering in Baltimore, and farmers were selling their beef to the British, and officers squabbled about promotions and rank, our Commander in Chief at least had the satisfaction that when springtime renewed the war, his regiments would be ready to march.

൬

Chapter Seventy-Seven

Benjamin, remembering the Oneida
named His Long Road.

On January 9, 1777, three days after we had arrived in Morristown, the snow in the village began to darken. Parlors darkened, shops darkened, headquarters darkened, as the light outside our windows faded. Baffled, frightened, people opened their doors and peered out. It was only natural to look up toward the sun in the pale blue winter sky.

We discovered a dark disk passing in front of it.

Some said it was naught but an eclipse. Others declared it was an ill omen.

The darkness deepened, until the snow at our doorsteps . . . and the two steeples reaching into the sky . . . had become dull white. Villagers looked across the green at each other, but no one called a cheery greeting. A flock of crows lifted from the branches of an ancient oak in front of Arnold's Tavern. Calling down to us with their evil laughter, the crows whirled over the village and disappeared to the west.

When the dark disk had fully covered the sun—the sky was now a strange hollow blue—some people stepped back inside and closed their doors. They would look no more. Perhaps they turned to their Bibles.

Then slowly, incrementally, the snow began to brighten. A growing yellow-white crescent reassured us that the sun would surely return. Officers crowded along the headquarters porch began to speak, as apprehension gave way to festivity. They appreciated a break in their work, a reprieve from their papers, especially since all was once more right with the world.

People stepped back inside to continue their dinners, their reports, their lessons in school, and the cobbling of another military shoe.

The villagers remembered that eclipse later in January, when the scourge of smallpox, brought into their homes by the Continental Army, began to spread.

By mid-February, the scattered cases had become an epidemic. First the Baptist Church, and then the Presbyterian Church, became hospitals filled with patients. The pews were moved, then the floors of both churches were once again covered with straw, so that hundreds of people, soldiers and civilians together, could lie in orderly rows as they struggled through their fevers.

General Washington issued an order that frightened many people more than the war itself: everyone who had not already survived the disease must be inoculated. His order included not only soldiers in the army, but civilians in the village and surrounding countryside where soldiers were billeted. Women and even infants were to be inoculated. He assigned Dr. Nathaniel Bond to oversee the inoculations in Morristown, in Princeton, and in all other garrisons in New Jersey where American soldiers were posted.

Whereas in previous years, doctors had sliced open a person's arm or thigh, then infected the wound with pus from a smallpox patient, Dr. Bond followed the new method of an English physician, Dr. Daniel Sutton. Dr. Sutton made only a small puncture, and thus infected the wound with a much smaller dose of pus. Most people in good health managed to maintain strength enough to survive their inoculation. They developed a rash within four days, then pustules which opened and drained. After three weeks, the open sores scabbed over and began to heal. The patients could look forward to a life of immunity.

When he was nineteen, General Washington had nearly died of smallpox on the West Indian island of Barbados; he was thus immune. Perhaps a quarter of his army was also immune. Those who had not survived their bout with smallpox were buried along the edges of every encampment and every march since the spring of 1775.

The General designated a number of houses in the village as sites of inoculation and, hopefully, of recuperation. Guards were posted around each house, so that no contagious patient might leave. Though he desperately needed new recruits, and knew that forced inoculation would scare away potential soldiers, General Washington ordered that all new recruits that spring must be inoculated before they entered the camp at Morristown.

By March, the region was less a widely scattered military garrison than a widely scattered military hospital. Though the inoculations were staggered (a new round every week or so) in order to keep some troops in camp healthy and on guard, the army soon had no more than a few hundred effective soldiers.

Had General Howe roused himself from Mrs. Loring's bed and posted a regiment, even half a regiment, to attack the Continental Army in Morristown in March of 1777, he could easily have won the war in less than an hour. He could then have planted the scarlet British flag in the middle of the Morristown green.

Like most people, I was as fearful of the inoculation as of the disease itself. When General Washington issued his orders, I suggested to Genevieve that we take Caleb home to Lincoln for the winter; I would accompany her in the wagon, then return immediately to Morristown to be inoculated. She could join me, perhaps leaving Caleb with her mother and father, in the spring.

Genevieve insisted on just the reverse: she and Caleb would be inoculated as soon as possible, to avoid catching the disease. Henry and I should wait until March. That way, a portion of the family would be healthy, while the others were struggling back to health.

We would not be able to take care of each other. Only soldiers already immune would be allowed inside the quarantined houses to care for the sick. Henry and I would have to wait for an entire month before Genevieve would emerge, hopefully with a living child in her arms.

She would have it no other way. "Benjamin, we are not going home to Lincoln," she stated firmly, "until the British go home to London."

We discussed the growing epidemic with the Peabody's, who astonished us when they volunteered their house as an inoculation hospital. Susanne with Robert, Genevieve with Caleb, and Ruth would submit to the first round of inoculations. Henry, Nathan, and I would move into the dance hall behind Arnold's Tavern, where we would sleep among the cobbler's benches. (We would thus make room for three more patients in the house.) In March, the women and children would emerge into the early spring sunshine, and the men would then take their turn. (Robert argued that he should be with the men; his mother insisted that her child would be with her.)

Never once did the Peabody's show any sign of resentment at the danger which our army had brought into their lives. Though many other families in Morristown now refused to quarter troops, Ruth and Nathan Peabody invited the scourge of smallpox into their very home.

We were not the only ones to volunteer for inoculation as soon as possible. Reverend Kesslaer appeared at headquarters to speak with the officer in charge of scheduling. He and his hospital staff were of no use during the epidemic unless they were immune to it. Thus he requested inoculation for himself and four others: Cato, Prince, His Long Road, and She's Carrying Flowers. He wanted the officer to understand that all four, especially the Oneidas, were taking a much greater risk than most of the soldiers took. The Oneidas considered smallpox to be the white man's disease, against which they had little power. But his four "nurses" had fled from no previous battlefield, and they would not flee from this one either.

"Does Colonel Askwith understand," asked Reverend Kesslaer, "that some measure of gratitude is due to these people?"

Colonel Askwith looked up with tired eyes from the papers on his desk. "Some measure of gratitude is due."

While the colonel added five names to his list, Genevieve stood up from her table and crossed the room. "They may stay with us at the Peabody house. We have room, and we begin tomorrow."

She's Carrying Flowers made one demand on the household. Throughout the month of their confinement, a strong fire burned in the fireplace day and night; and several times a day, several times a night, the soldiers on duty opened every window, upstairs and down, until all the air in the house was swept out, and the new air was cold and fresh.

Henry, Nathan and I bedded in the cobblers' shop and boarded at the tavern. Every day we walked around the green, then called from a distance of fifty feet to a guard at the Peabody's door, and every day the guard told us that all was well within.

During that month, I cobbled shoes. Henry fulfilled the promise he had made in New York: in Nathan's blacksmith shop, he crafted not a cradle (for Caleb was rapidly growing), but a sturdy child's bed that could ride in the wagon.

Robert was the first to emerge from the Peabody house, on the third of March. Henry was the first, from out in the road, to shout his name. Robert, squinting at the bright snow, walked toward us as quickly as he could on his weakened legs. I do not know if Henry had ever hugged anyone before in his life, but he picked up that boy and held him with his feet dangling a foot off the ground for a full minute.

Robert told us that the others would be out in a few days, but he could stand the confinement no longer. He had been the healthiest, his mother had been the sickest, but all were now up from bed and beginning to stir about the house.

Caleb had wailed day and night with the rash. But as long as he wailed, and did not sink to a whimper, they knew he would survive.

The three of us walked for a mile or so in the sunshine along the Newark Road, until Henry was afraid that Robert would tire himself. On the way back to the village, Robert told us that His Long Road had sung the same strange song over and over while he lay sick in bed. But as long as he was singing, they knew that he too would survive.

On the seventh of March, I watched as Genevieve emerged from the door, with Caleb in her arms. We hardly spoke to each other for the first few minutes. I held my wife and stared into her exhausted, jubilant brown eyes. I could muster nothing more than tears and an unrelenting smile.

Henry held Susanne in his arms for at least as long as he had held Robert. The two of them had never truly courted. Most likely they had not yet spoken of marriage. But as they walked with Robert across the melting snow on the green, the three together were far more a family than any ceremony could fashion them.

On the following day, as if each had waited until all five were ready, the hospital staff stepped together out the door of the white man's house, back into the world of the living.

Cato and Prince no longer cobbled with me in the shop. Instead, they worked with His Long Road and Henry to build a village of dome-shaped healing lodges in a hay field west of town, where the melting snow had revealed patches of grass.

In much less time than it would take a team of soldiers to build a hut with logs, then roof it with split shingles, His Long Road cut beech saplings in a nearby woods with his hatchet, stripped off the branches and sharpened the bottom of each trunk. He stood a dozen poles in a circle about eighteen feet in diameter, forcing their points into the thawing ground as deep as he could. With help from the others, he bowed the pliant saplings over and lashed their tops together with strips of walnut bark, forming the graceful frame of a dome. He strengthened the dome by lashing poles crosswise, in five horizontal rings from bottom to top.

His Long Road peeled sections of cedar bark from nearby trees, then lashed each section in an overlapping manner over the dome. (Though beech saplings were plentiful near the village, cedar trees were sparse; Reverend Kesslaer therefore asked Colonel Askwith if wagons could be sent to the Great Swamp, so that cutters could gather roofing for thirty lodges.)

Henry became especially adept at lashing together the graceful domes. Prince and Cato built rings of stones on the grassy floor of each lodge for a central fire. The smoke would vent through a small hole at the top of the dome.

As soon as the first healing lodge was finished, His Long Road and She's Carrying Flowers moved in. They were joined by Cato, Prince, and Reverend Kesslaer. The first lodge thus became the quarters of the hospital staff. Henry, Nathan, and I moved from the dance hall into the second lodge. Within five days, despite a flurry of mid-March snow, all thirty healing lodges were completed, ready for one hundred and eighty newly inoculated soldiers, six to a lodge.

I thought the primary benefit of His Long Road's unusual village would be that the pace of inoculation could now be increased. We were no longer limited by the few designated houses in the village and the two greatly overcrowded churches. We discovered, however, during the course of the spring, that though many people died in the churches (where only those sick with smallpox itself were taken), and though a scattered few of the inoculated died in the homes, almost every soldier who spent a month in one of the healing lodges was able to emerge as a healthy man.

Perhaps the difference was in the bark-flavored teas prepared by She's Carrying Flowers. Perhaps it was the strange, rhythmic chants which His Long Road sang while he moved from hut to hut, preparing each meal.

But in my judgment, the difference was in the cold air. We slept, wrapped in blankets on our bed of soft evergreen boughs, with our feet toward the fire and our head toward the wall, six men like six spokes of a wheel. Even a small fire, tended by Prince and Cato, kept the lodge warm. The smoke vented remarkably well through the hole at the top. But the great secret in the lodge's construction were the vents in the round wall, about two feet above the ground, where cold fresh air seeped in toward the fire. Unlike most hospitals, where the windows are closed and the stench alone can sicken a man, the healing lodges let Nature's clean air fill a man's lungs every time he breathed. We were warm; we never choked in the smoke; no man coughed upon another man's face, nor even touched his shoulder. And as March melted into April, we could smell—we could breathe—clean air scented by the awakening pine.

(These healing lodges proved so successful that during the second encampment in Morristown two winters later, Dr. James Tilton ordered them built in even greater numbers. He was certain that the lodges greatly reduced the rate of death among his patients because they were "completely ventilated.")

Henry, Nathan, and I suffered our fevers together, our rash, and the hideous open pustules. Though we never learned the words, Henry, at some point deep in his sickness, began to hum, weakly at first, the rhythmic chant of His Long Road's unrelenting song.

၈၃

Chapter Seventy-Eight

Genevieve.

ENTER THE FRENCH

Despite the epidemic, March of 1777 brought some encouragement to the Continental Army.

Early in the month, Lady Washington arrived by carriage (over muddy, rutted roads) from Virginia. She greatly improved the spirits of General Washington, who had been gravely ill for ten days, not from smallpox but the exhaustion of work and worry. Even the officers were cheered by her presence at headquarters, for she welcomed them all as members of the General's military "family." (She had been inoculated during the previous summer in Philadelphia, so she took no risk in coming to Morristown.)

Second, we received the news in March that Congress had returned to Philadelphia. Thus the nation's government resided once more in the nation's capital.

And third (information known only to General Washington and his scribe, as well as a few officers at headquarters), France had secretly shipped six thousand, eight hundred muskets, with powder and balls, to Philadelphia. The French captain had managed to evade the British blockade along the Atlantic coastline. This treasure of weapons traveled from Philadelphia to Morristown in Conestoga wagons that usually brought us blankets and corn. General Washington was now in the unusual situation of having more muskets than soldiers.

Most Americans had great difficulty feeling any friendship for the French. In 1755, as a young colonel, General Washington had fought with the British against the French in the Pennsylvania wilderness. He was therefore now receiving aid from a former enemy. However, that enemy had for centuries been the enemy of Britain, and it had the world's second most powerful naval fleet. Our Commander in Chief, and Congress, were required by present events to put the French and Indian War behind them.

Congress had sent its ablest ambassador to France, with the hope that he could establish a military alliance, secure financial credit, and obtain recognition by the court of King Louis XVI at Versailles of the United States as a new and independent nation.

Our ambassador was the renowned scientist and man of letters, Benjamin Franklin. He was seventy years old when he sailed across the Atlantic in the late autumn of 1776 (at the same time that General Washington and his army were retreating across New Jersey). Franklin faced an almost impossible task: to convince the French foreign minister, the Count de Vergennes, and the twenty-three-year-old king, that the United States would ultimately win the war, and that we would then become a highly profitable trading partner.

The Count de Vergennes was already dubious. When he learned, before Franklin's arrival, that General Howe had forced the Americans from Long Island, and then from Manhattan Island, he ordered four frigates laden with weapons and gunpowder for the American army to remain in their French ports. The Count did not want France to become entangled with a failed rebellion.

Benjamin Franklin arrived in Paris on December 21, 1776 (while Trenton was still filled with Hessians). Our ambassador wore a plain brown suit without medals or adornments, and a hat of marten fur. To the French people, he represented simplicity and equality; he was the American democrat, and as such, they honored him. Franklin's book, a collection of his epigrams known as "The Way to Wealth," had sold well in translation. He was recognized as a man both clever and honest in business; his nation was thus viewed as a worthy trading partner.

Equally important to the French, Benjamin Franklin, even at the age of seventy, was skilled at charming the ladies. The King's wife, Marie Antoinette, and her multitude of courtiers were soon inviting Monsieur Franklin to every soirée.

Benjamin Franklin did more than charm the French and promise trade. He suggested that after the war, the United States, if victorious, would help France to clear the British out of the West Indies. Most of the immensely profitable sugar islands in the Caribbean would then be in the hands of the French.

Franklin was quick to recognize British spies in Paris; he slyly enabled them to pass on certain urgent information to London. Perhaps when King George III heard that the Americans were negotiating with King Louis XVI, he would declare war on France, and thus compel the French to enter the war on the American side.

France had lost Canada and other vast holdings of land in North

America to the British in 1763. Ever since, France had sought a return of her land and a restitution of her honor. Although King Louis XVI was not yet ready to join the Americans in their war, he was willing, secretly, to support an enemy of the British. He allowed the Americans to purchase some weapons on credit; that first shipment arrived in Morristown in March, 1777. When the King and his foreign minister learned about General Washington's victories in Trenton and Princeton, they allowed the four additional ships laden with weapons to sail for Philadelphia.

King Louis XVI and the Count de Vergennes waited for news of further victories before they committed France to war. Meanwhile, Benjamin Franklin was invited again and again to dinner in Paris, and at the royal court in Versailles.

∞

Chapter Seventy-Nine

Benjamin York, master bootmaker.

Henry, Nathan and I survived our ordeal with smallpox. We emerged from the healing lodge to an April sun warming the brown and sodden earth. That evening, we savored our first dinner in over two months with all eight of us around the Peabody table.

The troops in Morristown were in excellent spirits, for they had weathered another winter. Neither desertions nor disease had managed to destroy the Continental Army. New recruits, inoculated in Philadelphia, arrived each week (they pitched their tents outside of the village), until General Washington commanded over eight thousand soldiers for the summer campaign. Most of the men had enlisted according to new terms set by Congress: they would serve for three years, or the duration of the war. Our Commander in Chief finally had troops who would not disappear almost as soon as they had been trained.

General Washington often went riding in the afternoon with Lady Washington, herself an excellent horsewoman. The troops knew that the General had been seriously ill, and they were cheered to see him back on Nelson, his favorite horse, cantering with Lady Washington and a cluster of officers along a lane into the countryside.

French dignitaries began to arrive in Morristown, claiming to be high-ranking officers with experience from European battlefields. Some brought military documents; others simply appeared at the tavern door in resplendent uniforms, surrounded by aides. The French "générals" stated that they had come to fight for "La Liberté," and requested the command of at least a regiment, with commensurate payment. Few of them spoke any English; our General spoke no French. While he wrote to Congress for instructions, he invited his guests to accompany him on the afternoon rides.

Once released from the healing lodge, I worked day and night in my cobblers' shop, fashioning a pair of boots. Two men were always present in my mind as I cut and stitched each perfect piece of leather: my father, whose instructions I remembered, and General Washington, who I hoped would do me the honor of wearing them.

I stitched the tall uppers, each with a cuff that could be pulled up to protect the knees. I waxed and blackened each boot until they shone in the lanternlight. When they were done—the finest footwear I had ever cobbled—I stood them together beside my bench.

I did not know how to present them to the General, in part because of a certain shyness, but primarily because I did not know whether the boots would fit.

So I asked Genevieve whether, in the morning, she would stand them outside the General's office door, where he might discover them, and perhaps try them on.

When she arrived at headquarters the following morning, she placed the boots on the floor outside the general's office. The Life Guard at the door picked them up and ran his hand inside each one, searching for any danger to General Washington. The guard informed Genevieve (speaking to her for the first time in four months, though he saw her every day) that he would deliver the boots to the General when the General was available.

Genevieve walked down the corridor to her office and began to copy some letters.

No more than ten minutes later, General Washington strode into her office wearing the shiny black boots. He bowed to her with all the grace of a Virginia gentleman (while Colonel Askwith stared), then said, "Miss Ebenezer, I would like to inform your husband that his boots fit my feet most astonishingly well."

"I believe, sir, that he is downstairs in his shop."

"Thank you."

I was working at my bench when I heard boots walking across the floor toward me. My heart thumping, I looked up, then I stood in my leather apron as General Washington approached.

"Master bootmaker York, I thank you for the finest pair of boots I have ever worn. Neither those made in Williamsburg, nor London, have ever been so precise a fit. Nor have any previous pair been made from such extraordinary leather. I commend you for your skill, and I thank you deeply for your generosity."

"You are most welcome, sir."

Once again we shook hands, as we had done at my wedding.

Then the General, with a nod of greeting to an audience of silent apprentices, walked back across the dance hall floor and disappeared through the door.

Returning to my work on a common vamp, I felt that I had finally made restitution to my father. I had lost his pair of boots to Hench, but I had crafted all that Papa taught me into another pair of boots that would serve the General, as I hoped, until we Americans had freed ourselves from Hench and his venomous ilk, forever.

Genevieve.

Toward the end of April, I received a letter from Judd, answering a letter that I had posted to Lincoln in January. He wrote that all was well on the farm. They followed news of the war closely. Mama and Papa longed for peace, prayed for it in their grace before every meal. They ached for the war to end so that Henry, Benjamin and I could come safely home. And so they could finally meet their grandson.

Judd's cattle would soon be calving. The Paterson's old barn had collapsed with the weight of so much snow on its roof, but fortunately no one had been in it, nor the stock either, just their wagon and some chickens.

Judd added that he had taken Benjamin's letter with him on market day to Boston, and had found a frigate bound for Dublin. The captain himself assured him that the letter would reach London. (Benjamin had written proudly to his family about his cobblers' shop and the twenty-five apprentices he was training.)

My brother signed the page, "With love from the family, Judd."

I kept all of his letters throughout the war and read them over and over. It was immeasurably heartening to know that Mama and Papa were well, and that the farm was flourishing.

Toward the end of May, the Continental Army prepared to depart from Morristown. We would march to a destination known as yet only to our Commander in Chief.

However, Caleb developed what Dr. Bond diagnosed as a case of measles. "The child must remain in bed," the doctor told us, "in a dark room, his eyes protected from light. He should breathe the steam over a pot of hot water."

I had no choice but to remain behind with the Peabody's (who insisted that of course I would stay with them until the child was well).

Then I would bring Caleb in the wagon to join the army at its summer encampment, wherever that might be.

PART V · 409

We could not know that the Continental Army would march almost continuously in a duet with the British for the next seven months, until our troops finally encamped close to Philadelphia.

Thus I said farewell to Benjamin and Henry on May 28, 1777 in Morristown, and would not meet them again until late in December, in the wooded hills of Valley Forge.

Benjamin.

My Genevieve, shy and discreet, has left out of her account one special evening. A springtime evening in May it was, lit by a waxing moon, and filled with the joyous songs of flirting birds. The soft warm air was fragrant with the scent of fresh white apple blossoms.

The orchard (just north of the village) was bounded on all four sides by a stone wall. Seated on a blanket beneath the trees, we saw only the lovely moonlit cloud of blossoms above us (and not a single lit window anywhere).

I am certain, counting back nine months from her birth during the brutal winter in Valley Forge, that our second child, our daughter Sally, was lovingly invited into the world by her mother and father in that hidden, fragrant, moonlit patch of American paradise.

‽

PART VI

The War Moves
to Philadelphia

Chapter Eighty

Benjamin, on the march
all summer, 1777.

During the month of June 1777, General Howe marched his army around the State of New Jersey, hoping to draw our troops into a major battle that would end the war. Though we marched as well, we stayed just out of reach. We never allowed the redcoats to challenge us on an open field.

Meanwhile, the British commenced a three-part maneuver in the north, designed to cut off New England from the rest of the States. General John Burgoyne invaded New York from Canada with a large army of British and German troops. He intended to sail down Lake Champlain, march to the upper waters of Hudson's River, then sail down to Albany. (The plan in all its details was no secret. Our spies had sent information south, even to the number of vessels the British had gathered on Lake Champlain.)

General Burgoyne's enormous army was accompanied by several hundred Iroquois warriors who would serve as guides, as soldiers, and (we anticipated) as butchers of American civilians. Of the six nations of the Iroquois, the Oneida, with the Tuscarora, had sided with the Americans, while the other four nations of the Iroquois continued their century-long alliance with the British. I was not surprised when His Long Road disappeared north to New York in June. Johannes told us that he "went home to the Oneida," no doubt anticipating a war within the war.

A second British army under Colonel Barry St. Leger had sailed across Lake Ontario from Canada, and was now marching in western New York toward the upper reaches of the Mohawk River. The Mohawk would carry them to its junction with Hudson's River, near Albany. St. Leger's troops would there join Burgoyne's troops, then sail and march south together along Hudson's River toward New York City.

The second army was also composed of British and German troops, guided by Iroquois warriors, most of them Seneca.

A third British army, now quartered in New York City, would sail up Hudson's River toward Albany. If the three-part plan succeeded, the

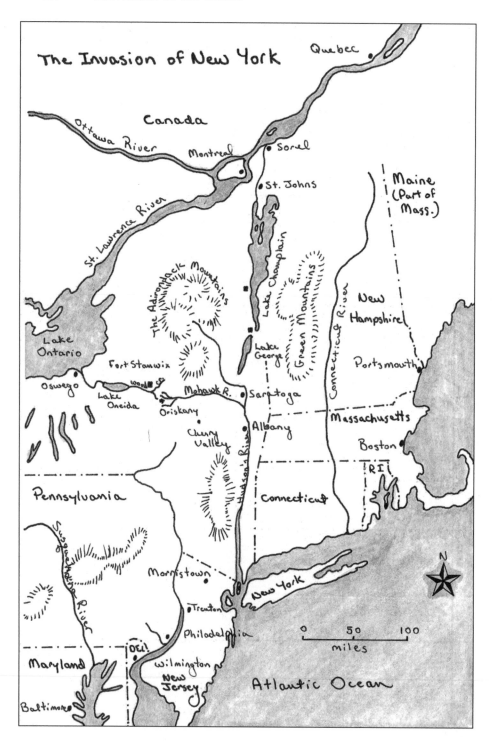

The Invasion of New York

entire waterway from the St. Lawrence River to New York Harbor would be controlled by the British. Hudson's River would serve as a barricade between New England and the southern states. Perhaps Burgoyne, St. Leger, and Howe expected a Loyalist uprising against the rebels. Certainly they expected that our military spirit would wither.

We were confident, however, that our troops at Fort Ticonderoga would halt General Burgoyne's advance down Lake Champlain. The upper Hudson would remain in our possession.

Our troops at Fort Stanwix in western New York, guarding the headwaters of the Mohawk River, would surely halt Colonel St. Leger's advance. The Mohawk would continue to serve as our American highway to the west.

With regard to the third army, we could make no predictions. Would General Howe send most of his troops up Hudson's River, or would he continue his effort to capture Philadelphia? While his army maneuvered back and forth across New Jersey in June, we knew where he was. But when General Howe realized that General Washington would not risk a major battle, he withdrew all of his troops to Staten Island. And then we could not know: would the redcoats head north in July, or south? Or both?

We waited in New Jersey, ready to dash in either direction.

On July 5, we learned to our astonishment that our troops had abandoned Fort Ticonderoga without firing a shot! The British had cut a trail to the top of a hill overlooking the fort. When they hauled several cannons to the hilltop, the American commander felt he had no choice but to abandon the fort. (Several American officers had previously recommended that our troops establish a post on that hilltop. But as the British had failed to build redoubts atop the hills overlooking Boston, so we had failed to built a redoubt overlooking our own fort.)

With British troops once again garrisoned in Fort Ticonderoga, the route south was now open—either by way of Lake George, or a march through deep forest—to the upper waters of Hudson's River, and thus to Albany.

General Washington immediately marched the Continental Army north across New York to the heights overlooking Hudson's River, where we would attempt to stop any British ships, or columns of troops, moving north from New York City. In addition, he ordered Colonel Daniel Morgan to sail up the river with five hundred riflemen: they would support General Horatio Gates and his small army as Gates attempted to block Burgoyne's march south. The riflemen, most of them experienced woodsmen from the mountains of western Virginia, were to halt any depredations by the Iroquois.

And then on July 24, we learned that a British fleet of two hundred and twenty-eight ships had sailed out of New York Harbor. There was little point in their sailing anywhere north. Almost certainly, the fleet was headed south for Delaware Bay and Philadelphia. Leaving troops garrisoned along Hudson's River under General Israel Putnam, General Washington marched the major portion of his army rapidly south across New Jersey, over the Delaware River, then down through Pennsylvania to the village of Germantown, six miles north of Philadelphia.

There we waited until we knew where the British would land.

News arrived that General Burgoyne had erred by not sailing south on Lake George, the route which would have brought him much closer to Hudson's River. His huge army, with a baggage train several miles long, was instead trying to cut its way through the immense forest south of Lake Champlain. The British troops were moving no faster than a mile a day, and the horses had little forage. The wilderness of New York had become our ally.

Then a tiny spark lit a raging fire. On July 30, halfway between Lake Champlain and Albany, a band of Iroquois killed and scalped a frontier woman named Jane McCrea. They paraded her long blond hair in front of the British troops, one of whom was the woman's horrified fiancé. News of this massacre spread throughout New York and New England (as well as the rest of America), where people blamed both the Iroquois and the British who had hired them. Throngs of outraged militia from the entire region were soon rushing to join General Gates in the coming battle against Burgoyne's struggling army.

On July 31, our troops in Germantown, Pennsylvania heard that scouts had sighted the British fleet off the capes of Delaware Bay. We expected the fleet to sail north up the Bay, to fight its way past our two forts on the Delaware River, and (if successful) to moor transport ships at the Philadelphia wharf, where thousands of redcoats would disembark to capture America's capital.

However, the fleet baffled us. The ships did not enter Delaware Bay, but disappeared back out on the Atlantic. Had their voyage been a feint to draw us south, before they raced back to New York City? The redcoats could then of course hurry north to rescue Burgoyne.

By now we had spent two full months marching hither and yon in the summer heat, without, aside from a few skirmishes, firing a shot. The shoes we had cobbled in Morristown were wearing thin.

On the last day of July, 1777, while attending a dinner in his honor at the City Tavern in Philadelphia, General Washington met a nineteen-year-old French aristocrat from the court of Louis XVI, who had never been on a battlefield, but who had sailed across the Atlantic to lend his services to the Continental Army.

Though a number of Frenchmen had tried to talk their way into high-ranking (and well paid) positions in our army, the Marquis de Lafayette was different. He brought with him a letter from Benjamin Franklin in Paris, who recommended the Marquis not as a soldier, but as the means of building a stronger friendship with both the French court and the French people. "He is exceedingly beloved," wrote Ambassador Franklin, "and everyone's good wishes attend him."

In addition, the Marquis stated that he would serve as a volunteer without pay. "I am here, sir," he told General Washington, "to learn and not to teach."

General Washington agreed that Lafayette could serve as an honorary aide in his camp. Thus began a profound and lifelong friendship between the childless General, forty-five years old, and the young Frenchman whose father had died when the boy was only three.

On August 22, 1777, our scouts finally sighted the British fleet: it was heading north up Chesapeake Bay. General Howe thereby avoided our forts on the Delaware River. He no doubt planned to march his troops from the northern tip of the Chesapeake to Philadelphia, a distance of about fifty-five miles.

General Washington issued orders that we would march south through Philadelphia on Sunday, August 24, to position ourselves (as we guessed) at some strong point between Chesapeake Bay and the capital.

General Howe would finally have his battle.

Genevieve, nursing a child back to health.

During the summer of 1777 in Morristown, I received brief letters from Benjamin, mailed whenever the army paused for a day or two near a town with a post office. Susanne received letters from Henry, in his handwriting, although (I did not tell her) Benjamin had clearly helped him with the spelling. They were well, they were marching; they were well, they were marching. And each one sent his love.

Caleb had recovered from measles by mid-July. On his first birthday, we went riding on Sir William, the boy snug in my arm. Susanne and Robert rode along with us. We had a fine supper on the bank of a stream.

We heard the news from the north, and thus my thoughts were often with my family on the farm. I wondered if General Burgoyne might not attack Massachusetts from Albany, and if General Howe might not sail his fleet back to Boston.

But above all, we worried, Susanne and I, about our men. We lived with a constant uneasiness that no prayers could ever banish. Perhaps Henry or Benjamin lay bleeding on some forlorn battlefield, calling our names into the wind, into the rain, into the darkness, while we drank our tea, or mended a shirt, or kissed our children good night.

∞

Chapter Eighty-One

Benjamin, on Chestnut Street.

The Continental Army did not simply march through Philadelphia on Sunday, August 24, 1777; we *paraded* through the city, so the city's patriots might be heartened, and the Loyalists dismayed, by the sight of so many sturdy soldiers.

Our troops were in high spirits, for the news had reached us from New York that St. Leger had failed to advance past Fort Stanwix. His Iroquois allies had abandoned him after the Battle of Oriskany, and his army was now retreating back to Canada.

In addition, a portion of Burgoyne's army had been captured while foraging for supplies near Bennington, Vermont. General Howe was now sailing his fleet up Chesapeake Bay and thus unable to rush to Burgoyne's rescue. We were whittling at the British in the north, and planning to make a blow with an axe here in the south.

The day before we paraded through Philadelphia, we washed our ragged clothing in a creek, laid trousers and hunting shirts in the sun to dry, then polished our muskets. Because we had no regular uniforms, nor even regular hats, we all plucked a sprig of greenery to wear as a cockade.

Early Sunday morning, we assembled in formation along the main road through Germantown. Each regiment employed a drummer and fifer in its ranks, so we might step lively, and so the music might never pause for the spectators in Philadelphia.

General Washington, mounted beside the Marquis de Lafayette (representing military support from France), led our column down Front Street along the Delaware River into Philadelphia. To our left stretched the two-mile wharf; we spotted the hull of one of the future frigates of the American navy, floating in a shipyard, though still without her masts.

Ahead to the right, towering high above Philadelphia's rooftops, we could see the white steeple of Christ Church. The brass weathervane on its peak wagged gently in a breeze off the river.

Further to the right (and thus in the center of the city) stood the red

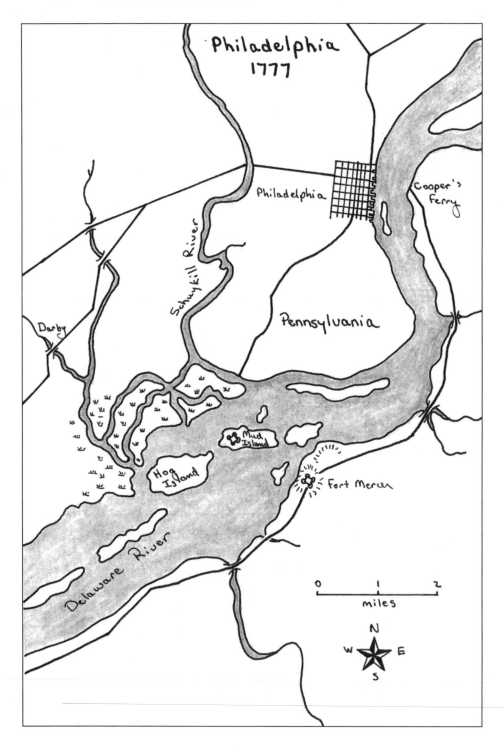

brick tower and even taller steeple of the Pennsylvania State House: the building where our Declaration of Independence had been signed. For the past several days, we had looked forward with keen anticipation to seeing that renowned building for ourselves. The sight of even its white steeple above the rooftops was enough for the men to whisper as they marched, "That's it!"

We paraded twelve abreast, our muskets shouldered at roughly the same angle, our well-worn shoes advancing roughly in step, while our drums rumbling boldly off the two- and three-story brick houses along Front Street. We were pleased at the number of people gathered to watch our proud procession. Even the Quakers in their broad-brimmed hats, who opposed all war and who thus had weakened our recruiting efforts, were gathered along the sidewalks to watch us pass.

We received an especially rousing cheer as we passed the London Coffee House on the corner of Front and Market Streets. Although the market stalls behind it were closed on the Sabbath, its front porch was crowded with patriots raising their morning cup of coffee to us.

When we swung our ranks to the right onto Chestnut Street—the central boulevard through the city—we discovered an enormous crowd along both sides of the street. Every citizen within miles, it seemed, had gathered to greet us. We heard a roar ahead of us as people cheered the approach of General Washington. (Last December he had stopped the enemy at Trenton, only sixteen miles from Philadelphia.)

The buildings along Chestnut Street were both solid and stately. The people who cheered us (some from their windows) were well dressed. The street was smoothly paved with cobblestones, and street lamps stood at regular intervals. We felt ourselves to be marching through a true metropolis, America's foremost city, where (as men in the Pennsylvania militia had boasted) the forty thousand citizens could walk the straightest, cleanest streets in America, read the news in seven different newspapers (one of them in German), borrow books from the nation's first library, or visit a doctor in the nation's first hospital.

Bells began to ring—every bell in the city tolled its welcome in a jubilant clamor of high clear tones and deep "Bong! . . . Bong! . . . Bong!"

We marched past Second Street, and Third, then we glanced to the right into a courtyard where Benjamin Franklin's brick house stood. We knew that he was in Paris, nudging the French into our war.

We looked to the left and admired Carpenters' Hall, with its handsome white turret, where the First Continental Congress had been held in the fall of 1774 (while I had been training as a redcoat in Boston). The gentlemen from Virginia had met the gentlemen from Massachusetts for the first time in that building; despite all they had heard about Samuel Adams and his mobs, they were pleased to meet a patriot nearly as reasonable as his cousin John.

Now we could see ahead on the left, set back from Chestnut Street between Fifth and Sixth, a long two-story brick building that was as much a shrine to us as any church could possibly be: the Pennsylvania State House. "There!" whispered the men as they pointed at the tall windows along the left end of the building. "Inside is Assembly Hall, where John Hancock penned his name to our Declaration."

"There's the very room where Colonel Washington was appointed our Commander in Chief."

Aye, to march so close to that sacred edifice, to hear our drums rumble against the long front wall, to see the granite steps leading up to the huge white door where Benjamin Franklin had walked in and out. And Thomas Jefferson. And of course our General himself. *That* was a treasured moment which we would take to our graves. Not a man among us whose heart did not beat with pride.

And with a strengthened determination. For two full hours, our troops paraded past the State House, and if the Revolutionary War had a turning point—when we were bound to persevere at any cost until the victory was won—it was then, on Chestnut Street, while we marched past the building where the common man's dignity had been born.

Inside those tall windows, our Congress had declared, "All men are created equal." As we marched past, muskets shouldered, we were determined to make it so.

Peering over my left shoulder down Sixth Street, I could see a park behind the State House where the delegates took a breath of air in the shade beneath the trees. And where private negotiations, impossible in the Assembly Hall, were quietly conducted and concluded before the gentlemen re-entered the Hall and a vote was taken.

Across from the park was the Walnut Street Prison, a building which few noted. Some of our men, after Brandywine, after Paoli, after Germantown, would become prisoners inside those walls—the most wretched of prisoners—during the eight months that Philadelphia was occupied by the British.

One block further, we looked to the right up Seventh Street and stared at the home of a prosperous bricklayer on the corner of Market: inside those windows on the second floor, Thomas Jefferson had labored over every sentence of our Declaration. More than one soldier promised himself as we marched past, "Once this devil of a war is over, I'm coming back to Philadelphia. Going to bring my family. Going to show them where Jefferson done his writing."

On along Chestnut Street we marched, westward, the morning sun warming our backs. I might have wished that Genevieve were with us, driving Sir William as she too paraded through the heart of our nation. However, General Washington had ordered the several hundred women who accompanied the troops to follow a route along the northern edge of the city, where few people would notice them. The General wanted the Continental Army to appear as strong as possible, unencumbered by the frailty and vice of camp followers.

(Genevieve would have refused to skulk past our capital. No doubt Miss Ebenezer, her hair tucked up into her hat, would have driven Sir William behind the artillery train, carrying, for all anyone knew, not a cobbler's shop but barrels of gunpowder in her wagon.)

A few blocks further, the city became a patchwork of pastures and scattered barns. Chestnut Street dwindled into a dirt lane that proceeded, with a surveyor's straightness, through a partly cleared forest. We spotted a flock of turkeys, but could not have said whether they were domestic or wild.

West of the city, the procession of wives and children, sweethearts and washerwomen emerged from the woods on a lane that was hardly more than a cart path. With a bit of banter, they joined the troops.

Together we crossed a floating bridge over the Schuylkill River, a much smaller waterway than the broad Delaware. Then we marched south, drums still thrumming and fifes still piping, toward our night's encampment at Darby.

Thus did we parade as General Washington's Continental Army, almost eight thousand strong, through the city first settled by Swedes and Dutchmen as a well protected port; the city dedicated by William Penn and his Quakers as a haven for men of all faiths; and finally, the city consecrated by our Congress as the birthplace of equality.

Forever would we remember the bells of Philadelphia: the bells that rang in every steeple as we marched among them. The troops would especially remember the huge bell in the tower of the State House, tolling above us with its deep rhythmic tone, more powerful, more vibrant, than even our drums.

∞

Chapter Eighty-Two

Benjamin, recounting

THE BATTLE OF BRANDYWINE

On that same Sunday in August, 1777, while we paraded through Philadelphia, British and German troops were disembarking at Head of Elk, the northernmost point of Chesapeake Bay. During the following week, we marched rapidly south, then blocked every road and bridge leading toward the capital. For the first time in the war, our cavalry, under the command of Polish Count Casimir Pulaski, showed its strength on the open farmland. In skirmish after skirmish, we let the British know that the taking of Philadelphia was going to be much different from the taking of New York.

But the enemy was strong. Thirteen thousand British and German troops pushed eight thousand American regulars (and a growing number of Pennsylvania militia) ahead of them, often by means of superior artillery. We made a stand near Wilmington in the State of Delaware, but the open fields gave the advantage to the redcoats in their European formations, and we drew back once again.

On September 7, the Continental Army camped about thirty miles southwest of Philadelphia. On that particular evening, a great number of the troops gathered in the fields along the edge of the encampment, beyond the flickering light of our dinner fires; the men did not face the enemy to the south, but stared instead toward the northern sky, where strange green ribbons of light rippled and pulsed. "Aurora borealis," said a fisherman from Boston. He had often seen shifting green ribbons while at sea off Nova Scotia.

I stood with a crowd of men in a recently harvested cornfield; our shoes, now no more than tattered shreds of leather, pointed their open toes north among the stubble of corn stalks. I wondered if Genevieve was at that moment watching a huge green fan that opened—with faint shimmers of pink—just above the horizon. Had she ever before seen such unearthly beauty?

Henry appeared beside me in the cornfield, though how he found

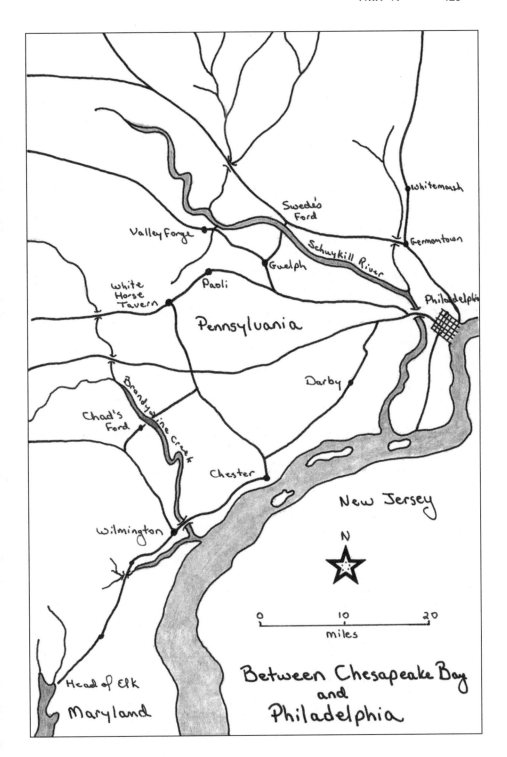

Between Chesapeake Bay
and
Philadelphia

me in that crowd of a thousand soldiers, I do not know. I had not seen him since early afternoon, for he had been summoned to headquarters. Neither one of us spoke. He stared up at those slowly undulating green ribbons, as fascinated by them as everyone else.

Then he said quietly, "I'm Captain Byrnes now."

I looked at him: his face, like the multitude of other faces around us, was faintly lit by the glow in the north. "Congratulations."

"Hmm." Unlike his sister, Henry did not readily say what was on his mind. Whereas Genevieve shared her thoughts with me while she pondered something through, Henry was more distant, more hidden. In part it was his shyness. But in part it was his instinctive determination to do what was right. Not what was comfortable, not what was profitable; what was right. And until he had it completely clear in his mind, he said not a word about it.

So when finally he spoke, my job was to listen.

"You know, Benjamin," he said, glancing back over his shoulder at the dark night beyond our hundred campfires, "the captain looks south, toward the enemy, waiting for the battle to begin."

We heard a murmur among the men, quiet talk about an especially bright ray of green beaming up from the horizon, like a fountain. The elms along the far end of the cornfield were silhouetted black against the green sky. A soldier standing near us wondered whether his folks up north in New Hampshire could see these lights—"these omens"—as well as we could. Maybe better.

"But the man looks north, toward a fine woman in Morristown, and toward her son. The man is waiting for life to begin."

Not a thing I could say to make the love and the loneliness, the worry and the fear, go away.

"What's waiting for us to the south, people have seen a thousand times before. Today we use muskets with bayonets. Folks in the Bible used swords and cudgels and the jawbone of an ass. Same blood soaking into the same earth."

Henry swept his hand across the green sky. "But what's waiting for us in the north, we've hardly taken the time to learn about. How much magic is in God's great sky? How much magic is in a woman's heart? Benjamin, I've only barely begun to learn."

An apprentice myself, I knew no way out of the dilemma between duty and love, between today's war and tomorrow's peace. Between being man enough to be chosen at headquarters as a commander of men, and being man enough to be chosen on a springtime evening as a future husband and father. Between marching beside a company of privates, leading them toward victory while protecting them from unnecessary death, and standing beside a bride in a church during the sacrament of marriage. Between offering himself as a target to an enemy sniper, and offering himself as a father to a half-orphaned boy.

"Tell them," he said, "tell Susanne and Robert . . . Tell them that I never hated a thing in my life as much as I hate this job. But I've got to do it."

Then Captain Henry Byrnes, attached to General Nathanael Greene, turned and made his way through the crowd of privates back to camp.

The British army advanced in two huge columns: one confronted us directly from the south, while the other angled toward the west. The second column clearly planned to outflank us, then either surround us, or race toward Philadelphia. Accordingly, the Continental Army shifted north. We crossed a thread of water, low now in the autumn, called Brandywine Creek, twenty-six miles from the capital. We spread our troops along the northeastern bank, commandeered every boat, guarded every bridge. Artillery was ranged along a ridge overlooking the main road to Philadelphia, especially where it crossed the creek at Chadd's Ford.

Relying on scouts for information, General Washington positioned his troops a short distance south along the creek, a greater distance to the north. Regiments under General Wayne and General Sullivan hid in the wooded hills. Troops under Brigadier General William Maxwell waded back across the stream and hid along the southwestern shore, where they would receive the first blow. The troops under General Greene (including myself in Henry's company) waited a short distance to the rear, as reserves. Wherever the British tried to cross the creek and force a breach in our line, General Greene's men would pour in as reinforcements.

Such was our deployment on the evening of September 10, 1777, when the British and German troops were encamped near the village of Kennett Square, a few miles southwest of the creek.

At dawn on September 11, German troops under General Wilhelm von Knyphausen fired upon General Maxwell's regiment along the western bank of Chadd's Ford, exactly where we thought the main attack would take place. Though our men repulsed two German charges, heavy musket fire forced them to retreat across the creek. While they waded slowly through the waist-deep water with their muskets held well above the surface, many were struck by a bullet in the back. The muskets splashed and sank to the bottom; bobbing corpses floated downstream. Wounded soldiers staggered toward shore, while the morning sun danced in the ripples around them.

Despite General Knox's artillery ranged on a hill above the ford, General Knyphausen managed to position his own fieldpieces on the heights across the creek. Our artillery horses had been driven to the rear last night, but one of our shells must have hit a German team, for we could hear a horse shrieking most horribly.

For the next several hours, cannons fired back and forth between the hills overlooking Brandywine Creek, all with little result. Black smoke filled the valley, though a breeze tended to carry most of it to our side, enabling our infantry to dash from one tree to another in the shifting skirmishes.

General Washington, accompanied by the Marquis de Lafayette, often rode from his headquarters at Ring's Tavern to inspect our lines. The men always cheered him, even while they loaded and fired. The lack of a German attack across the ford, and the prolonged dueling of artillery through the morning, caused us to suspect that the enemy troops were much weaker than they had initially seemed. We therefore expected an order from our Commander in Chief to sweep forward across the ford in a full attack.

But General Washington took no such risk.

The sun had passed its noon zenith when we began to hear firing far to the north. From shouts relayed down the lines, we learned that despite our scouts along the creek, a British column had managed to march undetected six miles to the north, then cross two branches at unguarded fords. The enemy was now marching south, on *our* side of the Brandywine, with such confidence that the redcoats were accompanied by a military band. General Howe no doubt planned to sweep behind us: we would then be caught between the British to our rear and the Germans attacking across the creek. The entire Continental Army might well be captured.

General Washington ordered the northern flank to pivot to the right; their hastily formed line now faced the onslaught. Count Pulaski led his cavalry around the right wing to hold back a sweep of British cavalry. General Washington galloped up and down our ragged front, ordering General Sullivan's troops into better positions at the edge of a woods, behind a wall, atop the crest of a hill. As at Princeton, the men were enormously heartened to see our General directing troops with his sword in the very heart of the battle.

But we had too little time to form a proper line, too little time to position artillery. And the eight thousand redcoats marching in precise ranks down Osborne's Hill, supported by artillery ranged on the heights behind them, were fresh troops, whereas our men had been fighting along the creek since dawn.

When General Sullivan's battered line began to collapse, General Washington galloped back through the woods to General Greene: he ordered the reserve troops to form a parallel line behind the front, as a wall through which Sullivan's troops could retreat. General Greene's regiment (Henry's company included) raced across the wooded hills, covering five miles through thickets and fallen timber in less than an hour. We formed our barrier behind a chaos of hand-to-hand fighting. My musket readied, I listened to the berserk roar of men clubbing and stabbing each other.

Henry was superb. Each company in our barricade performed two contradictory maneuvers: we had to open our ranks to let the retreating troops rush through, yet we had to close our ranks to stop the British attack, all without shooting our own men. Henry scanned the smoke-obscured field ahead of us, then shouted to his sixty men ranged behind the brambles of a hedgerow: he directed some of us to fire to the left, some to the right, while others held their fire and thus opened a channel for the regulars dashing toward us. Wherever that channel of escape crossed the hedgerow, that's where Henry stood, waving his hat and beckoning, both a beacon and a target. If a wounded man reached the wall of stones and briars and could not scramble across it, Henry—I saw him do this at least five times—leapt over the wall and hoisted the soldier, bleeding with bayonet wounds, over the rocks to safety, all the while with his own back to the British bullets.

We could now hear a moving roar of artillery and muskets behind us: the German troops had forced their way across Brandywine Creek. We had no more than half an hour before they would be upon us.

A year ago on Long Island, facing a bayonet attack and the threat of encirclement, our soldiers had fled in terror. But today we did not flinch. We met British bayonets coming over the hedgerow with French bayonets mounted on French muskets. We had reached that state of military madness that is only part courage, part discipline, and the rest a berserk determination to shoot or stab or bludgeon every red-coat within reach.

I myself became no less a madman than I had been on Breed's Hill. I thought nothing of stumbling over writhing, shrieking bodies until I reached a wounded redcoat struggling with blood-smeared hands to re-load his musket. I wrenched the weapon from his clutching fingers, then paid no heed to his cry for mercy as I drove the man's own bayo-net into his mouth, pinning his head against the earth while he kicked and shivered and died.

Aye, as with the jawbone of an ass did I slaughter mine enemy.

The British brought forward their artillery. We fell back, but no further than to the edge of a woods behind us. General Greene's line thereby ensured that our retreat remained a retreat and never became a rout.

I do not know about other companies, but I do know that Captain Byrnes' company never drew back to the next woods, to the next wall, until we had gathered all our wounded. If we found anyone crumpled but still breathing behind a tree, in a clump of ferns, in a ditch, we brought that soldier with us. Henry's men never forgot that at Brandy-wine, though the British ultimately gained the field, we left not a single living private behind us.

The early darkness of a September evening, and the exhaustion of the British troops who had marched fifteen to twenty miles that day, prevented General Howe from pursuing us. Nor did the German troops threaten us. We heard their distant huzzah, heard their victory volley, as we withdrew toward Chester, a village on the Delaware River.

General Greene's rear guard became a gathering party: along the twelve-mile march, we collected men lost from their companies, men staggering from their wounds, men looking for their chance to desert. As we plodded along that cluttered country lane, the night still warm, the stars hazy, I could hear Henry's encouraging voice, often calling out to a man by name.

By the time we marched wearily into the encampment of scattered dinner fires near Chester, Henry had twice the number of men under his supervision as he had commanded that morning. He reported to headquarters, somewhere in the village. Then he returned to the pasture where his troops had collapsed in their blankets.

He stood beside me at a campfire and devoured the firecakes which three of his soldiers had prepared for him. His face was blackened with powder. His hunting shirt was smeared with blood and dirt. His hands were torn from reaching through the brambles.

No one spoke, until the three privates each tossed a final piece of wood on the fire, then turned to Captain Byrnes and said, one by one, "Thank you, sir."

They disappeared into the night to find a place to sleep.

∾

Chapter Eighty-Three

Benjamin, recounting

THE PAOLI MASSACRE

As our sturdy troops had stood up to the ranks of redcoats and had not fled in a rout, so we stood up to our small defeat at Brandywine Creek and did not lose our determination to strike again. On the day after the battle, we marched north from Chester, crossed the Schuylkill River to the protection of its far shore, then camped close enough to Philadelphia that our wounded could be carted to the city's hospital. Congress rewarded the troops with an unexpected gift: wagons arrived in camp loaded with thirty hogsheads of rum.

During the two-day respite, General Washington dispatched Colonel Alexander Hamilton into Philadelphia to find shoes for the troops. At the General's recommendation, Colonel Hamilton asked me to accompany him. I was to inspect the goods with a professional eye before we purchased them.

Following breakfast on September 14, we rode together into the city. Though we spent long hours visiting a dozen shops, we discovered that most of cobblers had become speculators. Our troops had battled at both Trenton and Brandywine to protect the citizens of Philadelphia, yet many of those citizens (secretly) looked forward to a British occupation of their city. They could then sell their goods for hard British specie rather than paper American dollars.

Colonel Hamilton and I were certain that several thousand pairs of shoes were hidden somewhere in Philadelphia, waiting to be sold. They had been unloaded from a French frigate only a month ago and stored in a warehouse by the wharf. Now the warehouse was empty. When a wily merchant shrugged his ignorance of what might have happened to the entire cargo, I wanted to drag him by the neck to our camp and show him our wounded soldiers, our barefoot soldiers, our farm boys who had written home about marching past the Pennsylvania State House.

Alexander Hamilton, a young fellow my own age—who later served as Secretary of the Treasury under President Washington and organized America's financial foundation—departed from Philadelphia that day with no more than fifty pairs of shoes, most of them so small that they would be allotted to the washerwomen.

When I told Henry that evening at the campfire about our failure, he said, "One day we'll send the British home. But it's the Devil among us that worries me. "

For the next several days, the British army and the American army repeated the same wary maneuvering that had frustrated both sides throughout the summer: General Howe wanted to draw us into an open battle, while General Washington held his troops just beyond reach. Our Commander in Chief positioned us between the British to the south and Philadelphia to the north, while staying far enough west that we could not be trapped against the Delaware River.

On September 16, we battled near the White Horse Tavern, twenty miles west of Philadelphia. As the British were threatening our flanks, a fierce thunderstorm burst upon us, drenching our powder. We had no choice but to retreat from what the men called "The Battle of the Clouds." The day had become so dark and wet, it seemed the clouds were sitting on our shoulders.

Although we retreated further westward—first to Yellow Springs, then to Warwick Furnace, where we obtained dry powder—we did not leave the road entirely open to Philadelphia. The British army had to cross the Schuylkill River before they could enter the city. General Washington accordingly posted General Anthony Wayne with fifteen hundred men near Paoli Tavern: should General Howe attempt to cross the river, General Waybe would attack the baggage train.

On September 20, 1777, Congress, watching the steady approach of the British, once again fled from Philadelphia. Our nation's government packed up its papers and hurried first to Lancaster, Pennsylvania, far to the west, and then to York, well beyond the broad Susquehanna River.

Though we grumbled about "our courageous delegates," we could understand their caution. What we could never understand, could never forgive, was the betrayal of Americans by their fellow Americans. Spies loyal to the King informed General Howe of our hidden camp at Paoli, and even gave him the password used by our sentries.

Shortly after midnight on September 21, 1777, three British battalions commanded by Colonel Thomas Musgrave approached General

Wayne's camp in absolute silence. Using their bayonets and swords, the enemy quickly forced their way through the sentries, then poured into the camp, bayoneting many of our troops while they were still wrapped in their blankets. Most of our men were sleeping around campfires, and thus were well lit victims. General Wayne had no time to organize a defense. Those who could run disappeared into the forest. Those who could not escape were butchered while they begged for mercy.

When the Paoli survivors staggered into our camp the following morning, we listened with horror and outrage to their tale. The "Paoli Massacre" repeated the vicious bayoneting of prisoners on Long Island a year ago. During the month since the British had disembarked from their ships on Chesapeake Bay, they had plundered a multitude of farms in Maryland, Delaware, and Pennsylvania; they had slaughtered livestock; they had dragged young women into barns and raped them. And now the vicious brutes had run their blades through our helpless men.

Aye, we were still determined to protect Philadelphia. But we now had another purpose in mind for the muskets we oiled.

The next time we battled with His Majesty's royal regiments, we would strike with raging ferocity.

ॐ

Chapter Eighty-Four

Benjamin, at

THE BATTLE OF GERMANTOWN

When General Howe tricked us, we thought we had lost our chance for revenge.

We were camped at Evansburg, north of the Schuylkill River, guarding several fords, while the British were camped south of the river on a broad grassy flatland called Valley Forge. General Howe marched his troops northwest as if toward our supply depot at Reading. We too marched northwest, on the opposite side of the river. But under the cover of night, General Howe left campfires burning (as we had done at Trenton) and reversed direction: the British troops slipped below us and crossed the Schuylkill at Flatland's Ford. As September 23 dawned, General Howe had an open road leading east to Germantown, then south into Philadelphia.

We had been outmaneuvered. But that mattered little, for we had prevented General Howe from capturing the Continental Army. Though General Cornwallis marched his infantrymen and grenadiers into the city on September 26, he could do no more with Philadelphia than the British had been able to do with Boston or New York. They held the cities, but we held the continent.

As we had paraded up Chestnut Street on August 24, so the British paraded a month later on September 26. Whereas we had worn tattered hunting shirts and ragged trousers, with a sprig of evergreen in our hats, the British troops wore their splendid scarlet uniforms with polished buttons. We had marched to boys playing a drum and fife, whereas the British marched to an entire military band. And whereas the patriots had cheered us, now the Loyalists had their turn to cheer.

In the northern theater of the war, the situation looked far more promising. An express rider brought news that our troops in New York had halted the British advance on Albany. Thousands of regulars and militia now confronted General Burgoyne in the hills beside Hudson's River. Winter was coming soon in the north country; British provisions were nearly depleted. Burgoyne must either attempt a retreat back through the wilderness to Canada, or surrender to the well-provisioned forces of General Horatio Gage.

Though embarrassed to learn of imminent success in New York at the moment of our defeat in Philadelphia, our spirits were nevertheless lifted. General Washington ordered the regiments to assemble in parade formation, then told us that we would soon show ourselves equal to our "northern brethren." The quartermaster thereupon provided every soldier with a gill of rum; we raised our mugs with a cheer while thirteen cannons fired a salute in celebration.

General Cornwallis found lodging in one of Philadelphia's elegant mansions, while his troops occupied buildings throughout the city. The major portion of the British army, however, camped in Germantown, five miles north of Philadelphia. General Howe displayed his scorn for the Americans by refusing to construct fortifications around the village, even though his own headquarters was near the main road.

Consequently, we had our target. We would pounce upon Germantown as we had pounced upon Trenton. Only this time, we would not surprise a few hundred sleeping Germans. We would attack the flower of the British army.

At dusk on October 3, 1777, we departed from our camp northeast of Germantown, prepared for an all-night march. Each soldier attached a bit of white paper to his hat, so we could see each other in the dark. We divided into four columns: we would enter Germantown by four different roads before dawn. We hoped to drive the surprised British ahead of us until we had trapped them with their backs against either the Schuylkill River, or the Delaware. The two rivers joined below Philadelphia, forming a perfect trap.

However, the cold October night and the still unfrozen streams in the region created a heavy fog that hid everything around us. Nor did the four columns arrive at their four points of attack on time. Our own column, under General Greene, was delayed by a report in the middle of the night that a regiment of British infantry was marching toward us on Limekiln Road. We halted, sent scouts ahead. After an hour of standing in the cold misty darkness—the men grumbled with burning impatience—we learned that the British regiment had returned to Germantown. Only then did we proceed.

Daylight brightened the thick fog, but we could distinguish nothing clearly beyond thirty yards. As the blizzard had hidden our approach to Trenton, so the fog now hid our march toward Germantown.

When finally we reached the North Wales Road into the village, we heard muskets south of us: the battle had already begun. We guessed that General Wayne's men, who had approached from the west, must have been sighted by British sentries.

The firing alerted the entire British camp. The road ahead of us was soon blocked by redcoats all but obscured in the fog. With excellent discipline, we drove them back with steady volleys from our muskets, until we reached the Germantown marketplace. There on the green we discovered pots of porridge still on the fires, tents with clothing and rucksacks in them, and most heartening of all, a multitude of cannons. For the first time in the war, the Continental Army was driving His Majesty's Royal Army ahead of it on an open battlefield. *And* we were capturing artillery.

The fog darkened with musket smoke. There was no breeze to clear the air. We became so obscured from each other that soldiers lost their officers; officers became separated from their commanders. General Adam Stephen's troops, discovering figures ahead of them in the fog, opened fire on General Wayne's troops. Horrified that the British had gained their rear, Wayne's men swung around and fired back.

General Sullivan's troops, battling their way into the southern part of the village, called to their officers that they had no more ammunition; they had used their forty rounds. The British, close enough (though hidden in the fog) to hear the American voices, immediately attacked.

Most baffling of all, we could hear the roar of a major battle to the west, near the main road into Germantown. Should we continue to drive the British toward Philadelphia, or should we fall back to rescue a column that perhaps had been surrounded?

We could not know that six companies of infantry under Colonel Musgrave—the same Musgrave who had led the butchery at Paoli— had taken refuge inside a large stone mansion, and that our troops had halted their drive along the main road to attack the house. In the smoke-blackened fog, American artillery on one side of the house fired at American artillery on the other side. Redcoats firing from the windows killed a great number of our men as they assaulted the door and lower windows.

That confused halt at the Chew House broke the strength of our four-pronged attack on Germantown. The roar of muskets and cannons in the west caused other bodies of troops—who had forced the British to retreat for two or three miles—to believe they had been surrounded. Our troops already in the village, and east of the village, began to panic. Soldiers separated in the fog from their companies encountered clusters of their countrymen racing westward, every cluster shouting its own rumor of disaster and defeat.

For no real cause whatsoever, our attack suddenly reversed itself and became a rout.

Once again, General Greene formed a strong rear guard, holding the British at a distance while our troops withdrew from the village. And once again, we managed to carry with us all of our wounded. We left no one behind for the British bayonets.

The British pursued us for nearly ten miles. Finally, at White Marsh Church, General Greene counterattacked with enough force that the British halted. We fired volley after volley at the misty red brutes, until they withdrew and disappeared into the fog. I was disappointed to find that I still had two cartridges left, and an unbloodied bayonet.

Despite our defeat, the troops were in good spirits. We had driven the enemy from its own camp. Had we not been hampered by the fog, we might well have driven the British to the river, or into Philadelphia.

Our troops garrisoned in the two forts on the Delaware could then have attacked from the south.

"Next time," we told each other, "next time, we'll drive them all the way to the Atlantic."

Much good came from the Battle of Germantown. General Stephen, who had been drunk when his men fired on General Wayne's troops, was later replaced by the brilliant young Frenchman in whom General Washington had much confidence: the Marquis de Lafayette. The Marquis proved through the remainder of the war to be one of the General's most dependable officers.

The news of our nearly successful attack on Germantown, only three weeks after our defeat at Brandywine Creek, convinced the French of our determination to fight and retreat and fight again until we had driven the British from our continent. French confidence in the Americans was further strengthened by a major British defeat in the north: General Burgoyne's entire army had been captured at Saratoga in New York. Though the Count de Vergennes and King Louis XVI did not yet declare war on England, they communicated to Ambassador Franklin their encouragement.

In November, General Howe drove our troops from the two forts on the Delaware River. In December, the British skirmished with us one last time north of Philadelphia. Then the British Commander in Chief, according to his custom in both Boston and New York, invited himself into Mrs. Loring's bed and left us alone until spring.

In Paris, Benjamin Franklin learned that Philadelphia had fallen to the enemy. He no doubt worried about his daughter and her family who lived in the city. But his public appraisal, reported to the world, showed no anxiety. At a soirée, he was confronted by a Frenchman who gloated, "Well Doctor, Howe has taken Philadelphia."

"I beg your pardon, sir," laughed Franklin. "Philadelphia has taken Howe."

As we had camped in Morristown to be close to New York City, so we now marched in the first snow of winter to an encampment about twenty miles northwest of Philadelphia. There on a broad snowy plain, cupped on one side by forested hills and flanked on the other by the Schuylkill River, we pitched our tents on December 19, 1777.

There was no village, no tavern, no warm and welcoming church. There was not even a main road passing through; what road we followed dwindled into a farmer's lane rising up a hill into his woodlot. We saw nothing in that remote and desolate spot but trees enough to build our huts, unless we were buried in a blizzard first.

But from the forested hills and broad plain of Valley Forge, we could watch, we could wait, to see what the British would do. And as we had done in Morristown, we would become a much stronger army than anyone thought possible.

ɞ

PART VII

A New Army is Born
at Valley Forge

Chapter Eight-Five

Genevieve, seven months pregnant
and reporting for duty.

We knew more in Morristown about the Continental Army in 1777 than Congress did. Certainly we paid more attention.

The Quartermaster's department remained in Morristown during the summer and autumn of 1777, though the Quartermaster himself never appeared at his desk in Arnold's Tavern. The lone supply clerk, who sat at a desk near mine, received word that someone named Thomas Mifflin had been appointed by Congress to administer the department. But Mifflin apparently preferred the niceties of Congressional life to the deprivations of a backwoods village. His absence, month after month, threatened, far more than did the British, the survival of the American army.

The clerk sent what few supplies he could buy, in what few wagons he could hire, toward the last known camp of the Continental Army as it marched through the States of New Jersey, New York, New Jersey again, Pennsylvania, Delaware, Maryland, then back into Pennsylvania. The three or four half-filled wagons which he dispatched every week would hardly supply a company of soldiers, certainly not a regiment, and never an entire army.

Express riders from General Washington's peripatetic headquarters frequently arrived with urgent orders. The Quartermaster's weary clerk listened with his head bowed, nodding as if he knew to the potato what was needed. He would then explain that there were not enough wagons, or even any wagons, to carry hay, or even straw, to the starving artillery horses in Wilmington.

From my desk, I listened to an exasperated courier roar a volley of ripe soldier's oaths at the helpless clerk.

"Go talk to the farmers," he would shout back, seething. "Talk to the damn wagoneers. They will neither sell nor rent a single wagon. Not for American dollars, they won't."

I doubly ached during those seven months to rejoin our troops. I longed to be with my husband (and the father of our soon-to-be second child). And I was fiercely determined to offer the services of one wagon and one well-fed horse.

We knew at Arnold's Tavern, a month before General Washington's troops knew, that the Continental Army would be encamped at Valley Forge for the winter. We knew because a courier arrived in the middle of November with orders to send all further supplies not to Reading, nor to Lancaster, but to a place no one had ever heard of, twenty miles northwest of Philadelphia.

Finally, I could join Benjamin.

That evening at supper, I told the Peabody's that I must soon depart, "to be with my husband in Valley Forge for Christmas."

Nathan immediately offered to escort me. Ruth stated that *she* had potatoes for the troops, even if many of her "shabby little countrymen" in New Jersey had hidden every basket.

Susanne told us that she had already found another teacher to take her place at the school. She explained, "All those children who follow the army with their mothers can certainly use a teacher." Robert stared across the supper table at his mother, astonished, then delighted: they were finally going to go find Henry.

Nathan had no trouble hiring two wagons and two draft horses. The Morristown farmers knew that not only would they see their wagons again, but if a wheel or an axle broke, Nathan would fix it better than before.

On the following Sunday, the ministers in both churches announced that the Peabody's would be taking supplies to the Continental Army in Pennsylvania. By Monday afternoon, our three wagons were loaded with potatoes and turnips, corn, carrots, and squash. We lashed a dozen bales of hay beneath the wagons for the three horses. We also carried burlap sacks filled with old shoes from the good people of Morristown, and a bushel basket of mended woolen stockings.

We loaded our bedding into the wagons; the little oaken bed which Henry had built for Caleb fit just behind the wagon seat. Ruth packed her pots and skillets, soon to be blackened over campfires along the seventy-mile journey to Valley Forge.

We departed on a day of wintry sunshine. Sir William was glad to be back in the harness. He pranced as he led our three-wagon parade. The roads in December were tolerable: frozen rather than mired with mud, though not yet drifted with snow.

We drove south for two days to Trenton, where we crossed by ferry over the Delaware. We then drove two days westward (well north of

Philadelphia) to the Schuylkill River, which we crossed at Swede's Ford. The British had apparently withdrawn completely for the winter into New York City and Philadelphia, for we encountered not a single redcoat along the way.

Robert drove the middle wagon in our tiny supply train; Nathan drove the third. Susanne, riding beside her son, filled the cold clear air with her laughter as she chatted with her boy.

She clearly did not realize how close he was to becoming a young man, in a nation at war. Susanne, unlike myself, had never seen a redcoat, had never heard a musket fired in battle. Her heart had never been shaken by the sudden thunder of a cannon. Her heart was with Henry, back in Morristown in the blossoming month of May.

In the village of Gulph, just south of the Schuylkill River, we were told by a sutler to follow the road west; Valley Forge was another five miles. We were bound to meet the troops, he said, for they had marched through Gulph just two days ago.

As we drove along, we could see that the snow-covered road had recently been trampled by a great number of feet and hooves. The wheels of heavy artillery carriages had rolled in long interweaving ruts. But we noticed something else on that final stretch of road to Valley Forge, something so strange that I reined Sir William to a halt, then stepped down from the wagon and knelt on the snowy road.

Yes, there in a footprint—not a boot print, but clearly the print of a naked foot—was a stain of blood. It was the print of a right foot; when I looked ahead to the next print, then stood and followed several more prints (most of them less distinct, for shoes had trampled upon them), I again saw that red stain of blood just behind the toes, every time the right foot stepped on the snow.

Once we knew what to look for, we spotted stains of blood so frequently along the road that we stopped looking for them. For we had but thirty pairs of old shoes in Nathan's wagon.

First, looking ahead across the rolling white countryside, we saw vertical black threads of campfire smoke. Then we heard the faint chopping of axes. When five sentries stepped onto the road and faced us with muskets, I felt a strange sort of happiness: for though I had never been here before, I was nearly home. Genevieve the soldier was rejoining her troops. My daily purpose could now reach beyond caring for Caleb; I would soon be back with sharp-minded officers, especially

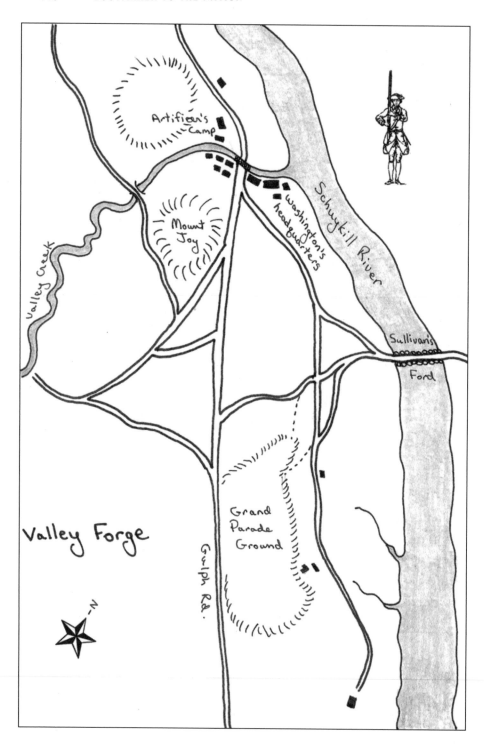

our Commander in Chief, whose urgent letters to Congress I would copy. Yes, I wanted Benjamin to wrap his strong, loving arms around me. But then I wanted to take my place in the midst of the orderly bustle at headquarters, where I would wrap my fingers around a quill pen.

I was undeterred by the cumbersome burden of seven months which I had brought with me. If I could drive a wagon for five days on winter roads from New Jersey to Pennsylvania, I could surely render General Washington's hurried handwriting into a legible copy.

I wanted to rejoin my husband. But as much, I wanted to rejoin my nation.

The wary sentries regarded me with suspicion while I explained that I had come from the army's former headquarters in Morristown, where I had been General Washington's personal scribe. But the guards relented when we showed them the potatoes and shoes in our wagons.

With permission to enter the encampment, we drove our wagons onto a long snowy plain cupped along two sides by forested hills, and flanked by the nearly frozen Schuylkill River. Hundreds of dirty white tents were scattered about the trampled field. Men in rags crouched around their campfires. We could hear a multitude of axes at work among the bare trees. A dozen men walked in a file down a slope with a log atop their shoulders. Along the foot of the hills—thus forming a broken ring around the snowy plain—stood the beginnings of log huts. The walls of the open rectangles were as yet no more than two feet tall. During our winter encampment in Morristown, we had lived in the warm, comfortable homes of the villagers; but here in Valley Forge, we would have to build our own village.

I asked a sergeant trudging with buckets of water from the river where General Washington had established his headquarters. Following his directions, we continued another two miles across the flats—we passed gaunt men in tattered trousers, the exhausted remnants of an army after seven months of marching—until we reached a crossroad that followed the shore of a frozen creek. Beyond a narrow bridge were more tents, more campfires, more clusters of men wrapped in ragged blankets.

We turned to the right, then drove along a lane for another hundred yards—past the largest barn I had ever seen—to a sturdy two-story stone house, built where the creek met the Schuylkill River.

Recognizing soldiers in the Life Guard stationed around the house, I knew that we had found headquarters. I reined Sir William to a halt, stepped down stiffly into the snow, then addressed a guard at the door.

"I am Genevieve York, a scribe to General Washington. Could you please inform the General that I am here to assist him?"

"The General ain't here, ma'am." The guard pointed toward the long valley we had just crossed. "He's living in his marquee until the last private has moved from a cold tent into a log hut. That's what the General said. You'll find him right close to General Knox's artillery park."

The General's marquee, I knew from our months of retreat through New Jersey, was a large oval tent. So the General would sleep in the cold with his men, until the last soldier had built himself a shelter.

I had spotted General Knox's orderly cluster of cannons, south of the road on a rise overlooking the rest of the encampment. I was about to drive back to the artillery park when another guard stepped toward me. "You Miss Ebenezer?" He cocked his head with a slight grin.

"Yes, I am."

"I'll send word to the General that you're here." He pointed to the enormous barn we had passed. "You put Sir William and them other two horses in the stables. Then you'll find Mister Benjamin," he pointed across the creek, "with the artificers. But we ain't got a lick of leather."

"I thank you."

We turned our wagons around in the farmyard, drove past the barn where I would later bring the horses, then crossed the bridge over a gray ribbon of ice. Reining left toward the colony of tents, I searched for Benjamin among the frozen scarecrows.

I was about to ask a soldier—he was limping toward camp with an armload of firewood—if he knew of a shoemaker named York, when Susanne's joyous voice called out from the wagon behind me, "Henry!"

Looking back around my wagon's canopy, I saw Susanne running across the snowy ground toward a man I now recognized as my brother. He whooped, "Susanne!" then he swung his axe into the chopping block where he had been working.

Whereas Delilah back in Concord had never bothered through the entire siege of Boston to make the short trip to Cambridge to visit Henry, Susanne had journeyed for five frigid days on winter roads to a remote—some might say desolate—valley between a freezing river and a forest verging on wilderness, so that Henry's arms could lift her from the ground as he kissed her.

Robert came running right behind his mother. Henry set Susanne on the ground so he could shake the boy's hand. But for the war, I might have called their happiness complete.

I set the brake, and was stepping down from the wagon when I heard Henry call, "Benjamin, come meet your family." Meaning, I knew, the bulging seven-monther I had brought with me.

Benjamin emerged from a nearby tent, a tent so tattered and patched that it might better have served as cannon wadding. His eyes looked at me, then at my swollen belly beneath the flaps of my coat. He looked again at my face as he strode toward me, his jubilant blue eyes confirming—after a separation of seven months—that as the war had not snatched away the man I loved, neither had it darkened his soul.

Our kiss (never mind the soldiers watching) was perhaps a bit more awkward than Henry and Susanne's, but not a whit less fervent.

On December 23, 1777, my third day in Valley Forge, I was sitting on a log beside our campfire, stirring a pot of potato and onion soup that drew a hungry stare from every soldier who passed nearby, when I heard the hooves of several horses approaching. Then I heard the strong Virginian voice that commanded both respect and devotion, and today a measure of delight, "Genevieve York, I have received the heartening news of your arrival."

I stood up with a ladle in my hand. "I am ready, sir, if your ink is not frozen in the ink pot."

General Washington in his black cape swung down from his horse, then he bowed as gracefully as if we stood in the ballroom of a Virginia mansion. I performed a slight but bountifully pregnant curtsy.

"I congratulate you," he said. I was glad to see a glimmer of humor in his otherwise exhausted eyes.

"You must wait until February, sir, and then you may congratulate the entire family."

"Ah, February. Then perhaps my irreplaceable scribe could give me at least a month of desperately needed work?"

"Your scribe can promise you six good weeks of work. After that, we must defer to the young American."

"Ha!" he laughed. I could feel a dozen ragged soldiers around me enjoying that laugh.

"Sir William is in the stables?" he asked. "And found enough to eat?"

"Yes, sir. Thank you, sir."

"Excellent." Turning for a moment, he pointed toward the stone house across the creek, two hundred yards from the artificers' camp.

"The Isaac Potts house shall be our headquarters. Though I am still quartered in a tent, we shall be at our desks tomorrow morning. May I count on you an hour after the drums at dawn?"

"With great pleasure, sir."

"Thank you." He swung back up into the saddle. Briefly, he noted the progress of our log huts: a dozen in a row now had walls waist high.

Then he reined Nelson back toward the bridge and cantered away with his retinue of officers.

I sat back down on the log, leaned forward toward the fire with my belly between my knees, and felt, as I stirred the potato and onion soup, profoundly at peace in the midst of my nation.

ॐ

Chapter Eighty-Six

Benjamin, citizen of the youngest town in America.

As a master carpenter of log huts, Henry labored every day from dawn to dark to help build a town for eleven thousand troops. Captain Byrnes showed the men of a dozen regiments how to choose and fell a tree, how to trim the log, how to notch its ends, how to split a length of oak to fashion a door. He ate his midday dinner wherever Susanne— with her basket of hot firecakes wrapped in clean linen, and her canteen of hot cider—could find him.

Robert, Henry's apprentice from dawn to dark, became adept at building a lathe-and-clay fireplace at one end of each hut. He built the chimney by increments, as the wall rose log by log.

Two years ago in Cambridge, the armed farmers besieging Boston constructed their jumble of huts with whatever boards and fence rails they could find. One year ago on the bank of the Delaware River, the troops built rude log huts as quickly as they could, knowing they would soon march again to some winter quarters.

But now in Valley Forge, we built proper log dwellings according to orders from General Washington: each hut was sixteen feet long by fourteen feet wide, with walls six and a half feet high (with a door but no windows), capped by a roof of split logs and shingles. Twelve men slept on bunks, six to a side. Their wet clothing, torn rucksacks, sodden shoes, as well as muskets and cartridge boxes and bayonet scabbards, were stored inside the hut, along with their stew pots and frying pans and kettles.

Each regiment built its huts in two parallel rows, with quarters for privates in front, quarters for officers in the rear. A sort of street thus ran in front of each row of huts; all doors opened onto it. The neat double rows were spaced in an oval around the edge of the long snowy field, so we might later use the field to practice maneuvers.

The "necessaries" were dug well behind the huts. They were moved once a week, and the old holes—according to stern orders—were filled with earth (not simply snow).

The artificers, or craftsmen (such as myself, a cobbler), built our huts in our own camp west of Valley Creek, a short walk across the bridge from headquarters, so that orders and reports could go quickly back and forth. We lived in a busy neighborhood with blacksmiths, carpenters, harness makers, and tinsmiths, men proud of their skills. They had little to work with, but they furnished the soldiers, as best they could, with ironware for the fireplaces, shelves and boxes for a man's few possessions, and a motley assortment of tin plates and cups.

Some of the soldiers dug a rectangular hole two or three feet deep inside the log walls, with the hope that their sunken hut might prove warmer with the earth itself as part of the walls. (However, because of moisture in the dirt floor, these dwellings remained excessively damp. Most of the men who lived in them became sick, perhaps because their clothes never completely dried.)

In addition to the eleven thousand soldiers encamped in Valley Forge, of whom nearly a thousand were Negroes, we had to build huts for roughly seven hundred women and their children. No huts were built to accommodate families; I lived with Henry and Robert and nine other men in one hut, while Genevieve and Susanne lived next door with ten other women. Caleb stayed with his mother, and with Susanne when Genevieve was at headquarters.

By mid-January, a month after we had arrived in Valley Forge, most of the huts had been completed. Smoke rose into the cold blue sky from nearly a thousand chimneys. (A great amount of smoke rose as well into the huts themselves, especially when a snowstorm clogged the chimney tops.)

Only after the last private had moved from his frozen tent into the moderate comfort of a smoky, crowded hut, did General Washington move from his marquee—it looked like a snow-covered haystack—into Isaac Potts' fieldstone house. His quarters were on the second floor, though his office was one of two rooms on the first.

Because the dining room beside his office was crowded with staff (including Genevieve) working at their tables, General Washington asked Henry to build a larger dining room as an addition to the house. Henry and his crew of apprentice carpenters fashioned a log cabin— four times the size of our huts—that extended from the farmhouse's back door. With smoothly planed lumber from a local sawmill, Henry crafted a handsome table—the chairs came from a schoolhouse—that could seat twenty officers and their Commander in Chief.

Genevieve, an angry patriot.

Benjamin has asked me to write about the farmers of Pennsylvania, because I was born an American, whereas he was born in England. He feels that it's not his place to find fault. I, however, still burn with anger at some of my despicable countrymen.

The Continental Army starved in Valley Forge during the winter of 1778. February was known as "the month of famine." During our six months in that barren encampment, roughly two and a half thousand soldiers, out of eleven thousand, died not of musket wounds but from disease. Our men sickened and died because they were eating less than would keep a child healthy.

Since the founding of Philadelphia almost a century ago, the surrounding countryside had provided abundant food for the residents of the port, through summer and through winter. Nowhere in Philadelphia's history might a person find a paragraph describing starvation, or even deprivation, on Chestnut Street. During the winter of 1778, the forty thousand inhabitants never missed a slice of bread, nor a roast of beef, because provisions were readily supplied by neighboring farmers. But during the same winter of 1778, the eleven thousand troops in Valley Forge, only twenty miles from Philadelphia, in the very heart of the fertile farmland, became so desperate with hunger that the entire army was close to disbanding. American farmers, not British redcoats, nearly caused the collapse of the American army.

During the British occupation of Philadelphia, many local farmers, merchants, craftsmen, and wagoneers traded only with the enemy, for the British paid them with hard specie. Speculators bought at one price from the farmers, then sold at a much better price to the British, while avoiding our encampment altogether. When our scouts went searching for food, they found almost nothing, for the farmers had hidden their cattle in the woods. Wagons too disappeared, and teams of horses. Our soldiers spoke with prosperous farmers on prosperous farms, where naught was to be found in the farmyard but a few chickens, which the farmer was loath to part with. He depended on the eggs, so he claimed, for his livelihood.

Nor were such greed and deceit to be found only in Pennsylvania. Our scouts rode north into New Jersey and New York, south into Maryland and Delaware, then returned with a few head of cattle, with a few worn-out drays, with enough corn for a company or two. I recall a letter which I copied that winter for General Washington: he complained that "Speculation, peculation, engrossing, forestalling" (devious methods used by our suppliers and merchants) "afford melancholy proofs of the decay of public virtue."

Congress, meeting through the winter in York, Pennsylvania, was absorbed in its petty squabbling. States argued with States about how much each should contribute to the national army, while none did so adequately. General Washington, increasingly outraged, wrote to the latest president of Congress, "The disaffection of the People is past all belief. . . . No Man, in my opinion, ever had his measures more impeded than I have, by every department of the Army." (These departments were the various committees in Congress itself.)

The General asked his officers for returns on their troops (a count of those healthy and those sick), then he reported to Congress, "We have, by a field return this day made no less than 2,898 Men now in Camp unfit for duty because they are bare foot and otherwise naked." Our soldiers had so few blankets that many were "obliged and do set up all Night by fires, instead of taking comfortable rest in a natural way."

General Washington did not hesitate to scold Congress, "It is a much easier and less distressing thing to draw remonstrances in a comfortable room by a good fire side, than to occupy a cold bleak hill and sleep under frost and Snow without Cloaths or Blankets." Contrasting the cold heart of Congress with his own tormented heart, he wrote to a delegate in York, "Although they seem to have little feeling for the naked, and distressed Soldier, I feel superabundantly for them, and from my Soul pity those miseries, which it is neither in my power to relieve or prevent."

Perhaps the most painful proof of our situation (to my eyes) were the frozen horse carcasses throughout the encampment. The poor beasts, after pulling wagons and artillery through the summer and autumn and winter of 1777, found no forage to reward them in Valley Forge. During the first weeks in camp, they collapsed where they stood. No one had time to bury them in the frozen ground, and thus we passed the carcasses wherever we walked, until their mouldering eyes and stark ribs were buried by the snow.

Sir William, as an express rider's horse (ridden by a dozen different couriers while I worked as a scribe), was provided with enough hay within the shelter of the barn to survive through the winter. (Without those twenty horses, our communication with the States north and south of us would have terminated.)

Meanwhile, the British troops enjoyed the food, wine, warmth, and splendid hospitality which they found in Philadelphia. Owners of the larger houses, including both Loyalists and Quakers, realized a fine profit by renting to the officers. Lesser merchants rented rooms and warehouses to the grenadiers and infantrymen. American hosts and British guests met frequently at the theater. They invited each other to a succession of elegant balls. So many of the Philadelphia belles were smitten by British and German soldiers that when His Majesty's Royal Army (to get ahead of my story) departed the following June, eight hundred young women marched out of the city with their husbands and fiancés.

Our scouts found a tanner in Germantown (from which the British had withdrawn). They offered to purchase a wagonload of hides, after the hides had been properly tanned. When our buyers returned with American dollars on the appointed date, the tanner apologized that he had been forced by circumstances to sell the entire lot to the British. Perhaps those hides became dancing shoes.

In my heart I am seething still, for our spies reported that American prisoners in the Walnut Street Prison were often seen out in the yard, digging through snow and grubbing into the frozen earth, that they might claw up the roots of grass to eat. Like our horses, many of those young soldiers died where they lay.

We asked ourselves bitterly, For whom are we fighting? For our greed-besotted and brutish countrymen?

Despite their grumbling, despite their threats, our troops did not mutiny. Often, when they spotted an officer walking along a street, they would call quietly from where they huddled around a campfire, "No bread, no soldier." "No meat, no soldier." But at muster the following morning, they stood before their officers, in their rags, holding a frozen musket.

Nearly every day, General Washington rode along the regimental streets of Valley Forge. He frequently dismounted to visit a man sick in his hut. After Lady Washington arrived in camp, she too visited the ill and impoverished, often with a basket of warm food. The men noticed; the men stayed on another day, another week, another month.

There came a time, somewhere in the depths of February, when a trace of wild humor began to replace the bitterness. One private would call to another as they emerged from their damp, gloomy, crowded, smoke-filled huts at dawn, "Good morning, Brother Soldier. How are you?"

A long-unwashed ragpicker with his empty pipe would answer, "All wet I thank'e, hope you are so too."

The men would caw like crows and hoot like owls, especially at night. They screeched and howled and hooted from campfire to campfire, from brigade to brigade, as if to affirm the fact that they *were* creatures in the wilderness.

Yes, every week, some of the soldiers deserted. But the rest of us felt that those who remained in camp were thus unburdened by the fainthearted. Let them trundle home to their hearths and their beds and their porridge. We shall huddle here and shiver with Thomas Jefferson in our hearts and Thomas Paine in our souls.

And when the war was over, when we had swept the British from our shores, we would all go home and do a bit of housecleaning there too. Let the scoundrels have their day. Our time would come, when with a proud heart we would take into our hands the reins of our nation. Some of us, we told ourselves as we wiped tears from our smoke-filled eyes, might one day take *our* seats in Congress. Or at least in the State legislature.

To declare our independence from Britain had not been enough. Now we saw that even to fight and win this war would not be enough. No war ever built a nation.

But when this war was over—we promised ourselves as we held our nearly frozen hands toward the warming flames—*we* would be the ones who would build a new and far better America.

As Henry said, "Aye, we're master carpenters all."

❧

Chapter Eighty-Seven

Benjamin, neighbor to an ancient nation.

But His Long Road was not allowed to become a master carpenter.

He had returned in early December from his Oneida home in New York; he rejoined the army just before we marched to Valley Forge. No one had seen him since he built his lodge beside the creek, about a hundred yards upstream from the artificers' camp. He covered a frame of saplings with sheets of cedar bark, hung a blanket over the door, then disappeared inside. Or so we thought, if we thought about him at all. For we were occupied with the building of our own huts, with the cutting of our own firewood, with the cooking of our own meager meals.

Lo Ha Hes (as Henry called him by his Oneida name) built no healing lodges. Soldiers too sick to remain in their tents were taken to a nearby schoolhouse, which, though crowded, was at least warmer than a blanket on the frozen ground.

On a Sunday afternoon in January, Genevieve went to speak with the midwife, She's Carrying Flowers, for Genevieve was by now in her eighth month.

Leaving our camp of two dozen log huts along Valley Creek, she walked south, crossing untrampled snow, toward the Oneida lodge at the foot of the hills. As she was approaching the lodge—she was close enough to see footprints in the snow around it, footprints leading to the creek, footprints fanning up the hill for firewood—She's Carrying Flowers pushed aside a gray blanket and stepped through the low door with a bucket in her hand. Genevieve called hello to her. She's Carrying Flowers glared at her with angry eyes, then disappeared back inside.

Genevieve did not know whether to proceed any further, and perhaps to apologize . . . but apologize for what?

She returned to our camp, where she found Henry and me shingling the roof of a neighboring hut. She told us what had happened.

"Damn me for a poor friend," muttered Henry, laying down his axe.

We climbed down from the roof, then walked with Genevieve through snow a foot deep toward the lone lodge with smoke rising from the top of the dome. We approached no closer than the spot where Genevieve's footprints turned around. Standing there, we listened, but though we could hear a multitude of axes and distant voices from across the valley, we heard not a sound from inside the cedar lodge.

Henry called, "Lo Ha Hes, your friend Henry has come to ask if you and Ka Tsi Tsya Ha would join us for supper. And the Reverend, if he is not occupied."

We had not seen Reverend Kesslaer for the past month either. Had he been working at the schoolhouse hospital?

We waited in silence for well over a minute. Brown leaves clinging to the oaks on the hill rattled dryly as a breeze swept through them.

"Lo Ha Hes," called Henry, "your friend has been a poor friend. But tonight we wish you to come to supper with us."

We heard a stirring inside the snow-dusted cedar dome, saw the gray blanket open. Johannes Kesslaer stepped out in his leather shirt and breeches. He walked toward us in tall fringed moccasins, beaded moccasins, beaded by the hands of his wife, Ka Tsi Tsya Ha. I was surprised to see that Johannes had grown a beard, a bushy reddish beard, darker than the long blond hair that touched his shoulders. He looked not like a Christian minister, nor like a physician, but like a hunter, a trapper, a voyageur, who had just stepped out from a forest far beyond the frontier.

Johannes stood ten feet from us, holding neither a Bible nor a cup of medicinal tea. His weathered face seemed older. His blue eyes stared at us with unhidden scorn.

"Do you know," he asked, glaring at Henry, "that the British came down from Canada last summer to attack your country?"

"Yes," answered Henry quietly, inviting Johannes to speak further.

"Do you know that the British attacked with two armies, one from the west and one from the north?"

"Yes," answered Henry.

"The army from the west marched from Lake Ontario toward the Mohawk River. The army from the north sailed down Lake Champlain toward Hudson's River. If those two armies had met and joined their forces, Albany and Boston would now be starving as you are starving."

"Yes."

"If they had met, all of your America above New York City would now be British."

"Yes."

"And you down here might wonder while you huddle in your paltry village, how long the British in Albany and Boston and New York and Philadelphia will wait until they sail their warships down the coast to capture Williamsburg in Virginia. Wilmington in North Carolina. Charlestown in South Carolina. And then Savannah in Georgia." Johannes sneered, "Where then would your great army have marched? Where then would your mighty Congress have hidden?"

He stared at Genevieve, then at me—whom in Cambridge he had married—as if we were the merest children, ill-mannered, both of us deserving a slap of his hand.

"Do you know," he asked, his voice rising with anger, "that of the six nations of the Iroquois, four fought with the British as their allies? Fought with the British army when they attacked from the west. Fought with the British army when they attacked from the north." He paused, then spoke with absolute clarity, "While *two* nations of the Iroquois, the Oneida and the Tuscarora, stood with the Americans. Stood with the Americans against their own Iroquois brothers."

"Yes," said Genevieve. "Yes, we knew that."

"Do you know that sixty Oneida warriors fought last August beside General Herkimer and the New York militia, to stop the British before they reached the Mohawk River?"

"I have not," I said, ashamed, "even asked Lo Ha Hes if he was at Oriskany."

"And do you know," continued Johannes with scorn, with incredulity, with rage, "that though the Oneida lost many warriors at Oriskany, they hurried to Saratoga—hurried as few of your white farmers from the Mohawk Valley hurried to Saratoga—to fight beside the Americans against the British under Burgoyne?"

"Yes," said Henry. "Captain Morgan's riflemen told us that the Oneida fought at Saratoga."

"You wait for your great ally the French to join you," said Johannes, spitting the word "French." "But your first ally, the first nation to offer its friendship and its tomahawk to your nation, you have forgotten like a withered vine in winter."

Henry was silent. As was Genevieve, as was I.

Johannes took one step toward us and pointed, "What trail through the snow do you see from the headquarters of your nation to the home of a warrior from the Oneida nation?"

We had more than wronged one man. We had wronged his people.

"Do not French officers dine at your General's table? Do not Polish officers dine at your General's table?"

Now Genevieve spoke. "Tomorrow morning, Monday morning, I shall inform General Washington at headquarters that his ally, the Oneida nation, awaits his attention."

Johannes nodded his acknowledgment, as if to a repentant child. Then he turned and walked through the snow back to the cedar lodge. He bowed down and slapped at the blanket; we had a glimpse of the fire. Then he disappeared inside.

No doubt his Oneida family had heard every word.

Genevieve, a witness who will never forget.

On Monday morning, I greeted the guard at General Washington's door. As he did every morning, the solemn guard turned without a word and tapped quietly on the door, then opened it enough to step inside. A moment later he opened the door fully, so that I could enter the office. General Washington glanced up at me, then returned to the paper he was writing. I knew to wait, until he was ready to hand me the letters and reports which I should copy.

A pair of logs burned in the fireplace upon a substantial bed of coals. The room was warm enough that the General had taken his coat off; he wore only his white shirt and buff waistcoat. Clearly, he had been at work for several hours.

"Yes," he said, reaching over his candlelit desk with papers for me to copy. He did not call me Miss Ebenezer, nor did his glance invite any conversation. Ordinarily I would have taken the papers and silently left his office.

However, as Benjamin Franklin dispatched his reports from France to America, so I brought my report from the Oneida nation. "Sir, I apologize, but I must bring something to your attention. It concerns the Oneida people of New York, whose warriors joined our troops at Oriskany in August, and at Saratoga in September and October. They feel that they haven't—" I stopped. It was certainly not for me to tell our Commander in Chief what he should or should not have done.

So I summarized as best I could Johannes Kesslaer's stern words. I omitted mentioning the lack of a path between headquarters and the Oneida lodge.

General Washington's distracted gaze slowly focused on me as he listened. When I had finished, he set down his quill, stood up from his desk and walked to the window. Glancing out, I could see a fence of split rails that crossed the rear yard in a dark zigzag against the snow.

"Please tell His Long Road that I shall be at his door in one hour. I shall speak to him within my authority as Commander in Chief of the Continental Army." He paused, then added, "of the United States of America."

"Thank you, sir."

I left the office, descended the stairs and hurried out the front door of the Isaac Potts house. Walking as quickly as I could with my eight-month burden, I followed the lane to the bridge, then crossed the frozen creek to our camp.

Benjamin and Robert were working on a chimney.

I called up, "They will meet in one hour," then I continued on my mission.

I walked through lightly falling snow until I reached the end of our footsteps on Sunday. There I stopped, with Henry's prints to one side, Benjamin's to the other. "Lo Ha Hes," I called, "warrior of the Oneida People. I come to tell you that General Washington will stand at your door in one hour, ready to hear your words."

I paused, waiting, unsure whether to say anything more. Was any-one inside? Should I wait for some reply?

A hand swept the blanket to one side, and Johannes stepped out.

"Genevieve York."

I waited.

"We shall be ready."

He turned, bowed down and stepped back through the door.

General Washington did not ride Nelson across the bridge over the frozen creek. He walked, in full uniform with his sword buckled on. He was not followed by his usual retinue of officers. He had come alone.

The soldiers in our camp, working on their huts, seated at their fires, mending a harness, fell silent as he passed among them, his face solemn, his eyes reaching far ahead.

Benjamin, down from the roof, and Henry, who had paused with his axe at a woodpile, looked at me with a question: Should we follow? I nodded. We ourselves had failed to offer our gratitude to the Oneida; we could not let our General stand alone to receive their reproach.

We walked through the snow about a hundred feet behind General Washington, Henry's hunting shirt flecked with sawdust, Benjamin's hands caked with mud. I could not walk as quickly as the General walked; my husband and brother kept pace with me.

General Washington's boots, the boots which Benjamin had made for him, reached a good six inches above the snow as the General strode across the meadow toward the Oneida lodge. Smoke rose from the dome, neither more nor less than yesterday.

General Washington walked beyond the cluster of our footprints, until he stood about twenty feet from the lodge door. We ourselves stopped fifty feet behind him. The falling snow whitened the blue shoulders and gold epaulettes of his uniform.

"Lo Ha Hes," he called, surprising me by using the man's Oneida name. "The poverty of this army camp, in goods and provisions, does not equal the poverty of my heart in its former lack of gratitude. Great has been my dereliction."

We could faintly hear, from inside the lodge, Johannes speaking as he translated the General's apology.

"Lo Ha Hes," called General Washington, "the Continental Army of the United States wishes to thank the warriors of the Oneida nation for your support last summer. Your strong arms helped us to stop the British on their march from the west. Your strong arms helped us to stop the British on their march from the north. I cannot speak for my Congress. But I can speak for its army. You have stood with us against the enemy, and we bring to you the honor and the gratitude that you so rightly deserve."

General Washington now stood in silence, while snow whispered down through dry oak leaves in the forest behind the lodge.

The gray blanket was pushed aside. Johannes stepped out in his fringed buckskin. He did not greet the General, but stepped to one side of the door.

Ka Tsi Tsya Ha now stepped out, dressed in buckskin. She held a large bundle wrapped in leather. She did not greet the General, but stepped to the opposite side of the door.

When Lo Ha Hes emerged, he wore a loin cloth of leather and a pair of moccasins, as a warrior might have worn last August. Three large feathers were fastened in his long black hair. He walked in the falling snow to within five feet of General Washington. Though we could not see the General's face, for we stood behind him, I saw in the dark eyes of the Oneida warrior a fierce dignity which I had never seen in any officer who addressed our Commander in Chief.

Lo Ha Hes spoke several sentences in his Oneida language.

Johannes translated in a steady voice, "When the British attacked last summer from Canada, we were your eyes. We were your ears. The Oneida spoke to Colonel Gansevoort at Fort Stanwix, warning him. The Oneida spoke to General Herkimer at his home, warning him."

General Washington answered not to the translator, but directly to Lo Ha Hes, "I thank you."

Johannes translated, "Yawah."

"The British surrounded Fort Stanwix at the head of the Mohawk River. They brought forth their many cannons, that they might become masters of the river. When General Herkimer marched with his eight hundred soldiers to break the siege, he was joined by our chief Tawah Angaragh Kan, who led sixty Oneida warriors."

General Washington answered with a slight bow, "I thank you for your sixty warriors."

Lo Ha Hes waved his arm abruptly. Never before had I seen any man gesture at General Washington with a demand for silence.

"General Herkimer did not reach Fort Stanwix. At Oriskany, where the trail passes through a forest, his soldiers were attacked by British soldiers in red coats, and by their New York brothers in green coats."

The Loyalists of New York. The hated Rangers.

Lo Ha Hes now walked to his sister, opened the flaps of the leather bundle in her arms, then held up a red British coat by its shoulders. The coat was smeared with dirt, darkened with powder. And it had a bullet hole through the chest. Lo Ha Hes laid the coat on the snow at General Washington's feet.

Returning to his sister, he held up a second red coat. We could see a cluster of cuts over the heart where a knife had stabbed again and again. Lo Ha Hes laid the second coat on the snow at the General's feet, so that the two slain soldiers might be clearly represented.

From his sister's bundle he now took a green coat, cleaner than the others, as if it had been little worn. He showed General Washington the front, the back: no bloody hole, no bloody gashes. "This man I killed with my tomahawk deep in his skull." He laid the green coat beside the two red ones.

From his sister's arms he took a third red coat, worn and stained from long use, with one yellow cuff torn and dangling. He walked a short distance and laid the third red coat in the snow, separate from the others.

"Saratoga," he said to General Washington.

Johannes had no need to translate.

Lo Ha Hes lifted the now empty deer skin from his sister's hands and dropped it into the snow. We saw that she held a second, smaller bundle. They spoke quietly with each other, then he opened the flaps and took in one hand a club with a heavy wooden ball at one end, and in his other hand a tomahawk with a black flint blade.

He said to General Washington as he held up the club, "Seneca, at Oriskany." He held up the tomahawk. "Mohawk, at Oriskany." He glared with rage and incomprehension at the General. "Do you understand?" We heard the unhidden anguish in his voice. "For you, the Oneida kills his brother Seneca. For you, the Oneida kills his brother Mohawk."

Johannes's words in translation were harsh.

"Before the white man," Lo Ha Hes spoke with contempt, "before the Dutch, the English, the French, and now the Americans," he waved the tomahawk as if he would banish all of them, "the six nations of the Iroquois lived beneath the white pine of peace. We were the people of the long house. Mohawk at the eastern door, Seneca at the western door. The Oneida lived between their brothers."

After Johannes had translated, Lo Ha Hes repeated, "The Oneida lived between their brothers."

In the long house along the Mohawk River. For centuries.

"Then came the white man with war, and war, and war, and war. With your beads and blankets and muskets and fire water. One Great Father, and another Great Father. And sickness, sickness, sickness."

Lo Ha Hes glared with accusation at General Washington.

The General stood absolutely still.

"Until our people turned upon each other like starving wolves."

This have we done to the people who *still* supported us. At least sixty Oneida warriors now camped in Valley Forge, ready to serve in future campaigns as they had already served at Oriskany and Saratoga. One of the cooks in the kitchen at headquarters was an Oneida woman named Polly Cooper.

"You fight your own English brother. You fight for land that is not yours. But for you, I fight my brother on the land we share. I fight my brother on the land of the long house. I fight my brother beneath the white pine of peace. Until the dying tree has fallen."

Lo Ha Hes stepped toward General Washington. He reached out one hand with the tomahawk in it, then said in English, "Take."

The General took the tomahawk from Lo Ha Hes.

The Oneida warrior offered the club with its heavy wooden ball that could break an enemy's skull. "Take."

General Washington took the club.

Lo Ha Hes told the General, "The blood of our warriors enters the earth with the blood of your warriors. The bones of our warriors are buried in the earth with the bones of your warriors. Remember this. When your British brothers go home in their boats with white wings, remember who your true brothers are."

General Washington held up both weapons. "This of the Seneca, and this of the Mohawk, shall find their place on my desk until the end of the war. They shall remain on my desk during the years of peace. Never shall I forget what the Oneida people have given to my nation."

Lo Ha Hes answered, "The Oneida people will fight beside you. We ask only this. That after your war, when you return to your farms, we too can return to our farms. And to our forests. To our river and to our lakes."

"I wish," General Washington's voice brightened with feeling, "all men peace upon their farms. And in their forests. Beside their waters."

The two men regarded each other for a long moment. Then Lo Ha Hes said, without harshness, "I have spoken."

He turned away and stepped back through the door of his home.

Ka Tsi Tsya Ha followed, as did Johannes.

We could hear someone adding wood to the fire.

General Washington turned and walked toward us, the club and tomahawk in his hands, and the burdens borne by a great chief in his eyes. "Thank you," he said to us, meeting our gaze one by one.

Then he walked alone across the snowy meadow, toward the head-quarters of the war he had never wanted.

മ

Chapter Eighty-Eight

Benjamin, remembering a gift of strength for Genevieve
in a wagonload of Oneida squash, beans, and corn.

The very next day, Lo Ha Hes built a lodge a quarter mile further up the creek, on the flats where the old forge had been. (The British had destroyed the forge during their depredations the previous autumn.) Working steadily, he built what came to be, for Genevieve and many other women in Valley Forge, the birthing lodge. Though Lo Ha Hes later built several healing lodges around the encampment, none of them were as distant from the regimental streets, nor as near flowing clean water, as the birthing lodge. During the winter of 1778, in that remote snow-covered dome, Ka Tsi Tsya Ha helped several dozen white and Negro children into the world.

We spoke of our Pennsylvania neighbors as "Ye who eat pumpkin pie and roast turkey." Desertion emptied a growing number of bunks. However, one evening in early February, a wagon appeared at the birthing lodge. By the next morning the wagon had vanished, but baskets of Indian corn stood in a circle around the inside of the lodge. While Henry and I tried to dull the ache in our bellies with hickory nuts from the forest, Genevieve, who had been invited to move into the lodge as soon as it was built, feasted on a variety of stews and breads from last autumn's Oneida harvest. The plentiful corn and squash and beans ("the three sisters," as the Oneida called them) had come in that wagon all the way from the Oneida longhouses in New York, whereas corn grown by our Pennsylvania neighbors stayed in their closely guarded barns.

On the sixteenth of February, 1778, Henry and I paced outside the birthing lodge on a cold gray afternoon, until we had trampled a ring around the cedar dome. We could hear Genevieve's tired voice inside, and Susanne's encouragement. We heard the calm voice of Ka Tsi Tsya Ha as she spoke Oneida. Johannes spoke both Oneida and English.

As the afternoon darkened, Genevieve began to shriek with pain. We heard a rising anxiety in the other voices.

Robert brought us some warm firecakes. But he could not endure the screams, and soon departed.

Henry and I grew so cold as we paced in the wintry dark that we considered building a fire near the lodge. He was about to hurry back to our hut to fetch his axe when we heard, among the other voices, a wail of victory. The child conceived in an orchard of blossoming apple trees in May, finally greeted the snowy world in a snug, warm Oneida lodge in February.

Ka Tsi Tsya Ha said something in Oneida. Johannes translated for the mother, then he called through the cedar-bark wall to the father and uncle outside, "A girl, a girl, a fine and beautiful girl."

Henry took my hand in both of his and shook it. I felt that every cannon in General Knox's artillery park should fire a salute.

When Johannes swept the blanket to one side and beckoned us, Henry and I crouched and entered the lodge. We saw the child, wet and red and wriggling in the uplifted hands of She's Carrying Flowers. I knelt beside Genevieve and held her hand. She laughed weakly and told me that my hand was nearly frozen.

Caleb had been born on the second floor of Pennington's boarding-house on Nassau Street in New York City. Our daughter had been born beside a warm fire, inside a bountiful ring of food, in a desolate valley in Pennsylvania.

We were becoming a most American family.

ॐ

Chapter Eighty-Nine

Genevieve, part of the "family"
of officers and staff.

Lady Washington, making her fourth pilgrimage to our winter encampment (Cambridge, New York, Morristown, and now Valley Forge), arrived in her carriage from Virginia in early February. She soon joined the other officers' wives in knitting what few stockings they could for the soldiers.

On February 22, 1778, General Washington's forty-sixth birthday, Lady Washington invited the "family" who worked at headquarters to a surprise birthday dinner in the log dining hut.

I had been back at my desk but one day, copying the General's impatient letters to Congress while Sally slept in Caleb's bed underneath the table. Most of the time, the infant remained serenely unbothered, wrapped in her blankets, by the thump of officers' boots as captains and colonels and brigadier generals hurried on business in and out of the office. (Whenever she awoke, I would set down my quill and carry her to the pantry, where in some degree of privacy I could nurse her.)

Lady Washington asked the officers and clerks to gather secretly in the dining room just before two o'clock in the afternoon. She herself would inform the General that Alexander Hamilton waited for him with a newly arrived Frenchman of great importance.

A few minutes before two o'clock, Colonel Hamilton (who eventually fathered eight children himself) carried Sally in her crib through the back door to the log-enclosed room without awakening her.

General Washington was thoroughly immersed in the forever delayed procurement of bayonets for the thousands of muskets which still had none. Thus when he followed Lady Washington out the door from his office, then through the back door, expecting to meet a French duke who claimed he could requisition the blades from Spain, he was utterly surprised to discover twenty members of his military family gathered around a table laden with roasted chickens and boiled parsnips.

He gave us the laugh we had all hoped for, then bid us be seated.

During our small feast (I thought of poor Benjamin as I savored a well-roasted drumstick), General Knox's artillery band formed at one end of the room and played with rousing vigor, "The Old Continental March." General Knox, whose girth had increased substantially despite the rigors of war, beat time with his fist on the dining room table.

General Washington, greatly pleased, invited the members of the band to partake of a gill of rum.

While the officers, clerks, and cannoneers raised their tankards with a toast to our Commander in Chief, I rocked Sally in my arms. The new American had been awakened by the fanfares of trumpets and drums.

&

Chapter Ninety

Benjamin, training with Baron Steuben's
company of one hundred chosen soldiers.

21 December, 1826
The shortest day,
the longest night,
as Valley Forge
was our longest night.

Though General Washington's military family toasted his health on February 22, 1778, on February 23, Providence delivered a birthday present of historic value.

During 1777, a number of French, Polish, and Austrian officers, some of them genuine nobility and some well-dressed imposters, had arrived in America to assist the Continental Army in its war against the British. Most of these foreigners expected positions of the highest rank, placing them above American officers who had been on the battlefield since 1775. By the end of 1777, General Washington had little desire to meet another "friend of liberty" who brought letters of introduction and an empty purse.

Thus when a Prussian officer named Friedrich Wilhelm Augustus Heinrich Ferdinand, Baron Steuben wrote a letter (translated by an aide from French to English) to General Washington, offering his services to the American army, the General may well have been skeptical. However, Baron Steuben enclosed letters of introduction from Silas Deane and Dr. Benjamin Franklin, America's ambassadors in France. He enclosed as well a letter from a Frenchman named Beaumarchais, who— as General Washington well knew—had secretly been shipping large quantities of muskets and gunpowder to the American army. Especially promising, Baron Steuben wrote in his own letter, "I had rather serve under your Excellency as a volunteer, than to be an object of discontent to such deserving officers as have already distinguished themselves." Clearly, someone had advised the Baron not to attempt to outrank the Americans.

Baron Steuben had already arrived in America (disguised as a Frenchman). He traveled from Portsmouth, New Hampshire to Boston, where he met John Hancock, who had recently retired as president of the Continental Congress. Hancock made arrangements for the Baron to travel along safe roads (far to the west of the British in Philadelphia) to York, Pennsylvania, where Congress could meet, and appraise, the foreign volunteer.

The Baron was well received by Congress, which sent a letter of approval to General Washington. Accordingly, on February 23, 1778, the General left his desk and rode several miles from headquarters to meet Baron Steuben on the road to Valley Forge. The Baron, who spoke German and French but no English, was accompanied by a suite of aides, and by an Italian grayhound. On the blue coat of his uniform, he wore gold epaulettes and an enormous jeweled four-pointed star. He claimed to be a lieutenant general who had been an aide-de-camp to the brilliant Prussian general, Frederick the Great.

General Washington might well have remained skeptical.

On the following day, at General Washington's invitation, Baron Steuben inspected the troops in Valley Forge. The Baron reported in writing that on one hand, he had never inspected such promising raw troops, while on the other hand, he had rarely encountered such disorder in every aspect of military life.

Impressed with the detail and accuracy of Baron Steuben's report, General Washington put the Baron in charge of bringing order to the Continental Army and its encampment, an all but impossible task at which he himself had never fully succeeded. The Baron, undaunted, soon proved to be an exceptionally well organized administrator, a gifted drillmaster, and a compassionate friend to every rank of soldier.

A broad gap existed in the Continental Army between officers and privates. In January, when General Washington ordered that sanitation be improved in camp, the officers wanted nothing to do with such an unseemly enterprise, while the undisciplined soldiers made do with things as they were. Consequently, when the multitude of "necessaries" filled up, new holes were rarely dug. Soldiers used whatever spot suited them in the woods. Disease threatened to sweep through camp with the coming of spring.

Baron Steuben organized major improvements in camp sanitation. New holes were dug in the frozen ground. The troops were ordered not to use the woods. The offal from butchered cattle was buried. And the dead horses gradually disappeared.

Few officers in the Continental Army would demean themselves by drilling their troops; they gave that lowly job to a sergeant. In contrast, Baron Steuben *himself* drilled the troops. General Washington formed a new company of one hundred soldiers, chosen from each battalion in

Valley Forge, whom the Baron would personally train. To give this company distinction, General Washington made it a part of his own Life Guard. However, since the existing Life Guard had been formed with soldiers from Virginia, the troops in Baron Steuben's company were selected from all the other States. Word quickly swept through the encampment: never before had a staff officer from the Prussian Army of Frederick the Great volunteered to drill mere privates in the American army. The Baron soon had the attention, and the gratitude, of every soldier in Valley Forge.

Henry and I were chosen by General Greene to train as recruits in the Baron's new company. We were selected not because we had proven ourselves to be exceptional soldiers, but exceptional teachers. (Henry as a carpenter, me as a cobbler.) Once the recruits had learned the Baron's military drill, we would in turn become instructors to every company in the encampment.

When one hundred soldiers from ten States, ranging from New Hampshire to North Carolina, formed into ranks on March 19, 1778, ready for our first lesson, we had no premonition that we would draw so many spectators.

None of us had ever before seen, or heard, anyone like Baron Steuben. The Baron roared his orders in French, which his young French aide Pierre-Etienne Duponceau then translated into English. (During the first day of drill, a captain from New York named Benjamin Walker stepped forward from the ranks and offered to help translate.) Baron Steuben did know one word in English, a word which he perfected with much practice, "Goddam!" While we bumbled and stumbled through our first exercises—some of us turning to the left, some to the right, while others nearly collided with each other, or stood motionless in a state of utter befuddled perplexity—Baron Steuben would roar volleys of Prussian oaths at us, mixed with a frequent "Goddam!" Finally he would turn to his two aides and say, "My dear Walker and my dear Duponceau, come and swear for me in English. These fellows won't do what I bid them." Walker and Duponceau would gladly oblige, enabling the Baron, an able student himself, to increase his vocabulary of oaths in English (though forever with a heavy Prussian accent). With little other entertainment in camp, men quickly gathered to watch the European drillmaster belaboring his company of struggling fools.

(However, when some of the spectators began to hoot and laugh and mock us, the Baron fired a volley of Prussian oaths at *them*. From that moment on, though the spectators on following days might number four or five times the number of soldiers in our company, they observed us with no more than a silent grin.)

Baron Steuben began his drill instruction with "the position of the soldier without arms," our initial stance when we formed on the parade ground. We then learned to face right and left, as well as to reverse the direction of our stance. We learned to march in formation, four abreast. Then how to wheel as a column. And how to halt without bumping into the fellows in front of us. The Baron increased our marching pace from the English sixty-two steps per minute to the Prussian seventy-five; thus everything we did, we did more quickly.

In general, Baron Steuben merged a simplified European drill with our own American way of thinking. Most important, when the men dared to ask him upon occasion *why* we were doing thus and such, the Baron would take the time to explain. Our affection and our respect for Baron Steuben accordingly grew, and we greatly looked forward to our morning and afternoon drills on the parade ground.

As we mastered the various positions, marched with proper order, and wheeled our column with some degree of grace, we could hear murmurs of approbation from the growing crowd of spectators. We soon developed an unexpected pride in our company of model soldiers.

On March 24, 1778, after five days of drilling, the members of our company began to instruct the troops in all fourteen brigades encamped at Valley Forge. Baron Steuben insisted that the officers throughout the camp not only learn the new drill, but help to teach it to their men. No longer would the gap of haughty disdain between officers and privates be tolerated. We heard the Baron say more than once to a reluctant colonel that though he himself was a gentlemen, an aide and personal friend to Frederick the Great, and a Baron in the Holy Roman Empire, he nevertheless took great pleasure in working with his men. General Washington's orders supported this new regime: the officers thus had no recourse but to comply.

During the following six weeks, our proud company continued to receive its own training for the first part of each morning and afternoon. Then later in the morning, later in the afternoon, we dispersed throughout the encampment to train the other troops. The Baron taught us, and we taught our students, how to *aim* our muskets (which few of the men had previously done in battle). We learned how to fire ordered volleys, and how to use our bayonets for something other than a roasting spit over a campfire. We then learned not only how to charge as a unified company with our bayonets, but how to form a defense against a British bayonet charge.

Gradually, and with great enthusiasm, individual soldiers moved within a company, companies moved within a regiment, and regiments moved within a brigade. Companies soon vied with other companies in their display of precision. Men cocked their hats, mended their shirts, and even, when the creeks thawed in April, washed their trousers. The Baron galloped from regiment to regiment, wearing his resplendent medals and the large jeweled star (the Star of the Order of Fidelity of Baden). The men looked forward to his arrival, for he would roar at them with his multitude of French, Prussian, and English curses. They would grin while they deployed ever more sharply.

Baron Steuben soon learned the ten exercise commands in English, from "prime and load" to "shoulder firelock." Thus he needed no interpreters when he put the men through basic drill.

He organized the riflemen into their own corps, then trained them to deploy not as scattered individuals, but as a unified force.

He demanded silence while the troops were marching.

And through it all, despite his thunderous cursing, he treated every soldier with respect.

Aye, the Baron proved to be a well organized administrator, and a gifted drillmaster. But he was also a compassionate friend to soldiers of every rank. Baron Steuben wrote an unprecedented booklet, detailing the responsibilities of every person in camp, from the highest-ranking commanders to the lowliest privates. The Baron provided far more than a list of military duties. He wrote, for example, that every captain, as the officer responsible for a company of sixty-four privates, must treat each of his soldiers in a way unknown to most military commanders:

> *"His first object should be, to gain the love of his men, by treating them with every possible kindness and humanity, enquiring into their complaints, and when well founded, seeing them redressed. He should know every man of his company by name and character. He should often visit those who are sick, speak tenderly to them, see that the public provision, whether medicine or diet, is duly administered, and procure them besides such comforts and conven-*

*iences as are in his power. The attachment that arises from
this kind of attention to the sick and wounded, is almost in-
conceivable; it will moreover be the means of preserving
the lives of many valuable men."*

In a later chapter, Baron Steuben repeated to his officers,

*"There is nothing which gains an officer the love of his sol-
diers more than his care of them under the distress of sickness; it is then he has the power of exerting his humanity in
providing them every comfortable necessary, and making
their situation as agreeable as possible."*

In a chapter entitled, "Necessary Regulations for Preserving Order
and Cleanliness in the Camp," the Baron wrote detailed instructions:

*". . . if any horse or other animal dies near the regiment,
(the quarter-master) must cause it to be carried at least half
a mile from camp, and buried. The place where the cattle
are killed must be at least fifty paces in the rear of the wag-
gons; and the entrails and other filth immediately buried."*

No detail was too small for the Baron's attention. In his "Instructions for the private soldier," the final item read:

*"He must always have a stopper for the muzzle of his gun in
case of rain, and when on a march; at which times he will
unfix his bayonet."*

Whether he was inspecting a soldier's well-polished musket, or
scolding a major for neglecting to visit a corporal in the hospital, Baron
Steuben never hid the warmth in his heart for his troops.

By the end of April, 1778, thousands of men marched and wheeled
and deployed across the Grand Parade in perfect order. The Continental
Army flourished with a new spirit, a spirit so proud and determined
that every soldier of every rank looked upon Baron Steuben as the man
who had created the army that would finally defeat the British.

During those weeks of daily training, Robert Peabody, now sixteen
years old, became a drummer in Captain Byrnes' company. His anxious
mother would not countenance his taking up a musket. So Henry found
him a drum. Enormously proud to have an official position, Robert

practiced for endless hours with the other drummers. In addition to field signals (a courageous drummer could be as important as an officer in directing the soldiers on the field of battle), Robert learned a dozen march cadences, some lively, some appropriate for a long march.

Every company needed a fifer as well as a drummer. (Though a drummer's "prime and load" might be lost in the thunder of cannons, a fife's piercing shrill could still be heard.) Because many of the fifers in the Continental Army were Negroes, Henry recruited a Negro boy from Virginia named Peter.

Robert and Peter, like the other apprentice musicians in camp, proved so earnest at their practicing that the troops began to grumble. Complaints reached headquarters. General Washington ordered that drummers and fifers were allowed to practice only between five and six in the morning, and four and five in the afternoon. When the daylong din was thus reduced to two hours, the troops were heartily grateful.

As Robert improved, he was allowed to join the more experienced drummers at daybreak when *reveille* awakened the camp, and at nine in the evening when tattoo sent the soldiers to bed.

☙

Chapter Ninety-One

Genevieve, savoring the exquisite balm of spring.

On days of poor weather, I nursed my daughter in the privacy of the pantry. But when the first warmth of spring finally arrived, I ached to be outside. I spoke with one of the Life Guards, the fellow I had known in Morristown; he spoke with the other guards, informing them of my request. Thus I was able to step outside headquarters, carry Sally in her blanket to the eastern, southern, or western sides of the stone house—wherever the sun was shining—then nurse her in the shelter of her blanket while the Life Guards stood steadfastly with their backs toward us. When Sally had finished, and had thanked me with her happy burp, I would pin up my blouse, then call quietly to the men, "Thank you."

During those short visits to the world outdoors, I was able to watch the return of spring. The sun rose noticeably higher each day as it passed in its arc behind the bare branches of the maples in the yard. A breeze from the south brought the lovely scent of damp earth. First a few, then suddenly a multitude of birds twittered in the yard, undaunted by the last brief snowfall of the winter. Perhaps most precious, as I leaned my back against a sun-baked stone wall and savored its warmth, my child was bathed in a freshness, a fragrance, and a promise that blessed as well our entire nation.

Susanne found her place in the army during that spring of 1778. Baron Steuben wrote his drills in French, then relied on his two aides to translate them into English, so that each lesson might be distributed to the regimental camps and copied into their orderly books. But Walker and Duponceau were far too busy in the field to keep up with translations at their desks. I therefore suggested that a French-Canadian schoolteacher named Susanne Peabody might be hired. The following morning, I brought Susanne to the stone house (just up the road beyond the artificers' camp) where the Baron and his staff were quartered. Within fifteen minutes, Duponceau had hired the abundantly skilled teacher to translate the Baron's drill into a draft that General Washington would then edit into proper military form.

With Henry a captain and Robert now a drummer, Susanne was profoundly gratified to find her own place within the Continental Army. She enjoyed working with the Baron, whose respect for his men was equaled by his charm with the ladies. She enjoyed as well working with Pierre-Etienne Duponceau, with whom she could discuss in the purest French her father's homeland, *la belle France,* a land she knew only in her imagination.

Their collective work proved to be a long-lasting success. Baron Steuben's *Regulations for the Order and Discipline of the Troops of the United States,* also known as the "Blue Book" from the color of its cover, was published in at least eight editions between 1779 and 1785. It continued in use until well after the war.

After the hard work of building huts in January, followed by the bitter famine of February, March and April brought several welcome improvements to life in Valley Forge.

On March 22, 1778, General Nathanael Greene became our new Quartermaster. He did not want the job: he protested vehemently to General Washington that he was a field officer who detested paper-work. Only his allegiance to the General compelled him to accept the enormous task. His skill in the field was soon matched by his skill at his desk: he quickly organized the entire supply system, with a string of depots reaching as far north as Hudson's River and as far south as Chesapeake Bay, so that cloth for new shirts and trousers, canvas for new tents, cattle and corn for the soup pots, and fresh forage for the horses began to appear in camp.

Shipments of clothing and arms from France now reached our warehouses in greater quantities. The sixty-four men in Captain Byrnes' company were greatly pleased when the Quartermaster's clerk provided them with new French uniforms, the woolen coats dark blue, their cuffs and facing white. The men turned in their battered muskets and drilled now with shiny French firelocks. Henry's privates proudly addressed each other as "monsieur."

The shad began their annual spawning migration up the Schuylkill River in April. When the weathered soldiers were not drilling, they be-came rollicking boys who could think of nothing but fishing. General Greene found nets in the barns of local farmers along the river. (We no longer bothered to ask, but simply searched, politely, until we found what we needed.) The soldiers stretched these nets from shore to shore, then the cavalry walked their horses in the shallows, herding the big silver fish until they were caught by their gills. When the nets were full, the men hauled them to the riverbank on the Valley Forge side. The two-foot shad thrashed in the soldiers' arms as the fishermen scampered whooping up the bank with that evening's feast.

We roasted the shad over campfires, then devoured them to their skeletons. The soldiers set down their plates; they sprawled in the fresh grass and groaned, too filled with fish to think of even budging toward their bunks.

Benjamin and I had no apple orchard that spring, but we had the wild thickets of shadbush. Their small white blossoms billowed above us as we lay on a blanket on a Sunday afternoon beneath a blue sky with our two happy children; beneath a pink sky on an April evening; and (once or twice, without children) beneath stars peeking down through shadbush blossoms on a deliciously warm springtime night.

During that spring in Valley Forge, some of the soldiers, no doubt from farms, turned the warming soil with their spades and formed a patchwork of gardens. Though they knew we would almost certainly leave our encampment before the potatoes were ready, they hoped at least for some peas and early beans.

I will close this chapter with a letter from headquarters. General Washington's profound compassion for his troops, and his appreciation for their endurance at Valley Forge, were expressed in his letter of April 21, 1778 to John Banister, a delegate from Virginia to Congress in York. General Washington wrote,

> *". . . without arrogance or the smallest deviation from truth it may be said that no history, now extant, can furnish an instance of an Army's suffering such uncommon hardships as ours have done and bearing them with the same patience and fortitude. To see men without clothes to cover their nakedness, without blankets to lay on, without shoes, by which their marches might be traced by the blood from their feet, and almost as often without provisions as well; marching through frost and snow, and at Christmas taking up their winter quarters within a day's march of the enemy, without a house or hut to cover them till they could be built, and submitting to it without a murmur, is a mark of patience and obedience which in my opinion can scarce be paralleled."*

☞

Chapter Ninety-Two

Genevieve, with a proper bit of history.

The rebellion which began with a skirmish in Lexington in 1775, became a war that reached halfway around the world in 1778. When France finally declared, in February, 1778, that she was a formal ally to the United States of America, and thus (once more) an enemy of Great Britain, the scope of the war suddenly extended from the Mississippi River to the disputed seaports of India. The Caribbean with its Sugar Islands, the Atlantic Ocean, the English Channel, the Mediterranean, and the long route around Africa to the Indian Ocean all became potential naval battlefields.

The confident British, who thought they could teach us a lesson in Boston, now found themselves entangled in a vast and complicated war with their ancient enemy. The King and Parliament initially attempted to collect a small tax on tea; by the end of the war in 1783, they had spent a national fortune on armies and navies which ultimately brought them naught but the loss of half their empire.

Defeated by the British in 1763 at the end of the Seven Years War, France had been quick to view the American rebellion as her means of revenge. During 1776, the French government secretly began to supply the American army with muskets, gunpowder and lead, cannons and round shot, and a small amount of clothing. In March, 1777, while the Continental Army was encamped in Morristown, King Louis XVI quietly contributed three million livres in silver to America's military budget, a loan without interest, not to be repaid until the end of the war. Of equal importance, France opened her ports to American privateers: our ships could now be supplied and repaired in harbors close to England, enabling them to raid British merchant ships with great efficiency.

America's three ambassadors to France, Silas Deane, Arthur Lee, and Benjamin Franklin, began negotiations with the French government in 1776. In addition to weapons and loans, they sought formal recognition of America's independence, and a military alliance against Britain. When the news reached Versailles on December 4, 1777 that American troops had defeated General Burgoyne at Saratoga (a victory to which French artillery had contributed greatly), the King and his skeptical foreign minister, Comte de Vergennes, realized that a British defeat in America might well be possible. Franklin nudged the French toward an open alliance by hinting that he might accept an offer of peace from Britain. On December 17, 1777, Vergennes promised, on behalf of the King, that greater support would soon be coming.

On January 7, 1778, while American troops were building their log huts at Valley Forge, France proposed a treaty of friendship and commerce. Our ambassadors were grateful, but continued to press for an open alliance. Another month of negotiations followed, during which French and British spies reported to their respective governments exactly what Ambassador Franklin wanted them to report. Finally, on February 6, 1778, during the grim month of famine at Valley Forge, Vergennes signed a Treaty of Commerce and Alliance, indicating openly that France would soon be at war with Britain.

The British were suddenly embattled with both an elusive colonial army in America, and the professional troops of France. The British knew that if they concentrated their naval forces in New York City and Philadelphia, the French might attack Britain's lucrative islands in the Caribbean. With an attack on Halifax in Nova Scotia, the French could attempt to recapture Canada. And while British ships guarded faraway ports, France might well invade England itself.

King George III sent a desperate peace delegation to treat with the colonials in America. The gentlemen from London arrived in June, 1778, but Congress in York voted unanimously to reject all proposals that fell short of a full and formal recognition of independence. General Washington refused to meet with the delegation at Valley Forge. One of the British ambassadors, William Eden, wrote despairingly, "It is impossible to see even what I have seen of this magnificent country, and not to go nearly mad at the long train of misconducts and mischances by which we have lost it."

News of the alliance between the United States and France, signed at the royal court in Versailles in February, reached Congress at their rustic outpost in York in April. Congress examined the details of the agreement, then ratified the treaty on May 4, 1778. An express rider galloped from York to Valley Forge to notify General Washington that the alliance had been formalized.

Our Commander in Chief followed his general orders on May 5 with an announcement of what every soldier in camp already knew:

France had finally joined the war on our side. Then he announced, in his reverent way, plans for a celebration.

> *"It having pleased the Almighty ruler of the Universe propitiously to defend the Cause of the United American-States and finally, by raising us up a powerful Friend among the Princes of the Earth, to establish our liberty and independence upon lasting foundations, it becomes us to set apart a day for gratefully acknowledging the divine Goodness and celebrating the important event which we owe to his benign interposition."*

The celebration would be tomorrow, May 6. Chaplains would "deliver a discourse suitable to the occasion." Then, "at half after ten o'clock a cannon will be fired, which is to be a signal for the men to be under Arms."

The activities thereafter would be directed by our drillmaster, Baron Steuben.

On Wednesday, May 6, 1778, the troops throughout Valley Forge assembled by brigades to listen to their chaplains read a summary of the Treaty. The reading was followed by a sermon. Chaplain John Hurt asked his soldiers, "Who is there that does not rejoice that his lot has fallen at this important period; that he has contributed his assistance, and will be enrolled hereafter in the pages of history among the gallant defenders of liberty?"

At 10:30 a cannon fired in General Knox's artillery park. The men, unarmed during religious services, returned to their huts to fetch their muskets and cartridge boxes (filled with blank cartridges). Then they assembled by brigades on the Grand Parade (as the broad meadow was now called) for inspection.

But here I must defer to a Continental regular who mustered on that day in Baron Steuben's model company of one hundred chosen soldiers. He was thus a member of General Washington's Life Guard. But above all, he was one of the five score teachers who planted the seeds of the Baron's Prussian genius in the hearts of over ten thousand soldiers in Valley Forge.

∞

Chapter Ninety-Three

Benjamin, on a day of great joy,
on a day of great promise.

23 December, 1826
The old farmhouse is
filled with Christmas.
The grandchildren
and great grandchildren
will soon arrive,
with Papa Caleb!

On May 6, 1778 at the Continental encampment in Valley Forge, I stood at attention with my firelock beside Captain Henry Byrnes. Both of us wore French uniforms with freshly polished buttons, and French shoes that my patriotic father would have scoffed at. To honor the French alliance, our hats were bedecked with sprigs of white paper (replicating, in our small way, the white flag of France). Henry, as the captain of Baron Steuben's company of one hundred, wore a red sash around his waist, and carried not a French firelock but a spontoon, a spear that he held upright beside him.

My firelock, like the ten thousand other firelocks shouldered in smart formation on the Grand Parade, was as polished as any firelock ever inspected by Frederick the Great himself.

Though that springtime morning was nearly half a century ago, I vividly remember the flapping of our regimental colors when a breeze swept across the broad field; the distant call of shouted orders as the fourteen brigades formed their lines from one end of the Parade to the other; the rumble of signal drums near and far; the sharp piping of fifes. (Those fifes: they sounded as if one bold species of birds twittering in the hills had flown down to the enormous field to see for themselves what we were doing . . . and now sent back to their compatriots the crows and cardinals a dozen lively reports.) And then we heard— though standing at attention, the men looked up—the sound of a flock of geese, honking high above us as their ploughshare, formed with less precision than our perfect regimental lines, flapped northward across a sky as blue as a robin's egg.

The Continental Army in its entirety was formed and inspected. Field officers were appointed to command the battalions. Then our

Commander in Chief rode his white horse—every soldier recognized Nelson—around the complete circuit of our lines.

He was followed by a cluster of mounted officers, including the Marquis de Lafayette, who wore around his neck a handsome white scarf. Baron Steuben, wearing his enormous jeweled star, regarded the troops in their well-formed ranks with unhidden pride (and perhaps a measure of well hidden astonishment).

But it was General Washington's face that the men watched most closely. We saluted our Commander in Chief as he rode past, and saw in his countenance, turned warmly upon us, his proud approval. We felt ourselves ready: we were the troops who would soon drive the British in full retreat from the streets of Philadelphia. We were the troops who would sweep the British out of New York City. We were the troops who would bestow upon America her freedom.

Identical shouts from commanding officers now echoed back and forth across the Grand Parade: we were ordered to prime and load our firelocks. We heard the slap of ten thousand hands on ten thousand cartridge boxes, then the rattling of ten thousand ramrods as we pushed our blank cartridges down the barrels of ten thousand weapons.

In the silence that followed, our firelocks once more shouldered, every man in Valley Forge must have felt that had we fired our volley toward Philadelphia, toward London itself, we would have rattled the chandeliers on Chestnut Street, and stood the hair straight up atop the head of poor King George.

We were ready. Buried in the soil of Valley Forge were the bones of over two thousand soldiers who had not survived the winter, as well as the bones of countless horses who had staggered until they died. But standing at attention that day, alive and alert in the ankle-deep grass, were over ten thousand soldiers—weathered veterans and new recruits—who knew in their determined hearts that we would win our country's freedom. We believed in our Commander in Chief, we believed in our officers, and we believed in ourselves. Though a few acres of corn went unplanted that spring in Massachusetts and New York, in Maryland and North Carolina, our farmer-soldiers would soon harvest a victory. We would provide the fruits of that victory to our families back home. To the villages where many had first drilled as Minutemen. To the States which had risen up from their colonial thralldom. And to the American nation, young, bold, determined, and vibrant, waiting to see what it might become.

More than that, we would offer the fruits of liberty to the entire world. We hoped that yeomen like ourselves might everywhere toss off the shackles of their ancient despots, and flourish with us in the warm springtime of freedom.

Aye, we were ready. When the signal cannon thundered—its roar rebounded from the hills wrapped around us: we heard one BOOM! and then a half-dozen scattered echoes—our officers marched us in the Continental Army's first review before our Commander in Chief. The brigades wheeled smartly to the right by platoons, then maneuvered so smoothly and swiftly across the Grand Parade, each platoon proudly feeling itself on display, that as ten thousand soldiers deployed in their units with skill and grace, we fairly amazed ourselves.

Our own brigade passed with well dressed ranks in front of General Washington. Though every soldier stared straight ahead, we felt his dignity, his strength, and his approval.

The brigade majors formed us once again across the Grand Parade, then ten thousand troops stood at attention, absolutely silent.

In April of 1775, only three years ago, seventy armed farmers had stood in two lines on Lexington green while seven hundred redcoats marched toward them. Those farmers had attempted to retreat; many had been shot in the back. Today, not even seven thousand redcoats would gain a foot of the sacred ground on which we stood.

The signal cannon fired. Its blast was followed by a stately volley of thirteen separate thunderclaps from thirteen six-pounders in the artillery park. Behind the steady parade of BOOM! . . . BOOM! . . . BOOM! . . . we could hear the rolling roar of echoes. As we listened to the cannon shots, and ghosts of cannon shots, it seemed as if the spirits of some ancient army had arrayed their phantom cannons around us, and now joined our military revelry.

After the thirteenth cannon had fired, we heard the last faint *boom*! from a hill beyond the flats of the Schuylkill River.

A lingering moment of silence . . .

Then a soldier in the First Virginia Brigade raised his firelock, and fired. The soldier beside him fired, then the next soldier, and the next: they commenced a running fire of musketry that continued along the front rank of the Army for almost half a mile. This *feu de joie*, as the French called it (fire of joy), allowed every individual soldier to announce, "I am here, I am ready," to his ten thousand compatriots, to his officers, to his Commander in Chief.

The steady, unrelenting progression of musket shots along the vast Grand Parade gave us bedrock proof that we were invincible.

When my moment came, I raised the stock of my firelock to my shoulder, pulled the trigger and savored the blast. I felt as if I stood front and center on the world stage: even my father, who had said so often, "No son of mine shall ever be a soldier," could see me. True, I hoped with all my battered heart that Caleb in his time would never become a soldier. But at that moment in Valley Forge (during an eight-year war when every time I fired a real cartridge, I knew I had committed a horrid sin), I fired my blank with more than determination, more than pride. I fired that shot with reverence: reverence for the ground we stood on, reverence for the cause we fought for.

And, if such a thing could be believed, I fired that shot as a sort of prayer: that once we had won this war for liberty, may there never be another war. May the cannons be forever stilled. May the hills echo with the bells of a dozen churches, ringing "Peace! . . . Peace! . . . Peace!" Forgive us, please, as we sin this one last time. Then let us sin no more.

The *feu de joie* became faint in the distance, then grew louder as it approached again along the second rank of troops.

When finally the running musketry had reached its starting point, the signal cannon fired. The entire Continental Army shouted with one voice in a grand huzzah, "Long live the King of France!"

Never had the boy in London thought the man in America would proclaim such an unpatriotic thought. But so I did, and I hoped that both kings heard.

We now reloaded. The thirteen cannons fired their stately salvo; the hills rumbled their echoes. Then a second running fire of musketry traveled along the huge meadow, and traveled back again, followed by the cheer, "Long live the friendly European powers!" (Meaning those nations which gave us gunpowder and loaned us money, or at least stayed out of the war on Britain's side.)

We loaded our muskets a third time, grinned at a third volley of thirteen cannon blasts, fired a third run of musketry. Then ten thousand voices roared with all their strength, "To the American States!"

A newborn child announces her existence to the world with a wail. In May of 1778, our newborn Continental Army announced its sturdy existence to the world with three times thirteen cannon blasts, with over thirty thousand separate firelock shots, and with a roar of voices that must have sundered the heavens.

Providence, the Almighty ruler of the Universe, the divine Goodness, may have peered down. Perhaps with approval.

Each battalion now broke into companies, which marched to their respective camps, where every soldier was treated to a celebratory gill of rum. Genevieve and Susanne, who had watched the review and *feu de joie* from a timbered knoll behind Captain Byrnes' company, joined us at the artificers' camp. Genevieve was full of praise, Susanne nearly speechless with admiration.

During a festive evening of fiddling, bagpiping, and dancing in the regimental camps, Henry and Susanne appeared shyly at our campfire. They asked, in the midst of boisterous carousing, if they might speak in private with Genevieve and me.

The four of us walked down to the edge of the gurgling creek. Bright stars shone above us; blinking fireflies drifted around us. Henry, holding Susanne's hand, announced that she had accepted his proposal of marriage.

Genevieve and I congratulated them. We felt—the four of us felt— in the midst of ten thousand soldiers who would soon march to their next battle, something so good, something so right, that I discovered tears running down my cheeks.

Susanne asked whether we would mind if the wedding were small and private—not, she and Henry had agreed, with Henry's company present, but just the family and a few close friends. Ruth and Nathan Peabody, of course, and Robert. Reverend Kesslaer to perform the ceremony. Ka Tsi Tsya Ha, and Lo Ha Hes. Cato and Prince. Peter. With Genevieve and me, Caleb and Sally, that would be five guests, seven members of the family, the minister, and the bride and groom.

"Yes, yes, wonderful," said Genevieve. "And *when* will you be married?"

"In ten days," said Henry, "on Saturday, May sixteenth. Until then, in the absence of a church, we are looking for the proper setting."

Genevieve, at home in Lincoln
on Christmas Eve.

24 December, 1826
Caleb and Mary
and their beautiful family
are all here.

Fifty years ago tonight, Benjamin, Henry and I were camped on the southern shore of the Delaware River, following months of retreat. The troops had not yet crossed back over the river to attack the village of Trenton. Christmas Eve, as we huddled in our cold smoky hut, was little more than a dream from the past: when family gathered by the warm hearth, read to each other from the Good Book, and reached beyond our daily cares toward our better selves. Toward the gift of divine love. And toward peace.

Today the old farmhouse in Lincoln is filled with family. A log of oak burns on the hearth, and the Good Book awaits our reading tonight.

God is Love, but He is also Mystery. A mystery perhaps as great as His love. Henry lies alone tonight in his Virginia grave. Susanne lives in France. Her son Robert is now a doctor.

And until I reach my own grave, I will always wonder, Why?

∞

Chapter Ninety-Four

Genevieve.

On the morning after the celebration, General Washington issued an unexpected order: "The Commander in Chief in a season of General Joy takes occasion to proclaim Pardon and Releasement to all Prisoners whatever now in Confinement."

This act of compassion was remembered by many men, especially those who became excellent soldiers after their release from the camp gaol.

Because our damp, dark, smoky huts had been the cause of so much sickness during the winter, General Washington ordered that at least two windows be cut through the walls of every hut to allow fresh air to blow inside. The mosquitoes came in too, of course, but the soldiers gradually stopped coughing.

The springtime sunshine, pouring in through rough rectangles chopped with an axe, made our small, crowded dwellings feel almost heavenly.

I was at my desk at headquarters, copying a letter from General Washington to General Smallwood at Wilmington, a long letter which detailed the measures to be taken before the troops in Delaware joined the main army at Valley Forge, when General Washington himself appeared before my desk. He wore no coat, no hat, no waistcoat, only his white shirt and neatly pressed blue breeches.

"Miss Ebenezer, I wonder if you and your fine Sir William would care to accompany me and Nelson on a tour of the grounds?"

All the windows at headquarters were wide open: the enchanting fragrance of shadbush, the jubilant songs of wood thrushes, and the occasional laughter of soldiers drifted through the house . . . beckoning us out. I saw before me a man who wished Pardon and Releasement from all further confinement, at least for a couple of hours on this afternoon in May. I set down my quill. "General Washington, with great pleasure."

Though he was a man of profound reserve, I saw in his eyes the glimmer of a schoolboy on the last day of school. "Then I shall have the horses readied," he said.

He glanced down at the infant, now three months old, sleeping in her bed beneath my table. "Is there someone who might keep an eye on your Sally?"

"Yes. Ruth Peabody. If I may take a few minutes to carry Sally back to camp."

"Of course."

The childless General watched with a smile as I knelt and gathered Sally into my arms.

General Washington and I walked together out the front door and down the stone steps; the Life Guard noticed, for they rarely saw the General without his cortege of officers. As we followed the lane toward the paddock, the midday sun shone warmly on our faces. Fresh green leaves in the oak trees along both sides of the road rustled in a breeze.

We could see our horses now, standing among twenty others in the fenced-in paddock beside the barn.

"Please attend to your little Sally," said the General, "as I shall require your company for a good three hours."

That meant that I should take the time to nurse Sally before I gave her to Ruth. The General would gladly wait in the paddock while the scribe became a mother, then the mother became a courier. "I shall be back, sir, within fifteen minutes."

He nodded, then whistled to Nelson.

I crossed the bridge over Valley Creek; freed at last of its ice, the water gurgled happily beneath my feet. Our hut was empty. I found Ruth with Caleb in a clearing in the woods behind our hut: napping in the sunshine, they almost disappeared in a sea of daisies.

When Miss Ebenezer, her duties as mother accomplished, returned to the paddock, she found the two horses saddled and bridled. General Washington sat mounted on Nelson with Sir William's reins in his hand. Five stable boys sat perched along the top rail of the fence, each one destined to tell his grandchildren, years hence, that *he* had helped General Washington to saddle his horse.

I swung up onto Sir William, took the reins from my Commander in Chief, then followed him at a trot out the gate and down the lane to Gulph Road, the main road through the encampment. Cantering toward the Grand Parade, we passed among soldiers who stepped to one side. Recognizing their commander, the men lifted their hats and cheered.

We rode between the huts of two brigades: General Conway's

"street" to our left, and General Maxwell's "street" to our right. Spring had surely come to Valley Forge, for ropes had been strung from hut to hut and between any standing trees; each line was draped with flapping shirts and trousers, blankets and socks. From women at their wash tubs, from children playing atop an earthen redoubt, from men splitting the eternal firewood, we were greeted with cheers.

Further along Gulph Road we reined to the left, then cantered north along a trace that descended toward the river. As we approached the Schuylkill, we could see great numbers of men along its grassy banks and in the water, enjoying perhaps their first bath in over half a year. Slowing to a trot, the General and I rode with a clatter of hooves across Sullivan's Bridge.

From up and down the river rose a cheer. (A dozen men without trousers dashed into the water.) General Washington acknowledged the men with a wave of his arm in both directions.

On the northern shore of the river, we surveyed several meadows where, as the General explained to me, he intended to set up tents for troops plagued by sickness in their huts. Here they could breathe "healthful air" and sleep "on fresh beds of straw." Satisfied that the rolling meadows were broad enough for the tents of three regiments (the Fourth New York, the Second North Carolina, and the Second Rhode Island, each with a large number of men unfit for duty), General Washington led me back across the handsome bridge (built during the winter by our engineers). Once again he waved to acknowledge the prolonged cheer from far up and far down the river.

As we headed southeast along a lane angling toward the Grand Parade, our horses cantered side by side: chestnut red, and white dappled with gray.

The General turned to me. "Miss Ebenezer, of some things I have no knowledge whatsoever. Therefore I must ask you a rather delicate question."

"Yes sir?"

"Are you able, only three months after the birth of your daughter, to gallop?"

I had wondered myself whether I would even be able to trot. But I seemed to have mended well after Sally's arrival.

"Sir, I believe I am quite able to gallop."

Ahead of us beckoned the broad green sweep of the Grand Parade, almost completely empty now of troops. Since his appointment as Commander in Chief during the spring of 1775, three years ago, General

Washington had labored day and night with the burdens of war upon his shoulders. Only within the last few weeks had he commanded, with the help of Baron Steuben, a genuine army. He had been on horseback almost daily during those three exhausting years, usually with a group of officers, always on business, often attending to problems that majors, adjutants, or wagoneers could easily have taken care of, but had left for him to solve. He daily did the work of a dozen men, and sometimes muttered at headquarters that his mind was "on the stretch."

With a touch of his heels, with a touch of my heels, we galloped. Nelson and Sir William seemed to have been waiting all winter for this vast, unencumbered heaven of rolling turf. Side by side, General Washington and I leaned forward in our saddles. His stern reserve vanished: he became a young man back on a Virginia plantation, the finest rider on the strongest horse, his muscular grace matching the graceful power of the thundering steed beneath him. His eyes—eyes that had too long focused on sheets of lamp-lit paper—now reached with eagerness far ahead across the open plain. The boy who grew up gazing across the broad Potomac, the man who later gazed across the even broader Ohio, the quiet prophet who saw his nation's future all the way to the Pacific, now galloped unfettered, as free as the springtime wind.

Dandelions sped in a yellow blur beneath us. The blue sky awaited our wings.

He looked at me, his face steady above Nelson's rippling white mane. His blue-gray eyes were exuberant, as if he had almost forgotten, but now fully remembered, the joy of galloping on a strong horse across a bountiful continent.

But more, far more than that: with the petty problems left behind, we knew, we understood without a word between us, that all this long and brutal struggle must end in victory. That we, all ten thousand of us, would fulfill our covenant with Providence.

That we would make real the American promise.

We galloped over land recently covered with snow. Snow spotted with blood. Land in which two thousand soldiers were buried; land which the blessings of liberty might have been buried as well.

But the army had not collapsed. It had not vanished.

The blessings it would bestow upon the millions yet unborn were a balm to an old warrior's heart.

General Washington never lost his compassion for us. He never lost his hope. And now, when like one of Papa's eagles he could finally spread his wings, the General smiled at me, and then he even laughed.

*   *   *

We had no need to speak as we completed our ride back to the barn. The General perhaps wanted to curry Nelson, as he had done when a lad with his Virginia horses: to walk him and cool him in the paddock and carefully water him.

But Lieutenant Colonel Hamilton waited at the gate with urgent news about British warship movements on the Delaware River, south of Philadelphia.

General Washington reluctantly gave the reins to a stable boy, then hastened on foot toward headquarters.

A short distance down the lane, he looked back at me and called, "Miss Ebenezer, I thank you."

Miss Ebenezer called back, "Sir, you are most heartily welcome."

ဢ

Chapter Ninety-Five

Benjamin, as best man.

Genevieve has asked me to write about the wedding, for it was a soldier's wedding, and a widow's wedding. Death accompanied the bride to the altar, and Death accompanied the groom when he and his wife departed from the church.

The sanctuary chosen by Susanne and Henry was the crest of a hill to the west of camp, where neither firewood nor logs for the huts had been cut. On a sunny Saturday morning, we walked westward along Gulph Road, then followed (just across from the Baron's stone house) a wagon trail that wound up a flank of the hill.

The higher we climbed, the larger the trees became. Astonished by the girth of some of the burly black giants, I surmised that these oaks were as old as Jamestown, the first colony in Virginia; as old as Plymouth, the first colony in Massachusetts. Some, their trunks over four feet wide, might well have been saplings when Columbus set sail from Spain. The trees formed a stately guard as we passed among them. Their spring-green leaves shaded us from the sun as we climbed, though patches of light dappled the ferns along the trail.

It was one thing to hear the birds in May down in the valley, where most of the trees had been cut. But as we now ascended through the forest, we heard hundreds of birds around us, their calls sharp and clear as they chirped and warbled and twittered with confident joy. Some were flirting; others no doubt sat on eggs in their nests. A few perhaps were already teaching their fledglings to fly.

Earlier that morning, before she put on the lavender wedding gown which Ruth Peabody had sewn for her, Susanne, with her apprentices Robert and Peter, had gathered dandelions in the fields around camp. She taught the boys how to fashion wreaths, poking the stem of each flower through a slit in the stem of the next, as she had done in Quebec when a girl. As our silent, thoughtful procession followed the trail up the gentle slope, the fifteen of us—even the minister—wore a bright, beautifully woven yellow wreath.

When Robert, and then Susanne, and then Sally in my arms, passed through a patch of dappled sunlight, each of them seemed for a moment to be wearing not a wreath, but a radiant halo.

The trail became a path which no one seemed to have followed in recent years. Robert pointed, and we watched the red tuft of a fox's tail before it disappeared a hundred feet ahead of us.

At the crest of the hill, we found our places. Reverend Kesslaer in fringed buckskin, a Bible in his hand, stood in front of a huge black oak. Henry and Susanne stood before him, as if walking up that trail had constituted walking down the aisle. Robert stood near his mother, watching everything carefully. He looked at his mother, who moved as serenely as if in a dream. He looked again and again at the man who was about to become his father.

The rest of us stood in a crescent behind the bride and groom.

Nathan and Ruth Peabody, watching another man replace their son, yet wishing the new family all possible happiness.

Peter, Cato, and Prince, a Negro boy and two Negro men, one a fifer, the other two skilled nurses.

Lo Ha Hes and Ka Tsi Tsya Ha, gifted at healing the sick and at bringing new life into the world.

And then Genevieve and me; Caleb, nearly two now, stood between us; Sally slept in Genevieve's arms.

It was, as well it should have been, a very American wedding.

A breeze rustled through the oak leaves above us; dancing spots of sunshine appeared and vanished around our feet. Reverend Kesslaer spoke the words of the ancient sacrament of marriage. Their voices hushed yet firm, Henry and Susanne each pledged their love, "until death do us part."

I remember thinking as we walked in our procession back down the path, husband and wife holding hands as they led the way, how right it would be if the fifteen of us entered, at the bottom of the hill, a land of peace. A land where every child, every woman, and every man were truly respected as an equal.

But I might as well have wished that General Knox's cannons had become a flock of cooing doves.

Genevieve, saying farewell to Valley Forge.

Winter may be a time of cold and famine, but with summer come the campaigns of war.

Our spies reported to headquarters that on May 8, General Henry Clinton had arrived in Philadelphia from New York. He would replace General William Howe as the commander in chief of the British and German troops.

On May 17, redcoats began loading artillery and other equipment onto ships moored along the Philadelphia wharf. The British were clearly preparing to evacuate the city.

On May 24, following a day of festivities in his honor, General Howe departed from Philadelphia aboard a frigate . . . bound for New York, or Halifax, or perhaps London.

Then on Thursday, June 18, 1778, the British Army, which had defended Boston against our siege for almost a year, which had fought battle after battle until it captured New York, and which had fought at Brandywine and Germantown to seize and secure Philadelphia, baffled us by abandoning Philadelphia without firing a shot. The Hessian troops departed aboard ships for New York, while the redcoats crossed the Delaware River aboard ferries, then marched northeast in a column twelve miles long through New Jersey.

The Loyalists in Philadelphia who had hosted His Majesty's army through the winter were horrified. They now faced the same brutal choice that Loyalists in Boston had faced: flee with the British, leaving almost everything behind, or await the retribution of Patriots who would soon pour into the city.

While the British were rowing east across the Delaware, our troops based in Wilmington marched cautiously into the western fringe of the city. General Washington had issued strict orders against any harm to the citizens or damage to their property. Our troops did, however, break down the doors to the Walnut Street Prison. Any American prisoners still alive were lifted from the floors of their cells and given more to eat than roots of grass.

The following day, Friday, June 19, 1778, after exactly six months in Valley Forge, General Washington ordered the main body of his troops, 11,800 strong, to march with firelocks and rucksacks out of the encampment in pursuit of the British army, 11,000 strong, as they hastened in their vulnerable column across New Jersey.

Our Commander in Chief was not satisfied with the simple liberation of Philadelphia. He was finally ready, with strong, determined, well-trained troops, to attack the British on an open field.

ജ

PART VIII

The Battle of Monmouth

Chapter Ninety-Six

Benjamin.

Leaving empty huts, the empty Grand Parade, and two thousand graves behind us, we marched east for nine days, from springtime into summer, and then from summer into the worst heat of the war. While General Henry Clinton led the British troops across New Jersey toward the coast (where Admiral Richard Howe waited with his fleet), General Washington led the American troops on a roughly parallel route, but further north. At some point, before the British reached the safety of a seaport, we would pounce.

Our Commander in Chief ordered General Daniel Morgan and his riflemen to flank the long British column. The six hundred snipers hid in the woods along the British route, signaled to each other with turkey gobbles, then fired with accuracy at targets much larger than a turkey. Whenever British flankers rushed into the woods, Morgan's mountain-men vanished.

Other detachments hurried ahead of the column: they destroyed bridges, felled trees across the road, and most devastating of all, they filled in village and farmhouse wells with earth. As the days grew steadily hotter, the redcoats, trudging through soft sandy soil in their woolen uniforms, their haversacks heavy on their backs, sent out men with buckets at every stream to fetch water. The water carriers, of course, became targets for our snipers.

The American troops marched in the same brutal heat, and drank just as greedily at every brook. Occasional thunderstorms cooled us for perhaps an hour; but then, as the sun once more blazed down from a hazy blue sky, the water rose from the sandy earth as steam . . . until the damp air was almost impossible to breathe. Men staggered out of our column to the shade of a tree, and there they collapsed. Other men fainted while they marched. Pulling them by their arms, we dragged the limp soldiers to whatever shade we could find.

By June 24, 1778, after six days of marching, we had reached the village of Hopewell, New Jersey, twenty miles north of the British. The enemy (as our scouts told us) were camped near Allentown.

While our troops lay in the parched grass that evening beneath

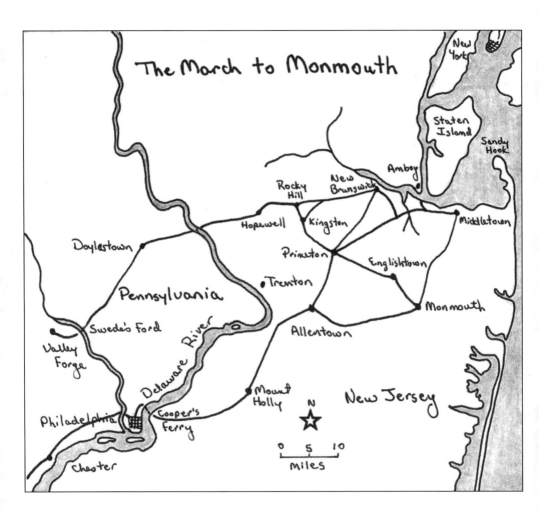

hazy stars (most were too exhausted to bother with their tents), General Washington called his officers together for a council of war. Genevieve sat just outside the General's marquee, under its canopy, copying by lamplight one of the General's many reports to Congress.

From her stool at a portable writing table, she could hear the thin, stubborn, self-righteous voice of General Charles Lee inside the tent, arguing with the other generals against any sort of major attack on the British column. The British had large troops of cavalry, he said; they had superiority in artillery. Furthermore, now that France had promised to support America, why not wait for the French navy to arrive? Why risk a major battle? We could lose the field, the Continental Army, and the war all in one day.

General Lee had no faith in Baron Steuben's training; our troops were still amateurs, while the British regulars were the best disciplined professionals in the world. No, much better to limit the engagement to skirmishing along the British flanks.

Arguing vehemently in opposition, Generals Wayne and Greene urged a full attack. Baron Steuben argued that a baggage train twelve miles long, with a divided army at each end, offered a rare target. And the troops were ready; the men were eager. They did not want to chase back and forth after the British for five months, as they had done all summer and fall a year ago.

General Washington listened to every officer, as was his practice throughout the war. However, because Lee was his highest ranking general (although he had never commanded troops on a battlefield), General Washington ultimately deferred to Lee's judgment. Rather than order a major attack, he would send forward only 1,500 troops under Brigadier Charles Scott "to act as occasion may serve on the enemy's left flank and rear." The main body of the Continental Army would continue "to preserve a relative position so as to be able to act as circumstances may require." Our troops would continue to follow the British, to harass the British, but no more than that.

Alexander Hamilton, disgusted, muttered that the plan "would have done honor to the most honorable society of midwives." General Anthony Wayne refused to sign the record of the meeting. The Marquis de Lafayette cursed in French.

After departing from the General's marquee, Greene and Wayne, with Lafayette, met at Baron Steuben's tent. Together they wrote a letter of protest, requesting once again a major attack against the British. All four officers signed the letter. Genevieve was still at her desk when a lieutenant arrived with a message for General Washington. A minute later, the General sent the lieutenant to summon his four officers. When they arrived, she heard the determination in General Washington's voice as he told them, "We shall attack."

General Clinton, no doubt aware that the Americans were camped just north of him, altered his route: rather than march north from Allentown toward New Brunswick on the Raritan River, he would march east toward Middletown, near the Atlantic Ocean. Admiral Howe would shift his fleet from Amboy to Sandy Hook, ready to ferry the British troops to New York.

General Washington accordingly marched us east, then southeast, as rapidly as we could walk in the unrelenting heat. On the night of June 27, we camped nine miles from Monmouth Court House, a hamlet at the junction of several roads: a junction through which the British column would have to pass.

Deferring once again to General Lee as senior officer, General Washington offered him the command of fifteen hundred troops who would advance during the night (as we had done at Trenton), then attack the British at dawn. (The General himself would stay back with the main army, ready to move wherever his troops were needed.) Lee declined the command, stating that such a small force was beneath his station. General Washington then gave the command to Lafayette, and increased the number of troops to five thousand. When Lee heard that the Advance Element was now a small army, he demanded his right to command it. General Washington, deferring once again to the etiquette of rank, returned the command to General Lee.

The Advance Element departed, without drums, right after supper. Captain Byrne's company remained in camp with the main army. We wondered, as did most of the nearly seven thousand men left behind, why our eagerness to attack the redcoats was so lamentably wasted.

The troops awoke on Sunday, June 28, 1778, to a morning as hot at dawn as most summer days became by noon. We stirred where we lay in the grass, then slowly sat up, with hardly the strength to stand. For the first time in the war, our officers allowed us to leave our haversacks beside the road as we marched the nine miles toward Monmouth Court House. (We would return at the end of the day to fetch our gear.) A farmhouse thermometer along the way read—a soldier called out to our column—"just over a hundred degrees." Walking southeast, toward the blazing sun, some of our soldiers began to stagger. In every company, two or three collapsed onto the sandy road. I dragged one of our lads off to the side, but then had to trot to catch up with my platoon. It was easier simply to step over the poor devils in the road.

At every stream, every brook, every warm and stagnant pond, we swarmed along the shore to drink, to dip our faces, to fill our canteens. Then quickly, quickly, we hurried back into the column, our faces cool for half a minute . . . until once more the sun burned our reddened brows.

Suddenly, to our astonishment, we spotted a crowd of American troops walking toward us in complete disorder. The soldiers—as we learned while they shuffled past—had been in Lee's Advance Element, but they were now in retreat! General Washington, mounted on Nelson, questioned the men, his voice sharp with anger. Then he galloped up the road toward what should have been Lee's position of attack.

We marched between a growing number of bewildered, disheartened, exhausted soldiers trudging along the fringes of the road. They had been on their feet all night; their officers had lost all contact with General Lee; they had retreated without any formal orders to retreat. From a mile or two ahead of us, we could hear random shots: nothing as coherent as a battle. We scanned the terrain, some of it hills tufted with pines, some of it swampy lowlands, for any sign of redcoats. Had we not been so well trained by the Baron, and had our hearts not been so determined to show that day what excellent soldiers we could be, a great number of our men, I am sure, would have faltered during that hour of enormous confusion.

However, not a single soldier from Captain Byrnes' company turned back. With Henry leading our little segment of the column, and Robert drumming in the rear, we were ready to battle the British all the way to Wall Street.

Then word swept back through the column: the regiment directly under Lee had fallen back early in the attack, though no one knew why. Other regiments then had to fall back as well, before the British could outflank them. Lee had failed to communicate with the other officers on the field. And now the British rear guard was attacking.

What should have been a surprise attack on the British, had suddenly become a British attack on our crumbling troops.

More news raced back through our column: General Washington had found Lee in the midst of the rout; the General had thundered at Lee in a rage; had sent him to the rear.

The firing increased ahead of us. Now we heard the booming of artillery, the first that morning.

Henry moved along our company as we marched steadily forward, telling us that General Washington had ordered Wayne (whose men were part of the Advanced Element) to halt his retreat and deploy his troops behind a hedgerow: that line would stand firm against the British until the main army (us) could rush to whatever defensive ground we could find.

Doubletiming at the Baron's hundred and twenty steps per minute, our shirts and trousers wet with sweat, we advanced in perfect order.

Then we heard—startling news that might be truth, might well be rumor—that General Cornwallis himself was leading his finest grenadiers to crush us.

&

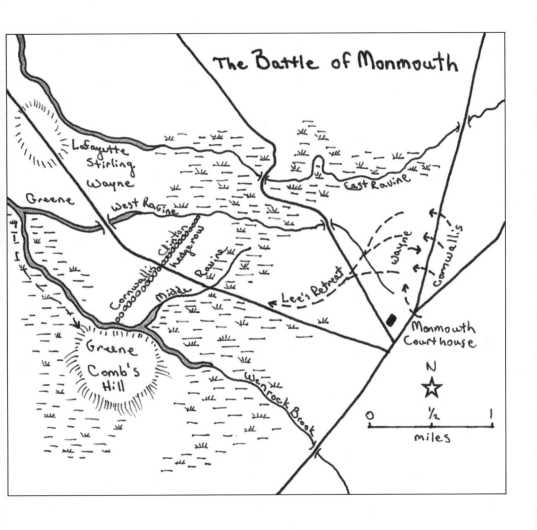

The Battle of Monmouth

Chapter Ninety-Seven

Benjamin.

THE BATTLE OF MONMOUTH

General Washington, now Commander in Chief on the battlefield, galloped to the head of our column of seven thousand troops. Pointing with his sword, he deployed General Greene's men to the right of the road, behind a rail fence part way up a sparsely wooded hill. With a shout from Greene, then from our officers, we wheeled to the right as smartly as we had wheeled on the Grand Parade.

While our regiment took its position along the flank of the hill, we could see General Sterling's regiment deploying to the left of the road. General Knox formed his artillery atop a hill above Sterling. Wayne's troops blocked the road half a mile ahead of us. Lafayette's troops blocked the road behind Sterling and Greene. The British had been chasing a ragged retreat, but they were about to confront a determined wall of Valley Forge warriors.

Looking down the slope through scattered pines, we could see a creek running along the foot of our hill. We spotted a narrow bridge where the road, a short distance beyond the bottom of the hill, crossed the creek. Beyond that bridge, General Wayne's courageous regiment held its ground behind a stone hedgerow as three brigades of redcoats, firing regular volleys, came advancing toward them. British cavalry now appeared from a woods much further up the road, preparing no doubt to gallop around Wayne's men so they could attack from the rear. Two more brigades of infantry paraded behind them, followed by a large troop of blue-coated Hessian grenadiers.

The Continental Army of twelve thousand (minus whatever number of men had retreated) faced an approaching force, each unit in perfect formation, that grew increasingly strong. But between us was not an open field, such as the British would have preferred. The battle would be fought on rolling irregular ground that dipped low enough in patches to become thick marsh and pools of black stagnant water: ground well suited for an army determined to turn a retreat into the hardest fought battle of the war.

As soon as Greene, Sterling, Knox, and Lafayette were in position, General Washington galloped forward, despite the constant blast of British musketry, to Wayne's line at the stone hedgerow. He apparently ordered General Wayne to fall back, for minutes later, Wayne's troops abandoned the wall in a well dressed column, bringing two artillery pieces with them. From our hillside a mile behind them, we watched the orderly maneuver with admiration.

(Talking later with Wayne's men, we learned they were outraged that *we* had not moved forward. They were extremely loath to give up their hedgerow.)

The redcoats advanced cautiously, perhaps suspecting a trap. Their line of scarlet was often indistinct, blurred by the shimmering heat on the plain.

When Wayne's troops reached the bridge, many of them left the road and scattered along the creek. Men with buckets brought water up to the artillery oxen. The regiment reassembled as quickly as it had dispersed, then continued a hundred yards further up the sloping road. The troops might well have passed between Stirling and Greene and then rested in the rear, for they had done their job: they had held back the first British charge until we had formed our line. Instead, to our astonishment, General Wayne's troops deployed into a line that blocked the road somewhat *ahead* of Stirling and Greene. They had given up their stone hedgerow, but damn if they wouldn't still take the brunt of any British attack.

The oxen were unhitched and led to safety further up the hill. The Continental Army now formed a roughly continuous line over half a mile long, some hundred feet above the British on their marshy plain. The last time His Majesty's Royal Army had fought us was at Germantown, when we had retreated through the fog in a rout. But that was way back last autumn, before Baron Steuben had ridden into camp.

I looked down again at the creek at the bottom of our hill. My mouth was so parched, my eyes so salted with sweat, that I could have sat right in the middle of that glinting silver streak and drunk a gallon or two. Could have floated face down in the cool current and guzzled. Then would have bobbed and splashed with the other lads until the British disappeared somewhere to the east and the sun disappeared somewhere to the west. Put the whole Continental Army down in that creek, and we'd probably drink it dry.

British cavalry now paraded across the bridge. They were clearly preparing for a direct charge. The pines were sparse enough that they could easily ride up the slope to where we stood behind our rail fence.

Three years ago, in June of 1775, General William Howe had learned on Breed's Hill how difficult it was to dislodge the Americans with a direct charge. But today he was on a ship somewhere at sea. General Clinton, fresh from the comforts of New York City and Philadelphia, apparently would have to learn the same lesson all over again.

And then suddenly, as two armies readied their swords, firelocks and bayonets, and readied their souls as well, for a clash on a horribly hot battlefield, a woman wearing a white blouse and bright red skirt emerged from the rear of General Wayne's line, carrying two buckets as she hurried, entirely alone, up the sloping sandy road. Despite scattered shots in the distance, we could hear her shout with a voice the equal of any sergeant's, "Water! Water! Where's the damn water? Don't you slugabeds see the men need water?"

⁓

Chapter Ninety-Eight

Genevieve.

The supply wagons followed the troops. Susanne sat beside me while I drove Sir William. She was in an almost unbearable (for me) state of worry, because for the first time since last December, she was separated from Robert and Henry. I had spent the past three years as a soldier's wife: a dozen times I had endured the nightmare of waiting at the edge of a battle for Benjamin, for Henry, and twice for Papa, to emerge alive from the madness. And now I had not only a worried wife but a frantic mother beside me, wringing her hands and fretting without stop as we drove in the dusty heat toward scattered irresolute firing: the early skirmish of a battle that had not yet really begun.

Caleb and Sally rode under the wagon's tarp. Caleb was awake but drowsy in the awful heat, while Sally wailed with frustration. I had bound her hands to her waist with a length of linen, because otherwise she would scratch the rash on her face.

Perhaps a quarter-mile behind the firing of muskets—no artillery as yet—a sergeant brown with dust ordered us to turn our wagons off the road into a field where the early summer corn was less than a foot tall. Without any shade, the sandy soil threw off heat like heat from the brick wall of an oven. While I considered what to do—I would unhitch Sir William and walk him into a nearby woods, then carry the children into the shade and fetch water for them with our tea kettle, then fetch water for Sir William with the wagon's bucket, while Susanne watched the children—Susanne announced as she climbed down from the seat that she was going to go find Robert.

"Susanne," I protested as I grabbed for her arm, but she was quickly beyond my reach, "Robert is with Henry. They're fine. Help me, please, with the children."

She stood in a state of severe agitation beside the wagon, looking first at me with wild desperation in her eyes, then toward the war that was just now finally becoming real. I knew I could not trust her with the children; she had a child of her own.

As I climbed down from my seat and unhitched Sir William, I searched the growing cluster of wagons for someone who might help.

With a surge of relief I spotted Amanda Dale, a washerwoman who had bunked with us in Valley Forge. "Amanda," I called over the rattle of wagons, "can you watch the children while I fetch water?" My fingers worked quickly at the last buckle on the harness.

"It's the men'll want water," she called back as she set the brake lever. "It ain't bullets, but buckets, that'll win the war today."

"Wait, wait!" I called to Susanne as she drifted toward the gunfire. She glanced back at me, frantic, her eyes begging me to come with her.

I hurried with Sir William into the nearby woods. Amanda, an ever reliable cooper's wife from Baltimore, climbed into the back of our wagon and soon emerged with Sally in her arms. Caleb squinted at the glare of the sun as he followed beside her.

I tethered Sir William to a crusty red pine. Amanda pulled at the knot of her apron, spread the square of brown linen on a patch of shade, then laid Sally, shrieking, on top of it. "Now you go," she said, looking up at me as she knelt beside my child. "I've water in a canteen, though it's as warm as soup. Don't worry about dinner. I'll find something for them." Already she knew I would not return before dark.

"Don't forget to water Sir William."

"Never forgot a horse in my life."

"Thank you, Amanda, thank you." I hurried back into the blazing sun, glanced about for Susanne—I did not see her but called her name—then climbed into the rear of our wagon for the bucket and tea kettle. Amanda was right: I'd best fetch water for the men.

When I tossed open the rear flap, Susanne was standing behind the wagon, waiting for me. I handed her the tea kettle and bucket. Turning back into the wagon, I unwrapped a piece of blackened burlap from around a blackened pot; I poured dried peas out of a smaller pot; then I climbed out from the heavy heat beneath the tarp into the fierce heat beneath the sun.

"Susanne," I said as I led her between parked wagons toward the road, "the men'll want water. Do what you can with your bucket while you're looking for Robert."

No longer filled with frenzied desperation, her dark eyes thanked me.

෴

Chapter Ninety-Nine

Benjamin.

The British cavalry paraded across the bridge, then formed a formidable scarlet line, shoulder to shoulder, along the bottom of the hill, about two hundred yards from General Wayne's troops, four hundred from ours. We had reinforced our rail fence with brush and branches and a few boulders small enough that the men could carry them. But when the cavalry drew their swords, we stared at the long ribbon of glinting blades and knew that our poor rail fence might as well have been built with straw.

Though the horsemen were still beyond musket range, our artillery could have reached them. But General Knox held his fire. Perhaps that was part of General Washington's strategy; or perhaps our Commander in Chief was gentleman enough that he would wait for the actual charge before (so we hoped) he ordered the cannons to fire their first volley.

The line of sabers began to advance, at a trot, up the gentle slope. The riders passed easily around the trees. We could hear the growing rumble of hooves as the cavalry began to canter; the jangle of bridle chains; a faint, indistinct order. Then we heard, from behind our line, the steady voice of General Greene, "Battalion! Make ready! Take aim!"

I raised my musket and sighted down its long barrel at the white belts that crisscrossed over an approaching red chest. We had orders not to fire until the British were forty paces from us: about eighty feet. My redcoat leaned forward in his saddle, holding his saber high. His mouth was open with a prolonged shout. His face—the face of a fury in a frenzy of rage—gleamed with sweat.

Then General Greene shouted the order, "Fire!" and I sinned once more against my English brother.

Genevieve, on the battlefield.

Walking as fast as we could over the crest of a hill, our bucket, tea kettle, and two pots still empty, we could see, looking down through the trees, the long double-ranked line of our men, their muskets raised. Three hundred yards beyond them—as we could see through the pine tops—a line of crimson cavalry came charging toward our troops. Their swords were so bright in the morning sun, so uniformly raised for the attack, that they blended into one giant scythe slicing toward us.

When the cavalry were thirty yards from our troops, a thousand muskets blasted at them. Artillery thundered atop a hill far to the left. Through heavy black smoke, I could see horses crashing to the ground. Some of the redcoats staggered up; others flailed and writhed where they lay. Horses thumped their heads against the earth. A second volley of muskets fired at the survivors. The few scattered riders still coming toward us jerked out of their saddles and tumbled into heaps. Their horses—those still on their feet—wheeled and fled in every direction.

A roar went up from our men, a brutal shout of victory. An officer shouted, "Front rank! Make ready! . . . Take aim! Fire!" Beyond the burst of smoke, I could vaguely see the red backs of soldiers running toward a bridge. A few riders galloped ahead of them. "Rear rank! Make ready! . . ."

Susanne gripped my hand. Between the musket volleys, and over the distant blast of cannons, I listened with horror to the wounded horses shrieking.

An express rider came galloping up the road toward us, a courier whom I knew, taking orders to the rear. I called to him as I stepped aside, pulling Susanne with me, "Where is General Greene deployed?"

"On the right flank," Daniel shouted as he rushed past, pointing over the reins. "Just above Wemrock Brook."

"Ahh," I said, as if I had already found my family and water both.

Susanne and I angled through the trees to the right, almost running now down the easy slope. Glancing again and again at the long line of our troops, I searched for Henry with his spontoon.

"Where'd you find water?"

Turning to the voice, I saw a woman in a red skirt running toward us through the trees, a bucket in each hand. She asked again as she slowed to a hurried walk, "Where'd you find yer water?" Her face was flushed with the heat.

"I . . . we haven't," I answered, holding my two empty pots.

She glared at us with disbelief. "Then what're you doin' , waitin' fer rain?"

"I'm told," I said, nodding toward a ravine far to the right, "that a brook runs somewhere near Greene's brigade."

"Well, if it ain't goin' to flow uphill, we better get on down there." She set off at a run toward the ravine, her legs kicking back her red skirt as she went.

"Susanne," I said, and then we were running too, about fifty feet behind the line of our troops.

(I had thought Susanne might scream and run when the cavalry charged; thought she might collapse with terror when our men fired their first volley; but she was right there with me, buckets in her hands, running to fetch water.)

The ground grew soggy as we descended into a gully beyond the end of our troops. The brook flowed not in a bed with a shoreline, but meandered through a broad marsh. If we wanted clean water, we would have to slog through wet sand that swallowed our shoes. We stumbled over tufts of swamp grass, waded through warm black water up to our knees—stagnant water with a scum on its surface—until finally we reached an amber brook about ten feet wide, with a slow but discernible current.

The first potful I poured over my head. I drank from the second potful, the water cool and clean. Then I dipped both pots, ready to carry water to the troops.

I glanced at Susanne: she had dunked herself completely under, and now she stood dripping, bucket filled, tea kettle filled, grinning at me and almost laughing.

"Goin' to wash yer petticoats too?" scolded our companion.

Carrying my pots by their handles, trying my best not to spill, I pulled my shoes up from the sucking sand as the woman—I remembered her from Valley Forge, a Mary somebody—waded toward shore in what Baron Steuben would have admired as doubletime.

My arms aching, my eyes stinging with sweat, I followed the red blur ahead of me behind the line of our troops until I realized that she was going to pass General Greene's regiment and take her buckets to whatever regiment it was that blocked the road.

"Susanne," I said, angling down the slope to the right. I could smell pine needles baking in the midday sun.

Because the drummer and fifer always stood behind the lines, I searched for a white boy and black boy standing near each other: Robert and Peter. There would be the company of Captain Henry Byrnes.

What comfort that would bring Susanne, I could not predict. For the next scarlet wave of war was surely gathering to break over us.

ଚ୍ଚ

Chapter One Hundred

Benjamin.

British infantry now defiled across the bridge, drums rumbling, flags flapping, as if on their way to celebrate the King's birthday in St. James Park. Wheeling to the right, they formed their precise ranks below Sterling's line. The Scottish Blackwatch in their kilts formed across the road; Wayne's men hooted catcalls at them. Grenadiers in tall bearskin hats formed directly in front of our line. Once again the bayonets glittered; once again, His Majesty was sending another wave of loyal subjects to their death.

Stepping out in front of us, Captain Byrnes addressed the sixty-four men in his company. We were to hold our position, no matter how hard the British attacked. Even if they turned Wayne, whose exhausted men must by now have used most of their cartridges, we were to hold.

Of course we would hold. Send the whole damn twelve-mile army at us. We would hold.

I could see about a mile of road crossing the battlefield, from our side of the bridge to a distant woods. That stretch of public thoroughfare was littered from one end to the other with scarlet bodies. Had those dead soldiers been able to rise up on their feet, they could have formed half a dozen companies.

And despite what had happened to them, they probably would.

Why does a man so easily relinquish his young life? Why does he so blindly believe that a king must be quite right in marching him with drums and flag to his death? Why does a man so willingly forget the excitement he once felt, as a boy, when awakening upon a summer's bright morn? How can he today toss away so heedlessly a lifetime of his woman's loving kisses? The joy of children who run to greet him? Why, why, why are we so willing to drink war's chalice of poison?

I heard a woman's voice—Genevieve's voice—calling, "Water, soldiers, water." Searching between the ranks of our company, I was astonished to see her passing a black iron soup pot—it might well have been ours—to a soldier who grabbed it with both hands. She looked toward me, looked toward where she knew I would be positioned, and called, "The pot's empty. I'll be back."

I had never before seen her on a battlefield, nor had I ever seen her so mud-smeared and disheveled. But then, she was like her brother: Genevieve never stopped growing.

As she hurried away with two black pots, she called, "Susanne!" A moment later, Henry's bride appeared from the ranks with a tea kettle and bucket, running to catch up with Genevieve. I was hardly surprised; I knew the woman had far more fire in her than anyone had yet seen. The two hurried behind the rear of our line and then descended a slope until I could no longer see them. They were headed, I guessed, toward a stretch of the creek safely to the west of us.

"Front rank! Make ready!" called Henry.

Looking forward, I cocked the firelock with my thumb, then held the musket upright to the left of my face.

The grenadiers were advancing toward us, marching over bodies as they had marched over bodies up the slope of Breed's Hill.

"Take aim!"

I stepped back six inches with my right foot for balance, dropped the muzzle down and brought the butt to my shoulder, shifted my left hand forward, then eyed along the barrel at a fellow wearing a bearskin hat in the hundred degree heat.

"Fire!"

Aye, we fired. And aye, my poor mate toppled backwards, while his mother back home wondered with a sigh when she would ever see her boy again. In a nameless grave he would lie, tomorrow, if anybody bothered to bury him.

The grenadiers still on their feet leveled their volley at us. Then they charged with their bayonets. A dozen times before in the war we had broken and run before a British bayonet charge had reached us. But today, not a man among us turned and fled. While Henry directed the firing, platoon after platoon made ready and then fired their volleys, thinning the redcoats that came lumbering toward us.

Still they came. "Goddamn!" shouted one of our men, as we had heard the Baron a hundred times shout, "Goddamn!"

When the grenadiers, like a pack of wolves, tried to break through the rail fence, we learned that though rails might not stop a musket ball, and certainly not a cannonball, they did bring a charging soldier to enough of a halt that one of us could bayonet him through the chest. Bodies soon hung over the rails like red rags hung out to dry.

At scattered points, the fence gave way and the maddened British poured through. But wherever our line weakened, General Washington almost immediately appeared, galloping on Nelson with his sword pointing there, and there, and there as he shouted orders to reinforcements. Our battle-weary troops needed nothing more than to hear that booming Virginia voice behind them; they unbuckled a cartridge box from a dead grenadier, reloaded their musket and fired anew for the General who had brought them through Valley Forge.

Every redcoat who managed to reach our line that day quickly became either a corpse or a wounded prisoner. We gave way not a foot, though Cornwallis shifted his attacks: center, left, and then right again.

Genevieve suddenly appeared at my side, no longer with two heavy pots but with buckets, borrowed perhaps from some wagon in the rear. She handed one bucket to me, the other to the lad beside me. I leaned my musket against the fence, then wrapped my hands around the wet wood and savored the sweetest, coolest, finest drink of water in all my life.

Beside me, behind me, I could hear other men hollering for their turn. I might well have swallowed half the bucket before I passed it on.

Then I turned to my wife. She wiped the sweat from my face with her apron, spoke my name with a voice from another world—the world of an apple orchard blossoming one evening in May, the world where children giggle and laugh, the world where Shakespeare speaks atop a hill overlooking Boston Harbor—and then she kissed me . . . I savored the sweetest, warmest, finest kiss in all my life. "Water!" shouted someone down the line. "The durn bucket's empty!"

I watched her leap in her blue skirt over a dead grenadier, saw her grab the empty bucket from a soldier's outstretched arm, heard her call, "Susanne!" Then I heard Henry shout from the opposite direction, "Prime and load!"

We slapped our cartridge boxes, seized a cartridge, bit off its end and shook a bit of powder into the pan.

As we readied our firelocks, we watched another brigade of sacrificial grenadiers form on the field at the bottom of the hill.

Genevieve.

Susanne found her Robert and her Henry, and a hundred other thirsty soldiers with her buckets that day. She stepped over the dead, knelt by the wounded, as if she had spent years on a battlefield. No man in her husband's company went without water for more than an hour. What would have happened had her son, drumming out orders from his post behind the second rank, or her husband, pacing among his men with a word of encouragement, been struck by a musket ball, I do not know. But as long as she could glance in their direction when she returned with fresh buckets, and see her boy, who listened sharply for every order from his father, and see her husband, who rarely took his eyes from the field beyond the fence, she moved with the agility and courage of a deaf person: a person who could not hear the blast of musket volleys; could not hear the six-pounders every time they split the sky with their cannonade; could not hear the gurgling cry of a man with a ball in his lung; nor the screams of berserk rage and demonic hatred when a British bayonet charge tried again to break through the fence. Her face was as dark from musket smoke as every soldier's face. Her apron was smeared with the blood she had wiped from soldiers' wounds. Her skirt was filthy with mud from the marsh where we dipped our buckets. But Susanne seemed not to hear the hellish bedlam. Her eyes never showed a moment of fear.

It was something far beyond courage. Nor was it some sort of faith, for she had already lost one husband and knew clearly that she might well lose another. But while she could—until her husband or her son or she herself was taken away in an instant by a musket ball or a cannonball or an exploding shell—she would fight not against the British, but against Death itself. She took the shock and the grief and the loneliness and the despair which she had already suffered, and she turned them into defiance.

ℭ

Chapter One Hundred One

Benjamin, in one of the war's
most brilliant maneuvers.

General Washington rode behind our line, no longer on Nelson, but now a bay horse with a black mane and tail. Cornwallis had moved his attack to the opposite end of the field, against Sterling's line, and thus I was able to watch the General as he rode up to General Greene. He pointed south with his sword, toward a hill about a mile away—to the right of British troops waiting to attack, and perhaps a bit behind them.

I did not know where Baron Steuben was then. I had not seen him since he had roared orders to our column in the midst of chaos that morning. But during the next half hour, I hoped that he was somewhere nearby, observing our sudden and secret deployment as the eight companies in General Greene's regiment performed the most difficult, and successful, maneuver in the Battle of Monmouth.

Leaving the fence to reinforcements from the rear, we marched to the right in a rapid column down the slope to the very spot where Genevieve and Susanne had been fetching water. Like most of the other men, I held my musket over my head in one hand and my cartridge box over my head in my other hand, then crouched down until my chest and shoulders and even my head were submerged in the cool, silent water. A moment was all I had, for other troops followed close behind. Yet a moment was enough for a gulp and a bath and a bit of boyish delight.

Hidden from the British by willows that grew along the edge of the marsh, our column waded toward higher ground. Then we wheeled left and marched double time across sun-baked sandy flats for about a mile. Moving parallel to a branch of the stream, we were hidden by both a long undulating stand of willows, and just above them, by a stand of scrubby pine. A few soldiers collapsed as we crossed the soft hot sand; most, however, kept the rapid pace.

Angling to the left, we climbed the back of a sparsely wooded hill. Perhaps the heat in the region, summer after summer, was too much for more than a few scattered pines to grow; perhaps the sandy earth never held water long enough for a seedling's roots to survive. Whatever the

522 • BOOTMAKER TO THE NATION

reason, the baked and barren hills of Monmouth made me long for, as I dragged my feet up that slope, the cold snowy hills of Valley Forge, with their thick forest of huge and abundant oak.

And then—as Henry and I had once climbed the back of Dorchester Heights and then peered over the crest at the enemy in Boston—our regiment, advancing in well dressed ranks to the crest of Comb's Hill, discovered that we not only looked down at the British assaulting our American line, but we looked down at their *backs*. We understood immediately what General Washington had foreseen: our five hundred muskets, and especially our cannons—the oxen had managed to drag a few six-pounders across the marsh—would enfilade the British troops, striking them from the rear. We now controlled a long stretch of the road running through the battlefield, and thus we could prevent any more British regiments from advancing. We might well turn a British retreat into a butchery and a rout.

Our cannoneers quickly ranged on the British line; their second volley of grapeshot blasted through the ranks of redcoats. We watched, and cheered, as the grenadiers, with astonishingly good order, withdrew by companies until they sheltered behind the very stone hedgerow where General Wayne's regiment had sheltered that morning, but on its other side.

Though the British swung their cannons toward us and soon ranged their artillery against our artillery, and though a battalion of infantry attempted an assault on Comb's Hill, they could not dislodge us.

We commanded the battlefield so completely that by late afternoon, General Wayne's regiment of incomparable warriors *advanced* toward the British rear guard. Their first early morning attack (under Lee's mismanagement), their orderly retreat, their defense at the stone hedgerow against Cornwallis' finest troops (at that point, they were General Washington's only hope), their second orderly withdrawal, and their long defiant stand across the road—ahead of Sterling's line, ahead of Greene's line—had not yet been enough for General Wayne and his inexhaustible men: they now defiled over the bridge, then spread out and swept slowly, steadily south across the battlefield carpeted with dead redcoats and the brown lumps of horses and the abandoned wreckage of artillery carriages. Though some of the men fell to British musketry as they advanced, Wayne's ragged patriots pushed the scarlet companies ahead of them, until by sunset they had almost reached the hedgerow where some of their own men had lain all day, dying and dead.

If it was heroes that America needed that day, she had them, in abundance.

When finally the ball of orange fire disappeared beyond the hills, leaving behind a heavy damp darkness, the musket firing down on the plain diminished . . . and then ceased. We could hear faint scattered orders as the British withdrew. We could even hear the artillery pulling back: the drovers cracked whips and called to their oxen.

In the full darkness of night, we could see the tiny orange sparks of British campfires two or three miles to the east, where the road curved toward Monmouth Court House. At the other end of the battlefield, we could see fires burning along the American line, and a few further up the hill. Wayne's men lit fires along the hedgerow, to which they had advanced in the dark.

We ourselves on Comb's Hill had no haversacks, no food, only the four buckets which Genevieve and Susanne had brought. Some of the men now used them to fetch water at the foot of the hill. Few bothered with a fire. We simply lay down on the warm earth—"slept on our arms," as we were ordered—and remained ready for any attack during the night. Or for the war to begin again tomorrow at dawn.

Genevieve lay down beside me. I held her in my arm as I stared up, a soldier still alive, at the hazy stars. For a while she cried, though she said not a word.

Nearby, Robert slept between his mother and father.

(We heard the next day, from the men in Sterling's regiment, that General Washington and the Marquis de Lafayette had slept in the open as well, side by side on the General's black cape. They were but two of the thousands of dark figures curled and stretched and sprawled on the ground behind the rail fence.)

The frogs croaked down in the marsh. Crickets rasped in the grass atop our hill. But neither the frogs nor the crickets were loud enough to hide the cries of wounded soldiers scattered across the battlefield. Some called out with words distinct in the night; some wailed with pain. While no one, no one, came to their aid with even a bucket of water.

༄

Chapter One Hundred Two

Benjamin.

When we awoke in the rude glare of the morning sun—even an arm laid over our eyes could not keep it away—we sat up, peered groggily down from our hill, and discovered that the British were gone. Scouts brought news to General Greene, news which he allowed to sweep through camp: the British had left their fires burning while they stole away toward the coast. (As we had done at Trenton.)

We did not pursue them. General Washington gave us two days of rest, while riders took his dispatches to the newspapers of the nation: the Continental Army had stood firm, in battle formation, against "the flower of the British Army." At the end of the day, we had held the field. The British, unwilling to risk another battle, had retreated to their ships.

Few soldiers beyond those in our company had noticed the labors of Susanne and Genevieve. The woman in the red skirt, however, had earned the gratitude of General Wayne's entire Pennsylvania regiment. Word passed through the encampment that a woman of German background, a farmer's wife named Mary Ludwig Hays, had carried buckets of water to Wayne's troops all through the sweltering day, no matter where they stood.

What was more, when her husband John, an artilleryman who sponged a cannon, was wounded in the leg by a British ball, she herself had taken over as the swabber, dunking a wad of lamb's wool into a bucket and running it down the hot cannon barrel to douse any sparks before the six-pounder was reloaded.

The Pennsylvanians called her "Molly Pitcher," a better name certainly than Molly Bucket, and more apt while they roared a rousing song to her as they raised a pitcher of ale.

The British marched to Middletown, then on to Sandy Hook, where they embarked onto Admiral Howe's fleet. The frigates ferried them to Staten Island, Manhattan Island, and Long Island. Thus "the flower of the British Army" was exactly where it had been a year ago, before it had sailed and marched to Philadelphia.

We ourselves marched north to New Brunswick on the Raritan River, where we took a bath. On July 4, 1778, the second anniversary of our Independence, we celebrated our victory at Monmouth with a double gill of rum and a boisterous night of dancing.

We learned from our New Jersey neighbors that during the night after the battle, while General Clinton was hastening toward the coast, nearly a thousand of the enemy had deserted, most of them Germans. The Hessian serfs had been sold by their masters to the British Army for the duration of the war. But they had been in America long enough—and especially in Philadelphia, where farmers in the market-place often spoke a dialect of German known as Pennsylvania Dutch— to decide that they wanted no more of King George's futile war.

Almost none of the deserters joined the Continental Army. Instead, they went off to work on farms where people spoke their language. And so they became American farmers themselves.

As for General Charles Lee, the troops who marched, and fled, in his doomed Advance Element were gratified to learn, some months later, that a court martial had found him guilty of three serious charges. Congress later dismissed him from any further service in the Continental Army.

From New Brunswick, we marched north into New York State. We crossed Hudson's River at King's Ferry, then set up our tents at a new encampment near the village of White Plains. Thus we were back to where we had been in October of 1776; once again we guarded the British, who were confined to the three islands of New York. (And one small island off the coast of Rhode Island.)

Genevieve copied a letter written by General Washington at his new headquarters, a letter in which he wrote with both amazement and his characteristic faith,

> "It is not a little pleasing nor less wonderful to contemplate that after two years maneuvering and undergoing the strangest vicissitudes that perhaps ever attended any one contest since the Creation, both armies are brought back to the very point they set out from, and that that which was the offending party in the beginning is now reduced to the use of the spade and pickax for defense. The hand of Providence has been so conspicuous in all this that he must be worse than an infidel that lacks faith, and more than wicked that

has not gratitude enough to acknowledge his obligations—
but it will be time enough for me to turn preacher when my
present appointment ceases, and therefore I shall add no
more on the Doctrine of Providence."

We had not yet defeated the British, but we had made clear to them that neither could they ever defeat us.

And now the French were coming. A French fleet under Count d'Estaing had been sighted off the coast of Virginia, and then New York.

From White Plains in October, 1776, we had retreated; but now back in White Plains in July, 1778, with our naval ally off the coast, with the training we had gained in Valley Forge, and with the victory that we had earned at Monmouth, we were ready for an entirely new stage of the war.

ജ

Chapter One Hundred Three

Benjamin.

But a new stage of the war did not begin.

For the next three stagnant years, from July of 1778 to August of 1781, General Washington and the Continental Army camped north of New York City, guarding Hudson's River and New England, while General Clinton dithered. Our several encampments formed a long crescent stretching from New Jersey to Connecticut; the men oiled their muskets while General Clinton attended concerts of Haydn and Bach, performances of Shakespeare's *Richard II* and *Othello.* Our regulars lived in log huts during the winters, in tents during the summers, while General Clinton, who had been raised in New York as the son of the British royal governor, traveled by carriage between his four elegant residences on Manhattan Island.

General Washington was never provided by the thirteen States with enough recruits to force the British out of New York. The French navy never cooperated in either an attack or a blockade. New York City thus belonged as much to England as Jamaica or Gibraltar.

The Battle of Monmouth in June, 1778 was the last major battle in the north. During the next three years, General Washington divided his army so that the Northern Department confined General Clinton to New York City, while the Southern Department struggled to prevent General Cornwallis from conquering the southern States. A third Department fought along the western frontier, where British and Loyalist troops, with their Indian allies, raided isolated farms and villages, especially in western Pennsylvania and New York. The war that began on Lexington's green had spread hundreds of miles across the continent, so that soldiers from the North saw with their own eyes the cruelty and poverty of slavery in the South. And soldiers from all along the eastern seaboard marched across vast areas of fertile land in the West.

In the North during those three long years, General Washington struggled to maintain some vestige of public support for his army. When Americans learned that France would send her army and navy to assist the Continental Army, many of them felt that the war was as good as won. Whereas every farmer near Lexington in 1775 had sprung from his bed to answer the alarm, many young men in 1778 felt no such urgency. They paid for others to fight in their place; the recruits who appeared in camp were often young boys, cripples, or slaves. Recruits collected the clothing, equipment, and firelocks that the army provided, then disappeared to sell their gear elsewhere. Other recruits deserted, then signed up again at a different location for a second bounty.

Recruiting was made especially difficult because soldiers were rarely paid, and only in Continental paper money, while the booming economy in America enabled war profiteers to become immensely wealthy. Why should a soldier leave his warm home to live unpaid in a cold, smoky hut, when he could be raising corn and cattle to sell to the Continental Army (or to the British) at prices that would surely never come again? Better, a man could sail along the coast aboard a privateer and share with the crew the plunder of every British ship they captured.

General Greene, still our Quartermaster, had to watch closely the wily merchants who supplied the Army. Wagons would arrive at the various encampments with barrels of rotten meat, because the pickling brine had been drained to lighten the load. Our cooks opened barrels only partially filled with flour: in the middle of the barrel was a hidden plug of wood. Blankets, when unfolded, were a yard short. Shoes were made from leather scraps. Desperately needed gunpowder often proved to be, when tested by the artillery, "bad and not to be depended on."

Cheating the Continental Army became so prevalent that several new phrases entered the American language: "mushroom gentlemen" were overnight aristocrats who sprang up like mushrooms after a rain; "to jockey" Continental dollars meant to spend them before they lost value; and "smart money" was the extra salary earned by a recruiter who manipulated his list of recruits.

General Washington witnessed firsthand the American greed for profit and luxury when he traveled to Philadelphia in December, 1778 to meet with Congress (which had returned from York). He discovered that delegates, as well as merchants, rode in elegant carriages, entertained each other at expensive balls, and dined around tables laden with more food than they could possibly eat. He was so shocked by the wartime fortunes earned and spent in Philadelphia that he wrote he would never "be again surprised at anything."

He and Lady Washington spent the weeks of January and early

February, 1779 in Philadelphia; they were the guests of honor at a party celebrating their twentieth wedding anniversary. He nevertheless wrote privately in a letter, "Speculation, peculation, and an insatiable thirst for riches seem to have got the better of every other consideration and almost of every order of men." The elaborate entertainment not only squandered money, but diverted people's attention from the war that he and his troops were still fighting: "an assembly, a concert, a dinner, or a supper that will cost three or four hundred pounds will not only take men off from acting in but even thinking of this business."

He was well aware that while the value of Continental dollars was decreasing daily, his hosts were manipulating the inflation to make a profit. He wrote to his brother Jack, back home in Virginia, that the "monopolizers, forestallers, and engrossers" made honorable men want to "curse their own species for possessing so little virtue and patriotism." He wished that "those murderers of our cause" could be hung in public on a tall gallows. "No punishment in my opinion is too great for the man who can build his greatness upon his country's ruin."

By the time he was able to leave Philadelphia, General Washington understood that many of his countrymen had no desire to end the war while they were making such grand profits: "It is now consistent with the views of speculators, various tribes of moneymakers, and stockjobbers of all denominations to continue the war for their own private emolument." He knew that many of America's former leaders had left Congress to work in their own State governments (Thomas Jefferson had returned to the Virginia legislature in 1776), and thus he recommended that the "ablest and best men" return to the Congress and there conduct "an entire reformation."

The troops throughout the army felt a growing resentment against both Congress, which rarely paid them, and the civilian population, which either cheated them or ignored them. Their brooding anger eventually led to threats of mutiny.

The winter of 1779-1780 was the coldest winter of the eight-year war. Hudson's River froze, and then the entire harbor below New York City froze as well. Cavalry rode back and forth between the Battery and Staten Island, a distance of six miles. Sleighs rather than ships brought supplies to the British troops.

Eleven thousand American troops were encamped, for the second time, near Morristown, New Jersey. The Army was now too large to be housed with families, so the troops were ordered to build log huts in a wooded area known as Jockey Hollow, three miles south of the village. The brigades were still building their huts when, in December, 1779, they were struck by a blizzard that nearly buried their tents. Before the roads could be cleared so that horses might push through with food, more snow fell on December 28. During three days in early January, a blizzard drove so fiercely through the encampment that sentries were blinded at their posts.

Joseph Plumb Martin, a private from Connecticut, wrote about that January:

"At one time it snowed the greater part of four days successively, and there fell nearly as many feet deep of snow, and here was the keystone of the arch of starvation. We were absolutely, literally starved. I do solemnly declare that I did not put a single morsel of victuals into my mouth for four days and as many nights, except a little black birch bark which I gnawed off a stick of wood, if that can be called victuals. I saw several of the men roast their old shoes and eat them, and I was afterwards informed by one of the officers' waiters, that some of the officers killed and ate a favorite little dog that belonged to one of them."

The winter of 1780 continued with storm after storm. As late as March 31, another eight inches of snow fell. General Washington, who had moved his headquarters to Morristown, wrote about his fifth winter as Commander in Chief, "The oldest people now living in this country do not remember so hard a Winter as the one we are now emerging from."

Even springtime did not bring a sufficient increase in provisions to the Morristown encampment. By May 25, 1780, two Connecticut regiments had reached their limit. Joseph Plumb Martin wrote about his fellow soldiers:

"The men were now exasperated beyond endurance; they could not stand it any longer. They saw no other alternative but to starve to death, or break up the army, give all up and go home. This was a hard matter for the soldiers to think upon. They were truly patriotic, they loved their country, and they had already suffered everything short of death in its cause; and now, after such extreme hardships to give up all was too much, but to starve to death was too much also.

What was to be done? Here was the army starved and naked,
and there their country sitting still and expecting the army
to do notable things while fainting from sheer starvation."

At evening roll call, the soldiers from Connecticut "began to show their dissatisfaction by snapping at the officers and acting contrary to their orders." The officers merely dismissed the troops and returned to their own huts.

The two regiments, however, did not leave the parade ground. One soldier angrily thumped the butt of his musket on the fresh green grass and called to his mates, "Who will parade with me?" Several hundred soldiers immediately formed in better order than they had formed for their officers; then with their muskets, they paraded on their own back and forth across the field.

Armed men drilling without orders posed a symbolic threat to the officers' authority. Troops from Pennsylvania were ordered to surround the unruly regiment from Connecticut. But when the Pennsylvania troops learned why the Connecticut regulars were demonstrating— simply because they lacked provisions—the Pennsylvanians threatened to join them. They were quickly ordered back to their huts.

The men from Connecticut ended their demonstration peacefully:

"After our officers had left us to our own option, we dis-
persed to our huts and laid by our arms of our own accord,
but the worm of hunger gnawing so keen kept us from being
entirely quiet."

Without their muskets, the soldiers gathered in groups back on the parade, where they spent the remainder of the evening

". . . venting our spleen at our country and government,
then at our officers, and then at ourselves for our imbecility
in staying there and starving in detail for an ungrateful peo-
ple who did not care what became of us, so they could enjoy
themselves while we were keeping a cruel enemy from
them."

The unsupervised drilling had its effect. Joseph Plumb Martin wrote, "Our stir did us some good in the end, for we had provisions directly after, so we had no great cause for complaint for some time."

In a letter to Congress, General Washington wrote that the unauthorized drilling "has given me infinitely more concern than any thing that has ever happened." It was the first tear in the fabric of our Army, a worn and threadbare cloth that might suddenly be ripped to rags.

In January, 1781, Pennsylvania troops mutinied for ten days, once again because of a lack of provisions and pay. One officer was killed, two others were wounded. However, none of the soldiers threatened to join the British. Once their grievances had been heard, the men returned to their duties.

Two weeks later, two hundred New Jersey regulars mutinied. To end the threat of a sequence of mutinies, General Washington responded with severity: two of the leaders were shot by a firing squad. The remainder of the men returned to their duty, and the spirit of rebellion vanished, at least for a while.

Despite these limited mutinies, a fierce and loyal spirit remained among the troops of the Continental Army. Though Congress and the American people had all but abandoned them, they themselves would continue to fight for the America in which they deeply believed.

ॐ

Chapter One Hundred Four

*Genevieve, dipping my quill
into a well of grief.*

Before General Washington and the Continental Army departed from Valley Forge in June, 1778, Lo Ha Hes, Ka Tsi Tsya Ha, and fifty-seven other Oneidas who had traveled and fought with the Army asked the General for permission to return home. The Iroquois people were still divided against each other; the Oneidas wanted to be with their own people, on their own land. General Washington agreed. To show their gratitude, both he and Lady Washington presented gifts to the Oneida people, including a woolen shawl from Lady Washington to Polly Cooper, one of the cooks at headquarters.

On July 3, 1778, an American Loyalist named Colonel John Butler led four hundred fellow Tories and five hundred Indian warriors from the Seneca and Delaware tribes in an attack on a cluster of settlements in western Pennsylvania. Most of the men from the settlements had joined the Continental Army; the families left behind in the Wyoming Valley were therefore especially vulnerable. Colonel Butler's small army slaughtered the defenders of three stockaded forts, plundered and burned nearly a thousand farmhouses along the Susquehanna River, and left hundreds of corpses, many of them women and children, strewn along the shore and floating downstream.

On November 11, 1778, a Mohawk warrior named Thayendanegea (known to white settlers as Joseph Brant) led two hundred Tories and five hundred Iroquois in an attack on Cherry Valley, a settlement about fifty miles west of Albany, New York. Once again, children and women were butchered, farms were destroyed, and prisoners were taken away to Iroquois villages, where some of the men were slowly burned to death.

In response to these and other frontier massacres, General Washington ordered a military operation against the Iroquois. During the summer of 1779, Major General John Sullivan led 4,400 hundred troops into western New York State. The soldiers destroyed about forty Iroquois villages, chopped down large orchards of fruit trees, uprooted extensive vegetable gardens, and burned great quantities of ripening corn. Most of the Iroquois had fled before General Sullivan's army arrived; the warriors who had attacked the white settlements were not captured. As Major Jeremiah Fogg wrote in his journal on September 30, 1779, "The nests are destroyed, but the birds are still on the wing."

Though Joseph Brant had led warriors from only four of the Six Nations of the Iroquois against Cherry Valley, and though the Oneida and Tuscarora had fought against their fellow Iroquois at the Battle of Oriskany, little distinction was made by white Americans between the two nations who had fought as their allies, and the four nations (Mohawk, Onondaga, Cayuga, and Seneca) which had supported the British. Accordingly, General Sullivan sent a detachment under Colonel Richard Butler to destroy every village between Lake Cayuga and Fort Stanwix: country that was predominantly Oneida. As General Sullivan wrote in his report after the New York campaign, his troops had "not left a single settlement or field of corn . . . this side of Niagara."

Johannes Kesslaer rejoined the Continental Army in October, 1781, in Yorktown, Virginia.

However, Ka Tsi Tsya Ha and Lo Ha Hes, the Oneidas who had helped to bring my two children into the world, vanished completely.

Perhaps they were caught in one of Joseph Brant's raids against Oneida traitors. Perhaps they tried to explain to an officer in General Sullivan's army that they had marched and camped for two years with General Washington. Perhaps a bitter settler in the Mohawk Valley sought revenge against any Iroquois who came near his farm.

Or perhaps She's Carrying Flowers and His Long Road, like most of the Oneidas who somehow managed to survive the war, were forced by land developers to resettle in the distant wilderness of Canada or Wisconsin.

⬥

Chapter One Hundred Five

Benjamin, chronicling briefly

THE WAR IN THE SOUTH

Brought to a halt in the North, the British command moved their military efforts to the South. British troops captured Savannah, Georgia in December, 1778, and then Charleston, South Carolina in May, 1780. The government in London expected Loyalists in the South to rise up in support of General Cornwallis' army. British troops should soon be able to control North Carolina, and then march north to Virginia, the largest of the thirteen colonies and the most heavily populated. With half of America in the King's grip, the northern half would no doubt beg His Majesty for a peaceful reconciliation.

In the South, geography had created three distinct populations.

The first settlers built their farms on the rich land along rivers that poured into the sea. Plantation owners along the eastern belt were now wealthy; they wanted minimal British interference in the form of taxation or regulation.

The next wave of settlers cleared the hilly land further west, far from the major seaports and capitals. Their argument was not with London, but with the coastal plantation aristocracy who regulated prices and controlled the economy.

The third wave of settlers were the Over-the-Mountain men and their families, pioneers who cleared the land beyond the Appalachian Mountains. They lived so distant from the Atlantic coast that they all but ignored laws passed by the legislature. Their argument was with the British, who with the hated Proclamation Line of 1763 had attempted to limit westward settlement. Worse, the British often incited the Indians to attack the most remote homesteads, causing daily fear and occasional terror all along the frontier.

Thus only a portion of the people in the South viewed the British as their enemy. A great number of Southerners in the middle belt viewed their American neighbors as their enemy. Into this mix of tinder, the British tossed a spark: they offered freedom to any slave who would join His Majesty's Army. When thousands of slaves disappeared from their farms and plantations, many Loyalists became Whigs, not because they supported independence from Britain, but because they were enraged at the British for stealing their property.

The war in the South became a civil war in which old grudges were settled. Farmers in one valley raided farmers in the next valley. Fierce battles were fought without a single British redcoat, without a single American regular, on either side. The conflict quickly became less a war of principle than a war of revenge.

As the British marched through Georgia, South Carolina, and then North Carolina, they continued, as they had done in the North, to burn and plunder. They gained no more support along their route than they had in Massachusetts. Instead, they intensified the civil war's fierce brutality.

One British cavalry officer, Lieutenant Colonel Banastre Tarleton, led his dragoons in an attack against a detachment of American infantry under Colonel Abraham Buford, at Waxhaws, South Carolina in May of 1780. As soon as the Americans had fired their first musket volley, Tarleton charged with his mounted soldiers into the line of infantrymen and slashed at them with their sabers. Colonel Buford waved a white flag of surrender, but Tarleton shouted to his men to give "no quarter." The British troops butchered Americans who had laid down their arms. Dismounting, the cavalry ran their swords through wounded Americans on the ground. Over two hundred and fifty of Buford's three hundred and fifty men were massacred at Waxhaws.

"Tarleton's quarters!" thereafter became the battle cry in the South, as Whigs of every sort attacked Loyalists of every sort.

The Continental Army initially suffered through disaster after disaster in the South. General Washington had managed to escape with his army from New York before the British captured the city in 1776; but when the British captured the strategic seaport of Charleston in May, 1780, they captured Major General Benjamin Lincoln and his 5,500 troops as well. The loss of Charleston and the army defending it was the most severe American defeat during the entire Revolutionary War. Though General Lincoln would later be exchanged for a British officer, most of his men were doomed to starvation and disease in the hideous British prisons.

Congress appointed General Horatio Gates, the officer who had defeated Burgoyne at Saratoga, to command the Continental Army in the

South. But on August 16, 1780, near the village of Camden, South Carolina, General Cornwallis, with help from Tarleton and his cavalry, outmaneuvered Gates and severely defeated him. Over eight hundred American regulars were killed or wounded; a thousand more were taken prisoner. The regimental commander under Gates, Major General Baron de Kalb (who had sailed to America with the Marquis de Lafayette), was wounded eleven times and died on the battlefield.

General Gates himself fled north on his horse until, after riding for three and a half days, he reached Hillsborough, North Carolina, one hundred eighty miles away. The nation, and the world, soon learned of his shameful flight.

Following this disaster, General Washington appointed his loyal Quartermaster, Major General Nathanael Greene, to take charge of the campaign in the South. Greene gladly left his desk at West Point on Hudson's River. Well schooled in military strategy by his Commander in Chief, he rode south toward a completely different kind of war than what he had known on the battlefields of Massachusetts, New York, New Jersey, and Pennsylvania.

(Although Captain Byrne's company had fought several times under General Greene, we remained in New York. Greene would command troops recruited mainly in the South.)

General Greene met with Congress in Philadelphia to receive final orders. When he continued further south on November 3, 1780, he was accompanied by Baron Steuben. The Baron trained a detachment of the Continental Army in Virginia (troops which he would later send south), while Greene reorganized the Army in the Carolinas.

On December 2, 1780, at headquarters in Charlotte, North Carolina, General Greene met General Gates and took over the command of the Southern Army. During the next four months, he exceeded General Washington's warmest hopes: first, his troops cleared the Carolinas and Georgia of every British outpost except the seaports of Charleston and Savannah, where the British sat as helpless as they sat in New York. Then he maneuvered Lord Cornwallis northward into Virginia, where General Washington and the main body of the Continental Army could catch him. General Greene thus proved himself to be, in the course of the entire war, General Washington's most brilliant field officer.

Nathanael Greene possessed several extraordinary qualities which enabled him to take the South back from the British.

When the war began in 1775, he faced three decisions, any one of which could have prevented many other men from enlisting. He had been raised as a Quaker in Rhode Island, and was forbidden by his faith to take up arms in a war. Between devotion to his church and devotion to his country, he chose his country.

Second, he and his brother had been running the family's prosperous iron works. Thirty-three years old in 1775, he could have used his skills and connections to seek out military contracts. Instead, he drilled with a company of Rhode Island recruits as the war approached, then marched with them to Cambridge when the war began.

And third, he had been married to Kitty, his eighteen-year-old bride, for less than a year. They shared a beautiful home in the countryside near New Haven. He might well have left Boston's conflict with the British for the Bostonians to fight. Instead, he wrote letters to Kitty from wherever his duty took him. When he joined the staff of General Washington's officers at headquarters, he invited her to join him. She became one of Lady Washington's closest friends. The General himself, as graceful a dancer as he was a horseman, always enjoyed Kitty as his partner, and once danced with her for three hours before they left the floor.

Nathanael Greene suffered expulsion from his church, turned his back on the promise of profits, and renounced the comforts of home. From the spring of 1775 in Cambridge to the summer of 1783 in Charleston, his devotion to his country never wavered.

As a boy, he possessed an unusual passion for reading. Unlike his brothers, who went to work as soon as possible, he insisted on staying in school. Even when stoking the forge fire or tending the grain hopper at a grist mill, he used his free minutes to read Euclid and Horace in their original Latin. During the evening, when the rest of the family gathered around the hearth, Nathaniel would disappear to an unheated room upstairs, where by the light of a whale oil lamp he could read without interruptions.

That passion for learning made him a superb student of military strategy. Throughout the war, General Washington encouraged his officers to read from a collection of military manuals at headquarters. In an extremely short time, the energetic Greene rose through the ranks and became a general.

Unlike several proud and calculating officers who attempted to thwart General Washington's leadership, Nathaniel Greene was absolutely loyal to his Commander in Chief. Though he hated to relinquish his field command, he accepted, out of loyalty to General Washington, the desk job as Quartermaster during the winter in Valley Forge. When Benedict Arnold, commander at the strategic fortress of West Point on Hudson's River, secretly attempted to deliver the fort into the hands of the British, General Washington trusted Greene so thoroughly that he appointed him as the new commander of West Point.

In every capacity, Greene showed himself to be a superb organizer. At Valley Forge, he managed to bring wagonloads of food and clothing and even shoes to the troops. In December, 1780, during his first weeks in Charlotte, he reorganized the entire Southern Army. On one hand he developed a system of supply depots and hospitals, while on the other hand he built up a military force that Cornwallis could neither defeat nor capture. Working night after night at the portable desk in his tent, he wrote a multitude of letters to General Washington, to Congress, to his officers, and to the local authorities in the South, maintaining clear communications with everyone.

Greene was able to work well with all of his officers, though they came from a broad range of backgrounds. Daniel Morgan, "the old wagoneer" who commanded the riflemen, was a former Indian fighter from the mountains of western Virginia. Colonel William Washington, a cavalry officer and cousin to General Washington, was a gentleman from tidewater Virginia. Greene respected his three local officers, Francis Marion, Thomas Sumter, and Andrew Pickens; he developed strategies which gave these men, who knew the South far better than he did, a great amount of independence. In return, rather than resent a superior officer from the North, Marion, Sumter, and Pickens coordinated their bands of partisans with Greene's small army of Continentals.

Greene never stopped being the student: when Daniel Morgan used a particular strategy with success at Hannah's Cowpens, and all but destroyed Tarleton's hated dragoons, Greene was willing to try the same strategy at Guilford Courthouse, and then again at Eutaw Springs.

As important as any other quality was Greene's unrelenting attention to the welfare of his men. His system of hospitals, his even temper, his mild punishments, and his steady leadership on the battlefield earned him every soldier's respect. Despite the hot, damp weather, the strange fevers, the snakes, the mosquitoes, the constant diet of rice (which men from the North did not consider to be any sort of food), and the savage civil war that raged around them, Major General Greene was able to hold his small army together, and to attack again and again, with such effectiveness that he outfoxed General Cornwallis and thus precipitated the final stage of the war.

Nathanael Greene won no major victories, but neither was he ever totally defeated. He had learned from General Washington to remain mobile, always just out of reach, though close enough to harass British foraging parties and supply trains. Maneuvering slowly northward, Greene drew Cornwallis away from his supply base in South Carolina. In March, 1781, he engaged the British in a battle at Guilford Court House which neither side won, but which cost Cornwallis a fourth of his troops. (The British were so close to defeat that Cornwallis ordered the British artillery to fire grapeshot into the battling troops, killing as many of his own soldiers as he killed Americans.) Cornwallis was forced to retreat to Wilmington, on the coast of North Carolina, where British ships could resupply his starving men.

Turning his back on the Carolinas, Cornwallis marched north from Wilmington into Virginia, where Baron Steuben and the Marquis de Lafayette were waiting for him. Greene, who might have pursued the British, chose duty over glory and returned to South Carolina, where on September 8, 1781 at Eutaw Springs, he fought the last battle in the South. By maintaining stability in the southern theater, he enabled General Washington to focus his full attention on Cornwallis in Virginia.

Toward the end of his campaign, Greene described his strategy in a letter to Thomas Jefferson, now governor of Virginia: "I have been obliged to practice that by finesse, which I dare not attempt by force." He said much the same in another letter, though he said it more bluntly: "We fight, get beat, rise, and fight again."

That was the strategy he had learned from General Washington, and that was the strategy which eventually won the war.

છે

Chapter One Hundred Six

Benjamin, chronicling
General Cornwallis' final march.

Lord Charles Cornwallis, one of Great Britain's most experienced generals, found himself, as was often the case within His Majesty's Army and Navy, completely at odds with his fellow officers, as well as with his fellow lords in London.

On April 10, 1781, while his troops were resting near Wilmington, North Carolina, he wrote an exasperated letter to a major general in Virginia:

> *"Now, my dear friend, what is our plan? Without one we cannot succeed, and I assure you that I am quite tired of marching about the country in quest of adventures. If we mean an offensive war in America, we must abandon New York, and bring our whole force into Virginia."*

On the same day, he wrote to his commander in chief in North America, Sir Henry Clinton, still comfortably riding his carriage to concerts in New York City:

> *"I am very anxious to receive your Excellency's commands, being as yet totally in the dark as to the intended operations of the summer. I cannot help expressing my wishes that the Chesapeak may become the seat of the war, even (if necessary) at the expense of abandoning New York. Until Virginia is in a manner subdued, our hold on the Carolinas must be difficult, if not precarious."*

Cornwallis was in the dark, without a plan, because Clinton had never formulated a strategy for the conquest of America. Further, both generals were under orders from the King and His various ministers, who assumed they knew how to run a war in America. Ministries rose and ministries tumbled in London while the colonials (as the British still viewed them) became increasingly unified.

Without clear guidance, but determined in his belief that a British conquest of Virginia would divide the North from the South and thereby lead to their surrender, Lord Charles Cornwallis marched his army north on April 25, 1781, toward Virginia.

General Washington had already sent Major General Lafayette with three regiments of light infantry to Virginia, in an effort to stop the depredations of Benedict Arnold, who fought now on the British side. When Cornwallis joined Arnold near Richmond on May 20, Lafayette began to play the same game with him that Greene had played: he stayed just out of reach, never risking more than a skirmish. Cornwallis said of Lafayette, "The boy cannot escape me." But as the boy wrote to General Washington on May 24,

> *"Was I to fight a battle, I'll be cut to pieces, the militia dispersed, and the arms lost. Was I to decline fighting, the country would think herself given up. I am therefore determined to scarmish, but not to engage too far, and particularly to take care against their immense and excellent body of horse whom the militia fears like they would so many wild beasts."*

As Greene had done before, Lafayette kept retreating northward. Cornwallis chased after Lafayette as he had chased after Greene and Morgan, and as General William Howe had earlier chased after General Washington: all without success.

In late June, Cornwallis marched his weary troops east to the town of Williamsburg, which had been the home of the royal governor of Virginia during colonial times, and which was close to a number of saltwater harbors where he might receive supplies and communication from New York. While in Williamsburg, he received a letter from Clinton, ordering him to send three thousand troops north by ship to help defend New York City, which Clinton believed the Americans and French together were about to attack.

Obediently, Lord Cornwallis marched and ferried his troops to Portsmouth, near the mouth of the James River, where most of his men prepared to embark for New York. But in Portsmouth he received, as ships arrived daily from the north, a series of conflicting and utterly confusing letters from Clinton. Cornwallis was instructed *not* to send his regiments to New York, but rather to Philadelphia; another letter ordered him to send troops to New York in all possible haste; another letter: establish a post at a deepwater port where the largest frigates in the navy might anchor; send reinforcements to New York, if you can spare them.

Finally on July 20, 1781, General Henry Clinton posted a letter with clear instructions to General Charles Cornwallis: establish a base at a deepwater port, the specific site to be chosen by Cornwallis.

After scouting several sites with his engineers, Cornwallis decided on the port of Yorktown, situated on a long irregular peninsula between the York and James Rivers, about eleven miles upstream from the mouth of the York and lower Chesapeake Bay. A village of seventy houses stood atop a bluff overlooking the deep river, which at that point was less than a mile wide. Across the river was Gloucester Point, where Cornwallis stationed a second body of troops, under Tarleton. When Clinton's fleet of warships arrived from New York, Yorktown would serve as an excellent harbor.

Major General Lafayette, bolstered now by General Anthony Wayne and his troops from Pennsylvania, moved cautiously down the peninsula between the York and the James. He was ready to block, with a force of almost five thousand men, any attempt by Lord Cornwallis to retreat inland. Lafayette knew that a French fleet of warships would soon come sailing up the Atlantic coast from the West Indies. If the fleet could blockade Chesapeake Bay, and if General Washington would send down reinforcements by land from the North, then the French Marquis would have the British earl caught in a perfect trap.

જી

PART IX

The Journey to Yorktown

Chapter One Hundred Seven

Genevieve, at New Windsor headquarters
on Hudson's River, summer of 1781.

Following the Battle of Monmouth in June, 1778, we lived for three quiet years near headquarters, guarding the British in New York City while we listened for news of the war in the South. We had no more than 3,500 troops, most of them unpaid and some near mutiny, in our blockade stretching from New Jersey to Connecticut. The British, however, had 14,500 troops posted on Manhattan Island, Long Island, and Staten Island, well supplied by ships arriving from England.

General Washington urged the French to block New York Harbor with a fleet of warships; a combined army of American and French troops could then attack from the mainland. But the French, despite the Treaty of Alliance, kept most of their ships in the West Indies, guarding their sugar islands from British attack.

Thus, the northern armies sat in their various encampments, while the British plundered the South.

Our men continued to suffer from ragged clothing, poor rations, and infrequent pay (in the all but worthless paper money). In December, 1780, at headquarters in the de Windt House in the village of Tappan, near Hudson's River, General Washington wrote, "We have neither money nor credit adequate to the purchase of a few boards for doors to our log huts." By January, 1781, our Commander in Chief had no funds from which to pay his couriers, or even to feed their horses; he thus could not communicate on a regular basis with the French Army now camped at Newport, Rhode Island. He was forced to use the postal system for his dispatches, knowing that the mail was often captured and read by the British.

As for ourselves: in March, 1780, during the second encampment at Morristown, though I lived once again with the Peabody's in their warm home while Benjamin and Henry endured the unrelenting blizzards in a cold log hut, I lost an infant son . . . stillborn, as if asleep. I believe that if Ka Tsi Tsya Ha had been with us in Morristown, then Johnny, my father's namesake, would be living nearby in Lincoln today.

*   *   *

The Continental Army was not entirely idle during those three years. Within our paltry limitations, we pestered the British as best we could.

In July of 1779, General Anthony Wayne led a nighttime bayonet attack on Stony Point, a promontory jutting from the shore of Hudson's River, about ten miles south of West Point. Advancing in three silent columns, Wayne's men slashed their way into the hilltop redoubt and captured the "Little Gilbralter."

A month later, Major Henry "Light Horse Harry" Lee led a similar attack against a British fort guarding the mouth of Hudson's River.

Although our troops soon abandoned both Stony Point and Paulus Hook—the outposts were too close to the British on Manhattan Island to be retained—their bold capture provided a bit of good news during that second summer of inactivity.

Then, in the spring of 1781, the mired war suddenly began to move forward.

General Washington received a letter informing him that the French were finally ready to offer concrete and substantial assistance. John Laurens, sent by Congress on a secret mission to Paris (his diplomacy bolstered by a letter from the Marquis de Lafayette to the Comte de Vergennes), wrote of his success at Versailles: a large French fleet would sail north from the West Indies, probably in July, bound for some unknown point along the American coastline. Further, and equally promising, the French government had contributed six million silver livres to the American Army; the money would be shipped in barrels to Boston.

Greatly heartened by the news, General Washington asked me to carry a message to Count Jean-Baptiste de Rochambeau, commander of the French troops at Newport, Rhode Island. The two commanders met in Wethersfield, Connecticut on May 21, 1781, to discuss how they could best use their two armies in conjunction with the promised French fleet. General Washington continued to argue for an attack on New York City. The Count de Rochambeau was not in agreement; he was well aware of the British strength inside their island fortress. He did agree, however, to bring his four thousand troops from Newport: they would join General Washington's troops at the encampment near Hudson's River. The two armies would then be able to maneuver together, in concert with the French fleet, as soon as Admiral Comte de Grasse signaled his destination.

On July 5, 1781, the four thousand French troops in their tailored white uniforms joined our three and a half thousand American troops in their hunting shirts and tattered coats. Camped between White Plains and Dobb's Ferry, French soldiers visited American campfires, and American soldiers visited French artillery practice, so that finally, three years after the formal alliance, the allies became acquainted with each other.

During the next several weeks, General Washington and the Count de Rochambeau searched for a weak spot in the British defenses on Manhattan Island, but they found none. Any attack was destined to be difficult and bloody.

I will pause here to mention that during the summer of 1781, while General Washington labored as Commander in Chief, he struggled as well as a husband. Lady Washington, spending her seventh encampment with him, was gravely ill with jaundice. She begged repeatedly that her son and only remaining child, John Parke Custis, ride north from Mount Vernon to see her. General Washington wrote an urgent letter to his stepson, but Jackie, who had spent the entire war as a gentleman of leisure, was unwilling to depart from the comforts of home.

On August 14, 1781, General Washington received two letters which determined his strategy.

Jacques Melchoir, Comte de Barras St. Laurent, commander of the French fleet in Newport, wrote that Admiral de Grasse was sailing from the West Indies to Chesapeake Bay; the Admiral expected to reach the Bay by September 3. De Grasse commanded an especially large fleet of warships: "between twenty-five and twenty-nine sail of the line and 3200 land troops." However, the Admiral could remain off the Virginia coast no longer than mid-October. Because of the threat of winter storms, he would then return to the Caribbean.

Thus General Washington now had only two weeks during which he would have to move the Continental Army—and the French Army as well—all the way from New York to Virginia. After three dreary years of sitting in camp, the troops must now march four hundred and fifty miles. And then, should the two combined armies succeed in such an enormous endeavor, they had only six weeks during which to battle the British, before the French fleet disappeared.

In the second letter, the Marquis de Lafayette wrote that General Cornwallis had finally settled his troops in Yorktown, a seaport (which

General Washington knew well) near Chesapeake Bay. Yorktown was no doubt intended to serve as a port for the British fleet, which would supply Cornwallis while he continued his efforts to subdue Virginia and the South.

So the British were on the Chesapeake, and the French would soon be there. It remained only for the Americans to arrive.

The troops would have to march through the August heat, which would worsen as they moved steadily south. The soldiers from the North had heard about the sweltering heat, the swamps, the snakes, and the fevers in the South; they might well refuse to march any further than Pennsylvania. And of course, most of our men had not been paid for months: entire regiments might mutiny at any point.

Further, General Clinton could easily ferry his troops from Staten Island to the mainland, then attack the Continental and French Armies as they marched in a long train toward the South. (As we had done when Clinton marched his troops from Philadelphia toward New York.) Our men might well have to battle their way through New Jersey.

Or, once the Continental Army had departed, leaving a much weakened guard above New York City, General Clinton might advance north into New England. What point in besieging Yorktown, if the British captured Boston again?

But the wildcat had waited for three tiresome years for his chance to pounce, and now he took the risk. The march to Virginia would be the longest maneuver of the entire war, and one of the most precarious, but he would attempt it.

General Washington issued two orders. The first outlined preparations for an attack on Manhattan Island. Pioneers cleared a new route through a woods toward King's Bridge, as if the Americans were planning to attack at that northern point. Other troops laid out an extensive encampment on the New Jersey coast across from Staten Island, as if in preparation for an attack from that direction. Firewood was gathered and openly stacked; forage for horses was brought in wagons from the countryside and heaped into tall haystacks; brick ovens were built, so the French could bake their bread. General Washington wrote detailed orders for an attack on New York, then made sure that his letters found their way into the hands of British spies. (Miss Ebenezer, as a courier, delivered one of these epistles into the hands of a well-known Loyalist post rider—we knew that the man *always* read the General's mail.)

In his second order, the General commanded his troops to prepare for an immediate march, with provisions for four days. No one knew our destination: not the soldiers, nor the officers. Haversacks were packed with diligent care; firelocks were oiled; blankets were aired, then rolled; real bread from real French ovens was distributed and then packed among the socks.

Lady Washington, well enough now to travel, set out by carriage with a guard of cavalry for Philadelphia. Because British troops aboard small vessels were plundering riverside plantations in Virginia, Mount Vernon was not safe.

On August 17, General Washington sent John Lally with a letter to Newport; the letter was thence carried south aboard a French frigate to Admiral de Grasse (by now at sea). It informed the Admiral in vague terms, which General Washington knew he would understand, "It has been judged expedient to turn our attention toward the South."

The gamble was enormous. What if a British fleet, racing north from the West Indies, prevented Admiral de Grasse from reaching Chesapeake Bay? What if a storm swept the French fleet out across the Atlantic? If the British managed to reach the Chesapeake first, they would control the rivers as well. Lord Cornwallis would command a replenished army. The American troops, finding that their wearisome march was all for naught, might rise up in an uncontrollable mutiny. The entire Continental Army, after six years of determined endurance, might simply fall apart.

On Sunday, August 19, 1781, only five days after receiving word of Admiral de Grasse's actual destination, General Washington ordered the Continental Army to march to King's Ferry, where they could cross Hudson's River. The troops were ready; the crossing was completed on August 20. We camped at Haverstraw on the western shore while we waited for the French to cross.

General William Heath remained at West Point with 2,500 troops to guard Hudson's River. With the army thus divided, we had only 2,000 regulars, and a body of unreliable militia, in our American camp. Though the Count de Rochambeau commanded a force twice as large, he never challenged General Washington as the overall Commander in Chief.

On Saturday morning, August 25, 1781, the combined French and American Armies, formed into three columns, began their march south. One regiment from New York, serving as rear guard, accompanied a train of large wagons pulled by oxen: atop each wagon was a boat with oars, clearly to be used in the attack on Staten Island. To encourage any

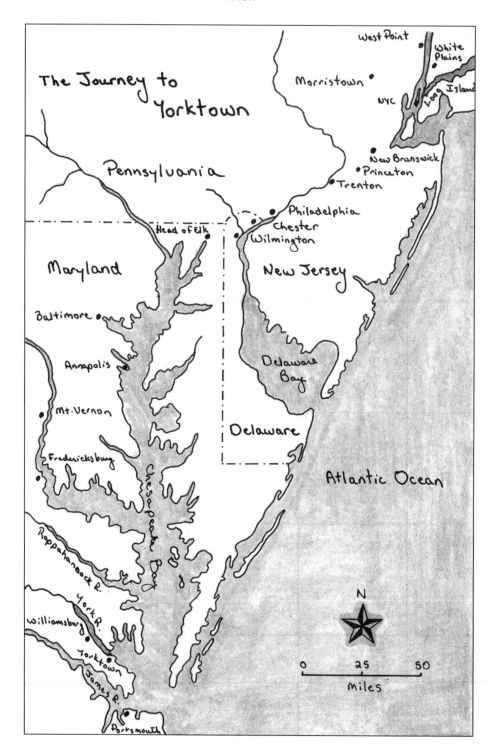

British spies along the route to spot the boats, a small but clamorous band of fifers and trumpeters marched along with the vessels, playing a proud "Yankee Doodle."

Benjamin and Robert marched with Captain Henry Byrnes in the column led by Major General Benjamin Lincoln. (General Lincoln had been the commander captured at Charleston, South Carolina in 1780; later exchanged for a British officer, he now served once again under General Washington).

Susanne rode beside me on the seat of the wagon. She was ready to take the reins should the children, or the Commander in Chief, let me know they needed me.

Caleb, now five years old, sat between us, staring with fascination at the long column of French and American troops ahead of us, and the occasional rider galloping past. Sally, now three and a half, napped in the wagon, or peered out the back at the train of artillery behind us.

It was certainly an odd way to raise children. Or perhaps it was the best way of all.

ଚ୍ଚ

Chapter One Hundred Eight

Benjamin, my feet pointed south.

Robert drummed the cadence, a quick and steady step which suited the spirit of the men. Though our destination had been the topic of un-relenting conjecture—bets had been wagered on a half-dozen points along the coast—we were glad to be marching almost anywhere. The men sensed that the approaching battle might perhaps be the final battle of the war. Bitter as most of the troops were at not being paid an honest wage for honest work, above all they just wanted to go home. "End the damn war," they muttered, "so I can go home and see to my corn."

On the third day south, our columns halted in the mid-afternoon; baffled by the pause, with several hours of daylight left, we could only mull over once again the ominous news we had heard that morning, that the British had ferried several thousand troops from Long Island to Staten Island: troops that might easily be ferried from the island's southern tip to Amboy on the New Jersey shoreline. Before we could attack the British, it seemed they were rushing to attack us.

But they did not attack. The redcoats remained on Staten Island, and not so much as a musket shot disturbed our camp that night.

We learned, however, the following morning at our breakfast fires—though what was news and what was rumor, a soldier could never determine—that someone had spotted a British fleet of warships as it sailed out of New York Harbor. We had already heard—news from the French while we were still back on the Hudson—that the French fleet at Newport was preparing to sail. Had the British set sail to intercept the French? What was happening out on the broad Atlantic, none of us knew.

We continued our march south, undisturbed. After crossing the Raritan River, we camped near New Brunswick. Every soldier knew that we could march no further south and still be maneuvering to attack Staten Island.

Awakened in the darkness at three in the morning by a rumbling of drums, and marching in the first glow of dawn at four—to the south— we knew that we had managed to outwit the British. The redcoats sat back on Staten Island, on Long Island, on Manhattan Island, waiting for our rowboats to begin the crossing, while we—with absolute faith in our Commander in Chief—went stealing toward some other prize.

News, rumor, had it that Lafayette had cornered Lord Cornwallis in Virginia. Near the Chesapeake. Maybe that's where the French and British fleets were headed. And us too. If so, that meant that as far as we had marched, we had barely gotten started.

Though we followed, passing through Princeton toward Trenton on the Delaware, the same route we had trudged during our retreat in 1776, this time Cornwallis was not on our tail, but somewhere ahead of us. This time we would catch him, and thereby send a major defeat to His Majesty King George III.

Then perhaps the King would call his scoundrels home.

❧

Chapter One Hundred Nine

Benjamin.

When we reached the Delaware at Trenton, it was the old story: not enough boats to carry the troops down the river to Wilmington, from which we would have had a short walk of twenty miles to the northern tip of Chesapeake Bay. There *were* boats, of course, hundreds of them all along the Delaware River, but they were as hidden in farmers' barns as the corn and cattle had been hidden in winters past.

So we took off our haversacks and loaded them into wagons. Still carrying our firelocks and cartridge boxes, we resumed our march at a much quicker pace, following a road along the river while Robert beat a sprightly cadence on his drum.

On Sunday afternoon, September 2, 1781, the American Army marched in a column two miles long through Philadelphia. The day was dry and hot; the dust kicked up by thousands of feet nearly choked us. How much grander it would have been to float down the river through the city, doffing our hats as we passed the spire of Christ Church.

But it was more than the dust that bothered the men. As we marched with a slow and solemn step past the Pennsylvania State House, the men glared at the windows of the room where our Congress met. Four years ago, on Sunday, August 24, 1777, we had marched past that same red brick building with its stately white spire. We had worn ragged shirts and ragged trousers, but we had also worn a sprig of greenery in our hats, as a symbol of hope. Now we still wore ragged shirts and ragged trousers, but no sprig of greenery. During those four years, we had been starved by Congress, we had been poorly clad by Congress, and we certainly had not been paid by Congress.

Profoundly insulting to us were the crowds along Chestnut Street, cheering us, for the people were well dressed and clearly prosperous. It was as if we were marching through some foreign country; or that two sets of people lived in our own country, with little in common between them.

We did not know it at the time, but as we were marching grimly through the streets of our nation's capital, our Commander in Chief was desperately searching the city for hard specie, so that he could pay each of his soldiers a month's wages. General Washington met with Robert Morris, the Congressional superintendent of finance, who in turn implored the French for an immediate loan. The Count de Rochambeau finally agreed to advance the American Army half the money which he carried in his war chest, knowing that he would soon be repaid from the barrels of silver which had been sent from Versailles, and which had recently arrived safely in Boston.

After marching through Philadelphia, the American Army crossed the Schuylkill River on a floating bridge, then camped on the far shore to wait for the French.

Susanne, driving the wagon near the end of the column, found Henry's company that evening. She told us that Genevieve had been summoned to headquarters (though we had no idea where headquarters might now be). When we would see her again, we could not possibly know.

The French Army, marching one day behind us, paraded through Philadelphia on September 3. They had paused north of the city to change into their dress uniforms, white with silk cuffs of various pastel colors. Whereas we had marched through the city with drums and fifes, the French entertained the cheering crowds with a full military band.

On September 4, the two armies marched together for eighteen miles, passing through Wilmington, Delaware, the town where we should have disembarked from our boats. We continued on the 5th, then finally on September 6 we reached Head of Elk, Maryland, at the very northern end of Chesapeake Bay. The troops had now marched two hundred miles in fifteen days.

And lo, we discovered once again that not enough boats had been found to ferry us south. We would have to march another sixty miles to Baltimore, on the western shore of the Bay, a port where a boat or two perhaps might be located.

At this point, on the threshold of entering the South, a growing number of men in a growing number of companies under Major General Benjamin Lincoln told their captains that they were not going a step further without a month's pay in specie.

Let all those cheering merchants in Philadelphia march south to the snakes and the heat and the redcoats.

Chapter One Hundred Ten

Genevieve, still in Philadelphia with Sir William,
at the beginning of the most extraordinary
journey of my life.

We had paraded through Philadelphia in the most appalling dust. The children of course insisted on sitting outside the wagon tarp on the seat, so they could see everything. And yes, I was glad that the four of us—Sally on Susanne's lap, myself, and Caleb between us—could take a good long look at the handsome brick building where our Congress had hurled back their challenge at the King. But Sally was coughing in the dust, and I had no idea when, or where, I might be able to give the children a bath.

The train of wagons was rolling out of the western end of the city, where brick houses trimmed with white gave way to wooden barns fringed with bright yellow goldenrod, when John Lally appeared beside me, leading by its bridle an unsaddled horse.

"Miss Ebenezer, the General needs you immediately. I've brought one of the artillery horses for your wagon."

I reined Sir William out of the column, then handed Susanne the reins. She lifted Sally from her lap to the seat, told Caleb to hold Sally's hand, then she wrapped the reins around the brake lever and stepped down to help John unharness Sir William. I fetched my saddle from the back of the wagon, as well as saddlebags and blanket. The General might need me for a day, might need me for a month, and I'd best be ready.

Sir William perked up his ears when I hefted the saddle onto his back. Though steady and strong when pulling the wagon, he never did like being a dray horse.

John and Susanne soon had the sorrel mare in the wagon traces. I mounted Sir William. With a brief good-bye to the children and a nod to Susanne—no more farewell than anyone ever gave anyone in the midst of a war—I followed John Lally at a canter along the edge of the road, passing regiments and artillery as we raced back into the city.

John Lally led me up Market Street to a mansion—a brick palace of turrets and tall windows—the home, as he told me while we tethered

Sir William and Shamrock to a wrought iron bar above an oaken water trough, of Robert Morris. (The house would later become the home of President and Lady Washington while the new federal government was located in Philadelphia.) We climbed the steps to a white door half again as tall as we were. John lifted a brass knocker and knocked. The door swung open. A servant in livery—his coat red with silver buttons, the collar trimmed with lace—bid us enter. And so the farm girl from Lincoln stepped into what seemed to be the palace of King George himself.

A raised hand indicated that we were to wait in the entryway while the servant took word of our arrival into an adjoining room—a room behind a closed mahogany door. A moment later the servant strode out; ignoring us, he hurried up a broad staircase, passing beneath the framed portrait of some ancestral dignitary. We heard urgent voices, then what sounded like someone pouring a bucket of water.

Now another servant, a woman wearing a blue dress and white apron, and a white mobcap as tall as a crown, came halfway down the stairs. "Mistress Genevieve York," she stated, as if I had better be that and none other, or I would be promptly scolded.

"Yes?"

"Come."

She turned and her blue skirt flapped back up the stairs.

"Well, Miss Ebenezer," said John Lally with a grin as he left me to my fate, "I'll be going now."

"Sir William . . ?" I asked, too overwhelmed to think any further.

"Will be with Nelson. Headquarters is in the saddle now."

"Mistress York!" snapped an imperious voice at the top of the stairs.

Lifting the hem of my dusty farm dress, I hurried up.

Not deigning to speak, but merely pointing with a regal finger, Queen Mobcap indicated that I was to step inside a nearby room. I pushed the door open, and found to my delight a copper bathtub filled with steaming hot water. The room was small, but elegantly paneled with dark cherry, and absolutely private. A bar of yellow soap. Two pale pink towels, neatly folded on a table beside a blue and white pitcher, itself full of steaming water.

And hanging from a brass hook on the wall, a deep blue robe that seemed—I reached out a dusty finger and almost dared to touch it— yes, it was made of silk!

"Ten minutes!" decreed Her Imperial Highness outside the door.

"The General is waiting."

Quickly, off came the dusty, bedraggled brown farm dress, and the limp petticoat beneath it. Off came the stockings that might, after a good boiling, have been better used as pillow stuffing, or as cannon wadding. Into the tub I stepped . . . then gradually I sat in the almost-too-hot water. I slowly submerged my shoulders, the back of my head, and now—holding my breath—even my face, until all of me was underwater. I felt most wonderfully poached. The dust and grime and sweat of New York, New Jersey, Maryland, and Pennsylvania washed away, and a great sigh of comfort bubbled to the surface.

I was scrubbing my arms with soap when a rap on the door from Queen Mobcap's iron knuckles made the yellow bar nearly leap from my fingers. "Yes mum!" I called, and scrubbed more quickly.

I washed and rinsed my hair, washed and rinsed again, then slowly poured the entire pitcher of hot clean water over my head. Suddenly I remembered, vividly, swimming in Walden Pond, a small lake really, between Lincoln and Concord. The water was so fresh in the evening, after I had spent the summer day at farm chores. I loved to wade in slowly, making the lone ripple that spread in an ever-widening ring across the lake. In the woods that wrapped around the shore, thrushes sang their evening vesper. In the turquoise sky, the first stars appeared, faint points of light, discernible only because I knew where to look for them.

Not since those lovely frolics in Walden Pond had I felt so clean.

The door latch turned, the door opened, the Queen's arm reached in and snatched my dusty clothes from the chair where I had laid them. The door closed with a thump, then I heard through the heavy wood her stern pronouncement, "You *will* not dally."

I stepped out of the copper tub, dried myself with both towels, and had just put one arm into a deliciously cool smooth sleeve of the blue silk robe, a robe that must truly have belonged to a princess, when I heard her sharp knock, followed by the command, "Come."

I slid my other arm into the second sleeve, felt the cool silk kiss my shoulders. Oh, I could have danced all evening with my prince on the grassy shore of Walden Pond.

Instead, I folded one flap over the other, tied a silken belt as light as gossamer across my waist, then opened the door and peered shyly out. The Queen was thumping down the long corridor toward a room at the far end. Seeing no one else in the hallway, or coming up the stairs, I hurried barefoot after her.

I admit that I hoped to find, waiting for me in that room, an elegant gown such as a princess would wear, perhaps wine red with lace at the cuffs . . . but I was less disappointed than baffled. For as I stepped through the door, I saw, laid out on an enormous mahogany four-poster bed, the uniform of General Washington's Life Guard: a blue coat with buff trim and silver buttons, a scarlet waistcoat, a white shirt, and buff trousers, all so clean that they must be absolutely new. And all, I now noticed, too small to fit the men who must be, by regulation, six feet tall. As I picked up the scarlet waistcoat, I understood that it was just the right size for Miss Ebenezer.

On the pillow was a black hat with the Life Guard's cockade.

"Ten minutes," decreed the Queen, as if I had that and not a minute more before I would be summoned to my beheading. "You will find a hair brush on the bureau."

I glanced at a brush and round hand mirror; both had silver handles. The Queen departed, as if to polish the axe.

With great reluctance, I untied the silken belt and took off the silken robe. Then I donned and buttoned the white shirt; stepped into and buttoned the buff trousers. Both fit as well as if my mother had stitched them. I put on the scarlet waistcoat, and felt quite dashing as I fastened the silver buttons. When I put on the blue coat, with decidedly more weight than the silken robe, I felt transformed. Into what, I did not know.

On the floor beside the bed, I discovered my freshly blackened and polished shoes. (She must have snatched them while I was underwater in the tub.) And on a chair, a pair of new black stockings. I sat on the chair and put them on: my pink feet felt most clean, comfortable, and properly shod.

I brushed my damp hair as best I could. I wished that I could have stood outside in the sun—perhaps in a rose garden behind the house— and brushed until my hair was properly dry. However, when my damp brown locks were free of tangles, I set the cocked hat squarely upon my head and regarded myself in the oval mirror above the bureau. Whoever I was, I was ready.

When I swung the door open, I saw Queen Mobcap thumping up the corridor toward me. She beckoned; I stepped forward. Without a pause she circled behind me, inspecting me, then she thumped back down the corridor. "Come."

At the head of the stairs, I was returned to the liveried servant, who barely noticed me, but descended the steps ahead of me. Opening the tall mahogany door, he ushered me into a sitting room nearly as large as the entire downstairs of our house in Lincoln. General Washington and another gentleman were seated at a long table covered with papers.

The General glanced up, then stood and regarded me with approval. It was the first time in our six years together that he had ever stood upon my entry into his office. "Mistress York," he said, "may I present you to Mr. Robert Morris, our financier."

Having spent the past few years with starving men who labored from dawn until dark, I could not help but note, as Mr. Morris stood up, that the portly aristocrat seemed never to have lacked his piece of cake. And yet, he was my host, the man who had provided that hot bath.

He nodded toward me, clearly preoccupied with matters upon the table. "Mistress York, you are most needed."

"Come around, please," said General Washington, gesturing to a chair beside him. "We need your sharp mind and fair hand. Every American dollar and every French *livre* must be clearly recorded."

As I stepped around the end of the table, I saw an account book open in front of my chair. Its blank page had already been dated at the top in what I recognized as the General's script: "September 2, 1781."

General Washington and Robert Morris sat down, I sat down, and we went to work. Writing as quickly as I could to keep up, I noted in the ledger every penny and pence and sou, every dollar and pound and silver French *livre* which Robert Morris had managed to gather from a multitude of sources in Philadelphia during the past few days. This was money, as the General briefly explained to me, which he would soon disperse as payment to the troops.

I spoke not a word, but felt, on behalf of the men, a deep upwelling of gratitude. If this is what it took——our Commander in Chief in the parlors of the rich—then I thanked him for what our Congress and State legislatures had unrelentingly failed to do.

Because every other clerk and officer was now laden with military duties in preparation for the impending siege of Yorktown, I became the Commander in Chief's sole secretary. Wherever he worked, I worked; wherever he traveled, I traveled. I was as continually with him as a member—which I had now become—of his Life Guard.

For the next seven weeks, until October 19, 1781, I would carry that ledger and a sheaf of blank paper in my saddlebag, along with a dozen goose quills and several bottles of ink, wrapped snugly in linen. I would write letters, reports, requisitions, urgent orders: about boats, wagons, artillery, and salt beef; about armies and fleets; letters carried by couriers, and a letter carried by the Marquis de Lafayette to Admiral Francois Joseph Paul, Comte de Grasse; letters insistent and letters diplomatic . . . until I penned, in General Washington's exact and careful wording, the stern conditions of the Treaty of Surrender at Yorktown.

છ

Chapter One Hundred Eleven

Genevieve.

Before we departed from Philadelphia, I copied an urgent letter from General Washington to the Marquis de Lafayette, whose five thousand American troops blocked any attempt by Cornwallis to retreat by land from Yorktown. The General had heard nothing since August 14, three weeks ago, about the French fleet sailing north from the West Indies. Nor had he heard anything for almost two weeks about the fleet sailing south from Newport.

> *"But my dear Marquis, I am distressed beyond expression, to know what is become of the Count de Grasse, and for fear the English Fleet, by occupying the Chesapeake (towards which my last accounts say they were steering) should frustrate all our flattering prospects in that quarter. I am also not a little solicitous for the Count de Barras, who was to have sailed from Rhode Island on the 23d Ulto. and from whom I have heard nothing since that time. Of many contingencies we will hope for the most propitious events."*

The General closed the letter with an unusually open revelation of his feelings. "Adieu my Dear Marquis! If you get any thing New from any quarter, send it I pray you *on the Spur of Speed*, for I am almost all impatience and anxiety."

On Wednesday, September 5, General Washington galloped out of Philadelphia toward Head of Elk, where many of the American troops, still unpaid, threatened another mutiny.

Riding along the western shore of the Delaware River, we were a few miles south of Chester when we saw a rider galloping toward us. He reined to a halt and handed the General a dispatch. Upon reading it, General Washington whooped with joy.

The Count de Grasse (the General announced to his staff) had sailed into Chesapeake Bay with twenty-eight warships. Already, three thousand land troops, commanded by the Marquis de Saint-Simon, had disembarked to support the small army under Lafayette. Thus the blockade of Lord Cornwallis by sea and by land was complete.

Rather than ride on toward Head of Elk, General Washington galloped back to the wharf at Chester, where the Count de Rochambeau
and his suite of officers, who had departed from Philadelphia by boat to
enjoy a tour of the river, would soon be docking.

General Washington strode out to the end of the pier and stared
north, searching for the vessel carrying his French allies. When he
spotted the white French flag atop an approaching mast, he not only
waved his hat, but took a handkerchief from a pocket and waved that as
well. Jumping up and down like a boy wild with excitement, he
shouted across the water, "de Grasse! de Grasse!" As the sloop neared
the dock, he announced, "de Grasse is in the Chesapeake!"

The French Count and his officers stared at the American General,
who had always been so rigidly composed. When their vessel pulled
broadside to the pier and Rochambeau stepped onto the wharf, General
Washington embraced him with an unprecedented hug as he announced
again, "de Grasse is in the Chesapeake!"

He handed the French commander the momentous dispatch:
twenty-eight warships, three thousand marines already on land. The
French had beat the British to the Bay.

The Count and his officers, now equally delighted, congratulated
our Commander in Chief, then celebrated with him, during a dinner at a
riverside tavern in Chester, the closing of the trap.

℞

Chapter One Hundred Twelve

Benjamin, a paid soldier!

On the morning of September 6, 1781, the regiments were mustered for general orders. Although none of the men had yet abandoned the encampment at Head of Elk, neither were they in any mood to march one foot further south. As companies assembled, men muttered with anger, with apprehension, for if the general orders stated that we would move today deeper into Maryland, no one could say for sure whether the Continental Army would march, or riot.

The lieutenant addressing our regiment announced that the day's orders were from the Commander in Chief (rather than from General Lincoln, as they most often had been during the long march south). Thus we listened with a bit more patience, a bit more hope.

> *"It is with the highest pleasure and satisfaction that the Commander-in-Chief announces to the Army the arrival of Count de Grass in the Chesapeak. . . . He felicitates the army on the auspicious occasion, he anticipates the glorious events which may be expected. . . . The general calls upon the gentlemen officers, the brave and faithful soldiers . . . to exert their utmost abilities in the cause of their country, to share with him . . . the difficulties, dangers, and glory of the enterprise."*

A murmur passed through the troops. The French navy was in the Chesapeake. Felicitates. Glorious. Brave and faithful. "But we still ain't yet been *paid*," shouted a soldier to the nervous lieutenant. "Damn yer glory!"

It was at that moment, on a warm September morning in northwest Maryland, at the very midpoint in our nation between North and South (and not far from where the capital city of Washington would later be built), that Philip Audibert, Deputy Paymaster General under Robert Morris, tipped the balance. He appeared on horseback in front of the assembled regiments—some of the men recognized him and whispered, "It's the paymaster!"—followed by a sturdy artillery wagon, a wagon guarded by a troop of cavalry, and loaded with wooden barrels.

The eyes of two thousand war-worn soldiers were on those barrels. The wagon halted. A table was brought forth from an officer's marquee. Philip Audibert dismounted, climbed into the wagon; then with help from a sergeant with an iron bar, he pried the lid from a barrel. The paymaster fetched a bucket from the bed of the wagon, then dipped it into the barrel, pushing and working the bucket until it was full. He passed the bucket to the sergeant, who passed it over the rear of the wagon to a major, who, to our astonishment and joy, poured a great glittering heap of silver coins onto the counting table.

A roar went up from the troops.

It was a roar just about loud enough for Lord Cornwallis to hear, way down in Yorktown. If he *had* heard it, he might well have decided that it was time to go home.

As company after company stepped forward in an orderly manner for the first Month's Payment in Specie in the history of the war, we realized that it was not Congress, nor any of our States, that was paying us, but the King of France. The coins were silver half crowns. They not only banished any further thoughts of mutiny, but bolstered our resolve to march south against Lord Cornwallis and rid our nation of his British plague.

The men stared at the coins in their hands, placed them in a pocket and took them out again, then showed them to each other, even though every man had exactly the same coins.

Though we did not know at the time the nature of the financial transaction, the money had come from the war chest of the Count de Rochambeau, loaned to Robert Morris in Philadelphia; Robert Morris would pay back the Count with money shipped from France to Boston, then hauled by ox cart to Philadelphia. Thus the French reimbursed the French, while the American troops marched south to war with a bit of weight in their ragged pockets.

I say marched, rather than sailed. Although a few more fishing sloops appeared at the docks of Head of Elk—lured perhaps by the scent of French money—they were far from enough to transport all of the troops. So we began our sixty-mile walk to Baltimore.

Genevieve.

General Washington inspected the few boats in the harbor at Head of Elk. He then wrote, and I copied, a multitude of letters to anyone at the northern end of the Bay who might have a vessel of any size for transporting troops south.

We crossed the Susquehanna River on September 8 and arrived in Baltimore that evening. Despite a celebration dinner in honor of the Commander in Chief, a great number of speeches, illuminations in many windows, and other festivities, General Washington and his aides eventually made their way to the wharf, where they spoke with every fisherman and schooner captain they could find.

෨

Chapter One Hundred Thirteen

Benjamin.

We arrived in Baltimore on a hot, damp September 9. We set up camp at the edge of town, then wondered less about supper than about boats. The captain of the Baltimore militia informed our regimental commanders that several small frigates from Admiral de Grasse's fleet were sailing up the Chesapeake to both Annapolis and Baltimore, in order to transport troops the final two hundred miles to the mouth of the Bay. The men received this news from their officers with a silent nod. We would believe it when we actually boarded the ships.

Nevertheless, as we lay on top of our blankets that warm evening, we told ourselves that since the ships were French, and not American, they would probably be there.

The following day, a regiment marched into Baltimore to embark at the wharf . . . and did not return to camp. Nor did we hear that troops had been seen marching out the southern end of the city. Perhaps that regiment actually was afloat.

On the evening of September 12, Captain Byrnes informed his company that we would sail on the morrow. We should accordingly prepare to decamp.

But no. As we were marching with our firelocks and haversacks into Baltimore the next morning, Captain Byrnes was told to order us back to camp. News, rumors, followed us as we returned to the still-warm coals of our breakfast fires and sat down on logs from which we had stood up two hours ago. The entire French fleet had sailed out the mouth of Chesapeake Bay, and thus no longer blockaded Cornwallis. A fleet of British warships had been sighted off the coast. Both fleets had vanished out on the Atlantic. Until the result of their battle was known, all transport of troops on the Chesapeake was halted.

Should the British prove victorious, and should they then sail into Chesapeake Bay, General Washington did not want his army scattered in a multitude of small boats. (Or so we surmised as we boiled a bit of salted beef for dinner.) And if the British fleet *were* victorious, we still had a long damn war ahead of us.

*   *   *

And where was Genevieve? With General Washington, who had, we heard, ridden south from Philadelphia to Chester, to Wilmington, to Head of Elk (though we had not seen him), then on to Baltimore ahead of us. He had departed from Baltimore early in the morning of September 9, the day we arrived. Had he, they, rushed south to join Lafayette?

With the French blockade now open, the British might well sweep into the Bay and up the rivers with fresh troops from New York. Their spies were everywhere. General Clinton would certainly make every effort to capture our Commander in Chief.

Now I was the one left worrying in camp, while Genevieve was out somewhere near the front line of this hateful war.

ℰℭ

Chapter One Hundred Fourteen

Genevieve, at Mount Vernon.

General Washington had last seen his home, Mount Vernon, in May, 1775, when Virginia was still a colony. He had departed from his plantation in a carriage drawn by four horses, with his retinue of aides and Negro slaves, as a delegate to the Second Continental Congress in Philadelphia. The muskets had already fired at Lexington and Concord. On June 14, John Adams, delegate from Massachusetts, nominated Colonel Washington, delegate from Virginia, as Commander in Chief of an army that did not yet exist. On June 15, Congress resolved that a general be appointed to lead the Continental troops, then elected Colonel Washington, now General Washington, with a unanimous vote.

General Washington had no time to return home. On June 18, he wrote a letter to Lady Washington (whom he addressed as "my dear Patsy"), informing her that

> *"It has been determined in Congress, that the whole army raised for the defense of the American cause shall be put under my care, and that it is necessary for me to proceed immediately to Boston to take upon me the command of it."*

He added,

> *"But as it has been a kind of destiny, that has thrown me upon this service, I shall hope that my undertaking it is designed to answer some good purpose."*

He enclosed with the letter his newly drafted will.

He sent his carriage and team of four horses back to Mount Vernon. On June 23, 1775, at the age of forty-three, he began the long ride toward Boston.

Now on Sunday, September 9, 1781, over six years later, General Washington galloped out of Baltimore before dawn, accompanied by his aide Lieutenant Colonel David Humphreys, his Negro servant Billy Lee (who had been at the General's side every day for those six years), and a troop of twenty Life Guards, including myself. The rest of his staff, and the suite of French officers, would catch up with him. But tonight, with sixty miles between Baltimore and Mount Vernon, the General intended to sleep in his own bed.

The General could risk a brief excursion home. The French fleet was still in Chesapeake Bay; it had not yet vanished out on the Atlantic to challenge the British. The Marquis de Lafayette was positioned to block any retreat by land. Lord Cornwallis, trapped in Yorktown, had made no attempt to fight his way free. The long column of American and French troops marching south would not reach Williamsburg, thirteen miles from Yorktown, for at least another week.

British marauders no longer cruised the rivers of Virginia. Lady Washington had accordingly been able to leave Philadelphia and return to Mount Vernon in July. Her son John Parke Custis was there, with his wife Nelly and their four children. General Washington's grandchildren had all been born during the war; he had never seen them.

Throughout the war, the General had written long letters to the managers of his plantation; he monitored the rotation of crops, the building of a new south wing on the house, and the collection of debts in the increasingly inflated paper money, as much as he had monitored beef and rum and gunpowder for his troops. His managers replied with long letters listing new problems.

Thus there was time enough and reason enough for a brief detour home.

With Colonel Humphreys, Billy Lee, myself, and a dwindling number of Life Guards (only five managed to bear the pace), we galloped along backcountry lanes that cut through the forests and farmland of Maryland. General Washington, tireless, rode in the lead. We cantered unannounced through tiny villages, the people along the road as stunned and flustered as their chickens when the nation's Commander in Chief suddenly appeared . . . and then disappeared.

As the cool fresh morning warmed into the heat of afternoon, my white shirt and scarlet waistcoat became damp with sweat. But after three years of waiting, waiting, waiting near New York City, to gallop on Sir William across the back roads of Maryland—a greater distance in one day than we had ever before traveled—was heaven itself.

Even when we halted in a village for a brief dinner (more to rest the horses than to replenish ourselves), after less than half an hour of porridge and corn bread, the eight of us were as ready as General Washington to mount again and ride (before someone who considered himself to be the village mayor took it upon himself to attempt a speech).

It was September now and the days were shorter. As we ferried on a barge with long sweeping oars across the Potomac River, the misty orange sun was low in the west ahead of our bow. A dancing copper sun on the dark water beckoned us, and welcomed us, to the State of Virginia. To the South.

We rode through the darkening evening, the General as silent as he had been throughout the long day. Locusts hummed in the summer heat, their airy thrumming surprisingly loud among the black, depthless trees. A whippoorwill called its distinct name from a dark meadow. The General turned his head to listen.

I felt that same jubilant peace I had known on my night rides as a girl: happy to breathe the sweet night air, happy to greet the mysterious stars, happy to feel Sir William pounding beneath me. But whereas before I had ridden the dark lanes without any real destination, tonight I was riding toward Mount Vernon, toward Yorktown, toward a new America, an America which one day I would bring home to Lincoln.

Now we slowed to a canter, passed in the night an orderly row of trees and shrubs along both sides of the lane. Then we spotted ahead what General Washington had no doubt seen in his mind when we had set out at dawn: a long, dimly white, two-story facade, its symmetrical windows brightly lit, its roof as black as the night above it. We heard a shout from a window, "De Massah home!" Almost immediately, while we slowed to a trot around the circular driveway, people began to pour out the large front door, some of the faces white, many of them black.

Lady Washington was among them, lit by a lantern held by one of the Negroes, her face radiant with far more joy than she had ever shown, or known, at the encampments. The General dismounted, took her hand, and bid her, "Good evening, Patsy."

A young man, elegantly dressed with a white bow at his collar, emerged from the door with his wife and four children. His face in the lanternlight was uncommonly pale; all the men I had known for years had faces burnt dark by the sun. General Washington bowed down as he looked closely at each of his four step-grandchildren. He shook hands with Jackie . . . rather formally, I thought.

Then with a sweep of his hand to the eight of us—we had all dismounted by now and given the reins of our horses to a growing number of Negro stable boys—General Washington invited us up the steps and through the handsome door into Mount Vernon.

I was invited to dine with General and Lady Washington at a large candlelit table. From my chair, I looked at a dining room window, hoping to see the grounds outside, but could discern nothing in the darkness. General Washington, noticing my curiosity, told me with evident pride that I would be able, at breakfast, to look out "upon the broad Potomac."

Though our host and hostess were cheerful in their conversation, for the meal was more a celebration than a supper, I knew that they surely wanted to be alone with each other. As soon as they could within the bounds of courtesy, I prepared to take my leave.

"Sir," I queried, "will you be needing me this evening?"

General Washington looked at me with a smile. (I loved to see that smile on his careworn face. It was rare. Some of his aides, who had worked with him for years, swore they had never seen the General smile.) "Miss Ebenezer, your good friend Lady Washington, who has known you through more winter encampments than she wishes to count, has suggested to me that perhaps you would appreciate a bath."

"Quite," said Lady Washington. She rang a small bell on the table; a white serving girl entered the room. "Would you show Mistress York to the bathhouse, please, and make sure she has all she needs."

A quarter of an hour later, I stood alone in a simple outbuilding, pouring buckets of cool water over my head. There was a copper tub (neither as large nor as well polished in the lanternlight as Robert Morris's tub), but I did not use it. Nor did I require that the water be heated. I bathed in bucket after bucket of well water drawn from deep in the Virginia earth, water as cool and sweet and clean as a Massachusetts rain in May.

Though I had been offered quarters inside Mount Vernon, in a room adjoining Colonel Humphrey's quarters, I requested, as much to please myself as to honor the privacy of my host and hostess, that I sleep as usual in my blanket beneath the stars. After checking on Sir William in the stables, where a Negro was grooming him, I fetched what I needed for the night from my saddlebags, then walked around the imposing white house—I nodded along the way to several of the Guards—to the flat, grassy yard outside the dining room windows.

I wanted, in the morning, to see the sun glimmer "upon the broad Potomac."

*   *   *

The General and I spent Monday, September 10, working in his study. He wrote a multitude of letters to officials in both Maryland and Virginia, urgently requesting that certain roads be improved at once. Because of the shortage of boats, a great number of troops and wagons would soon be using the roads south to Williamsburg. Ruts were to be filled, bridges repaired, and fodder gathered for the horses.

Sunshine poured in through the two office windows. Broad beams of sunlight slowly swept across the General at his desk. His blue-gray eyes glinted handsomely whenever he looked up from his papers.

While he conferred with Colonel Humphreys as to the whereabouts of General Knox and his artillery, I recalled, seated at a small writing table, that it had been Bookseller Knox, an epoch ago, who had sold to Benjamin the books from which he had taught Nathaniel to read. And it had been Librarian Knox who had found enough paper at Cambridge that Benjamin could teach me to write. I felt I had lived a dozen lifetimes since those early days, and we had not yet reached the end of it.

The Count de Rochambeau and his officers arrived on horseback that Monday evening. General Washington, delighted in his role as host, fêted his French guests with a grand dinner in their honor. The banquet table became a display of Virginia's bounty: roast venison, wild and domestic fowls, greens of a dozen kinds from the Mount Vernon gardens, roasted fish from the river. We drank tankards of cold sharp cider, then wine from bottles long unopened. The General apologized that his Madeira, an amber wine, was from neither Virginia nor France, but from the islands of Portugal.

On Tuesday, the Chevalier de Chastellux, third in command in the French army, arrived at Mount Vernon with his retinue of aides. General Washington walked with both the Count and the Chevalier along the brick-paved paths of his gardens, proudly showing them his well-tended orchards of fruit trees (the apples now at the peak of ripeness), his neat plots of herbs, his enormous tomatoes. He ordered the stable boys to lead his finest horses across the paddock, so that his guests—and no doubt he himself—could admire them. Then he took the French officers on a tour of the front and back lawns, pointing out a variety of trees—many with a girth of a foot or two—which he himself had planted.

At dusk, the General walked with his guests to a bluff overlooking the river. The serene Potomac, silver-gray in the twilight, at least a mile wide, seemed to embody a dream of peace. After an absence of six years, the General became silent as he gazed upon his beloved river.

His detractors had often whispered that he harbored secret ambitions of becoming America's king, with the army as his base of power. Those misguided fools never watched him gaze with such longing at that river. I recalled his words to the worried citizens of New York City in 1775, while on his way to take command of the army in Cambridge:

> *"When we assumed the soldier, we did not lay aside the citizen; and we shall most sincerely rejoice with you in that happy hour when the establishment of American liberty upon the most firm and solid foundations shall enable us to return to our private stations."*

After a brief but immensely busy visit of two days and three nights, General Washington departed from Mount Vernon at dawn, with an entourage of about thirty riders. He planned to reach Williamsburg within three days, on Friday, September 14. He was especially anxious to meet with the Marquis de Lafayette and to receive a full report on the situation at Yorktown.

In addition to the French officers and their staff, the General's entourage now included his stepson, John Parke Custis. Unlike most men of his generation, Jackie had never fired a musket in battle, nor had he even witnessed a battle. But now that victory was imminent, he wanted to dress in a blue uniform of his own, so he could ride with the elegant French generals as one of his stepfather's aides. He had convinced his mother to let him go, then he had asked for and received the General's permission. Waving proudly goodbye to his wife and four children, he rode with the rest of us out the long driveway in the first pale glow of sunrise, bound for Yorktown.

Billy Lee had rejoined us, riding once again at the General's side. A throng of slaves lined the driveway, waving farewell to the General.

A stableboy who groomed Sir William had told me one morning— though I asked no questions, he proudly revealed the information—that earlier in the year, when a British warship sailed up the Potomac and anchored within sight of Mount Vernon, twenty-seven of General Washington's slaves rowed out during the night to seek their freedom. Taken on board, they had vanished with the frigate.

We had not ridden far before a rider came galloping toward us. The courier handed General Washington a dispatch.

As he rarely displayed his humor, so the General rarely displayed, his face a stern mask, his "impatience and anxiety." Turning to the two French generals, he said evenly, "Admiral de Grasse has departed from Chesapeake Bay. British sails from the north have been sighted. Apparently the Admiral went out to meet them on the Atlantic."

The news had enormous import, which we absorbed in silence.

Were Admiral de Grasse to be defeated, our efforts on land would crumble. The French government, after three years of delay and disappointment, might well decide to withdraw from the war completely. Were the British now able to reinforce Lord Cornwallis from New York with supplies and fresh troops, while the French disappeared, our own troops might say, "Enough."

Aye, if Admiral de Grasse were defeated, our Commander in Chief might well find himself with neither an ally nor an army.

The Count de Rochambeau was the first to speak. "Ça ira bien."

The Chevalier translated, "It will go well."

General Washington did not respond. He had withdrawn deep into his own grave thoughts, as I had often before seen him do, whether at his desk or in the saddle, or even while walking among a crowd of men: we simply vanished for him, as if he and the great dilemmas of the war had set the rest of us at some great distance.

He turned around in his saddle and addressed a soldier in the Life Guard, one of the five who had kept up with him on the gallop to Mount Vernon. "Ride immediately to Annapolis and stop all of our boats moving south. Then ride north to Baltimore and do the same. Continue north to Head of Elk and stop any remaining troops. At every port, send couriers onto the Bay to stop every vessel."

"Aye, sir." The Guard headed his horse to the north and galloped back up the road we had just followed.

The General now turned to the Count de Rochambeau. "I must be in Williamsburg as soon as possible. The gate by sea is open. We must keep closed the gate by land."

Understanding that his host was about to ride for the next three days at a pace which few could match, the Count nodded his assent. "Allons-y."

"Then let us," said the Chevalier, "be on our way."

And so we rode, through that Wednesday, September 12, and Thursday, September 13, and Friday, September 14, pausing to rest our horses, pausing to sleep no more than six hours in a night. The French and American entourage stretched back for miles behind the General. Various riders arrived at taverns, at inns, at various hours; few were in the saddle with us when we departed at dawn.

By the time we reached Fredericksburg, we had become our former contingent: the General on Nelson, his tireless servant Billy Lee on one of the finest mounts in Virginia, four Guards (the fifth was by now in Annapolis), and the General's tireless scribe on *the* finest mount from Massachusetts. We thundered across the bridge over the Rappahannock River; we did not pause to visit the General's mother, who lived in the village and who, as the General once told me, cared naught for the war but instead scolded her son whenever he visited her for neglecting her.

A thunderstorm followed us south on Friday morning, the black clouds rumbling above us. Bolts of lightning crashed into the woods beside us, while sheets of rain turned the road into a long strip of mud. The mud of course came flying up from the hooves of our indefatigable horses; though the General in the lead was soaked with rain but still fairly clean, those of us behind were so splattered that any distinction between Billy Lee and myself had virtually vanished.

We reached Williamsburg on Friday afternoon. Although built during the peace and prosperity of colonial America, Williamsburg had engendered some of America's most radical resolves during the angry months leading up to our Independence. Thus it seemed appropriate that Continental troops now camped on the once-tranquil greens. As we rode along the main street, I spotted, flapping above neat rows of tents, the flag of the Virginia militia, of General Wayne's Pennsylvania regulars, and of Baron Steuben's division.

The French troops which had disembarked from Admiral de Grasse's fleet were encamped near the College of William and Mary. Though the General cantered past the Virginia militia without halting to meet with their officers, he reined Nelson to a halt at the edge of the French camp, where several officers in white, no doubt informed of his approach, stood ready to greet him.

But before General Washington had time to dismount, a lone rider came galloping toward him from a side street, a young man with a long narrow face, wearing a blue coat with white trim and gold epaulettes: the Marquis de Lafayette. He halted so close to the General that one horse nearly collided with the other, then he leaned from his saddle and wrapped his arms around the General. Billy Lee and I watched, stunned (the entire French regiment was watching too), as Lafayette kissed the General from one muddy cheek to the other, and then back again, as if not the Commander in Chief but his beloved wife had just ridden into camp.

Lafayette then sat back in the saddle and explained, as rapidly as he could speak in his admirable English, where he had deployed various bodies of troops throughout Williamsburg and the nearby countryside. What information his scouts had brought from Yorktown: "The British dig and wait." The need for supplies was urgent, especially food—

"What have you heard from Admiral de Grasse?" asked General Washington.

"Sir, I am sorry. Nothing since he sailed out to sea on the fifth."

Then, at least no news of defeat.

The remainder of the afternoon was spent with a review of French and American troops, all of whom appeared to be in good spirits.

That evening, the Marquis de Saint Simon, commander of the French troops from the West Indies, hosted General Washington at a banquet in his honor. The General, though clearly exhausted, not only attended the banquet, but stood at the front door of the white frame house which Saint Simon had requisitioned, and shook the hand of each officer, French and American, who entered. The Count de Rochambeau had by now arrived; looking much less fresh, he stood beside General Washington and greeted the officers as well.

The Marquis de Saint Simon had brought with him his own staff of chefs, who prepared the finest of French cuisine. The several different wines that evening were not from Portugal, but from "la belle France." We might have been dining, as the Marquis de Lafayette remarked to the General, at Versailles itself.

From the initial soup to the final salad, a small orchestra played music from French operas, including Grétry's "Lucille," in which a trumpet fanfare celebrates the return of a father to his family. General Washington, thus saluted with Gallic panache as the father of the allied armies, acknowledged the honor with a bow to Saint Simon.

Departing from the festivities shortly after a church bell had tolled the hour of ten—the September night was warm and the windows were open—General Washington and his staff walked through the dark lanes of Williamsburg to his quarters at the home of George Wythe, an old friend who had signed his name to the Declaration of Independence.

Since we were in a town, I could not simply unroll my blanket and sleep beneath the stars. I was therefore quartered in a small, second-floor room in the Wythe house, with a lovely gabled window looking out on tranquil rooftops and a steeple. I had just lain myself down on the bed—and was marveling at how fine it felt to stretch out on a mattress, without clumps of earth and nubs of rocks beneath me—when I heard a voice down in the street demanding to speak immediately with General Washington. I heard the door latch open, heard boots thump up the stairs, heard a knock on the General's door down the hallway.

I heard the General's door latch . . . and waited . . . then I heard, we all heard, the General call out, "de Grasse is back in the Chesapeake! The British fleet is battered and sent home!"

My feet had hardly touched the floor when I heard the General call, "Mistress York, your pen is wanted."

We spent half that night drafting dispatches: Admiral de Grasse had outmaneuvered the British and had damaged a portion of their fleet. The French fleet was now back in the Bay, forming its blockade. Further—surely a stroke of Providence—while the two fleets were out on the Atlantic, Admiral de Barras and his fleet from Rhode Island had successfully entered the Bay, bringing heavy siege artillery and great quantities of salted beef.

These dispatches were carried north by riders galloping through the night to every port along Chesapeake Bay. The news was accompanied by an order from headquarters: all troops were to proceed south immediately, aboard every available vessel.

To General Benjamin Lincoln, commander of the American troops somewhere at the top of the Bay, General Washington wrote, "Hurry on then, my dear General, with your troops upon the wing of speed."

છ

Chapter One Hundred Fifteen

Benjamin, aloft in the rigging!

On Sunday morning, September 16, 1781, Henry, Susanne and Robert were walking with me and the children—Sally walked on one side, holding my hand, while Caleb walked on the other side, too old now to hold my hand—as we started back toward our campsite after a particularly dreary Sabbath sermon—the somber mumblings of the minister would have darkened the mood of a funeral—when a rider cantered past, calling again and again to every corner of the encampment, "Muster to move out! Muster to move out! The ships are sailing south!"

"Hurrah!" I shouted. "The ships are sailing south!" I knelt and said to Caleb, who during these last seven days in Baltimore had been as baffled and bored as the rest of us. "Help your Aunt Susanne to hitch up Rosie. Be sure all the pots and pans are in the wagon." For if the troops were about to sail, surely the wagons would be rolling south.

"Yup," he said, already talking like some west Virginia rifleman.

I turned to Sally. "You help your Aunt Susanne. It'll be just the three of you now, for a little while."

A great kisser lately—following her Aunt's example—Sally puckered. With a laugh, I gave her a kiss (and could have swung an iron fist into King George's nose for what he was doing to my unknowing little girl).

Then I stood. Henry was kissing his bride—they still behaved as if they had been married yesterday—then he dashed away through the Sabbath crowd to find our colonel and clarify his orders.

I gave Sally's hand to Susanne. "We'll meet you in Williamsburg."

'Or thereabouts,' I could have added. We had no definite destination, other than Yorktown, which promised to be a battlefield.

Taking Sally's hand, Susanne stared at me with her dark eyes, silent.

She had been born a generation too early, or too late, for she was a pioneer, a settler, who asked only to nurture her family and to nurture the earth. She wanted nothing to do with soldiering.

"Susanne," I told her, "you'll be home with Henry in Lincoln by Christmas." As I said it, I believed it. "You'll have the best carpenter in all of Massachusetts to build a house for you. A home that you two will never again in your lives have to leave."

Still she was silent, and still she stared at me.

"Susanne—"

"Go," she said, almost angry with me. As if those seven days in Baltimore had been a paradise, and now the mad fools were off to war again.

With haversack and musket, I marched with my company through the streets of Baltimore to the wharf, where, to my astonishment, I was ordered to board not some rowboat or fisherman's sloop, but a French frigate! Sent north from Admiral de Grasse's fleet, the vessel—a sixth class frigate, as was the *Lively*—had sailed the length of Chesapeake Bay in order to carry us beneath wings of canvas to our destination. A frigate!

I stood with Henry and Robert at the forecastle's larboard gunnel. Looking beyond the bow, I saw that Baltimore's harbor swarmed with small craft paddling or sailing southeastward toward the main body of the Bay. Aye, well we might have been aboard a crabber's scow.

Turning to survey the length of our deck, I listened as the captain called out orders in French, then watched as we cast off lines to the wharf. The bosun piped up to men in the rigging: I watched the first white sails open their bellies to the wind. We had a fine northwest breeze, no doubt stronger out on the water. I watched as the clews were drawn taut, as each sail was properly trimmed, and felt the hull begin to roll beneath my feet with a majesty that even the finest horse could never replicate. Aye, we seemed to ride on the back of a huge white swan, gliding serenely, while a host of skittering black waterbugs scrambled out of the way.

Glancing up at my particular spot, I pointed nearly straight up so that Robert and Henry could watch as well when the "t'gallant," as I told them, was shaken loose from its gaskets. My spirit soared when I heard the sail rumble in the wind. Then it bellied, silent, as the skilled crew quickly trimmed it.

"That's where I worked with the lads," I told Robert, pointing at a sailor standing barefoot on the Flemish horse a hundred feet above the deck.

"Naw," said Robert, incredulous.

"Aye, up there, we hated to come down."

*   *   *

Once we were well out into the Bay, the frigate swung to starboard and held a course which I gauged by the midday sun to be due south. I watched the lads on deck as they trimmed the sails to our new heading. The bosun piped up; with the vessel settled upon her course, the lads aloft scurried down the ratlin's. They glanced with a grin at the dozen Americans vomiting over the rail, then disappeared below.

Thinking I would take a walk around the frigate's deck, I asked Henry and Robert if they would join me. But Henry, clutching the gunnel, was feeling a bit green, and Robert, clutching the gunnel beside him, allowed that he might best keep Henry company. So I set out alone to compare a French frigate with its British counterpart.

They were remarkably similar. The French and English coastlines stared at each other across the narrow Channel. During the centuries of naval warfare, captured vessels were no doubt brought back to port for shipbuilders to examine. Adam, proud of the frigate he sailed, once told me that the *Lively* had been designed by the greatest of all British shipbuilders, Sir Thomas Slade, in 1756. Slade had clearly adopted the best of what he found in captured French frigates. Or, more likely, the French had adopted the best of what they found in Slade's masterful ships.

As I approached the quarterdeck, I noticed a tall officer standing near the wheel who wore a uniform neither French nor American. He was translating back and forth between the French captain and an American major, and though his English was extremely clear, it was spoken with a distinct accent. The discussion concerned whether or not a meal would be provided to the American troops. The major argued that his men had not eaten since dawn; the captain argued that because so many Americans were either at the rail or on their knees around a bucket, any meal "would only be throwing our good French bread into the sea." No matter how vehement the captain and the major became, the tall fellow in the middle remained remarkably cheerful. He passed the tirades back and forth with a lilting voice and affable smile, perhaps in a stalwart effort to keep the two from coming to blows.

When finally the American major, outranked, disappeared angrily down a hatch, I stepped forward to take advantage of a translator on deck. I asked the tall officer if he would ask the captain whether I, a seasoned sailor, might climb into the rigging.

With a cordial nod, he translated my request. The French captain glared at me, then snarled, "Je m'en fou!" Our translator said congenially, "It is all quite the same to me."

"Then may I ascend," I pointed, "to the fore t'gallant, my customary position?"

The French captain listened with officious impatience, then snapped, "Merde!" Our translator rendered this as, "But of course."

Then with a slight bow, he asked, "May I join you?"

Here was a naval officer asking a soldier if he might join me in the rigging. In the t'gallant rigging!

I replied, almost with a laugh, "But of course."

As we walked along the starboard gunnel toward the foremast, the gentleman introduced himself as Count Anders Inghage, of Sweden. He was an officer aboard Admiral de Grasse's flagship, the *Ville de Paris*, but he had elected to join this excursion north in order to view the Bay. He found it far less dramatic than the waters leading into Stockholm, but "most definitely warmer."

Count Inghage took off his coat and waistcoat and set them in the bow of a cutter on deck. He unfastened his dress sword and laid it in the cutter. Then he placed his hat with its white plume beside the sword. Wearing a white shirt with frill at its neck and cuffs, he pointed up the foremast and queried, "Shall we get a bit of wind in our ears?"

I took off my own coat and waistcoat (both French, but exceedingly worn and soiled since I had been issued them over three years ago at Valley Forge), and laid them in the cutter. I set beside them my battered hat, which had no white plume.

Then with a nod to Robert and Henry, who stared at me over their shoulders while they clung to the plunging, heaving prow, I grabbed a shroud and swung my feet up to the gunnel. Looking down with a grin, I saw the surging blue water directly beneath me. Then up the ratlin's I climbed, like a boy bolting free from a schoolhouse door at the bright, bold beginning of summer.

I felt the faint jolt of Count Inghage stepping onto the ratlin's below me. He was soon beside me, matching me step for step up the rolling rope ladder. A count he may or may not have been, but a Swedish lad born to the Swedish sea, he was without a doubt.

Scorning the lubber's hole, we climbed the futtock shrouds around the fighting top, then paused on the platform to stare ahead at the broad blue stretch of Chesapeake Bay. My poor, threadbare, sweat-stinking shirt began to flap in the breeze. With a French "*Pardon*,"—which I had learned from Susanne when she reached across Henry's plate for the salt—I lifted the shirt over my head, tied it as a bulky overhand knot around a shroud . . . and felt with great pleasure the fresh wind on my back.

Up the topmast shrouds we climbed. I invited Count Inghage to lead as the ratlin's narrowed to a point. How quickly my feet found their way; how easily and gracefully my hands moved upwards.

With barely a pause to peek over the tops'l, we continued up the t'gallant shrouds. I was back on that rope ladder so narrow that it twisted while I hugged it to my chest. I was puffing for breath now, but seven years it had been!

Count Inghage insisted that I take the lead as we stepped onto the larboard foot-rope. The t'gallant was handsomely bellied beneath us. With my arms wrapped over the spar, I worked my way out to the end, until I stood, enormously pleased, once again on that loop of foot-rope called the Flemish horse.

I had not been aloft since the lads and I had struggled to gather the madly flapping sail in the storm—when the spar had jumped against my jaw and Nathaniel held me with his arm. I felt a most powerful wish that Nathaniel could be standing beside me now.

But it was Count Inghage, a new person in a new time, who took his place beside me. As the ship gently rolled—far less on the Bay than it would have at sea—we gazed at the blue Chesapeake spread ahead of us, sprinkled with a hundred vessels heading south.

ॐ

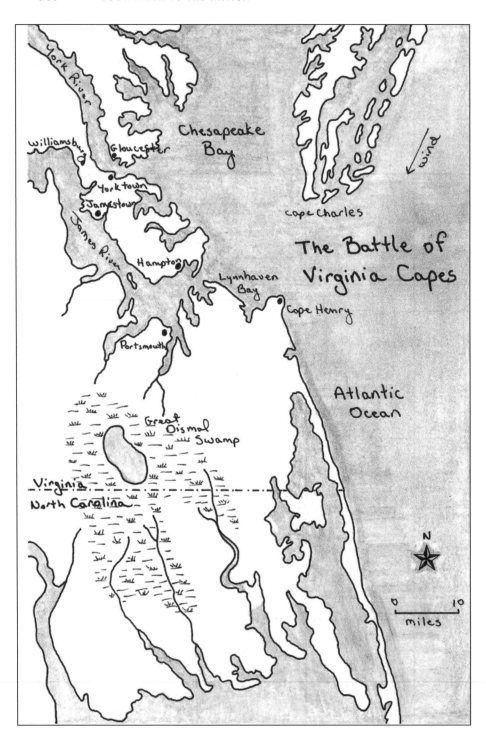

Chapter One Hundred Sixteen

Benjamin, chronicling

THE BATTLE OF VIRGINIA CAPES

"Were you," I asked, "aboard Admiral de Grasse's flagship when the French sailed out to meet the British."

"I was."

"And did you witness the battle out on the Atlantic?"

"The Battle of Virginia Capes, on September the Fifth. I did."

If I was to be grateful to the French, then I wanted to know what to be grateful for. "Then tell me, please, about that day, so I can tell my children."

"Jaaaah," he said. "I don't know that even a single American fisherman saw what the French did for you that day."

Count Inghage rode through a slow roll, as a topman will do before speaking. Then he began, "As a sailor, you would ask, of course, about the wind. It blew as it blows today, from the north, tending toward northeast. Such a wind favors a fleet sailing from the north, as were the nineteen ships of the line under British Admiral Thomas Graves that day, coming down from New York. But what did Graves do when he rounded Cape Charles and discovered a French fleet anchored— *anchored*, mind you—in the mouth of Chesapeake Bay? Did he blast his way into them before they could even get their topsails trimmed? Did he fire nineteen broadsides at their helpless hulls?"

Count Inghage shook his head with a laugh of contempt. "You see, Benjamin, these admirals of the ocean sea operate under two great laws. The second is to sink or capture your enemy's ships. But the *first* law, by far more important, is to be sure that nothing happens to your own ships. Admirals do not seek to fight with their proud warships. They seek to hoard them, just like a clucking hen with all her little chickens. And so . . . did Graves set his sails for the attack? Nei, he luffed."

He let the wind out of his sails. Exactly as General Howe had done in Boston, in New York, in Philadelphia. As General Clinton had done for the past three years. All in the great British tradition.

"Of course, Admiral Graves was following naval code. The Royal Navy's *Fighting Instructions* are clear on this point: he was to 'form line ahead' in a battle line parallel to the enemy's battle line, and only *then* to attack. But of course the French had no battle line. They were anchored in Lynnhaven Bay inside of Cape Henry. So Admiral Graves—even though Britain had been fighting this war for six and a half years—chose to wait for another few hours, while the French hauled anchor and sailed out onto the Atlantic to form their battle line."

Count Inghage paused through a long and especially pleasant roll of the ship.

"The French were at first unable to accommodate. They had the incoming tide against them. I was aboard the *Ville de Paris*, swinging on its anchor cable. We had twenty-four ships of the line in Lynnhaven Bay. The other four warships, and most of the smaller frigates, were then transporting troops up the James River. The fleet was thus weakened by the absence of four vessels, which together carried over two hundred cannon. We were weakened as well by a substantial loss of crew. With both the wind and tide against us, the British could have shot us like ducks in a tub."

Count Inghage pointed: a flock of large white birds, more slender than swans, flapped across the water ahead of us.

"But François Joseph Paul, Comte de Grasse was no duck in a tub. What did he do?" The birds, like a thin white cloud, skimmed over the water toward the distant gray-green shore. "He must of course prevent the British fleet from reaching Yorktown, where Lord Cornwallis was desperately waiting for them. He must prevent the British fleet from controlling any part of Chesapeake Bay. And, knowing that a small French fleet under Admiral Barras was somewhere out on the Atlantic, making its way south from Newport, he must prevent the British fleet from attacking his brethren."

Barras with the siege cannon. As important to the impending siege of Yorktown as the cannons from Ticonderoga had been to the siege of Boston.

"Admiral de Grasse ordered his twenty-four warships ready for combat. Men spring to the rigging, others open the cannon ports. But when the tide begins to turn in the early afternoon, the Admiral does not sail his entire fleet out to the Atlantic—although he tacked against the northeast wind as if that were exactly what he proposed to do. No, instead . . . he sends out one ship around Cape Henry, and after a while, another ship, so that his decoys are not in a tight battle line, but have a great distance between them: the first five ships are stretched out across a mile of the Atlantic.

"The greater part of the French fleet waits. We wait to see if the British will follow our bait. Or will they now attack our even smaller fleet in the mouth of the Bay, then dash west to reach Yorktown before we can stop them?

"Through his brass telescope, Admiral de Grasse watches all nineteen British ships swing their prows to the east. Following Royal Naval Code, they will match our expected battle line with their own battle line. They will make no attempt, until they have properly vanquished us, to capture Chesapeake Bay.

"Accordingly, Admiral de Grasse feeds his ships out one by one, leaving a portion of his fleet still inside Cape Henry until he is certain that all of the British ships are sailing well to the east.

"Once out on the Atlantic, we tighten our line of twenty-four ships. The British, well over a mile north of us, upwind, tighten their line of nineteen. Our fleet is heading east by southeast, a tack that gives us good speed—and increases our distance from the coast of Virginia.

"At six bells in the afternoon—staring at the distant line of British warships, I imagined their bells ringing at the same moment as ours—Admiral Thomas Graves finally hoisted his blue-and-white checkered flag, signaling 'bear down' to the rest of his fleet. However, he did not take down from the mizzenmast of his flagship the earlier flag, still signaling 'line ahead formation.' While 'bear down' indicated an attack, 'line ahead formation' indicated, to the baffled captains of the fleet, that every ship should remain in the present battle line."

"Admiral Graves forgot to take down his first flag?"

"Oh, it was a bloody muck up. And worse: because the British line was not parallel to the French line, but angled at about thirty degrees to it, only a few ships in the British van came close enough to the French that their cannonballs could reach a target. *Most* of the British frigates, though perfectly lined up, were too far away to fire even a single cannonball through a French hull.

"The British second in command, Admiral Samuel Hood, had been in the van when the fleet had first discovered the French at anchor. Hood had no doubt counseled Graves to attack. Not only had he been ignored, but when the British vessels pivoted from a starboard tack to a larboard tack, then sailed out to sea, Hood found himself no longer at the front, but the *rear* of the line. Seething with impatience (so we may surmise), he could only stare through his telescope toward the point far to the southeast where the two battle lines converged. When finally, an hour and a half into the battle, Graves pulled down his 'line ahead' flag, Admiral Hood had only half an hour of daylight left.

"The coming of darkness suited Admiral de Grasse perfectly. Able to retreat more easily with the wind than to advance against it, he drew his line back further and further, until firing ceased on both sides. The two fleets drifted through the night, within sight of each other: we could see their lanterns, and they could surely see ours. We learned, as reports came aboard our sail-rigged cutters to the *Ville de Paris*, that fifteen of our twenty-four ships had been engaged in the battle, though none were badly damaged. (We later learned that only eight of the nineteen British ships had fought, and that several had been severely crippled.)"

The Battle of Virginia Capes, on September the fifth. On that day, the Continental Army had been verging on mutiny at Head of Elk. We had been paid in silver on the sixth. So the French had outmaneuvered the British on the fifth, then paid us on the sixth. And thereby trapped Lord Cornwallis, and kept the army alive. After three and a half years of documents and dithering, our allies—our brothers in arms—had suddenly given us the strength to end this tedious war. France had long ago acknowledged on paper America's independence from Britain; but now she lent her sword to help us cut the knot. For that generosity, for that wisdom, for that strength, I felt profoundly grateful.

"When the orange sun rose," continued Count Inghage, "over the Atlantic on the following morning, every French sailor stared north to see how many of the nineteen British ships might still attack. But not a one, it seemed, was brave enough to assault again the French *fleur de lis*. Admiral de Grasse, looking through his telescope at the shattered British rigging, mentioned to me with great satisfaction that today, the sixth of September, was the Marquis de Lafayette's birthday.

"Aboard the French fleet—and aboard, we assumed, the British fleet as well—carpenters and riggers and sail menders went to work. All through the day, we drifted, drifted, drifted in the steady north wind further away from the mouth of Chesapeake Bay. We did the same on September 7. Both the French and British lines were still remarkably straight, though by now we were no longer off the coast of Virginia, but the coast of North Carolina."

Admiral de Grasse did exactly the same as General Washington had spent over six years doing, and as General Greene, General Morgan, and the Marquis de Lafayette had also done: they maneuvered just out of reach of the enemy, leading the British further and further from a supply base, from a line of communication, from an initial objective, slowly wearing the British out, without themselves ever losing a major battle.

"For five days, the two fleets maneuvered and drifted within sight of each other. Once, we beat northwest, preparing to attack their van, but the British turned their sterns to us and retreated. Our lookouts counted again and again all nineteen ships; none ever attempted to race back to the Bay. Then on September 9, the men aloft shouted that a British warship was going down. It was the *Terrible*, heavily damaged; she sank with seventy-four cannon. Our lookouts thereafter counted eighteen.

"The weather, which had held so steady, abruptly changed. Squalls swept our fleets apart. Because we could no longer see the British, Admiral de Grasse ordered an immediate return to Chesapeake Bay. We dropped anchor in the Bay during the night of the tenth, and discovered at dawn on the eleventh—*Merci, bon Dieu!*—that the fleet from Newport was safely anchored further inside the Bay. The French now had, with both fleets combined, thirty-five ships of the line. The British could only watch from outside the mouth of Chesapeake Bay as Admiral de Grasse renewed his blockade."

Ever since Henry Hudson had navigated up his river, the British had sailed unchallenged from Nova Scotia to Florida, from Halifax to St. Augustine. But now that the French had closed one particular bay, the British empire in America was threatened. Though they held New York City, and Charleston and Savannah, all that mattered now was Yorktown.

"Poor Admiral Graves had nothing to do but sail back to New York, where he would inform General Clinton that the naval effort to rescue Lord Cornwallis had failed. Today is Sunday, September 16, if I am correct. Admiral Graves might at this very moment be sailing into New York Harbor, preparing in his quarters the exact wording of his little speech."

Count Inghage and I rocked high in the rigging in silence. Grateful for his firsthand account, I told him, "Thank you."

"Nei." He waved a dismissive hand at me. "When we return to the deck, tell the captain and his crew, *'Merci.'* "

☙

Chapter One Hundred Seventeen

Genevieve, aboard the Queen Charlotte.

General Washington spent his first days in Williamsburg struggling with problems in Maryland, problems in Virginia, problems at sea. As always, we lacked adequate supplies, adequate wagons, and adequate money.

The British troops under Cornwallis had plundered every farm in the region, often with extraordinary brutality. They stole the best horses; they slaughtered the others. Barns laden with tobacco and forage were set afire. A French officer visited a nearby plantation, seeking fresh vegetables for his men: he discovered a young woman bayoneted to death in her bed. Her breasts had been sliced off and her belly cut open. On the bedroom wall, the British brutes had written, dipping their fingers into the mother's blood, "Thou shalt never give birth to a rebel." The child she had been carrying was found outside, hanging by a noose from an apple tree.

The village of Williamsburg was already crowded with refugees from the surrounding countryside when thousands of French and American troops, arriving daily from the north, set up encampments in nearby pastures and fields. Once again, General Washington sent out the old order that necessaries were to be dug, and *redug* when needed.

We were at our desks in the Wythe House on Saturday afternoon, September 15—I was copying orders to local fishermen for baskets of fresh fish (to be purchased on credit)—when a French officer in the cleanest white uniform I had seen in weeks arrived with a message for General Washington. Escorted into the General's office, Capitaine de la Loire introduced himself, then announced that Admiral de Grasse had sent four chests of money, to be used to procure food and supplies for the American troops. Three of these chests, he explained, contained a loan, in silver *livres*, from French citizens in the West Indies. The fourth chest, however, contained a gift in gold *reales* from the people of Havana. The Cubans earnestly supported the American cause. "Further," he added with a knowing whisper, "they wish to even an old grudge against the British pirates."

General Washington, his reserve intact, followed Capitaine de la

Loire out the door of Wythe House, then he stared—as did we all—at four ox-carts in the street, each cart bearing an oaken chest wrapped with wrought iron straps. A troop of three dozen French marines stood along both sides of the street, guarding the carts.

General Washington stepped through the marines and placed his hand atop one of the chests. The French had paid his troops at Head of Elk; the French had blockaded Chesapeake Bay; and now the French, and the Cubans, would feed his troops until the battle at Yorktown had been won.

General Washington returned to Capitaine de la Loire and told him warmly while shaking his hand, "*Merci. Merci.*"

The captain saluted, handed the General a folded document, stated that he must now return to his ship, and departed with his marines.

Twenty members of the Life Guard were immediately deployed around the four carts. After some discussion, the General agreed that the chests would be stored in a brick house down the street where the French commissary, Claude Blanchard, was quartered. I was to assist Monsieur Blanchard by keeping a tally in my ledger of all payments made from the four chests.

The oxen pulled their load in a short but extraordinary parade down the street. Members of the Life Guard carried each chest—eight men staggered with the weight—into the brick house. Moving a table, they set the four chests in a compact row in the dining room near a cold hearth. The drovers, their duty done, drove away their empty carts.

I returned to the Wythe House to fetch my ledger. General Washington was already back in his office. While inspecting my quills to find a freshly sharpened point, I heard a crash that was clearly not the blast of a cannon, but nearly as loud. Racing down the street to the commissary's house, I peered in through the door and stared at a jagged hole in the floor. All four chests were now in the cellar.

Although not a single chest had burst open (the oak and wrought iron had done their job), the dozen privates from Delaware (recruited on the spot as they were walking down the street in search of a tavern) had a most difficult job as they hefted the chests back up to street level.

Later that afternoon, a letter arrived at headquarters from Admiral de Grasse. In a condescending tone to our Commander in Chief, the Admiral stated that he was "annoyed" with the slowness of our troops as they marched south. The storms of autumn would soon arrive. "The season is approaching when, against my will, I shall be obliged to forsake the allies for whom I have done my very best and more than could be expected."

The Admiral was threatening to sail away! The French blockade would disappear. What sort of ally was this?

General Washington conferred with the Count de Rochambeau. Together they sent a polite letter requesting the pleasure of a meeting with Admiral de Grasse.

The Admiral's cordial invitation arrived at headquarters on Sunday evening. He was sending a captured British vessel the following day to Jamestown. The cutter would carry both General Washington and the Count de Rochambeau, with their staffs, down the James River to the flagship *Ville de Paris*, aboard which they would meet on Tuesday.

General Washington spent much of Sunday night at his lamp-lit desk, writing a list of questions which he would present to Admiral de Grasse.

On Monday morning, September 17, our group of seven stepped out of two carriages onto the bank of the James River, near the remains of what had once been the village of Jamestown. On this small marshy peninsula, with its protected cove for a harbor, the English had built their first settlement in America, in 1607. Within twelve years, their crops, and their confidence in each other, had grown to the point that the colonials were able to establish the first representative government in America: in 1619, one year before the Pilgrims landed.

And here, on this very stretch of shoreline along the river, the first African slaves had been unloaded from a Dutch ship and sold to the Virginia colonists, in 1619. Thus we stood that morning on the site where the English first established their way of life in the New World.

The *Queen Charlotte*, a thirty-foot cutter with a single mast, was waiting for us alongside a pier. On board stood a French officer in a white uniform, and, on a small elevated quarterdeck at the tiller, a river pilot wearing a filthy shirt and breeches. The officer wore shiny black boots; the river pilot was barefoot. As Capitaine Boulanger welcomed us on board, he attempted to repeat in his best English each of our names as we introduced ourselves. He was especially pleased to meet "Général Vasheentun." When I boarded, the last of the seven, Capitaine Boulanger bowed with pleasure and told me, "Enchanté!" He took my hand and kissed it.

The pilot at the tiller gave General Washington a sullen nod, then looked to his sails. A boy on the pier cast off the lines. The cutter had a

"Queen Charlotte"

long bowsprit (here Benjamin is helping me with the names) with a sail attached to its end; that sail now swung the bow away from the pier and pulled us toward the center of the river. The farm girl from Lincoln was sailing aboard her first sailboat!

After days of urgent business at headquarters, we found ourselves standing in a row along the gunnel, gazing peacefully across the brown water of the James River. No one spoke, not even the affable Capitaine Boulanger.

General Washington stood nearest the bow. The river, several miles wide (and thus unlike any Massachusetts river), was not the Potomac, but nonetheless, it must have offered him some measure of peace.

The Count de Rochambeau stood beside him, and then Colonel Louis le Beque Duportail, the brilliant French military engineer who had designed the vital fortress at West Point.

Standing fourth along the gunnel was the Chevalier de Chastellux, more a philosopher than a soldier, and thus supremely French.

Beside these three aristocrats stood General Knox, a bookseller, a philosopher in his own right, a master of artillery, and, were we to need his three hundred pounds to balance a gust of wind, the best ballast we had on board.

Sixth in the row was Colonel Tench Tilghman, the General's aide, who had been at the General's side during Lee's rout at Monmouth.

Last in that row stood the scribe with her satchel of paper, freshly sharpened quills, and bottles of ink. Being furthest to the stern, and thus closest to the pilot at his tiller, I could smell, even with the breeze on my face, what might have been a barrel of fish heads standing in the hot Virginia sun, or a mud flat at low tide, had it not been him.

After my eyes had rested long enough on the tranquil water, I turned around to inspect my first sailboat. It had four sails, all of them speeding us along so nicely that the water gurgled off our stern. The triangular jib was rigged to the bowsprit and lower half of the mast; reaching far forward, it caught the wind in front of the cutter.

A smaller staysail, also a triangle, caught the wind passing over the forward third of the vessel.

Rigged to the mast and stretching sternwards between an upper gaff and a lower boom, was a four-sided sail with not a single right-angled corner. The boom was low enough, I noticed, that should it suddenly swing across to our side of the cutter, all seven of us would be swimming, or bubbling, in the James.

The fourth sail was the highest, draped from a horizontal spar at the top of the two-part mast.

With so much canvas spread to catch the wind, in front of the cutter, along the length of the cutter, behind the cutter, and well above the cutter, the *Queen Charlotte* raced along in what was merely a steady breeze. Were a real wind to catch our sails—a good strong norther off the open sea—we would gallop.

The voyage from Jamestown to the mouth of the James River was about thirty miles, as Capitaine Boulanger estimated. We would then have another twenty miles across the mouth of Chesapeake Bay to the *Ville de Paris*, anchored in formation with the other thirty-four ships of the line in the fleet.

"When, then, shall we arrive?" asked General Washington, facing forward now, his boots spread against the gentle roll of the cutter, one hand gripping a black shroud that supported the mast.

"*Eh bien*, the Admiral is expecting us at ten o'clock tomorrow morning," replied Capitaine Boulanger, his eyes on the scattered white clouds to the northwest.

"Ah," said General Washington, then he turned and walked toward the stern. I could see immediately—for I had spent over six years with him—that he was furious with impatience, but showing his temper to no one.

Only with great reluctance had he left his desk at headquarters in Williamsburg. Two entire armies were assembling for their first battle under one command. We had artillery, but a shortage of gunpowder. Wagons were still rolling south along the Virginia roads; many were waiting their turn to ferry across the Potomac River, and then the Rappahannock. The Virginia militia had arrived, bringing many more stomachs than firelocks. And of course, at any moment, Cornwallis and the bloody Tarleton might try to slash their way through the disorder in Williamsburg toward the back country of Virginia. Or they might attempt an escape across the York River. General Clinton might well be heading south with every ship in New York Harbor. And no one knew what reinforcements might be sailing from London.

With all this to challenge his weary mind, General Washington had no need to spend what could well be three days away from his desk, away from reports arriving with express riders every half hour, away from scouts who reported day and night from Yorktown . . . so that he could visit an imperious French Admiral who threatened to sail back to his Sugar Islands. As Doctor Franklin had courted the French nobility at Versailles, so General Washington was now called upon to court the

French nobility in America, with all politeness possible, wherever and whenever they chose to meet with him.

Yes, the voyage was a pleasant one. And yes, Capitaine Boulanger provided an excellent dinner, served in a small cabin beneath the raised quarterdeck on which the tillerman stood. But when, at dusk, we sailed out the mouth of the James, then raced in a much brisker wind toward the shelter of Lynnhaven Bay, and anchored there for the night, well within sight of one end of the French fleet, General Washington was seething. Surely we could have sailed out to the *Ville de Paris*, for the wind was steady and every ship of the line in the blockade had its lanterns. A two-hour meeting, even at midnight, and then we could be off again, half way up the James by dawn.

But no. The Admiral expected us at ten o'clock tomorrow morning.

Capitaine Boulanger invited General Washington to share the cabin with him for the night. The General replied that he preferred the sea air under the stars. All seven of us accordingly slept on cotton pallets on the hard deck, with a cape or a blanket drawn over us. Our tillerman slept up on his quarterdeck, which suited us well; because the cutter swung at the end of its anchor line, he was always downwind.

As I lay on my gently rocking bed, listening to the unfamiliar cry of a sea bird, listening to the gentle slap of a line against the mast, listening to small waves lap against the hull, I wondered where on the roads of Virginia my two children and Susanne might be. I wondered where my husband and brother and Robert might be. Thinking again of Sally, whom I especially missed, I could have wept, had I allowed myself such unmilitary behavior.

And then I thought, that when the war was over, and we were all back on the farm in Lincoln, how fine it would be if we all rode on horses and in the wagon into Boston on a clear, bright, breezy summer morning, rode right through the city, past the marketplace, to the wharf. We would look for a cutter or a schooner or a sloop at the pier, with a captain willing to take us out on the Atlantic for the day. (Never mind what it might cost.) We would load the family aboard, with baskets of dinner, Mama's ham and Papa's cider, then sail and sail and sail far out from land, on a craft as sleek and swift as the *Queen Charlotte*, where the waves and the wind and the sun were all as the Creator first meant them to be.

☙

Chapter One Hundred Eighteen

Genevieve, almost in Paris.

On the following day, Tuesday, September 18, 1781, I felt like an American peasant in disguise, visiting the French King at Versailles. General Washington, however, never let them know for a moment that he felt like anything other than Commander in Chief.

In the morning aboard the *Queen Charlotte*, Capitaine Boulanger provided us each with a "*baguette*" of bread which had been baked in an oven aboard the *Ville de Paris* by the Admiral's personal baker. He apologized that the bread was not absolutely fresh, but now two days old. He need not have apologized; the bread, though with not a bit of butter or strawberry jam, was remarkably good. Standing along the gunnel in the morning sunshine, the nine of us—including the captain and the silent, sullen river pilot—broke off fluffy white chunks and soon devoured our slender, two-foot loaves.

Capitaine Boulanger offered us as well a number of strange fruits from the West Indies, of which the orange papaya, cut in half and eaten with a soup spoon, quickly became my favorite.

But the *piece de resistance* (as Susanne would have called it) was the Cuban coffee which the captain served in elegant blue and white cups on a tray. We drank our coffee—from the first sip, we *savored* it—while gazing across the silver-blue water at the distant blockade of French warships. The morning was cool and fresh; the wind had swung around so that it now swept in from the sea, smelling no longer of tidal flats but of brine. Portly General Knox, sipping his coffee, began to deeply hum.

The tillerman readied his sails, coiled his lines, then stood at the tiller while Capitaine Boulanger and General Knox hauled in the long anchor line. (Despite his rank, Capitaine Boulanger—captain of his own French warship, not of this captured British cutter—seemed to enjoy lending a hand.) I watched with fascination as the tillerman, filling the jib with wind while the other sails luffed, swung the prow of the cutter to the north. Then by tightening his lines—he called gruff orders to Capitiane Boulanger, who tightened them—he caught the wind in his four wings and quickly had us leaning steeply as we skimmed from the shelter of Lynnhaven Bay out onto the long smooth waves rolling in from the Atlantic Ocean.

We formed our row of seven once more along the uphill side of the cutter, some of us facing the morning sun as it cast a yellow sheen across the Atlantic, some of us facing the enormous flocks of white birds that drifted over Chesapeake Bay. When Capitaine Boulanger stepped out from the cabin with his silver pitcher and poured for each of us, including the tillerman, a *second* cup of coffee, life was absolutely complete.

We sailed north for several miles, just inside the row of anchored French ships. Their bare masts and spars formed a towering fence across the mouth of the Bay. Each ship of the line was as large as the largest vessel I had ever seen in Boston Harbor. Each flew a white flag with three gold *fleur-de-lis*; the flags were so huge, flapping valiantly in the wind off the sea, that we could hear their rumble. General Washington walked back from the bow until he stood beside me. "Do you remember the good Doctor Franklin at your wedding in Cambridge?"

"Of course," I said, surprised that the General would now be thinking about my wedding.

He swept his hand toward the blockade of men-of-war, a line so long that the ships furthest north became misty and faint. "There is the work of our good Doctor Franklin. He finally got the King to see that we are serious."

Our pilot tillered sharply to the right, toward the largest and most elegant of all the ships. As I read *Ville de Paris* in gold lettering across the stern, I heard the faint ringing of three bells from high up on deck. No doubt we were right on time.

Three levels of tall windows wrapped around the stern, each level framed with ornate scrollwork, painted gold. Long balconies, fringed with elegant balustrades, stood outside the two upper rows of windows. Had Marie Antoinette stepped out in a pink gown to gaze at the Bay, I would not have been surprised.

A shrill whistle piped some signal. Men in white gathered along the towering side of the ship to look down at us. One of them called down through a trumpet a greeting in French.

As our tiny cutter approached the great flagship, Capitaine Boulanger told us proudly that the *Ville de France* was the largest warship in the world. Our mast barely reached as high as the man-of-war's deck. General Knox pointed with admiration at three rows of square porthole covers along the length of the ship. "Gunports," he told me. "Over fifty cannons to a side. Much easier than driving oxen over a snowbound mountain."

A long line came uncoiling down. Capitaine Boulanger caught it, then tied it to our tiny bow, so that we drifted back and settled with our hull parallel to the warship's hull. Our pilot hung half a dozen ingeniously woven bundles of rope over the side, which kept the two hulls from scraping even as waves lifted us lengthwise and lowered us again.

Working together, Capitaine Boulanger and the tillerman dropped the luffing sails and folded them. Both men were astonishingly quick. The pilot had probably spent his school days on the river; the captain, as a boy, might well have sailed his own little skiff along the coast of France.

The question now forming in my mind was answered in a most unsettling way when a rope ladder with wooden steps was lowered over the ship's side, until its bottom rung reached the gunnel just aft of our mast. Henry had been the tree climber when we were children, not I. Looking up the side of that towering ship, I felt as if I were looking up the steeple of Old South Meeting House in Boston.

The Count de Rochambeau led the way. Standing on the gunnel, bracing himself with a grip on a shroud, he waited until the cutter rose and hovered on the back of a wave, then he stepped onto the ladder, quickly gripping its ropes with both hands before the cutter dropped away beneath him. We watched as he climbed at a steady pace up the blue-and-yellow hull.

General Washington followed, his boots—the polished, well-worn boots which Benjamin had cobbled—moving just as steadily up the ladder.

General Knox waited . . . until Chastellux, Duportail, and Tilghman had all disappeared from the ladder onto the ship's deck . . . before he placed his weight on the first step. I shifted safely toward the cutter's stern; Capitaine Boulanger, I noticed, moved safely toward the bow. Whether General Knox, or a loose cannon, came crashing down on us, it would make, in my estimation, little difference.

Once General Knox, without a pause in his long ascent, had stepped onto the ship's deck, Capitaine Boulanger gestured to me: my turn. Never before had I truly appreciated Benjamin's tales about his ventures up into the rigging. But as I stepped, with great trepidation, onto that gently swinging ladder, then made my way upwards, past the first row of gunports, past the second row of gunports—not a soul above me was bothering to watch—I felt that I was proving myself as one of Benjamin's sturdy topmen.

When finally my eyes peered level with the windy deck of the ship, I beheld a scene of pomp and ceremony. French sailors stood as neatly in formation as if Baron Steuben had cursed them into rank-and-file perfection. Toward the stern, General Washington in his blue-and-buff uniform was speaking with a French officer equally tall, wearing blue-and-scarlet: Admiral de Grasse.

I placed my feet gratefully on the steady deck, straightened my Life Guard's coat and cocked hat, then crossed the broad deck until I stood, as inconspicuous as a duckling among swans, beside and just slightly behind Colonel Tilghman—within sight of General Washington, should he need me. As the General was introduced to one French officer after another, each of whom made a formal bow, I wished that my father could see us; my father, who had only once in his life been aboard a ship, in order to throw its tea into Boston Harbor. How far America had come since that early day! His face blackened with lamp soot, Papa had chopped open the crates with his axe; his daughter now stood on the flagship of the most powerful assembled fleet in the world, listening to French aristocracy speaking their best English as they addressed our Commander in Chief as "Your Excellency."

Following the introductions, Admiral de Grasse invited General Washington to join him in his cabin. A bell rang four times as they passed through an elegant doorway at the rear of the deck. The French officers waited politely while their American counterparts followed. Number seven once again, I stepped over a mahogany door jamb into the most extraordinary room I had ever entered.

The Admiral's day cabin, as wide as the ship, was wrapped with those same stern windows which I had seen from the cutter. The bright morning sun shone through the windows to the left, lighting a writing desk and a red leather chair. At that desk, no doubt, the Admiral had written his letters to our Commander in Chief.

The long row of tall windows across the stern—I counted nine of them—faced the broad, silver-green expanse of Chesapeake Bay. We seemed not to be aboard a ship, but in a royal palace beside the sea. The windows to the right faced the line of men-of-war in the blockade to the north. Beyond them, I could see, miles away, a faint gray wisp of shoreline: Cape Charles.

It was as if a bit of Europe had come to gaze upon the wild shore of America. As if European royalty wanted to know where all the poor and discontented peasants had run away to. Or perhaps, as if royalty wanted to know how the world had once been—big, open, green, fresh, and free—before anyone had gilded it.

The Admiral beckoned us with a sweep of his arm to be seated around a long table in the center of the room. One end was covered with sea charts, some of them rolled, some spread open and anchored at their corners with brass candlesticks. Admiral de Grasse and General Washington sat beside each other in two leather chairs; thus both were at the head of the table, in cooperation rather than contention. The rest of us took our places along both sides, the Count de Rochambeau at the far end with his hands folded on a chart.

Scribe York reached into pockets which she had sewn inside her coat and took out several sheets of folded paper, a short and frazzled but well-sharpened quill, and a tightly corked bottle of ink. She opened the slightly damp sheets of paper and flattened them on the table, then she carefully loosened the black cork. After dating a sheet of paper, "SEPTEMBER 18, 1781," she was ready for the negotiations to begin.

General Washington, speaking through his interpreter, Colonel Tench Tilghman, opened with a statement that emphasized in broad detail the importance of the present campaign. Both "the peace and independence" of America, and "the general tranquillity of Europe" were threatened, should their allied efforts not meet with success against the British forces at Yorktown. Crucial to the campaign was the presence of the French fleet, closing all escape by sea, and all reinforcement by sea, until "the reduction of Lord Cornwallis's position" was completed.

General Washington asked, with smooth diplomatic skill, whether Admiral de Grasse could inform him of the date upon which his orders required him to depart.

Admiral de Grasse stated that his orders indicated he should depart for the West Indies by October 15, but that he, on the basis of his own judgment, would prolong the presence of his fleet until the end of the month.

I could see in the General's eyes that he calculated in a flash: six weeks. Far better than four.

He glanced at me, halfway down the table. "For my own notes and remembrance, please record that Admiral de Grasse will support us with his fleet until the thirty-first of October."

And so, for the General's "remembrance," we had the precise date in writing.

General Washington now inquired whether the three thousand

French troops which had been landed under the command of Marquis de Saint Simon might be recalled back to the fleet, and if so, when might that be?

Admiral de Grasse assured General Washington that the three thousand marines would remain under the General's command during "that period for the reduction of York."

I noted the information under Point Two.

General Washington thanked Admiral de Grasse and the gathered officers "once again" for their skillful victory against the British fleet on the fifth of September. (He had of course thanked them when he first arrived on deck.) That victory, the General continued, enabled French ships to control Chesapeake Bay, as well as the Atlantic outside of Cape Charles and Cape Henry, and the James River to well above Jamestown and Williamsburg.

However, the British still had a few ships anchored near the port of Yorktown, and thus they controlled the York River. They might attempt a sudden escape, either by crossing over to Gloucester, where Tarleton already had several hundred troops, or by sailing to the upper end of the York River, well beyond Williamsburg, a point from which they could continue their flight by land.

Would it be possible for Admiral de Grasse to send a number of smaller ships up the York, to guard against any untoward navigation by the British?

"Far too dangerous," replied the Admiral. "Our scouts indicate that the British have substantial artillery along the western shoreline, which could be brought to bear against any invading frigate."

General Washington pushed the point slightly.

Admiral de Grasse remained firm.

I wrote, "Point Three: no French ships in the York."

Proceeding to the next question, General Washington turned from the regional conflict to the entire southern coastline: he asked whether, should the campaign at Yorktown end with sufficient expedition, the French fleet might be able to assist American land troops in an attack on the British-held ports of Wilmington, North Carolina, or Charleston, South Carolina. The defeat of those two garrisons would free the Carolinas entirely from any British occupation, and accordingly, any further threat to Virginia.

Again the Admiral said no. His ships were not of the proper design for the besieging of seaports. He explained no further.

"Point Four: Yorktown only. Neither Wilmington nor Charleston."

General Washington now raised the problem which had plagued him since his first days in Cambridge in 1775: would the Admiral be able to loan him additional heavy artillery, and especially, gunpowder?

Admiral de Grasse stated that his ships had expended a significant amount of both shot and gunpowder during their engagement with the British. However, he would confer with his officers. Turning to his staff, he gathered information from several of them. Then, addressing both General Washington and General Knox, he specified the number and size of cannons, and the number of barrels of gunpowder, which his transports would ferry to Jamestown within the next three days.

I noted every barrel.

General Washington completed his list of questions. He included a few minor requests; some were honored, some not.

He then summarized our agreements point by point, and warmly thanked Admiral de Grasse for his willingness to support the siege of Yorktown to the inevitable triumph.

The Admiral was grateful for these warm sentiments of friendship from his American ally. Perhaps to show how strongly he believed in the American cause (or perhaps to have the final word), he surprised us by offering two thousand additional troops, should General Washington need them for the final "coup de main"—a slap of the hand—against the British.

The General and the Admiral now stood up from their chairs—everyone stood—and shook hands. I do not know whether Doctor Franklin ever shook hands with King Louis the Sixteenth, but I do know that General Washington gripped the hand of Admiral de Grasse, and that he no doubt wanted to maintain that grip . . . until he let go in order to receive Lord Cornwallis's sword of surrender.

The table was cleared of papers and maps. A multitude of stewards suddenly streamed into the cabin, to serve dinner: fresh sea bass "*a la française.*" Sweet potatoes from the West Indies, glazed with raw cane sugar. And the finest of wines. Scribe York, her duties now completed, increasingly appreciated both the delicate flavor of the white wine and the handsome young steward who poured it.

As we finished our *tartes*, the westering sun shone no longer off the starboard quarter (as Benjamin would say), but directly through the stern windows. We admired its copper sheen on the Bay. That a war awaited us on the mainland seemed unthinkable.

Following the leisurely banquet, Admiral de Grasse invited General Washington on a tour of the *Ville de Paris*. The General was surely anxious to return to our cutter, so that we might sail with what little daylight remained for the James River and Williamsburg. But of course the honored guest must visit the three decks of cannons.

When finally he returned to the quarterdeck, General Washington was informed that during the afternoon, every captain of every man-of-war in the fleet had come aboard. Each Count and Duke and Marquis now wished to make the cordial acquaintance of General Vasheentun. Our Commander in Chief, a Virginian of the highest order, showed his redoubtable skills by responding to every courtesy with an equal if somewhat reserved courtesy.

Finally, in the last glow of daylight, we climbed down the ladder to our cutter. The descent was made under much darker conditions than the ascent, and the ladder dangled much further out from the rolling hull of the *Ville de Paris*, then clattered against it, for the wind seemed to be increasing.

Capitaine Boulanger cast off. The tillerman swung the prow with his jib, then set us on a course toward the distant mouth of the James. The sun had by now disappeared; above the western horizon, horsetail clouds blazed a radiant scarlet.

My eyes were on the beauty of that sky, and the colors it rendered across the broad Bay, when suddenly a cannon blast from behind jolted me severely.

Staring back toward that thunderclap, we discovered that hundreds of sailors stood in the rigging of all three masts of the *Ville de Paris*, their white uniforms distinct against the darkening sky. Now a second cannon fired, sending a plume of red sparks from a gunport. One by one, in a dignified series, nineteen more cannons fired, honoring our Commander in Chief with a twenty-one gun salute.

General Washington lifted his hat and waved it to the tiny white figures of crew in the rigging and officers along the stern rail. Perhaps with a telescope, Admiral de Grasse could see him.

We thought of course that we had now received the French salute. But to our amazement, a sailor at the end of a spar fired a musket, and so commenced a naval "*feu de joie*," a running fire of musketry such as we had fired on the Grand Parade at Valley Forge, when we celebrated our alliance with the French. We watched with growing admiration as their muskets fired smartly all through the rigging, from spar to spar, from mast to mast, high above the magnificent *Ville de Paris*.

I wished that the Baron could have been with us.

After the final shot, we all waved our hats and shouted, "*Huzzah!*"

Then we sailed away in a rising wind and deepening dark toward the protected waters of the James.

◌

Chapter One Hundred Nineteen

Benjamin.

I remember clearly that threatening evening in September, 1781. Count Inghage and I were on the third day of our grand voyage down Chesapeake Bay, at our customary station in the rigging. Just after five bells, the boson's pipe sent teams of topmen aloft to furl the t'gallants and double reef the topsails: weather was coming. Searching the sky, we discovered a bank of black clouds far to the southeast, belying the tranquillity of a beautiful crimson sunset to the west.

The smaller boats on the Bay, loaded with our troops, began to scurry toward the eastern shore. The American pilot at our helm must have convinced the French captain to seek shelter for the night, for even as the sails were reefed, our frigate veered east as well.

The pilot knew his business. He steered us around a hook of land, then ran with the rising wind off our starboard quarter up a surprisingly deep bay . . . to the most perfect anchorage a sailor might ever find. The topmen were lashing tight the sails along every spar (the lads welcomed Anders and I to gather canvas and secure our gaskets) when sudden gusty sheets of rain almost blinded us.

Anders and I followed the last of the topmen down the ratlin's as the battering storm and the full darkness of night made every step a cautious one.

A jagged flash struck the shore nearby; the thunderclap an instant later shook every timber in the ship.

Genevieve, that same night.

My grandchildren, please keep deep in your hearts that tillerman, a Chesapeake fisherman who smelled as if he stored yesterday's catfish in his pockets and a crab under his hat. For without him, your mother would not be sitting here now at this table in Lincoln, nor, I believe, would General Washington have returned to his desk in Williamsburg.

Our tillerman and Capitaine Boulanger both spotted the wall of black clouds as soon as it appeared above Cape Henry. The French captain had his coat off in a moment, then his waistcoat; off came his boots and stockings, all of them tossed down into the cabin. Now barefoot in his fine white shirt and knee breeches, he showed Duportail and Rochambeau which lines to release on deck (he wasted no time with those of us who spoke no French), then up the ratlin's he climbed to the topsail. He shouted down; Rochambeau released his line: he let it out slowly, while Boulanger gathered the flapping sail along the length of its spar, then lashed it tight. He was clearly doing the work of several men—perhaps a team of four spread along the spar—but he was doing it alone, and exceedingly well.

As he was coming down the ratlin's, the tillerman shouted to Knox to take the tiller. (No time to waste with those who spoke no English.) General Knox hastened up the two steps to the quarterdeck, stood where he was told to stand, then took hold of the long heavy bar of the tiller. He stared at the compass in its binnacle, lit by a whale oil lamp, while the tillerman shouted the course he was to follow. "Two sixty-five! Never mind she swings a bit. Keep her at two sixty-five!"

General Knox laughed that he would hold two sixty-five until they reached New Orleans.

The tillerman jumped down to the deck. He and Boulanger, without a word, had the gaff mainsail down, gathered, wrapped and tied in less than three minutes.

The wind was rising: dark waves slapping the hull tossed their spray across the deck.

The two men now lowered the jib, leaving only the fourth sail, the small staysail on the bow of the cutter, to catch the wind.

The job done, the tillerman bounded back to the quarterdeck and took the tiller from Knox (who stepped down to the deck with a swashbuckling stagger).

Gripping the gunnel, our faces wet with a cold driving mist, we watched a line of white froth racing toward us across the black water. Like the British cavalry charge at Monmouth, I thought. Then a blast of wind heaved the cutter nearly onto her side, while we gripped the rail . . . someone shouted something . . . I felt my feet slide . . . and then our shuddering cutter rolled back up and pounded forward. The staysail pulled us with at least as much speed as all four sails had driven us that morning. Whitecaps reached toward us like desperate ghosts, then swept past the stern.

The mast bent forward. The shrouds were as tight as the strings on a fiddle.

I looked at the tillerman, faintly lit by the compass lamp as he held his course. I expected a look of grim resolve; but no, his face was filled with an expectant eagerness. Like every good sailor, he wanted to see what his vessel could do.

The *Queen Charlotte* was—I suddenly remembered the feeling—racing across the black water like a sled racing down a long snowy hill, thumping and lurching at the edge of balance, but always skimming so fast that no accident seemed able to catch it. The hull heaved and pounded beneath our feet. Something loose clattered about in the cabin. Spray lashed across the deck, salty when I licked my lips.

A bolt of lightning cracked nearby, startling me as much as that first French cannon. In the moment of its flash, while the thrashing sea gleamed silver-black and the blowing foam glowed unearthly white, I glanced again at the tillerman's face. No longer sullen, our American was grinning. His hat was gone, his fair hair flew back in tangles. He seemed to be hollering something, though not to any passenger on board, nor to Boulanger, who stood at the bow near a line to the staysail. Perhaps our tillerman was hollering to the *Queen Charlotte* herself, as I at full gallop would call to Sir William above the thunder of his hooves.

I could not hear the tillerman's voice. The wind was shrieking in the rigging. Then a thunderclap muted even the screaming wind.

Five of the seven, I noticed, had gone below to the cabin. General Washington and I remained out in the storm. He stood on the jouncing deck near the bow, one hand on the gunnel. His woolen cloak was no doubt as wet as mine. The hat in his hand, like the hat in my hand, was drenched with rain and spray. With every flash of lightning, he glanced up the steady mast . . . at the straining triangular sail . . . at the raging sea beyond our bow. He seemed, with a sturdy sailor at the tiller and a sturdy sailor at the jib, as confident as a man can be in time of war.

With the hand of Providence perhaps on the tiller as well, we found an anchorage about two hours later, in a sheltered bay just inside the mouth of the James River. The tillerman knew the bay was there (as he told us the following morning) because the roar of the sea along the shoreline had become quieter: there was open water into a cove.

He swung the prow into the wind, then shouted "Anchor!" into the darkness, which was close enough to "Ancre!" that we soon heard the splash. *Queen Charlotte* drew back against her anchor line. Boulanger and the tillerman brought down and silenced the wildly flapping staysail. And then, despite the storm lashing through the trees on shore, despite the rain drumming on the deck, despite a thin wail high in the rigging . . . the night seemed wonderfully calm, the deck wonderfully level.

Dark creatures emerged from the cabin door; peering through the rain at the tranquil vessel, and at the haven of a calm bay around them, they muttered prayers in English and French.

General Washington stepped up to the quarterdeck. In the glow of the lamp, he reached out his hand to shake the tillerman's hand. "To whom do I have the honor of extending my gratitude, sir?"

The tillerman gripped the General's hand. "I am Charles Cooper, sir. Sorry if you're a bit damp."

"Mister Cooper, your name shall be made known to the gentlemen in Congress."

"Thank you, sir."

Long and dreary would be the log of the remainder of our voyage. The storm gradually abated to a drizzle, until by midmorning the next day, after we had sailed no more than two or three miles, the wind died completely and we were becalmed—utterly becalmed—not far inside the mouth of the James.

On the 20th, we struggled against another gale. The day brought us blinding rain, constantly shifting winds, and a sandbar that caught hold of our bow and held it . . . until the tide lifted us off again.

We were greatly cheered, however, on the evening of the 20th, by an easing of the weather, and the appearance of a French frigate which anchored nearby for the night. It carried, as we learned when we hailed it, American troops who had embarked in Baltimore. The crowded ship was bound for Jamestown. A flock of smaller boats was not far behind: troop transports from Head of Elk, from Baltimore, from Annapolis. General Washington was greatly heartened.

The frigate disappeared into the rain on the morning of the 21st. But as we beat our way up the river, a growing number of vessels, some under sail and some paddled with oars, joined us in the struggle up the James. Despite his impatience with the unsteady weather, General Washington would cup his hands and call out to every new craft, "What regiment are you?"

Recognizing the voice of their Commander in Chief, the astonished soldiers would hail back, "Fourth Massachusetts!" "Second New

Hampshire!" "First New Jersey!"

Three hundred and fifty miles south of his former headquarters on Hudson's River, General Washington was finishing the longest of his army's marches, the longest of his army's voyages, and the greatest of his army's gambles, on the James River in the State of Virginia. He and his men would land together on the very shore where, one hundred and seventy-four years ago, the British had landed to build a new colony. But now, we would build a new nation.

"Second Pennsylvania!" "Second New York!"

A Negro voice called proudly through the rain, "Rhode Island!"

Queen Charlotte finally reached the Jamestown pier on Saturday morning, September 22, after an absence of five days, during which the General had spent no more than eight hours aboard the *Ville de Paris*.

General Washington learned, however, within minutes of stepping into the Wythe House in Williamsburg—he had not yet taken off his sodden cloak while he read reports and spoke with his scouts—that during those five days, Lord Cornwallis had done next to nothing.

❧

Chapter One Hundred Twenty

Benjamin, waiting.

After Henry, Robert and I had found our assigned encampment, a soggy field east of Williamsburg, Henry reported to our colonel with an accounting of his company: we had not lost a single soldier between Hudson's River and Virginia. Then the three of us walked through the unrelenting drizzle into the village to see if we could find our wives, mother, and children.

We located headquarters, where a clerk told us that Mistress York was with General Washington (where, he would not say), and that both had been expected back several days ago.

As for the supply wagons, some had arrived and some were still on their way. The quartermaster had posted officers along the roads from the north; every wagon was tallied, then directed to its regiment.

We returned to our camp. (None of us had any desire to stroll in the rain through Williamsburg.) Henry spoke again with our colonel. He requested and received permission to ride north in search of the regimental supply wagons. Captain Byrnes hoped to hurry them along.

That left Robert and I waiting in our damp tent near Williamsburg, Virginia, which was, perhaps, better than waiting in our sun-baked tent near Baltimore, Maryland.

Genevieve, forsaking a roast of beef.

Shortly after I returned with General Washington to headquarters at the dry, warm, snug Wythe House, Alexander Hamilton informed me that my husband Benjamin had been there about an hour ago, looking for me.

General Washington peered up from the sheaf of reports in his hands. "Mistress York, I think you have been wet enough and starved enough and without sleep long enough to take a little time to visit your husband." He paused, closing his eyes for a long moment. "Tomorrow is the Sabbath." He seemed to savor that thought . . . then he opened his eyes and looked at me again. "Let us say, you are furloughed until Monday morning?"

"Yes, sir. If Lord Cornwallis has waited this long, he will surely give us until Monday morning."

I went upstairs to my room, took off my sodden, rumpled uniform and handed it out the door to a maid. As I put on my old farm dress, wonderfully dry, I could smell a roast of beef turning on a spit over the fire in the cookhouse next door: dinner for General Washington and his staff. I gazed at my bed, with a lavender quilt spread over it. I could so easily have eaten three plates of beef and potatoes, then climbed into bed and slept through the entire Sabbath.

But Benjamin was somewhere nearby. Perhaps our children were too. I ached to sleep, but I wanted to sleep with my family in my arms.

Benjamin.

I was just getting a fire going in front of out tent—wet wood, wet kindling, but somehow I managed—when Genevieve walked into camp with a rain cape over her shoulders. I stood up, a stick of wood still in my hand. Her face was lit by the firelight as she approached without a word. The look in her eyes told me, Let us never again for a single day be parted.

I took her into my arms and squeezed her—squeezed life itself—as I pressed my face against her wet hair. She said my name and I said hers, and so we had bedrock beneath our feet again.

Then she asked, "Sally and Caleb?"

"Genevieve!" called Robert's voice. We looked at him: he carried a basket filled with potatoes and carrots. "Have you seen my mother?"

"Have you seen my children?" she answered.

"Henry went to find them. Not even half the supply wagons are here yet."

Though neither one of us had known Robert to ever so much as boil an egg, he prepared a pot of carrot and potato soup over the smoky campfire, with one leg of chicken borrowed from Peter, who joined us for dinner.

Genevieve sat on a log beside me, soon leaning against me while we watched Robert at work. She never spoke a word while the soup boiled, never spoke a word while she ate three bowls to my two.

Then she peered behind her and asked, "Our tent?"

She held my arm as I walked her to our new white tent, with not a hole in it, provided by the State of Virginia upon our arrival. I held open the flap; she took off her rain cape and shook it, then she stepped inside. My blanket was already spread on a bed of dry straw. She lay down; I took off her shoes, then lay beside her and pulled the other half of the blanket over us.

She snuggled into my arm. Then she mumbled, already half asleep, "Benjamin, I want to bake an apple pie."

About ten minutes later, I heard Robert whisper outside the tent, "Benjamin, may I come in?"

"Of course, of course."

He lay on his blanket beside us in the darkness, and within minutes he too was asleep.

But I lay awake, my arm around the soldier without whom the peace would be meaningless.

℘

Chapter One Hundred Twenty-One

Genevieve.

When I returned to my desk on Monday morning, I learned that on Saturday night (while I slept in Benjamin's tent), the British forces at the port of Yorktown had attempted to open the French blockade. They set four schooners on fire and sent them drifting with the tide down the York River toward the French fleet. The French, however, seeing the flaming hulks drifting toward them in the dark, had time enough to slip their anchor lines and sail out of the way.

The British provided a grand spectacle for the French, but caused no damage. The four schooners drifted out to the Atlantic, where they became four sparks in the night . . . then disappeared one by one.

On Tuesday morning, I learned from an exasperated Alexander Hamilton that Admiral de Grasse had once again changed his mind: he intended to sail away with his entire fleet as soon as the wind was right.

"What!" I exclaimed, dumbfounded. "Sail away?"

He explained that General Washington had received a dispatch from his spies in New York, informing him that British Admiral Robert Digby had arrived from London with six warships, as well as transport ships carrying troops. With this additional strength, Admiral Graves would almost certainly return to Chesapeake Bay. General Washington immediately sent a message to Admiral de Grasse, informing him of Admiral Digby's arrival in New York, while expressing confidence that preparations for the siege were progressing well.

But Admiral de Grasse did not share that confidence. His reply had arrived at headquarters late Monday night. "Our position has changed," he wrote. "The enemy is now nearly equal to us in strength and it would be imprudent in me to place myself in a situation that would prevent my attacking them should they attempt to afford succor."

Admiral de Grasse intended to leave a few of his smaller ships at the mouth of the James River, and the York. He would sail with his thirty-five warships out onto the Atlantic, where he would have room to maneuver in battle. He might perhaps sail his fleet up to New York and there, if possible, trap the entire British fleet in New York Harbor.

(General Washington had been asking the French to do just that for the past three years, while his troops were encamped in a crescent around New York. With a French blockade, he could have attacked the city. But now his troops were in Virginia . . . and Admiral de Grasse wrote of sailing for New York!)

The Admiral concluded his letter, "I shall set sail as soon as the weather permits me." He would, however, be willing to consider any further thoughts which General Washington might have.

When I entered General Washington's office to pick up letters to copy, he handed me only one. It was dated "September 25, 1781." That was today's date: he must have been working well before dawn to write this letter. He stood up from his desk when he handed it to me, something which he rarely did. He might have made some bitter comment, especially since I too had dined amidst the prolonged camaraderie aboard the *Ville de Paris.* But he said only, his tired eyes brightening for a moment, "You saw your family?"

"Benjamin, yes. The children are somewhere along the way."

His blue-gray eyes stared at me for a long moment, as if he would say something more, about the children. As if he were struggling to turn his attention away from the difficulties and complexities and the enraging stupidities of war, to the beliefs and the principles, and the children, that we were fighting for.

At last he said, with his reserve, with his confidence, fully in place, "They will be fine."

I took his letter back to my desk. It was one of the longest he had written during the entire war. He began, "I cannot conceal from your Excellency the painful anxiety under which I have laboured since the receipt of your letter with which you honored me on the 23d inst."

He continued, his handwriting clear, never rushed, as if he had thought through every sentence before he wrote it:

> *"The enterprise against York under the protection of your Ships is as certain as any military operation can be rendered by a decisive superiority of strength and means; . . . The surrender of the british Garrison will be so important in itself and its consequences, that it must necessarily go a great way towards terminating the war . . .*
>
> *"Your Excellency's departure from the Chesapeake by affordg an opening for the succour of York, which the enemy*

wd instantly avail himself of, would frustrate these brilliant prospects, and the consequence would be not only the disgrace and loss of renouncing an enterprise, upon which the fairest expectations of the Allies have been founded, after the most expensive preparations and uncommon exertions and fatigues; but the disbanding perhaps the whole Army for want of provisions. . . .

"I most earnestly entreat Your Excellency farther to consider that if the present opportunity shd be missed; that if you shld withdraw your maritime force from the position agreed upon, that no future day can restore us a similar occasion for striking a decisive blow; . . . the epoch of an honorable peace will be more remote than ever. . . .

"Upon the whole, I shd. esteem myself deficient in my duty to the common cause of France and America, if I did not persevere in entreating Yr. Excellency to resume the plans that have been so happily arranged . . .

"Let me add Sir that even a momentary absence of the french fleet may expose us to the loss of the british Garrison at York . . .

"The Marquis de la fayette who does me the honor to bear this to Yr. Excellency will explain many peculiarities of our situation which could not well be comprised in a letter; his candour and abilities are well known to Yr. Excellency and entitle him to the fullest confidence in treating the most important interests. I have earnestly requested him not to proceed any farther than the Cape for fear of accidents shd Yr. Excellency have put to sea; in this case he will dispatch a Letter to Yr. Excellency in addition to this. I have the honor etc."

General Washington asked the Marquis de Lafayette, a close friend of the French King and thus the most persuasive messenger on the American continent, to leave a bed where he lay sick with a fever, in order to sail the same difficult route which General Washington had just spent five days sailing.

The Marquis of course agreed to deliver the General's urgent letter to Admiral de Grasse, and to argue with all fervor possible against the departure of the French fleet.

*   *   *

We then waited, on Tuesday, on Wednesday, and on Thursday, while the last of the supply wagons rolled into Williamsburg; while the French siege cannons from Rhode Island were unloaded at the tiny port of Trebell, across the slender peninsula from the enemy's camp; and while the French and American troops, seeing their strength grow by the day for the final attack on the British, grew increasingly restless for the final thirteen-mile march to Yorktown.

Even the rain stopped. The sun shone brightly from a clear blue September sky upon our preparations.

ℬ

Chapter One Hundred Twenty-Two

Benjamin, with the seven of us.

Genevieve meant what she had said about baking an apple pie.

Henry and Susanne rolled into camp on Wednesday, September 26, with Caleb and Sally riding on the seat between them. Everyone was safe, the children were healthy, and now the seven of us were together again.

We each had a rousing tale to tell around the campfire that evening: Caleb told us how Susanne had taught him to drive Rosie in the slow-moving wagon train. Susanne told us that Sally had sat for much of the trip on the seat of the next wagon back, beside a drover from Maryland, an ancient fellow with three teeth and a white beard who taught her every song he knew. With her bright voice, Sally sang for us, "Soldier, soldier, won't you marry me?"

Then the other four of us—"three by land and four by sea," as Genevieve noted—each told our part in the story of the French frigate, anchored one entire night on the James River within fifty yards of the *Queen Charlotte.* Neither Benjamin nor Robert nor Henry, standing in a row along the frigate's gunnel as they stared across the black water, nor Genevieve, standing at her gunnel and staring back, had known that after three weeks apart—"Weeks as long as *months*," I said—they were so close that they could have hailed each other from deck to deck.

Once again I thought that never had I seen a more handsome couple than Susanne and Henry. They sat together on a log in the firelight, his arm wrapped around her shoulder, her arm snug around his waist. Never mind the war; glancing at each other every time they laughed, they were still celebrating their honeymoon.

Robert was a changed lad since his mother and Henry had returned. Now a young man of nineteen, he had fared well enough with Genevieve and me during the days the three of us had been together. He had helped with firewood, helped with dinner. But he had not played a single flam on his drum, and took no notice of the other drummers at either reveille or the musters. However, once he had greeted his mother as she stepped down from the wagon, and shook the hand of Captain Henry Byrnes, the world was back under his feet. The drumhead was tightened and the sticks once again beat their vigorous tatoo.

The dinner fire settled to a bed of orange coals that brightened with each quickening of the evening breeze. We, too, settled into a silence. Our bellies were filled with a sumptuous feast of boiled crabs (which Robert had found—alive in a basket—at the encampment market), and our hearts were filled with peace.

It was then that Genevieve announced, seated beside me on a log with our Sally on her lap, "I want to bake an apple pie. *Two* apple pies. September at home: the apples are ripe now. We'll pick the best, the seven of us, and Mama and Papa and Judd make ten. Then I'll bake two beautiful apple pies, and we'll move the table outside by the red sumac in the sunshine, and have nothing for dinner but hot apple pie."

That's what Genevieve wanted. That's all any of us wanted. To sit together as a family of ten, each with a plate of steaming hot pie and a glass of Papa's cold cider. We'd let the pie cool a bit, until Henry tasted and savored and nearly swooned over the first piece.

Just that, in a country that was free.

In a country where the war had finally, finally ended.

Genevieve, at headquarters.

On Thursday afternoon, September 27, the Marquis de Lafayette galloped from the Jamestown landing to headquarters in Williamsburg. Exultant, he raced up the stairs to General Washington's office, where he announced, "The Admiral will stay."

He handed Admiral de Grasse's letter to the General, who read it through once to himself, then—something he had rarely done—read it aloud to his gathered staff. The Admiral had written, "The plans I had suggested for getting underway, while the most brilliant and glorious, did not appear to fulfill the aims we had in view."

"Brilliant and glorious indeed," growled Hamilton.

General Washington wasted no time on such reflections. He immediately sent out a general order: the combined French and American Armies would march tomorrow morning, Friday, September 28, at 5:00 a.m.

℅

PART X

Victory at Yorktown

Chapter One Hundred Twenty-Three

Benjamin, one of sixteen thousand.

At four in the morning, when the stars were still bright, the men gathering around their breakfast fires were in excellent spirits. We had begun our march from Hudson's River a month ago, and now we were packing our gear in preparation for the final thirteen miles to Yorktown. The combined armies, fully assembled under General Washington's command, amounted to sixteen thousand troops. We had 5,500 regulars in the Continental Army, bolstered by 3,500 militia, totaling 9,000 American soldiers fit for action. The French supported us with 7,000. While the Americans fielded a greater number of men, the French fielded a greater number of professionals. Their troops included a strong artillery corps of six hundred gunners, armed with eighty heavy siege cannon. As we folded our tents that morning, checked once again our cartridge boxes, and savored a plate of fried Virginia ham, we felt our strength.

Lord Cornwallis, however, had only 7,500 troops huddled in the tiny village of Yorktown, many of them sick with fevers and smallpox. They were sleeping, our scouts told us, in tents made from the sails of their trapped frigates.

We had marched for one month in one direction with a powerful purpose, whereas the British had been marching for over a year in the South, chasing hither and yon after General Greene, General Morgan, and the Marquis de Lafayette, all to little purpose.

The approach of autumn had brought an end to the sultry days of summer. The weather was now cool and clear. Nights were colder, but better to wrap a bit more snugly in a wool blanket than to march in the sweltering heat.

Thus when we assembled with our companies in the first glow of dawn, then heard the drummers roll the command to march, we stepped forward with greater readiness than ever the Continental Army had stepped forward before.

The drum roll seemed to strengthen with every mile as we marched east toward the rising sun. The sandy road cut through a forest of pine,

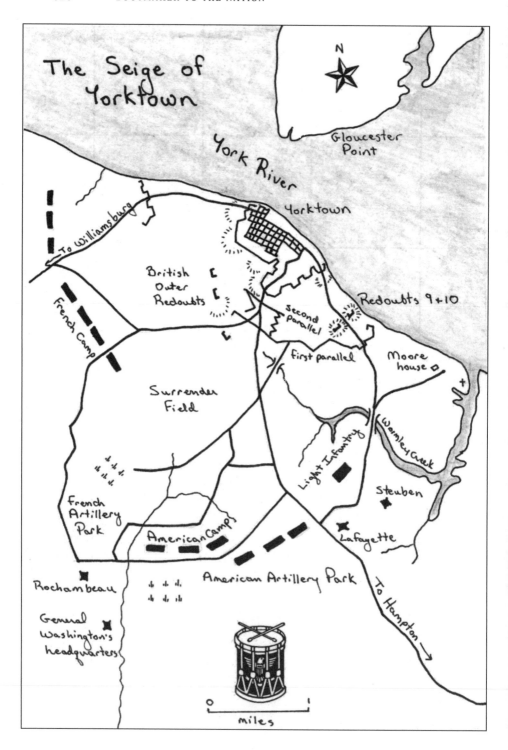

then skirted patches of marsh. The twittering of birds in the first hour of daylight reminded me of that April dawn on the road to Lexington, when chirping birds had greeted the day while men marched past in steadfast determination to kill each other. That had been my first march into war, whereas this was hopefully my last.

The road passed many abandoned farms between Williamsburg and Yorktown. Their owners had been driven away in July and August by marauding British troops. The yards were littered with bits of clothing and broken furniture; kitchen gardens were overgrown with weeds, doors hung open. Troops had trampled through a cornfield, toppling the five-foot stalks. Fence rails lay strewn on the ground. Near a broken water trough lay the rotted remains of a horse.

We were in General Washington's home country now. He had been a member of the colonial House of Burgesses in Williamsburg, and had surely ridden this road many times to the port on the York River. No doubt he knew well the owners of these plundered farms. We could only guess the thoughts of our Commander in Chief as we approached the enemy.

Though most of our regulars now wore uniforms which had been shipped from France—blue coats with a variety of regimental facings—the several hundred riflemen under Colonel William Lewis looked as if they had stepped out yesterday from their mountain wilderness. And though most of our regulars now marched in sturdy French shoes, many of the riflemen, scorning the footwear of cities and towns, marched in leather moccasins.

In contrast, the First Rhode Island Regiment always distinguished itself as an especially professional body of soldiers. Even the French officers noticed them. An aide-de-camp to the Count de Rochambeau observed to an American officer, "The Rhode Island Regiment . . . is the most neatly dressed, the best under arms, and the most precise in its maneuvers."

This regiment was unique in another respect: three-quarters of its troops were Negroes. Many had served for five years or more, and few ever deserted. Cato and Prince, after Reverend Kesslaer's departure with the Oneida, had joined the First Rhode Island as medical aides, and thus they found a degree of security with their brethren.

Because the British might possibly attack us along the short road to Yorktown, our artillery train did not follow at the end of the column, but rolled at intervals between the regiments. Should British cavalry suddenly gallop out of the forest, hoping to slash our flanks with their sabers, they would be stopped with both musket fire and grapeshot.

But we encountered no enemy troops. Our van sighted not a single red-coated picket. After three months of plundering and brutality along the roads of Virginia, leaving behind them a trail of wreckage and rage, the British now offered us an open road to their door.

I occasionally saw Genevieve as she rode with General Washington and his staff up and down our column. Susanne drove the wagon in the supply train, with Caleb and Sally riding on the seat beside her. We had been a family at war for so long, that driving a wagon with two children in it toward a battlefield seemed completely normal. Several dozen children accompanied the hundreds of women, who in turn accompanied the combined French and American armies of sixteen thousand troops. The British had fielded an army at war, but the Americans had fielded a people at war.

We paused at mid-morning to eat a quick dinner of bread and dried beef. The absence of any sign of the British led us to wonder, uneasily, if perhaps they had somehow managed to escape.

Called by drums back into the column, we marched but a mile or two further, then divided our forces. The French followed a fork to the left, toward the western end of Yorktown. The Americans followed a fork to the right, toward the countryside south of the village. We thus formed, well before nightfall, a crescent of troops and artillery about five miles long, facing, at a distance of two miles, the earthen wall of British redoubts wrapped around the village. The French anchored their line on the shore of the York River. We would have marched a mile further, until we had reached the river east of Yorktown—thus forming a half-circle around the enemy—but the British had destroyed the bridges over several creeks. Our engineers went immediately to work; they spent much of the night building bridges strong enough for men, horses, and artillery.

The British had not escaped. Our scouts reported a multitude of redcoats manning the cannons behind the earthen redoubts. The trapped frigates were still anchored in the harbor.

On that first night outside of Yorktown, we slept under the stars. General Washington slept, as Genevieve later told me, wrapped in a blanket beneath a mulberry tree.

It was odd to think, as I lay near Robert and Henry and stared up at the tranquil autumn stars, that sleeping two miles away were thousands of young soldiers, completely surrounded by powerful land and naval forces and virtually doomed to defeat . . . and yet, we would fight and men would die until that final, irrefutable defeat was forced upon them.

If a soldier seeks to understand the logic of war, then he must first attempt to understand the mysterious evil within his own soul. We are compelled to kill with honor; but we refuse, until the dead are heaped at our feet, to agree on some form of peace, with dishonor.

⮒

Chapter One Hundred Twenty-Four

Benjamin.

The following morning, we marched over the new bridges across Wormley's Creek and thus completed our half-circle around Yorktown. Lord Cornwallis could no longer escape by land unless he wanted to wage a major battle, his seven thousand troops against our sixteen thousand. We, however, could steadily tighten our siege line, moving the batteries of French and American cannons ever closer.

General Washington rode along our seven-mile line, checking to be sure that every company was in place. Mounted on Nelson, he studied the British fortifications through his brass telescope. The British had cut down every tree in the broad fields outside their earthen redoubts, giving themselves a clear shot at any approaching troops. However, the besieging army had its own strategy. We could approach the British fortress by digging long trenches through the sandy soil. The trenches must be angled so that no cannonball could be fired into them, and deep enough that the diggers would be completely hidden. Such a strategy would bring us right to the British doorstep.

The American troops had little experience with siege engineering, but the French soldiers were professionals in every aspect of warfare. And Baron Steuben, as an aide to Frederick the Great, had participated in several Prussian sieges. If the Baron could teach us to march, he could certainly teach us to dig.

Henry's company encamped at the far end of the American line, near a road that followed the bluffs above the river to the eastern edge of Yorktown. Before the road could enter the village, however, it was blocked by two British redoubts. We thus pitched our tents beside the road that led directly to our future battlefield.

The Marquis de Lafayette and Baron Steuben both pitched their marquees to our rear. A farmhouse nearby was readied as the American hospital. In an empty pasture behind it, Cato and Prince quietly set up a dozen healing lodges.

When the men took their buckets to fetch water from Wormley's Creek, they found deep black muck along the shore. But they also found, hiding in thickets, a surprising number of hogs: hogs which had escaped from their farms after the British had broken down the fences. Saturday evening at supper, we dined on potatoes boiled in black water, and feasted on fresh roast pork.

On the morning of the Sabbath, the last day of September, news raced along our line: during the night, the British had withdrawn from their outer line of redoubts. The enemy was now crowded inside their inner ring of fortifications. We would of course occupy the vacant redoubts as quickly as we could, for they were only half a mile from the village. Thus a mile and a half of battlefield (since we were two miles away) had just been given to us, *uncontested.*

(Only later did we learn that Lord Cornwallis had received a letter from General Clinton in New York, promising that twenty-three ships with five thousand troops would soon be sailing for Chesapeake Bay. Believing that he would be rescued by sea, Cornwallis saw no need to lose valuable soldiers on an unimportant battlefield. He consequently withdrew his troops into the safer confines of the inner fortification.)

Cornwallis clearly had no knowledge of the French siege cannon. When rolled forward to the abandoned redoubts, they would be able to send their cannonballs crashing through every rooftop in Yorktown.

On that Sunday morning, the troops watched anxiously from the edge of our encampment as General Washington and his engineers rode across the open terrain, scarred with stumps, to inspect the empty outer works. Though the British ranged their artillery on the small party, our Commander in Chief inspected every position.

Early Sunday afternoon, hundreds of American troops began to dig long angled trenches out to the vacant redoubts. When we reached them, we connected the small earthen forts with additional trenches. The redoubt walls facing our line were well reinforced with beams and sod; we now built up the sandy walls facing Yorktown.

French engineers showed us where to dig broad platforms for their artillery, which by now had been hauled from the port of Trebell on the James River to the French artillery park. Teams of oxen would later pull the heavy cannons out to the redoubts in the darkness of night.

The British fired their artillery at us while we worked. But as the French had predicted, the cannonballs merely sailed over our heads. The British gunners could not see us working, nor could they clearly see, at a distance of half a mile, the growing trenches themselves, and thus they had no target to aim at.

Though the men worked hard in the grit beneath the afternoon sun, tossing their shovels of earth up over the top, they were in high spirits. The abandoned redoubts enabled us to advance as much in one day as might otherwise have taken weeks. On that fine Sabbath at the end of September, and on the night and days that followed, we dug our way toward victory. And home.

With the network of trenches nearly completed, the second stage of the siege now began. In a woods far to the rear, American troops worked with French troops to make *gabions* and *fascines.* (Some of our men had already learned how to weave these baskets when we built our wintertime redoubt atop Dorchester Heights.) Together we cut saplings less than an inch thick, trimmed off the branches, then wove the pliant trunks into bottomless baskets about two feet in diameter. The sturdy cylinders, called gabions by the French soldiers, would later be carried forward to the trenches, placed along the upper edge of the wall, then filled with earth, thus forming a wall that grew taller and thicker as the trenches grew deeper. Sand tossed up from a shovel was loose—and often poured back into the trench—whereas sand contained in ordered rows of baskets would stop a cannonball (or so the French assured us). Without an abundance of large rocks, we would gradually weave our fortress wall.

Fascines were long bundles of sticks, some up to twelve feet long, wrapped and tied with vines. These bundles would be laid lengthwise along the inside slope of the growing wall, then held in place with stakes, so the troops would have something solid to grasp and climb on. During the darkness of night, fascines would be laid along the outer slope as well, giving the wall additional strength.

The sides and top of the entire fortress wall would then be covered with earth—and if possible, with squares of grassy sod. A system of trenches fortified in this manner, the French told us, would enable an army to bring forward not only artillery, but entire regiments of hidden troops, rested and fully armed for a sudden attack.

Our men became extremely adept at driving fifteen four-foot sticks into the ground in a circle, then weaving pliant branches around and around, higher and higher, until, after no more than ten minutes, they pulled another gabion out of the sand and handed it to a runner, who took it to a growing stockpile. (After a little practice, we could cut and weave even at night.) During the first five days of October—sunny days in a woods where the trees and ground were bright yellow with autumn—the allies constructed thousands of such gabions and fascines.

The two armies became increasingly close. The Americans quickly adopted French words, and the French adopted ours. As the soldiers wove their sticks together, the troops were woven together as well.

Henry led a detail of carpenters. With French guidance, they built the components of artillery platforms. The heavy beams and planks would later be carried into the trenches, then assembled upon platforms of flattened earth. The cannons and howitzers and mortars would be hauled by oxen at night to their positions. The artillery barrels would poke through the fortress wall, though the gunners would be completely hidden. Kegs of gunpowder, and the cannonballs and shells, would be stored along the edges of the trenches. Everything would be in place, and every soldier would be ready, for the sudden commencement of the allied artillery barrage.

Aye, the art of war might appear ingenious . . . save for the fools who employ such a crude and brutal art.

Such was my contemptuous thought late at night, while Genevieve slept near General Washington's marquee at headquarters, and I stared alone up at the stars. But by day, the philosopher once again became a soldier who wove bottomless baskets.

The British, meanwhile, had their own grim work. During their long march through the South, they had stolen a great number of horses. Now, trapped without forage in Yorktown, the horses were starving. Some were set loose to cross the desolate plain toward our lines; barely able to walk, the horses shuffled toward us and grazed on bits of grass along the way. When a gaunt stallion reached our pickets, it was led with a rope halter to the rear, where it could graze peacefully in a meadow.

Most of the horses, however, were slaughtered at the edge of the river. The British walked the poor beasts into the water and then slit their throats. Our scouts on the river's bluff, watching for the possible arrival of a British fleet, reported that hundreds of dead horses floated out with the tide.

The British were capable of far worse than that. During their march through the South, they had collected slaves as well. They of course promised the runaways that they would be free, if they would volunteer for service in His Majesty's Royal Army. Most of the British fortifications in Yorktown, including the abandoned redoubts, had been dug and built by slaves.

But now that supplies from New York had been blockaded by the French, the British had no more provisions for their slaves than they had for their horses. Accordingly, the British drove the Negroes out of Yorktown. But before they did so, they infected them with smallpox. The British knew that as the Americans would rescue a few starving horses, we would rescue the starving Negroes as well.

When our soldiers went searching for saplings and vines, they found clusters of Negroes hiding in the woods. The slaves were too weak to travel, yet they were afraid—especially those from Virginia—that their former masters were in the American camp. Some of them found corn cobs in a field and had managed to build a fire; they tried to roast the ears of corn, then gnawed the blackened grains.

Cato and Prince gathered the wretched outcasts into their healing lodges. Negro soldiers who had been inoculated against smallpox volunteered to care for these refugees from American plantations, refugees from a British war camp.

Because smallpox was spreading among the troops in Yorktown, General Washington issued orders that all British and German deserters who reached our lines were to be escorted directly to a hospital, where they would be confined. Our troops were ordered not to touch a British canteen, nor even a shovel, should we find one lying near one of their redoubts.

We were to assume that our English brothers, after six and a half years of war, were capable of every barbarity.

☙

Chapter One Hundred Twenty-Five

Benjamin.

By Friday, October 5, our troops had prepared enough gabions and fascines to begin the third stage of the siege. We would dig a different sort of trench, one that did not connect the abandoned redoubts, but ran parallel to the southern wall of the British fortress. Our "parallel," as we called it, would be a trench over a mile long, running about half a mile from the redcoats crowded behind their ramparts. We would place more siege cannon along this parallel, then commence the digging of a second and closer parallel. Ultimately, the British would either surrender in their hopeless situation, or we would assault their walls and butcher them.

The night of October 5, rainy and exceedingly dark, served our purposes perfectly. French and American engineers were able to inspect every rise and ditch on the broad plain south of Yorktown, then to lay down pale strips of wood outlining the future trench. General Washington, riding a black horse and wearing a black surtout, approved the position of every gun emplacement.

On the following night, a detachment of a hundred men built campfires to the southwest of Yorktown, where the British could clearly see them. The men marched back and forth in front of their fires throughout the night, as though thousands of soldiers were making some urgent preparation. Those brave fellows thus drew the British artillery fire . . . while over four thousand French and American troops advanced from the south with entrenching tools.

General Washington swung the first pick into the soft sandy earth. Then he handed the pick to a private from Connecticut. All through the night, our General walked along the deepening trench, inspecting each cannon platform, each hollow where supplies would be stored. He often climbed atop the front bank, where gabions, arriving in a steady flow, were swiftly put into place, three rows deep, then filled with earth. The fascines arrived as well, with stakes to hold them in place.

The British artillery, firing grapeshot at the bonfires, made such a roar that the enemy never heard our picks and shovels. It was only at dawn—an hour after we had withdrawn from our completed parallel—

that the British discovered a raised embankment over two thousand yards long, a mere half-mile from their walls. They blasted our night's work with their cannons, but their bombardment served only to prove to the Americans that the French had been correct: the long earthen rampart with its hidden skeleton of gabions and fascines was astonishingly sturdy.

On Sunday, October 7, our company, as part of Lafayette's division of light infantry, marched forward at noon along the angled approaches, then manned our posts in the first parallel. Despite the steady barrage of British artillery, we did not lose a man. The British simply could not see us. They *could* see, however, our banners when we raised them on poles above the rampart. One flag stated, for every redcoat and Hessian to read, "HAEC MANUS INIMICA TYRRIS." ("This company is an enemy to tyranny.") The banner drew several unsuccessful cannon shots; the men roared with delight as each cannonball sailed overhead.

The British then watched something extraordinary, something mad. Colonel Alexander Hamilton, our commanding officer that day in the first parallel, ordered the entire division of light infantry to climb with muskets and fixed bayonets onto the top of our new embankment. We were stunned. Was the order in jest? No, the order stood firm. We were compelled to obey. At first a few, then increasingly more of the baffled, terrified infantrymen climbed to the top of the rampart. As we stood at attention, the British, no doubt astonished, ceased their firing. Then, for no more than a minute—but a horrid minute it was—Colonel Hamilton ordered his thousand men through the commands of Baron Steuben's drill. We proceeded smoothly and swiftly—every man's heart pounding as he waited for a blast of grapeshot—then we grounded our arms. Profound silence stretched across the battlefield . . . until, given the order, we scrambled back down into the trench.

Some of the men thought the maneuver was a brilliant insult to the British. But Captain Byrnes was furious. Colonel Hamilton, he told me with disgust, had no right to risk his soldiers like that. There had been nothing military about the drill; it had simply been Hamilton's private little show. Henry had no use for officers who strutted a rooster.

During the next two nights, oxen brought up the artillery. Cannons, mortars, and howitzers were positioned in batteries along the French and American sections of the long trench; artillery crews readied their wormers, sponges, and rammers, their linstock with its cotton rope soaked in saltpeter, their priming horns. And kegs of French powder.

The British continued a nightlong cannonade—their shells sailed over us in blazing arches—with little effect. During the second night their firing diminished, as if the British gunners were saving the last of their shells for the moment of our attack.

By midday on Tuesday, October 9, 1781, the combined French and American artillery was in place. (We had brought forward, however, only half of the ninety-two siege guns. The rest waited in reserve, until we had dug the second parallel.)

At three in the afternoon, beneath a clear blue sky, the flag of the American nation, with its thirteen red and white stripes, and thirteen stars in a field of blue, was hoisted on its pole—the men roared a cheer—above the American artillery battery at the right end of the line. It flapped proudly in the breeze off the river. The French flag, with three gold *fleur-de-lis* on a field of white, appeared above the French battery toward the left end of the line.

The French Army and their American Commander in Chief now shared a mutual honor: General Washington would fire the first shot, from a French cannon. Everyone in the first parallel, everyone in the encampment, heard the French sixteen-pounder roar with the opening blast—it echoed that first mysterious musket shot in Lexington six and a half years ago. We heard as well the cannonball an instant later as it crashed through one, two, three houses in Yorktown. British officers seated around a dining table in the first house (we later learned) were killed by the blast of bricks thrown across their table.

From their several batteries, the French gunners shouted together, "Huzzah for the Americans!" They then opened fire all along their line, blasting a barrage of shells into both the fortifications and the helpless village. A British frigate in the harbor, the *Guadeloupe*, quickly hoisted anchor and ran on its jib to the far side of the York. Those who could not escape, however, soon realized that every house, barn, and tavern in Yorktown was within reach of our cannons. Only in caves along the waterfront were the British able to find any true shelter.

The American artillery now opened fire, shaking the earth beneath us, searing the sky above us. Though I had heard cannons firing all through the war, never before had I heard such a broad and orderly thunder. We fired hour after hour though the remainder of the day, through the evening, and into the night. Our shells flew like arching meteors beneath the stars, the flames of their fuses trailing behind. Our mortar shells flew the highest, dropping almost straight down upon their targets. In all of this, there was a hideous beauty.

General Washington ordered the forty allied guns to fire without pause throughout the night; thus the British had no opportunity to repair their targeted batteries. Flames reached up into the darkness from scattered points in the village. Though the British shells arched across the stars toward us—sometimes passing our own shells high in the heavens—they landed not on homes and warehouses, but on empty land. Only occasionally did a British shell burst in any of our trenches, killing and maiming in an instant a dozen men.

The firing continued all day Wednesday, while gun crews replaced each other in orderly shifts. The infantry stood guard at intervals along the first parallel, in case the desperate British should decide to attack. Food was brought forward, and buckets of water. Some of the troops regretted having to trudge back through the angling trenches to the safe encampment when their shift was up. They *liked* the thundering blast of those cannons.

On Wednesday night, the French fired red-hot cannonballs at the *Charon*, a British forty-gun warship which had not retreated from the harbor. The frigate caught fire; then the blaze, fanned by a breeze on the river, spread to a pair of transport frigates anchored nearby. Asleep in my tent at the time, I barely stirred at the additional roar of cannons. But thousands of soldiers sat upright with a jolt in their dark tents when an enormous blast shook the night: the blaze had reached barrels of gunpowder in the *Charon's* hold.

The burning ships drifted free of their anchors and floated across the dark river to its far shore: a cheering message, no doubt, for the British troops trapped on Gloucester Point.

By sunset on Thursday, October 11, only a few scattered British cannons continued to fire at us: we had destroyed almost every enemy battery. That night, Baron Steuben's division marched out with shovels and gabions to construct the second parallel. Though shorter, seven hundred fifty yards long, it was much closer to the British ramparts— only three hundred yards from their walls. Once again, the work was completed by dawn, without the loss of a single Allied soldier.

On Friday morning, the riflemen moved into the second parallel. They were close enough that they could aim their long barrels at the chest of any redcoat who showed himself above the battered rampart.

Throughout the war, the leather-clad riflemen had signaled to each other from their posts in a forest with a turkey call. At Saratoga, the woods surrounding Burgoyne's beleaguered army had been filled with wild turkeys. Though ranged now behind an earthen wall, within sight of each other, the mountain men continued their practice. Soldiers in the first parallel could hear the faint but unmistakable gobbling of wild turkeys in the second parallel, mocking the British.

෨

Chapter One Hundred Twenty-Six

Genevieve.

Headquarters at Yorktown was different from every other head-quarters during the war. That was in part because we did not work and sleep in buildings; our quarters were tents. General Washington slept on a folding bed in his marquee, while his staff slept in a cluster of tents nearby. Headquarters was in a forest clearing far to the rear, at the midpoint between the French and American camps; officers from both lines accordingly had an equal distance to walk to their morning meetings in the General's dining tent. A spring bubbling up from the earth provided fresh, cool water, though with a coppery taste. And the trees provided shade, especially in the afternoon when even the dappled sun on the tents made them unbearably warm.

But above all, the Yorktown headquarters was entirely different from all the others because we were not waiting. We were not waiting for the British in New York to attempt a march toward New England or Philadelphia; we were not waiting for food and supplies; we were not waiting for the French government to make a decision. Instead, we were attacking the enemy with everything we had, and we had everything we needed. Day and night, our cannons thundered without mercy. Whenever the wind blew off the river, dark sulfurous smoke drifted heavily over our encampment, yellowing the sun. The throng of French and American officers laboring at headquarters ordered their regiments forward, ordered artillery forward, more powder forward, until over a thousand shells were fired at Yorktown every night.

I was not able to leave headquarters, unless I rode with General Washington as part of his staff. I worked from before dawn until ten o'clock at night, eleven o'clock, sometimes midnight, when my eyes were too tired to write any longer. I would stand up from my table in the dining tent—where a dozen other scribes and officers might still be working in the glow of their lamps—then walk along a path through the dark woods to the staff tent. Although I was ready to collapse among the slumbering scribes and couriers on my own bit of blanket, I hoped that Benjamin would be standing near the flap of the tent, waiting for me, his uniform the same as a thousand others, but his smile entirely his own. Some nights I would find him asleep in the grass beside the tent ropes (if he had been digging all day, or all of the night before, and could no longer stay awake while he waited for me). Then I would lie beside him and gently kiss him, until he awoke and showed me what a real kiss was all about.

Then he would tell me about Sally and Caleb. They were safe with Susanne, in the big wagon camp to the rear of the quartermaster's tent. Either Benjamin, or Henry, or Robert tried to visit Susanne every day. But it was "most strange," Benjamin told me, to stand with his musket in the second parallel, close enough to the British batteries that he could hear the screams of their wounded, then to visit his children that same day after supper. Sitting by the campfire, Caleb on the log beside him and Sally in his lap, he tried to reassure them that soon the war would be over and all the family would be together again.

Robert had become as skilled a drummer as any in the army, and Susanne was grateful for that, for as long as her nineteen-year-old son was beating Reveille and Assembly and March, no one handed him a musket.

She was knitting something, Susanne was. Benjamin had seen her quickly put something down as he walked toward her; she untied her apron and laid it over whatever it was she wanted to hide. Benjamin pretended not to notice, but later in the evening, when she was putting Sally to bed in the wagon, he lifted the apron and sat a tiny yellow cap. Yellow, like sunshine.

Yes, headquarters, and the entire allied encampment surrounding Yorktown, were different from any we had known before. We knew that probably never again would we be able to assemble sixteen thousand French and American soldiers together. Never again would we roll into position so much artillery. And, certainly, never again would the French fleet remain day after day at their anchor cables, guarding the gate to the sea.

We were down to our last hope and our last prayer, and wanted so desperately to wake up to a new American morning.

ℬ

Chapter One Hundred Twenty-Seven

Benjamin, on the Sabbath.

The first parallel reached, at its right end, all the way to a bluff overlooking the York River. The second parallel, however, reached only part way; its full length was blocked by two British redoubts southeast of Yorktown. Both were still occupied by British and Hessian troops. If those two small earthen forts could be captured, we could extend the second parallel to the river, then fire our cannons at the easternmost wall of the fortifications, and more: at the beach and harbor beyond the wall, the last refuge of safety in Yorktown.

If we could capture redoubts nine and ten (as the British numbered them), our battering ram would be at their door.

Early Sunday morning, October 14, General Washington ordered batteries of artillery to fire throughout the day at those two redoubts. Perhaps the British and Hessians would abandon their posts under such heavy fire. Perhaps they would give them to us, as they had given us all the other forward redoubts on Sunday, September 30.

Then, with Allied artillery at point-blank range, perhaps the British would surrender Yorktown as well.

And then . . . might the war not be won?

On that Sabbath morning, with several hours free before I reported for duty, I washed and shaved in preparation for the Christian service at nine. The artillery was especially loud that morning; the minister would have to speak up if we were to hear his sermon.

I had just buttoned up my waistcoat, and was putting on my blue coat with white Massachusetts trim, when Cato and Prince appeared some twenty feet from me.

Cato beckoned to me with a quick wave of his hand. Leaving the other privates—a group of us were nearly ready to walk together to the service at a flagpole—I walked over to the two men whom I had not seen for several weeks.

"Mistah Benjamin, you must come," said Cato. He and Prince were dressed in the blue coats with white facing of the Rhode Island Regiment, coats much like mine. On the upturned brims of their miter hats, however, they wore the insignia of an anchor.

Prince, as silent as ever, stared at me with dark eyes that revealed nothing, but saw everything.

"What is it?" I asked Cato. We had never lost the friendship that we had enjoyed in Morristown when I taught them both to cobble shoes.

"Johannes Kesslaer," said Cato. "Bring a shovel."

Johannes Kesslaer. I had last seen him when he departed with She's Carrying Flowers, his Oneida wife, on the day the Continental Army marched out of Valley Forge. All of the Oneidas serving with the army had gone home, to protect their people from the Iroquois who had sided with the British. That had been in June of 1778, over three years ago.

I fetched my entrenching shovel, leaning against the trunk of a pine with a dozen others, then I called to the cluster of privates who had been watching us with curiosity, "You go on without me."

Reverend Kesslaer. Wherever it was that Cato wanted to take me, it would be—I knew with growing dread—a different sort of Sunday service.

The three of us followed the road west. We soon crossed the main highway leading north toward Yorktown; I say "toward," not "into," for the two parallel trenches had been built right across that highway.

Continuing west, we passed to the rear of a half-dozen regimental camps. The New Jersey flag fluttered in the morning breeze, as did the flags of Rhode Island, New York, Pennsylvania, Virginia, and Maryland. These were the camps I passed every night on my way to visit Genevieve.

But whereas I would usually cross a bridge over a creek, then turn left on a trail toward General Washington's headquarters, we crossed the bridge, then turned right and followed a path along the creek in its deep gully. We could see, behind the six regimental camps, a broad meadow: an enormous sweep of pale brown grass. During this walk of well over half an hour, neither Cato nor Prince said a word.

Now we left the path and entered a woods of scrubby trees and undergrowth. I could smell the smoke of a campfire, though we were well upwind of the American encampment. And the French were far off to our left.

Then I saw him, in his buckskin, face down and clearly dead. His long fair hair spread in a tangle across one leather shoulder. As I stepped toward Johannes, I saw that he lay across a young Negro woman whom he had been carrying in his arms; she too was dead.

"We ain't yet touched him, " said Cato.

I leaned my shovel against a willow, then I knelt down and reached for the broad, leather-clad shoulders of the man who had married Genevieve and me. I had some difficulty lifting him, and then turning him over, for his arms were wrapped snugly around the woman who lay crosswise beneath him. I was finally able to lay him a short distance apart from her on the brown leaves.

He had a red-stained bullet hole in the leather over his heart. He had been shot by a capable sniper. By a rifleman.

"We come into the woods this mornin'," said Cato, "to collect more of the sick." He nodded deeper into the woods. "Twenty, thirty every day, dyin' with smallpox. Another hundred starvin'. And maybe two, three hundred already dead." He knelt beside the young woman, her face covered with the familiar red sores of smallpox. "They ain't got but two shovels."

The woman was dressed in filthy rags. Cato straightened her head, then he placed one of her hands on her chest, and the other. She was old enough, I saw, that she might well be the mother of children.

Cato stood up. "We heard about a white man," he told me, "who brought sick people from along the creek up here to the woods. Who searched along the road west of Yorktown for people thrown out the gate. Who brought what food he could. And we thought," he glanced at Prince, "Mistah Benjamin, we wondered, Johannes come back?"

Aye. Sixteen thousand soldiers, and seven thousand soldiers, and a thousand dying Negroes, and one white man down there in the gully searching along the creek, hoping to help somebody.

"When we come into the woods, we see him walkin' toward us with a woman just barely alive in his arms. He would have carried her all the way—we would have led him—to a healin' lodge far back in the rear. But before I could even say 'Johannes,' a rifle behind us, out in that open field, told him all the white man wanted him to know."

I had met Johannes on the neck leading from Bunker's Hill to the mainland. He had been carrying a nearly dead British infantryman in his arms. No sniper had stopped him then.

The shock, the grief, the anger were in that moment next to nothing beside the shame that gripped my soul.

Where was his wife?

Where was her brother?

Dead somewhere near the Mohawk River in the State of New York? Killed by a Seneca tomahawk? Or by a musket belonging to one of General Sullivan's soldiers, as they drove away the Iroquois in 1779?

Is this what a husband does in his grief? Finds the most wretched of the wretched, and offers them what little he can give.

Where had Johannes first come from? The man who could preach, the man who could heal. The man willing to do both, never mind those who reviled him.

I remembered another man, the man I had known before Johannes.

Nathaniel, build your church here. While the cannons thunder and rage and roar, build your church here.

We took turns, the three of us, digging two graves in the sandy earth. We lowered the two bodies to their place of rest. Prince had brought two pieces of linen, clean scraps he might otherwise have used as bandages, to place over the face of Johannes, over the face of the nameless woman.

We came to the moment when a minister should have said some words over the dead. The three of us were mute. Then Prince knelt; he scooped his hands into the pile of loose sand, and poured the sand over the woman's crossed hands.

Cato and I knelt beside him, and in this way we filled the two graves. Our hands scooped and poured and finally smoothed and patted with silent respect.

When we were done, we stood, and Cato looked at me with some measure of gratitude. But Prince . . . he stared at me, as if he could see ahead, beyond the end of this war, beyond the flag-waving, beyond the last march home. He stared at Caleb more than at me, at Caleb's son and grandson, as if he knew, better than all us fools busy with our war, what was coming.

Then the two of them took my shovel and disappeared deeper into the woods. They would find those twenty or thirty today whom they would lead, and carry, to their healing lodges far to the rear.

If, of course, the sniper allowed them to pass.

I turned and walked alone out of the woods. Then I followed the path beside the nearly dry creek toward the Maryland encampment. I saw no rifleman in the empty brown meadow.

The Maryland flag fluttered in the Sunday morning breeze.

∽

Chapter One Hundred Twenty-Eight

Benjamin.

That Sunday did not relent. It had me in its teeth and it would not let go. So much during the Revolutionary War happened on a Sabbath. Maybe that was part of the overall plan. Maybe Providence wanted us to think.

Every war, of course, must finally have its end. But even that is a part of war's curse: those who fought, forever carry a battlefield in their soul.

Despite the fierce, daylong bombardment of redoubts nine and ten, the enemy would not abandon those two key forts. Our scouts reported to headquarters that redoubt nine was manned by a hundred and twenty British and Hessian soldiers. Redoubt ten was manned by seventy men, all British. The rectangular earthen ramparts of each redoubt were made all but insurmountable by what the French called a *fraise*: a fringe of horizontal poles, sharpened at their outer ends and close enough together to stop any attack, at least long enough for the British to butcher the attackers. Beneath the *fraise,* the enemy had built a thick *abatis*: a tangle of trees and limbs with sharpened branches. The heavy bombardment may, or may not, have opened trails for assaulting troops through that briar patch.

On Sunday afternoon, General Washington issued orders to both the French and American camps: the redoubts would be attacked that night. Four hundred French soldiers under the command of Count Guillaume de Deux-Ponts would assault redoubt nine. At the same time, four hundred American soldiers, chosen from Lafayette's division of light infantry, would attack number ten.

Captain Byrnes' company was on the list of the chosen. To a man, all sixty-four of us were ready for the mission that night. Perhaps a few of the men were encouraged by dreams of glory. Most, however, knew the job had to be done; we did not want to shirk our duty at some other soldier's expense.

And as battered as the British were, they might well surrender the moment they saw us.

We ate our supper early. Toward dusk, Captain Byrnes inspected every firelock to be sure that all were unloaded. The attack would be silent, with bayonets only.

Genevieve.

Late that Sunday afternoon, October 14, 1781, Colonel Hamilton galloped into headquarters, dismounted, then handed the guard a letter for General Washington. The guard took the letter into the General's marquee. Colonel Hamilton stood close by in a silent fury, awaiting an answer.

General Washington emerged from his marquee, glanced at Colonel Hamilton, then gave a message to a courier and sent him galloping. Without a word to Colonel Hamilton, the General went back into his tent.

Within minutes, the Marquis de Lafayette came riding into headquarters. He too glanced at Colonel Hamilton, pacing a short distance away. The Marquis hurried directly into the General's tent.

Shortly afterwards, the guard called to Colonel Hamilton: General Washington would confer with him. Hamilton strode past the guard and disappeared into the tent.

Those of us watching from the dining tent later learned—for such a drama could not hide its secret—that Lafayette had given the command of the attack on redoubt ten to his aide-de-camp, Lieutenant-Colonel Jean-Joseph Sourbader de Gimat. Colonel Hamilton, outraged, insisted that *he* should command the attack. It was his tour of duty, and he was the senior of the two officers. In his letter to General Washington, he strongly requested that he be appointed the commanding officer in the American attack on redoubt ten.

General Washington granted him the command.

When the three officers emerged from the General's marquee, they were most cordial toward each other.

Now the war could continue.

ॐ

Chapter One Hundred Twenty-Nine

Benjamin, with Captain Henry Byrnes.

At dusk, our column of four hundred infantrymen entered the trenches that angled in a zigzag toward the first parallel. We passed men bringing out empty buckets, empty barrels. To them we were just another battalion moving forward to stand guard during the night.

When we reached the deep, broad parallel, we walked—through clouds of black, choking smoke around each thundering cannon—to its eastern end, near the river. There we stood in our long column, out of the way of the gunners, while we waited for the evening sky to darken completely.

The officers moved among their men, quietly inspecting, calmly encouraging. Captain Byrnes spoke with each of his sixty-four privates. When he came to me—once a captured redcoat whom he had deeply mistrusted—he gripped my shoulders with firm hands and whispered, "Thank you."

The men were greatly heartened when General Washington himself appeared at the far end of our column. Walking slowly along its length, he spoke with the troops. His stern face was faintly visible in the fading turquoise glow in the sky, in the flash from the cannons, in the flickering light of shells arching overhead. He told us that the key to the siege of Yorktown was the capture of redoubts nine and ten. After this final blow against the British, they would be rendered helpless. He told us that our country would never forget our courage. Few men, he said, had the opportunity to render so much service to the generations that would follow.

Walking within a few feet of every soldier, General Washington looked briefly into each man's face. When he paused to meet my eyes, I could see—despite his look of stern determination— a tinge of pain, of regret, of early grief. Ours was the only mission at Yorktown forward of the trenches, the only mission that would almost surely take us into hand-to-hand combat with the desperate British.

At the end of our line, he looked back at the silent column of four hundred chosen Americans, and gave us a confident nod. Then he passed again in front of us, staring forward along the deep trench, his coat blue when a cannon flashed, and otherwise black.

In the full darkness of night, we climbed with our empty firelocks, bayonets fixed, up the wall of fascines to the top of the rampart. Our column then advanced in absolute silence across flat open ground toward redoubt ten, half a mile away. The terrain was pocked and torn with bomb craters, strewn with shattered branches. No drummer beat a cadence; Captain Byrnes had ordered Robert to remain in camp.

Peering to the left, we tried to see the column of French infantry, advancing parallel to our column, a hundred yards away. Perhaps, for a moment, in the light of a soaring shell, we could discern a fragmentary line of something dark. But nothing the enemy would notice.

Fifty yards from redoubt ten—we could see its elevated wall—we lay flat upon the earth, holding our firelocks above the grit while we waited for the signal to attack. The French had commenced an artillery barrage on the opposite side of Yorktown, drawing British fire toward what seemed to be the opening of an attack. Fiery arches laced back and forth in the west, beneath the peaceful canopy of sharp bright stars.

Low in the western sky, amidst all the clamor and flame of war, shone silver Venus, brighter than any star. Above her and to the left shone silver-yellow Jupiter. Venus, the evening beauty, and Jupiter, the god of strength.

I had not been able to visit Genevieve before our company entered the trenches. Nor had Henry spoken with Susanne. Maybe that was better. Both women could believe this evening that their men were sitting on a log by a campfire, waiting for the soup to simmer.

Then we heard the signal: three quick shots from a French artillery battery, followed by three more. We sprang to our feet. A corps of men advanced ahead of us: "the forlorn hope," one soldier from every company, led by Colonel Hamilton. They were accompanied by sappers with axes. The sappers would chop through the sharpened branches and poles around the redoubt, opening gaps where the forlorn hope could climb—or attempt to climb—with their bayonets and spontoons to the top of the ramparts. Captain Byrnes had of course volunteered to be among the first wave of men. Silhouetted now against the flash of our shells, that brave detachment looked like dark souls with long sticks, racing toward the flames of hell.

"Rush on, boys!" We heard the urgent whisper from Lieutenant-Colonel Gimat. "Rush on, boys!" Now it was our turn. There was no thinking, only the years of training; the accumulation, large or small, of hatred in a soldier's heart for the enemy; and the bond of loyalty, friendship, even love for the other mad fools running along with you toward the brutes that together you will destroy.

As we charged in silence toward the redoubt, we could hear shouts, and shots, from atop its wall. The British had discovered us. Then the earth vanished from beneath my feet and I tumbled with a half-dozen other men into an utterly black hole. A hole blasted by our own shells earlier in the day. We scrambled up the loose wall, climbing over each other in our rush, then we dashed again toward the flames of British musket fire flashing down at the sappers chopping with their axes.

Our men were roaring now, urging each other on. Far to the left, we heard shouts in French. The forlorn hope pushed like demons past the sappers, unwilling to wait for the tangle of branches and poles to be cleared. Muskets blazed down at them. British bayonets jabbed at them. Grenades burst among us with such brilliance that I could see twenty frenzied faces in a flash, the Americans shrieking upward, the British glaring down with terror and rage.

Colonel Hamilton, his boot on the shoulder of one of his men, was among the first to reach the top of the wall. The firing diminished—the British had no time to reload. I could hear the clatter of gun barrels blocking bayonets, the thud of wooden stocks against a face, a skull, and the screams: screams that reached up and seared the stars with their agony, whenever a bayonet drove deep into a living man.

Now I myself was climbing up that wall. I scrambled through the jumble of jagged branches like a bull on a rampage through a briar patch. The sappers, despite the bedlam pouring upward over them, and crashing down upon them, kept chopping with their axes. They flailed at that fringe of horizontal poles, cutting gaps two feet wide that we could clamber through. With one hand gripping my musket, the other grabbing anything by which I could pull myself up, I finally stepped onto a pole, hoisted myself further up, then peered over the top of the wall to see if anyone stood there whom I might kill. Yes, but too far back, and engaged with somebody already inside the redoubt.

I kicked and crawled up the last of that shell-blasted wall. Saw a redcoat jabbing his bayonet into a dark corpse at his feet—with berserk rage, he stabbed the body again and again. I raised my musket and drove its bayonet into the back of that redcoat. He shrieked, arched his back . . . I pulled out my blade and would have stabbed him again, but he fell, a black heap, and never moved.

I climbed into the redoubt, stepped over both corpses and stared in the darkness for the next redcoat I might send home to his King . . .

Then I realized that the struggle around me had ceased. The British were surrendering.

"Hold your arms!" ordered Colonel Hamilton. "The redoubt is ours."

Halting where we stood, wary of any British treachery, we listened to the French still battling in the darkness for redoubt nine.

As Colonel Hamilton gathered the British prisoners into a cluster, guarded by a dozen of our men, we learned that the British commander, Major Campbell, had been captured as he tried to escape. An American detachment of two companies, led by Lieutenant Colonel John Laurens, had circled behind redoubt ten to prevent the escape of the garrison; they had captured Major William Campbell, although about forty redcoats managed to flee to Yorktown.

Our troops still climbing into the redoubt gave a sudden cheer. Shouts of jubilation ran back along the short column. Now the cheer was taken up by our dazed men in the redoubt: they had captured the key to Yorktown . . . and were still alive.

I myself partook in no festivity; I wanted to find Henry.

Of course, I could have called out his name, as any soldier might seek his captain.

Mute, I peered at the triumphant faces of our men guarding the prisoners. I searched among the victorious officers gathered around Colonel Hamilton.

The redoubt was filled with a clutter of crates, kegs, and scattered haversacks, the equipage of various patrols who had stood guard here for weeks. I thought to find Henry seated on an upturned crate, perhaps injured by the abatis he had climbed through.

Now we heard cheers from the French: they had captured redoubt nine. Our men cheered across the dark plain in answer.

"Doctor Thacher, here, please," said a voice near the front rampart. Apparently the doctor had accompanied our column, ready to begin his work as soon as we had finished ours. I felt a surge of deep gratitude toward the man, for he had served with the Continental Army through most of the war. In New York City, he had—

"Never mind him, sir. The captain's gone. But this one here is still breathing."

The doctor stood up from a corpse at the edge of the wall, then stepped to another man nearby, groaning as he gripped his leg.

Toppling a barrel as I shoved past it, I dashed across the crowded redoubt and knelt beside the man whose bruised face in the flickering light of a shell was Henry's face. The British bayonet was still in his chest, at the end of a firelock that leaned almost but not quite to the ground. His throat, his chest, one arm, had been stabbed at least a dozen times.

Lifting the stock of the musket as I stood, I gently drew out the blade. I tossed the weapon into the dirt. Then I knelt again, reached my arms around a man a thousand times better than me . . . and out of my mouth came a wail that walled away even the blast of cannons.

‽

Chapter One Hundred Thirty

Genevieve.

The capture of redoubt ten cost the Americans eight men dead and thirty-two wounded. The British lost eight men killed; seventeen, some wounded, were taken as prisoners.

The French suffered much greater losses. Forty-six of their men had died. Sixty-eight were wounded.

No one seemed to have counted the number of Hessians who died in redoubt nine.

While the prisoners were brought through the trenches toward the rear, hundreds of our own troops rushed forward with shovels and picks to extend the second parallel eastward to redoubt nine, and then to ten. Despite a sudden rain storm, they worked all night, bringing the right flank of the second parallel to within two hundred and fifty yards of the British fortifications. By noon the following day, the remainder of our artillery had been rolled forward. The two captured redoubts became batteries of howitzers.

During the uneventful three-year encampment outside of New York City, General Knox had trained his gunners to fire their howitzers with such accuracy that they could drop a shell, with a steep trajectory, just behind a stone wall. The gunners liked to boast that they could drop a shell into a bucket a quarter of a mile away.

General Knox's gunners were now able to drop their shells directly onto every British battery still firing. The enemy's cannons were soon all but silenced.

That was the military view of things.

In a meadow overlooking the York River, a mile to the rear of the first parallel, where that summer's hay had not been cut and the tufted grass was nearly waist deep, several hundred troops and their officers gathered on Monday afternoon for the funeral of the eight men who had died at redoubt ten. Most of the troops who stood in solemn silence were from Lafayette's division of light infantry; they had known for months, for years, the soldiers whom they would bury today.

The French had buried their forty-six soldiers that morning in a clearing behind their lines. Several French officers, Rochambeau, Deux-Ponts, Duportail, the Marquis de Lafayette, now stood in a row with Colonel Hamilton, Baron Steuben, and our Commander in Chief, facing eight rectangular gashes in the earth.

On the other side of those eight waiting graves stood eight open wagons—wagons recently unburdened of barrels and shovels and sacks of potatoes—wagons which now carried eight coffins hastily built that morning with weathered planks torn from an old barn.

Our family that stood near one of those wagons.

Officers, troops, and family—we were there to honor the men who would never see, never celebrate, never benefit from the end of the war.

I told myself, while standing between Susanne and Benjamin, that at least Henry had not died of some fever in a cold, smoky hut. He had not been left dead on a field for the British to bury, as so many men had been left on Long Island. He had not died in anguish in some British prison. And he certainly had finished better than the many cowards who ignored the war, or earned their profit from it.

Could I write a letter to Mama and Papa, a letter that would enable them to move beyond their grief, to the balm of being proud of what their son had done?

But how was I ever to comfort the poor devastated woman beside me, who had already lost one husband, and now, so richly in love, had lost another?

And the boy, who lost a father, a hero, and the reason for his every drumbeat, every heartbeat?

As for myself, I had watched Henry grow. I had watched him change from the silent, sullen, hidden man who went from chore to chore on the farm with rarely a glance, much less a warm glance, to the man in Cambridge who stood watch and ate supper and talked long into the night with more true friends than most of us ever found in a lifetime. In Lincoln, he had walked into church and out of church with his neighbors from Lincoln. And he had done business with merchants at the market in Boston. But in Cambridge, in New York, in Morristown and Valley Forge, he had shared his soul, he had shared his carpentry, and he had shared his purse with every possible kind of American. Henry had grown, until the boy who had once courted a girl with no more heart than a rabbit's, became the man who offered his heart to a deep, passionate widow and her earnest son.

Henry had grown, until a quiet farm in Lincoln became a part of the embattled Colony of Massachusetts; until the Colony became a State; until that State had brother States in New England; and until, from New Hampshire to Georgia, we all became one Nation.

Many men had stayed on their farms, where the war was little more to them than strife and scandal in a newspaper. But Henry had stepped out into the larger world; he had marched with unwavering resolve in that world; he had fought—at first—against kings and royal governors and taxes on tea. Until he had grown enough that he fought, as we all fought, for a freedom that belonged to no one person alone, but to all of us together.

He had wanted to show Robert and Susanne the farm in Lincoln, of course. And he had wanted, master carpenter, to build a home for his family on the southwest corner of Papa's acreage, a ten minute walk from what he liked to call "the old homestead."

He had wanted as well to show Robert and Susanne the streets of Boston, the wharf, and the Common where Samuel Adams had spoken to the crowds and had been the first to truly stir up the soul of America. Henry had wanted to walk the streets of New York City with Susanne and Robert, to show them where he had stood guard as a sentry, staring out at night at a harbor filled with the most powerful navy in the world.

He had wanted to visit the Peabody's in Morristown. He had hoped, he told me one night, to convince them to move to Lincoln, because for Susanne, they were forever family. Then Robert would have two sets of grandparents. Henry liked Ruth and Nathan; he wanted them to live nearby, the same as he wanted every one of the sixty-four men in his company to live nearby.

I do not remember what General Washington said at the funeral. Nor what the Count de Rochambeau said, and Colonel Hamilton then translated. I held Sally in my arms and stared out at sailing vessels—French, British, American, I didn't know—leaning with the wind as they appeared and disappeared in the mist on Chesapeake Bay.

After an honor guard had lowered the eight coffins into the graves, we picked some wild daisies, and little purple flowers like pea flowers on a vine. Caleb picked his own flowers; Robert picked some for both himself and for Sally.

Cato and Prince stepped forward in their handsome blue-and-white uniforms. From somewhere—perhaps from the garden of an abandoned farm—each of them had brought a cluster of red roses.

The eight of us stood at the edge of Henry's grave and tossed our flowers—Sally mimicked the rest of us—down onto the warped and weathered planks of Henry's casket.

We left before the earth was shoveled in. The troops, standing at attention with rested firelocks, took their hats off and opened their rank to let us pass through them.

We could still hear the cannons, of course, and the mortars and the howitzers and the shells exploding somewhere among the streets and homes and gardens of Yorktown.

৪১

Chapter One Hundred Thirty-One

Genevieve.

Where do people go after they have buried half their reason for living?

We were crossing a bridge over a creek when Benjamin turned to Susanne and asked her, "Will you come with me to the French camp? I want to find the soldiers who were in redoubt nine while we were in ten. Will you help me, Susanne, to talk with them?"

She nodded that she would.

So, with something of a purpose now, we walked past Lafayette's light infantry encampment, past the state regimental camps, and past the lane—forever busy with officers hurrying back and forth—that led to headquarters.

At the edge of the French encampment, Susanne spoke with a wary sentry . . . spoke with a shattered whisper, but made herself understood in French. Led by one guard and then another, we were taken through a camp of troops cooking their meals beneath a white flag emblazoned with three gold *fleur-de-lis.*

We came to a campfire where no one was cooking. The men sat around it on logs, staring at the flames and thinking what soldiers think after they have been to a funeral that morning. We were two women, an American soldier in a blue uniform, a young man in a drummer's uniform, and two small children, who suddenly appeared before them. Our escort said something to them, but of course he could not know who we were. The soldiers stared at us, as if we were intruding upon their grief.

Susanne began to explain, gesturing toward Benjamin. The French soldiers immediately stood up. Several of them walked around their fire and shook Benjamin's hand. "Thank you," they said. "Thank you."

He replied as best he could, "Merci. Merci. Merci."

Then Susanne struggled to say something, something with broken words but with a tone of enormous pride, "Henri . . . Henri . . ." The soldiers understood that Henry had been her husband, that he too had been in redoubt ten, had been killed in redoubt ten. One of the French soldiers reached out his hand to her. He was weeping.

I do not know what graciousness, what civility, Doctor Franklin found in Paris and at the court at Versailles, but it could not have been as profoundly genuine as the kindness and compassion of those French soldiers. They found bread, cut off thick slices and toasted them over the flames—browning each piece with masterful attention—then they offered the bread to us with apologies that there was no cheese. One after another, they spoke at length with Susanne. I heard the word "Quebec" several times; the conversation had wandered all the way back to the French Canada of her girlhood.

One of the soldiers disappeared into a tent. He returned with a sword in a sheath. It had been, he told Susanne (and Susanne told us) their captain's sword. Unable to speak further, he handed the sword to Robert.

We walked home in the darkness of evening. The night promised to be clear. Though I wished that the family could sleep in that meadow by the sea—the cemetery by the sea—I knew the pickets would never let us go beyond the edge of our encampment.

We found a corner of grass behind the tents, and there we lay, the six of us, bundled in our woolen blankets. Sally and Caleb, exhausted by the strange day, and glad to have both their father and mother lying beside them, fell immediately asleep.

Lying in Benjamin's arm wrapped around me, I stared up, beyond the black, heart-shaped leaves of a mulberry tree, at the bright stars. What could a sister whisper except, "Thank you, and farewell."

ॐ

Chapter One Hundred Thirty-Two

Benjamin.

While we slept that night, three hundred and fifty British soldiers under Lieutenant Colonel Robert Ambercromby attacked the weakest point in the Allied line, the junction between the French and American trenches. The attack at three in the morning was unexpected; many of the French soldiers, one night after the successful capture of redoubt nine, were asleep at their posts. The British, pouring silently into the trench, quickly bayoneted seventeen Americans and over a hundred French. They also managed to spike several cannons by jabbing their bayonets into the touchholes, then breaking off the blades.

Perhaps the honor of His Majesty's Royal Army required that they make one last heroic assault before their capitulation. If so, there was little heroism and little honor in the final massacre of the war. A boy of fifteen, an attendant to one of the French officers, had been sleeping against the wall of the trench despite the roar of cannons. After the British attack, his body was found with fourteen bayonet wounds.

Twenty hours later, at eleven o'clock on Tuesday night, October 16, Lord Cornwallis attempted a second maneuver. He replaced any British troops still manning the fortifications with Hessians, then tried to ferry his redcoats across the York River to Gloucester Point in sixteen rowboats. The plan was to evacuate all the British troops in three crossings, leaving behind the sick, the wounded, and the fools still guarding the ramparts.

The first crossing was successful: several hundred infantrymen reached Gloucester Point. But during the second crossing, a sudden squall swept over the river. Rain poured down, the water churned with whitecaps, and a fierce wind scattered the sixteen boats along both shores of the river and out into the Bay.

Only at dawn did the wind diminish. Lord Cornwallis ordered all the troops to return to Yorktown. While the dozen remaining rowboats (several had disappeared) ferried back and forth between Gloucester Point and the Yorktown beach, the French, seeking vengeance for the British butchery the night before, aimed their artillery at the boats paddling like ducklings across the channel. Many redcoats ended the war that day with a sixteen-pound shell skillfully ranged on their tiny craft.

From the second parallel, our men dug additional angled trenches even further forward, until, as one sergeant boasted, he could now throw a rock at the British. The last of the heavy French siege artillery were rolled forward. We now had ninety-two cannons, howitzers, and mortars firing day and night at the tiny village of Yorktown. That was more artillery than we had fired in the spring of 1776 at all of Boston.

��

Chapter One Hundred Thirty-Three

Benjamin.

On Wednesday morning, October 17, 1781, nineteen days after the Allied Armies had formed their half-circle around Yorktown, and eight days after our siege cannons had opened their barrage, those of us in the forward trench—now less than two hundred yards from the ruins of the British earthworks—watched with astonishment, then a glimmer of hope, as a British drummer appeared atop the remaining hump of a wall and beat on his drum.

He wore the reversed uniform of a drummer: a yellow coat with red trim, and a tall bearskin hat. He was beating a yellow drum, also with red trim.

But we could not hear whatever cadence he was playing. Our unrelenting cannons, which had been firing all night, had increased their roar at sunrise. While cannonballs arched over the pocked and blasted plain between us, where every tree was now no more than a shattered stump, that lone drummer stood atop a ruined parapet and beat on a drum that no one could hear.

The artillery in redoubts nine and ten, behind us, became quiet. They had spotted the drummer.

Gradually, the batteries along the second parallel ceased firing. Now the French cannons grew silent as well. The American guns along the first parallel were the last to halt their cannonade, for they were over half a mile back from the drummer. But finally they too became silent . . . silent for the first time in over a week.

Now we could hear, faint and crisp in the midst of that stunning silence, a sound that for thousands upon thousands of weary soldiers— American and French, English, Irish, Scottish, and German—was the most beautiful military music they had ever heard: a drum beating "the parley." The drummer played it over and over, with the steadiness of a man whose job, at that moment, was the most important job in the world: speaking for Lord Cornwallis, and thus speaking for the British King and Parliament, he informed the rebels, listening on behalf of their new nation, that the British were ready to talk.

A British officer now appeared on the parapet. He stood beside the drummer and waved a white handkerchief. That tiny white speck, fluttering like a moth, imparted its message of one word: "Surrender."

We were watching a miracle.

An American officer appeared atop the rampart of the second parallel, a short distance to our left. He walked in his blue uniform with white trim across the wasteland toward the British officer in his red uniform with yellow trim. The British officer and drummer now began to walk toward the American officer. As they approached, we could see that the drummer was a boy of maybe fifteen.

Our colonel spoke with the British lieutenant, then blindfolded him with the white handkerchief. He sent the drummer back to his line, then guided the lieutenant around the shell holes toward the second parallel.

We could see, even without a telescope, that the British lieutenant carried a message in his hand: no doubt a letter from Lord Cornwallis to General Washington.

Genevieve.

Working at our tables inside the dining tent at headquarters, the scribes and officers heard the artillery grow quiet. We lay down our quills and stepped out the open flap. General Washington emerged from his marquee and stared toward the silent lines.

It was like a thunderclap in reverse: instead of being warned that a storm was approaching, we heard a deep stillness, telling us, perhaps, that peace was approaching.

General Washington ordered a courier to General Rochambeau's headquarters, asking the French commander to join him at once.

Baron Steuben and Colonel Hamilton stood beside each other near their Commander in Chief; the steady old warrior and the brash young officer both stared toward the lane along which a messenger should—at any moment—come galloping.

During the next few minutes, three riders arrived. The first was a major from a New York regiment, who called to General Washington even as he reined his horse to a halt that the British had waved a white flag.

Shortly thereafter, two riders cantered into the clearing: General Wayne from Pennsylvania, and a blindfolded redcoat. General Wayne led the other man's horse by its bridle. As they slowed to a halt, General Wayne called out, "A message for you, sir." The British officer—a lieutenant, as I could see from the epaulette on his left shoulder—held up one hand with a rolled piece of paper in it.

General Washington stepped forward and took the paper. He read it while his entire staff watched in utter silence. Then we heard him say, as if to all of us, "This has come at an earlier period than my most sanguine hopes had induced me to expect."

He asked the captain of the Life Guard to offer the British lieutenant some water and refreshment; he would speak with the man shortly. Then he invited his senior officers to join him in his marquee.

During the next three days, I kept a record of every missive which arrived at headquarters, and every letter which General Washington sent out. He wanted, as he said, no mistake or misinterpretation as the terms of surrender were negotiated.

The message brought by the British lieutenant read as follows:

> *"Sir, I propose a cessation of hostilities for twenty-four hours, and that two officers may be appointed by each side to meet at Mr. Moore's house to settle terms for the surrender of the posts of York and Gloucester.*
> > *I have the honor to be, etc.,*
> > *Cornwallis."*

Knowing that the British fleet from New York might arrive at any hour, General Washington did not grant the British a full day's reprieve. At noon, he sent the lieutenant back to his lines, and he sent an order forward to our own lines: as soon as the lieutenant was safely behind the wall of the British fortification, the Allied artillery was to commence firing. Thus after about four hours of a mutual cessation, our guns resumed their bombardment of Yorktown.

At about three in the afternoon, our guns again quieted, so that an American officer could deliver the following letter to Lord Cornwallis:

> *"I have had the Honor of receiving Your Lordship's Letter of this Date.*
> > *"An Ardent Desire to spare the further Effusion of Blood, will readily incline me to listen to such Terms for the Surrender of your Posts and Garrisons at York and Gloucester, as are admissible.*

"I wish previous to the Meeting of Commissioners, that your Lordship's proposals in writing, may be sent to the American Lines: for which Purpose, a Suspension of Hostilities during two Hours from the Delivery of this Letter will be granted."

An hour later, another British officer was escorted to headquarters with a second letter from Lord Cornwallis:

"I have this moment been honoured with your Excellency's letter, dated this day.

"The time limited for sending my answer will not admit of entering into the detail of articles; but the basis of my proposals will be, that the garrisons of York and Gloucester shall be prisoners of war, with the customary honours. And, for the conveniency of the individuals which I have the honor to command, that the British shall be sent to Britain, and the Germans to Germany, under engagement not to serve against France, America, or their allies, until released or regularly exchanged. That all arms and public stores shall be delivered up to you; but that the usual indulgence of side-arms to officers, and of retaining private property, shall be granted to officers and soldiers, and that the interest of several individuals, in civil capacities and connected with us, shall be attended to.

"If your Excellency thinks that a continuance of the suspensions of hostilities will be necessary, to transmit your answer, I shall have no objection to the hour that you may propose."

Lord Cornwallis's request that his troops be allowed to return home replicated the same request made by General Burgoyne at his surrender in Saratoga, New York, on October 17, 1777, exactly four years ago. However, whereas General Gates had granted that request, General Washington did not. British troops who returned to England would replace other British troops guarding the coastline against an invasion from France; the relieved troops could then be shipped to fight in America.

General Washington did not answer Lord Cornwallis' second letter that day. He did, however, maintain the cease fire throughout the night. The silence enabled the soldiers in the encampment to hear the evening songs of whatever birds we had not frightened away, as well as the gentle rasp of crickets. The absence of shells burning across the sky enabled the men to admire a multitude of exceptionally clear stars. Many of the troops concurred—as Benjamin later told me—that never before had they witnessed such a brilliant Milky Way.

Jupiter and Venus seemed to savor the tranquillity as they shone together in the west.

Early in the morning of Thursday, October 18, General Washington sent to Lord Cornwallis a long letter which listed in detail his terms of surrender. It read:

> *"To avoid unnecessary Discussions and Delays, I shall at Once, in Answer to your Lordship's Letter of Yesterday, declare the general Basis upon which a Definitive Treaty and Capitulation must take place."*

General Washington stated that the request to send British and German troops to their respective countries in Europe "is inadmissible." He continued:

> *"Instead of this, they will be marched to such parts of the Country as can most conveniently provide for their Subsistence; and the Benevolent Treatment of Prisoners, which is invariably observed by the Americans, will be extended to them."*

He concluded this paragraph with a demand which the British had surely never expected:

> *"The same honors will be granted to the Surrendering Army as were granted to the Garrison of Charles town."*

At the American surrender of Charleston, South Carolina in May, 1780, following a British siege which had lasted a full month, General Clinton, and Lord Cornwallis as his second in command, had intentionally humiliated General Benjamin Lincoln and the American troops by requiring them to march to the surrender field with their flags furled. Now General Washington, with General Lincoln as one of his officers at headquarters, would humiliate the British in the same manner.

The terms of surrender covered British shipping: all vessels in the Yorktown harbor, or across the river at Gloucester, would be delivered to the French navy.

British artillery, arms, and accoutrements would be delivered to the American army.

Officers and troops could retain their "Baggage and Effects," but any plundered property "will be reclaimed."

General Washington offered no leniency toward Loyalists who had sought protection or profit from the British Army:

> *"With Regard to the Individuals in civil Capacities, whose Interests Your Lordship wishes may be attended to, until they are more particularly described, nothing definitive can be settled."*

Given the great number of British soldiers sick with fevers and smallpox, General Washington stipulated that they would be cared for by British doctors:

> *"I have to add, that I expect the Sick and Wounded will be supplied with their own Hospital Stores, and be attended by British Surgeons, particularly charged with the Care of them."*

General Washington concluded firmly:

> *"Your Lordship will be pleased to signify your Determination either to accept or reject the Proposals now offered, in the Course of Two Hours from the Delivery of this Letter, that Commissioners may be appointed to digest the Articles of Capitulation, or a Renewal of Hostilities may take place."*

With a clear threat to renew the Allied artillery bombardment, General Washington sent his letter across the wasteland to the British.

Lord Cornwallis sent his response back that same day: he would dispatch two British officers to meet with two Allied officers, "at any time and place that you think proper, to digest the articles of capitulation."

General Washington agreed on the Moore House, as Cornwallis had first proposed; it was a white wooden farmhouse owned by Augustine Moore, situated near the river less than a mile behind the first parallel. (The meadow where we had buried Henry was the farm's hay field.) The General asked me to accompany the two Allied negotiators, so that the record of positions and agreements would be complete. Thus on Thursday, October 18, mounted on Sir William, I rode with Colonel John Laurens, who had been with General Lincoln at the surrender of Charleston, and Viscount de Noailles, brother-in-law to the Marquis de Lafayette, to the farmhouse which the eight wagons had rolled past three days earlier.

In the early afternoon, we met with Lieutenant Colonel Thomas Dundas and Major Alexander Ross. Though we had expected the negotiations to be completed within an hour or two, it was almost midnight before the two British officers would agree to surrender with their flags furled, and their band playing a British or German tune, rather than (as for some reason would be more honorable) an American or French tune.

We returned after midnight to headquarters with a surrender document containing fourteen articles. General Washington read through the fourteen, and penned "granted" after ten of them.

Loyalists would not be immune from punishment for their support of the British Army.

Deserters from the Allied Armies who had joined the British forces in Yorktown would not be immune from punishment. (At the beginning of the siege, General Washington had stated, in his general orders, that any deserter later found in Yorktown would be hung.)

Merchants who had accompanied the British Army would be treated as prisoners of war.

British doctors would attend to the British sick and wounded. (General Washington wanted no smallpox in the Allied camp.)

The final draft of the ten articles of capitulation was sent to Lord Cornwallis on Friday morning, October 19, with instructions that the articles were to be signed and returned to the American line by eleven o'clock. The British and German troops were then to march out from Yorktown to a designated field at two in the afternoon to surrender their arms.

Negotiations were over. The hour of defeat had come for the King's professional soldiers.

And the hour of victory had come for the farmers and shopkeepers and cobblers of America.

ᘒ

Chapter One Hundred Thirty-Four

Benjamin.

The British surrendered on October 19, 1781, exactly six years and six months after the skirmish at dawn in Lexington, on April 19, 1775. During those six and a half years, thirteen Colonies had become one Nation, and three million widely scattered people, more than one-fifth of them slaves, had become united in their thinking of themselves, to some degree, as Americans. Thus the British surrendered not to Boston or New York or Philadelphia, nor to a Congress, but to a People.

Shortly before eleven o'clock that morning, General Washington honored the American troops who had captured redoubt ten by walking through the trenches to that redoubt: he would receive the final terms of surrender, signed by Lord Cornwallis, not at his headquarters, but at the very spot where our men had fought so bravely.

He was accompanied by General Rochambeau, representing the French land forces, and Admiral de Barras, who had successfully avoided the British fleet and thus delivered the French siege artillery, and the salted beef, to the Allied forces at Yorktown.

The long ramparts of both parallels were crowded with soldiers who had climbed upon them in order to watch a British officer as he walked across the desolate plain with Lord Cornwallis's final letter for General Washington: his surrender. The battered fortifications around Yorktown were crowded with redcoats, who were as silent on their side as we were on ours.

The British officer in his red coat and dress sword walked the two hundred and fifty yards to redoubt ten. He climbed its earthen wall to the top of the rampart, where General Washington stood, as if upon a stage a hundred feet long. By receiving the British letter in full view of thousands of his troops, our Commander in Chief let us know that the letter was delivered to us as well, and to the nation.

General Washington read through the terms of surrender once more. The letter was signed by Lord Charles Cornwallis, and by Captain Thomas Symonds, senior British naval officer in Yorktown. The General asked his aide, Jonathan Trumbull, to add a line at the bottom:

"Done in the trenches before Yorktown in Virginia, October 19, 1781." Beneath that line—which honored our troops—our Commander in Chief signed his name, "G. Washington."

We watched as our General climbed down the rampart into redoubt ten. We watched the lone British officer as he walked back to the silent redcoats and the devastation behind them in Yorktown.

Our men did not cheer. We were not yet done. At two o'clock in the afternoon, we would watch the British and the Germans march out of their fortifications and lay down their arms.

The cool October day, with a bright sun shining down from a nearly cloudless blue sky, promised one more unprecedented scene in this day of extraordinary drama.

☙

Chapter One Hundred Thirty-Five

Genevieve.

THE SURRENDER AT YORKTOWN

During the ceremony of surrender, Benjamin and Robert stood with their company in the column of American troops. Susanne, with Caleb and Sally, stood with the thousands of spectators who had gathered from farms and towns as far away as Richmond.

I, as a member of General Washington's staff, was mounted on Sir William near the American officers who awaited the surrender of the British sword.

I shall give the quill first to Benjamin. We both endured through six and a half years of America's war; but though I was never far from the thunder of cannons, never was I forced, by public duty or private conscience, to pull a trigger and end a man's life.

Benjamin.

In a field as large as Yorktown itself, halfway between the village and the American encampment, the Allied Armies assembled at noon in two parallel lines, the Americans to the west, the French to the east. We thus formed a passage between us, about fifty feet wide and three-quarters of a mile long. At two o'clock, the British would march out of Yorktown on the Hampton Road; their column would turn off the highway onto a lane that led to the field, then pass between our lines toward General Washington, waiting for them at the end of their long gauntlet of dishonor.

The French wore their white dress uniforms with silk facings in a variety of pastel colors. Their hats were decorated with plumes, and their boots were well polished. They might well have been parading in a park in Paris on a Sunday afternoon.

The American regulars wore their variety of uniforms, now three years old and stained with dirt from New York to Virginia. In our hats, we wore turkey feathers and sprigs of Virginia holly. We brushed the dust off the worn shoes that had marched from the North to the South.

News of the surrender had raced across the countryside. By one o'clock, thousands of people had arrived in carriages and wagons, on horseback and on foot, to witness the capitulation. The British troops would have to march between two lines of enemy soldiers, and two vast crowds of civilians whom, during the past year, they had plundered.

While we waited in the warm sunshine, the French band of fifteen musicians played a repertoire of lively tunes. Our men noted an instrument which few of us had heard before, a timbrel, or tambourine.

Our fifers replied as best they could with a few tunes of our own.

And then the word swept down our two lines, "Listen! *Ecoute!*" The band stopped playing; the troops and spectators ceased all conversation. We could hear the faint, slowly approaching sound of drums, back behind a grove of trees that bordered the field. They beat a slow march . . . not the lively cadence to which I myself had marched on the road from Lexington to Concord.

When the British emerged from the trees—first officers on horses, then ranks of soldiers in a growing scarlet column—every French and American soldier stared to see Lord Cornwallis. But as the cluster of grim-faced officers approached and then passed by, we were baffled and disappointed: the British commander in chief was not at the head of his army.

The British band played a piece which few of our men knew, but which I readily recognized as "The World Turned Upside Down."

The redcoats marched with little order, their ranks poorly formed. They carried their muskets with an insolent and slovenly carelessness, for never would they fire them again. With sullen faces, they looked, almost to a man, toward the French line rather than toward the line of Americans. They would not deign to turn their eyes upon the rabble who had defeated them, and who now made them carry their flags rolled in cases.

Observing this ill-mannered insolence toward the soldiers of his light infantry, the Marquis de Lafayette spoke to Peter, our fifer, who stood beside Robert with his drum. Peter immediately raised his fife and played, above the melancholy dirge of the British drums, a lively rendition of "Yankee Doodle." Robert took up the cadence on his drum. Other fifers and drummers joined them. In less than a minute, "Yankee Doodle" swept in both directions along the American line until every fifer and drummer was boldly taunting the British with the same song which the British, an epoch ago, had mocked us in Boston.

The redcoats turned their scowls upon us. We grinned back at the butchers of Long Island, who had chased us from Manhattan Island, and all the way across New Jersey. Our men whistled "Yankee Doodle" to the brutes who had forced us to winter in Morristown and Valley Forge, while they idled and danced and whored in New York and Philadelphia. We were most pleased that the redcoats passing before us would spend the coming winter in prison camps, without His Majesty's monthly shilling.

When the British officers neared the end of our two parallel lines, and thus approached General Washington, our drummers and fifers fell silent. Though thirty thousand or more spectators were then assembled around the field, not a soul spoke. The British drumming ceased; their column halted.

Looking beyond the end of our two lines, we could see General Washington and General Rochambeau, mounted on their horses and facing the British. Mounted near them were General Knox, General Wayne, Baron Steuben, General Lincoln, and Colonel Hamilton.

Between the British officers, and the cluster of Allied officers, flew two flags. To the left, at the head of the French line of troops, fluttered a white flag emblazoned with three gold *fleur-de-lis*.

To the right, at the head of the American line of troops, waved a flag only four years old: it had thirteen red and white stripes; the blue field at its upper corner contained thirteen white stars in five short rows. The British thus confronted the flag of our new and victorious nation.

Genevieve.

Though it was clear to every officer that Lord Cornwallis had failed to find the courage to lead his troops today, General Washington made no comment. He sat with stern dignity upon his Nelson. He showed no sign upon his visage of triumph, nor of scorn. He seemed to preside not at a victory, but at a judgment.

General Charles O'Hara, an Irishman leading the British officers, rode his horse to one of the French officers and asked, "Where is General Rochambeau?" The French officer pointed to his commander.

But when General O'Hara then tried to offer his sword to General Rochambeau (in an attempt to surrender to the aristocratic French rather than to the American rebels), General Rochambeau pointed to his Commander in Chief and said, "We are subordinate to the Americans. General Washington will give you orders."

General O'Hara now walked his horse the short distance to General Washington. He apologized for Lord Cornwallis, who was, he said, too ill to leave his quarters.

General Washington answered with a brief nod.

General O'Hara offered his sword to General Washington. Our General replied, as he refused the sword, "Never from such a good hand." Even as he declined to accept the sword from the British second in command, he did so with great courtesy.

Directing every step of the surrender with absolute control, General Washington pointed to his own second in command, General Benjamin Lincoln, who had been humiliated at the surrender ceremony in Charleston, South Carolina. General O'Hara was thus forced to render the British sword, in defeat, to General Lincoln, who accepted it, his honor restored.

General Lincoln now directed the British to proceed to a nearby section of the field, where the Duke de Lauzun and his mounted hussars had formed a large circle: the British troops were to lay down their arms inside that circle, then march back between the two Allied lines toward Yorktown.

This process began well enough. But soon, as each British platoon officer marched his troops into the circle of French horsemen and gave the command, "Ground your arms," the soldiers threw their muskets onto the pile with such force that all dignity was lost—and the firing locks might well have been broken. General Lincoln rode into the circle and ordered the British to ground arms with care . . . which thereafter they did. The redcoats took off their cartridge boxes, and any knives, swords, or bayonets as well, leaving them in rapidly growing heaps.

The German troops, when their turn came, marched with greater order and dignity. The Hessians had little interest in the fate of the British empire. Perhaps some of them were already thinking of their escape from prison camp to some German farm in Pennsylvania, where they could earn enough money to purchase a bit of land of their own.

By the time the last of the British and German troops had laid down their arms, three thousand five hundred soldiers had surrendered. The other half of the Royal Army had been too sick in Yorktown to march in the procession; their weapons would be collected later in the village.

On Gloucester Point across the river, seven hundred British troops laid down their arms. Banastre Tarleton, who had led the slaughter of so many American prisoners in the South, was forced to give up his bloody sword to the Marquis de Choisy, while a troop of gloating Virginia militia watched his humiliation.

And then it was over. Once the British had departed from the field, we ourselves returned to the encampments. As a show of respect, our Commander in Chief invited the British and German officers to dine with the French and American officers that evening.

I was not present, nor did I take part in the revelry in the American camp.

Benjamin was on duty in Yorktown.

Susanne and I took the children for a long walk past Moore's House, so we could pick fresh flowers in the meadow for Henry.

∞

Chapter One Hundred Thirty-Six

Benjamin, in Yorktown.

Directly following the surrender ceremony, I marched with my company into Yorktown. We patrolled the few streets in the village, maintaining some degree of order while other Allied troops gathered British arms and supplies, moved the sick to hospital tents outside the village, searched for Loyalists and deserters, and—one grim detachment from which we kept our distance—carried off unexploded shells.

I would not wish upon any man in his lifetime what I experienced in those few hours. Of the fifty or sixty houses in the village—some of them handsome dwellings made of brick—most were damaged with ragged holes where cannonballs had crashed through them. Many homes were missing part of a wall, part of a roof, because a shell had exploded inside. Furniture and papers were strewn in the yards, with shreds of clothing and random shoes.

The destruction of property, however, moved me far less than the sight of blasted men, or pieces of what had once been men, still lying in the streets. A Negro hand rested, palm up, at the edge of a garden. Shreds of burnt red wool from a soldier's uniform littered a doorstep; the door itself was blasted open and partly burnt. Toward the end of one street—a tranquil spot overlooking the river—a shell had burst among a platoon of redcoats; their bodies, ripped by jagged pieces of shell casing, had been thrown to all points of the compass.

We stared at the carcasses of horses, at the mangled bodies of dogs, at scraps of flesh and feathers that had once been a chicken.

Here is your war, King George. Here is your war, great august body of lords in Parliament. Come walk these streets and know forever the work of your decrees and proclamations. Of your pride and your greed and your arrogance. Of your unrelenting ignorance, your eyes forever closed to people who want but to live a decent life in a decent world. People who speak more truth in ten words to a neighbor than you do in a speech of a thousand words to your "colonials." Aye, come see, Your Majesty, the work of your empire, and your tax on tea.

*　　*　　*

Hundreds of Negroes, too sick with smallpox or fevers or simple starvation to leave the village, were huddled or lying among the ruins. By nightfall, teams of American soldiers hired by Virginians were searching through Yorktown for runaway slaves. We later heard that two slaves from Mount Vernon, both young women, had been found and returned to General Washington.

The harbor afforded a view of devastation of a different sort. The British Navy had scuttled its ships, rather than surrender them to the French. The York River was deep enough to carry sloops, schooners, and frigates, but not deep enough to swallow them. A dozen masts, some with crosswise yards, stood above the surface of the river. The shrouds and ratlin's still reached up to their peaks, twenty feet above the waves. As a former topman, my heart ached for those beautiful ships, gone forever in a pointless naval cemetery.

And what about the British fleet which General Clinton, safe in New York, had promised that he would send to rescue Lord Cornwallis?

Admiral Graves, after his cautious little battle with the French on September 5, followed by several days of fruitless maneuvers, finally sailed back to New York to confer with General Clinton. His damaged fleet arrived on September 24; various ships were docked for repairs.

Despite the increasingly desperate letters from Lord Cornwallis (letters carried in boats small enough to slip at night past the French blockade), General Clinton dithered. Unsure whether to attempt some sort of rescue, or perhaps to recapture Philadelphia, he decided to wait for a fleet sailing from England under Admiral Robert Digby.

Admiral Digby arrived with his fleet of three ships on September 24, the same day that Admiral Graves arrived from Virginia. The two fleets might have been quickly combined and ordered to sail at once to Chesapeake Bay, laden with troops, supplies, and food, but Admiral Digby had brought on his flagship the King's eldest son, Prince William Henry. Prince William Henry planned, once the rebellion was over, to become Governor of Virginia. General Clinton and the Loyalists of New York entertained Prince William Henry with a tour of the City, elegant dinners, inspections of British and German garrisons, and a concert performed by the Royal Military Band.

Meanwhile, Admiral Graves was unwilling to risk his precious fleet in another battle with the powerful French. He insisted that his ships be repaired to the final line and spar. When a storm in New York

Harbor blew one warship into another ship's bowsprit, cracking it, both vessels were again docked for repairs.

Finally, on Friday, October 19—the day of the British surrender at Yorktown—the combined fleet sailed out of New York Harbor with twenty-five ships of the line (each vessel carried over fifty cannons) and ten smaller but well-armed frigates. The fleet carried not only seven thousand fresh British troops to the rescue, but Sir Henry Clinton himself.

When, following a rapid voyage of five days, they arrived at the mouth of Chesapeake Bay on October 24, General Clinton and Admiral Graves, aboard the flagship *London*, were informed by fishermen who sailed out to them—hoping, no doubt, to sell every fish they had on board—that Cornwallis had capitulated. The General and the Admiral spent the next few days confirming that information. They peered through their telescopes into the Bay, where Admiral de Grasse's fleet of thirty-six ships of the line stood guard.

On October 29, after prowling the mouth of the Bay for ten days with seven thousand troops and countless kegs of gunpowder on board, General Clinton ordered the frigate *Rattlesnake* to sail for London with the news of Lord Cornwallis' surrender.

Admiral Graves then, for the second time in two months, came about and sailed his fleet from the treacherous waters off Virginia to the safety of New York Harbor.

No one seems to have noted in the ledger of history any particular comment from Prince William Henry.

ॐ

Chapter One Hundred Thirty-Seven

Genevieve.

In his general orders on October 20, the day after the surrender, General Washington congratulated the American and French Armies on their victory. Always mindful of his men's behavior, he praised them for their courageous and honorable conduct during the siege.

The General pardoned all American soldiers who were presently under arrest in our encampment. (This pardon did not extend to deserters, several of whom were hung at a public gallows in Yorktown.)

The General made note, as he had so often done, of the role of Providence:

> *"Divine service is to be performed to-morrow in the several brigades and divisions. The commander-in-chief earnestly recommends that the troops not on duty should universally attend, with that seriousness of deportment and gratitude of heart which the recognition of such reiterated and astonishing interpositions of Providence demand of us."*

On that Sunday, October 21, 1781, Benjamin and I began our sixth wedding anniversary at a divine service, thanking the good Lord for peace. For the *first* peace we had known in our marriage.

As the returns from all three armies arrived at headquarters, we learned that we had taken 7,247 enemy officers and soldiers as prisoners, including those who were sick. Eight hundred and forty British sailors, from the sunken ships in the harbor, were also taken prisoner.

During the siege, the British had lost 156 killed, 326 wounded.

The Americans and French armies together had lost 75 killed, 199 wounded. The death of seventy-five soldiers in a combined army of sixteen thousand troops may seem very few, unless one of them was your brother.

The most gratifying letter which General Washington wrote and I copied during the entire war was his letter from Yorktown to Congress, dated October 19, 1781:

"Sir: I have the Honor to inform Congress, that a Reduction of the British Army under the Command of Lord Cornwallis, is most happily effected. The unremitting Ardour which actuated every Officer and Soldier in the combined Army in this Occasion, has principally led to this Important Event, at an earlier period than my most sanguine Hope had induced me to expect."

The General entrusted this momentous letter to one of his aides, Lieutenant Colonel Tench Tilghman, with instructions that it be delivered to Thomas McKean, the president of Congress in Philadelphia. Departing immediately, Tilghman sailed the first portion of his journey: down the York River, and then north up Chesapeake Bay. But after his sloop had run aground, had finally been set free by the rising tide hours later, and then had idled in a windless calm, Tilghman asked the captain to row him to the nearest dock on the Maryland shore. As soon as he reached shore, he borrowed the first of many horses and galloped the rest of the way north to Philadelphia.

Though weak with a fever, Tilghman finally rode into the city after midnight on October 24. The only person up at that hour was a German watchman patrolling the streets with his lantern. The watchman guided Tilghman to President McKean's house, where Tilghman pounded on the door. First a servant, then McKean himself appeared in the doorway to hear the messenger's news.

Upon reading the dispatch from General Washington, President McKean ordered the bells of the Pennsylvania State House to be rung. The citizens of Philadelphia were thus awakened in the middle of the night to the news of victory.

The German watchman with his staff and lantern continued his rounds, calling up to windows that had swung open, "Basht dree o'glock und Gornvallis ist gedaken!"

ᜧ

Chapter One Hundred Thirty-Eight

Benjamin.

During the next two weeks, the men spoke, day and night, of going home. Though the war had not officially ended, surely the British knew they were beaten.

Our Allied encampment rapidly shrank to a few thousand men. The French troops from the West Indies returned to their ships, ready for the voyage south. General Rochambeau divided the remaining French troops between Williamsburg and Yorktown, where they would spend the winter guarding against any renewed attack on Virginia. General Washington sent two thousand American regulars on a march south to join General Greene, who kept a body of British troops trapped inside Charleston, South Carolina.

Several regiments from the northern States prepared to depart on November 3. They would sail on up the length of Chesapeake Bay to Head of Elk, then march—victoriously—through Philadelphia to their winter encampments in New Jersey and New York. Once again, they would confine the British to the helpless outpost on Manhattan Island.

General Washington planned to depart from Yorktown, as he told Genevieve, on November 5. He would ride first to Mount Vernon, then to Philadelphia to meet with Congress, and then north to New York. He invited most of his staff to accompany him. He told Genevieve, however, that since she had served in the Continental Army for over six years, and since the winter was generally quiet, she and her family might return home to Massachusetts until spring. He would expect her at headquarters on Hudson's River in April, to help him as he prepared for the summer campaign of 1782.

Private Benjamin York was accordingly granted leave from his regiment, until the following April. Genevieve and I—it was hard to imagine, hard to believe—would drive Sir William and the wagon all the way home to Lincoln, where her parents could finally meet their grandchildren. Susanne and Robert would of course ride with us, to see if Lincoln might become a home for them.

Susanne told us, and announced to Robert too, one evening at the campfire that she was with child. Henry's child. Conceived during the long march south, the child would enter the world next May. From that evening on, Genevieve and I—and eventually Susanne herself, as her happiness balanced with her grief—spoke about Little Henry, already a member of the family.

Though war is a journey through hell, when the time arrives that a soldier must say farewell to the men who have eaten the same burnt firecake, and breathed the same choking smoke, and sheltered behind an earthen embankment from the same exploding shells, it is a hard thing to do. I would see most of the men in my company again, next spring at New Windsor, and that was a great satisfaction to me. But the others, the friends from Pennsylvania and Maryland and Virginia: most of us would never share another campfire supper.

In the course of this war, I had lost my family in London; I had lost Nathaniel; I had buried close friends for six and a half years, until I had buried Henry too. And now once again I was saying farewell, to people whom Genevieve and I would forever keep in our hearts.

ଌ

Chapter One Hundred Thirty-Nine

Genevieve.

General Washington knew that the British were far from defeated in America. Though they had lost over seven thousand troops in York-town, they still had thirty thousand troops, both British and German, stationed along the Atlantic coast: in Halifax, Canada; Penobscot, Maine (a province of Massachusetts); in New York City; Wilmington, North Carolina; Charleston, South Carolina; Savannah, Georgia; and St. Augustine, Florida.

General Washington wrote a letter to Admiral de Grasse, asking once again whether the French fleet, on their way south, could support Allied land forces in a siege of Wilmington and Charleston. The Admiral replied that he had obligations in the West Indies; his fleet would hoist anchor on November 4. General Washington graciously made another trip out to the flagship to personally thank the Admiral, and to present him with two fine Virginia horses as a gift of gratitude.

The General was well aware, of course, that had Admiral de Grasse been willing to sail north with his fleet rather than south, a combined attack on New York City in late November would have ended the war before Christmas.

The real danger now in America, the General knew, was a growing complacency among the people, and in Congress. He wrote in a letter to a friend before he departed from Yorktown:

> *"My only apprehension (which I wish may be groundless) is lest the late important success, instead of exciting our exertions, as it ought to do, should produce such a relaxation in the prosecution of the war, as will prolong the calamities of it."*

A farmer at heart, he understood profoundly how much the soldiers just wanted to go home.

The Marquis de Lafayette, suspecting that the war would now be in the hands of diplomats rather than soldiers, requested leave from his Commander in Chief to return to France for the winter. Lafayette had served on the General's staff, had been wounded at Brandywine, had slept on the ground beside the General after the triumph at Monmouth, had returned to France for fifteen months as the General's ambassador to the King, and had, upon his return to America, commanded the troops defending General Washington's home state of Virginia. An ever-capable officer, Lafayette had managed to corner Lord Cornwallis in Yorktown.

After more than four years of service, the adopted son was leaving the adopted father. General Washington rode with Lafayette to the wharf in Jamestown, from which the Marquis would sail to Head of Elk, then ride to Philadelphia, where he would report to Congress—and perhaps take some communication to the King at Versailles.

On November 4, General Washington cleared the portable desk in his marquee. Into oaken boxes he packed his papers, his private journal, and two gifts which had been on his desk at every headquarters since the winter in Valley Forge: an Iroquois club with a round wooden ball, and an Iroquois tomahawk with a black flint blade.

On Monday, November 5, 1781, at the General's invitation, my family and I, riding in our wagon, accompanied General Washington and his staff to Williamsburg, where he visited a hospital filled with soldiers wounded during the Yorktown campaign. Inside the red-brick Governor's Palace, he walked slowly up and down long aisles of beds, talking with the men. The soldiers were clearly heartened that their Commander in Chief had stopped to visit them before he departed for home.

General Washington dined at a tavern in Williamsburg known as Bird's Ordinary. Because several French officers were riding with him to Mount Vernon, he asked Susanne if she would sit among them as his interpreter. (Though at least two of his aides could well have served in this role, he thus honored the widow.) Susanne, greatly pleased, showed the first glimpse of her former vitality since Henry's death. Her French, claimed the admiring officers, was impeccable; her English, claimed General Washington, was impeccable as well.

Outside the tavern after dinner, in the fading light of a November afternoon, General Washington in his black cape shook Benjamin's hand; shook Robert's hand; shook young Caleb's hand (a moment which Caleb, then five and a half, can still remember).

With the grace and dignity of a Virginia gentleman, he turned to

Susanne, took her hand in his, then bowed and kissed it. The French officers murmured with approval.

He now turned to me, glanced at me for but a moment, then looked away. I could see in his eyes that this farewell was as difficult for him as it was for me.

He walked over to Sir William in the wagon harness. He spent a long minute stroking the horse's chestnut neck. Then once again he turned to me, with greater composure, and said, "Miss Ebenezer, from deep in this old soldier's heart, I thank you."

"And I sir, thank you." I maintained far less composure; tears were streaming down my cheeks.

With a nod to all of us, General Washington turned and walked toward Nelson, who would carry him home to Mount Vernon.

We joined the train of supply wagons heading north.

Four days later, while waiting as wagon after wagon was ferried across the Rappahannock River, we heard the news from John Lally, riding north with General Washington's dispatches for Congress.

Jackie Custis, Lady Washington's son, who had wanted at Mount Vernon to dress in a military uniform and accompany his stepfather to Yorktown, had become sick at the encampment with a fever. He had watched the surrender from a carriage. General Washington had sent the boy—accompanied by Dr. Craik, the General's own physician—to Eltham, the estate at the head of the York River of Lady Washington's brother-in-law, Burwell Bassett.

When General Washington departed from Williamsburg, he rode directly to Eltham, where he arrived late at night and found Lady Washington and the boy's wife in despair: John Parke Custis, twenty-eight years old, was on his deathbed. He died that night, leaving four young children.

General Washington had planned to entertain the French officers at Mount Vernon following their allied victory at Yorktown. Instead, he turned his attention to his distraught wife, who had already lost her other child, a daughter of seventeen, to epilepsy. Though surrounded by family, the General found himself in charge of making preparations for Jackie's funeral.

ೞ

Chapter One Hundred Forty

Benjamin.

Genevieve posted a letter from Williamsburg to her family in Lincoln, telling them about Henry, and that we were on our way home. We did not know whether the letter would reach the farm before we did, but we hoped that Henry's parents, and his brother Judd, would have some time alone with their grief, before we arrived with Susanne and Robert and the grandchildren.

Traveling north in November, we encountered weather that grew steadily colder. Just above Trenton, we drove through one especially harsh day of cold rain. By the time we parted from the supply train at Peekskill and continued toward our State of Massachusetts, Susanne was knitting mittens and scarves against the first gusts of snow.

We followed the same road that we had followed, heading south, in April of 1776, after the British had abandoned Boston and General Washington ordered his army to march to New York. As we passed through Connecticut in early December, and then Rhode Island, we were surprised—and greatly comforted—by the hospitality of farmers and villagers along the road. They had heard the news from Yorktown, but they were too far north to cheer the troops marching back to New York. As soon as they learned, when we halted in a village to purchase potatoes and oats, that we had come all the way from Virginia, that we had been at the battle of Yorktown, that I (still wearing my uniform) had fought there, the good people of Connecticut and Rhode Island took us in as if we were long lost family. Never did Congress feed us as well as the poorest farmers, the poorest fishermen, who harbored us along the road. As they served a feast upon their table, and a mug of the autumn's best cider, all they asked in return was news from the war: How had the British behaved at the surrender? Were the gallant French soldiers as handsome as folks said? Did we ever catch a glimpse of General Washington himself?

In Providence—where we stopped to purchase skeins of yarn for Susanne, who was now knitting sweaters and woolen caps and good heavy stockings—when Genevieve mentioned to the merchant that I had fought in General Nathanael Greene's regiment at Brandywine,

Germantown, and Monmouth, the merchant sent a lad running to the newspaper. Soon the editor himself arrived to write down "the details and particulars" of our story about Rhode Island's famous general. We told him as well about Rhode Island's Negro regiment, and how well it had fought in every engagement.

But it was after we had crossed the border into Massachusetts, that we might well have been crusaders returning home from the Holy War in Jerusalem. We were welcomed and hosted at nearly every village tavern. Veterans from the siege of Boston at the war's beginning wanted to meet a regular who had been in Virginia at the war's end. (We finally stopped repeating that the war had not yet ended.) People wanted to know, How had the Fourth Massachusetts fared at York-town? Was the French fleet, so recently at Newport, sailing back to Rhode Island? Families who had not seen their sons for years asked if we had news of a soldier from Braintree, from Dedham, from Milton.

Snow covered the ground as we drove our wagon up the road from Newton. Close to home, we paused for dinner early in the afternoon in Water Town. We did not want to arrive hungry, needing a meal. We would have preferred a quiet bowl of stew, but a farmer recognized Genevieve, and soon we were treated to the customary thirteen toasts.

The pale orange sun, low in the December sky, had swung well to the west as we drove the last stretch of road, the eight winding miles from Water Town to Lincoln. Ebenezer York had once galloped on Sir William along this same stretch of road, in the race to become one of General Washington's couriers.

I was at the reins, although Sir William knew the route now all the way to the barn. Caleb sat between Genevieve and me, staring at the snow-topped stone walls and the unpainted farmhouses in this State of Massachusetts that he had heard so much about. Sally was bundled in a blanket in Genevieve's lap; nearly four now, she was old enough to understand that we were finally going to a place where we could stay for a while: she would have her own bed, in a room inside a house.

Robert and Susanne sat on a seat which Henry had built in Valley Forge, just behind the driver's seat, under the open tarp. They peered ahead on that wintry afternoon at a snowy road laced with the tracks of two or three wagons: a road that for them did not lead home, but they knew not where.

Genevieve had been quiet all day. She stared at the farmhouses, perhaps remembering who lived inside. A woman of twenty-five now, she had been a girl of nineteen on the day we buried Nathaniel. And I, now twenty-six, had been a lad of twenty. I can say today, at the age of seventy-one (soon to be seventy-two in April), that we lived more in those six and a half years than most people live (riding in a wagon back and forth between a farm and the marketplace in Boston) in a lifetime.

Genevieve suddenly pointed with her gray mitten. "Sally, look. Caleb, look!" She had spotted the white steeple of the Lincoln Meeting House, almost indiscernible against the gray-white sky. "That's your mother's church."

The meetinghouse came slowly into view as we approached the center of Lincoln. Its tall white spire capped an open bell tower; the bell inside had rung on the night of April 19, 1775, calling Henry to his first battle. The church stood on the village common, now covered with trampled snow. At one end of the common were horse sheds; at the other end, a fenced-in pound for runaway pigs. Someone was walking across the broad field, wearing a black coat and hat. A small dog ran back and forth ahead of him.

When we reached the junction of the South Great Road, which we had been following from Water Town, with the Bedford Road, which led north to the pike between Lexington and Concord, and south toward the farm, Sir William pulled left and snorted, ready to gallop. But Genevieve raised her hand, and I reined Sir William to a halt.

She stared in the December twilight at a huge chestnut tree that stood on the common, its enormous trunk nearly as broad as our wagon was long. Its black branches were so tall and broad, limned with white from a recent snowfall, that the tree might well have been a round snow cloud that had settled to the earth.

Then she turned toward a modest, one-story clapboard house that stood in the northern corner of the junction. Its front door was adorned with a simple pediment above it. "There," she told Susanne and Robert, "is where Henry went to school."

She waited a long moment while they peered around the edge of the canvas at the school. Then she looked ahead and made a clucking sound to Sir William. He lurched forward, swung the wagon to the left, and broke into a canter along the last mile to the farm.

Genevieve, home.

I took the reins from Benjamin and let Sir William gallop in the traces. Had our letter reached home? How could I explain to them the man who had become Captain Henry Byrnes? How could I possibly tell them all that had happened?

Even in the dusk, I could see snow in the air. The weathervane atop the meetinghouse steeple had been wagging with gusts from the west: a storm was coming.

Sir William slowed just before the turn through the gate, then he lunged toward the farmyard. The two downstairs windows flanking the door were lit: two rectangles of amber. The three windows upstairs were dark. Behind the house, on the far side of a stone wall, I could just barely discern the gnarled black trees in the apple orchard.

Sir William clattered to a halt. I sat on the wagon seat, not knowing whether to call out, or to climb down and knock on the door.

A large dark figure stepped out from the barn with a milk pail in each hand. He stopped and stared at me. It was Judd, but I couldn't utter a single word. Then I heard him say, "Thank the good Lord, it's Genevieve."

"Judd!"

"Mama!" he roared toward the house. "Papa! It's Genevieve!"

The house door swung open; there stood Papa, the orange firelight from behind him pouring out onto the snow. I handed poor Sally to Benjamin, bounded down from the wagon, saw the great man running toward me in a white shirt and no coat, and then I was in my Papa's arms. A lifetime ago, the war had begun when I had ridden with him on Lady Rose, his arm snug around me while we cantered all the way to Boston and the Green Dragon Tavern. Codfish chowder, the manly smell of tobacco burning in the white clay pipes, and the vehement talk that surged up and down the table, Samuel Adams indignant, James Otis adamant. Then cantering home beneath the stars while Papa tried to explain to his little girl what was meant by the word Liberty.

Now Mama pulled me from his arms and squeezed me in hers. She told me through her tears, "We got your letter, but you're home, you're home. My precious Genevieve is home." She smelled of ginger and treacle and bread in the oven.

Then, standing in falling snow lit by the glow from the doorway, I introduced my parents to their grandchildren. Mama knelt and shook

Sally's hand; the child was too shy for a hug. Papa reached down and shook Caleb's hand. Suddenly Judd with a laugh scooped me up from behind, held me in his arms . . . and with a whoop of joy tossed me into the air—as he had done when he had been a man at fifteen and I was but a slip of a girl at ten.

When he set me down, I introduced Susanne and Robert, waiting shyly beside the wagon, to Caroline and John Byrnes, and to Judd. Papa, with no less pain in his heart than they felt in theirs, told them, "I am sorry that we have lost our Henry. But you are welcome here as our daughter and our grandson."

"Yes," whispered Mama with a tremble that kept her from saying anything more . . . until she swept her hand toward the door and said, "Come in, come in."

Judd and I put Sir William in the barn while Benjamin accompanied our guests into the farmhouse. Papa filled nine mugs with cider, and Mama, whether or not we had eaten in Water Town, set out a feast.

I think we should now lay down our quill. Benjamin tells me that we are not done yet, that we must finish the war, write a Constitution, and elect a President. But I tell him that even General Washington went home to sleep in his own bed for awhile.

Let me savor, for a week or two, what we did in those six and a half years. And then maybe I can write some sort of Epilogue.

Benjamin, home.

I shall conclude with a memory forever clear.

While a sentry stands at his post in the hours after midnight, staring over the windswept black ice in Back Bay toward the few scattered lights in Boston, he hears footsteps crunching in the snow as someone approaches from behind. The sentry glances over his shoulder, expecting a messenger with fresh orders. Instead, he sees a tall figure wearing a long black winter cape with snow on the shoulders. He recognizes the stern and yet benign face of his Commander in Chief.

The General stands for long minutes beside the sentry, scanning the ice and the city in front of them.

Then the General speaks quietly to the sentry, "Keep a sharp watch, my high Son of Liberty."

General Washington turns and walks away into the darkness.

No sentry ever dared to sleep at his post. And no sentry ever forgot the burning pride in his heart when his Commander in Chief called him "my high Son of Liberty."

I know, because it happened to me, twice.

℘

Epilogue

Chapter One Hundred Forty-One

Benjamin.   *16 April, 1827*

Today is my seventy-second birthday, a day which I claim to do with as I like. I shall accordingly take up my quill and begin the long neglected Epilogue.

Genevieve has instructed me to be brief. Spring is here and she has gardens to plant. (Meaning that I must first turn the soil.)

Then brief I shall be, with one exception: I shall withhold no detail of my four hours of duty aboard the British frigate *Jersey.*

Following our victory at Yorktown, two years passed before Britain finally signed a peace treaty with the United States. During those two years, American merchants prospered from the informal renewal of peace, while soldiers and officers became increasingly impoverished. General Washington was challenged by another threat of mutiny: not of soldiers against their officers, but of officers against the Congress itself.

In March 1783, General Washington met with the bitter officers at their encampment in New Windsor, near his headquarters in the State of New York. Many of them had served for over six years with little pay, and now they faced—whenever peace was formally declared—having to walk home as beggars. The General asked the officers not to stain their honor with a revolt against the nation's government. He promised that he would write, once again, to Congress on their behalf. But they remained sullen, unconvinced.

Only when he put on a pair of spectacles—something that most of the officers had never seen him do—and explained that his eyes had grown weaker in the service of his country, did they relent. Their love for General Washington greatly outweighed their financial grievances.

In any case, Congress could do no more than ask the thirteen States for funding. And the States, as always, felt little obligation to tax their citizens on behalf of a national army, especially now that peace seemed to have returned.

On March 23, 1783, a French warship arrived in Philadelphia with a dispatch from Paris: the preliminary peace treaty between France,

Britain, and the United States had been signed on January 20. Congress sent a courier galloping to headquarters at Newburgh with the news. General Washington wrote back, asking for instructions regarding the future of the Continental Army. Congress replied that until the formal peace treaty had been signed, the army could not be dismissed. However, soldiers and officers could be released on furloughs, in a gradual manner, most likely never to be recalled.

General Washington asked if the troops might, in the stead of any payment, take home with them their uniforms and firelocks.

A munificent Congress agreed that the troops might take home with them their uniforms and firelocks.

Mustering the regiments at New Windsor on April 19, 1783, eight years to the day after the skirmishes at Lexington and Concord, General Washington announced to the men the preliminary signing of a peace treaty. Then, as he had done so often throughout the war, he spoke to us in terms of what we had accomplished for our nation, and for all of mankind. Before we departed for home, he wanted us to understand that we had "assisted in protecting the rights of human nature and establishing an asylum for the poor and oppressed of all nations and religions."

We were forever to be an honored group of men:

> *"Happy, thrice happy, shall they be pronounced hereafter who have contributed anything, who have performed the meanest office in erecting this stupendous fabric of Freedom and Empire."*

For eight years, General Washington had required the highest level of conduct in the camps and on the battlefield. He now encouraged that same dignified behavior as the troops went home:

> *"Nothing now remains but for the actors of this mighty scene to preserve a perfect, unvarying consistency of character through the very last act, to close the drama with applause and to retire from the military theater with the same approbation of angels and men which has crowned all their former virtuous actions."*

Though most of the men had not a pence in their pockets, they would take home with them—and treasure for the rest of their lives— the General's praise and gratitude.

Four days later, on April 23, 1783, the first group of furloughed soldiers departed from camp. Although regiments from Massachusetts were released in early June, Genevieve chose to remain at headquarters for as long as General Washington needed her. We would wait, as we had said all along, until the last British warship had finally sailed back to England.

During that summer of 1783, I was promoted (at the instigation of the men in our dwindling company) to the rank of captain. I wore an epaulette on my right shoulder and a red sash around my waist. I felt a bit nonsensical, a character on a stage without a role.

As General Washington always addressed his troops in a manner which lifted our thoughts to a higher level, so the Commander in Chief now addressed the entire nation. In a circular letter to the governors of the thirteen States—a letter which he knew would be published in newspapers and broadsheets across the nation—he spoke directly to the American people.

He began by honoring his promise. Unlike virtually every military commander in the history of human warfare, he would soon resign his commission back to the civil authorities who had granted it.

"Head Quarters, Newburgh, June 8, 1783

Sir: the great object for which I had the honor to hold an appointment in the Service of my Country, being accomplished, I am now preparing to resign it into the hands of Congress . . ."

His retirement passed a great and enduring responsibility to the American people. They must become more than what they had been before the war, yeomen tilling the soil, and merchants working within the limited world of commerce.

"The Citizens of America . . . are, from this period, to be considered as the Actors on a most conspicuous Theatre, which seems to be peculiarly designated by Providence for the display of human greatness and felicity."

We were reminded, once again, of the role of Providence.

"Heaven has crowned all its other blessings, by giving a fairer oppertunity for political happiness, than any other

Nation has ever been favored with."

Our fortunate nation was born, the General told us, at a time unique in human history.

> *"The foundation of our Empire was not laid in the gloomy age of Ignorance and Superstition, but at an Epocha when the rights of mankind were better understood and more clearly defined, than at any former period . . ."*

Our future felicity, however, was not guaranteed. The job was not yet finished. After struggling for eight years with a weak Congress, which in turn had struggled with thirteen bickering States, General Washington advised the American people to create an enduring Union. Four full years before delegates (from only twelve States) met in Philadelphia to draft a Constitution, he wrote:

> *" . . . this is the favorable moment to give such a tone to our Federal Government, as will enable it to answer the ends of its institution, or this may be the ill-fated moment for relaxing the powers of the Union, annihilating the cement of the Confederation, and exposing us to become the sport of European politics, which may play one State against another to prevent their growing importance, and to serve their own interested purposes."*

All that we had fought for could now be preserved, or lost.

> *"According to the system of Policy the States shall adopt at this moment, they will stand or fall, and by their confirmation or lapse, it is yet to be decided, whether the Revolution must ultimately be considered as a blessing or a curse: a blessing or a curse, not to the present age alone, for with our fate will the destiny of unborn Millions be involved."*

Those were the stern words that farmers and shopkeepers, North and South, read quietly to themselves and aloud to their families. Those were the words discussed in taverns and after church. Had that war of over eight long years, and had the decade leading up to it, brought us the blessing of a unified and healthy nation, or the curse of bickering children without their King?

And what sort of Union would it be? We had promised ourselves, through eight grim winters, through countless skirmishes and battles, that we would be something more than a Union of merchants and landowners. We would be, somehow, what Providence intended us to be.

Today in 1827, though no drum musters me at dawn to my duty, I still ponder that fundamental question. Do we continue to march, fifty years later, toward the fulfillment of our bold and unprecedented declaration that "All men are created Equal"? Or have we taken a seat, each citizen at his own private table—whether plentiful or meager—our thoughts on a bit of mutton?

Something good there was in Morristown, when so many of us were cobblers. Working together, we made shoes that the army might march.

I learned, after eight years of watching the best lads on earth die around me—I saw the shell-blasted limbs and fever-shrunken bodies on both sides—what it means to be a citizen of this new nation.

God required the price. He wanted to know that we were serious in our brave undertaking before He bestowed His blessing.

And the British, damn 'em, required a terrible price as well, though they paid dearly in the end.

Aye, we soldiered for eight long years while hope and despair never gave up their well-matched battle in our hearts. Until the French sailed their mighty fleet into Chesapeake Bay, and General Washington wrapped his cannons around Cornwallis. And then my soldier-bride and I saw the end of it all.

Nay, not the end, but a beginning, that no true American should ever forget.

છ્ર

Chapter One Hundred Forty-Two

Genevieve.

Before Benjamin takes us aboard the *Jersey*, I must interrupt with a measure of happiness.

Susanne and Robert fared well at our quiet farm in Lincoln. Robert enjoyed working with Judd in the barn, and Susanne was profoundly grateful, as she became heavier with her child, not to be rolling through some strange state in a wagon.

My parents became very fond of the woman and her son who had provided Henry, for three and a half years, with the joy of being both husband and father. Mama got out her old knitting needles and sat for hours with Susanne. Papa saddled a horse for Robert. We lived through that tranquil winter with a fire blazing on the hearth and snow drifting deep outside; and we lived as well with a grief that slowly lessened its grip. Many homes in America must have confronted a balance between what the war had taken from us, and what we hoped our new nation would provide.

Benjamin and I prepared to depart in March, 1782, for Newburgh, New York, I to resume my duties at headquarters, Benjamin to resume his duties with his company at nearby New Windsor. My parents asked Susanne to stay with them on the farm until her child was born in May. She agreed, though reluctantly. The farm without Henry could never be her home.

On the day before Benjamin and I departed from Lincoln, Susanne spoke with me outside the house: she asked me to promise that if the French Army ever returned from Virginia to New York, I must let her know. She would say no more, but it was then that I knew her heart. She hoped to find a refuge from America, from war, from the deaths of two husbands, with a French soldier. He was no doubt one of the men at the campfire on the evening after Henry's funeral: a soldier who had been battling in redoubt nine while Henry was fighting in redoubt ten.

Susanne had nothing more to believe in that the look in a stranger's eyes: not a look of love, certainly not of passion, but of an anguish and an understanding which few others could share. War had ravaged them both; in that, neither would be a stranger to the other.

She had been born in French Canada; her father had been a French officer in Quebec, her mother a Quebecoise. If she and Robert could sail with a French soldier—a new husband, a new father—to France, they would be, in a way, home.

In February, 1782, a new government gained control of Parliament in London. Overruling the King, the Whigs halted any further military action in America.

Accordingly, during the quiet summer of 1782, General Washington agreed with General Rochambeau that the French Army could now march north from Williamsburg to rejoin the Continental Army outside of New York City. I wrote to Susanne in August, telling her that the French would arrive in Newburgh in September. I also wrote to Judd, asking him to bring Susanne and her two sons—Henri was now three months old—from Massachusetts to New York in the farm wagon. I mentioned to Judd in my letter that his former officer, General Henry Knox, was still serving at New Windsor.

My parents said farewell to Susanne and Robert. Their hearts were broken by the departure of their grandson.

Judd arrived with his three passengers—our family, it seemed, was always arriving or departing in different combinations—in early September. General Washington, expecting the French Army within days, was greatly pleased that Susanne, his ablest translator, had returned to headquarters.

On a bright September afternoon, the arriving French regiments marched with their band between two parallel lines formed by cheering Americans. During the next several days, soldiers and officers of every rank hosted each other at campfire dinners (though once again the French provisions proved far more abundant than our meager American rations).

Susanne found her Jacques DuPlaix on the very first evening. She brought him to our campfire and introduced him to Benjamin and me. Robert was as quietly happy as his mother, for Jacques was the soldier who had given him the French captain's sword.

The following morning, Susanne spoke with General Washington. She received permission to transfer her services as translator from the American Army to the French.

The British in New York City, now under the command of Sir Guy Carleton, no longer ventured beyond their cluster of islands. General Rochambeau accordingly received orders from Versailles to march his troops to Boston, where they would embark for the West Indies.

Susanne, Robert and Henri departed with them. We never saw them again, although Susanne and Robert, and eventually Henri, have continued to write faithfully to us from their home in Tours on the Loire River in "la belle France." Susanne is eighty-three now. Her "venerable Jacques," as she calls him, has been, for almost forty-four years, "the kindest of husbands."

Robert became a physician. He remained in Tours, which may well account for his mother's longevity. Henri, however, moved to Paris in 1800, at the age of eighteen, where he apprenticed as a journalist. A child of war, he became a chronicler of Napolean's widespread wars in Europe. He was also, perhaps in deference to his mother, one of the few young Frenchmen of his time who never served as a soldier.

Brave and beautiful Susanne. To their graves, Mama and Papa thanked you for the happiness that you brought to Henry.

଼ଠ

Chapter One Hundred Forty-Three

Benjamin, aboard

THE PRISON SHIP *JERSEY*

The Peace Treaty was finally signed in Paris on September 3, 1783. On behalf of the United States of America, the document was signed by John Adams, Benjamin Franklin (now seventy-six years old), and John Jay. The British Crown recognized the independence of the United States, extended the western boundary of America to the Mississippi River, and acknowledged the right of New England fishermen to fish for cod and haddock off the coast of Newfoundland. British troops had already withdrawn from Savannah and Charleston. They promised to complete their evacuation of New York City by November 25.

On that Sunday morning, my company of twenty-two men was camped on the northern end of Manhattan Island. We were a small part of a detachment of five hundred troops from West Point, under the command of General Knox. Following a breakfast at dawn, our column marched south from Harlem Heights toward the city; we would observe the departure of the British troops, and maintain order as New York once again became an American port.

In the countryside north of the city, every tree had been chopped down, no doubt for firewood. Where once a forest had grown on the rolling land, there was now a devastation of stumps. Nearly every farm house stood in a field of weeds. Fences, barns, and chicken coops had all been torn down for wood. During their seven years in New York City, the British had ravaged the countryside—as if they had been a swarm of locusts with axes.

I had often dreamed, after our retreat in 1776, of returning to New York, to walk the streets I knew so well, to admire the multitude of buildings, and to marvel at the array of people from a dozen nations who daily bustled about their business.

But as our column now marched along the Broad Way into the city itself, we stared, appalled, at the vast charred ruins to the right of the road, where a third of New York had burned in the autumn of 1776. Blackened chimneys stood above block after block of burnt timber and beams. Patches of weeds grew on open remnants of what had once been a street. Brick steps climbed above the charred wreckage and there ended in the empty air. A breeze off the river stirred up a swirl of ashes. The conflagration might well have been no more than a month ago.

We paused, five hundred somber troops, in front of the ruins of Trinity Church. The remnants of four stone walls, enclosing no longer a sanctuary for the spirit, but the rubble of a collapsed roof, formed the four sides of an enormous coffin.

Aye, war is the vilest of all sins.

Our troops ascertained that the British troops were embarking in an orderly manner from the Battery. We inspected and secured every block of the city. We stared with silent accusation at every Loyalist peeking out a door, peering down from a window; for seven years they had profited from the British occupation. But their neighbors, patriot refugees during those seven long years, would soon be returning home.

My company had one further duty to perform, our last of the war.

We marched (all of us volunteers who had suffered and survived every camp illness) down Wall Street to Queen Street, which we then followed south, just above the warehouses of the East River wharf. At a fork, we followed Cherry Street down to the docks. We were now so close to the British that we could see, further along the wharf, a parade of redcoats crossing a gangplank to board their transport ship. The "lobsterbacks"—as the taunting boys in Boston had once called us— were finally going home.

At the end of an otherwise deserted pier, we found a dozen cutters waiting for us. Manning the oars were sailors from Marblehead; they were the same men who had ferried our wet, starving, exhausted troops from Long Island to Manhattan Island on that foggy night of August 29, 1776. They had thus rescued General Washington's army from almost certain capture. Today they would help us to rescue several hundred patriots who had been far less fortunate.

As my company (more a squad) climbed down the pier's ladder and stepped into the boats, I searched the cutters for Adam, and Ethan, and Michael and Hank at the oars. The lads had found work in Marblehead, had rowed through the fog that night, had rowed through the drifting ice across the Delaware. I had hoped they might be here today, but I did not see them.

During the summer of 1782, General Washington had received a letter from an American naval officer held prisoner aboard the *Jersey*, a British prison ship. The old warship was anchored in Wallabout Bay, just above Brooklyn. The hulk had roughly a thousand prisoners on board, most of them sailors captured on privateers and navy frigates. The prisoners were locked in the holds below; they were allowed up on deck at the whim of their British and Hessian guards. Hot and airless in the summer, unheated in the winter, and indescribably filthy, the holds festered with every sort of disease. The naval officer begged General Washington for some measure of help.

Throughout the war, General Washington had written to various British commanders about the treatment of American prisoners, with little success. The British were sometimes willing to exchange officers, but privates and sailors died by the hundreds in cold and filthy prisons in Boston, Halifax, England, Philadelphia, and New York. As long as the Royal Navy controlled New York Harbor, neither the General nor Congress could offer any aid to the wretched men aboard the *Jersey*.

When Sir Guy Carleton notified General Washington that he would evacuate New York City on November 25, the General wrote immediately to Marblehead, requesting sailors willing to fetch the prisoners from the *Jersey*. (Many of the prisoners were known to have Marblehead as their home port.) Three physicians from Boston brought enough medical supplies to set up a hospital in a warehouse on the Manhattan wharf. Because the citizens of New York feared what they called "the *Jersey* fever," the prisoners would not be allowed within the city itself.

I had survived my few days in the *Lively's* dungeon. Adam and the lads had spoken about sailing their own privateer. Therefore I volunteered for this mission to the *Jersey*.

Church bells in New York City were ringing their call to worship as our dozen cutters pulled away from the pier. The November morning was sunny but cold, with none of autumn's last warmth, but rather the bite of winter's first chill. Several cutters were laden with coats and blankets; the sailors had prepared well to bring their brothers home.

Our little fleet rowed about a mile up the East River, then hooked south into Wallabout Bay. We spotted the *Jersey*, a black hull without masts, anchored a quarter-mile offshore from the bay's long beach. Nearby were anchored three smaller frigates, known as "hospital ships." From these four floating dungeons, we were to receive—consigned to us by British officers still on board—an unknown number of prisoners. Our cutters would ferry the newly freed men to the Cherry

Street Wharf, making as many trips as necessary throughout the day. Once we were certain that every prisoner had been transferred into our boats, the British crew were at liberty to join their fleet at the Battery.

As we approached the black hull, encrusted over the years with every sort of filth, we could see a half-dozen redcoats on deck, but no prisoners. A long narrow gangplank angled down from the deck to a large raft. How many thousands of men had trudged up that gangplank, to a ship that never took them home?

Two hundred feet from the raft, we began to smell the stench. Each oarsman paused to tie a length of white linen over his nose and mouth. My men and I did the same; the physicians from Boston had prepared us all with ample bandages for this purpose. Our masks would make little difference, however; throughout the day, we would breathe and speak and curse and work in the penetrating stench.

The redcoats stared down in silence as we approached. A rowboat was tied to the raft: their transport to the British fleet. We did not hail the crew, nor did we ask for permission to come aboard. We simply drew alongside the raft, then I and twelve of my men stepped onto it. The rest of our company would inspect the hospital ships.

The sailors in eight of the twelve cutters tied their painters to the raft. Though they had no orders to accompany us on board the *Jersey*, they quietly shipped their oars, stepped onto the raft, then with a grim and determined nod, put themselves under my command.

The ship until now had been absolutely silent. But as we walked up the long gangplank in our blue uniforms, carrying muskets—a boarding party of Continental regulars—we heard first one voice, and then a sudden desperate clamor, calling to us from small square holes cut on two levels along the black hull. Peering into a tiny window with iron bars across it, I discerned a haggard face staring out. The stench was by now so horrid that several of us, sailors and soldiers both, vomited over the side of the gangplank.

An officer wearing a long blue coat and plumed hat stood at the top of the gangplank, glaring down at me. I thought, as I approached, that I would have to push him aside in order to board the ship, but he stepped back at the last moment.

I recognized him immediately. But because I wore a blue Massachusetts uniform with a captain's epaulette on my shoulder, and a white cloth over most of my face, he did not recognize me.

"Are you David Sproat?" I asked, knowing that he was not.

"Nay," he growled with contempt, "the Commissary of Prisoners has departed for the Admiral's flagship."

"Then to whom do I have the honor of speaking?"

"To Assistant Commissary Hench," he replied, clearly proud to be the vessel's commanding officer. "I am in charge here, and shall sign any papers you might have."

"When our accounting is completed, Assistant Commissary Hench, I shall be grateful for your signature." I glanced around the empty deck. "Where are the prisoners I am to receive?"

With a sly grin, Hench jangled a ring of keys. "They're under the gratings, they are."

"Then in the name of the free and independent United States of America, I order their immediate release."

Hench spat, not over the gunnel but onto the deck. Then he turned and limped—yes he limped, and I remembered with pleasure the night I cut the soles of his feet with my knife—toward a hatchway aft of the stub of the mainmast. As I followed Hench down the ladder, I left the bright sunshine behind . . . and entered an underworld that no fire-and-brimstone preacher could ever have imagined.

The prisoners were confined to the berthing and orlop decks. Looking down through the lattice of the locked wooden grating that covered a hatch, I could see crowded faces staring up at me. I could smell the poisoned air. I could hear the cries and wailings and supplications of countless voices. I stood at the threshold of His Majesty's hell.

Hench rattled the ring of keys so his prisoners could hear the jingle of liberty. "Down, rebels, down!" he shouted with glee through the grating. Then he knelt, stiffly, fit a key into a padlock and released the latch.

When he stood up, he stood with his feet still on the grating, and so he kept the wretches imprisoned below for one moment longer.

Then he stepped surprisingly quickly toward the ladder. As he climbed back up to the weather deck, I noticed the boots—stolen boots, no doubt—on his feet.

The sailors from Marblehead quickly lifted the grating. Then we stared at an orderly throng of cadavers rising from their grave. They staggered weakly up the steps, some with joy in their haggard eyes, some with a look of numb astonishment. The sailors called gently to them, "Up with you, lads. We've a boat waiting for every one of you. We're going home, lads. Home!" We reached out to brace many men so feeble they seemed ready to collapse. We saw tears running down their cheeks into filthy matted beards.

I called up to my dozen soldiers, who peered down the weather deck hatchway as if from the land of the living. They quickly stacked their muskets, then reached down to steady the prisoners emerging into blinding sunshine.

The parade of human wretches, some sobbing their gratitude in French, some in Spanish, some jabbering incoherent English, continued for ten, fifteen minutes as hundreds of men, and boys, slowly climbed the steps toward our guiding hands. "There's more below," one told me, "what cannot walk."

The sailors went searching for lanterns. We stood on what had once been the cannon deck, but was now the berthing deck for the British crew.

A cluster of Negroes, one with a boy in his arms, staggered up through the hatchway. They stared at me, stared up at the light through the hatch above us. I remembered that dawn in Lexington, when one Negro had stood among his neighbors in their line across the village green. He had stood as sturdy as every other man against the redcoats.

A sailor returned with a lit lantern. "Sir, I think you should see the officers' quarters."

"Yes," I said, turning to follow him. He led me toward the stern. We passed through the cook room, where a huge empty pot sat on a cold stove. We passed through steerage, where the guards had slept in their hammocks, and where a dozen sailors were now lighting lanterns in preparation for their descent into the holds.

We then entered the officers' cabin, serving in part as quarters for Hench and his brotherhood, and in part as a storehouse for the treasure they had stolen. Lit by sunshine through open portholes, heaps of winter coats and woolen blankets lay piled against the walls. On a table lay a dozen pocket watches, pen knives, coins from France, from Spain. I picked up a locket and opened it, then stared at a small oval picture of someone's wife.

After half an hour, the last of the prisoners who could walk had climbed up the ladder from below. I followed the undaunted men from Marblehead down the ladder into the dimness of the middle deck. The sailors dispersed fore and aft with their glowing lanterns; they knelt beside prisoners who cried out to them, or moaned, or lay silent. We found over a hundred prisoners in every stage of sickness and agony, many of them lying near the tiny windows that let in a wisp of fresh air, a beam of sunlight.

Voices called from the deck below. Several of us descended through the hatch, taking lanterns into a dark damp hold just above the waterline. The orlop deck contained a plague of smallpox. Most of the prisoners had to be lifted from their filth. The sailors, coughing, choking, retching, carried their burdens up the three ladders to the weather deck.

After those still alive had been brought up to the sunshine and laid upon blankets, we carried up thirteen corpses: eleven men and two boys. We wrapped the dead in blankets and laid them separately on the bow.

The cutters departed with all the prisoners they could carry. I looked across the bay at the hospital ships, the *Hunter*, the *Strombolo*, and the *Scorpion*: their decks appeared empty. Their cutters had already departed for the Cherry Street Wharf.

That left about two hundred prisoners waiting aboard the *Jersey* for the boats to return. Some lay upon the deck, raving in delirium. One man crawled back and forth, calling for someone who never answered. But most of the prisoners stood silently along the gunnel, staring across the river toward the distant shore of Manhattan Island. They could see a few buildings at the northern end of the city.

Five redcoats stood near the gangplank. They had been the final crew of guards, and were clearly ready to hurry down to their rowboat. Six of my regulars stood with muskets and fixed bayonets to block the way.

On the poop deck, aft of the quarterdeck—ordinarily the captain's private realm—Assistant Commissary Hench stood in his long blue coat, his plumed black hat, and now, as I noticed, an officer's dress sword. Beside him were several trunks, filled, no doubt, with enough plunder to provide him with a life as Squire Hench back home in England. He paid no attention to the rest of us, but stared toward the river. Perhaps he was waiting for the Admiral's flagship barge to come fetch him and his property.

I walked around the deck, tallying in my mind the grim details of the report that I would write for General Washington. Near the bow, I noticed two men facing not north toward the river, but south toward the long curving shore of Wallabout Bay. I recognized one man by his shoulders, and the other by his slender frame: Adam, and Ethan. As I approached, I was able to see their faces as they stared at the beach a quarter of a mile away. Yes, it was the lads from the *Lively*, though twenty years older and a third of their weight thinner. Untying the white cloth from my face, I stepped toward them.

"Ethan," I said quietly, "it's Benjamin." I looked at the shriveled giant beside him. "Adam, it's Benjamin."

They stared at me; their eyes lit with recognition. Ethan greeted me with a faint smile.

Adam pointed across the water. "Michael and Hank are buried on the beach."

I looked again at the long crescent of sand, bounded by a tall bank. A house stood at one end, and a dock.

"Eleven thousand men were buried in that beach," said Adam. He spoke like a dead man who had returned to deliver the truth.

"Eleven thousand!" I whispered. No one in the Continental Army, not a person at headquarters, had known that the *Jersey* had delivered so many men to their final port.

"But not that many are there now," said Adam. "Seven times the British bastards rowed me to that beach. Seven times I dug a trench in the sand and lay the bodies in it. Seven times I saw where the tide or a storm had washed part of the beach away. The sea took some of the men, left others half buried." He stared toward the beach, the cemetery. "I saw an arm once, as if the man were digging his way back into the world."

Ethan looked toward the stern of the ship. He pointed at the blue figure of Hench. "On the Fourth of July, some of the men sang a few songs, It was all we had for some sort of celebration. Hench shouted down through the grating, 'Silence, you damn rebels!' But we still kept singing. That night, he and his guards opened the hatch and came down the ladder into the hold. It was so black that we couldn't see them, only hear that something was up. Suddenly they were slashing at us with cutlasses. Hench was shouting, 'Sing now, you rebel bastards, sing now!' They chopped and butchered while the men climbed over each other in the black hold to escape. Then the scurvy devils went back up the ladder and locked the grating."

"All that night," said Adam, "Michael was shrieking with half his face cut away. I could not see him, but I could feel the meat and bone of his jaw. He was dead in my arms long before any light came through the window. Hench would not let me bury him. Would not let me even get in the boat to the beach."

We stared along the length of the ship at Officer Hench. A breeze off the river stirred the blue and yellow signal flag above him.

Turning again toward the beach, Ethan told me, "The fever took Hank. He was a gunner who could throw a cannonball almost as far as he could fire one. But at the end, even I could pick him up."

I knew then what I would do. I would sin one last time.

When the boats returned, the remaining prisoners—all save Ethan and Adam—were helped down the long gangplank to the raft, then into the cutters that would carry them to the clean beds of a hospital. I spoke briefly with Sergeant Hartley; at a signal from me, he was to allow the five British redcoats down the gangplank to their rowboat.

Then, with the white mask tied once again around my face, I climbed the steps to the poop deck to speak with Assistant Commissary Hench. I told him, "My men would be honored, sir, to convey you and your baggage to the Battery."

"Won't be necessary. My own crew will take me."

"Very well. But I must insist," I stepped over to the flagpole, untied the rope from its cleat and began to lower the signal flag, "that you, as commanding officer of this vessel, accompany me on a final inspection of all decks. Your signature must verify with full authority that every prisoner has been released."

Hench sneered, "Signature for who?"

"For Congress. For the Commander in Chief. For the people of the free and independent United States." I goaded him a bit further, "For the brave people of the world's newest nation." I unfastened the blue and yellow pennant from its rope.

Hench spat on the deck. "Then let's be about our inspection." He seemed a bit pleased. Perhaps he appreciated the thought that his signature would be delivered to Congress, to General Washington himself.

I drew a knife with which I had sliced countless potatoes. I cut the loop of the rope, pulled it free from the pulley at the top of the pole, then coiled the rope as I followed Hench down the steps to the weather deck.

He glanced at the five redcoats waiting to ferry him to the Battery. Then he limped to the hatchway and descended the ladder. I followed behind. Just before I left the sunshine for the shadow below, I signaled to Sergeant Hartley.

We inspected the middle deck, and though we found it filthy, and littered with rags of clothing, battered tin cups and unwashed bowls which the prisoners had left behind, we discovered no one, living or dead, from bow to stern.

710 · BOOTMAKER TO THE NATION

We climbed down the third ladder to the orlop deck, where we again searched for anyone who might have been overlooked. The sun, now low in the west, shone through the row of tiny square windows; a nearly horizontal row of pale red beams, visible in the damp and dirty air, struck the opposite side of the hold and formed a row of distinct red squares just above the deck.

Our inspection completed, Hench mumbled, "Aye, all accounted for." He limped in a hurry toward the ladder.

But two men were now coming down the steps, two sailors brave enough to re-enter the tomb from which they had but an hour before been freed. "Officer Hench," said Adam, "I come to speak on behalf of the men of Wallabout Bay."

Hench glanced at me: clearly as a fellow officer, I would order this ruffian back up the ladder.

"Officer Hench," said Ethan, "we would like to show you their signatures."

Hench grabbed for the hilt of his dress sword, but my knife was out of its sheath, its point nudging into his back, before he had drawn his blade even six inches. "Take your plumed hat in your hands, Officer Hench," I told him, "and hold it tightly."

As Hench raised up his hands, Ethan stepped forward and drew the sword from its scabbard. Then he pointed the curved blade toward the planking of the ship's hold . . . where a square of red sunlight shone on the dark wood. "Officer Hench, please follow me."

Hench limped toward the planking. "I am an officer in the service of His Majesty King George the Third. You have no right—"

Adam grabbed Officer Hench by the neck of his coat and dragged him like a sack of flour across the deck until he shook Hench's terrified face about a foot from the square of red light. "Do you see their signatures, Officer Hench?" Adam roared. "Do you see the names of the men you murdered?"

I could see, inside that square of light, a dozen names carved into the wood: the names of prisoners who wanted to leave, before they made the journey to Wallabout Bay, something of themselves behind. Looking beyond the red square, I could discern more names; large, small, jumbled together, they covered every inch of planking. Carved into the inner hull of the *Jersey* were probably eleven thousand names, maybe more.

"You can't blame all of this on me!" shrieked Hench. "There's Commissary Sproat. There's General Clinton. Admiral Graves. There's the King himself."

"Aye," said Adam, throwing Hench face down on the floor and stepping with one heavy foot on his back, "there's the King himself."

I gave Adam the coil of signal flag rope. With the skill of a sailor long at sea, Adam lashed Hench's hands behind his back; he drew Hench's feet (in their fine stolen boots) up behind him and bound them as well; then he passed the remainder of the line around Hench's neck with a running bowline: if Hench kicked sufficiently, he would hang himself.

Hench screamed a volley of curses, some of which, despite my months aboard the *Lively*, I had never heard before. The three of us stood for several minutes watching him rage, listening to him choke.

The square of red sunshine crept along the wall, lighting new names.

"Farewell, Officer Hench," said Adam. "We hope you enjoy your voyage."

"Farewell, Officer Hench," said Ethan. "At eight bells, they'll be bringing the raw meat and maggots."

As we climbed the ladder to the middle deck, we could hear his curses and screams and yelps of rage. We could hear him still as we climbed to the upper deck, then up through the hatchway to the weather deck—where we breathed the welcome air off the bay. All three of us stared at the huge scarlet sun hovering over Manhattan Island.

The five redcoats and their rowboat had vanished. They were clearly little concerned with the fate of Assistant Commissary Hench.

Adam, Ethan, and I, followed by Sergeant Hartley, walked down the long gangplank to the raft. Through the small square holes of the lower deck, we could hear—we paused for a pleasant moment while we listened—Officer Hench roaring his curses at us.

We climbed into the last of the cutters, uncleated the line, then watched those fine lads from Marblehead as they dipped their oars into Wallabout Bay and pivoted our bow toward home.

While we crossed the bay toward the river, the shrieking aboard the *Jersey* became increasingly faint.

And then we could hear only the waves washing along our craft, and the rhythmic dip of the oars.

Officer Hench might survive through the night. He might survive for a week. But we doubted, Adam and Ethan and I, that he would see another Christmas.

∞

Chapter One Hundred Forty-Four

Genevieve.

Nine days later, following a peaceful evacuation by the British, and the restoration of civil order in New York City, General Washington prepared to depart for home. He would stop at Annapolis, Maryland, where Congress was presently assembled, to return his commission as Commander in Chief. Then he would ride on to Mount Vernon, where he planned to fulfill the dream he had maintained all through the war: to become a farmer again.

On Tuesday, December 4, 1783, General Washington met with his officers at noon at Fraunces Tavern, on the corner of Broad and Pearl Streets, to say farewell. During the previous summer, while the army was slowly disbanding, a group of officers at the encampment in New Windsor had invited the General to a farewell dinner. Then, angry at Congress because they had still not been paid for their years of service, they canceled the dinner. General Washington was stunned, and profoundly disappointed.

No such disappointment occurred today at Fraunces Tavern, where General Knox, a bookseller who had brought the train of cannons from Fort Ticonderoga to Cambridge, and Baron Steuben, a Prussian who had transformed a collection of starving, ragged soldiers into an army of professional troops, and twenty other loyal officers gathered with their Commander in Chief in the Long Room on the second floor for a final meal together.

Seated next to Lieutenant Colonel Benjamin Talmadge, I watched as General Washington stood up at the end of the table with a glass of wine in his hand, to propose a toast. His officers filled their own glasses, then raised them in silence. I had heard General Washington speak with friendship, with impatience, with compassion, and with rage, but never in all my years with him had I heard his voice tremble with such profound emotion. He told his officers, "With a heart full of love and gratitude, I now take leave of you. I most devoutly wish that your latter days may be as prosperous and happy as your former ones have been glorious and honorable."

Not a man spoke as they drank the toast which honored them more than Congress ever could.

The General set down his glass, then said, "I cannot come to each of you, but shall feel obliged if each of you will come and take me by the hand."

General Knox was the first to step toward his commander. General Washington did not merely shake his hand; with tears running down his face, the General embraced his chief of artillery and devoutly loyal friend.

One by one, the officers who had remained at their posts to the last days of the war stepped forward to receive their Commander in Chief's grateful embrace. They knew of his intention to depart forever from public service, and thus believed they would never see him again. The men in their blue coats with gold epaulettes felt more than sadness; they were weeping tears of a great and irreparable loss.

After he had thanked every officer in what he had always called his "family," General Washington walked out of the room. Leaving our meals, we followed him the short distance down the street to the pier at Whitehall, where a boat waited to row him across Hudson's River to Paulus Hook, New Jersey. (Benjamin stood with an honor guard of infantrymen at the wharf.) The General climbed down the stone steps to his barge, while a crowd of officers, civil authorities, soldiers, sailors, and the people of New York City watched in absolute silence.

As the oarsmen rowed the barge away from the Battery and into the river's current, we quietly waved our hats. General Washington stood up, took off his black hat and waved back.

Benjamin and I, with Sir William in the harness and Caleb and Sally in the wagon, departed from New York City on the same day. As we headed north, we read the accounts in various newspapers about General Washington's journey south. After stopping in Philadelphia, Wilmington, and Baltimore, he arrived in Annapolis, where Congress was assembled. (Congress had recently been chased out of Philadelphia by mutinous Pennsylvania regulars who had not been paid.)

On Saturday evening, December 22, General Washington attended a ball given by the governor of Maryland in his honor at the State House. One reporter noted that the General "danced every set, that all the ladies might have the pleasure of dancing with him." The belles, as they put it themselves, wanted "to get a touch of him."

At noon the following day, Sunday, December 23, 1783, General Washington returned to the State House to do something that no Caesar had ever done: he would return his military commission to the civilian authorities. Unlike a multitude of predecessors throughout history, the General would not dismount from his horse to settle upon a throne.

No more than twenty members of Congress were present in the Senate Chamber; the rest had already gone home for Christmas. But the large gallery at the back of the room was crowded with people who had gathered to witness this unprecedented moment.

The General was escorted to his seat. Thomas Mifflin, president of the Congress, (and formerly the Quartermaster who had never reported for work), addressed him, "Sir, the United States in Congress assembled, are prepared to receive your communications."

General Washington rose from his chair and took a folded piece of paper from his pocket. He had prepared a short speech.

> *"The great events on which my resignation depended having at length taken place; I have now the honor of offering my sincere Congratulations to Congress and of presenting myself before them to surrender into their hands the trust committed to me, and to claim the indulgence of retiring from the Service of my Country.*
>
> *"Happy in the confirmation of our Independence and Sovereignty, and pleased with the oppertunity afforded the United States of becoming a respectable Nation, I resign with satisfaction the Appointment I accepted with diffidence. A diffidence in my abilities to accomplish so arduous a task, which however was superseded by a confidence in the rectitude of our Cause, the support of the Supreme Power of the Union, and the patronage of Heaven."*

The General reaffirmed "my gratitude for the interposition of Providence."

He then asked Congress not to forget its debt to his officers:

> *"Permit me Sir, to recommend in particular those, who have continued in Service to the present moment, as worthy of the favorable notice and patronage of Congress."*

He concluded,

> *"Having now finished the work assigned to me, I retire from the great theatre of Action; and bidding an Affectionate farewell to this August body under whose orders I have so*

long acted, I here offer my Commission, and take my leave
of all the employments of public life."

From an inner pocket of his coat, he took out and unfolded a second piece of paper: the commission which had traveled as far north as Boston, and as far south as Yorktown. He handed the paper to Thomas Mifflin, and thus guaranteed that the government of the United States, whatever form it took, would be civilian and not military.

The president of Congress now read a letter of gratitude written by Thomas Jefferson in Paris. Early in the war, Jefferson wrote the sacred phrase which had become the essence, the soul, of America: "All men are created Equal." General Washington had fought and won the war which gave that eternal dream of equality the opportunity to take root and flourish. Thus, one giant now spoke to another.

"Called upon by your country to defend its invaded
rights, you accepted the sacred charge before it had formed
alliances and while it was without funds, or a government to
support you. You have conducted the great military contest
with wisdom and fortitude, invariably regarding the rights
of the civil power, through all the disasters and changes.
You have, by the love and confidence of your fellow citizens,
enabled them to display their martial genius, and transmit
their fame to posterity. You have persevered until these
United States have been enabled, under a just Providence,
to close the war in freedom, safety, and independence."

President Mifflin handed Jefferson's letter to General Washington, who tucked it into a pocket.

The General shook hands with each member of Congress. Then he strode out the door to where Billy Lee was waiting with his horse.

With a fifty-mile ride ahead of him to Mount Vernon—in December, when the days were short—General Washington set off at a gallop. He and his two aides, Walker and Humphreys, spent that night lodged at a tavern. Billy Lee, whose commission into slavery began on the day he was born and continued until the day the General died, slept in the servants' quarters.

On Monday, December 24, 1783, the foursome crossed the Potomac River on a ferry, then galloped the remaining distance to Mount Vernon. Home on Christmas Eve, General Washington was welcomed by Lady Washington, who had been at his side during the encampments at Cambridge, New York, Morristown, Valley Forge, Middlebrook, Morristown a second time, Tappan, and finally Newburgh.

She had shared the war with him, and she hoped that the world would now allow her to share the peace.

☙

Chapter One Hundred Forty-Five

Genevieve.

I lay awake last night with an anxious feeling that, though we have now filled ten ledgers, we have not yet finished.

I recalled a letter which General Washington wrote in February, 1783 to the most capable of all his generals, the trusted officer whom he appointed to command the entire southern campaign of the war, General Nathanael Greene. This letter, written during the last winter of the war, expressed the General's astonishment at what his Continental Army had accomplished.

> *"If historiographers should be hardy enough to fill the page of history with the advantages that have been gained with unequal numbers (on the part of America) in the course of this contest, and attempt to relate the distressing circumstances under which they have been obtained, it is more than probable that posterity will bestow on their labors the epithet of fiction; . . ."*

I wonder myself whether my grandchildren, and those who come after them, will believe all that we have written, will value all that the troops have endured.

> *". . . for it will not be believed that such a force as Great Britain has employed for eight years in this country could be baffled, in their plan of subjugating it, by numbers infinitely less, composed of men oftentimes half starved, always in rags, without pay, and experiencing, at times, every species of distress which human nature is capable of undergoing."*

My children, the starvation was true, the rags were true, the sickness was true. The worry and the fear and the grief were everlastingly true. And if you believe us not—if you value not—then I am certain, as Providence is just, that you yourselves shall soon come to starvation and sickness and grief.

America is more than a nation; it is a gift. Cherish this gift. Pass it on as a treasure greater even than the treasure which you have received.

For as your hearts grow, or wither, so shall your country grow, or wither.

And long, I warrant, shall you wait before another Samuel Adams tells another young girl, "You're the equal of a king. With your braids and bib apron, you're the equal of a king."

∽

Chapter One Hundred Forty-Six

Benjamin.   *15 May, 1827*

As I said to Genevieve last night, we could write a second book about the Constitution and the Presidency. But as Genevieve said to me, we'll do no such thing until the potatoes are planted.

Sitting now by the open window, breathing the fresh warm air of spring, and beckoned by the scent of apple blossoms in the orchard, I admit that I feel like a schoolboy restless at his desk.

Caleb is coming today with Mary and their grandchildren. No room at this table then for papers and ink, and no quiet in the house for the distant voice of history.

So I'd best push my pen toward that final period.

For three and a half years after the war, the thirteen states bickered and squabbled about borders, navigation rights, customs duties, old debts, and whose money could be used to pay those debts. The nation attempted to function under the Articles of Confederation, adopted by Congress during the war, but as the Articles had never compelled the states to tax their citizens and thus support the national army, so the Articles, following the war, never compelled the thirteen states to work together toward any form of Union.

The nation's debts remained unpaid to France and the Netherlands, and to British merchants (debts from before the war). Further, Britain demanded full compensation to the Loyalists who had abandoned their homes in America. As long as America refused to pay its debts, Britain maintained her troops in several western forts—and thus threatened further battles. The last of the redcoats had not yet gone home.

Fearful that the fragile Union was soon to break apart into regional clusters, fifty-five delegates from twelve of the states (Rhode Island refused to attend) met in Philadelphia in May, 1787, to repair the faulty Articles of Confederation. They quickly decided to replace the Articles with a completely new Constitution. The smaller states argued with the larger states over representation; the southern states argued with the northern states about slavery. But all agreed on the structure of a three-part government, with a legislature, judiciary, and executive, which would check and balance each other. After four months of debate in the same room where the Declaration of Independence had been signed, the delegates voted, on September 15, 1783, to accept a Constitution which began with the words, "We the People." The foundation of this novel system of government would be the citizens of the nation, who would vote on a regular basis for their representatives, and for their President.

Between the initial gathering of the first Continental Congress in Philadelphia in September, 1774, and the signing of the Constitution on September 17, 1787, thirteen years had passed. The feisty colonials had matured: the rebels had become republicans. But we were not yet done learning. Like Henry, the citizens kept growing.

During the autumn, winter and spring of 1787-1788, the proposed Constitution was examined, article by article, in every tavern and home from New Hampshire to Georgia. Each state held a convention, in which delegates debated whether or not to adopt the Constitution, and thus whether or not to join the Union. Newspapers carried a multitude of articles that examined every aspect of the Constitution; some of the finest essays were written by Alexander Hamilton. During nine months, from September to June, the American people studied government: the nation became a school, with classes offered to everyone. Probably never before in human history have so many people learned so much in such a short period of time.

The American people decided to accept the Constitution, but with a specific Bill of Rights. On June 25, 1788, Virginia became the ninth state to ratify the Constitution, thereby making it "the supreme law of the several states," and the framework for the nation's new government. The other four states eventually ratified as well.

The first election for the President took place in February, 1789. General Washington became, at his inauguration in New York City on April 30, 1789, President Washington. (His administration commenced two and a half months before France was shaken by the beginnings of its own Revolution). During its first session, Congress passed into law ten amendments to the Constitution which comprise our Bill of Rights.

As important as the *beginning* of this first presidency was its *ending*, for George Washington willingly allowed another man, who had been elected by the people, to take his place at the head of government. On December 23, 1783, General Washington had relinquished power as Commander in Chief; almost fourteen years later, on March 4, 1797, he relinquished power as President of the United States. The peaceful transition of leadership to John Adams set the young nation firmly on its course.

Now, in 1827, under the leadership of our sixth President, John Quincy Adams, and with twenty-four States presently in the Union, we have become a sturdy nation, and a far more powerful nation. But have We the People fulfilled our original promise? A fifth of our nation's people remain enslaved. The original peoples of this continent have been brutalized, forced from their land, and slaughtered. The Negro and the Indian have suffered far more, and far longer, than the colonials ever did because of a British tax on tea.

The time must surely come when the Constitution's one great and lingering flaw, the acceptance of slavery and its spread ever westward, must bring this nation to its reckoning. We have lived with the snake for so long, that we don't hear it hiss any more. But we are raising a crop of apples, and when the harvest comes, we are going to eat from that tree of knowledge until we've got a belly full.

With gratitude that we lived when Providence gave us a nation to build, and with the hope that our children's children will offer peace and liberty to *all* the peoples who work the sacred American soil, I now lay down my quill.

In its place, I want to hold the hand of my beloved Genevieve, while we walk together in the springtime sunshine upon the land that once demanded the finest in the human mind, the finest in the human heart.

Caleb, at the old homestead in Lincoln.

They are out in the apple orchard now, the two old patriots. Their labors are done. As they walk hand in hand among the blossoming trees, a scented breeze sprinkles white petals upon them.

Thank you, thank you, for your gift.

&

About the Author

With a doctorate in literature from Stanford University in 1974, Dr. John Slade has taught high school and university English in the United States, the Caribbean, Norway, and Russia. While teaching in St. Petersburg and Murmansk during the difficult 1990s, he discovered that though the Russian economy was in complete upheaval, and though many of his students lived with two well-educated but newly unemployed parents, the students nevertheless had the solid foundation of their proud history. Because they knew their history, their literature, their music, they knew their Russia, and could never lose it. Despite the whirlwind of current events, they had a foundation on which to build.

American students, and the American people in general, after the trauma of September 11, are looking with a loving and yet probing eye at their country. Who are we, as a nation, and as a good neighbor in the world? What is our future path?

The author hopes that by returning to the birth of our nation—by reliving the rich and powerful years from 1763 to 1783—we can better understand the events, and the values, of our own American foundation. By clearing away the clutter and the neglect, by returning to the granite bedrock of our Revolution, we can find a more solid footing, and thus can build together a national edifice perhaps less commercial, but instead more generous in spirit.